Two Crimes

TWO CRIMES :
The Omnibus Murder
The Ferry Murder

by
Fortuné du Boisgobey

Translated, introduced and annotated by
Nina Cooper

A Black Coat Press Book

Acknowledgements: Thanks to Charles Griggs for his reviews of all drafts and his helpful critique of each. Thanks to Kitty Werner of Distinction Press for making it all possible. Thanks to the Henneveux Family for their loyal support, as well as to Daniel Auliac for his always invaluable help.

Le Crime de l'Omnibus (1881)
Le Bac (1882)
English adaptation and introduction Copyright © 2017 by Nina Cooper.
Cover illustration Copyright © 2017 by Daniele Serra.

Visit our website at www.blackcoatpress.com

TABLE OF CONTENTS

Introduction

Even though Fortuné du Boisgobey, *feuilletoniste,* novelist, paymaster for the French army in Tunisia, traveler, Paris *bon vivant,* friend of Edmond de Goncourt, ardent Catholic, and one time President of the *Société des gens de lettres,* began his serious writing career when he was over 40, from that point until he was 70, he produced an astounding number of novels. The estimates run from 60 to over 100. They were immensely popular in France and were translated into English and reprinted by Scribner's in the United States, and Vizetelly & Company in England. They were even translated and published in Japan.

Du Boisgobey was born in Granville, France, in 1821, and died in Paris in 1891 at the monastery of the Brothers of Saint-Jean-de Dieu, then located in the Rue Oudinot, at the rear of the Invalides, where, because of the paralysis of his lower limbs, he had moved shortly before his death. According to General Reid, a supporter of Abraham Lincoln and Cultural Attaché to France after the War of Secession, du Boisbogey's family in Granville was an old one, comprised of bourgeois lawyers and civil servants. His father had been mayor of that provincial town, which had existed as far back as the 10th century, and was later a Deputy to the National Assembly. The day after Fortuné du Boisgobey's death some French newspapers began circulating a false story concerning his origins, a story which exists to the present day. The original story said that du Boisgobey was a pseudonym and that his surname was really Castille. The story was almost immediately debunked by General Read and by du Boisgobey's obituary that appeared February 28, 1891 in the *New York Times.*

General Reid was given the post of Consul General to France as payment for his services to the Union. In his *Autobiography,* General Reid states that he was President of a dinner/conversation club called the *Dîner des Spartiates,* to which du Boisgobey also belonged. General Reid called the club "an academy of conversation," adding that it certainly was not Spartan in food or drink. He remembered:

The death of M. Fortuné du Boisgobey has brought to my mind the interesting symposiums held at Brabant's the year after the termination of the Franco-Prussian war (1870–1871), for it was at those charming gatherings that I first met this remarkable man...It is a curious circumstance that one of the journals of the 27th February 1891, the day after the death of M. du Boisgobey, stated that his real name was Fortuné Castille, and that he was born at Granville, while another paper declared that he was the son of M. Abraham Dubois of Nantes. I was even told that he cut his father's name in two, making it Du Bois, and added the last part, Gobey, which was his mother's name, thus making it du

Boisgobey. There is no truth in any of these assertions. M. du Boisgobey simply bore the name to which he was entitled, and which was one of prominence in the last century as well as in this.[1]

Du Boisgobey's obituary in the *New York Times* February 28, 1891, is not only an obituary, but also an indictment of Ponson du Terrail and other *feuilletonistes*. But, although the writer's disapproval of du Boisgobey and other *feuilletonistes* is apparent in almost every line, the obituary is one of the few sources of an accurate list and date of publication of du Boisgobey's major novels. The author of the obituary writes:

One of the greatest writers of the penny-dreadfuls died in Paris yesterday in the person of Fortuné Hippolyte Auguste du Boisgobey. He was born at Granville (Manche) in 1824, and was graduated at the Lycée Saint Louis. His parents were wealthy and the du Boisgobeys are an ancient respectable aristocracy of magistrates in the Avranchine. But Fortuné du Boisgobey took to writing fiction as to any other money-making avocation.

At twenty he was a clerk to the Treasurer of the French troops in Africa, at twenty-four he went to Paris to attain distinction as a young man of the Haute Noce[2] *and he was successful. In 1861 he traveled in the Orient. At the age of forty he began to think of adopting a profession. As Ponson du Terrail was earning a fortune with his horrible feuilletons, Fortuné du Boisgobey sent a novel of similar quality to the* Petit Journal. *It was entitled* Les Deux Comédiens *and appeared in 1868.*

It was detestable enough to please M. Dallez of the Petit Moniteur, *who straightway signed a contract with the author for seven years at 12,000 a year. Fortuné du Boisgobey was worthy of the editor's confidence.*

The author then lists 47 novels and du Boisgobey's second book of travels with dates of publication and ends his obituary with:

There are others, and all are popular and translated in all the living languages, but the entire catalogue, as literature, has no other merit than the evenness of its mediocrity.[3]

The popular-literature-reading public was not of the obituary writer's opinion because du Boisgobey continued in popularity, some critics saying in notoriety, until well into the 1920's. During his lifetime, New York publishers did not respect his copyrights and published his novels shortly after they appeared in Paris, although they were sometimes considered scandalous or somewhat sensational. An article in *The Literary News* of New York for September 1887 printed an article on second-hand book stores selling uncopyrighted editions of popular

---

[1] General Charles Meredith Read, "The Spartans of Paris, Leaves from my Autobiography," pp. 81-103, *The Magazine of American History*, Vol. XXVI. August 1891. No. 2.

[2] Refers to dandies and young men of dissolute life.

[3] Du Boisgobey obituary. *New York Times*, February 28, 1891.

authors, mainly to boys and sailors.

The author of the article reported:

The business is at its best in the summer and the boys look for sensational literature to satisfy their taste for novelty. Among French authors, Fortuné du Boisgobey, who writes detective stories such as The Vitriol Throwers, *is in the largest demand. His books are ground out at the rate of one every month. The bookseller says that his customers are so anxious to see the current number of du Boisgobey's works that they scarcely contain their impatience...The reading of sensational novels is not as harmful as is generally reported, in the opinion of the dealer.[4]*

The British publisher, Vizetelly & Company, in advertising "New Books and New Editions," in *Publishers' Weekly*, for September 1887 lists twenty-seven of du Boisgobey's novels already published or soon to appear at a price of two shillings per volume. They preface their advertisement as: DU BOISGOBEY'S SENSATIONAL NOVELS and end it with this poem from the "Ballade of Railway Novels":

Ah! Friend! How many and many a while They've made the slow time fleetly flow, And solaced pain and charmed exile, Boisgobey and Gaboriau![5]

Robert Louis Stevenson found it "solaced pain and charmed exile" when, after the failure of his first literary work, he left for Davos, to spend the winter and, he wrote, *"bury myself in the novels of M. du Boisgobey."[6]*

Before beginning his career as a *feuilletoniste* and novelist, du Boisgobey, at 18, wrote an early travel book, *Voyages en Bretagne*, published in 1839, based on a walking tour he took before rejoining his parents at their summer home near Mont Saint Michel. The book was reprinted in 2001, but went through only one printing and is now out-of-print. The *Introduction* says:

At the end of July 1839, a young man, 18-years-old, his bachelor's diploma in his pocket, took the Orleans fast train to make a tour of Brittany, after having gone down the Loire and before rejoining his parents at their property near Mont-Saint-Michel. Alone, or with some temporary companion, he was to make his way, most of the time on foot, to look at, to listen to, and to note down carefully his impressions at each stop: architecture and "druid monuments," but also local industries, naval activities, anecdotes and stories old people had dug up from family archives, sprinkled his unedited notes. Salt works, the Brest penal colony, Huelgoat silver productions give us an interesting description taken down quickly.[7]

Gaboriau's interest in travel never left him. Before returning to France

---

[4] *The Literary News*, New York, September 1887.
[5] "New Books and New Editions," Vizetelly & Company, Publishers Weekly, 1887.
[6] Robert Louis Stevenson, *My First Book; Treasure Island*.
[7] *Voyage en Bretagne*, Paris: Ouest France Éditeurs, 2001.

from Africa, somewhere about 1863, he traveled extensively in Africa and the Orient as well as in Germany, Austria, Greece and Palestine. He published his impressions in *From the Rhine to the Nile: Notebook of a Parisian*.[8] In the Foreword he says:

These notes, written daily, were done on the spot before 1870. Since the war (Franco-Prussian War 1870–1871), Berlin's appearance is no longer the same, and since the International Exposition of 1874, Vienna's appearance has significantly changed. So only after some thought did the author decide to publish his somewhat too retrospective travel impressions. But he told himself that ultimately Berlin has only changed in ugliness, that Vienna has stayed charming and the Orient has lost nothing of its unalterable beauty. Saint Sophia and the Parthenon, Jérusalem and the Bosphorus are today what they were ten years ago, what they will still be in a century. This account has, moreover, no other claim but that of being sincere. The author tells only what he saw and what he did, and he tells it as if talking to a friend by the fireside.[9]

There is little contemporary truthful information about du Boisgobey. What there is usually begins the statement that he was a follower of Émile Gaboriau, the father of the detective story, or that he was a member of the Gaboriau group of writers. There is indeed some small justification for such a classification, since du Boisgobey wrote two volumes continuing the history and biography of Émile Gaboriau's detective, Monsieur Lecoq: *The Old Age of M. Lecoq* and *The Nabob of Babour, Sequel to the Old Age of M. Lecoq*. He also mentions Gaboriau in passing in *The Omnibus Murder*, calling him "the late lamented novelist." Although he borrowed liberally from Gaboriau, his style and technique differ considerably from that of Gaboriau. In *The Omnibus Murder*, he borrowed not only the setting of Paris as reconstructed by Baron Haussmann, who, under Napolean III tore down buildings, demolished the medieval city walls, widened streets and constructed a new water and sewage system to create modern Paris, but he also borrowed the extended carriage pursuit across Paris streets and bridges. Since at least one bridge has been renamed, the careful reader may have trouble following the chase. In addition, he used a mysterious man in disguise similar to a role Gaboriau frequently gives Monsieur Lecoq.

However, the most obvious difference between du Boisgobey and Gaboriau is that du Boisgobey's plots tend at least as much, and sometimes more, toward romance as toward the pursuit of crime and criminals. That is not to say that love interest is lacking in Gaboriau. Lecoq is motivated by it in *File No. 113* and Old Man Tabaret (aka Tire-au-clair) considers it at 60 in *The Lerouge Affair*. In Gaboriau, although it provides motivation, it does not monopolize the plot. Du Boisgobey, particularly in *The Ferry Murder* has no plot

---

[8] Paris: Décaux Librairie, Illustrée, 1876; Plon:1880.
[9] Fortuné du Boisgobey, *From the Rhine to the Nile: Notebook of a Parisian*, Paris: Décaux *Librairie Illustrée*, 1876; Plon: 1880.

without the love interest. The mystery and the love affair are so intertwined that one cannot be worked out without the other.

In *The Omnibus Murder* and *The Ferru Murder*, for example, the love story takes up at least as much of the exposition as does the crime, which in *The Ferry Murder* is actually a mystery as to whether or not there is a crime. Because the love story takes up so much of the plot, the criminals are not as dyed in the wool, outright villains as are those of Gaboriau. The villains of the latter are wicked through and through, passionate, determined, and believable in their wickedness. Du Boisgobey seems to want to excuse the wicked, has other characters apologize for them or blames their sins on their age or on personality flaws. Perhaps it might be said that he was ahead of his time in the use of psychiatric analysis. Many of his plots resemble contemporary soap operas more than crime stories. The titles of some of the translations into English will serve to illustrate:

The Felon's Bequest: A Novel Of The Prison And The Boudoir, The Convict Colonel: A Romance, The Sculptor's Daughter, The Husband And The Diva, Le Demi-Monde Under The Terror, The Youngest Soldier Of The Grande Armée.

Although the love interest is sometimes paramount in du Boisgobey's novels, the sensational is rarely absent. An article in the *New Princeton Review*, describing those "eager to look into his peep show," says:

Give him a murder, a mutilated body, a fast young man with a good heart, a selection from the demi-monde, an ingénue, a duel, a diving bell, and game of baccarat—with these and a villain (who generally cheats at cards), M. Fortuné du Boisgobey and his public are content...It is not very high art—far from that—but you go on reading because things really do occur in the tale, because you are curious, and because your curiosity makes you forget your work, forget your sorrow, forget "problems," metaphysical, social, financial or religious." [10]

In Gaboriau's novels, characters are introduced and described by the author as they lend their personalities to the plot and the action moves quickly; narration and exposition support or balance dialogue. Du Boisgobey, on the contrary, uses dialogue to carry the plot along and, as a result, the plot unfolds slowly. The author's intended humor or irony within dialogues is sometimes almost lost and banal conversations are not infrequent.

The novels of both authors are what Dorothy Sayers calls "fat," and du Boisgobey merits Charles Dickens' criticism:

There is something which we must, some of us, admit, that M. du Boisgobey is, on the whole, amusing. For my part I can forgive a great deal to the man who amuses me. And, unfortunately, there is another thing which we must, some of us admit, that M. du Boisgobey is long. What a sensational novelist that sensational novelist would have been if he had only 'boiled it down'! Of

---

[10] Hodge, et al. "Theology," *The Princeton Review*, 1888, p. 150.

course, the exigencies of the 'feuilleton' method of publication precluded any suicidal tendencies of that description.[11]

But, perhaps, one of the greatest differences between Gaboriau and du Boisgobay is the level of society in which they moved and from which they drew their plots. This fact comes through in the novels of both. Gaboriau, in his relatively short life, moved in the police and *feuilletonistes* working circles: crime and crime scenes, the morgue, the judiciary. Sprinkled throughout his novels are satirical comments on the judicial system, the penal system, the double standard in matters of sex, as well as on the vanity, pomposity, and duplicity of minor government officials. His experience, as well as his social and intellectual contacts, were thus more limited than those of du Boisgobey. Wide travel, contact with international society and intimate friendship and intellectual exchange with Parisian literary society provided du Boisgobey with greater insight into social life and problems outside the criminal and judicial worlds. As an intimate friend of Edmond Goncourt, he met socially and intellectually the literary great of the day. His prestige was such that he was able to prevent a young novelist, Harry Alis (pseudonym of Jules Hyppolyte Percher, killed in a famous duel in 1895) from gaining entry into *La Société des gens de lettres,* an honor which others, notably Guy de Maupassant, thought Alis well deserved. (The following two years du Boisgobey was President of that group.) Du Boisgobey found Alis' novel unrealistic. Guy de Maupassant, in *Les Croniques*, gives this account of du Boisgobey's satirical speech to the committee:

And then M. du Boisgobey is astonished to find lack of realism in the novel of his young colleague. And I'm astonished in my turn, and even more than he, at his astonishment! He exclaims, "How unbelievable!" because a young Japonese of noble race enters the most aristocratic drawing rooms of the Faubourg Saint-Germain, those drawing rooms whose doors M. du Boisgobey considers impassable, although he has revealed its society, its manners and its love affairs to all the doorkeepers and greengrocers in France.

Maupassant ends his defense of Alis with these ironic comments:

There you have it! There's the French language defended by M. Fortuné du Boisbobey. Oh, what a marvel! Lack of reality condemned by M. du Boisgobey. Oh, a second marvel! And The Sun Queen, *the book of an artist, well thought out and written, interesting and true, thrown in the trash can by M. Fortuné du Boisgobey with* L'Assommoir *and* Germinal. *Oh, a third marvel!!!*[12]

That du Boisgobey's criticism could influence the decision of a literary committee could have had as much to do with his friendship with Edmond de Goncourt as with the committee's respect for du Boisgobey's judgment. In an entry from the *Goncourt Journals* (Troisième Série, deuxième volume, vendredi, 14 mars 1890) Edmond Goncourt notes the following conversation with du

---

[11] Charles Dickens, *All The Year Round, September 25, 1892*, p. 296.
[12] Guy de Maupassant, "Les Académies," *Les Chroniques, Tome V.*

Boisgobey, a conversation indicating that Goncourt ranked du Boisgobey as "one of our colleagues," these being: Léon and Alphonse Daudet, Pierre Loti, Guy de Maupassant, CharlesMarie-Georges Huysmans, and other literary men mentioned frequently by Edmond de Goncourt at that period.

A government, which could be expected to have a few more honest people in the ministry and a few more police in the street; that's today's government. Boisgobey, speaking to me about the mental incompetence of one of our colleagues, compared him to a latrine worm peculiar to Africa, and whose mistress, in that country, couldn't say the Arab name without spitting on the ground.[13]

As noted by Maupassant, du Boisgobey places some of his plots in an unrealistic world. On the other hand, he is also a social critic of contemporary life in France, noting the inferior position of women even in rich bourgeois families, the unrealistic sexual education given to women prior to marriage, the pretentiousness of the artistic community, as well as that of the Parisian and provincial bourgeois, the strength of gossip, the "qu'en dira-t-on," the worry of "what will people say," in the life of the bourgeois, even as he gives a perhaps false and overly sympathetic picture of the life of the aristocracy in the Faubourg Saint Germain.

Throughout the 1920's du Boisgobey's novels, both in English translations and in the original French went through not only many editions, but many and varied translations by several different publishing houses. In 1882, 1883, and 1885, *Le Bac*, for example, was translated as: *The Ferryboat: Who Died Last? Or The Rightful Heir: Was It a Murder? Or Who Is The Heir" Or Love's Triumph: The Tragedy of the Ferry.* Beginning in the 1930's both Gaboriau and du Boisgobey's works were eclipsed by other kinds of detective stories, although they were still important enough to be reviewed, and sometimes apologized for, by major critics such as T. S. Eliot and Dorothy Sayers in England and André Gide in France in the 1930's and even into the 1940's.

Today, approximately shortly before the year 2000 to the present, Gaboriau and du Boisgobey are being re-edited and published again in French by well-known established presses and newer, smaller presses. Sorbonne professors are holding conferences on XIX Century popular literature, analyzing and reappraising the work of both writers. Magazines such as *Le Rocambole* are publishing articles on XIX century popular literature in general. An article in "Actualites" of *Le Monde* for Friday, May 12, 2006, summarizes the current state of publication of and interest in popular XIX century literature in France under a headline reading:

THE NEW GOLDEN AGE OF THE POPULAR NOVEL
French editors seem to be again interested in popular literature of the XIX

---

[13] *Journal Des Goncourt* (Edmond Goncourt), Troisième série, deuxième volume, vendredi, 14 mars, 1890.

Century. After the BIBLIOTHEQUE POPULAIRE of the ENCRAGE editions, which has published Ponson du Terrail, Fortuné du Boisbobey and Eugène Sue, it's the turn of the L'AUBE editions to launch a very nice pocket-book presentation entitled POPULAR WRITERS. For its part, ALTERDIT is launching a collection entitled HERO, CAPE AND SWORD which recalls that former series published by Tallandier in the 1930's, "The Novels of the Cape and Sword."[14]

But, for modern readers, unaccustomed to formality in manners and in family life, to arranged marriages, to the control of parents over children, to extended and tight-knit family groups, to females as pawns in money matters, du Boisgobey will present a challenge to belief. Were such situations real? Boisgobey's novels will persuade them that they were. And, after all, as Dickens says, can you not forgive a lot to the man who amuses you, and, it might be added, to a man who "solaced pain and charmed exile?"

Nina Cooper

---

[14] "Actualités, *Le Monde*, Vendredi, 12 mai 2006.

THE OMNIBUS MURDER

I. Death in the Omnibus

In the evening, about midnight, have you ever missed the last omnibus on the line which passes by your house? If you're not on a budget and don't have to strictly watch expenditures, you have only to take a cab. But, if, on the contrary, your modest fortune forbids such a small extra expense, you have to return home on foot, going across Paris, sloshing in the mud, sometimes in a driving rain. You've grumbled a hundred times about the Company. After sixteen hours of work, it gave its horses and its employees a little rest. It couldn't do anything else.

There are several ways to miss it, that helpful vehicle, the last hope of people who're late. When you try to catch it, standing on the street corner, having hailed the coachman with fruitless signals, you see the dreaded, hopeless word full appear in white letters standing out against a blue background, you're furious. But, after all, you half expected it. You accepted fate with good will and continued to walk. You vaguely flattered yourself that another one would pass by. Sustained by that illusion, you finally arrived, on foot, at your lodgings without being too aware of fatigue.

The worst way is to go to the station, the first vehicle in line, just at the moment when the only outbound omnibus has just filled up. There is no way to make a mistake. It really is the last one. The clerk who is turning the handle to close the office ticket window has answered you that there are no more. The travelers who came before you laugh in your face when you politely ask if there isn't one single little place left.

There is no way out of the situation. You have no other means of transportation but your legs. They have to carry you all the way to your destination, because you won't catch up with it on the way, that damned vehicle you were counting on to avoid a long walk.

Thus it was that on one evening of this winter at a quarter to midnight at the corner of the Boulevard St. Germain and the Rue du Cardinal Lemoine, at the exact moment that the coachman of the green omnibus which goes from the wine shops of the Halles to the Place Pigalle was climbing up to his seat, a woman, properly dressed and still young, as well as you could tell by her get-up, because a thick veil covered her face, arrived out of breath. She came from the

15

direction of the Jardin des Plantes, by way of the Quay St. Bernard, and she must have run a long time, because she was exhausted. She had some trouble articulating the question people who're late anxiously ask the employee charged with giving the signal to depart.

"Everything is full, Madame, and there's none after this," said the conductor, who was busy looking over his papers.

"Ah! *Mon Dieu*. I'm going to Montmartre! I'll never get there."

And, really, at that hour and at that season, a trip on foot of four to five kilometers could certainly frighten a person belonging to the weak sex. There was a dry cold and a north wind which made this cold even more piercing. There was snow in the air. The streets in this area were deserted; no one passing by on the wide sidewalks, not a *fiacre* on the horizon. The inside of the omnibus was full, but no one had dared brave the temperature by mounting to the upper level, where, for three *sous* you were almost sure of catching a big cold.

The lady lifted her eyes toward the "seats in the air," as they're called by the conductors. She must've had a very great desire to take advantage of the last departure, because a gesture she made indicated clearly that she regretted not being able to climb up on the top despite the wind and freezing temperature. Then, knowing that such a climb is not permitted to ladies, and that the employees did not compromise with the rules, she stuck her head into the long carriage where there was no longer room for her. Probably she wasn't without hope of making some gallant traveler take pity on her situation and give over his right as first occupant of a seat. There was a very faint chance, because there was hardly anyone but women travelers. Women don't willingly give up a privilege. However, she had the much unexpected good fortune to interest someone in her fate. A gentleman seated at the back got up and slipped toward the exit door.

"Get in, Madame," he said, jumping lightly to the pavement.

"Oh! Monsieur! You're too good. I can't take advantage of your kindness," exclaimed the woman.

"Not at all! Not at all! Don't give it a thought. I'm going to get myself installed up on top. It's not warm, but I have thick skin."

"Truly, Monsieur, I don't know how to thank you."

"It's nothing. It's not worth mentioning."

"Let's go, Madame, let's go, please," said the employee. "We're leaving."

The lady already had her foot on the step. She didn't need to be asked any more; but instead of relying on the conductor for the step up, she accepted the help graciously offered her by the man who had just rendered her a service. She put her hand in his, and perhaps left it there a few seconds more than was necessary. That was certainly the least she could do for such a polite gentleman. This contact wasn't at all compromising. Both of them wore gloves. They were wearing heavy fur-lined gloves with a leather exterior.

However, the gentleman who had just given up his seat was neither handsome nor young. He could have been forty years old and even more. His mustache and his sideburns cut in the military fashion were very heavily grey. He was wearing a loose-fitting overcoat made by a cheap tailor and a derby hat of hard felt, the hat of an independent man who made no effort to follow the fashion. He had, in addition, rather regular, but hard, features, as if carved out with hatchet strokes.

He climbed to the top of the bus with remarkable agility, and he took a position at the entrance on the first seat, very near the exit stairs. While he was getting himself situated there, raising the collar of his overcoat, the woman he had just helped slid into the vacated seat at the back of the omnibus, on the right, between an old woman totally covered with a wool hood and a young girl very simply dressed. Further on, against the back window, there was an old gossip in a bonnet that should have paid for two because she literally overflowed on her neighbor to the left.

Across was seated a man, the only one in the vehicle: a tall boy, thin and brunet with lively eyes and a smiling mouth, the true head of an artist, but a successful artist. He had neither the slovenly dress nor the aggressive behavior of the young art students who haunt the brasseries of the outlying boulevard. The other travelers belonged to the different categories of those who take the omnibus, middle class women returning home after an evening spent at the home of relatives living at the other end of Paris, mothers carrying a child wrapped in a blanket, women returning from night work, collapsing with sleep.

The heavy vehicle moved off. The silver bell rang sixteen times for the interior and once for the upper deck. The conductor called for ticket payment, and the *sous* passed from hand to hand. The tall brunet began to examine the travel companions that chance had given him. He found only two there that were worth his trouble to study their face and their appearance, and those two were exactly across from him. He hadn't forgotten anything of the little scene that had preceded the departure. To do him justice, he was about to offer his seat when the man in the derby hat had stood to give up his. He had certainly noticed the hand squeeze exchanged between the lady and the kind gentleman. He told himself that could be the beginning of an affair, and, if he couldn't hope to see the end of it, he promised himself to at least observe the incidents which might happen during the trip. It already seemed to him that the two people of this traveling drama formed a rather badly contrasting couple. The woman, who had agreed a little too quickly to become indebted to an unknown man, evidently wasn't from the same social class as her second-hand knight, because her dress was almost elegant. She seemed to have a pretty figure and her eyes shone through the dark blonde veil that she stubbornly refused to lift. It didn't take anything more for an inquisitive mind to occupy itself with her, and the artist seated in front of that mysterious person had an inquisitive mind.

He divided his attention between the veiled lady and the young woman seated beside her. That person also had lowered the veil attached to her maroon velvet cap, and one could hardly see anything but the lower part of her face, a

17

dimpled chin with a somewhat wide mouth, but with a very clean outline, and pale cheeks of a lusterless pallor.

"A Spanish complexion," the tall brunet said to himself. *"I'm sure she's charming. What a pity the cold keeps her from showing the tip of her nose. However little the thermometer descends, they all now have the mania to mask themselves when they go out. When you want to meet a pretty face you have to wait for summer. Still, if there was light in this devil of an omnibus, but one of the lanterns is out and the other is smoking like a tallow candle burned out. You can't see a thing. We're in a rolling cave. You could commit crimes here that nobody would know about."*

Continuing to observe, the tall brunet recognized that the young girl couldn't be rich. In the middle of January she was wearing a little short coat without sleeves, called *une visite,* of a black material so thin and so worn out that you froze just looking at it, an alpaca dress, Corinth grape-colored, that long wear had made shiny. She was hiding her hands in a skimpy muff which had lost some of its outside cover, a muff that in the past must have been bought for a twelve-year-old girl.

"Who is she? Where does she come from? Where is she going?" the young man wondered. *"And why is the woman sitting next to her looking at her out of the corner of her eyes. Does she know her? No, because she's not speaking to her."*

However, the omnibus had made good time. It was now rolling along the Pont Neuf, and the coachman, who was in a hurry to finish his day, whipped up his horses to a fast trot up the incline which descends toward the Quai du Louvre. Public transportation vehicles don't have such good suspension as the eight-spring *calèches*, and this sudden movement had the effect of greatly bouncing the travelers about. The young woman was thrown against her neighbor, the one last arrived, and clung to her arm, uttering a weak cry that was followed by a deep sigh.

"Lean against me, if you aren't feeling well, Mademoiselle," said the veiled lady.

The other woman didn't answer, but she let herself fall on the shoulder of the compassionate woman who offered to support her.

"That young woman is not well," exclaimed the tall brunet man. "The bus must stop, and I'm going..."

"Not at all, Monsieur; she's sleeping," the veiled lady said calmly.

"Pardon! I thought..."

"She was already sleeping when the jolts suddenly woke her up. But she's already going back to sleep. Let's let her rest."

"Leaning on you, Madame! Aren't you afraid..."

"That she'll tire me? Oh! Not at all. And she won't fall, I'll answer for it, because I'm going to hold on to her," continued the lady, passing her right arm around the sleeping girl.

The tall brunet man bowed without insisting. He had good manners and he thought he had already done too much in getting mixed up in what didn't concern him.

"Young girls today, they're pitiful," the fat woman in the bonnet said between her teeth. "Me, I've pushed my cart all evening selling oranges, and, if it was necessary, I still have legs strong enough to climb on foot right to the top of Montmartre. Ah! If that girl there was going dancing at the *Boule Noir* or at the *Elysée*, that would wake her up. But to go home to mama, *bernique*! There isn't anybody who can do that anymore."

She didn't get any reaction to her comments. The young girl she was talking about didn't move at all. The neighbor whose shoulder served as her pillow pretended not to have heard, and the artist, seated in front of the two women, didn't say a word, although he really wanted to rebuke that badly informed old gossip somewhat sharply.

He began to observe again and he was almost softened when he saw the veiled lady gently take hold of the naked hands of the sleeping girl and put them back in the worn muff that poor girl carried tied to her shoulder by a frayed string.

"A mother couldn't have taken better care of her child," he thought. *And me, who took that excellent woman for someone trying to start an affair. Why? I wonder. Because she accepted a gentleman's seat? Because she thanked him by letting him squeeze the tips of her fingers? Well, that's what the gallant man got for his politeness and maybe a chest cold, because he must be freezing up there. So much for that. I'd really like to see the face of that girl who's sleeping so soundly. The lines at the bottom of the face are perfect. She must not be rolling in gold, that little girl, to judge by her clothes. I would bet she would willingly consent to a head pose. If she stops on the way, I'll amuse myself by following her. But as we get off, if she goes as far as the Place Pigalle, I'll suggest to her that she sit for me some time. Let's hope she opens her eyes before the end of the ride."*

The omnibus was still traveling at a speed which would put *fiacres* to shame. The two vigorous Percheron horses pulling it outdistanced all the nags that those who rent vehicles on the street harness up as soon as the sun goes down. When no passenger is pulling the bell to get off they go even faster. The coachman, who doesn't have to hold them back to let someone descend, pushes them as much as he can. He hardly halts at the required stops. There was no one to pick up on the Rue du Louvre; nobody either at the office on the Rue Croix-des Petits-Champs. But the Place de la Bourse there was some change. Three women seated at the entrance of the vehicle were replaced by a middle-class family, a father, a mother, and a little boy. But the travelers at the back didn't budge.

The young girl was still sleeping, leaning against her charitable neighbor. The woman who sold oranges had finally dozed off. Some other women were dozing too. After the station on the Rue de Chateaudun, when the team, rein-forced by a third horse, began to climb the hard side of the Rue des Martyrs, the inside of the omnibus resembled a dormitory. The massive machine was rolling along like a ship balanced on a swell. It rocked the passengers so gently that almost all of them, little by little, let their head nod and closed their eyes. There was hardly anyone but the tall brunet who was sitting upright. The conductor walked up and down to stretch his legs and the coachman cracked his whip to get warm.

At the last third of the ascent, the fat gossip woke up with a start, and shouted that she wanted to get off. The spot was not convenient to stop because the slope is so steep that the horses slide and go backwards as soon as they stop going forward. Women who insist on putting their feet on the ground before getting to the top of the escarpment must have the conductor's help. This is what the obese woman did, not without grumbling, using not very gracious words to the good employee who didn't come quickly enough to catch her in his arms. She rushed toward the exit, crushing her neighbors' toes. When she had touched the pavement she started to yell out that she had gotten off too soon, that she should have waited until the Avenue Trudaine because she lived on the Clignancourt carriageway, and 100 other recriminations which didn't move any-one.

However, she decided to walk and the omnibus, which was almost at the top, continued its climb.

At this moment, the artist, who was still thinking about the two women seated in front of him, was brusquely distracted from his reverie by a noise which came from the top of the omnibus, the noise of three boot heel taps, three successive vigorous blows separated by a short interval.

"Well!" he said to himself, *"that's the traveler on the upper deck who's giving foot signals like a master at arms. It seems he's still there. There's one that ten degrees below zero doesn't bother. Ah! But he's had enough because he's deciding to come down."*

In fact, the boots which had just brought about this rumbling appeared on the upper stairway, the legs followed, then the torso, and finally the man, after having thrown a rapid glance into the inside of the omnibus, jumped down to the pavement. The painter, who had watched these movements, saw him walk away hurriedly down the Rue de la Tour-d'Auvergne.

"So," he thought, *"That good man with such heavy boots doesn't have the intention that I thought he had. I was supposing that he'd wait at the exit for the lady who'd accepted his seat and that he'd almost try to make her accept his arm. Not at all. He's going quietly away, alone. He's right, because that lady doesn't seem to me to be in the mood to become friendly with gentlemen of his type.*

While he was holding this judicious discourse with himself, the omnibus reached the point where the Rue des Martyrs crosses two other very busy streets, the Rue de Laval on the left, and the Rue Condorcet on the right. It always stops there in order to unhitch the extra horse, and also because on that stretch of the line, it often happens that the carriage empties. The male travelers, and above all the female travelers, get off en masse. And that evening it was exactly the same. Almost all the women stood up at the same time, and it was a question of who would get out first. There was such a general and complete rush to the outside that no one remained in the interior but the tall brunet and the two women seated in front of him. Still, the woman supporting the sleeping girl seemed to be getting ready to leave also.

"Monsieur," she said quickly, "That poor child that was leaning on me is having such a good sleep. I would reproach myself if I woke her. However, I have to get off. I live near here and it's late. Do I dare ask you to take my place in my function as an altar of rest?"

"With the greatest pleasure," answered the young man, sitting down in the seat the fat orange merchant had just left.

"Wait just a moment, please," cried out the charitable lady to the conductor, who was about to give the signal to depart.

At the same time she lifted, with infinite precautions, the head of the young girl who was leaning on her shoulder. She placed it gently on the shoulder of the tall brunet, ready to receive it. The sleeping girl let this be done without giving a sign of life and collapsed so completely that the neighbor to whom she was confided thought it necessary to hold her by the waist.

"I thank you, sir," said the veiled lady. "I don't like to leave her alone, but since you're going to the end of the line, I can leave her. If you could take her right to the door of the house where she's going, you'll surely do a good deed, because, at this hour this neighborhood is dangerous for a young girl."

And without waiting for an answer from the man to whom she directed the request, she slid rapidly out of the omnibus, which had just started up the Rue de Laval. The conductor was leaning in the corner, at the entry to the vehicle, above the ticket meter, and he was busy verifying, by the fleeting gas light, the last checks on his list. The painter remained then completely alone with the beautiful sleeper. No one could have kept him from saying sweet things to her or asking her to sit for a portrait, but to do that, it was first necessary to wake her, and he wanted to behave properly. He pulled her discretely against his chest and he hoped that increasing that decent pressure a little he would manage to bring her out of her torpor. He was wrong. In vain he pressed a little more. His hand couldn't feel the heartbeat of that child, who, nevertheless, must not have been, accustomed to letting herself be hugged in this way. Then the thought came to this bad boy that she was not so much asleep as she wanted to appear, that she wouldn't ask anything better than to become obligated to him. He was a Parisian. He had experience and intuition. So he believed very little in the virtue of young girls who get in omnibuses all alone at a quarter to midnight, and who go, at that untimely hour, toward the outside boulevards.

21

He wanted to know how he should act. He leaned forward a little to see the face of that stubbornly sleeping girl up close. But the last lantern, the one that had been sputtering since the departure, had finally gone out, and the interior of the vehicle was plunged in complete darkness. He leaned forward close enough to almost touch the young girl's face. He saw that she was pale as alabaster and that no breath was coming out of her partially open mouth. He took one of her hands which had remained in the muff, and he found that hand was icy.

"She has fainted," he murmured. "She needs help."

And he called the conductor, who answered him without moving.

"We're coming to the station. It's not worth stopping for such a small thing."

In fact, driven rapidly by a coachman in a hurry to go to bed and by horses that smelled the stable, the omnibus has gone down the Rue Frochot in a wink and was coming into the Place Pigalle. Frightened, the young man tried to lift the unfortunate child who had collapsed in his arms, but she fell back, inert, and only then did he understand that life had flown out of that poor body.

"Here we are, Monsieur," said the conductor, who took them for two lovers. "I'm very sorry to wake your lady. But we don't go any further. You have to get off, unless she wants to sleep in the carriage."

"It's in the grave where she'll sleep," the tall brunet called out to him. "Don't you see that she's dead?"

"So! You're joking to amuse yourself. Well, there, really, that isn't lucky, you know, that kind of joke. You should never laugh about death!"

"I have no desire to laugh. I tell you that woman has flesh as cold as marble, and she's no longer breathing. Come help me get her out of the omnibus. I can't carry her by myself."

"She shouldn't be very heavy. Nevertheless, if she's really sick, I'm going to give you a hand. We can't leave her there, that's for sure."

With that conclusion, the conductor grudgingly decided to get into the vehicle, where the tall brunet was doing his best to support the unfortunate child. The employee got in also and with the three of them they had no trouble lifting the frail body. The station waiting room hadn't yet closed. They carried her there and stretched her out on a bench. With a trembling hand, the young man lifted the veil which hid half of the dead girl's face. She was wonderfully beautiful, with the true face of a Raphael virgin. Her large black eyes no longer had any luster, but they were still open and her contracted features expressed an unspeakable pain. She must have suffered horribly.

"It really is true that she's passed on," murmured the conductor.

"During the trip! And you didn't notice it?" exclaimed the employee.

"No, and the lady sitting next to her didn't see anything either. That's strange, but that's how it was."

"Apoplexy, then…or it could be something gave way in her chest. "

"As for me, I think someone killed her," said the tall brunet.

"Killed!" repeated the conductor, "what do you mean! There's not a drop of blood on her."

"And then," added the employee, "if someone had struck her in the carriage, the other travelers would certainly have seen it."

"She's eighteen years old, at most. At that age you don't die suddenly," said the young man.

"Are you a doctor?"

"No, but,…"

"Well, then, you don't know any more about it than we do. And instead of useless talking, you should go look for the police. We can't keep a dead woman in the office."

"There're two of them coming."

And in fact, two policemen making their rounds were approaching with measured steps. The employee called to them and they came forward without very much haste, because they thought the case was hardly worth getting in a hurry. And when they saw what it was about, they were not unusually upset. They let the conductor tell them about the situation, and the older of the two gravely pronounced that these sorts of accidents weren't unusual.

"However, there's a gentleman who claims that somebody murdered her in the omnibus," said the man wearing a helmet with a capital O affixed.

"I'm not claiming anything at all," said the tall brunet. "I only swear that that death is most extraordinary. I was at first sitting across from that poor girl, and I..."

"Then you'll be called tomorrow to the police station and you'll tell what you know. Give me your name."

"Paul Freneuse. I'm a painter and I live in that big house that you can see from here."

"That one where there are nothing but artists. Good! I know it."

"What's more, here's my card."

"That's enough, Monsieur."

"The Commissioner will hear you tomorrow morning, but you can't stay here. They're going to close the office while my colleague goes to alert the post so they can send a stretcher. Fortunately it's not the kind of weather to sit outside in front of the cafes on the Place Pigalle. If it were summer, we would already have a crowd at the door."

That old soldier spoke with such assurance, and he must have had similar experience with tragic events, that Paul Freneuse began to doubt the validity of his own judgment. The thought of a crime had come to mind without his knowing very well why. He had to recognize that the facts absolutely contradicted it. The cadaver bore no apparent wound. Nothing had happened during the trip which allowed the supposition that the unfortunate child had been attacked.

"Obviously, I have too much imagination," he said to himself as he left to obey the wise injunction of the policeman. *"I see a mystery in a situation which*

happens every day. That little girl had a heart disease..., an aneurysm which broke and she was struck down. That was a pity because she was admirably beautiful. I can't do anything about it. I'd be very good and noble to waste my time opening an investigation about a simple short newspaper article. I have my painting for the Exposition at the Salon to finish. It's already too much that I interfered so as to be interrogated by a police commissioner to whom I have nothing serious to say. He'll very probably make fun of my extravagant ideas if I should decide to speak to him about the possibility of a murder... committed by whom, Bon Dieu? By that charitable lady I replaced at the corner of the Rue de Laval... and how?

Without a doubt by breathing on her young neighbor... That's absurd! Life isn't snuffed out like a candle."

The employee was already closing the shutters and the younger of the policemen was running to find some men to carry the body. The other one had placed himself in front of the office door to send away the curious, if any presented themselves. The conductor, who was talkative, was explaining to him how at the departure he had noticed that the young girl already looked sick. The coachman had remained on his seat, and he was having a great deal of trouble holding back his horses, impatient to return to the company's depot.

"Do you need me any more?" asked Freneuse.

And as the policeman made him a sign indicating no, he started on his way to his dwelling, which wasn't far away. He hadn't taken three steps when he remembered having let his cane fall in the carriage. That cane was a pretty rattan one that one of his friends, an officer in the navy, had brought him from China, and he was fond of it. The omnibus was still there. He climbed in, and, as you could scarcely see, he lit a match so as not to have to feel about with his hands. The cane had rolled under the bench. In stooping down to pick it up, he saw a paper which had also fallen and a golden pin, one of those women use to hold on their hat.

"Well, look here!" he muttered, "The poor dead girl lost this. I'll have something left to remember her."

Paul Freneuse picked up the cane, the paper and the pin, put the cane under his arm, the paper and the pin in the pocket of his overcoat, slowly got out of the omnibus and went away without turning around, for fear the policeman might decide to call him back. He now thought no more about getting involved in the following events of that sad adventure. He was promising himself to rest easy if the Commissioner didn't require his testimony.

Paul Freneuse had talent and a great many likeable qualities, but he somewhat lacked continuity in ideas. His head got fired up too easily and grew cold again even more quickly. He constantly threw himself into the most risky conjectures, a little like children chase after all the butterflies that fly in front of them; but he soon tired of chasing wild dreams. When he had become himself again, he thought only about his art, about his work, and also a little about his pleasures, although he led a rather regular life.

So that evening he had just gone through very lively emotions and he was already calmer. He had constructed a whole novel about the death of a young girl, and this novel grew dimmer and dimmer in his mind.

He was eager to get home, to see his studio, and he was going straight there, when, in a café which stood out like a cape of land between the Rue Pigalle and the Rue Frochot, he saw one of his friends, an artist like himself, sitting at a table in front of an empty glass and a stack of saucers. The saucers indicated the number of beers absorbed by that thirsty painter. That friend was alone in the first section of the café, a sort of glass cage, where you were as much in view as if you were drinking outside. You had a perfect view of the people passing by. He recognized Freneuse. He began to make telegraphic signs to call him and Freneuse decided to go in, knowing full well that if he dared to continue on his way, comrade Binos was going to run after him.

His name was Binos, that beer amateur, mediocre artist, but incomparable talker, practical philosopher, lazy as a dormouse, busy with everything except painting, although he always had two or three paintings in progress; in short, the best fellow in the world, the most helpful, the most disinterested, and above all the most amusing.

Freneuse, who never agreed with him on any point, couldn't do without him, and gladly consulted him for the pleasure of hearing him contradict everything and go off into bizarre paradoxes.

"There you are!" Binos yelled to him. "I've been chasing you all evening. Where're you coming from?"

"From an expensive neighborhood. I had dinner at the house of one of my cousins who's an intern at the Piété and who lives on the Rue Lacépède," answered Freneuse.

"And you got off the bus at the Halles wine market, when you should've come back on foot through a wonderful freeze. You will never be anything but a bourgeois."

"A bourgeois if you like, but a strange thing has just happened to me."

"In the omnibus? I see what it was. You missed the connecting omnibus."

"Don't joke. This is very serious. Look down there at what's happening."

"Well, what? The conductor is holding forth in the middle of five or six loiterers in front of the office door."

"There is a dead woman in that office…a ravishing young woman who was traveling with me…across from me at first and then beside me."

"Did she give up the ghost in your arms?" asked Binos still joking.

"Almost. And nobody was aware that she'd died."

"What tale are you telling me there?"

"I'm telling the truth. It's the most extraordinary thing, so extraordinary that a while ago I had almost come to believe that the death was not natural."

"A mystery to solve. That's my business. I was born to be a policeman. I would show the cleverest Sûreté police a thing or two. Tell me the story and I'll give you my conclusions as soon as I know the facts."

"The facts! But there aren't any. Everything happened the simplest way in the world. When I arrived at the Boulevard St. Germain station, the young girl was already in the car. I noticed that she was pretty and I sat down facing her. A fat woman was seated to her right, a gentleman to her left...a gentleman if you want to call him that...he looked like a former national guard drummer."

"Good! That's already one suspicious man."

"Suspicious or not, before the omnibus left, he gave his seat to a lady who'd arrived late...a real lady, that one...elegantly dressed and not at all ugly, as well as I could judge through her little veil."

"If she didn't raise it, that was because she had a reason to hide herself. And she accepted, without hesitating, the courtesy of the individual you've just described to me? Do you know what that proves? That they know each other and that the thing was agreed on between them in advance. The man was holding the seat. The woman took it and she's the one who struck the blow."

"But there was no blow," Freneuse cried out.

"You think that because you didn't see anything," said Binos, who was following his idea with imperturbable persistence. "I maintain once more that that exchange of seats isn't natural. Now I have a basis; that's enough for me. Continue. It was the last bus, wasn't it?"

"Yes. I ran from the Rue Lacépède in order not to miss it."

"One more reason that the man didn't get off. If he stayed, it was because he didn't want to leave."

"He didn't stay. He climbed to the upper level."

"Several degrees below zero make a cold wind that cuts the face. I get the picture now; he perched himself up there because he wanted to be sure that his accomplice completed the operation."

"Not at all. The man stepped to ground at the entry to the Rue de la Tour-d'Auvergne, and the woman a little further on...at the corner of the Rue de Laval."

"That is to say, three minutes afterward. They wouldn't have had any trouble rejoining each other. I am sure that in getting off the man stopped an instant on the pavement so that the woman could see that he was leaving."

"No, but I noticed..."

"What?"

"That before coming down from the upper level the man gave three or four taps with his heel so strong that everybody in the interior heard them."

"*Parbleu!* That was the signal."

"I admit that thought came to me."

"Ah! You see very well that you suspected them! Only you don't have the courage of your opinions."

"And you, when you start to ride an idea, you go a great deal too far. I admit, if you wish, that these people were in agreement, but not to kill an unfortunate girl they didn't know."

"How do you know?"

"I'm at least certain that she didn't know them, because she didn't do them the honor of looking at them. I'm rather inclined to think that the man was hoping at the beginning that the woman would pay him back for his courtesy by allowing him to accompany her. In getting on, she let her hand be squeezed."

"Better and better. I don't have the shadow of a doubt. That handshake meant: *Kill her!* "

"But you're crazy! I told you there wasn't the least incident during the trip."

"Well, the girl who's dead was living when she got in the omnibus, wasn't she?

"Oh! Very much alive. She was wearing a veil too, but her eyes were shining through the veil like two black diamonds."

"Good! And when she got here they were extinguished. When was it noticed that she had passed on?"

"I was the one who noticed it, at the moment when we arrived at the station in the Place Pigalle. For a short while she had been leaning her head on my shoulder, and I thought she was sleeping. I wanted to wake her, and..."

"What! On your shoulder! Then you were seated beside her? I thought that you were sitting across from her."

"The veiled lady who was her neighbor on her left supporting her from the Pont Neuf, thought as I did, that she was sleeping. When that lady got off on the Rue de Laval, she asked me to take her place. I didn't mind at all serving as a pillow for a young and pretty girl. The bench on her right was empty. I took it and the lady passed me a burden which seemed sweet to me."

"And you didn't find this sleep that nothing interrupted stupendous? Paul, my boy, you can dash off a genre painting quickly; but your naiveté goes beyond limits."

"I admit it; and, however,..."

"The lady knew perfectly well that she was putting a cadaver in your care, and she wasn't holding her except to keep her from falling. She had judged by your face that you weren't aware of anything. As soon as she could, she left you to get out of it by yourself. That was pretty daring, what she did there, and she might have played you a very bad trick. How did you get out of it when you arrived?"

"Ah, that. Are you insinuating that they could've accused me of murdering the woman beside me?"

"He! He! More extraordinary things have happened."

"Come now! I've just spoken with the police who verified the death. The body didn't have even a scratch."

"Well! There come some men from the police station with a stretcher to take her away."

"They asked me my name, that's all."

"They asked you for your name, and you gave it?"

"No doubt about it. Why would I've hidden it? Besides, I couldn't do anything else."

"That's a reason. It's certain that if you'd refused to say who you were, your refusal would've seemed shady. They would've suspected you."

"Suspected of what? I've already told you that girl died with a ruptured aneurism. Everybody who saw her had no doubt in that regard. The police, the station employee, the conductor..."

"All these people are as competent, one as well as the other, in matters of death! Don't say stupid things. You know as well as I do that a doctor will examine the corpse and that only he can settle the question. And whatever he decides, you can expect to be called to the commissioner's office."

"All right, I'll go. And I'll be sure not to take you with me. With the things you imagine and with your logic, you would upset the head of the most sensible man. Ah! You would make a terrible Investigating Magistrate! You see crimes everywhere."

"I see them where there are some, my friend. You've just witnessed a perfectly good murder, cleverly set-up and masterly executed. There'd be enough in that to supply newspaper copy for all the Paris newspapers for three months."

"You're crazy. Tomorrow the newspapers will print that a young girl died suddenly in an omnibus, and after tomorrow nothing more will be said of it."

"If the public is no longer interested in it, I'll make it my business."

"You want to act like the police for your amusement! You didn't need anything more than that. That does it."

"You have to use your free time to do something, and I have some time to spare."

"And your painting, wretched man, your painting, which should be ready for the Exposition and which is hardly begun!"

"I'll enter it for the spring. In the winter I'm never in the mood. So I have two months ahead of me, and inside of two months I'll have found the woman who pulled off this wicked deed."

"You mean the woman who was sitting beside the poor child?"

"Naturally."

"Pardon. There were two of them, one on the right, the other on the left of the poor little thing."

"The one who stayed on the bus right up to the Rue de Laval, and who so cleverly passed the cadaver to you."

"Will you please be good enough to explain to me how she was able to kill her neighbor without anyone noticing it."

"Gladly...as soon as you answer the question I'm going to ask you. You told me the girl was leaning against the veiled lady..."

"Yes. I even think the lady was holding her by the waist."

"Just when did she start to charitably put her arm around her?"

"Well, it seems to me it was after the downward incline of the Pont Neuf. The omnibus was going very fast, and a wheel must have gone over a big rock, because there was a very violent jolt. The little girl uttered a cry... oh! a very weak cry. She put her hand on her heart; she fell backward... probably the shock broke a vessel in her chest. She died without suffering...and almost without moving."

"That, in fact, couldn't be more like reality," Binos said ironically. "And then, after this light spasm, her head fell down...the good lady offered her shoulder...she put her arm like a belt around the child who no longer moved."

"You're describing the scene exactly as if you'd seen it."

"And you, who did see it, you just thought that young girl had suddenly gone to sleep and hadn't waked up."

"At first I didn't pay a great deal of attention. You couldn't see very well at the back of the carriage. The lanterns had almost gone out."

"*Parbleu*! I was sure of it. That rascal counted on the obscurity."

"But, once again, what method did she use to send into the next world, in less than ten seconds, a girl less than twenty-years-old and who could be expected to live? You're not going to maintain to me, I suppose, that she stabbed her?"

"Stabbed, oh! no. There are surer and less noisy methods."

"Which?"

"Well...poison, for example...with a drop of cyanide you can strike down the healthiest man."

"When you pour it in his eyes, or on his tongue, yes..."

"Or on a simple scratch on the skin. You're shrugging...All right! I don't claim I'll convince you this evening. Maybe tomorrow you'll realize I'm right. I'll come up to your studio in the afternoon. Until then, I'm going to leave you. There are the stretcher-bearers carrying away the body. I'm going to stroll around outside the station to find out a little concerning what they're saying about this story. I know the police sergeant. He'll tell me what he knows."

And the policeman by calling dashed out of the café, yelling out to his friend: "You can pay for my drinks. I had only fourteen beers."

29

II. The Painter's Studio

Days follow days and none is ever like the other, says the proverb. The day following that sad omnibus trip which ended in a catastrophe, a beautiful winter sun lit up the Place Pigalle. The temperature had suddenly turned mild, the fountain, no longer frozen, launched its gay jet of water toward the blue sky, and the Italian models, seated on the steps around its basin, smiled with wellbeing in the rays of the star which warmed them during the long wait in front of the art studios.

Paul Freneuse was as joyous as the weather. A night of rest had calmed his emotions of the previous evening and chased away the gloomy visions. He thought no more of that adventure except to pity the poor dead girl and to congratulate himself for not having taken seriously the ridiculous imaginations of his friend Binos. In the morning he'd received the visit of an inspector sent by the Commissioner, more to talk with him than to interrogate him. The accidental death had been completely and duly confirmed by the doctor charged with examining the body, which bore no trace of violence. The young girl must have succumbed to an internal hemorrhage and, while waiting for the doctor's conclusions to be confirmed by an autopsy, had been sent to the morgue to be laid out there, because no mark of identification had been found on her which could be used to establish her identity. In addition, the facts didn't allow any supposition that a crime had been committed. The testimony of the conductor was very clear. In giving a deposition before the Commissioner, he didn't hesitate to mock the passenger, who, arriving at the station, cried out that someone had just murdered the young girl. He had easily demonstrated that this gentleman's opinion was not based on common sense.

The passenger was Paul Freneuse, whom the Commissioner knew quite well by reputation, because his name was already well known and he wasn't hard to find, since he had left his address with the policemen.

But Paul Freneuse had completely changed his opinion, so much so that he judged it absolutely useless to report to the inspector the absurd logic which that fool Binos had regaled him with while drinking beer. He limited himself to telling what he had seen without afterthought and without commentary. And, everyone being in agreement, Freneuse, freed of a rather disagreeable preoccupation, had eaten lunch with a good appetite and had begun work with enthusiasm. He was at that time finishing a painting which he was counting on a great deal to carry off, at the up-coming Salon, one of those successes which definitively establish an artist: a figure of a woman, just one, a young Roman girl watching over a goat at the foot of the tomb of Cecilia Metella.[15] And he had had the good luck to discover a model that God seemed to have created expressly to furnish him with the type he was dreaming of.

She was a very young girl, almost a child, that he had met one day coming down from the top of Montmartre, who had asked him the way to the Jardin des Plantes. Freneuse had spent four years in Rome and he knew enough Italian to answer the little girl in the only language she understood well. Then he inquired what she was doing in Paris. Without embarrassment she answered him that she had just arrived, brought by one of her countrymen who made a living collecting models of both sexes in Italy. He lodged them on the Rue Fosses-Saint-Bernard, near the wine merchants of the Halles in a big house full of accordion players and other wandering musicians. She was born in Subiaco, in the Sabine mountains. She had spent her childhood herding goats across the rocks of that savage land. Her mother, who had died the year before, posed in the artists' studios in Rome. She had never known her father In Subiaco she was thought to be the daughter of a French painter, who, after having lived several years in Italy, had left without giving any thought to her. She had had an elder sister, but that sister had been taken away when she was very little by a man who recruited students to teach them to sing and to place them in Italian theatres.

Paul Freneuse, marveling at her beauty, at once had the idea of confiscating this totally unknown model for his profit—the child hadn't yet worked for any artist. He had immediately come to terms with the leader of her group. In consideration for a rather large sum, the leader of the group had signed a contract with him to lodge Pia—that was the little girl's name—separately and properly, and to send her every day to the Place Pigalle to pose, and to refuse offers which other painters might make. And for five months, Pia hadn't missed arriving at Paul Freneuse's at noon a single time. He treated her a great deal less like a paid model than like a friend.

Pia's beauty wasn't commonplace. The child didn't resemble those Italian "*bambines*" who all have the same big black eyes, the same somewhat full red lips, the same light brown complexion, to the point that you would have said they were poured from the same mould. She was certainly from the race which has furnished models for painters in all centuries, but she had an expression which is almost always lacking to girls from her country, a mobile and intelligent expression, something personal and alive. And that countenance wasn't deceptive. Pia had an open mind and an astonishing facility to understand everything, to assimilate everything. In a few months she had managed to speak French very well, which she didn't know a word of when she came to Paris. She

---

[15] Cecilla Metella, daughter-in-law of Crassus, the richest man in Rome, and daughter of Consul Creticus, the Roman general who crushed the Spartacus slave rebellion. Built between 40 and 50 B. C., her tomb is the finest surviving monument on the Appian Way.

amused Freneuse with her naïve remarks and her unexpected retorts. She astonished him by the accuracy of her ideas about everything in life and even in the arts, for which she had a very keen appreciation. She astonished him even more by her wisdom. That little marvel, who never showed herself anywhere without being admired, hadn't the shadow of coquettishness and knew how to keep too eager admirers at a distance. She had kept her native costume, without spoiling it with additions from Parisian fashions, which girls like her willingly permitted themselves. No shawl had ever covered her still somewhat thin but charmingly curved, shoulders; shoes had never imprisoned her feet, accustomed to tread naked on mountain thyme.

And she lived like a saint, never going out except to come to Freneuse's studio, not associating any more with her countrymen than with the other women who followed the scabrous modeling profession in Paris. Thanks to Freneuse's generous advances, she was no longer reduced to living that communal existence which poverty imposes on poor girls brought from Italy by a master who exploits them. She still lived in the house on the Rue Fosses-Saint-Bernard, but she was completely separated from the vagabond colony which camped in that sort of dormitory life. She lived alone in a small bedroom under the roofs, a narrow attic room with whitewashed walls, where the only furniture was an iron bed, three caned bottom chairs, and a broken mirror. Whatever time remained to her there, after posing in the studio, she spent reading and singing songs from her mountains, and dreaming...about what? Freneuse sometimes amused himself by asking her. And she answered him that she didn't really know herself. Maybe she was dreaming about her fifteenth birthday which had just passed.

What she earned posing for her benefactor was enough for her, and even more, because she hardly ate any more than a bird, and she spent very little money for personal expenses, although she was very careful about her person and her clothes. And she was gay, as Roman women seldom are, gay with that open gaiety which contentment with oneself and absence of cares bring. When she came into Paul's studio, joy entered with her. However, for about a month, Freneuse thought he had detected that she laughed less, was more reserved, more pensive, less of a child, to sum it up. She no longer played with the studio's favorite cat, a superb angora that had taken a liking to her and that always jumped into her lap as soon as she sat down to pose. These symptoms seemed serious to the artist. He knew some personalities like that, these little girls transplanted from Italy to France, who languish when they are first in our cold climate and who mature suddenly at the first rays of the sun. And he suspected the beginning of a little love affair.

To clear up the matter, he had gently questioned the little girl, who began to cry instead of answering, and he hadn't wanted to insist, although the idea which came to mind saddened him. Freneuse had become attached to that child and it distressed him to think that she was perhaps going to stupidly fall in love with some coarse shepherd come from Abruzzi to Paris to earn a lot of money playing the hurdy-gurdy. He wondered sometimes if he was not jealous of her, and he reproached himself for forgetting that he was twenty-nine, almost the double of Pia's age. Then he became grave, almost cold, and the session of the pose went by without his saying a single word to the poor child, who went away with a heavy heart.

But the day following his omnibus adventure, Paul Freneuse had one of his good days. The certainty of not being mixed up, even indirectly, with a judicial inquiry made him completely joyous and he chatted gaily with the little female goatherd at the back of the studio half leaning against a high step ladder meant to represent a block of marble standing out from Cecilia Metella's tomb.

"Pia, my beautiful one," said Paul Freneuse, laughing, "you don't know that yesterday evening I almost climbed your six floors to surprise you. I had gone to dine in your neighborhood."

"And you didn't come to see me," exclaimed the young girl. "I would've been so happy to show you my room...It's so pretty now. I have three pots of flowers and a bird that sings really well. I owe all that to you."

"I. was afraid of disturbing you. Your attic room is hardly any bigger than your bird's cage. And then, to drop in on you, without telling you... *ma foi*! I didn't dare. I might have run into your lover."

Pia turned pale and her eyes filled with tears.

"Why do you say that to me?" she murmured. "You know very well that I don't have a lover."

"Come now, little girl," Freneuse continued gaily. "Don't cry. The makes you ugly and destroys the pose. Did you cry when you took your goat to pasture, down there, in the mountains?"

"No, never, and not here either, except when you try to vex me. You're the only one who makes me cry."

"And also laugh. Come on now, laugh a little, or I'll think you're angry with me. I was not speaking seriously."

"All right! See, I'm not thinking about it any more. But, please, don't say that I have a lover. Where would I get one, *Mon Dieu*? Down there, in the house, all the boys who work for Old Man Lorenzo are ugly and mean as monkeys. Then on the Place Pigalle? On the fountain steps? But if you look out the window when I'm coming, you'll see that I never stop there. I'm in too much hurry to get into your studio to get warm and to hug my friend Mirza; he's my lover."

The angora purring near the stove heard his name and jumped with a bound into Pia's lap. She, laughing, continued. "He really loves me, that one. He comes without my calling him and he never causes me pain."

"You're right, little one. Mirza is a good cat. He's better than I am and than that animal Binos, who never comes here except to torment you."

"Oh! Him. I don't care...but you, Monsieur Paul, as soon as you make fun of me, I can't keep my head, or the pose. See! I haven't moved since the beginning of the sitting, and now that you've upset me, I don't know how to pose."

"As you were a while ago...your head back a little more. Look at me... put Mirza down and don't move."

Pia did as Freneuse told her and the cat went back to sleep in his favorite place.

"That's perfect like that," the painter continued, "and because you're nice, you can learn that I didn't go tell you good evening yesterday because it was too late when I passed near your street...a quarter to midnight... everybody was asleep in the barracks where Lorenzo lodges his "*pifferari.*"

"Me, I wasn't asleep," Pia said very low.

"At that untimely hour! That's really very bad, little one. Little girls your age should go to bed like the sparrows, with the *Ave Maria*, as they say in your country."

"That's what I do every evening, but yesterday..."

"No explanations, Mademoiselle. You'll change positions again if you start to chat, and I have no time to lose. The light is already going and so that you won't be tempted to talk, I'll tell you a story of what happened to me...coming back from your accursed neighborhood. "

"Oh! Monsieur. Paul! I swear to you that I won't say a word."

"All the same! All the same! You may not talk, but my story will make you cry again...and right now I need your eyes."

"Nothing bad happened to you, I hope!"

"No. No. You can see that. I have never made so much progress working. If I continue working like this, my portrait will be finished in two weeks."

"And afterward...I won't come anymore?" Pia asked quickly.

"There you go! Your face has changed expressions again. Strike the pose, youngster, back to the pose! After this portrait I'll make another one...where you'll be standing...three hours on your feet. You'll be so tired you won't want to talk."

At this moment the studio door opened brusquely, and Binos came in like an exploding shell, crying out:

"I saw her, my friend. She is wonderful!"

"Who?" asked Freneuse.

"*Parbleu!* The dead woman. I've come from the morgue. She's been laid out there for an hour...and is there a crowd!"

Binos had no sooner gotten out the words: "I've come from the morgue," than Freneuse started to motion to him in a way that the meaning was very clear. But Binos never stopped once he had started, and he again picked up the thread of his discourse.

"You were right. She was admirable," he continued. "If she had wanted to pose while she was alive, she would have been paid twenty francs an hour. Pia is a model like you seldom see, right? Well, she doesn't come close to that one. I tried to make a rapid sketch while passing by the glass window, but the police made me circulate. There was a bourgeois there who said stupid things to me. He called me heartless, that imbecile. I have more heart than he does. What I was doing was in the interest of art. Fortunately, they're going to photograph her. Besides, when I saw that they were going to throw me out, I said to myself: *'There's just one thing to do,'* and I went immediately to ring..."

"Will you shut up, you damned blabber mouth?" Freneuse shouted at him. "If you say another word, me too, I'm going to throw you out."

"Why? What's the matter with you?" asked the second-rate artist with an amazed air.

"What's wrong with me is that you're keeping me from work and, next, you're frightening the little one with your vile stories."

"What! Because I'm talking about the morgue? Ah! she's nice, that one! But that will amuse her, on the contrary. I'll bet she never passes in front of that establishment without going in, and as she must pass it almost every day to come from her house..."

"Binos, my boy, for the second time, I order you to be quiet and I'm warning you that at the third warning, if you don't obey...you know how under the Empire they broke up public assemblies."

"Threats? Violence? What side of the bed did you get up on this morning? Yesterday evening all you could do was talk about your adventure."

"Again!"

"All right! All right! I didn't know that Pia was so impressionable. But from the moment Mademoiselle has hysterics, I'll be silent as the grave... until she leaves. However, afterward, I have a lot of things to tell you."

"Until then leave me alone. I don't have any time to waste. Get back into the pose, my dear Pia, and if this fool lets himself open his mouth, please me by not listening to him."

"The morgue, that's the building where they expose the dead?" the child asked, upset.

"That's enough! You too, you're getting mixed up in it," exclaimed Freneuse.

"So you've both sworn that I won't do anything today."

"I know where it is," continued Pia;" but I haven't dared to go in, and I'll never dare...oh! no, never! ...never!"

"*Parbleu*! I should hope not. If you took a notion to, I'd never have you back here. But you don't seem to me to be in the mood to stay quiet on your stepladder, and I'm going to shorten the session. Three more minutes of immobility, and it'll be finished, little girl. Just a touch to give, ...I was beginning to catch the expression when that animal Binos came to disturb us. Ah! I've got it now...Don't budge any more."

Pia was careful not to. She had become thoughtful and her big black eyes had lost all expression. They stared vaguely at Mirza, that had just awakened and was arching his back.

Binos, to console himself for not talking any more, poked around in all the corners of the studio, turning pictures backward on the wall, opening paint boxes, and upsetting the easels.

He did this so long that Freneuse, impatient, called out to him.

"Will you stop moving around? What are you looking for?"

"Some tobacco. I forgot to buy any," answered the scoundrel, shaking a long pipe which seldom left him.

"The jar is at the foot of the mannequin, under the window."

"Good. You're not going to carry your hard-heartedness to the point of forbidding me to smoke? Thanks for your kindness, my prince. Ah! But what about this? That's a bad joke; the jar's empty. There's no more tobacco in it than there are brains in the cranium of my bourgeoise in the morgue."

"Haven't you been enough of a pain! Go look for my tobacco pouch in the pocket of my overcoat, hanging over there."

"I'm obeying, my lord," Binos answered gravely, carrying both his hands to his forehead in imitation of an Oriental salute. And he began to rummage around in the coat while Freneuse, who was wiping his brushes, was saying to Pia:

"That's enough for today, little one. I can't see anymore."

"What a joke! What a joke!" grumbled Binos. "I've wasted my time looking in the depths of this luxurious piece of clothing. I don't see your joke. I don't find anything at all...that is to say, yes, I do. My searching fingers have found an object which I could use to clean my pipe...after I've smoked it. Let's look at that a little...What do you know...a woman's hat pin!"

Binos, delighted with his find, triumphantly brandished the golden pin which he had just taken out of his friend's overcoat.

"Ah! my boy," he exclaimed. "You stuff your clothes with objects useful to the fair sex! Who is the princess which left you this token of her love?"

Freneuse had completely forgotten that pin he had picked up in the autobus, and he found inappropriate the remarks his comrade Binos allowed himself apropos of an object which had, in all probability, belonged to the dead woman.

"Please put that pin back where you found it!" he shouted to him.

"You think I'm going to profane it by using it for vulgar purposes," the incorrigible jokester said ironically. "Don't worry! I won't use it. You could still carry it over your heart. Ah, well, you've fallen in love now? Since when?"

"Binos, you really are irritating me."

Pia had suddenly gotten up and had run to look closer at the pin.

"What do you say about that, mountain child," the scoundrel asked her." You never wore anything like that at Subiaco...and you've had the good taste not to wear it in Paris. The bourgeoise who planted this trinket in her hair is unworthy to love an artist...and Paul should be ashamed of holding on to this pitiful relic...the ridiculous product of Parisian manufacturers, bought in a bazaar for fifteen *sous*. Help me, little girl, to shame our friend for his grotesque adoration for the owner of this deplorable ornament. What! You're crying! Why the devil are you crying! Could it by chance be that you want it? Could you have the misguided fantasy to dishonor your beautiful hair by ornamenting it with that gold plated, imitation needle?"

"I'm not crying," murmured the young girl, trying to hold back her tears.

"Binos, you're insupportable." Freneuse exclaimed. "I forbid you to torment that child. You're the one who put her nerves on edge with your wild talk. Let her leave in peace. Put on your coat, Pia, and go quickly toward the Rue des Fosses-Saint-Bernard. Night's coming on and the streets aren't safe for you after sundown. Try to come tomorrow exactly at noon. I'll barricade my door so that one of my annoying acquaintances...and yours...doesn't disturb us and we'll have a long sitting."

Pia was already ready, and, as Freneuse held out his hand to her, she leaned over to kiss it, after the Italian custom. He quickly drew her up and kissed her on the forehead. The child turned pale, but she didn't say a word and she left without looking at Binos, who was laughing in his beard.

"My friend," he began as soon as she had disappeared, "I've made in one day more discoveries than the most famous navigators have made in a century, and the last is the most interesting of all. I've just discovered that the transplanted shepherdess is madly in love with you. She was crying because she thought that pin had been forgotten in your pocket by your mistress. She's jealous. Therefore she adores you. Refute this logic, if you dare,...and if you can."

"I don't refute anything at all, but if you go on like this, I assure you we're going to have a falling out."

"Well, where does it come from, this skewer that a forty-franc restaurant could use to serve kidneys? Is it a souvenir of the beloved woman? I believed you were thinking of taking one for the right reason. People say they've seen you recently in elegant drawing rooms, where they show off well brought up young ladies who would gladly marry an artist, provided he earns 40,000 francs a year, and you must be coming close to this imposing figure. You shouldn't hide it like that. If you want to abandon your comrades, say so."

"Binos, my friend, you're ranting and I ought not to answer you, but you have to answer fools. I must tell you that I found that pin yesterday evening. I kept it as a souvenir. It must have been attached to the hat of the young girl who gave up her soul during the trip."

"That! Well! This is a piece of jewelry cooks put on for their Sundays off. I can tell you that the marvelous creature reposing now on one of the morgue slabs never cheated her employers by inflating the shopping receipts. I would rather believe that it was lost in the omnibus by one of her neighbors."

"Then I make you a present of it," said Freneuse.

"I accept," Binos exclaimed. "That's a clue. It takes the least thing. It doesn't matter what, to convict a murderer...a nothing...a piece of paper... a sleeve button forgotten at the scene of the crime. In melodramas they call that the finger of God."

"Well! There you go with your craziness again."

"Craziness as much as you like. An idea just hit me, and I'm going to do an experiment under your eyes. Where is Mirza? Come here, Mirza!' Mi! Mi! Mi!," Binos purred in a caressing voice.

"What do you want with my cat? Don't bother him, please."

Mirza, tempted by the gesture of the scoundrel, came toward him slowly, sedately, as is proper for a cat that respects himself.

"Don't go, Mirza," said Freneuse. "You find out very well this gentleman is teasing you. He doesn't have anything to give you."

"I didn't bring him a treat, that's clear," grumbled Binos. "I don't allow myself to take care of my friends' cats, but I can certainly pet them. Mirza's a disinterested animal. Mirza loves me for myself. Let him show his affection by rubbing up against me."

While talking about one thing and another to distract his friend's attention, the devilish scoundrel had sat down on a stool and held out a treacherous hand to the too trusting angora that was coming forward with careful steps. Freneuse, although he saw Binos' movements, did not see that he held the gold-plated pin between his fingers, He hid it so well that only the end of it went out further than his thumb and his index finger, a sharp point like that of a sewing needle. Mirza himself saw it, but he was a gourmand and curious,—these are the least faults of cats living in a good household—and he came forward to smell what a friend of his master was offering him. His muzzle came in contact with the pointed object. Binos took advantage of the situation to lightly stick the pink nose of the poor beast, who took one step backward, just one. His head fell back on his shoulder, his long silky hair stood up, his shoulders slumped, his paws spread apart and became stiff, his jaws opened up, his eyes became dim. But he didn't give that prolonged *miouw* which is the cats' moan. He didn't jump. He remained motionless and mute. Then a convulsive trembling shook his whole body, and, at the end of twenty or thirty seconds, he fell all at once.

"What have you done to Mirza?" Freneuse cried out, rushing to lift up the household animal he was fond of. And as soon as he had touched it:

"It's dead," he said, very upset.

"Yes, just like the young girl in the omnibus," Binos said tranquilly.

"You killed it," the artist said again, angrily. "This goes beyond joking. Leave here and never set foot here again."

"You're throwing me out?"

"And you certainly deserve it, because you've taken everything I love. It hasn't been a half hour since you came in here, and you've done nothing but wicked things. Pia left in tears, and you were the cause of it. The only thing left for you to do was to murder an unfortunate beast that was the joy of my studio. Really, if I didn't know that you're three-quarters mad, it wouldn't be enough just to throw you out. I would ask you the reason for your odious behavior."

"That would be amusing," laughed Binos,"excessively amusing! Drag me along the ground and thank me by sticking a sword through me because I saved your life. That's the limit."

"You saved my life, you!"

"Neither more nor less, my dear fellow."

"I'd be curious to know how. Are you going to maintain to me that my cat was rabid?"

"No. Mirza was a good angora and if he had any faults...as, for example, tearing my trousers to sharpen his claws...his death redeemed them, because he died for his master...and so that a great crime would not go unpunished."

"Some more of your wild imaginations!"

"Will you listen to me before throwing me out? I just ask you for ten minutes to prove to you that if I hadn't this genius idea, some misfortune would have happened to you."

"Ten minutes, all right! But after that..."

"Afterward you can do as you like...and me too, I'll do what I want to-Do you see this pin?"

"Yes, and if I'd known that you were going to use it to pierce Mirza's heart..."

"I didn't pierce his heart with it...look! There's not a drop of blood on his white fur. I hardly touched him on the muzzle...and he fell down stiff. Now do you understand what happened yesterday evening in the omnibus?"

"What? Do you mean to say...?"

"The poor girl who's in the Morgue was killed the same way that I've just killed Mirza, only they stuck her in the arm."

"With that pin?"

"*Mon Dieu,* yes. It didn't take anything more. And that little girl's suffering wasn't any longer nor any more painful than that of your cat."

"What! The pin would've been..."

"Poisoned, dear fellow, and you carried it in your overcoat pocket. Feeling around for your handkerchief and your tobacco pouch in that pocket, your fingers sooner or later would have encountered the point of that instrument and at the next exposition there would've been one painting and one medal fewer. It's a miracle that I'm still alive," Binos continued. "If I'd picked up the pin by the point instead of by the golden ball which crowns the other end, I'd be at this time stretched out on your studio floor, and you wouldn't have anything else to do but have me buried. My death wouldn't be a disaster, and art wouldn't lose a great deal by it, but even so, I prefer that the accident happened to your cat."

"Me too," murmured Freneuse, troubled so much he didn't know where he was.

"Thanks for that good word," said the scoundrel, with an ironic grimace. "I can state with pleasure that you're no longer angry with me for having saved you...and I sincerely congratulate you for having picked up this little instrument in the omnibus. It will help me find the ones who made it."

"A pin which can kill! That's unbelievable."

"The facts are there."

"But these poisons that can strike one down, those doesn't exist except in novels or in plays."

"And among the savages, dear friend. They dip the end of their arrows in it when they go hunting or to war, and all the wounds made by the arrows are mortal. That's well known."

"Yes, I certainly have read that somewhere, but..."

"And the poison they use is well-known also. It's curare. It's claimed they make it with the venom of the rattlesnake and they know it can be kept indefinitely when it's dry. Look! See that coating which looks like varnish and which is spread over the point of that pin. There's the chemical product with which you could destroy a Prussian regiment in less than five minutes. I've always regretted that we didn't rub our bayonets with it during the siege..."[16]

"Speak seriously now. There's nothing to joke about, if what you imagine is real."

"Are you still in doubt? You have only to examine Mirza to convince yourself. He was marvelously healthy. A slight prick was enough to snuff out his life. And you saw that he died without shaking and without a sound. Scarcely an almost imperceptible tremor...an instant of immobility...then the fall, and it was all over. Exactly the scene in the omnibus."

"That's true. She only cried out very faintly,...she stiffened..."

"And her head fell on her neighbor's shoulder, after which she didn't budge. The deed was done."

"What! That miserable creature on her left would..."

"I'm going to tell you all about the situation! You can throw me out, if you want to, after I've finished."

Freneuse showed by a gesture that he no longer was thinking about throwing his friend out, and that he pardoned him for Mirza's death.

"The instrument," Binos began again, "must have been made, prepared, and carried by the man who climbed up on the second story of the omnibus. A woman wouldn't have known how to manipulate the poison, and probably she wouldn't have dared. Examine, please, this portable dart. It is completely new, and it is difficult to imagine anything more ingenious. It looks like a hat pin. It looks innocent and if anyone had snatched it from between the hands of the wicked woman who used it, no one would have taken it to be what it was. It has a little ball on one end so that some one could give it a hard push without harming himself. It's short enough so that it could be hidden in a lady's muff, long and pointed enough to go through the thickest clothing...and the little one was wearing a dress whose worn material hardly protected her any better than a spi-

---

[16] Reference to the Siege of Paris 1871—the fall of Paris to the Prussians.

der's web. To sum it up, everything was foreseen by that man, who must be a very great villain. And it's the woman who was in charge of the execution."

"Why her? Then, this miserable man was too cowardly to do the deed himself!"

"It wasn't that. He'd calculated that the woman would draw the attention of the other travelers a lot less. They wouldn't have found it natural that the young girl would lean her head on a male neighbor's shoulder; whereas on the shoulder of the woman sitting next to her, that was quite simple."

"He guessed then that she would expire in that way..."

"Perfectly, my friend. Curare's effects are as well known as those of arsenic. They've experimented in the laboratory of the *Collège de France* a hundred times with this pretty poison. The animal that's pricked stops, leans to the right and the left and falls, ...if there's no one there to support him. The plan then was to support the dead girl right up to the time there was an opportunity to get rid of her without any danger. Impossible to leave her there. She would have fallen full length, and there would've been a scene the killer didn't want to get involved in."

"Then you think the man didn't settle on a location in the omnibus except to save a seat for his accomplice?"

"Not only do I think so, but I'm sure of it. Did you get in the omnibus before he did? Did you see him enter?"

"I was one of the first to arrive. The girl followed me a little afterward, and she had hardly sat down across from me when the man got in."

"And, of course, he went directly to sit down beside her."

"Yes, although there were other seats not occupied. For a moment I even had the idea that he knew her. But I soon saw they didn't speak to each other."

"Here's how the rascal must have operated. He stood in wait for the little girl outside the station. His accomplice, who'd been given his orders, waited a little further off."

"Then they knew the girl was going to take the omnibus?"

"Probably. How did they know it? That's what I'll find out later on, when I've tracked down these miserable creatures."

"Then you hope to find them?"

"*Parbleu*! I'm telling you that they were waiting until the little girl got in just so as to settle themselves in the seat next to the one she occupied. The accomplice, herself, waited until the bus was full. And then they acted out the comedy they had cooked up between them...the woman, distressed at not being able to leave, the man gallantly offering to give her his seat. We can bet the woman didn't hesitate to accept."

"She did, for form's sake. She exchanged some polite comments with him; but she got into the omnibus. She even allowed him to help her. She put her hand in his...a little hand, *ma foi*! and in a nice glove. She even left it there, so far as I could see, a little longer than was necessary."

"All right! That settles it."

"Do you mean to say that familiarity proves they were in agreement? *Ma foi*! It's certainly possible."

"It's certain, so much more certain since they left the omnibus at almost the same time. The man got off at the Rue de La Tour-d'Auvergne, and the woman on the Rue de Laval. But the prolonged hand squeeze proves something else, dear fellow."

"Then what?"

"The man was wearing gloves too, wasn't he?"

"Yes, heavy, fur-lined gloves, which must have been bought in an English shop. I noticed that detail."

"There was a reason for that. Those gloves were expensive, and the man, you told me, didn't seem to be well off."

"Not poor either. He looked like a non-commissioned middle class officer."

"Well! If he had gloves as thick as that, it was because he was afraid of pricking himself."

"How's that?"

"He was holding the pin, and he passed it on to the woman by lovingly squeezing the end of her fingers. Both of them knew that the least scratch would be fatal, and they had taken their precautions against accidents."

"So, according to you, at that moment the woman received the pin from her accomplice's hand... And she used it."

"Very cleverly, because no one saw anything. She waited for an opportunity, which came at the descent down the Pont Neuf. There was a jolt there, a jerk which threw her against her neighbor. She took advantage of it to drive the point of the instrument into the arm. On this point I don't have the shadow of a doubt. And I don't need to remind you of what happened afterward."

"Yes," Freneuse murmured. "All these events seem to follow each other logically. It's true you have a method to link them one to another."

"It's not a method; it's logic."

"Then explain to me how that terrible woman forgot, in the omnibus, that poisoned pin that would have betrayed her."

"You must believe she didn't do it on purpose. The pin dropped from her hand; a start from the unfortunate girl she had just killed made her drop it. And the wicked woman was careful not to bend down to pick it up. In the first place, she was afraid of pricking herself, and then she was no longer free to move about, because she had to support the dead woman. When the time came to descend, she couldn't wait to get out, and she left, might say, without asking for her belongings."

"She could've foreseen, however, that someone would find that concrete proof of her crime."

"Bah! She'd hope that the man charged with sweeping out the omnibus would push the object outside. What would follow hardly bothered her. What did it matter to her that the pin would bring death to people who'd have the fatal idea of picking it up and using it! A criminal of this kind, doesn't care about one murder more or less."

"The fact is that woman must be a monster. To kill a poor child she doesn't even know in that way; that's the coldest villainy…pointless cruelty."

"What!" Binos exclaimed. "Do you imagine she killed her just for the pleasure of killing her, or to try out her pretty instrument…just like the Marquise de Brinvilliers distributed poisoned cake to the poor people who begged her for charity, just to see the effect of the poison she was using! Freneuse, my friend, you're going too far. Those types of experiments have gone out of fashion because they're too dangerous. That creature knew very well what she was doing in using the pin against her neighbor. It was that girl she wanted to do away with, and not any other."

"But why! What had the unfortunate girl done to her?"

"That question I'm not yet in a position to answer. I need time to find out. I'll manage to do so, and we'll know later what we're dealing with. For the moment, I'll limit myself to swearing that the crime had a reason. There is always a reason to get rid of a woman, and there's more than one reason of this kind…revenge…jealousy…cupidity…"

"But why comment this crime in an omnibus in front of fifteen people…instead of…"

"Instead of waiting for the victim on a street corner, or going to kill her at her house, or still, dragging her into a house to strangle her. That seems bizarre at first, but that can be perfectly explained, however. Murder in a private house is a dangerous business. Suppose that woman or her accomplice had presented themselves at the girl's lodgings. The concierge or the neighbors would have been able to recognize them. That's a chance they didn't want to take. Suppose, on the contrary, the girl went to their house, or to the house of one of them, and she didn't come out again. That would have been still worse. How could they get rid of the cadaver? That's the stumbling block for murderers. To do the job in the street, that would have been easier, on condition of not doing it in full daylight. But, probably the girl went out very seldom in the evening. And, what's more, the victim would have to be alone and the street deserted. And what proves to us that girl was not accompanied by someone, a girlfriend or a boyfriend, who left her only very near the station? It was probably then that the wicked couple, who were perhaps following her, and who surely had been stalking her, decided to operate in the omnibus. Given the ingenious instrument they used, nothing was simpler. The hard part was to get away before anyone saw that the victim was dead, and you saw how they did that."

"Then you're going to locate them in Paris now! You wouldn't recognize them if you saw them. I might recognize the man. And yet, …I saw him only a short time…but the woman… I saw nothing but her eyes through a veil…"

"That's not enough. It's true you heard her voice."

"Yes, a well modulated voice, grave rather…a Parisian accent, it seemed to me, nothing else in particular. But if I couldn't manage to recognize them, I would really like to know how you, who've never seen them, you can flatter yourself that you can lay your hands on them."

"Oh! Me, I have my system. I will proceed from the known to the unknown, like mathematicians. When I find out who that young girl was, I'll look for the people she frequented. I'd be very stupid if, among those, I didn't discover someone who had an interest in getting rid of her."

"You're forgetting that the man and the woman on the omnibus were unknown to her, because she didn't say a word to them during the trip; therefore she didn't visit them."

"They acted for others."

"That's a very dangerous supposition. And, besides, your plan doesn't have a solid foundation. Nobody knows either the name or the residence of the dead woman."

"Pardon! She's laid out at the Morgue, and…"

"That certainly proves they found no identification on her."

"None, that's true. I found that out from the clerk of the establishment. I was going to tell you about my conversation with this public servant when you thought it proper to interrupt me under the pretext that I was frightening Pia. He told me that in her pockets he had found only a worn-out change purse which held the sum of fourteen *sous* and a little set of keys attached to a steel ring. Her underclothes bore no distinguishing mark. As for the rest, there was not a calling card, which isn't astonishing, and not the smallest bit of paper. "

"A bit of paper! You remind me that I picked one up yesterday in the omnibus."

"You found a piece of paper, and you didn't say so?"

"*Ma foi*, I wasn't thinking about it any longer."

"What were you thinking about then?"

"About my portrait, and you should be thinking about yours. That is to say, about the one you've been planning to do for a year, and that you've not even begun."

"Don't bother me. You're only talking about work. Me, I have a passion for the unknown. I see that there is decidedly nothing to be done with you."

"Oh! Nothing at all!"

"So, I'll work all alone. If you help me, it'll be without knowing it…and without wanting to. Let's see! What did you do with this paper? You didn't burn it, I hope!"

"No, but I might have lost it."

"All right, where did you put it?"

"I put it the pocket of my overcoat, with the hat pin…which you used to poison my cat. Poor Mirza!" the artist sighed, looking at the already stiff body of the unfortunate animal.

Binos still held that dangerous pin in his hand, and as he was gesturing a great deal while he talked, Freneuse observed his movements with certain unease.

"Please do me the favor of putting your dangerous instrument down somewhere," he said. "You'll wind up doing something unfortunate. It's enough that you killed an innocent animal."

"Don't be afraid; I'm aware of that," answered the art dauber, who nevertheless thought he should get rid of the murderous instrument. He placed it gently on the stove, and ran over to the overcoat which he had taken it from. He stuck his hand into the open pocket and took a crumbled up piece of paper from it."

"*Dieu merci*! It's still there," he exclaimed. "This is it, isn't it?"

"I think so. But I'll have to admit to you that I put in my pocket yesterday evening without looking at it."

"Ah! You want to pride yourself on not being curious. That's unheard of! Then why did you pick it up, if it wasn't to look at it?"

"I intended to, but you called me. I went into the café and your extravagant talk made me lose my head. Anyway, you have it now. Tell me what it is."

"It's a letter," said the dauber triumphantly.

"Without the envelope and, consequently, without the address," Freneuse observed.

"That doesn't matter. The letter will tell me a lot of things. Ah! the devil! It's torn almost in the middle lengthwise. That's going to hinder my understanding...but I'll manage, even so. They finally guessed what the beetles and the birds engraved on the obelisk mean. That was more difficult than completing the missing ends of the lines. And also, there are two of us. Listen to this."

"*My dear*,"...the following word is torn...*my dear friend*,[17] or my dear, some sort of short name. It's too bad it's not there, but we already know the letter's addressed to a woman."

"By a man, it seems to me. The handwriting is very masculine."

"Yes it's strong, large and rather irregular. That's not business handwriting. Let's see what follows."

"*Finally we're ready. I've been sure of my —— arrival for a month. She lives Rue Des ——. Seldom goes out, but goes out sometimes in the evening —— I don't yet know to whose house, but —— I return to my first plan because it is more —— not that is put off. So please be kind enough to —— not a word to anyone, not even to —— discover that those living in the house become suspicious... Then until tomorrow, my dear Z...*

"Ah! The lady's name begins with a Z. That's already something."

"And the signature?" asked Freneuse.

---

[17] Using the female gender.

"Absent. Torn... There's not even a syllable left," said Binos, who had read the letter aloud, stopping after each break in the sentence.

"*Parbleu*! That certainly tells you a lot! That letter is absolutely unintelligible. All it tells us is that the dead woman was named Zelie, or Zephyrine, or Zenoble, or..."

"Then, you think she's the one who lost this paper?"

"I don't know, *ma foi*! But if she didn't, then who did?"

"It was the other one, the hussy who used the pin. And do you want me to tell you what she used this fragment of a letter for? She used it to wrap up the poisoned pin. You can see that easily. Look at how it's crumpled. The hussy was afraid of pricking herself, and she took her precautions."

"Yes," Freneuse murmured. "She tore the letter carefully. It's impossible to understand anything whatsoever about what's written on this scrap of paper."

"You think so?"

"What can you infer from these mutilated sentences?"

"For me, it's as clear as if nothing were missing."

"Then you will oblige me by explaining it to me, because I don't get it at all."

"Because you haven't taken the trouble to think about it. However, there is something that jumps out at you. It's that the letter was written by a man and addressed to a woman."

"Whose first name begins with a Z. There's no doubt about that. But after that? What's it about?"

"To send into the next world the poor girl who is now sleeping on a slab at the morgue."

"Where the devil do you see that?"

"On each line. I'm going to go over them again one by one to convince you. The note begins with these words: '*Finally, we're ready!* That means: 'Finally, the time has come to act.' *Arrived a month ago.*' Who? The girl obviously! '*Arrivée*' is written in the feminine. And that agrees very well with what we know. She wasn't French. I examined her closely. It wasn't our pale sun that turned that complexion golden."

"That's true. She had a Spanish complexion."

"Let's assume, if you will, that she came from the depths of Andalousia. What did she come here to do? The author of the letter probably knew, and the first thing he did was spy on her. First of all he stated that she sometimes went out in the evenings—to whose house? He doesn't yet know, but it was enough for him that she went somewhere. He had a plan and he wanted to put it in operation without delay. This plan, we know about it now; it was the prick with the pin. '*It mustn't drag on,*' this inventor of expeditious procedures wrote. This familiar language suits very well the man that you described to me, this traveler on the bus upper story. And he added: '*They want everything finished by...* There's an end to the sentence which clearly establishes his position. He's being

46

given orders. He's working for another person. This scoundrel is only a paid assassin. *They* want...

Who is this *they?* Probably a man interested in doing away with the girl and too prudent to compromise himself by acting himself."

"Yes," Freneuse murmured, "Your logic is not bad, but you're not any further along, because all that is very vague."

"Pardon, on the second line, there is a rather precise clue. *'She resides... She* is certainly the newly arrived girl... *'She lives on the Rue des...'* "

"Well, the name of the street isn't there. Do you hope to guess it? That would be harder than all the rest."

"Notice, dear friend, that it's not Rue *de*...it's Rue *des.* This plural will help my investigation immensely. How many are there in Paris of streets *des?* Very few, right?"

"But you're mistaken. There are a lot of them. If you wish, I'm going to repeat a dozen of them from memory...Rue des Amandiers...Rue des Bons-Enfants...Rue des Blancs-Manteaux...Rue des Canettes...Rue des Quatre-Vents...Rue des Deux-Ecus..Rue des Mauvais-Garçons..."

"Enough! Enough! You'll wind up reciting the Bottin Address Book from one end to the other. I'd rather consult it at my leisure. Whatever you say about it, you can count those streets, and even if there are fifty of them, I'll investigate them all. I'll go from door to door asking if a young girl has disappeared from the house."

"And at the end of three or four months, maybe, you may finally get some information," said Freneuse, shrugging. "It would be a lot simpler to go turn over the pin and the torn letter to the Police Commissioner, who will open an investigation and, with the methods at his disposal, quickly discover the victim's domicile"

"Very well. You're going to accompany me the magistrate's office."

"Me! Ah! Amazing! Oh, no! I've already told you. I don't have any time to waste."

"As you wish. But I can't do anything without you. I mean, nothing official. If I go before the Commissioner, I will certainly have to tell him where I got the things that I brought him. I will also have to tell him about the death of your cat. I think he will even ask to see Mirza's cadaver. They will do an autopsy on the poor beast."

"Never on your life!" Freneuse exclaimed. "I don't want them to dissect my cat. It's bad enough you killed him."

"Then it's useless for me to go see the Commissioner to tell him the story," Binos replied. "The ends justify the means, my dear fellow. If we put the situation in the hands of the police, you must expect to be extensively and frequently interrogated."

"That's what I don't want."

"And that's what would happen, without a doubt. Right now, nobody believes there was a crime. Thus, they haven't bothered you. But if Mirza's poisoning is made public, things will change face quickly. They will experiment on other animals with the pin. They will sacrifice dogs and rabbits. Doctors will write fat reports on the effect of curare, and they will no longer doubt that the young girl on the omnibus was murdered. They will mobilize all the police agents, and as you were the only one who saw and observed the killer and her companion on the bus upper story, they will very likely ask you to go with these Sûreté gentlemen on their rounds, just to identify the guilty persons, if they manage to flush them out."

"All right! Does an individual citizen have to give up his private life in such a situation? You're making fun of me."

"I agree that I've painted the picture a little thick, but you can be sure they will call you every time they've put their hands on a man or a woman suspected. You're the one who'll decide if they have to be released or if the arrest must hold."

"A charming perspective! I'll be under police orders all day. Not at all, not at all! Do whatever you intend to, my dear friend. Provided that I won't have to get mixed up in anything. That's all I ask of you."

"Then, you'll give me the pin and the torn letter; you will give me a free hand, and you will never try to control my operations?"

"Never! On one condition. That's if you will keep me informed."

"You can count on it. I won't be busy with anything but chasing down the villains. Since I see you everyday, I won't have anything better to do than tell to you, or relay to you what I did the day before. We're agreed, aren't we? We'll do without the Commissioner."

"Yes,…however…"

"What then?"

"I wonder if we have the right to keep to ourselves what we know. A good citizen's duty is to shed light on justice. You want to leave, as they say, our light under a bushel."

"Pardon! I expect to spread light on justice when the moment is right! That means when I catch the villainous couple. Justice will owe me thanks, because I will have done its job, and these villains' trial will be more than half finished when I turn them over."

"Really! I admire you. You have confidence in your talents. And you probably intend to act all alone."

"Not completely. I have a lot of aptitude for becoming a first-class bloodhound, but I lack practice. At the beginning, I'll need a guide, an instructor, not for the main principles, I've instinctively guessed them, but to show me the little tricks of the trade. I have such a man in mind."

"Ah, bah!"

"*Mon Dieu*, yes. He's a man I meet often in the café…not in this neighborhood. He became a friend because one evening I made a crayon sketch of him, for free. He talks about the police rather willingly, and he talks very well about them. I'm almost sure he was one in the past."

"The devil! You have nice acquaintances."

"What do you expect? I can't spend my evenings in the Saint-Germain drawing rooms. They always forget to invite me. But if you knew this fellow Piédouche, you would understand why I enjoy his company. He's very clever…and tells amusing stories."

"I don't doubt it, but you don't have to introduce him to me, and I even ask you not to speak to him about me. And now that we've come to an agreement, take away everything that would remind me of that gloomy story. Take the letter, the pin, and even Mirza's body."

"I don't ask for anything better," said Binos. "And at the same time I'm going to let you get rid of me. I have something to do at my place."

"One last recommendation," added Freneuse. "Never say a word of this business in front of Pia. She's very sensitive, and I'd be afraid…"

"And then she would talk about it. Have no fear. I won't say anything to her. And if she asks me what became of your cat, I'll tell her he died because he licked some paints with arsenic in them off your palette."

III. Paul Freneuse

Paul Freneuse had his reasons for not wanting to prolong a conversation with Binos which would never end, not wanting very much to get involved in the ideas of this whimsical and enterprising amateur art dauber. Binos would like nothing better than to draw him with him into the criminal chase he was dreaming about, but Paul Freneuse had less imagination and more common sense than his comrade. He now recognized that the young girl in the omnibus might have been murdered. The experiment which had cost Mirza his life was decisive. But from that to believing that it was possible to find the criminals again, was far off. Freneuse was not at all interested in embarking on an enterprise which would have taken his time and disturbed the tranquility of his spirit, which he needed for his work.

Without being ambitious, Freneuse was determined to conquer an independent position, and he was well on his way to doing that. He already possessed the celebrity which leads to fame, sometimes even to glory. The only son of a business man who should have been able to leave him a sizeable inheritance, Paul found himself at nineteen without support and without resources. Completely ruined by one of those commercial crises which overturn the most solid businesses, his father died of grief and left him only a good name, because he had sacrificed everything to meet all his commitments. Paul, who had lost his mother at his birth, was alone in the world, having no other relative but a distant cousin, who lived in the country. The cousin thought he'd done a great deal for him by putting at his disposition 1,000 francs meant to allow him to search his fortune abroad. Paul, who had absolutely no taste for the profession of Australian gold prospector and who felt he had great aptitude for painting, had used that charity to take himself off to Rome. He had remained there five years, working to earn a living, and, above all, educating himself. He had left a student; he returned a master, a very young master, still challenged, but very respected by artists and very appreciated by the buying public. At the same time they were discussing him, the critics respected him and he had trouble filling all the public's orders, so honor and money were coming to him at the same time. He thought more highly of the honor, but didn't forget that in this world, it's money that guarantees freedom, and he tried to reconcile everything. He told himself, *"When I'm rich, or just comfortable, I can devote myself entirely to art. That means more to me than anything. Wealth is not the end, but it's the means."*

And to arrive more quickly to the independence which was his aim, Paul Freneuse sometimes thought about getting married. He certainly had everything it took to please a young lady. He was tall, thin, and had a good physique. His features somewhat lacked regularity, but his face was expressive and handsome. A pleasant and intelligent speaker, without the slightest pretension, and with perfect manners, Paul possessed still other advantages; an excellent heart and an open and happy personality. One could easily believe that opportunities to settle down had not been lacking. The last two or three years especially, no winter went by without his receiving some favorable invitations: dances and dinners where he was introduced to marriageable young ladies. He gladly accepted and he was even somewhat attentive to some young ladies who were what was called good catches; but he hadn't yet found what he was looking for. Freneuse had got it into his head that he would marry only a woman that he could love, and he didn't want to fall in love except with his eyes wide open. But he wanted a great number of morale qualities, and what's more, he had particular ideas about beauty, artist's ideas.

However, he had noticed, at the beginning of the season, the daughter of a gentleman who in the past had had business dealings with Monsieur Freneuse senior, and who eagerly welcomed the son, since the son was on his way to becoming rich and famous. And certainly Mademoiselle Marguerite Paulet merited being noticed and even being paid court to. First of all, she was marvelously beautiful, as beautiful as Pia, although she didn't resemble her anymore than day resembles night. Pia was pale brown. Mademoiselle Paulet was rosy blonde. Pia was rather petite and her delicate shape was as yet just a promise; Mademoiselle Paulet was tall, and although she was barely twenty years old, her opulent beauty was already full blown. Pia resembled a Raphael virgin; Mademoiselle Paulet resembled a Rubens Flemish model. Paul Freneuse, who loved the masters of all schools, although he preferred the Italian masters, greatly admired the charms of the lovely heiress, who had done him the honor of dancing many waltzes with him since the beginning of winter.

Because Mademoiselle Paulet *was* an heiress. After having been in business—That's the accepted term to designate a man who got rich by speculation—her father enjoyed a nice fortune, honestly acquired, they said, and had no other child. Her mother had died leaving her 200,000 francs, which she would acquire at her majority.

Monsieur Paulet, owner of three houses in Paris, was thought to have a 70,000 pound income, and would probably leave more than that after his death, since he saved some every year, although he lived on a very respectable scale.

His daughter liked society; he took her out often, and he loved to have guests. He especially gave exquisite dinners. He invited Paul Freneuse, who accepted them with pleasure, less for the superiority of the cuisine than for a taste for the beauty of Mademoiselle Marguerite. He had gone there so often that winter that, not being able to return the favor, since he lived as a bachelor, for a long time he had been looking for an opportunity to do something considered as a return courtesy to Monsieur and also to Mademoiselle Paulet.

Now, at the last dinner, Mademoiselle, who was seated next to Paul Freneuse, had expressed a desire to see *Les Chevaliers du brouillard,* a play that had just opened at the Porte-Saint-Martin.[18]

And Paul Freneuse, knowing that the richest Parisian bourgeois didn't at all mind to the theatre for free, immediately thought of making them the gift of a theatre box. He was careful not to offer it himself, but he cleverly learned what Monsieur Paulet intended doing with his next evenings, and having learned that two days after that was not committed to a social engagement, he procured a nice box on the first tier, not by paying for it, which might have offended Monsieur Paulet's sensibilities, but by obtaining one from a journalist friend. And that evening was precisely the day of Mirza's unfortunate death. Binos, his murderer, had just left the studio when Freneuse received a gracious note from Monsieur Paulet, thanking him and inviting him to join him in the box, where he intended to take his daughter that evening.

The artist was hardly in the mood to enjoy the pleasure of spending a few hours in the charming company of Mademoiselle Marguerite. The omnibus tragedy had saddened him; Binos' plans had upset him. He was already reproaching himself for having promised not to reveal the discovery of that poisoned pin, which he should have given to the police commissioner with some explanations and some support for them. He was even beginning to fear finding himself compromised sooner or later by some indiscretion of his imprudent comrade. However, without seeming ill-bred, Freneuse could hardly avoid entering the theatre and going to greet the father and the daughter who had expressed the desire to see him there. And, in addition, it was an excellent opportunity to chase away the unpleasant thoughts tormenting his mind. So he decided to get dressed, and about 6:00 p.m., he went out on foot to go dine on the grand boulevards with a group he was part of and where he was somewhat rarely seen. It happened that those there were not boring and their gaiety cheered up Freneuse, who actually had no serious cares. He chatted a great deal on subjects he liked and when the moment came to start toward Porte-Saint-Martin, he had completely forgotten his preoccupations. He was thinking only of Mademoiselle Paulet and he was preparing himself to be pleasant. But fate decreed that a chance encounter reminded him of the unpleasant memory of a sad adventure. Arriving in front to

---

[18] Theatre de La Porte Saint-Martin, 18 Boulevard Saint-Martin; it was, with the Chatelet Theatre, home of large scale, spectacular melodramatic productions. Jack Sheppard's *Chevaliers Du Brouillard: A Romance*, novel by William Harrison Ainsworth, based on the exploits of Jack Sheppard (4 March 1702–16 November 1724), a famous London burglar. It was adapted for the stage by John Baldwin Buckstone, who also took the staring role. English title: *Old London*. The French Almanach for 1859, page 520, says: "*Les Chevaliers du Brouillard* was being enacted night after night at the Porte Saint-Martin with a success quite unparalleled." Jean Renoir in *My Life and my Films* calls it his favorite play in his youth, (p. 14). A *New York Times* review, April 18, 1873 noted: "The play, as represented, was the apotheosis of rascality."

the theater's peristyle, he stopped a moment to finish an excellent cigar. He was not a little surprised to hear himself addressed in these terms:

"For sure, I'm not mistaken; it's really you."

The person who spoke to Freneuse was a fat woman, with a muffler wrapped around her head and a basket of oranges strapped to her waist. Freneuse didn't recognize her at first, but she didn't give him time to try to remember.

"You don't remember me," she continued in a hoarse voice. "Me, I recognize you very well. You were the one sitting across from me, yesterday evening, in the *Halles aux vins* omnibus."

"Ah! Of course, I remember now," stammered the artist, dumbfounded.

Ordinarily the people that fate gives you as traveling companions in public transportation vehicles don't stop to speak to you when they meet you in the street the following day. Obviously, if that old gossip called out to Freneuse on the Boulevard Saint-Bernard sidewalk, it was because she wanted to talk to him about the sad event which happened during the trip. However, she wasn't in the omnibus when it was noticed that the young girl was dead. How did it happen that she was so well informed? She wasn't long in explaining that.

"What do you know," she began. "Now there's a story. It was the little one, right? She passed on during the trip. Who would have thought it? Me, I would've put my hand in the fire that she was sleeping. That must have had a strange effect on you to have held a dead woman on your shoulder without knowing it."

"What! You know..."

"They told me that at the Place Pigalle office this morning. I take the bus every day to go buy my oranges on the Rue des Halles... That's how all the ticket collectors at the station know me...and when they told me a tall brunet helped take the body out, I guessed immediately it was you. That must have been difficult, seeing that you were the only man inside the omnibus."

"What's even more difficult is that you remembered my face," murmured Freneuse.

"Oh! Me, when I've seen a face, I never forget it. So, you see, the person who was sitting beside the little one, and who gave up his seat, you may think I didn't pay attention to him. He didn't stay with us five minutes. Well, if I met him again, I wouldn't have to look at him very long to say: 'That's him.'"

"If Binos were here," Freneuse said to himself, *"He'd link up with that orange peddler and he'd go out with her very day in hopes of using her memory for faces. I don't have the least desire to do the same, but I'm curious to know what she thinks of yesterday's adventure."*

And he continued aloud:

"And would you also recognize the lady who took advantage of the gentleman's courtesy?"

"Ah! That one, no, of course. She didn't even show the end of her nose.

With the veils that women these days wear, it's worse than if they were masked. It ought to be forbidden to hide themselves like that…because… suppose a woman did something bad…once she'd left, there'd be no way to pick her up. Wait! That reminds me that the station agent told me that at the time you got the idea that the little one had been killed on the trip. What would anybody have killed her with, I ask you? It seems she didn't even have a scratch."

"Yes, but that death seemed so extraordinary to me…"

"It's true she didn't make a lot of noise. What do you expect! At that age you're not very tough."

"Then you don't think that the woman sitting next to her…"

"The lady whose little face nobody stared at? Just think about it! If she had done anything wrong, we'd certainly have seen it. And then, that's not all. The doctors examined the girl's body and they didn't find anything. For me, it doesn't astonish me that she met her end without making any noise. Her paper-maché face told very well that she was sick."

"Her face…then you saw it? But she was veiled also."

"That's true. I haven't told you yet that I went to the morgue. I knew she was there, and from Sainte-Eustache to Notre Dame isn't far, and once there, I went to look, like everybody else. There was a line at the door… wouldn't you know! That's understandable. They hardly ever show anybody but those who've drowned themselves. A drowned person isn't very pretty, while the little girl was as pretty as day, and death hadn't changed her. She seemed to be sleeping. Also, I recognized her. It didn't take very long."

"Then you knew her?" Freneuse exclaimed.

"I know,… I certainly did know her!" said the fat woman. "I've met her ten times at the market in Place Saint-Pierre, in Montmartre. I have to tell you, I live at Chaussées Clignancourt."

"Then you know who she was?"

"As for that, no, seeing that I never spoke to her. You understand that at my age you don't pass the time of day with young people, especially when you don't know who you're dealing with. But as for having seen her, ah! yes…and if I live a hundred years, I'll never forget her face. She had black eyes that shone out at you…that made you want to light your cigar with them…and a skin as velvety as white satin…without color, don't you know. You would've said she didn't have a drop of blood in her veins."

Freneuse was, for a moment, upset. He was not, like his friend Binos, passionate about the job of investigator, but the mystery of the omnibus preoccupied him a great deal more than he admitted to himself and he had thought the orange peddler was going to clear it up. But the information he'd hoped for hadn't come out. He told himself, however, that perhaps some useful news could be drawn from that chubby woman, and he continued:

"But if she came often to the Montmartre market, that's because she lived in that neighborhood."

"Oh! That's for sure," answered the fat gossip.

"And it's possible that, among the merchants who sold things to her, someone might be able to tell in what street, and even in what house she lived."

"That's very possible, but nevertheless I'd be surprised at that. They probably didn't pay attention to her, because she didn't buy very much from them. Some eggs, some vegetables, some salad greens. She didn't spend thirty *sous* a day. Then, you see, customers like that don't matter. And, in addition to that, she was proud as a little queen. She never spoke to them except to ask: 'How much?' and when she thought it was too expensive, she didn't bargain. She left without saying a word."

"However, she couldn't have been rich?"

"Rich? Oh! no. I saw her always wearing the same threadbare camisole and the same black wool dress worn right down to the strings."

"And she was always alone?" asked Freneuse, who in spite of himself was letting himself follow the investigation like a simple Binos.

"Always. The maids who came to market with their sweethearts made fun of her because she didn't have a lover."

"Pretty and well behaved…that's unusual…especially when a young girl doesn't have a fortune, no relatives, and is forced to work for a living."

"Relatives,…I really think she didn't have any, but I got it into my head that she wasn't a common worker."

"Then what do you think she did?"

"She must have given lessons at twenty *sous* for a set number. That job doesn't bring in very much."

"Then she went to a number of people's houses, and it's very likely someone will recognize her corpse."

"Who knows?" answered the fat woman, shrugging. "Not everybody goes to the morgue and she's laid out there for only three days."

"But you went there, and you could probably tell the custodian what you've just told me."

"Me! There's no danger of that. I don't have any time to waste. I have to go about my business. Consider the fact that I have to think of my man, who's been in bed four months with rheumatism he got as a dock worker. If I don't take care of him, then who will take care of him? And if I'd told what I know to the supervisor, I would've been there two hours, and tomorrow I'd still be obligated to go speak with the dog of a commissioner. No, thank you! Besides, what good would that have done? I don't know the little one's name, nor her address."

Freneuse had to admit that the orange merchant wasn't wrong. He had done just as she had. He hadn't gotten involved, although he knew a good deal about that sinister event.

"That doesn't mean that, if you needed me," the fat woman continued, "I'm at your service. Virginie Pilou, Chaussées Clignancourt, at the corner of the Rue Müller. You'd just have to inquire about me at the fruit seller's. I can certainly see that this poor girl's fate interests you…, and I'll try to get you some information. No later than tomorrow morning I'll ask about her around the neighborhood. Now, excuse me, my prince. While I'm chatting, I'm not selling my oranges. You're not the one who'll buy them, are you? My merchandise isn't for gentlemen."

And leaving Freneuse, the old gossip started shouting again:

"For three *sous*, beautiful Valencia oranges! Three *sous*!"

Paul judged it would be useless to insist. Mother Pilou wouldn't have told him any more, for the excellent reason that she didn't know anything else. And besides that, it was time he went into the theater. The first act was over. He counted on arriving for the second in the box where Monsieur Paulet had reserved a seat for him. In such a case, not to hurry was almost impolite.

Now, the intermission was coming to an end. Freneuse thought it better to arrive before the curtain was raised. Therefore, he followed the spectators who were going back in after having smoked their cigars outside. He gave the usher the number of the box and he slowly climbed the stairway leading to the corridor of the first-tier boxes. He had left his circle of friends in excellent spirits, ready to make the best of everything, and to show off his important occasions' pleasant personality. But that encounter with the orange seller had changed his mood. She had just confronted him with problems which charmed Binos so much and which amused him so little. It really seemed that that unfortunate omnibus situation was following him everywhere. He would have liked never again to have heard about it. Everybody, even people he didn't know, talked to him about it. And what irritated him most of all was that he couldn't stop thinking about it no matter what he did. It interested him in spite of himself. He told himself in vain that that young girl's death was not his business and that his dear comrade's observations didn't make sense. He had involuntarily listened to a gossip's words. He took pleasure in questioning her, and the information she furnished him at random piqued his curiosity.

"Decidedly, *this is too stupid,*" he muttered to himself, letting himself be carried along by the crowd flowing back into the theatre. *"I'm deliberately creating problems for myself when I would just have to go on with my life to be perfectly happy. I've succeeded in making a name for myself and earning a great deal more money than I need. I'm coddled everywhere and it's only up to me, perhaps, to make an advantageous marriage, while at the same time marrying someone I'm attracted to. Why would I need to burden myself with what happens following an event where I just happened to be present? That's all right for Binos, who's an idler and wild, to go out looking for criminals who can't be found. As for me, I have better uses for my time. Women who sell oranges and poisoned hat pins can go to the devil! This evening it's a matter of pleasing that admirable creature named Marguerite Paulet. If I could just get her permission and her father's to paint her portrait for next year's Salon, that success would console me very well for never having discovered the man and woman who plot-*

ted this murky business."

While holding this level-headed discourse with himself, Freneuse was forcing himself through the wave of humanity surrounding him, and barely succeeding. There was a tall and strong fellow right in front of him whose broad shoulders barred his way and who seemed deliberately not to hurry just to make those following him impatient. After several attempts to slide between the wall and that individual, Freneuse finally tried giving a little push, to make him decide to move a little faster. The man turned around, muttering some impolite words. He thus revealed his face to the artist, who felt a bizarre sensation on seeing him. It seemed to him that play-going amateur resembled the traveler on the top of the omnibus. He had the same rough-cut features, the same graying mustache, the same sideburns cut in the military fashion, the same hard face. Only, the dress was completely different. Instead of the overcoat with pockets and a derby hat, this gentleman was wearing a black frockcoat of fine cloth and a new silk top hat.

His eyes examined Freneuse rapidly, very piercing black eyes, shaded by thick eyebrows, and he probably thought him not worth his anger, because, instead of a harsh remark, he turned back into the crowd and quickened his step so that he broke through and was promptly lost in the orchestra corridor.

"You'd swear that he recognized me and that he stole away," Freneuse thought. *"If Binos were here, and if I told him what I thought, he would stick to that person's heels. But I'm not Binos and I'm not going to amuse myself by running after him."*

On that wise reflection, he continued on his way and he had less trouble getting to the first tier of boxes, almost all the people crowded at the entrance having their seats downstairs. He looked for the box, which was a box facing the stage. When he found it, he called the attendant, without thinking any more about the encounter he had just had. The vestibule attendant came hurrying when the well-dressed gentleman called her and let him into the box occupied since the raising of the curtain by the father and the daughter.

Freneuse had the pleasure of seeing Mademoiselle Marguerite's cheeks blush pink, which seemed to him a good sign. Monsieur Paulet welcomed him in the most flattering way. He took the trouble to stand up and hold out both hands to him and brought, himself, a chair for the newcomer, who didn't seat himself until having paid for his entry by a well-turned compliment to which the girl answered with a gracious smile.

"I knew you wouldn't refuse to keep us company," Monsieur Paulet exclaimed. "And I thank you for giving us your evening."

This landlord was a neat little old man, with a pleasant appearance and good manners. He had quick movements, ready speech, an engaging personality and his face would have been more sympathetic if it had been more candid. His eyes spoiled it a little. They almost never looked at you directly and they had a disturbing mobility. And then, his lips smiled too much, and the smile was banal. But the whole wasn't displeasing and Monsieur Paulet would have made a most presentable father-in-law.

Mademoiselle Marguerite, fortunately for her, didn't resemble him at all. She undoubtedly inherited from her mother her shape, her complexion, and the somewhat nonchalant grace which gave her whole person a particular charm. She was, as they say, a thoroughbred and Monsieur Paulet was a simple, good-natured fellow somewhat lacking distinction, but he admired his daughter and what he was satisfied him. Freneuse had been able to please him by showing him regards which artists don't lavish on bourgeois. He carried his condescension even to flattering his mania, which was talking at random about painting. He listened to the judgments about ancient and modern masters formulated seriously and didn't think himself too good to answer them. Mademoiselle Marguerite didn't know any more, perhaps, than her father, but she had tact. She knew, thanks to Freneuse, not to make fun of him.

"My dear fellow," Monsieur Paulet said point-blank, "You arrive just in time to settle a question about art."

"I'm disqualifying myself in advance," Freneuse said modestly. "I'm convinced that you're right and Mademoiselle is not wrong."

"Oh! Don't try to get out of it by a polite evasion. You are very competent to decide between us, and it's absolutely necessary that you give us your opinion. Besides, it's because of you that the problem arose."

"I'm very proud to learn that you and Mademoiselle have wanted to think about me."

"Please believe, my dear Freneuse, that we often do that. You aren't among those one can forget when one knows you as we know you. If we didn't know you, we would at least know your works, which are well worth the trouble to get to know. Your name is on every one's tongue and in all the newspapers. They're talking a lot about the painting you're going to show this year. It will be a great success at the Salon, they tell me, and I believe it. Well, it was precisely this painting that was the cause of our difference..."

"But," the artist objected timidly, "I'm sorry you haven't done me the honor of coming to see it. You would be able to judge..."

"I know what it is; that's all they're talking about in the artistic world... a young girl goat herder in the Roman countryside seated at the foot of the tomb of ...Metella...no, of Cecilia...anyway, of a tomb...but, between us, you ought to have chosen a happier subject...because tombs, you see,... you don't have to be an amateur of painting..., people don't really like to see that in one's drawing room. That might negatively affect the sale..."

"Oh! Cecilia Metella has been dead such a long time!" seriously replied Freneuse, who wanted to laugh in Monsieur Paulet's face.

"That's an excuse, but that wasn't what it was about. I was maintaining a while ago to Marguerite that all you artists, you're wrong to keep reproducing Italian men and women on your canvases. And I claim, for female models, especially, our French women furnish marvelous types."

"You are right a thousand times over, Monsieur, and I wouldn't have to go very far to find one," Freneuse said quickly, looking at Mademoiselle Paulet.

"There! What did I tell you?" Monsieur Paulet exclaimed. "Freneuse thinks you would make a superb model."

"I can't really see myself as a shepherdess in the Roman countryside," said Mademoiselle Marguerite.

"You would be beautiful in any kind of costume," Freneuse said warmly.

"Still, I would have to portray the character you've chosen. Now, Italian women aren't blonde, so far as I know, and I have the misfortune to be so. The sun hasn't made my complexion golden, nor darkened my hair, and my features absolutely lack character."

"Bah!" said Monsieur Paulet, cutting off Freneuse, who had a compliment on his lips. "You are very nice as you are, and I know many people who agree with me."

"I beg you to count me among those people," added the artist, delighted to seize the opportunity to affirm his admiration of Mademoiselle Marguerite's beauty.

"And what's more," the father continued, "I admit I can't get ecstatic about these heads artists go to look for so far away. They're really pretty, your Roman women, with their skin the color of lemons and their eyes with dark circles under them! And the things they wear! Rags that a cook wouldn't dare put on to go walking out at Mardi Gras. It should be illegal to go out in garbs like those."

"You're very hard on these poor girls," Freneuse murmured. "They really must do their job, and to pose they can't dress like engravings of Parisian fashions."

"Right! I understand that. You need local color. I know what that is, even though I'm only a bourgeois. But if I were a painter, I would do it another way. I would have a dressing room at my studio, and when I needed any sort of *Fornarina*, I would choose a French woman, and I wouldn't have to do anything but disguise her to have a model."

"But. Father, that wouldn't be at all the same thing," said Mademoiselle Paulet. "The type is so different!"

"Don't talk to me about your type. What the devil! Beauty is beauty!"

Freneuse looked down and didn't say anything. He didn't care to argue with a man who put forth such ridiculous statements. He was beginning to wonder if he could endure a father-in-law so lacking in artistic feeling. But Marguerite had guessed what he was thinking, and she favored him with a look which made him forget for an instant his prejudices against

M. Paulet. This look said so many things; it was tender, almost begging. It asked pardon for the bad taste of a father, who didn't resemble his daughter.

"And what's more," said the capitalist, "I have particular reasons for detesting the Italians. Can you imagine that those rascals might very well cost me a nice inheritance which should come to me...the inheritance from my brother."

"Really?" Freneuse asked, somewhat astonished. "I didn't know you had a brother."

"Nobody knows it, because he lives in the country and we don't have the same name. My mother married twice. That brother is from her second marriage. But I am now his only relative and, as a consequence, his heir. We had a falling out a long time ago. He decided to go live in a little village in the south of France, claiming that the Paris climate didn't suit him. Marguerite doesn't know her uncle."

The artist, whom the information hardly interested, murmured distractedly, "That's not a reason to disinherit you."

"No, but here's the bad thing. That animal, who's always been a first-class eccentric, decided in his youth that he had talent for painting. He spent some years in Italy smearing some canvases, the best of which wouldn't sell for fifteen francs. If the only thing he left was these paintings, I would've mourned about it a long time ago, but he is rich, as rich as I am, if not more so. And it's not impossible that he made a will in favor of a child he had in the past in Rome."

"Then he married there?"

"It's said so, but it hasn't been proved. It's claimed that he was stupid enough to marry, I don't know what creature, who posed for painters. I myself don't think he went quite that far. But he's free to dispose of his fortune and he's capable of leaving it to his illegitimate daughter. Now you can understand, my dear Freneuse, why I hold Roman models in horror. And what's even more curious in that story," Monsieur Paulet continued, "is that my fool of a brother never took an interest in the pretty family he created down there. After having arranged his affairs so as to end his days in Rome, he suddenly changed his mind. He took a whim to return to France. He went to live 150 leagues from Paris, in a country hole where he lives alone like a recluse. When I was informed of that fine resolution, I wrote him to suggest that we reconcile. I offered him a place to live here, with me. I'd willingly have made the sacrifice to go get him in his desert to bring him back here. Ah! Well, yes! He answered me with a very dry letter which refused any kind of reconciliation and even to see me. That's where we've been for ten years. But you can well imagine that I had him watched without his knowing it. His lawyer took my side, and he's kept me up to date. Now, I've lately learned that Monsieur my half-brother has been talking about naming foreign individuals as his heirs, and I'm very worried. I've taken some preventative measures, as for example to find out..."

"But, Father," Mademoiselle Marguerite interrupted gently, "I don't think these details interest Monsieur Freneuse very much. And besides, they're about to raise the curtain. Please allow me to see and even to hear."

"You're right, little girl. I must've considerably bored our friend telling him about my family affairs; but he'll forgive me. It's for your good that I get so upset, because my hare-brained brother's fortune must revert to you after me. And then," Monsieur Paulet continued, "I was trying to explain to this dear Paul why I can't endure Italian women. That won't keep me from going one of these days to see his painting."

Paul nodded as a sign of agreement, and as the curtain was going up at this moment, he didn't have to answer. To tell the truth, he had hardly listened to the rather confused story that Marguerite's father had just told him. But he had to recognize that this millionaire's conversation lacked charm and that he professed absurd opinions in matters of art. Freneuse didn't think himself strong enough to argue with him the merits of models who made the trip from Rome to Paris to pose for French painters. He preferred a great deal more to admire in silence his daughter's beautiful head, that he saw three quarters of, and which seemed to have been cut from the canvas of some Flemish master. The artist engrossed himself in that contemplation, which Mademoiselle Marguerite appeared to lend herself to willingly, while Monsieur Paulet, armed with an enormous pair of opera glasses, ogled the downstairs audience crammed with male spectators and, above all, female spectators.

Freneuse thought, examining with the eyes of a connoisseur the lines of that very pure profile, *"I believe she has intelligence and heart. The man she loves will not be unhappy, and, after all, the man who marries her won't be forced to live with the father. I would prefer that she were less rich and this father less middle class. He has ideas which exasperate me. I'm astonished that he doesn't perceive that we wouldn't be able to agree on anything. He shows me enough that he likes me, and I wonder why, because I haven't done anything to cause it.*

"Maybe he's not too unhappy to show me off to his friends as you exhibit a rare bird. That sort of vanity is wide-spread among people like him. He likes to pose as a comrade of artists. And, however, no. It seems to me there's something more and that his advances have a motive. He wouldn't act any differently if he was thinking about making me his son-in-law. For me, the question is to know, first of all, if I please his daughter. I don't like the thought of venturing myself on this terrain to end up with a disappointment. I'm not in love with Mademoiselle Marguerite, but I don't belong in becoming so, if I spend a lot of evenings with her. I must take advantage of this one to risk a trial."

While holding this very sensible discourse with himself, Freneuse devoured with his eyes Mademoiselle Paulet, who appeared to give all her attention to the play, but who was well aware of the effect she was producing on her young neighbor. A moment came when she felt bothered by the persistence of the stare. To put an end to it, she borrowed her father's opera glasses and she pointed them toward Jack Sheppard who was coming on stage. Freneuse understood the intention and began to look at the orchestra seats, just to save face. But his eyes soon rested on a man standing up at the first row of seats, leaning against the wall of the stage boxes of the ground floor. That man probably

61

wouldn't have drawn Freneuse's attention, although he was standing while all those around him were seated, but just then he was looking at the box at the front of which Monsieur Paulet and his daughter were enthroned. The artist's eyes, which were excellent, met those of the spectator in the orchestra seats, and he recognized him also. It was the gentleman he had bumped into on the stairway, after having passed the ticket taker, and who had appeared to him to look vaguely like the traveler on the omnibus bus. This time Freneuse could examine him at his ease, because the face was directly across from him, in full light, and he didn't look away, having nothing better to do while Mademoiselle Paulet was amusing herself looking at the actors and the décor. He took less pleasure in staring at the unknown man than in contemplating the beautiful Marguerite, but his curiosity was excited by this current problem. He began to try hard to recall the features of the man seen the evening before in the omnibus. He almost succeeded and he again confirmed the resemblance; but he didn't reach an absolute certainty. Paris is full of people who wear toothbrush mustaches and sideburns cut level with the ear. The physique was the same, the shoulders also, and a certain abruptness in the movements.

From time to time the individual made jerky gestures which seemed to be addressed to someone. Not to the persons who occupied the Freneuse box, because neither the father nor the daughter paid any attention to the insignificant individual who was observing them at a distance. But that didn't prove anything, and Freneuse, less zealous than Binos, was going to give up further examination, when he saw the gentleman in the orchestra section lean over to speak to a woman sitting beside him. The thing in itself was very natural. However, the artist immediately had the feeling that woman must be the creature who had manipulated the poisoned hat pin. If so, it was a chance guess, whose accuracy it was impossible for him to verify, since the woman sitting next to the poor dead woman hadn't shown her face a single time during the trip from the Boulevard Saint-Germaine to the Rue de Laval. However, at the first words the man standing up said to her, she quickly raised her head to look at the box that the man had probably just pointed out to her. The light from the chandelier was falling directly on her face, and Freneuse saw she had large features, somewhat regular, but too pronounced, and a complexion with some acne. The whole, however, wasn't displeasing and the expression of the face didn't lack distinction. Her age was somewhere between 35 and 40.

"*Am I the one she's looking at so persistently?*" Paul wondered. "*I doubt it, because seated where I am she can hardly see me. And then, if it's not me, it's Monsieur or Mademoiselle Paulet...Mademoiselle, actually, because she's beautiful enough to be stared at, and nevertheless, that's unusual... a woman who comes to see a play and who continues looking at a pretty young girl instead of paying attention to the drama.*"

Neither was Monsieur Paulet himself paying much attention to the exploits of Jack Sheppard in the Pie Borgne cabaret.[19] He had struck a triumphant pose, and nonchalantly leaning against the partition of the box, he was flaunting the heavy watch chain, which wound around his vest like a snake, and the diamond buttons which shone like stars on his shirt. He was looking for people he knew in the audience. He finally spied the couple quartered in a corner of the orchestra seats. The woman immediately again faced the stage, but the man greeted the capitalist. He didn't greet him with a wave of the hand, as you greet a friend. He bowed respectfully, and at that distance such a humble courtesy was a little ridiculous. Monsieur Paulet answered it with a rather dry nod. The man, probably satisfied with having been seen, quickly sat down and began to chat with his companion.

"*Parbleu!*" Freneuse said to himself, "*It's just up to me now to find out who this person is I've been preoccupied with for the last half-hour.*"

Mademoiselle Marguerite forestalled the question he was going to ask her father. She had just put down her opera glasses and she had seen the exchange of greetings.

"Who is this gentleman?" she asked. "Is he one of your acquaintances? I don't recall ever meeting him."

"Yes, he comes in the mornings to my study sometimes," Monsieur Paulet answered, swaggering, "but not to my drawing room. I'd certainly be careful about introducing him to you. He's a business agent."

"Exactly what is a business agent?" asked the beautiful Marguerite distractedly.

"My dear child, it would take too long to explain it to you. It wouldn't interest you very much, I suppose, to learn that these gentlemen...I mean to say these people...take care of, for a moderate price, the jobs one wants to give them. They take charge of difficult recoveries, tangled settlements, investigations of all type; their specialty is things in law suits."

"That's a word that doesn't tell me very much."

"Because you don't know the language of business. It's true you don't need to know it, because I take care of, and will always take care of, yours... at least as long as I live... After me, that care will go to your husband, who, I certainly hope, will be a hard-working and organized man. As for the agent who has just allowed himself to greet me across the whole room, the first time I used him, I asked him to be less demonstrative in public. He's a clever man and I think he's honest, but that's no reason to give himself airs and greet me in front of 1,500 people...especially as I know his intention. To greet a capitalist like myself, that's an advertisement for a poor devil like himself. I really want to use him, because his services can be useful to me, but I won't tolerate familiarity from him."

"He is, you say, expert at his profession?" the artist asked.

---

[19] Blind Magpie.

"Oh! Very expert, from what they say. It was one of my business acquaintances who recommended him to me. I recently employed him for certain delicate business, and I haven't had time yet to judge him by the results, but it seems he has no equal for information."

"Then, sir, I'd be very obliged to you if you'd put me in contact with him. I have right now a debt to recover, and the man owing me has disappeared... If your agent could..."

"Very well. As soon as I see him, and that'll be soon, I'll put him in touch with you."

"Oh! You don't have to take that trouble. I'll write him to come to my place if you'll be good enough to tell me his name."

"His name? I seem to've forgotten it. You can understand that names like that aren't those you retain. But I have his card at the house, and you'll know tomorrow where he lives."

"I thank you in advance," said Freneuse, slightly disappointed.

He had flattered himself that he would astonish Binos by reporting to him precise information about an individual who resembled the omnibus traveler and he would have to wait until Monsieur Paulet was willing to send it to him. If it so happened that he thought about it.

"Well!" said the capitalist, "They're already lowering the curtain. They make plays scandalously short now. You don't get very much for your money."

"It seems to me, father, that's just the end of an act," answered Mademoiselle Marguerite. "Yes...look! They've tapped the stage floor three times to indicate the next act, and no one has left his seat."

"That doesn't matter; we can still chat. Nothing bores me as much as being obliged to whisper for fear of bothering the play," said Paulet, who liked to show off his vocal organs. He had a deep bass voice, the voice of the legendary Monsieur Prudhomme.

"So, my dear Freneuse," he continued. "You have money, because you're owed some. That's good. That's very good at your age to have some debtors instead of creditors. I wasn't wrong about you. You live comfortably, and that doesn't prevent your setting some aside. It's true you must put enormous sums in the cash box. Paintings are rising in price and you're in vogue. Is it indiscrete to ask you what you earn each year?"

"But...it would be difficult for me to state an exact sum," Freneuse stammered, blushing a little. "That depends on a number of things."

"Go on! Give an approximate figure."

"Last year I set aside nearly 50,000 francs...and if I wanted to paint portraits..."

"You'd earn a lot more. You should do so, my friend. You should do so. I'm giving you good advice. There's no better profession than yours today. And an expert that I know assured me the other day that it's going to be even more productive. America is beginning to buy and..."

64

The usher cut short Monsieur Paulet's enthusiastic estimates. She entered discretely, and said, addressing him:

"There's someone outside who asks Monsieur to come out an instant... someone who brings Monsieur a very urgent message."

"A message!" repeated M. Paulet. "That's strange. I didn't tell anyone I was going to Porte Saint-Martin, and here's a telegram come to be delivered to me here."

"But, Father, your valet de chamber knows you're here," said Mademoiselle Paulet.

"That's true. I didn't think about that. He even knew that I was expecting important news, and as he's very intelligent... Please allow me, my dear Freneuse, to leave you an instant...Marguerite will talk painting with you... She knows more about it than I do."

Monsieur Paulet hastily followed the usher, who closed the door of the box after him. This was the first time in his life that Freneuse had found himself alone with Mademoiselle Paulet. In society, tête-à-têtes are rare. Some words exchanged at the piano, while turning the pages of a musical score, around a table, while a young girl pours with her white hand a cup of tea for the most elegant of her father's guests. An unforeseen incident furnished the artist an excellent way to leave the ordinary banalities of conversation, and he had only to take advantage of it. Mademoiselle Marguerite, on her side, probably desired it, because she was the one who began the conversation on a more intimate footing.

"I'm afraid my father shocked you by forcing you to reveal the amount of your revenue," she said in her softest voice. "You mustn't hold it against him. He has a consideration for money—that I don't have at all...but it's on my account that it's important to him. He adores me, and he claims I couldn't be happy without an enormous fortune. I admit I understand happiness in an entirely different way. I wouldn't be upset if my husband were rich, but I want, most of all, to like him."

"And I, Mademoiselle, I'd be able to console myself very well in marrying a girl without a dowry, if I loved her."

"So, then we can agree," Mademoiselle Paulet said gaily. "Let's see if we're in agreement on the rest of the program. What pleases you? You're a painter. You must dream of a type."

"I've found it."

"Can one know where?"

"Do you ever go to the Louvre Museum?"

"Not often. My father doesn't like modern painting...and there are some days that I agree with him."

"Ask him to take you into the Grand Gallery; in the fifth bay on the left look for a portrait painted by Rubens. The master has been dead for some centuries, but the woman who served him as a model is alive. You know her...and I won't need to tell you her name when you've seen that marvelous canvas. The resemblance is striking and you will know then what my ideal is like."

"But, if I'm not mistaken, Rubens painted only Flemish women...and Flemish women are blonde."

"My ideal woman is blonde."

"That's unusual. You never paint anything but brunettes."

"Because brunette models are on every street corner... You just have a hard time choosing, while blondes are rare as fine pearls."

"Italy really does furnish very few of them. Then, if I agreed to pose for you..."

"I would be too happy, Mademoiselle."

"But then I would have to go to your studio every day."

"Your father could come with you."

"Oh! He wouldn't like anything better. Only..."

"What is it?"

"I would like to be sure of not meeting anyone there, especially not brunette Italian women. I don't have the same reasons as my father for detesting them, but I have a great failing... I'm horribly jealous."

That statement was certainly a declaration. The artist, who understood the meaning of all that intimate language was about to increase his own, when Monsieur Paulet brusquely entered.

"My dear friend," he said with an agitated air, "You'll have to excuse me. My daughter and I must leave you. The telegram which I've just received, tells me that my brother died today at three o'clock."

"Believe me, Monsieur, that I'm very sorry for your loss," Freneuse stammered.

"The telegram tells me he has disinherited me. What I was afraid of has happened. He leaves all his fortune to I don't know what foreign streetwalker. But, even though I don't have any reason to bless his memory, I can't remain at the theater. That would be indecent. Come, Marguerite. My valet is going to have a carriage sent and we're going to finish our evening at the house."

Freneuse surprised, and a little troubled, by that news, had gotten up and stood at the front of the box. Mademoiselle Paulet had risen also, and her facial expression showed not profound sadness but a very obvious annoyance. Obviously she was less affected by the death of an uncle she had never seen, than she was vexed by leaving so quickly company which pleased her. Monsieur Paulet appeared upset, and assuredly this was not because of a brother he regretted losing. He hardly knew him, and he scarcely loved him. But, even if you are a millionaire, you don't easily resign yourself to losing an important inheritance.

Freneuse looked at the situation from the point of view of his continuing relations with the father and the daughter. It seemed to him that he shouldn't distress himself too much. The inheritance which they had missed getting would perhaps have doubled their fortune, and the richer Marguerite became, the more the chances were that Monsieur Paulet would become more demanding concerning the advantages his son-inlaw would bring to the marriage. But this wasn't the moment to think about that. The father was in a hurry to leave, and the usher, whom he had told they were leaving, brought the young girl's hat and cloak. Freneuse, leaning on the box partition, not knowing very well what to say, watched them, and the three of them formed an easily seen group. It was the intermission, and in the downstairs audience, a great many opera glasses were trained on Mademoiselle Marguerite.

"Stay here, my friend," Monsieur Paulet said to the artist, who was preparing to accompany them to their carriage. "You're not in mourning; and it's certainly a small thing that you take advantage of seeing the end of the play that we must leave so as not to violate society's rules. I assure you we'd prefer to finish our evening with you."

And as Freneuse started to protest:

"Don't insist, my dear fellow," continued the capitalist, "You will disoblige me. Besides, we'll see each other again soon. As soon as I'm free of the worries that I'm going to have to assume following the death of my unfortunate brother, we'll come surprise you one day in your studio, I warn you."

Freneuse couldn't do anything else but bow. He shook Monsieur Paulet's hand; Marguerite held hers out to him, in the English fashion, and she underlined that gracious gesture by giving him an encouraging smile.

Freneuse remained alone, but he had something to console him for the beauty's departure. His affairs had started out well and he hoped they weren't going to remain there. The father had just shown the greatest good humor and the daughter, in a three minute tête-à-tête, had just gone as much forward as the reserve imposed on young ladies by their up-bringing allowed her.

"This is becoming serious," the artist told himself, *"and I'm beginning to believe that it just depends on me to possess an adorable wife before long and a father-in-law graced with a 70,000 pound income. The question now is to find out if all this good fortune is worth the sacrifice of my freedom. I don't make much use of it, except to work from morning to night, but I work as I like. If I marry Mademoiselle Paulet, I would be condemned to paint nothing but blondes. She pointed that out to me. Poor Pia, I would have to close my studio door to her, and she's capable of dying of sadness Bah!"* Freneuse, summed up, *"I could be free of her by sending her back to Subiaco with a handsome sum that would help her find a fine husband down there in her country."*

While reflecting thus, he put on his hat preparing to leave, since he didn't at all care to see the end of the *Chevaliers du brouillard*. He looked vaguely at the audience. Few of the spectators had left their seat during the act which had just finished and the one about to begin. In the orchestra seats, everyone was seated, except one woman. That woman was going toward the exit, just at the moment they expected the curtain to raise, and she was maneuvering so as to rejoin a gentleman standing at the entrance to the corridor, motioning her to hurry.

"*Well! Well!*" murmured Freneuse. "*That's the business agent and his companion who're leaving in the middle of the play. Why are they in such a hurry to clear out? Could it be because they saw me in Monsieur Paulet's box? That's possible because I stayed seated in the back until the moment the father and daughter got up. Then they might be afraid to leave the same time as I do. Well! I'm going to foil their calculation. I'll arrive at the exit before they do and I'll meet them face to face. Oh! Binos what foolish acts the ideas you've stuffed my head with make me commit.*"

Bringing to mind that art student dauber, the hunter of clues, Freneuse went rapidly into the corridor and ran to the stairway, without taking the time to put on his overcoat, which the usher had just given him. He cleared the stair steps descending from the second tier boxes four at a time. He ran so well that he was ahead of the two suspects he was trying to examine up close. It was also important for him to see without being seen. That was why, in order to make himself less noticeable, he hastened outside the theater and took a position a little to the right of the exit door.

A minute later, the man and woman appeared under the peristyle. They were arm in arm and they stopped a moment on the threshold. The man looked in one direction, the woman in the other.

"*Good!*" Freneuse thought. "*They're cautious. They don't dare step out onto the sidewalk without being sure I'm not watching them. Obviously, they're afraid of running into me. Ah! She's put down her veil... That was a mistake because now she reminds me exactly of the woman on the omnibus. What's more, I don't think she's noticed me yet. Wait! There's the orange merchant going up to them.*"

In fact, the old gossip had come to plant herself in front of them and was harrying them with loud offers of merchandise.

"Three *sous*, beautiful Valencia!" she yelled, barring their passage with her tray of oranges. "Buy some oranges, my prince. Treat your lady. That will cost you less than at home."

Her proposition had no success. The man shoved her away without a second thought and quickly passed on. He led his companion and they went down the sidewalk arm in arm toward the monumental door that gives its name to the theatre. Freneuse immediately left his hiding place, and in three steps the joined the orange merchant, who greeted him with this exclamation:

"*Hein!* The proverb has a lot of truth to it; '*When you speak of the Devil,*' you know the one... Didn't I tell you I'd recognize him if I saw him again..."

"The man on the omnibus top?" Freneuse interrupted. "That really was the one, wasn't it?"

"Ah! I can guarantee you he was the one. And the particular woman he was dragging about seems to me to be the woman he helped yesterday evening at the Halles wine merchants stop. He made her acquaintance when he got off... You know... He gave her his seat. That's what comes from being polite to ladies. It's always the same. He's not generous, that gentleman. He could have treated his princess to my Valencia oranges. That wouldn't have ruined him."

Freneuse was already far away and the fat woman was still talking. Armed with that strong affirmation, which confirmed his suspicions, he had already dashed in pursuit of the couple in front of him who were slipping away. He wanted absolutely to know where these people lived.

And he had decided to follow them all the way to their lodgings, so as to be able to point out their domicile the next day to Binos, who would take it on himself to complete the investigation. He was immediately aware that they suspected his intentions. The woman turned around often and the man maneuvered so as to be hidden, mingling themselves with the theater-goers leaving the Renaissance Theater to stretch their legs during an intermission.[20] But Freneuse, who had good eyes, didn't lose sight of them. He had good legs, too, and he soon caught up with them. But as he didn't want to get too close to them, he slowed his steps and began to trail them at a more convenient distance. Without a doubt they felt him on their heels. They no longer looked behind them and they quickened their steps.

Freneuse saw them rapidly go past the omnibuses stationed near the entry to Saint-Martin, pass between the entry and the neighborhood, reach the Boulevard Saint-Denis, which began a little further on, and finally reach the large sidewalk where a long line of vehicles for rent were lined up.

"They're going to take a fiacre; that's clear," the artist said to himself. *"Diable! I didn't think about that. Well, I'll take one also. I don't intend to lose their trail, right up to the door of the house where they live."*

Freneuse wasn't mistaken. The man and his companion approached a vehicle and entered into a discussion with the coachman, who had gotten down from his seat. The carriage at the head of the line was near the entry to the Rue Saint-Denis, and the *fiacre* they'd chosen was the fifth in line from the head of the queue. Freneuse took the last one, in order not to draw their attention. He put his hand on the carriage door-handle and to give the suspected couple time to get into the carriage he pretended to look for a cigar in his case.

"Are we ready to go?" asked the coachman, from atop his seat.

"Do you see that gentleman and lady who're talking over there with your comrade? As soon as they are in the carriage and it starts off, follow it."

"Understood. Then, when you're ready."

"Yes, and there's a good tip for you if you don't lose them."

"Me, a *Camille*, let myself be outdistanced by a rattletrap like the *Général*? There's no danger of that. Get in, sir, and rely on me not to lose the woman you're shadowing along the way... I know about these things," said the coach-

---

[20] Alexandre Dumas, père and Victor Hugo were instrumental in constructing this theatre built to stage the Romantic dramas of the era. The building at #20 Boulevard Saint-Martin resembles that of the Opera.

man in the white hat.

Freneuse, delighted to have come across an intelligent man, was watching out of the corner of his eye, the couple parleying a little further away, and was astonished that the discussion of terms was taking so long.

"The orange merchant was right," he thought. *"This gentleman from the omnibus roof is a skinflint. He's bargaining about the cost of a trip. Ah! He's deciding to pay in advance. He's putting the money in the coachman's hands. He's opening the door. He's helping the lady in...and he's getting in after her. Now's the time to do the same. They think they've thrown me off the track. They don't suspect that I'm going to chase them down."*

"Are we ready, Monsieur ?" asked the coachman. "They're all inside, the colleague down there has just climbed up on his perch, and he's already tapped his nag to make him start."

"Go on," said Freneuse. "And don't follow them too closely. We must not let them know that we're following them."

"Don't worry. They won't see anything but the lights."

Freneuse jumped into the carriage, and, looking out the window, he was pleased to note that the other carriage had just left the line and was rolling slowly down the Boulevard carriage way. The *Camille* driver hadn't exaggerated. His horse was fast and he didn't need to push him to keep up. He took his place ten feet from the Général Company's four-seater, and maintained the pace without any trouble.

"Where are they going?" Freneuse wondered. *"Into my neighborhood, very probably. Yesterday evening the man got off at the Rue de la Tour d'Auvergne and the woman on the Rue de Laval."*

He was surprised to see the *fiacre* carrying them turn obliquely to the left and go down the Boulevard de Sebastopol,

"I was wrong," he murmured. *"It's the opposite. They're turning their back toward Montmartre. And, actually, nothing proves that they live there. They took the Place Pigalle omnibus to make their strike. After that, they could very easily go back across the bridges to return to their house. It doesn't make any difference if they live on the Left Bank. I'm free the whole evening. It wouldn't be the same thing if I were married."*

That last thought made him remember Mademoiselle Paulet, whom he had somewhat forgotten since leaving the theatre box. And he also remembered that the father of that adorable person knew the man with the toothbrush mustache. He even knew him extremely well, since he employed him as a business agent.

"Parbleu!" he said to himself. *"I don't need to go to so much trouble. I can find out whenever I like the name and address of that person. Monsieur Paulet didn't remember them, but he had them written down on his card and he promised to give them to me. I would really like to give up this chase, which doesn't tell me anything Monsieur can't tell me."*

He raised his hand to push the call button to stop the coachman, but some other ideas occurred to him.

"Yes," he thought to himself, *"Monsieur Paulet will tell me as much as he knows, but it could be that this unusual fellow introduced himself under a false name and gave him a false address. A man of that type is very capable of having two domiciles. And it would be interesting to see if the wench accompanying him lives with him. And besides that, when will I see Monsieur Paulet? His brother's death is going to keep him busy. I don't dare present myself at his house until several days from now. In the circumstances he finds himself, I can't decently write to him asking for such insignificant information. So I'll save time if I continue to end the chase I've begun,"* concluded Freneuse. *"The question is to know where this nice couple is going to lead me. On the other side of the river; that looks very probable. We're coming up on the Place du Chatelet. The carriage is rolling toward the Pont au Change...still straight ahead. If he continues like this, he'll take me to the St. Jacques gate. We won't be there in an hour because he's traveling like a tortoise."*

That was true. The carriage that the couple had gotten into wasn't going fast. The two horses pulling it were lolling along as if they were following a funeral cortege. And it was somewhat astonishing that the business agent had chosen to return home in one of those enormous two bench *fiacres* with a grill on top which is hardly ever used for anything except for transporting to the train station travelers weighed down by baggage. The respectable vehicle was traveling so slowly that Freneuse's coachman had all the trouble in the world preventing his horse from passing the calm team trotting in front of him.

"These people aren't in a hurry," the artist said to himself. *"That certainly proves they don't know I'm following them. What a look they'll have on their faces when they see me get out the same time they do... But, really, will I get out? It seems to me that would be completely useless. My intention isn't to ask them for explanations. It will be enough for me to know where they live. As soon as they've returned to their home, I'll return to mine."*

So, as he had foreseen, the carriage, after having gone across the Place du Chatelet, went across the Pont au Change; but instead of continuing straight, it turned left, onto the Quai de la Cite and soon arrived at the tip of Notre Dame.

"Ah! What about that! Are they going to the morgue?" Freneuse wondered, recognizing the municipal building where the unidentified dead are laid out. *"That would be a bit too much! But no, at this hour the building is closed. The carriage isn't stopping. They're going over the Pont de l'Archevêche. Obviously the couple lives on the Left Bank...and probably in the same neighborhood as Pia because the carriage is now rolling along the Quai de la Tournelle."*

It was rolling along so well that it arrived at a middling trot at the crossroad where the Boulevard Saint-Germain ends, at the entrance to the Pont Henri IV.[21] There the coachman walked his horses, swerving a little to the right, and

---

[21] Now called Pont de Sully.

71

halted them in front of a house which formed an angle between the Boulevard and the Rue des Fosses-Saint-Bernard. Freneuse gently lowered the front window and pulled on the sleeve of the *Camille* driver, who turned around and said to him in a low voice:

"If Monsieur will let me choose my place to stop, Monsieur will be able to see without anyone seeing him."

At the same time, he maneuvered so as to park along the sidewalk, behind the first carriage. This was done very quickly, and Freneuse immediately leaned against the door, in order not to miss the exit of the man and woman traveler. To his great astonishment, no one appeared. The coachman of the four-seated *fiacre* had just linked the reins to the whip guard, and got down heavily from his seat. He unbridled his horses, attached the feedbag to their necks, and started to light up his pipe without being in a hurry, like a man who knows he'll have a lot of time to smoke it.

"What does that mean?" Freneuse muttered. *"They've arrived at their destination. Why don't they get out? Do they suspect that I'm spying on them? No, because if they suspected it they could've gone further trying to throw me off the track.*

At the end of five minutes' uncertainty and anxious wait, the painter heard the coachman say very low:

"I have an idea that the lady in question has played a trick on us, and there's nobody in the carriage."

That comment was a moment of enlightenment for Freneuse. He opened the door, jumped to the sidewalk and approached the carriage, shut tighter than ever. The windows were rolled up, but, by looking sideways, it was easy for him to assure himself that the interior was empty.

"And your passengers," he asked, trying to assume a disinterested air. "Did you scatter them on the way?

"My passengers?" laughed the coachman. "I'm waiting for them, but I don't think they're going to come. It's all the same to me, seeing that I'm paid to stay here until 10:30 p.m. The quarter hour has just sounded and when my beasts have finished their oats, I'm going back to the company depot. My day is done. I got a hundred *sous* tip."

"But the gentleman and the lady who got in at the Porte Saint-Martin…?

"What! You yourself saw that…and you followed them from that point? Ah! well, they played a good trick on you. They got in my rolling box on one side and they got out of it on the other. That was agreed with the bourgeois. He handed me over ten francs in advance for my letting them pass through, the lady and himself, and for dragging along empty to here. It was just a matter of making you run to the Halles wine market while they rush about on the grand boulevards. I see that now, and I believe it's not worth the trouble for me to pose in front of this door. They knew you were following me. They aren't stupid enough to come get picked up here."

Freneuse understood perfectly the justice of this reasoning. He didn't say a thing. He turned around, his head lowered, ashamed of letting himself be fooled, and swearing he would never again be taken in following trails.

"Well!" he muttered to himself, getting back to his carriage, *"Everyone to his own job. I was no more born to do the job of the police than Binos was created to be a painter. But I'm now very sure that the man and the woman were in the omnibus yesterday evening. If they hadn't recognized me, they wouldn't have taken so much trouble to escape me. And if they feared me so much, that's because they don't have a clear conscience. Fortunately, Monsieur Paulet will give me their address, and then we'll see..."*

"Place Pigalle, driver, and hurry!"

IV. The Bouvelard Rochechouart; Binos and Piédouche

The Boulevard Rochechouart is the neighborhood par excellence for dingy bistro cafés which in Paris slang they call *caboulots*. There are also respectable cafés there and some licensed shops where honest workers come to drink a liter at the counter; but the first kind of establishment is in the majority. In addition, the *caboulots* aren't frequented exclusively by people of low life. Bohemians, who seldom work, come there, it's true, but only those who've never had any trouble with the police. Painters' studios abound in these neighborhoods and the art students strolling about aren't too particular about the quality of the drinks and the choice of society. It's enough for them that the proprietor extends credit to his regular customers and that he doesn't show himself too demanding about dress. They could come wearing open-collared working class dress, and play dominoes all day, or all evening, without being obliged to have their glasses refilled too often.

Friend Binos was one of those. He had for a long time been a regular customer in one of these nice places. He roosted on the top floor, Rue Myrrha, and the *Grand-Bock* was situated between the Rue Clignancourt and the Boulevard Ornano, two steps from his lodgings. This privately owned bar didn't look like much from the outside. Its tile front wasn't washed too often, and the dirty curtains hid the mysteries of the room at the back from passers-by. There was a billiard table full of holes and some wooden benches stationed about so that drunks could sleep on them in comfort. But the inside was decorated with frescoes due to Binos' imaginative paint brush that had covered the walls with strange and incongruous figures. This work, done for free, had gained him the good graces of the master of the house, Old Man Poireau, better known by the name Old Poivreau, because of his taste for absinthe. He regularly drank a half-liter a day, and he held it not too badly, although he was tipsy beginning at daylight and he went to bed drunk almost every evening.

Binos was at home there. He had an open tab, and he enjoyed almost unlimited credit. He spent about twelve hours out of twenty-four there and he had, you might say, influential standing. When it pleased him to hold forth on great art; the regular customers didn't understand anything about it, but they listened to him as if he were an oracle. And he'd made friends he was sure of meeting there, because they hardly ever left. They thought it an honor to buy him a drink when he was thirsty, since he didn't associate with everybody. He stayed away from those pretty gentlemen, regular dancers at the *Boule-Noire* and the *Reine-Blanche,* who got together convivially to play pool at Old Man Poivreau's bar. He even shunned the little neighborhood merchants who sometimes came in to play piquet. He became friendly only with very steady people: a marble tombstone maker for the Saint-Ouen cemetery, for whom he designed extravagant tombstones; a retired man named Monsieur Piédouche, who had a very distinguished air; a druggist retired from business, who didn't show up very well in conversations, because he was deaf, but who admired artists in general and Binos in particular. This man was, to tell the truth, the scapegoat of the malicious amateur artist. Binos never spared him the bar expenses, but the good man never got angry, and persistently searched out the company of his persecutor.

On the contrary, Binos had for Monsieur Piédouche a sympathy deepened by a certain respect. Monsieur Piédouche's frank and determined manners attracted him. His speaking charmed him. Monsieur Piédouche was a most agreeable talker. He had seen a great deal and retained a great deal. He knew a great number of countries and a great many people. He talked about everything like a sensible man, and he gave good advice. With that, he was discreet to the point of never telling what he was doing, nor what he had done in his youth. Binos thought that he'd served in the army, but he wasn't sure. In trying to find out what that amiable companion might be, he had finally imagined that he was attached to high political or diplomatic police. And he liked him even more. The police, that was his monomania and he never missed an opportunity to direct the conversation to this interesting subject. Nevertheless, Piédouche never dealt with that topic except with extreme reserve.

But for three days, Binos futilely waited for his preferred partner at the *Grand-Bock*. Monsieur Piédouche had stopped coming there. That unexpected vanishing enormously annoyed Bino, who was burning with desire to consult him about the omnibus affair. Piédouche had become invisible, precisely on the day after that tragic happening.

Binos bitterly deplored this annoying event and asked all those at the *Grand-Bock* about his Piédouche. Nobody had seen Piédouche and Old Man Poivreau wasn't in any condition to give any news about this faithful customer of his establishment. They knew Piédouche lived in the neighborhood; some said in the Place d'Anvers, others said Rue de Dunkerque; but he never invited his acquaintances from the café to his house. Binos himself did not know his address, although he had asked him for it several times. Piédouche had always avoided giving it exactly, and the mystery with which he had surrounded his life hadn't contributed a little to persuade the amateur artist that he was a member of the police. His unexplained absence had only confirmed Binos in his opinion. He was convinced that Piédouche had just been charged with some secret mission and that he wouldn't be seen again for some time. And he was extremely sorry about that, because he had counted on his knowledge, and even on his help, to clear up the very complicated story that he had bragged about unraveling.

To Paul Freneuse he had solemnly sworn to discover the woman who had used the pin and her accomplice riding on the bus top. He understood now that he had taken on too much and that by himself he couldn't do anything. He admitted his powerlessness to himself. That admission humiliated him to the point that he couldn't show himself at his friend's in the Place Pigalle. Now, Freneuse wasn't a man to go out looking for Binos. When Binos came to the studio, Freneuse made him welcome, in memory of a former camaraderie, born at the School of Fine Arts, in the already distant days of their youth. But, since they entered life by the same door, they had followed such different ways that the bounds of that camaraderie had somewhat relaxed. Freneuse went about in the fashionable world, and was perfectly at home there. Binos, with his slovenly dress and appearance, would have been out of place in a drawing room. Freneuse held bistro-cafés in horror, and Binos seldom left them. As a result, they hadn't seen each other in three days.

Binos had firmly established himself at the *Grand-Bock*. He never went far from it except to take a turn through the morgue. His only object was to see if the young girl from the omnibus was still there or if someone had recognized her. He always came back from that gloomy trip without having learned anything new. No one had come forward to claim the body and the time fixed by the regulations had just expired the morning of the third day.

The registrar clerk said they were going ahead with the burial. The poor corpse was going to be thrown into the public grave pit. The secret of the crime was going to be buried with the victim in the paupers' cemetery. The certainty of this very close denouement dismayed Binos and made him remorseful. He was at the point of asking if it would just be better for him to carry the poisoned hat pin to the Commissioner and to tell the Commission about the scene on the omnibus, without taking into account the repugnance of his friend Freneuse to get mixed up in that business. But he would a great deal more preferred to do the work himself, in collaboration with that Piédouche, who, in his estimation, was cleverer than all the policemen in the world.

While the imprudent dauber cooled his heels waiting for this personage, Paul Freneuse, who could have furnished Binos with important clues, stayed quiet in his studio, and didn't want to see him at all. Paul Freneuse, after thinking about it, had taken the position of remaining quiet until there was new information, that is to say, until Monsieur Paulet gave him the address of that business agent who had so subtly hidden himself the evening of the *Chevaliers du brouillard* play. Paul Freneuse worked furiously and thought a great deal more frequently about Mademoiselle Marguerite than about the suspicious couple he had chased.

So, the third day, toward noon, after having dined on a plate of sauerkraut, washed down by several glasses of beer, Binos, melancholy, walked across the main room of his favorite *caboulet.* His forehead troubled and his pipe between his lips, with every turn he went to glue his face against the glass door, always hoping he would see Piédouche come up the boulevard. It was the time he usually arrived to play billiards or dominoes. But Piédouche didn't appear.

Old Man Poivreau was asleep on his counter between a bottle of absinthe and an empty glass. The retired druggist, who answered to the name of Pigache, was reading a newspaper in a corner, and probably was very interested in what he was reading. He was not saying a word and was as immobile as a stone, although Binos had already thrown several jibes at him, which hardly touched him, since he was deaf. Binos, exasperated by the boredom of waiting, was getting ready to play a dirty trick on him by setting fire to his newspaper with a match, when suddenly the bistrocafé's door opened.

"Good day, friends! Hello, Father Poivreau!" said a loud voice which awakened the owner of the establishment and made the druggist, deep into reading his newspaper, raise his head.

"Piédouche!" exclaimed Binos. "Finally, you're here! That's not unfortunate. I've been asking everybody about you for three days."

"To offer me a glass of *fine,* I'll wager," the illustrious Piédouche, who seemed to be in a happy mood, said, laughing.

"That, first of all...and then for something else. And so, where have you been? Then have you been sick?"

"Me, sick! Look at my torso! Do I look like a draftee who's been exempted because of a weak constitution?"

"No, *parbleu!* but even if you are healthy, you aren't exempt from being indisposed. I often have a hangover, me, who's as strong as the Pont Neuf. And when I saw you didn't come three days in a row, I was worried. If I'd known your address, I'd have gone to inquire about you."

"Oh! That wouldn't have been worth the trouble. I never go back home except to sleep. I left on a trip Tuesday evening, and I just returned this morning."

"Then that explains everything. Did you go very far?"

"No, only 15 leagues from Paris...on business...about a little inheritance which dropped from the skies."

"That's better than a tile or a paving stone...my compliments, old boy, That's an accident that never happens to me."

"Bah! Who knows? But while we're waiting, I'm buying drinks this morning. Father Poivreau, a small decanter and some glasses! ...and hurry up, *hein*? Well! He's guessed what I wanted, the old devil...the cognac is already open...and he's put the tray on the table, beside the respectable Pigache. That's so I'll invite this old fellow. Bah! I don't ask for anything better than to stand for one drink more. Today I'm on a spree."

"*Parbleu!* If I'd gotten an inheritance, I'd invite everybody who passed by. But I don't hold with drinking in the neighborhood of Old Man Pigache."

"Why's that? What's he ever done to you, the poor old fogy?"

"Oh! Nothing. Only I have a story to tell you, and advice to ask you... just for myself."

"All right. He won't hear us chat. He's deaf as a post."

"That's true. I wasn't thinking about that. By speaking low I won't be afraid he'll catch a single word. We can sit near this druggist."

"Intimate confidences! Secrets! That's certainly something new! Are you

77

conspiring against the government? The devil! That won't do at all."

"Oh! I understand that," said Binos, who took this statement for an admission. "I understand that you can't get mixed up in things like that. When you're part of the administration... But it's not about that... It's about a private affair."

"An affair! That's for me. Explain it to me, but let's drink first," said Piédouche, who had filled the three glasses and seated himself shoulder to shoulder with Pigache.

"To your health, papa," he continued, patting his neighbor's shoulder.

"All right, and you?" answered the old man, bewildered.

"He thinks I've asked him about his health," Piédouche laughed. "He must have crushed some of those drugs to be so hard of hearing. Leave him alone and tell me your story. He'll drink if he takes a notion to, and if he doesn't, we'll empty the carafe by ourselves"

Binos, already leaning on the table, wanted nothing but to get to the subject. He began the story of the omnibus trip, starting the beginning, without omitting any detail. Everything was there, from the episode of the seat given up at the start to the catastrophe of the arrival. He described in colorful language the three characters of this drama, the two accomplices and their victim, the silent scene which had taken place at the descent on the Pont Neuf, the amazement of the employees at the moment it was established that the young woman passenger had died during the trip. Nothing was missing in this moving tableau, except that he put himself in the scene instead of speaking about his friend. He attributed outright to himself the role Paul Freneuse had played. His egotism was part of it, and he judged it useless to compromise a comrade who didn't care to be involved in an affair of this kind.

Monsieur Piédouche listened to him with close attention and marked interest. He allowed himself, however, to smile two or three times, and he finally exclaimed:

"Now there's an adventure! But how the devil did you find yourself at a quarter to midnight in the wine merchant Halles?"

"I had spent the evening looking for a woman who lived in that vicinity...a model," stammered Binos, who hadn't anticipated that question.

"Ah! Well! It really has to be said; the story of that sudden death, that's very interesting, but what do you want to consult me about?"

"I want to know what you think about that strange accident."

"But," answered Piédouche, shrugging, "I don't think anything at all. "I'm not a doctor."

"Me neither. And however, I'm sure that poor girl was assassinated in the omnibus."

"All right! By whom and how, please?

On that, Binos took up the second part of the account that he'd been preparing for three days. He recounted the discovery of the poisoned hat pin and the fragment of the letter, the experiment that had cost a cat's life, then his multiple visits to the morgue, his uncertainties and the solutions he had drawn after he had thoroughly reflected. He concluded by begging Piédouche to help him, giving him the benefit of his knowledge and to join him in the battle to locate the abominable couple who had perpetrated that dastardly work.

Piédouche had become serious. He shook his head in an understanding way at each observation Binos formulated, and he downed, one after the other, three small glasses before answering.

"Ma foi!" he finally said. "I'm beginning to believe that death wasn't natural. Have you set out the facts to the Police Commissioner?"

"I've been careful not to, because I want to avoid him. It'll be time to bring him up to date when I know how to lay hold of the woman who did the murder and her accomplice."

"You're right. Commissioners often do stupid things. They would suspect you. But, tell me....You've kept the hat pin and the torn letter?"

"Oh! I can tell you I have! I carry them over my heart. Look."

Saying this, Binos drew from his jacket pocket a case in which he usually kept his favorite pipe. He opened it and he took out the two clues that Freneuse had given him: in the case, the hat pin in the place of the absent pipe stem, and the letter in the place of the bowl.

"That's an ingenious hiding place," Piédouche said, laughing.

"You can understand that I was afraid of losing the objects, and above all of sticking myself," the artist exclaimed." But I'm not preventing you from examining them; and I even ask you to. Only handle the hat pin with caution."

"I won't handle it at all; that would be the safest thing. I'll be content to decipher, if you'll permit me to, what's written on this piece of paper."

"What! If I'd let you! I've been wanting for some time to know what you think of it. As for me, I find the proof of the crime is at the end of each line."

While Piédouche unfolded the crumpled up piece of paper, Binos, looking up, saw that Old Man Pigache was smiling wickedly. The fellow hadn't been distracted from reading his paper by a conversation his deafness kept him from hearing, but he had good eyesight. The exhibit of the hat pin seemed to cheer him up infinitely.

"Ah! My fine fellow," he said, pointing to it with his finger, "You're making relics of your girl friend's finery! That's what it's like to be young. She's pretty, *hein!* The pretty girl who holds her hat on with that?"

"Don't touch! That bites," Binos yelled at him.

And for more safety, Binos closed the case.

"Good! Good! Don't be jealous my boy," continued the deaf man. "There's no more of that at my age, those silly things."

"Read your newspaper and let us alone, you old fogy," grumbled Binos.

"You say I'm well conserved...you flatter me young man; but I don't hold it against you," answered Pigache, going back to his newspaper. He always devoured it to the last line.

"Obviously, we don't need to be worried. He's deafer than I thought, and Old Man Poivreau has started to snore on his counter. You can continue with your opinion about the letter, old man."

"The letter doesn't prove very much," murmured Piédouche."There's not one sentence which has a complete meaning."

"No, but you can read between the lines. *'She arrived a month ago... She,* that's obviously the little one they pierced in the omnibus. *I'm returning to my first plan...*the plan to kill her with the hatpin, that's clear. *She goes out very little, but she goes out sometimes in the evening...*still the little one. The scoundrel who wrote that doesn't know to whose house, but he knows where...in the wine merchant Halles area, *parbleu!* and he waited for her on her return."

"Dear friend, you're very good, better than I am, because I'd never have found all you're telling me in that. But, as for the hat pin, I can find out, if you want to know what poison it was dipped in. I know a chemist who's first rate in those matters. He will conduct experiments, analyses...all the devil and what goes with it."

"That suits me!" Binos exclaimed.

"Only, you have to entrust me with the object," added Piédouche.

"Give you the hat pin!" said Binos. "But I don't ask anything better. I'm sure you won't make bad use of it. It will be as safe with you as with me."

"I'd ask you to be present at the tests," Piédouche continued, "But that might upset my chemist...because...you understand, he's an expert certified by the courts, and this is not a matter of a legal experiment. If I told him the story of the omnibus, he would perhaps be afraid of compromising himself by putting his knowledge at the service of an individual he doesn't know. As for me, his friend, he won't ask for any explanation...or at least he'll be satisfied with the one I invent."

"That's right. Take the hat pin, dear fellow, and the case in the bargain...on one condition, however..."

"What?"

"On the condition that you promise to work with me. I've sworn to find the guilty persons, and without you, I can't do anything worthwhile."

"How does it happen that you have such a high opinion of my talents as an investigator?" Piédouche asked, laughing.

"*Ma foi!* At the point we are in the matter, I can certainly tell you," Binos exclaimed "I imagine that in the past you've worked in that sort of profession."

"That's very flattering to me...above all if you're not like a lot of people who're prejudiced against the police and against all those connected with them."

"Me! If I were not an artist, I would like to be a secret agent, that is to say, let's understand each other, not a paid informer. I'd like to hunt down men as an amateur...for my benefit or for the benefit of my friends...like Monsieur Lecoq in Gaboriau's novels."

"Monsieur Lecoq, if I'm not mistaken, was a professional."

"Me, no. I missed my calling. But I don't hold it against you that you've been one."

"However that may be," Piédouche said with a discreet smile, "I ask you to believe that I'm not one now."

"That's another reason for you to work on my affair. If you were attached to the Prefecture, that would hamper your going along with me; while, free as you are, you can take the investigations in the direction I want to undertake."

"There's nothing hindering that, in fact, but if they end with a result, what will that mean for us?"

"The pleasure of avenging the death of a poor girl assassinated by scoundrels."

"That's something, I agree. The question is to know if we have a chance of succeeding. You told me, I believe, that the victim hasn't been recognized at the morgue?"

"Unfortunately, no, and they are burying her this evening."

"The Devil! There's not a minute to lose. If we don't discover who she is, we won't find those who murdered her. And I admit that I don't know at all how we can find out her name."

"There's one way; that's to find out where she lived."

"If you think that's easy..."

"No, but it's not impossible. We already have a clue. Read the torn letter again. On the third line, there's rue *des...* and not rue *de..."*

"Actually, this plural is a starting point."

"Perfectly...And I would already have gone through all the streets with names in the plural if I hadn't been kept here in hopes of meeting you. For the last three days I haven't, you might say, been out of the *Grand-Bock*. Poivreau could vouch for it, if he wasn't drunk, and I'd call on Old Man Pigache's testimony, if the creature wasn't deaf."

"Nothing can be done about it! I was busy with my inheritance. This delay is nonetheless very annoying, and we must try to make up for it. By consulting the Bottin address book, we'll have the complete list of the streets that interest us, and then we can divide the work between us. You'll visit half of Paris, while I visit the other. Besides, there's a method to follow to shorten the search. That unfortunate girl, didn't you tell me, took the last omnibus from the wine merchants of the Halles?"

"Yes, the one that doesn't get to its destination until past midnight."

"Therefore, she was going home to bed. Therefore, she must have lived in the vicinity of the Place Pigalle. Therefore, it would be logical to begin with this neighborhood. Do you know a street *des* there?"

"I know several of them: the Rue des Martyrs...the Rue des Abbesses..."

"All right, let's look at these two before all the others."

"Hum! The Rue des Abbesses is terribly long. It starts at the Notre Dame de Lorette church and goes up hill right to the Butte Montmartre."

"What!" Piédouche exclaimed, laughing, "You're already shirking work!"

"No, but I'm afraid of losing time."

"Then, let's start with the Rue des Abbesses."

"It's very near here, the Rue des Abbesses," said Binos, "and it's not very long. There's no reason that we shouldn't start with it. I say *we* because you seem inclined to accompany me. That fits me like a glove. Without you, I wouldn't do anything worthwhile. I still don't know how to talk to doorkeepers. You'll teach me the job, and when I possess the basics, you'll see that I won't do too badly on my own."

"I'm convinced of it." Piédouche pronounced gravely. "Besides, you'll find it's not very difficult. It's only a matter of having self-confidence and a little mental discernment. But if you want your apprenticeship to profit you, you must get information for yourself. I'll be there, and I'll prompt you."

"Perfect! Then let's get to work immediately."

"I like that noble enthusiasm, and I'm completely in agreement. You'll allow me to take the poisoned hat pin?"

"The hat pin and the letter if you like. I'll be a great deal easier when they are in your hands, because, in my lodgings there's not one piece of furniture with a lock, and all my pockets are more or less full of holes."

"The devil! It would be annoying to lose clues as precious as these, and since that's how it is, I'll keep everything, in trust, of course, and agree to return the objects to you as soon as you ask," said Piédouche, putting the torn piece of paper in the case where the hat pin already lay.

Old Man Pigache, who had finished reading his newspaper, watched him do it, smiling in a silly way.

"Does it astonish you, papa, that I'm pocketing these knick-knacks," Piédouche said loudly. "There's nothing to be surprised at. That just clearly proves my friend Binos has confidence in me."

"What are you saying?" asked the old man, turning his ear to him.

"Nothing at all, old fool," laughed Binos, who was already standing up.

Piédouche went over to shake the owner of the establishment, woke him, paid for the drinks, and left. Binos followed him out to the boulevard. They walked side by side toward the Place Saint-Pierre, which runs from the foot of the Butte Montmartre. You can take that route to go to the Rue des Abbesses, and Piédouche probably had his reasons for adopting that itinerary. Piédouche was always very properly dressed and he probably wasn't anxious to take the more frequented ways while going about in the company of an art student dressed in an extremely dirty jacket and wearing a soft hat with extravagant brims.

"My dear fellow," he said, just as they entered the Rue d'Orsel, "I imagine that poor girl must not have had a home of her own. I thought that to myself from to the description you gave me of her dress."

"It's true her get-up wasn't brilliant," murmured Binos. "Dressed like Jenny the worker. She must have lived in an attic room."

"Yes, in a rooming house. I'm asking you that because my opinion is to begin our investigation with private houses."

"Good idea! Excellent idea! Ah! You have talent! Me, I would never have thought of that. And since you reason so well, tell me a little about why they killed the little thing...assuredly not to rob her... They found only fourteen *sous* on her."

"What! You haven't guessed? It was a woman's vengeance. She'd taken the lover or the husband of a lady who took it badly."

"That's possible..., but she didn't have a face that would steal other women's men."

"Pardon! You told me yourself that she was remarkably beautiful."

"Yes, but with the modest and reserved air of a girl who's never left her mother."

"*Peuh!* You mustn't always believe appearances. Well-behaved young ladies don't wander around alone at midnight in omnibuses. Besides, we don't have to worry about that until later. When we know who she is, it'll be time enough to try to find out why someone did her in."

"Brigadier, you're right," said Binos, who always agreed with Piédouche.

They were walking quickly, and they had already gone past the Montmartre theatre. The Rue des Abbesses, which goes right up to the Rue Lepic, begins a little further on. It's one of the best of this area and rooming houses, which abound on the outside boulevard, are somewhat rare here. The houses have a middle-class, respectable appearance; the city hall and the post office of the 18th arrondissement are there. It is, in addition, very little frequented. You can chat there comfortably without bothering passers-by. Soon Piédouche stopped in the middle of the carriage way, and pointing out to Binos an intermediate door surmounted with a projecting window.

"My dear fellow," he said. "There's a cheap hotel that doesn't look like anything special. Precisely because of that, you're going to go in there."

"With you," added Binos.

"Oh, no, without me."

"What! You want me to go in alone to that rooming house!.... and question the person who runs it without you! The devil take me if I know what to say to him! To ask information from a landlord whose name I don't know, that's not very easy."

"You're making much of something that's a very little thing. There are three or four ways to go about it."

"Which one would you take?"

"The simplest. I would take a shiny 100 *sou* coin out of my pocket, and I would let the owner of the establishment see it. If you're doing business with a simple porter, a two franc coin will do. I would politely ask to know if he doesn't have as a lodger, a girl of such and such a type. It's a good bet he won't refuse to answer you. And if any one answers you no, that will be the truth, because these sorts of people know what talking means. They will certainly see that you won't turn loose of the coin except in exchange for useful information."

"It seems to me that you'd act that comedy better than I."

"No, because I've never seen the girl whose name you want to know. I'd describe her very badly. While you who've examined her at your leisure, you'll draw a portrait so resembling her that they'd recognize it immediately."

"The fact is that I could paint her from memory. I've even thought about painting her...lying on a slab in the morgue, a realistic subject for next year's Salon."

"Well, then, go ahead. What's holding you back?"

"*Ma foi!* I can certainly confess it to you. What's holding me back is that I don't have a five franc coin on me, nor a forty *sou* piece. I forgot my billfold at the house."

"Is that all? Here's mine," Piédouche said, taking from his pocket a nice leather purse. "There's enough in there to loosen the tongue of all the Montmartre landlords and please don't worry about paying me back."

Binos hesitated a moment for form's sake, but he accepted, saying:

"This is just a simple advance, dear friend, an advance that I'll pay you back one of these days. Besides I'm going to try to save you some money. I may get the information for thirty *sous*. But come to think of it...once I have it, if I have it, I won't be any further along. Suppose they tell me the person in question lived there, but she disappeared three days ago. What should I do?"

"You'll cleverly get information about her habits, the people who came to see her. You'll ask if she left baggage in her room...papers...what name she gave when she entered, ...and when you know all that, you have only to run to the morgue and make your report to the clerk, who will alert the police. The person renting rooms will be called. He'll recognize his lodger, since she hasn't yet been buried. From that point you'll have a base of operations, and you can begin a serious investigation."

"With you, I hope?"

"With me, if you insist. I don't care very much about getting mixed up in it openly, but I won't bargain with you about my opinions, if you think you need them."

"Piédouche, old man, we're together in life and in death," Binos exclaimed in an excess of enthusiasm. "I'm going to clear the threshold of this premise, which doesn't at all resemble a palace, and make my debut in the private detective field under your auspices. Then I'll come back to give you my report. I'm counting on your waiting for me."

"Gladly, up there on the square that's in front of the registry office. And don't hurry. I have time. If we've found the right place, carry the investigation further. Get complete information. Above all don't forget to ask if the missing lodger had any papers. It's important for the rest of your operations that her identity be established by authentic documentation."

"I understand, dear friend. And now…on to the Tour de Nesle," declaimed the amateur artist, hurrying toward the rooming house pointed out by the wise Piédouche, who began to slowly ascend the Rue des Abbesses.

The door to the hallway was open, and Binos went in with a firm step.

"What a man!" he murmured. "If the little girl really lodged here, Piédouche is the greatest policeman of modern times. He's led me directly to the right place. My word of honor, I'd almost be persuaded that he knew where it was."

The hallway wasn't large. Two men walking side by side would have had trouble walking through it. Neither was it very well lighted. Binos went forward cautiously, holding out his arms to touch the walls on either side. He finally felt a side corridor opening on the left, and a voice shouted:

"What do you want?"

"I'd like to talk to the concierge," Binos replied.

"There's no concierge here," said the voice, that of a woman.

"To the proprietor, then."

"I'm the proprietor. What do you need? Are you here to rent a room?"

"No, I'm here to find out about one of your women lodgers."

"Don't know any. I lodge only men."

"However, I was told…"

"What? Explain yourself…and first, come forward so I can see you."

Binos didn't ask anything better than to show himself, but he couldn't see a thing. He didn't know which way to turn to join the cantankerous person questioning him so rudely. By groping about with his fingers, however, he finally located a glassed door with an open louver. The door was ajar. He pushed it and entered a small room that was not much better lighted. Light came in only through a frosted glass bull's eye window that softened the dim light coming from an interior courtyard. He had trouble seeing a very shriveled little old woman who was warming herself in front of an almost extinguished coal fire.

"All right! Now talk," she shouted to him. "I know who I'm dealing with."

Binos would've liked to have been able to say as much, because he didn't understand anything about that reception. Disconcerted, Binos was wondering where he should begin. It was impossible to use the method recommended by Piédouche. Showing a five-franc piece wouldn't have produced any result. The old woman he was trying to coax by showing it to her wouldn't have been able to see the metal shining between the fingers of the stranger who was going to question her. But Binos never stayed very long in a difficult situation. If diplomacy wasn't his strong point, timidity wasn't his failing. He had a natural tendency, as they say, to put his foot in his mouth.

"You claim you know who you're dealing with," he began audaciously. "Let's bet you don't."

"If we bet, you would lose, my little man," replied the lady in the office, fixing on him two grey eyes which shone in the obscurity like the pupils of a cat's eye.

"I know you like the back of my hand."

"Ah! Bah! Tell me what my name is."

"I don't know your name, but I know you smear a good canvas with bad colors. You're a painter, my boy, and not a sign painter. I've met you fifty times on the Boulevard Clichy with your color box."

"Ah! I admit it, mother, and I'll paint your portrait whenever you like."

"I don't need my portrait. I've been looking in the mirror for fifty years. That's enough for me. And I forbid you to call me 'mother,' seeing that I have no children...nor husband either, thank God!"

"All right! I'll say Mademoiselle."

"No studio caricatures, youngster. I don't like them. What do you want?"

"To know if you haven't had in you lodgings a young woman I'm interested in."

"Well! There you are, my boy. I guessed that you came about her."

"About whom?" asked Binos, somewhat taken aback.

"About the Italian woman, *parbleu!* About Bianca."

"Ah! If you've guessed it...it's not worth while for me to contradict you," murmured Binos, who wanted to let the old woman talk.

"Then you're the one who seduced her...filthy bastard? That's what I suspected...that the silly girl had given in to the art students. She had rotten taste there. You took advantage of it, but you did a villainous thing. That little girl didn't have two ounces of vice in her. I would've gone through fire that she was innocent when she had the bad luck to find you in her path. Where did you pick her up, tell me, you monster? Was it in the Saint-Pierre market, where she want every morning to buy herbs for her dinner..., or in the evening on the Place Pigalle, when she was coming back from her singing lesson?"

"I swear on your head that I didn't seduce anyone."

"Shut up, you serpent! She hasn't been back in three days, she who's never stayed out all night. You dare tell me you didn't take her to your hovel."

"I'd hardly dare to," Binos exclaimed, delighted to hear these unmerited reproaches, because he had learned he'd found the right place. That Italian girl who'd disappeared three days before could only be the dead young girl in the omnibus. He already knew her name was Bianca, and it was just up to him to find out more.

"All right, it's useless for you to act the rogue with me. That won't work. Let the little girl be wherever she likes, I don't care. But you've come to claim her *baluchon*, haven't you? Well, you can tell her for me that if she wants it, she'll have to take the trouble to come get it. She can certainly take the trouble," the old woman continued. "She hasn't become a princess since she's with you."

"Pardon!" Binos stammered, "I've already told you..."

"Oh! I have no doubt she doesn't care to see me again, because she knows

I don't mince words when I have truths to tell. I would treat her like a street-walker, and she would deserve it, because it's shameful, what she's done. If I'd known that it would end up like this, I wouldn't have given her a room."

"But, good lady..."

"There's no 'good lady' here. When I think about it, it turns my stomach. Oh! The holier than thou. You can bet she didn't tell you how she came to me. Well! It was in the evening, and it was raining so that you wouldn't let a dog sleep outside. There she arrived at my rooming house with a boy carrying her bag. You should have seen that...a case in white wood which wouldn't have held two dresses and six chemises. —'Madame,' she said to me in a funny accent, 'could you give me an inexpensive room? I don't have a lot of money, but I'll pay by the day.' Me, when she said that, I took a look at her face, and I immediately saw that she wasn't a fly by night. There're enough of those in this neighborhood. I asked if she had identification papers. She took out an Italian passport. Astrodi, Bianca, eighteen years old, singer. I ask you!...a singer...a poor devil who arrives on foot from the Gare de Lyon to save the expense of a carriage! That's like your saying you're a painter, you who're good for nothing but cleaning palettes and wiping off paint brushes."

"Thanks!"

"You may be going to claim to me that you paint canvases that can be exhibited at the Exposition! Go tell that joke to Bianca, if you dare. That may work because you've already made her swallow that you'll make her happy, but with me, no, there's no way. I know what you're worth, dauber, and that's why I hold it against you for having seduced the little girl. When I think that during the month she was here, no man came to her room... nor woman either. She didn't know anyone. And she never went out except to go to a singing teacher from her country, so she said. Afterwards, it could have been to run to the perfect lover in your attic."

"Never in my life! I didn't know her..."

"Possible. But you made her acquaintance. If I could understand, for instance, why she went crazy over your puss! You must have bamboozled her, singing to her: 'I'm an artist; so are you. We're made for one another. An attic room and my heart.' She believed that! In the name of God! How stupid girls are!"

Binos protested with a gesture. He interrupted the old woman just enough to excite her to continue chattering, and this system served him very well, because in five minutes of monologue, she had just told him almost all he wanted to know, and that without his even questioning her.

"But I'm wasting my time," continued the testy landlady, "and I have other things to do than to chat to birds of your feather. I think I've already seen enough of you. Get out!"

"Not until you've told me..."

"What! What more do you need? Have you gotten it into your head that

I'm going to give you the little girl's clothes? Not so stupid. You'd be capable of taking them to the pawn shop. They wouldn't give you even the six francs she owes me for three days' rent; but that doesn't matter. I have her suitcase and I'll keep it. You can tell her for me that if she wants to come reclaim it, I'll give it to her without withholding my six francs. She doesn't have too much money, the poor girl, especially now that she's going to be obliged to feed you."

"Ah! Wait a moment. I'm a nice fellow, but I don't allow anybody to..."

"To throw what you are in your face? Whether you permit it or not, it's all the same to me. You can tell her also that her room is rented and I wouldn't take her back as a renter if she gave me twenty francs a day. I don't want trouble-makers in my rooming house...nor any loafers either. That means that if they ever throw you out of your pigsty, there'll be no room for you here."

"Eh! *Sacre bleu!* I don't have any desire to become your lodger. I'd rather sleep outside. But if you'd let me speak, you would know that's not at all what it's about. But I haven't been able to get a word in. Will you finally listen to me...yes or no? I didn't come here for trivial things."

"No, because you come for Bianca."

"About her, yes; but she's not the one who sent me; she's dead."

"Dead!" The old woman cried out. "That kind of joke is too much."

"It's not a joke. The girl you call Bianca is dead, and if you think I'm lying, you have just to go to the morgue. She's there."

"At the morgue!" repeated the landlady, rising brusquely. "You're messing with me. That's not possible."

"Go there and see," answered Binos. "Only hurry. She's been there three days and they're going to bury her."

"For three days! ...Since she didn't come back here... Then it really wasn't you..."

"Because I told you I didn't know her. I saw her for the first time in my life stretched out on a marble table behind a glass window."

"Then how did you guess she lodged with me?" asked the old woman looking Binos straight in the eyes,

"I didn't guess anything at all. I thought she must live in this area, and that she didn't have her own furniture. I decided to visit all the rooming houses. I began with yours, and I was lucky. You told me right off her name. I didn't know that."

"Ah! Well, you, so you're with the police? And me who took you for..."

"For what I am, mother. Jacques Binos, artist, painter. I went to the morgue. I saw the unfortunate girl laid out. She is so beautiful that I was moved...and when I found out that no one had recognized her, I began investigations as an amateur. I did well. At least now they can put her name on the death certificate, and on the wooden cross I'll place on her grave."

"Her name! Her name! It still has to be proved that it's really my lodger, Bianca Astrodi, that they carried there."

"But you're the one who'll prove it. You'll really have to go identify her."

"Me! Never! I'll get sick. Just thinking about a drowned man's casket gives me goose bumps."

"I understand that, my dear lady, but there's no way you can avoid this burden. I'm going right now to give my deposition to the Commissioner, and he'll send for you immediately."

"Ah! You scoundrel, if you do me that turn, you'll pay for it."

"I can't keep to myself what I've learned. You yourself wouldn't want them to throw your lodger in the same hole they throw the dead they've dissected in the amphitheatre."

"Be quiet. You give me chills. Ah! *Mon Dieu!* The poor girl! How did that happen to her? She didn't throw herself in the water, I hope. No. Then she was run over by a vehicle."

"They found her dead in the omnibus at the Place Pigalle station."

"What! She was the one! I saw that in the *Petit Journal,* and to think I didn't suspect anything. However, it happened the evening she didn't come back. And me who imagined that she was walking the streets!"

"That proves people can be mistaken. Now you won't accuse me anymore."

"For having seduced her, no. But it doesn't make any difference. That death was suspicious. Bianca didn't weigh very much, but she was as strong as an oak. Someone must have poisoned her."

"Maybe so. But who? You told me she never saw anyone."

"Here, no, but she went out every evening and sometimes in the daytime."

"Where did she go? That's what it's necessary to know."

"I'm certainly not the one who'll tell you. Bianca wasn't talkative and I'm not curious. Because of that, I don't know anything at all. She did talk about a singing teacher who gave her lessons and who lived in the Jardin des Plantes area,...although that appeared odd to me, seeing that in that direction there are only accordion players,...and unless that was to learn to sing in courtyards or on the street... One time also, when she first started lodging with me, she told me she had relatives in Paris, but she didn't know where they lived. I thought she was bragging."

"But she wasn't lying in saying she went to the Jardin des Plantes area, because she died in the omnibus which came from the Halles aux Vins. What's astonishing is that her teacher, or her relatives, if she had any, didn't go check at the morgue. They must have read the newspapers. They should certainly have been worried about her disappearance."

"Oh! They hardly took any notice of her. They never set foot here in the month she was here."

"She arrived at the Gare de Lyon," murmured Binos, talking to himself. "It's strange she didn't go rent lodgings at Montmartre."

"That's not strange at all. She didn't know Paris, and an Italian I had as a

89

roomer last year, pointed out my house."

"Then she came directly from Italy?"

"From Milan. It's on her passport."

"And you have it, her passport?"

"Of course I have it, my little man. It's upstairs in her case with other papers: her worn out clothes and all her worldly goods, which couldn't be very much. She locked her baggage and she carried away the key."

"The key! They found it in her pocket with a coin purse which contained only some *sous*."

"*Parbleu!* She wasn't rich, the poor girl. And even so, she was distrustful; when she went out, she was always careful to lock her case. I could, of course, have had it opened by a locksmith when I saw she hadn't come back, but I liked her, that little girl, and, then, I believed she would return. I wouldn't have thrown her out if she had come back. I would have been content to lecture her, because, you see, my boy, I'm not mean. You only have to ask about in the neighborhood. They'll tell you that Sophie Cornu has never been hard on her lodgers."

"I can believe it, although you were hard on me, a little while ago."

"Don't hold it against me, my boy. I took you for one of those goodfor-nothings who hang about on the boulevard to pick up poor girls they meet. It's neither your fault nor mine, but you come across badly. And I have it in my head that you don't often work."

"A little every day, my dear lady."

"I want to believe you, if that pleases you. And from the moment that it wasn't you who seduced Bianca, I have nothing more against you. I'm even happy to have seen you, although you brought me bad news. At least I know what happened to the little girl. I'll keep her from being put in the communal grave, although it'll cost me fifty francs to buy a plot."

"Very good! I was right in guessing you had a good heart. Now, you're going to take yourself to the morgue."

"*Saperlipopette!* That's something I don't look forward to."

"Nevertheless, you have to do it. I'd like to spare you that trouble, but if I went in your place, it wouldn't be the same thing. Me, I didn't know that girl, while you, who lodged her and have all her papers..."

"Yes, I could tell her name and prove I'm not mistaken. Are you at least sure she's still there?"

"I'm sure she hasn't been buried. If she's not still on display, you will only to speak to the clerk, who'll show her to you."

"Brr! That's going to make my blood run cold. And after I've identified her, what will happen next?"

"You don't have to worry about anything. The police Prefecture will send someone to your house to pick up her baggage. They'll examine this poor dead woman's papers, and who knows? They may find the relative she spoke to you about."

"That I wouldn't count on. And, then, what good would that do? Strange relatives, those are. They didn't worry any more about her than about a lost dog.

"But, my boy, that's not the only problem. If I leave, somebody has to watch my house and my maid is out doing the washing. I'm going to ask a neighbor woman to go get her, and I can't lock you up here. Be off and come back to see me tomorrow, if you will. I'll give you a better welcome than I gave you today. And if your heart tells you to, you'll go with me to the burial."

"I certainly believe my heart will tell me to, but if I go, that will be on one condition; that is if we share the expense."

"Share the expenses, you say. You don't have a *sou*. And me, *Dieu merci,* I have enough to pay for her to have a first-class funeral. We'll talk about that tomorrow, little one, but be off. I don't have time to loaf about."

Binos asked nothing better than to disappear. If he outdid himself in graciousness and in generous offers, it was because he felt the necessity of getting on the good side of the owner in order to lay the foundation for projects that he hadn't breathed a word about to her. Binos had fully succeeded in his errand; Binos triumphed; Binos believed himself first-rate in diplomacy, absolutely like those people who have won at gambling because they had winning cards in their hands, and who imagined that their success is due to their skill.

Binos took leave of Sophie Cornu and dashed down the street. The illustrious Piédouche had said he would meet him in front of the Montmartre registry office. He ran to meet him there and approached him, lifting both his arms above his head to announce to him from afar that he was bringing good news. It wouldn't take much for him to throw his hat in the air to show his joy.

"Well?" Piédouche, who was a great deal calmer, asked him.

"Well," Binos answered. "I've found what we were looking for. Your clues were right, my dear fellow, and I proclaim you a great man. The little girl had been lodging here since here since she arrived in Paris, that is, for a month. And the crazy old woman who keeps the rooming house is about to put on her tartan to go identify her at the morgue. She told me the name of the dead woman and all..."

"Then she has the papers?"

"The papers, the old clothes, everything is in the baggage. And everything will be given to the Commissioner of Police as soon as the identity has been verified."

"That's perfect. —But did you tell her what you thought about that death in the omnibus? Does she know that the little girl was murdered?"

"She doesn't suspect it. I am more artful than I appear. I understood immediately that if I talked to her about a crime, she would hang back. She would be afraid of being compromised. By letting her think her lodger died naturally, I was sure she wouldn't have to be begged to go identify her."

"All my compliments, dear fellow. You've handled it like a real professional. And I think that now you can do without my cooperation. You know as much as I do."

"Ah! No," Binos exclaimed. "Without you I will do only stupid things. So I don't see at all where I should begin, unless I decide to go recount our business at length to the Commissioner of Police."

"Anything but that," Piédouche said quickly. "The Commissioner would take you for a fool. Those people don't deal in imagination, and you have nothing positive to tell them. The landlady told you that the girl never had a visitor, no matter who. Therefore you can't suspect anyone."

"She told me the girl had relatives in Paris and that she went out everyday to take a singing lesson."

"Relatives in Paris, that's very vague. And the singing lesson was possibly only a pretext. Where would you go to look for this singing teacher?"

"The old woman never knew."

"Well, it's necessary, first of all, to discover the address of this teacher in question."

"It seems he lives beside the Jardin des Plantes. And you are the only one in the world capable of finding him."

"I will try, and I may perhaps succeed, but investigations take time. It's a miracle that we located right away the lodging house where she was living, a miracle that won't happen again."

"The Devil! But they're going ahead with the burial. Once the poor child is buried, how can it be verified that she was poisoned by a pin prick?"

"That's what my scientist friend will tell me when he's experimented with the pin. If he confirms that the poison the assassin used doesn't leave a trace, there's nothing more to do, neither now nor later. If, on the contrary, it leaves traces, there will always be time to verify them. Then the moral proofs that I've been able to collect will have some value. The first point is to know who had an interest in doing away with the girl."

Binos lowered his head and didn't seem too convinced.

"My dear fellow," Piédouche continued, "if you don't have confidence in me, don't be afraid to say so. It's not at all important to me to get mixed up in this affair."

"Oh! But I do! I do! I have unlimited confidence in you."

"All right, let me work in my fashion. I ask you for carte blanche."

"Oh! Very gladly. I will take your orders and I will report absolutely to you."

"Good! That way I can work with some chance of success. On one condition, however,..."

"I agree to it in advance."

"On condition that you won't talk about me to anyone. If people knew that I was undertaking this campaign..."

"They won't know it. Who do you think I would talk to about it?"

"To your friends, *parbleu!* You have some in all the studios of the neighborhood. And I suspect them of not being discreet. I even suspect that you've already talked. During the three days you've been searching for me, you haven't kept the story to yourself, I'd be willing to bet."

"I swear to you, Piédouche, that..."

"Don't swear, dear friend. I can read in your eyes that you've talked to someone. Tell me to whom; I'd prefer that."

"*Ma foi!* You can't hide anything from you. Yes, I had a confident, but this confident is a serious boy who won't talk, I'm sure. This adventure doesn't interest him at all, and he already thinks no more about it. He has something else to do. Besides, he doesn't believe it's a crime. It's Paul Freneuse, a painter. He will perhaps have the grand medal at the next Salon, and he earns 60,000 francs a year.

"Oh! I know him by his reputation, and by sight. Have you told him you're relying on me?"

"No, he doesn't even know you exist; I give you my word of honor, and I also give it to you that I will never utter your name in front of him. He will believe that I'm acting alone, without a helper."

The prudent Piédouche thought a moment. Binos's last statements had cleared up his expression, which the admission of an indiscretion had darkened, and after a short silence, he said in a decided tone:

"I have your word and I accept it. That's why I willingly take on your affair. Rest easy and come tomorrow to the *Grand-Bock*. I may have news for you. Now we must separate."

"I obey, illustrious master," Binos said gaily, shaking hands with Piédouche, who started immediately walking toward the outside boulevard.

V. Monsieur Paulet and Marguerite

While the enterprising Binos and the wise Piédouche, were locating the domicile and the name of the poor dead girl, by one of those chances which only happen to clever people, the capitalist Paulet had worries other than that of pursuing the authors of the omnibus crime. That was for several reasons, the first of which was that he was completely ignorant of that story. Monsieur Paulet hardly ever read anything but financial newspapers, and when he flipped through the pages on politics, he disdained the small contemporary news items. Monsieur Paulet prided himself on being a serious man and in being interested only in serious matters. He bragged that he had never opened a novel. If for some time he had been interested in artists that were because he had acquired the certainty that in our time the profession of painter is one of the most lucrative there is, if one is successful at it.

It wasn't without some trouble that he'd formed that conviction. He has spent his life despising bunglers, as he termed them. He considered them to be starvelings—that was his word—or to be spendthrifts who would wind up in extreme misery. But one of his friends had informed him late in life. That friend, who'd made a fortune selling unusual things, antiques, and even paintings, had proved to him by figures and by examples, that the artists in vogue made an enormous amount of money and some of them even became millionaires.

"They never do anything risky, and they're certain never to go bankrupt." This last argument had greatly impressed Monsieur Paulet, who, for nothing in the world, would have been willing to expose his daughter's fortune to disappearance in a commercial disaster. Now, he had right at hand a painter with a future. He already sold his canvases for a great deal of money and was on the way to selling them for even more, a hard-working, thrifty, and organized boy, whose background and family he knew, well disposed, well brought up, and well situated in the world, a real phoenix of a son-in-law, pleasing to Marguerite. Nothing was missing.

Monsieur Paulet had, therefore, settled his choice on Paul Freneuse. He was only waiting for him to make direct overtures, for which an opportunity to present itself would soon not be lacking. At the theatre, during the *Chevaliers du brouillard* play, the interview narrowly missed taking place. But that understanding had been interrupted by an incident which, since that troubled session, had caused the father of the blonde Marguerite to spend many sleepless nights.

The telegram which told him his brother had just died disinheriting him, was drawn up in the usual style of telegrams, that is to say, that the person who sent it had economized words so well that it was hardly intelligible. Monsieur Paulet had immediately telegraphed to ask for additional explanations. His correspondent, who was the dead man's attorney, had answered him with this la-

94

conic sentence: "I'm leaving tomorrow for Paris."

Monsieur Paulet was impatiently awaiting that good attorney, who had always protected his interests and who probably wouldn't have undertaken such a long journey without serious reasons. The testator had died at Amélie-les-Bains, a city 250 leagues from the capital, at the foot of the eastern Pyrénées, where the sick took healing waters. The ministerial officer who had written down his last wishes, would certainly not have undertaken a trip if it hadn't been a question of bringing the disinherited brother a copy of the document which dispossessed him.

Thus, Monsieur Paulet had lived the last three days alternating between dejection and hope, which seemed very hard to him. His rest was almost as important to him as the fortune, and the uncertainty troubled him to the point of making him lose his appetite and his sleep. His daughter, a great deal less agitated than he, no longer recognized him. He had become almost unapproachable. She had tried to remind him that Paul Freneuse was expecting their visit to his studio. He had taken her reminder very badly. He had even told her curtly that he wouldn't go out without having met with the attorney, who might arrive at any time. Marguerite had to give up trying to persuade him. She consoled herself by trying on mourning attire, which suited her very well.

Monsieur Paulet didn't leave his study. He spent his time going through old correspondence he had exchanged with his brother, before their definitive falling out. He tried to discover in these letters, written during his brother's sojourn in Italy, some clues relative to the marriage he suspected he had contracted in Rome, and he could find nothing positive there. The essential question was to find out if the dead man had had legitimate or natural children there, and, above all, what had happened to those children. Monsieur Paulet had therefore had inquiries made, which until then had yielded only incomplete results. Since his brother was dead, it was more essential than ever to clear up these important points.

The fourth day, after a melancholy lunch, where Marguerite had not appeared, under pretext of a migraine, the disinherited father had just sat down at his desk when one of his servants came to tell him a gentleman was asking to speak to him.

"What's the name of this gentleman?"

And when he learned that the visitor hadn't wanted to give his name:

"I don't receive people I don't know," he continued.

"He says he's come to take up a very important matter with Monsieur," murmured the valet de chamber.

"Oh! Oh!" thought Monsieur Paulet, *"What if it's the notary downstairs? These country people don't know how to behave. That man thinks that people come into my house as they do into his law office. He thought it wasn't important to present his calling card."*

"All right, let him come in," he said aloud.

95

He arose to meet this person so impatiently waited for. A minute afterward the door opened. An individual entered who was neither a lawyer nor a countryman; that was easy to see.

"What! It's you!" the capitalist said to him, frowning, "I ordered you not to come back unless you were bringing me certainties instead of vague probabilities."

"I have followed your orders, Monsieur," answered the visitor. "You haven't seen me for some time, because I had nothing new to tell you, but today I have my hands full of certainties."

"Well see if you do. But first of all, remind me of your name. I've completely forgotten it." Monsieur Paulet said disdainfully.

"Blanchelaine, Monsieur, Auguste Blanchelaine."

"Very well. I remember now. You claim to be a business agent and you live beside the Saint-Honore market?"

"Rue de la Sourdière, 74."

"Right! I must have put down your address somewhere, but it's gone out of my head. Just recently someone asked me for it, and I couldn't give it to him. You should have left me your business card."

"I don't have one on me, but if you will point out the address of the person who wants to see me..."

"In a while...when you've told me the news you're bringing me...and first of all, I must tell you that the other evening, you allowed yourself to greet me in the theater...across the whole audience. I did not authorize you to take such liberties with me."

"You didn't forbid them to me."

"That's possible, but I ask you not to do it again. Now, let's see what you have to tell me. Where are you with your investigation?"

"They're finished."

"How's that?"

"I have at hand that Bartoloméa Astrodi, who died last year in Rome, had, in 1862, a daughter named Bianca."

"In 1862!" repeated M. Paulet, whose face visibly turned gloomy.

"Yes, Monsieur, the 24th of December. I was able to procure a copy of the act of baptism."

"Show it to me."

"I don't have it on me, but I'll give it to you at the proper moment."

"You must at least know what the act contains. That Bartoloméa Astrodi, was she married?"

"No, Monsieur. Her daughter Bianca is listed as being born of an unknown father."

"Ah!" Monsieur Paulet breathed, relieved of one worry. "What became of that daughter? She probably disappeared?"

"That is, she left her mother ten or twelve years after her birth. But her mother always knew where she was. At the beginning of this winter, that Bianca was singing in the choirs of the La Scala theatre in Milan."

"And,...she's still there?"

"No, Monsieur, she left for Paris a month ago."

"For Paris! Why did she come here?"

"To look for her father, who is French."

"Well!" exclaimed the capitalist, visibly upset. "This is fiction you're telling me."

"It's the truth, Monsieur. My information is perfect, believe me, so complete that I can tell you the name of this Frenchman. His name is Francis Boyer. He had that child in Rome, where he was then living. He now lives in the Pyrénées-Orientals Department."

"That's none of your business," Monsieur Paulet said quickly. "I didn't hire you to get information about the father."

"No, but I never do things half-way. While getting information about his daughter, I wanted to know why she left her country...and I found out."

"How did you find out?"

"That, monsieur, is my business. If I revealed my professional secrets to those who employed me, they would no longer need me. I know it. I will prove it... And I know even more things."

"What more do you know?" asked M. Paulet, trying to assume an indifferent air.

"Monsieur," said Auguste Blanchelaine, "I can protect myself by concealment and limit myself to giving you an account of the way in which I acquitted myself of the mission you confided to me. I was charged with finding information about a child a certain Bartoloméa Astrodi had in Rome about twenty years ago. I'm bringing you this information. I'm able to back it up with legal proof. Nothing else remains for me to do but to ask to be paid for my care and trouble, if I want to stop there."

"I'm not refusing to pay you."

"I'm persuaded of that, but you wouldn't estimate my services at their true value, if I stopped there. And I think the moment has come to put my cards on the table."

"What do you mean, '*put your cards on the table?*'"

"I mean that I'm not ignorant of why you're interested in knowing what became of the daughter of the Astrodi woman, who posed for painters."

"My interest? But I don't have any."

"Let's be serious, please. If you didn't have any, you wouldn't have promised me 1,000 francs for exact information. Well, monsieur, that interest, I allowed myself to look for it. I didn't have very much trouble finding it. Bianca Astrodi, daughter of Bartoloméa Astrodi, is your niece."

"That's not true! I don't have a niece."

"Oh! She's your niece, but not legitimate..., and what's more, Monsieur

Francis Boyer, her father, is only your brother on your mother's side,…your half-brother, as it's commonly called. You are nonetheless his natural heir for that part of the fortune which he had from your mother, and that part is well worth having, because it represents a very important sum."

"And even if this were so," Monsieur Paulet exclaimed, "the existence of that girl doesn't concern me. You've just told me yourself that she wasn't recognized as legitimate in Rome. Therefore, she has no right to the inheritance."

"No right to reclaim it legally, no, certainly not. But, monsieur, you are not ignorant of the fact that brothers are not heirs to whom an inheritance cannot legally be denied. Nothing prevents Monsieur Boyer from leaving his estate to the first man who comes along…or the first woman…as, for example, to Signorina Bianca Astrodi. It's even luckier for that young lady that Monsieur Boyer didn't recognize her because he would then not have been able to dispose his total fortune in her favor. Our civil Code decrees it thus."

"If my brother had had the intention of making a foreign woman his sole heir, he would have taken some interest in that person. And he never searched her out during the many past years."

"Perhaps he lost her from view and nevertheless had never forgotten her."

"He would at least have expressed a desire to find her again. He would have, in whatever fashion, have manifest his intentions..."

"But he did manifest them…and it wasn't his fault that he didn't see his daughter again."

"You know more about it than I do, it appears," Monsieur Paulet said with irritation.

"Not more, but as much," Monsieur Auguste Blanchelaine answered calmly. "I was privileged to tell you that I clear up fully the business people are willing to entrust to me. I therefore had to gather information in the area where Monsieur, your brother, settled a short time after his return to France. I have a connection in Amélie-les-Bains."

"Ah! This is too much! And I'm astonished at your audacity... You dare tell me to my face that you spied on me. Do you also claim I'm paying you to get mixed up in what doesn't concern you?"

"I don't claim anything. I limit myself to laying out the facts to you. It's up to you to consider the consequences."

"Go to the devil with your consequences!" screamed Monsieur Paulet, carried away by anger. "I don't need you now. My brother has just died."

"I knew that."

"You knew it?"

"Yes, since yesterday. And I also know that he disinherited you in favor of Bianca Astrodi."

"You're also going to tell me you saw the will?"

"No. And you haven't seen it either. But the notary who received it must have written to you. You're trapped."

"Whether I am or not, I no longer need your services."

"On the contrary, my services to you are more necessary than ever. What would you give to whoever brought you proof that Bianca Astrodi is dead?"

"How dare you say that girl is dead? I think you're making fun of me. A little while ago, you claimed she was in Paris."

"Eh!," laughed Blanchelaine, "People die in Paris like anywhere else."

"And you have proof of the death?"

"I have it and I'm ready to give it to you…not for nothing, of course."

"I'd be very stupid to pay you for it, because I don't need you to get it."

"Try."

"I would only have to consult the state civil registries, in all the Paris mayorial offices."

"You're free to do so. People who die aren't always registered under their real name."

"If that Astrodi girl was registered under a name other than her own, how could you furnish me a death certificate, establishing her death?"

"That's my business."

"And then, even if you furnished me one, what good would it do me? If that Italian girl inherited, her own descendents would inherit."

"Certainly, but what day did Monsieur Francis Boyer die?"

"Wednesday, at three o'clock."

"Well, if the Astrodi girl died on Tuesday, what would happen?"

"That wouldn't change the situation any."

"I thought, Monsieur, that you knew the civil law Code better."

"I suppose you're not going to give me a lesson in law. As for me, I don't have any time to lose. Explain yourself and let's get on with it."

"I don't ask anything better. In order to inherit from someone, you have to survive him, don't you?"

"Without a doubt."

"Therefore a will made in favor of a dead person is null and void."

"That's evident, but…"

"The will becomes *caduc*…that's the legal term."

"So?"

"Therefore it becomes as if it never existed; the succession comes back in is entirety to the natural heirs."

"You're sure of what you're claiming?"

"Absolutely sure! If you doubt it, consult your notary, or your lawyer, or any one who knows the law."

"That means that if that girl died one day before my brother…"

"A day or an hour, it doesn't matter. She can't inherit if she died before the will became effective. It's only a question of date. And to clear it up, it's enough to produce the two death certificates."

"My brother's and the girl's."

"Precisely. You can get Monsieur Francis Boyer's whenever you like, if you don't already have it. It's up to you to try to secure that of Bianca Astrodi."

"Then you're here to suggest selling it to me?"

"*Mon Dieu,* yes."

"Do you know, Monsieur, that you're making an unusual business deal?"

"In this world, you do what you can. If I were a property owner like you, I wouldn't amuse myself by selling wills. But one job is the same as another, and my clients have never had reason to complain about me. You yourself, Monsieur, will only congratulate yourself if, as I hope, we come to an agreement. Because of me you'll have a nice fortune, and it won't cost you but a relatively modest sum. Besides, I remind you that you're the one who sought me out."

"Pardon! I heard about you through one of my friends who assured me that for a fixed price you undertook investigations of people and that you were a clever man. I called you and I entrusted you with finding information concerning a woman named Bartoloméa Astrodi. But I didn't say a single word about an inheritance."

"Oh! Agreed. But I would've been very stupid not to know that was what it was about. So I began by gathering information about inheritances that you would eventually receive. And I didn't have very much trouble establishing your situation and that of your brother."

"If I'd known that you were going about it like that, I'd never have gotten in touch with you."

"That's what it pleases you to say now. You must allow me to think the contrary, and to remind you of a conversation I had with you...not the first, the second, because you really received me twice. In the course of our last interview, when I asked you what I should do if I acquired the proof that Bartoloméa Astrodi had had a child, you shouted that if that child existed, it would be hoped it died."

"I hope you're not going to claim that I ordered you to kill it."

"For shame!" Monsieur Auguste Blanchemaine said, shrugging, "Does a man like you give such a commission to an agent he employs? He limits himself to expressing a wish, and that's what you did. You told me—I remember the words verbatim—you told me: 'The man who brings me information that child is dead, brings me good news.' And I remember very well I answered: 'Good news costs a lot.' To that you answered: 'The cost means nothing to me.'"

"You have, Monsieur, an extraordinary memory," grumbled Monsieur Paulet, visibly troubled. "It seems to me that one has to be careful with the expressions one uses in a conversation with you."

"You have to be careful also with what you write to me. I won't hide the fact from you that I have carefully conserved a letter from you with detailed instructions. In the terms of that letter, I must, in case Bartolomea Astrodi had a child, find out what happened to that child, and when I did, do everything possible to prevent it from coming to France. You even added that if by chance it had come and was still here, it was necessary, by whatever means, to prevent its staying here. Do you understand, *by whatever means?*"

"I meant *what could be acknowledged*," Monsieur Paulet said quickly. "If I didn't add that, it went without saying. Honest people never have recourse to such methods, and I'm an honest man."

"I have no doubt. But it's no less true that you gave me carte blanche to get rid of a person who inconvenienced you."

"*To get rid of,* these aren't the right words. You're choosing odd terms to use."

"I'm choosing those that best express my thoughts."

"Then I ask you to explain your thoughts. You would think, to hear you, that you'd killed that girl, and that you're trying to make me your accomplice."

"You're going too far," Blanchemaine laughed. "I didn't kill anybody; I beg you to believe it. I only wanted to show you that I didn't act without orders and that I was working on your behalf. Besides, that's evident. I had no personal interest in the disappearance of Bartoloméa Astrodi's daughter."

"But, then, how did she die?"

"If I told you, you wouldn't need me, and that's what I won't do. I've gone to enough trouble for you to pay me adequately. Think about all I've done the last month. I've directed two or three investigations at the same time, and I've directed them successfully: Investigation of Bartoloméa, respectable mother of Bianca; investigation of the aforementioned Bianca; investigation of Monsieur Francis Boyer, your half-brother."

"Oh! That one, I don't owe you gratitude for that," Monsieur Paulet said between his teeth.

"I don't require gratitude from you," replied Blanchelaine with ironic gentleness. "I limit myself to proposing that you buy the death certificate of Bianca Astrodi."

"I understand that, and after thinking about it, I refuse."

"That's up to you, dear Monsieur. Would it be indiscreet to ask you to let me know the reason for this refusal?"

"Absolutely not. I am refusing because the death certificate is completely useless to me."

"You mean to say you'll do without me to procure it for you?"

"Not at all. I admit, on the contrary, that, without you, I won't be able to have it delivered to me. I don't even intend to try."

"Then you are renouncing the inheritance from your brother? That's unselfishness I wasn't expecting."

"Pardon! The heiress is dead, isn't she?"

"Dead and buried."

"Then she won't come to claim the inheritance."

"No. But if you claim your part, you won't get it. The will has been turned over to the local President of the Tribunal. I can tell you that the natural heirs can't take possession so long as the death of Bianca Astrodi hasn't been verified by authentic documentation. A conservator will be named to administer the fortune until the heiress or her death certificate is found. And that fortune will continue to grow indefinitely because no one will take advantage of it. That's one consolation, but it's a small one. So, next, you'll tell me that in thirty years from now the title will revert to you. Not to you... to your grandchildren, because in all likelihood you won't still be in this world. And it may even be that Mademoiselle, your daughter..."

"That's enough!" Monsieur Paulet cried out, pushed to the brink by this irrefutable logic. "How much do you want to deliver this certificate to me?"

"Finally! You've become reasonable, Blanchemaine exclaimed. "We'll come to an understanding at last, because I'm only proposing reasonable conditions to you, and my claims are very moderate."

"State them then," Monsieur Paulet said with spite.

"Gladly. Your brother left approximately 1,200,000 francs."

"A lot less than that."

"I don't think I'm off by 50,000. My information came from a good source."

"In any case, I have a right to only half of that fortune."

"I know that. The other half reverts to the heirs on your father's side, since Monsieur Boyer was only your half-brother. There is even some business to be done, it might be said in passing, with these heirs who have as much interest as you in establishing that the heiress of the entire estate is dead. I didn't take them into consideration and I won't do so. But you could, when dealing with them, recover part of your expenditures, because it would be fair for them to reimburse you half of the commission you're going to pay me."

"Maybe," murmured Monsieur Paulet, "but go on. State the figure."

"I could demand an equal share, but I will be content with a fifth... let's say 100,000. You see I'm figuring with the minimum, because your brother left you closer to 600,000 francs than to 500,000 thousand."

"A hundred thousand francs! You have the impudence to demand 100,000 francs! I would rather renounce everything than give them to you."

"As you like, Monsieur," Blanchemaine replied coldly. "I will have lost my work, but you will have lost a fortune."

Monsieur Paulet made an angry gesture and began to walk up and down his study.

"I don't intend to try to convince you that you're wrong," continued the agent. "However, I advise you to think again before making a definite decision. If I leave your study without our coming to an understanding, I won't set foot here again, I warn you. I like business to be done promptly, and I have no time to lose. This evening, what I've done for you will be erased from my list. If you call me tomorrow, I won't bother to come."

"But, after all, Monsieur," Marguerite's father said, stopping his pacing up and down, "you don't, I suppose, claim to get hold of 100,000 francs today?"

"No, because I don't have a copy of the death certificate on me. Tit for tat. You'll give them to me when I bring it. Or rather... you're going to see how fair I am,...when you have taken possession of your inheritance."

"On that basis, we can come to an understanding, if..."

"But I want a contract in writing."

"What! You distrust me?"

"In no way, but business is business. You never know who will live and who will die. If by chance you pass on before everything is settled, I would have a difficult time reclaiming from Mademoiselle Paulet the execution of a contract she didn't execute."

"Still, I must know the form you intend to give to this contract, because you're describing an agreement beyond the usual."

"It's enough for me that it have no stain of illegality. You will simply agree, by a notarized document, that in remuneration for certain acts undertaken by your orders, you owe me the sum of 100,000 francs, payable the day you come into your part of the inheritance of your brother's estate. There's nothing immoral in that. Courts certainly sanction engagements contracted with matrimonial agencies."

"Besides, if I sign, I can't sue you," murmured Monsieur Paulet. "Is that all?"

"*Mon Dieu!* Yes...except for one condition which I don't doubt you'll accept, and for which I'll be satisfied with a verbal promise."

"Then what is it?"

"I'll ask you to give me your word of honor not to speak to anybody about our agreement."

"Oh! If that's all it is. I don't have any wish to brag about it."

"Without bragging, you could take it up with one of your friends...as, for example, the one who asked you for my address."

"The person who asked me for your address, has nothing to do with all this," said Monsieur Paulet. "My affairs don't concern him, and I don't intend to bring him into them."

"I believe it," answered Monsieur Blanchemaine, "but I want to be certain."

"You're not going to require, I think, that I make a notarized document swearing to keep silent."

"I've already had the honor to tell you that your work of honor would be enough for me."

"All right, you have it."

"I accept it, and I rely on it. Dare I now ask you to tell me the name of your friend, the one who wanted to know where I live?"

"To what purpose? You don't know him."

"But I would be delighted to meet him. He probably needs my services. I make my living by my work. That's why it's important for me to add to my clientele."

'That's understandable. And I'll send you this gentleman. It's a question of tracking down a debtor."

"That's my specialty and I'll do my best, if your friend wants to employ me. Then he's a business man? A man from high society doesn't come to an agent to collect a debt."

"He's not a businessman. He's a painter."

"A painter! Oh! Then I know who he is. You were with him the other evening at the Porte-Sainte-Martin Theater. He's Paul Freneuse."

"Ah!" murmured Monsieur Paulet with astonishment. "Is he an acquaintance of yours?"

"An acquaintance, no. But he was pointed out to me and I run into him frequently in the street and at the theater. That's a face you don't forget once you've seen it…an essentially Parisian face. He has a great deal of talent and as much reputation as talent."

"Then there's no reason for me to refer him to you."

"No reason at all. I would gladly put myself at his service if my services could be useful to him. But I would be particularly obligated to you if you didn't send him to me."

"Why?"

"Because I don't believe he seriously intends to employ me. An artist who owes money, that's rare. But an artist who tries to collect from a debtor, that's never seen. That idea might have passed through Freneuse's mind, but I'll bet it didn't stay there…or, if by chance he still has it, he will probably change it. Since I don't have any time to waste, I prefer not to get mixed up in an affair I would perhaps have to drop some fine morning. Therefore, I ask you, if he persists in wanting my address, to tell him you've forgotten it."

"Agreed. I promise you not to give it to him. But you did well to warn me, because I wouldn't have kept it from him. It's probable that I'll see him very soon. But let's get back to important things. When will you bring me the death certificate of the Astrodi girl."

"Tomorrow, or the day after tomorrow at the latest…if you sign today the contract which guarantees my right to a commission."

And as he saw that Monsieur Paulet wasn't in a hurry to pick up the pen to commit himself, Blanchemaine added:

"What are you afraid of? The wording I suggested to you leaves no place for any equivocation. You won't reimburse me until after you've inherited. Between us there's no possible misunderstanding…no difficulties either. We have interests in common and we can take care of them very easily when our ends are attained, and this fortunate moment won't be far off. Two days from now, you will be able to establish that Monsieur Francis Boyer's heiress was no longer in this world when he had the will drawn up and signed. Inside of a month you'll gain possession of your part of the inheritance."

That agreeable perspective put forth so conveniently, decided Monsieur Paulet. He sat down at his desk, opened a drawer, took a piece of officially stamped paper from it and drew up in his most beautiful handwriting a contract composed in the terms indicated by Monsieur Blanchelaine, who read it attentively and enclosed in his wallet with evident satisfaction.

"Now, monsieur," said this merchant of inheritances, "it's as if you had a half-million more and me 100,000 francs, which would mean a great deal more in my modest fortune than 500,000 or 600,000 in yours. Nothing remains but for me to take leave of you and to ask you to give your servants orders to give me entrance whenever I come. I hope to give you the death certificate day after to-morrow before noon. It will be up to you to do the rest."

"Very well. I will expect you," murmured Monsieur Paulet.

He showed out the middleman, who left without saying anything else. He was returning, very thoughtful, toward his study, when a slight noise made him lift his head. His daughter Marguerite had just partially opened a door which communicated with the drawing room, and was standing on the threshold of the study.

"May I come in?" she asked, smiling.

"Yes, since I'm alone," answered Monsieur Paulet.

"For only ten seconds. I thought this gentleman would never leave."

"Then you knew I was with someone."

"I was coming to see you and just as I was about to enter, I heard two voices. So I waited."

"I at least hope you didn't listen at the door?"

"Not exactly, but I have a keen ear and you were talking very loudly."

"And you understood what we were talking about?"

"Not a great deal. I picked up a name in passing."

"What name?

"Paul Freneuse's name, and I was completely surprised. What did this gentleman say about him?"

"You are certainly curious!"

"Oh, no, not too much. I'm sure it wasn't a secret."

"You're mistaken. I was dealing with matters which don't concern you."

"Then you have business with Monsieur Freneuse?"

"Marguerite, you're annoying me. Tell me what you want to say to me and leave me alone."

"I want to ask you if the house arrest you've imposed on me for the last four days is almost at an end."

"What! House arrest! Have I padlocked your apartment? Aren't you free to do as you like, as you've always been?"

"*Mon Dieu!* I know very well I'm not under arrest, like a first lieutenant who didn't follow orders. I can come and go from one end of the apartment to the other. Nothing keeps me from going to the window and watching people go by in the Rue de la Ferme-des-Maturins…where nobody goes by. And if this recreational spectacle wasn't enough to distract me, I could choose to go out with Miss Betsy, my governess, who'd take me for a walk in the Champs-Elysées and to eat cake in the English *patisserie* in the Rue de Rivoli."

"What more do you want?" asked Monsieur Paulet, shrugging. "Do you think I'm going to give dinners or take you to the theater while we're in mourning…and a very recent mourning? You know my brother has just died."

"He died 200 leagues from here, and I've never seen him. You can't require that I mourn, and you're right, because it's impossible for me to fake a sentiment I don't feel."

"I understand that, and I myself, I don't think I'm obliged to weep for this unfortunate Francis, who for years has given no sign of life and who's done his best to disinherit me. But there are social requirements that nobody can avoid. If I didn't follow them, everyone would throw stones at me."

"Oh! I'm not asking you to go out in society. I'm even doing what's expected. You can see I'm dressed in black from head to toe…and in wool at that. But these are the customary accommodations. I don't think we're forbidden to go see our friends."

"No, of course not. Only I don't know if my friends are capable of amusing you."

"It's certain that you have a lot of them that don't amuse me at all. But it seems to me that the other evening, at the Porte-Saint-Martin, you promised Monsieur Paul Freneuse you'd visit his studio."

"Ah! That's what you're getting at, crafty little girl. You'd have done better to tell me frankly that you're dying to go."

"Then you don't see any reason not to?"

"Why we shouldn't…not exactly. This young man is very nice… He has none of the drawbacks of artists…if he did, I wouldn't invite him to my house. And since I told him we would go visit him, we'll go…one of these days."

"Why not immediately?"

"Because I'm expecting at any moment the notary who has my brother's will."

"What! This notary is coming to Paris? I thought that Monsieur Boyer had disinherited you."

"He intended to…, but something happened. This would be too long to explain to you, and, besides, you don't understand anything about business. Be satisfied knowing everything is going well. I will leave you a nice fortune, and you won't lose, as I feared, that of your uncle. You'll be richer than I hoped, my little Marguerite," Monsieur Paulet concluded, rubbing his hands together.

"So much the better! I'll be able to marry whomever I like," exclaimed the young girl. "I'll have enough money for two."

"Good. I understand. That means, doesn't it, that you've gotten it into your head to marry Paul Freneuse?"

Marguerite blushed a little, but wasn't at all upset.

"Well, what if that were true?" she said. "You haven't forbidden me to think about Monsieur Freneuse."

"Absolutely not," answered Monsieur Paulet. "You can even add that in welcoming this young man as I have welcomed him, I have let you know that it wouldn't displease me to grant him your hand…if he asked for it."

"He'll ask for it, father."

"How is it you're so well informed of his intentions?...Ah! I know…the other evening, at the theatre, I left you alone with him for an instant, and he took advantage of my absence to propose to you. He would've done better to come to me first… That's the proper thing in such a case…I know artists believe they are authorized to behave differently from other people."

"But, Father, Monsieur Freneuse hasn't made me the slightest proposal."

"Then, how is it you know his intentions?"

"I wouldn't be a woman if I hadn't guessed them."

"And, you encouraged him to go forward?"

"Encouraged? No...that would be saying too much. But I didn't discourage him."

"Then, you love him?"

"I like him a great deal," murmured Marguerite, lowering her eyes.

"That's not an answer," said Monsieur Paulet, who didn't like equivocation. "You're astonishing, all you young girls; as soon as marriage is mentioned to you, you think you must take on a silly air. You can't get a sensible word out of you. Come now! Are you or are you not in love with Freneuse?"

"Do you want the whole truth?" Marguerite answered after hesitating a little.

"*Parbleu!* Who could you tell, if not your own father?"

"Well, I don't know if I love him or if I don't love him."

"Well, that's certainly something new! I think you're making fun of me. It's impossible that you don't know your own feelings."

"That may be strange, but that's how it is. You're asking me if I love him… You must first explain to me what you mean by the word: *love*."

"Ah! If you think I'm going to give you lessons on these matters! Finally, would you willingly marry Paul Freneuse?"

"Yes, very willingly. And, of all the men you've introduced to me, he's the only one I'd accept as a husband."

"Finally! That's clear," Mosieur Paulet exclaimed, laughing. "You didn't need to go to so much trouble to tell me what you feel. You chose this young man without consulting me; but I don't blame you for having chosen him. I've studied him since I invited him; I informed myself about him; and now that I know him well, I think he'll suit you. He doesn't have a fortune; his father didn't leave him anything…but he earns a lot of money, and I know he has enough good sense not to spend all he earns. It's good for a young man to economize. That's a guarantee of wisdom, and when someone behaves as he does, you're always ready to set up housekeeping. I'm persuaded he'll make you happy."

"Money doesn't make happiness," Marguerite said very quietly.

"Not always, but it contributes to it greatly," answered her father, who was a practical man. "That's all that needs to be said. The matter is settled. With your dowry and the money Paul Freneuse earns from his paintings, you would be rich enough. His appearance should please you. He's a very handsome boy. He has intelligence and good manners. It remains to be seen if his character suits you."

"How do you think I could know it? I don't know his character any more than he knows mine."

"However, you've met rather often."

"On social occasions, yes; but that's not where one shows his faults."

"No, obviously not. And nevertheless marriages aren't made any other way. Without trying it out, which isn't practical, you just have to rely a little on appearances. As for me who's talking to you right now, I married your mother on faith, and I didn't do too badly. I hadn't seen her ten times in all before the marriage ceremony; whereas you..."

"As for me, I'm more demanding. I'd like to know my husband totally..., to share his life."

"The Devil! If you think that is easy!"

"There is a very simple way."

"Show it to me; I'd like to hear that."

"Have you forgotten that Monsieur Freneuse offered to paint my portrait?"

"No, but I don't see..."

"A portrait isn't painted in a day. It takes a lot of sittings."

"So?"

"So! If I go pose in his studio, I'll get to know what goes on there."

"But I suppose nothing happens in Paul Freneuse's studio which isn't proper. If I thought anything to the contrary, I would close my door to this young man. Have you learned that he leads a disorderly life?"

"No, but I know that he has models come in."

"Naturally. It seems that, for painters, they can't be done without."

"Right now, for example, he's painting a picture where there's a young girl."

"Who's guarding sheep. He's chosen a strange subject. Why not a young girl herding geese, while he's at it? These artists have strange ideas. But what's that to you?"

"It seems the Italian girl who's posing for that figure is wonderfully beautiful. Monsieur Freneuse spoke to me about her with admiration... with enthusiasm."

"Well! Are you imagining that he's in love with that creature?"

"I don't say that, but I'd be curious to see her."

"Pardon me! I hope you're not thinking about making her acquaintance. These wenches who come to Paris to rent themselves out to studios are girls hardly to be recommended. And I like to think that if Paul Freneuse undertook your portrait, he would arrange it so that you wouldn't meet his goat herder in his studio."

"I think as you do, father, but that wouldn't prove anything...on the contrary."

"Ah! That's it. Then are you jealous? I didn't know you had that fault."

"That's because, right up to now, I never had the opportunity to show it. I was indifferent to all men."

"And now it's not the same thing. There's one you're set on. I don't have anything else to add, since I'm thinking of making him my son-in-law. But, really, you're getting jealous a little too soon. At least wait until you're married."

"One doesn't prevent the other," Mademoiselle Paulet answered, smiling. "What do you expect? That's how I'm made, and I can't change. I know it's not usual for a girl to worry about the life before marriage of the man she's going to marry. As for me, I want to know about it, and I maintain I'm not wrong."

"In principle, no. But I'd be curious to know what you mean to do to achieve your purpose. You'd have to be a little bird to spy on a man without his knowing it..., and besides, birds don't go into artists' studios. Do you imagine that you'll be able to find out anything about Freneuse's morals when I've taken you to his studio?"

"Perhaps. I have keen eyes, and I'll see a number of things that escape you. As, for example, if we meet the Italian girl, I'll know immediately if he values her only as a model."

"I, myself, would answer for it. These girls who run around in red skirts can't seduce a boy who has taste. And artists are less often taken in than simple middle class men. They've seen so much!"

"It happens, however. Didn't you tell me that my uncle..."

"Your uncle never did anything like other people."

"I would like to be sure that Monsieur Freneuse wouldn't do as he did. And to be sure of it, I must, first of all, know if the little goat herder girl from the Abruzzes is as beautiful as he says."

"All right, but he'll be very careful not to have her there when we go to see him, and he'd be right."

"That's precisely why I want to surprise him. He knows that you've just lost your brother. He thinks you're busy with the business of inheritance. He won't expect our visit. Today the weather is superb; the weather is excellent for painting. He won't want to lose such a good opportunity to work on his painting, because he's behind and the Salon opens the first of May. I'm certain his model's there and this is the posing time. So, if you will, we'll go take a walk, which will take us, as if by chance, to the Place Pigalle."

"Eh! And we'll go knock on his door without an invitation. Hum! It seems to me that would be a little risky. First of all, he might not answer the door, as is his right, because we didn't give him notice. I've heard that artists never answer the door when they're working with a model, for fear of disturbing the pose."

"When we're at the door, I'll speak to you very loudly. He'll recognize my voice, and he'll be willing to leave his paint brushes to let us in. If he leaves us outside, I wouldn't pardon this behavior. That's agreed, isn't it, dear father? You see I'm ready to leave. I just have to put on my hat and my coat. You, also. And you haven't put your feet in the street the last three days. The fresh air will do you good."

"Ta! Ta! Ta!" said Monsieur Paulet. "And the notary from the country that I expect from one moment to the next?"

"The notary?" Marguerite repeated disdainfully.

"Of course," Monsieur Paulet said. "He's supposed to bring me a copy of my brother's will and you know I can't wait to see it. The telegrams he sent me are too laconic. He likes to draw them up in pidgin French to save on words. These country people are stupid."

"It seems to me that if he were in Paris today, he would have come already. Trains arrive only in the morning and in the evening. Since this notary didn't arrive on the day train, he won't come in the daytime."

"The express trains...but I suspect he took an omnibus train...still to save money. Down there they don't know the British expression. *Le temps c'est de l'argent.* How do you say that in English?"

"*Time is money,* and to put the expression into practice, I'm going to finish dressing. If this gentleman descends here while you're out, your valet will come get you. You'll just need to give him your instructions and Monsieur Freneuse's address."

"That's an idea. Thanks to that arrangement, I believe I can be away for an hour without inconvenience."

"And even two," Mademoiselle, who certainly intended to extend the visit to the studio, said in a very low voice.

"But," said her father, "What pretext will we use for dropping in on Freneuse without notice?"

"First of all, we don't need an excuse. He's invited us several time to go see his studio."

"Agreed. But when you invite people, you'd really like to know in advance the day they're coming, so as to be ready to receive them properly. Freneuse wouldn't be very happy to show us a studio in disorder."

"But, I intend to surprise him."

"Then we'll have to explain why we're coming unexpectedly, and since you can't give the real reason..."

"You'll tell him you've come about my portrait. He offered me to begin it whenever I liked."

"Hum, that's serious, that's very serious!" said Monsieur Paulet, shaking his head.

"How is this very serious?"

"You aren't thinking about the fact that if I accept his proposition, it's almost as if I commit myself to giving him your hand."

"How's that? It's his profession to make portraits, since he's a painter. He's already done so. I saw one by him last year at the Salon…a portrait of a woman precisely…and it was a masterpiece."

"It's probable that he's already been paid for it, and even paid very well. Do you think he would agree to being paid for yours?"

"No, I don't think so."

"Then that's as if you were receiving a gift of about 10,000 francs from him. He sells portraits at that price, I know. Now a young girl can't decently accept a gift except from her fiancé."

"All right, if I don't marry Monsieur Freneuse you can buy my portrait, and in that way you won't be obligated."

"He'll refuse to sell it to me; you've just said so yourself. And your face would remain hung on his studio walls. That would be nice!"

"He wouldn't insult me that way; I'm sure of it. Besides, I hope I won't see anything at his studio which would decide me against continuing a project…"

"That you desire…admit it, and that I approve. I hope as you do that he'll succeed. However, you never know what will happen…and you should foresee everything."

"I am foreseeing everything, but I hold to my test. I'm going to run the risk."

"Think about the fact also that the time is very ill-chosen to ask Freneuse for sittings. If he undertakes your portrait, he won't finish his portrait for the Exposition."

"That's exactly what I'm hoping."

"Because then he'll have to send away the Italian girl he's using as a model. Really, my dear Marguerite, I no longer recognize you."

"That's because I am, in fact, very changed, " Mademoiselle Paulet said resolutely.

"Well! I can see you're crazy about this boy. If I stand in your way, you'd be capable of becoming ill because of it. Go put on your hat while I give François my orders."

Marguerite didn't have to be told twice. She knew perfectly well that she would get what she wanted, and her maid was waiting to give the last touches to her outfit. Her father was accustomed to giving in to her and he was in a good mood since Monsieur Blanchemaine had told him of the death of Bianca Astrodi. So, he had given in with good grace. He gave clear orders that they be ready for the notary, if by chance he came, and that they come immediately to tell him of the arrival of that important person. Ten minutes later, Monsieur Paulet and his daughter started out, arm in arm, toward the Place Pigalle.

VI. *After the* Chevaliers du Brouillard

Since the representation of *The Chevaliers du brouillard,* Paul Freneuse had lived like a hermit. Or, what came to the same thing, he was living like an artist who is late in sending his picture to the examination judges and who is working frantically for fear of missing the opening of the Salon. The first day had been hard. His chase of the man ran through his head. He reproached himself for having come back empty-handed, and he planned to renew the quest as soon as the opportunity presented itself. He also thought about Mademoiselle Paulet a little more than was reasonable. And when he sat down in front of his easel, the image of the beautiful Marguerite, brought about by his amorous painter imagination, often came between his eyes and his canvas. But that was only at one sitting. From the second, the passion for art took the upper hand. The memory of the *fiacre* chase receded into the background, the phantoms evaporated and he thought of nothing but creating a masterpiece.

The moment was well chosen to finish it. Monsieur Paulet, kept away by his mourning, could not for some time bring about the projected visit to the studio, which had been vaguely talked about, and he wasn't even accepting visitors. Freneuse limited himself to sending his card and wasn't afraid of being disturbed from that direction. And to crown the good luck, Binos no longer came roaming around his friend. Binos, who spent his life wandering around the studio, smoking interminable pipes, Binos had become invisible. Freneuse wasn't worried about him. He really thought this dreamer had set up his tent at the *Grand-Bock* or in another friendly *caboulet* unless he was amusing himself playing policeman, running after the authors of the autobus crime. Freneuse knew he would come back when he had any news to tell him, or just because his credit had run out in the cafés where he drank on credit. And Freneuse wasn't at all sorry about his absence. Binos was an insupportable companion for a hardworking artist. Binos moved about constantly, touching everything and not staying one minute without talking. Apropos of anything, he launched into far-out theories, sprinkled with extravagant paradoxes which would have exasperated the most patient man. There was no way to silence him. Since that restless man no longer came to stand behind Freneuse and criticize his work, the painting was going twice as fast.

Pia posed five hours every day. She came before noon and she didn't leave until night fall. She posed with assiduity and exemplary perseverance. Never a movement, never a word. She never asked to rest. Freneuse had to suggest she do so before she would agree to rise from her pose to relax from her tiring immobility. In the past she had been less calm and she had taken advantage of the interruption in the sitting to stretch her legs and untie her tongue. She took extreme pleasure in visiting the studio. She made real voyages of discovery, lifting the canvases and sketches Freneuse had turned against the wall, exclaiming with joy when she recognized the model who had posed, finding unexpected comparisons, asking intelligent questions, and chirping like a bird. But her gaiety had vanished little by little, and for several days the poor child seemed to have completely changed character. She no longer chattered; she no longer flitted about. Getting down from where the requirement of the pose held her, she went to set sadly in a low stool in the corner, and she stayed there silent, immobile, her shoulders on her knees, her chin resting in her hands.

Freneuse hadn't been aware at first, absorbed as he was in retouching; but the third day, he noticed Pia had red eyes, and he asked the reason for her sadness. The child answered that she missed Mirza, whose tragic end she had just learned. Freneuse absolutely refused to believe that she was weeping for the angora Binos assassinated. But, as he no time to lose, he had given up trying to make her confess, while promising to question her in depth as soon as his canvas was finished. Unfortunately, at the fifth séance after the death of the cat, he had to recognize that Pia was no longer holding the pose, and he had to tell her so.

"Little one," he sighed, "That's not right at all. Right now you're posing like a Virgin Mary at the tomb or a Mary Magdelaine in the desert, and not at all like a Subiaco shepherdess. Come now! My girl, when you watched over your sheep down there, you didn't have that graveyard expression."

"At Subiaco," the child said, "I didn't have any troubles."

"Then what trouble do you have now?" exclaimed Freneuse. "Love trouble?"

"You know very well I don't."

"Right. You told me you didn't have a lover, and I believe it. You are too wise to fall in love with the boys you meet in Lorenzo's house or in the Place Pigalle. So what's wrong?"

"Nothing's wrong, Monsieur Paul."

"Don't tell me that. I know you too well. I can read your face like an open book, and I can tell you're not at all the same. You no longer laugh; you don't hold your head right; you let your arms fall, as if you were posing for a statue of sadness. It's come to the point where I can no longer do anything good. If you continue to cry, I can't finish my painting. My little goat herder will look like the daughter of a brigand that's just been shot. There's only one way to get you back to the pose, little one. Tell me your problems. That will give you relief and I'll find a remedy. Come on, talk. Old Man Forenzo, where you live, has he given you any trouble?"

"No, he almost has respect for me since you recommended me to him. He never comes up to my room without permission."

"Very good. I'd give him a nice *bonne-main* the first time I saw him, and I'd go to see him on purpose. And do you need money?"

"Oh! No. I earn two times more with you than I can spend."

"Are you homesick? Do you miss the mountains?"

"What would I do there now? I have nobody there now," murmured the poor girl.

"That's true," Freneuse said, very moved. "You're an orphan."

"My mother died last year."

"And you never knew your father?"

"I saw him when I was just a child, but I hardly remember him."

"He was a Frenchman wasn't he?"

"People told me so. My mother never talked to me about him."

"And you have no other relatives?"

"Oh, yes I do, a sister. I thought you knew that."

"Yes, I remember now that you told me she had left Subiaco when she was twelve. She was older than you."

"I was nine years old when she was twelve."

"And your mother let her leave?"

"My mother was so poor she could no longer take care of her."

"Hum! My countryman behaved very badly. You don't abandon your wife and your daughter if you have any heart."

"As for me, I earned my living by watching sheep," continued Pia, without denying that severe but just analysis of her father's conduct.

"My sister was more delicate than I. She couldn't endure poverty. She had a good voice and a singing teacher looking for students passed through our area. He offered to teach her music and later to place her in an opera troupe. She went with him."

"And you never heard any more about her?"

"She wrote every year to a man in Subiaco, who gave us news of her. My mother never learned to read, and I learned to read only in France, thanks to you."

"Well, what happened to her, that sister? I've never thought to ask you about her. Did she make her way in the theater?"

"She sang in several big Italian cities and last autumn she was in Milan...and she sang at La Scala."

"As a *prima donna?*"

"No, as a member of the chorus."

"The devil! Then she must not be a millionaire. How did you learn all that, since you left Subiaco?"

"They wrote her from there that our mother had died and Old Man Lorenzo brought me to Paris. Where we live everybody knows Lorenzo and they know where he lives. Six weeks ago, I received a letter from my sister, a letter addressed Rue des Fosses-Saint-Bernard. That was the first time in my life that anyone ever wrote me."

"But that won't be the last. You answered your sister, didn't you?"

"Yes, once. But then a second letter from her arrived that told me she was going to come to Paris."

"Ah! Bah! And she came here?"

"Yes, a month ago."

"What, little one, you hide that from me?"

"My sister had forbidden me to speak of her. She didn't want anyone to know she was here."

"But you yourself saw her?"

"It's because I don't see her any more that I'm crying," said Pia, breaking down in tears.

"What! You don't see her any more?" exclaimed Freneuse. "You've already had a falling out?"

"A falling out! Oh! No," sighed the little Italian. "We love each other tenderly...as two sisters alone in the world love each other."

"Well, then, why have you stopped seeing each other?"

"Because she hasn't come to my place any more."

"What keeps you from going to see her?"

"I've never known where she lives."

"Well, honestly! Ah! That's just too much! What! Your sister arrives in Paris, just to find you, and she doesn't give you her address! But first of all, it seems to me that she could have lived with you."

"No, Old Man Lorenzo's house wouldn't suit her. They don't bother me there, me, because I'm still only a child, but my sister is eighteen years old and she's beautiful."

"Do you think you're ugly? But that's not it. I can concede, if I absolutely must, that she didn't want to take up shelter in that *caravanserai* in the Rue des Fosses-Saint-Bernard. That's no reason not to tell you where she lives."

"She had a reason she didn't confide in me and I didn't ask her. I only know she didn't want to have anyone come to see her."

"But she came to see you?"

"Yes, every evening."

"Why in the evening?"

"Because she knew that I posed for you during the day."

"Ah! You spoke to her about me?"

"Oh! Very often."

"And her, what did she talk to you about?"

"Of our mother, of our childhood, of our country..."

"Did she miss it, your country?"

"Yes, she told me her dearest wish was to live there with me!"

"Then she'd given up the theater?"

"Without regret. She didn't like the profession of singer."

"And you, would you be willing to give up posing?"

"I don't know," replied the young girl, lowering her eyes.

"It will certainly be necessary for you to give it up sooner or later. You can't spend your life going from one studio to another. You'll marry."

"I don't want to marry," Pia said quickly.

"Well, you'll change your mind. Let's get back to your sister. She at least told you why she came to Paris. I suppose it wasn't to go on the stage, since she didn't like the theater."

"Oh! No."

"Why, then?"

"She made me swear not to tell anyone."

"The Devil! It was a great secret then? And she forbade you to tell me?"

"She didn't mention you. She didn't know you allowed me to talk during the séance."

"She didn't know either that I'm your friend. If she'd known it, she would've made an exception in my favor. She didn't want Old Man Lorenzo to know her business. I understand that. But, me, I'm not Lorenzo...I'm not even Italian...and I'm sure she'd have judged me worthy of her confidences. You should've brought her to me."

"I wouldn't have dared."

"All right! But now that you're upset about knowing what's happened to her, you can certainly tell me what she came to do in France. That could perhaps help me find her."

"If I thought that..."

"You can believe it. And you don't distrust me, I hope!"

"Oh! No.

"Well, then, talk. I've already almost guessed your secret. Your sister was looking for someone, wasn't she?"

"That's true."

"When I know who, I'll get to work, and I won't work haphazardly. I know a great many people, and if your sister had contacted me, I could probably have given her some useful clues."

"Do you promise me you'll keep to yourself what I'm going to tell you?"

"Who the devil do you think I'd repeat it to? Of all my friends, only Binos knows you, and I don't have any intention of taking him as a confident. He talks too much, and in addition to that, he couldn't be of any use to me. This fellow spends his life in cafés. I don't think that's the place to find the person your sister's looking for."

"No, Monsieur Paul, it's not there...because my sister is looking for... our father."

"Your father!" repeated Freneuse, who wasn't at all expecting that statement. "Ah! Yes. He was French. I wasn't thinking about that any more. But you told me a while ago that you hardly remember ever having seen him."

"My sister remembers him perfectly," said Pia. "She's three years older than I am, and when our mother was abandoned, she was already old enough to understand."

"Then she must have told you later what happened, and why your father

117

deserted his children. Just between us, he behaved himself very badly. Because, after all, he never denied his paternity,...and there was a time when he treated you as his daughters."

"I have only a very vague impression of that time. I know we were living in Rome and that we went to see him everyday in an old house in a square a lot larger than the Place Pigalle, across from a large stairway. At the top there was a church with towers."

"Good! The Place d'Espagne, at the foot of the Trinité des Monts. And you suddenly stopped going there?"

"Yes. He left suddenly. He went back to France. Then we went back to Subiaco. My mother could have continued earning her living posing in studios. She was so beautiful! But she didn't want to any more. She brought us back to the mountains."

"How did you live?"

"My mother had saved a little money...a very little...by modeling for painters."

"What! Your father didn't leave her anything?"

"No, nothing."

"That's abominable."

"My sister thought he couldn't take care of us because he was poor."

"That's a nice reason. He had enough to live on because he came from France to Italy to study painting. If he wasn't in a position to give you an income, he should at least not have left you in poverty. And God knows how you suffered! Did you at least have shelter?"

"My mother had rented a cabin outside the village the shepherds no longer wanted. She washed at the fountain the linen of two or three rich families. My sister and I, we herded sheep."

"And your father never let you hear from him?"

"No. Once the priest told my mother that someone wrote him from France to ask if we were still in Subiaco. She asked him to answer that we had left the country. Did he do it? That's what we never knew."

"So, the poor woman didn't want to hear anything more about him. She must have hated him."

"A bitter word never came out of her mouth. She never even pronounced his name in front of me."

"But you know his name?"

"My sister knows it."

"And she told it to you?"

"I didn't ask her what it was. I saw it would cost her too much to let me know what it was. Every time I mentioned the reason for her trip to Paris, she started to cry."

"All of that, dear little girl, is very extraordinary. But now's not the time to comment on you story. It's a matter of locating your sister. What day did she stop coming to see you?"

"Last Wednesday. I waited for her all evening but she didn't appear."

"And you saw her the evening before?"

"Yes, Monsieur Paul. She stayed with me later than usual. She told me when she was leaving she'd come back the following day."

"How did she arrive?" Freneuse asked after thinking a moment.

"But, …on foot…I really believe. And she went away the same way. She wasn't rich."

"Then probably she didn't live far from you. You didn't see her on her way when she left you?

"No, she wouldn't let me."

"And you never met her in the street?"

"Never. I go out so little. To come to your studio and return, I take the omnibus."

"Tell me, little one, did your sister, like you, keep your Subiaco dress?"

"Oh! No, Monsieur Paul. Since she was singing in the great theaters of Italy, she dressed like French women."

Freneuse was going to follow this investigation into the habits of the lost sister, when a peculiar noise attracted his attention. Something was softly scratching at the door and soon a plaintive *meow* was heard.

"Ah! Mon Dieu! It's Mirza," the young girl exclaimed.

"Mizra!" repeated Freneuse. "Come now! You know very well he's dead. Cats don't rise from the grave."

"It really is a cat, nevertheless. Listen! He's scratching at the bottom of the door."

A second *meow* even more plaintive than the first made her shiver.

"The poor beast is dying of hunger. May I let him in?"

"*Ma foi!* Please do. If it's not the soul of my angora that's come back, it's another companion for us. It's lonely here since there're no more animals. I was about to buy a monkey or a perroquet, but I prefer a cat... They're less bother... And since Providence is sending me one..."

Pia was already at the door, but she had hardly opened it when she jumped back in surprise, almost in fright. Binos was standing in front of her, his hat pushed back, his hands in his trouser pockets, his eyes joking, his pipe in his mouth.

"What! It's you!" Freneuse exclaimed. "What does this stupid joke mean?"

"My dear fellow," answered the amateur artist, gliding into the studio, "I suspect you're angry with me. If I had knocked 'toc, toc,' as usual, you would've recognized my way of knocking. I knew you were capable of not opening the door. And as nature has endowed me with a particular talent for imitating animal cries, I imitated Mirza's voice. Wasn't it remarkably like him?"

"You should be ashamed of bring up the memory of your victim."

"It had to be. It had to be," said Binos, moving his arms about like a melodramatic actor. "It succeeded, because here I am in your studio. Now that I'm here, I'm staying here, my excellent friend. Good morning, little one. You're as beautiful as can be this morning."

Pia didn't answer this compliment. She sadly returned to take up the pose on her stool, to make Freneuse understand that she didn't want to talk further about her sister in front of this visitor whom she didn't like very much. But Freneuse, whom the surreptitious entry of Binos has put in a bad mood, didn't hesitate to tell him what he thought about him.

"I ought to throw you out," he grumbled. "We haven't seen you in four days. You were probably stranded on the benches of a cabaret. You're taking refuge here because they won't give you any more credit. We'll forget about that this time. I'll tolerate you here, but on one express condition: that you don't open your mouth. I must talk with Pia before going back to work, and I forbid you to get mixed up in our conversation."

Pia threw him a begging look, whose meaning he understood.

"Don't be afraid, dear child. I won't put your secret at the discretion of this drunk Binos, but I still have one or two questions to ask you. Let's see! Today is Monday; five days have gone by since the disappearance which is upsetting you. What do you think happened to…that person? An accident?"

"Alas! Yes. Paris is so dangerous…especially in the evening. I've been imagining terrible things. She could have been run over by a carriage…or murdered... I thought more than once about going to the morgue. But I didn't dare. I was afraid of finding her there."

"Well! The morgue! They know me there!" exclaimed Binos, who was cleaning his pipe in a corner.

"Silence over there!" Freneuse yelled.

"I'm not talking to you. I'm talking to myself. Do you claim you can keep me from having a talk with myself?"

"I forbid you to do anything. Go sleep off your absinthe and let us alone."

And lowering his voice he said to Pia:

"Listen, little one. I promise to do anything necessary to find her. In this country, it's not like in your mountains where people disappear without leaving a trace. Just bringing this to the attention of the Prefect of Police will be enough for him to start searches and they'll find something. I can answer for it. A stranger who arrives must take shelter in lodgings. Those who operate lodgings are obligated to ask their lodgers' names and inscribe them in a ledger that the police inspectors have the right to examine whenever they please."

"Her name is Bianca," murmured the young girl.

"That's her first name, but the other one?"

"It's the same as mine."

'Yes, you both go by the name of your mother. You told me that a while ago, but I've forgotten it, and it's indispensable that I know it, in order to ask for an investigation. Remind me."

"Astrodi," answered Pia.

She had spoken very low, but Binos had keen ears.

"Astrodi!" he exclaimed. "You want information about the woman named Astrodi! I can supply it."

"Why are you butting in?" Freneuse shouted at him. "I've already told you to let us alone."

"All right, I'll be quiet," grumbled Binos. "But you're wrong not to let me talk, because I could tell you some interesting things."

"About what?

"About the person Pia has just named."

"You were listening to us! You were spying on us! Obviously I was very wrong to let you come in here. You will please do me the favor of leaving."

"I was not listening. The proof is that I didn't hear a word of what you said to the little one, but she raised her voice at the end of your conversation. Since I neglected to close my ears, I overheard a name I know."

"How do you know it?"

"What's that to you? I have my secret and you'll be glad that I'm keeping it. Continue your conversation, my friend. I won't interrupt any more. I'll be silent as a mouse. May all academicians die instantly if I say a single word."

"That's enough. I want to know immediately what you know about that Astrodi."

"That female Astrodi! Then it's a woman?"

"Don't pretend to be innocent. What do you know about her?"

"Nothing at all."

"You're lying. You've just told me you could give me information about her."

"That's possible, but I'll keep it to myself."

Pia listened attentively to the questions and answers. She didn't dare take part in the dialogue, but she looked at Freneuse, trying to read in his eyes what he thought of the words thrown out by the fool Binos.

"Listen!" he said to the dabbler. "I've endured you up to the present, but I tell you if you don't explain yourself categorically and right now, I'm going to ask you to leave and I'll never again see you."

"Are you serious?"

"Very serious. I give you my word of honor on it."

"Then I'm going to start confessing. What I'm saying is completely in your interest. You'd regret breaking off with me. I don't want your existence to be poisoned with remorse."

"Will you stop joking?"

"I've finished. You're asking me for information about a certain Astrodi woman. To begin with, I can tell you that you knew her."

"Me! You're crazy!"

"Not crazy at all. You saw her only once, but you spent an hour with her…near her to be more exact…"

"Where was that?"

"Don't you have some idea?"

"Not the least in the world."

"Come now! You have a short memory. Get your thoughts together. How did you spend your evening, last Tuesday?"

"Tuesday?" murmured Freneuse, who hardly remembered how he'd spent any day of the preceding week.

"I'm going to help you. You were going back home when you saw me through a café window…where you condescended to enter."

"When I got out of the omnibus?" asked Freneuse, very moved.

"Precisely. And it was in that omnibus that you met that *signorina* that you're asking about with such solicitude."

"What! That girl who…that…that would be…"

"That's girl's name was Bianca Astrodi. I discovered that yesterday. I dare say that discovery does me honor, because it's due to my perseverance and wisdom."

"How could you be sure that was really her name?"

"I found where she lived. She lived very near here, Rue des Abbesses, in Montmartre. I talked with the landlady, who gave me the most precise information and who was willing to go identify the body. That respectable lady's name is Sophie Cornu. She has a good heart, because she paid the expenses for the burial, which took place this morning. I went to the graveside with her."

"Be quiet!"

It was too late. Pia had heard everything. She stood up straight and took a step toward Binos, who didn't understand anything about the effect his words had produced.

"My sister is dead," she murmured.

And she fainted where she was.

"Fool! You see what you've done," Freneuse shouted at him.

"How could I know that little one was also an Astrodi?" Binos said between his teeth. "I knew only her first name of Pia."

Binos lacked tact and good sense, but he had a good heart. While justifying himself as well as he could, he helped his friend lift up Pia. With the two of them, they got her back on her feet, but she had lost consciousness. Freneuse had to lift her in his arms and put her down on a divan at the end of the studio.

"Her sister!" her murmured, totally distraught, "It was her sister! I should've suspected that, after I heard her story. That girl disappeared Tuesday evening, the evening of my adventure in the omnibus."

"Me, too, *parbleu!*" exclaimed Binos. "I should have guessed it. Every feature of the dead woman resembled Pia. Why didn't I think about that? The age…the Italian features, everything was there. I have to say I didn't know Pia had a sister. She's very secretive, that little girl."

"Be quiet, you beast! Bring me that bottle of smelling salts, over there, on the console, near the bust."

"I'm going…while I do, open her blouse, she can't breathe."

Freneuse followed this advice, and the young girl's brown shoulders emerged from her red dress.

"Here's the bottle," Binos exclaimed. "Hold her up while I put it under her nose. It shouldn't take long. I don't know what's in this English bottle, but that would raise the dead. It stings your head."

Pia, stretched out on the divan, was leaning her charming head against Paul Freneuse's chest. Her hair had come undone and was falling in long tresses on her pale cheeks; her eyes were closed, and a faint breath came with difficulty out of her half-opened lips.

"You've killed her," Freneuse said to the dabber who was kneeling to administer the smelling salts to the poor girl.

"Oh! No. She'll come around in a minute, and I'll try to comfort her. Who the devil would've guessed she was so sensitive. That's not a fault of Italian women. I knew an Italian woman who lost her husband one morning and threw a drunken party at noon in Henner's studio. After all, that was only her husband."

"That's enough! I can excuse your stupidity, but I forbid you to tell Pia how her sister died. That would be enough to carry her away."

"Don't worry about it. I'll make up a story, and so she'll forgive me, I'll take her to the place we took her sister this morning. Sophie Cornu did things very well, a very nice service at the Montmartre church and a five-year grave rent at the Saint-Ouen cemetery.[22] As for me, I contributed a wreath of long-lasting flowers and a big vase of violets from Parma."

While talking, Binos was waving the smelling salts about with very little success. Pia shook convulsively but she didn't regain consciousness. Freneuse wanted to strangle the incorrigible dauber who couldn't hold his tongue, his damned tongue, the cause of all the trouble. At the most critical moment of that strained situation, someone rang the bell.

"Give me the bottle, and go open the door," said Freneuse with annoyance. "If I don't open up, they'll ring again. But when you find out who it is, you'll please slam the door in the face of the imbecile who allows himself to disturb me."

"If you had any creditors, I'd believe that this was one," grumbled Binos, going toward the door. "That ring was commanding and means to be answered."

Pia must have heard it, and she was so nervous that she was afraid. She had thrown her arm around her friend's shoulder and drawn him to her so closely that the artist's lips brushed the child's forehead. There was no doubt they formed a pair that an artist would have liked to paint. They were a picture al-

---

[22] Grave sites in France are not in perpetuity, but paid for periodically.

ready posed. Binos, who didn't see them, half opened the door and stuck his head out. He had prepared a statement to scare away the intruder he thought was in the hallway. He wouldn't have had any trouble finding one, because he possessed a vast repertory of impertinent and insolent remarks. The commission Freneuse had just given him was one he'd like to fulfill. But the words stayed in his throat when he saw a young woman of remarkable beauty flanked by a well-dressed, opulent looking gentleman. Binos made a cult of Rubens, the king of color, and it was a Rubens before him in full light. The impression was so startling that, in his enthusiasm, he opened the door wide instead of closing it. He was thinking;

"Freneuse can say what he likes. I can't leave a masterpiece on the stairway."

At the same time, he doffed his hat and bowed very low, retreating three steps to make way for that triumphant person, who entered very deliberately without even honoring him with a look. The gentleman accompanying her followed, hesitating a little. Binos, carrying is hand to his forehead, took the 'at attention' position of a soldier whose superior is passing by. Freneuse let out a cry of surprise, which made Pia open her eyes. He had just recognized Monsieur Paulet and his daughter.

The divan where Pia was half lying, her head leaning against Freneuse's chest with one arm around his shoulder, this badly situated divan was placed right in front of the door, and precisely below a large square window which as a consequence let full light into the studio, right in front of the eyes of the people entering. Monsieur Paulet stopped short, seeing this graceful picture, mumbling incomprehensible words. His daughter, however, a great deal less intimidated than he, hesitated to come forward. She frowned and the blood rushed to her face.

Binos had closed the door and was looking with a sort of ecstasy at that scene which delighted his artist's heart. But Paul Freneuse's situation was cruelly ridiculous. The poor boy couldn't push away the young girl strangling him and then come to greet Mademoiselle Marguerite.

Pia got him out of his embarrassment. She had regained consciousness. She drew herself out of his arms. She even had strength to readjust her blouse, to straighten her hair, and to stand up. And she stayed there, pale and trembling, looking steadily at the beautiful stranger examining her with a disdainful air.

"I see that we are interrupting you," Monsieur Paulet finally got out. "If I had known, please believe me, dear sir, I wouldn't have entered."

"I would greatly have regretted being deprived of your visit," Freneuse answered with effort, "and I beg you to excuse me. This young girl has just become ill while posing..."

"And you came to her aid. That was very natural. But our staying here is disturbing you. We're going to take leave of you."

"Oh! Monsieur," Binos exclaimed. "You can't be so cruel as to leave so soon. If Madam leaves, it would seem to me that the sun has stopped shining."

The odd fellow had come to plant himself shamelessly in front of the beautiful Marguerite, and was staring at her, miming the expressions of a man dazzled.

This trick didn't seem to displease Mademoiselle Paulet, because she was smiling, but Freneuse was choking with anger.

"The little girl is on her feet," continued the impudent amateur artist. "An instant of rest on the green couch and it won't come back. Isn't that right, *Carissima*," he said, speaking to the child, who was crying.

"No, I'm leaving," she said, drying her tears.

"You're right, my girl. Fresh air will do you good. Take a turn around the Place Pigale. You can come back when you feel you feel able pose again."

"I will not come back," murmured Pia. And she started walking unsteadily toward the door. Freneuse started to run to her to hold her back, but a look from Mademoiselle Marguerite nailed him to the spot. Pia saw that commanding look with surprise. Her pale cheeks turned purple, her sweet face contracted sadly. She was wounded to the heart. But she didn't stop. This time Freneuse didn't hesitate. He passed in front of Mademoiselle Paulet. He met Pia just as she was putting her hand on the door knob.

"Go back home, my dear Pia, and take courage," he said loud enough for Monsieur Paulet and his daughter to hear. "I will come see you tomorrow and together we'll go take flowers to the cemetery."

"Good-bye," said the Italian girl, holding back a sob. And she left, leaving Freneuse remorseful. And he really was so, because he lacked energy in certain situations, but he assuredly did not lack sensitivity. Pia's sadness touched him. If he'd been more master of himself, he wouldn't have let her leave like that; but Mademoiselle Paulet's presence made him lose his head.

"I'm really upset," exclaimed Marguerite's father. "You must have wanted to go with that little girl..."

"That would be completely useless," interrupted Binos, "I know her. She has a will of iron. From the moment she decided to leave alone, no one could make her change her mind. Besides, she's not ill. She's full of grief, that's all."

"What grief?" Mademoiselle Marguerite asked dryly.

"Oh! A great sorrow. She has just learned that her sister is dead."

"She learned it here?"

"Yes, madam, and by chance...an unfortunate accident. I had never heard anything said about that sister and I was telling my friend Freneuse that I had just been present at the burial of a young girl I don't know at all...except for seeing her corpse at the morgue. I only knew her name. I was imprudent enough to say in front of the little one that the unfortunate woman was named Astrodi."

"Astrodi! The girl you were talking about was named Astrodi!" exclaimed Monsieur Paulet.

"Yes, Bianca Astrodi," answered Binos, rather surprised to see that his questioner was somewhat emotional.

"And you have proof that she is dead?"

"Absolutely. Yesterday, that would have been difficult, seeing that no one had as yet recognized her, although she had been laid out at the morgue for three days."

"Then she died by accident?"

"Yes, monsieur, by an accident, …an unusual one…"

"Could you tell me where she was living?"

That question, thrown out unexpectedly, had the effect of immediately stopping Binos' confidences. He didn't like bourgeois. He called everybody who wasn't an artist that—and he was always on his guard with them. Now, he had recognized right off that Monsieur Paulet was a first class bourgeois. If he hadn't already acted badly toward him, that was because Mademoiselle Marguerite fascinated him by her opulent beauty. Since the illustrious Piédouche had made him promise not to talk to anyone about it, he cared even less about telling her the tragic story of the omnibus.

"I don't know anything," he answered with confidence. "But if you want to know where she lived, you can get information at the Prefecture of Police."

Freneuse had been on pins and needles since Pia's departure. He could clearly see that Mademoiselle Paulet was looking at him out of the corner of her eye, and he could guess why. He would have wished to explain to her how he'd been forced to take the young Italian girl in his arms. From another point of view, he felt it wasn't up to him to first answer a question which hadn't been asked. To try to justify himself without being asked to would almost have been presumptuous. That would have been the same as saying: 'I know you're jealous of me, and it's important to me to prove I've given you no cause.'"

But the beautiful Marguerite was not accustomed to hiding her impressions and she brought up without hesitation the subject Paul Freneuse didn't dare mention.

"She's pretty, that little girl," she said in an offhanded way. "Is she the one who comes to pose every day?"

"Since I began my painting, yes, Mademoiselle," the artist, who never lied, answered.

"That is to say, for four months, if I'm not mistaken."

"Four and a half months, Mademoiselle."

"I can understand that you can't go more quickly, if you must often interrupt the sitting as you have interrupted the one today."

"This is the first time that's happened, Mademoiselle. Usually, that child holds the pose admirably. When you came in, she had just suddenly gotten such sad news that she fainted. I had to pick her up and carry her to the divan."

"That was as it should be. How could you not be interested in her? You see her every day for three or four hours. Besides, it seems to me she's much attached to you. She had tears in her eyes when she said: 'I'm leaving.'"

"She was crying because she has lost her sister."

"Ah! That was her sister who died?"

"Yes, Mademoiselle."

"What! Bianca Astrodi was the sister of that model?"

"Yes, Monsieur, didn't I tell you that?"

Marguerite's father had had a pleasant surprise in learning from Binos' mouth that Monsieur Blanchelaine had told him the truth. There couldn't be two Bianca Astrodis in Paris, and the only one there had just left for the next world. There could be no doubt about it, since people with no interest in the question confirmed it. That excellent Monsieur Paulet's conscience had rejoiced. He had even wondered if it wasn't possible to get out of completing his contracts vis-à-vis the business agent. Why did he need to pay for a copy of the death certificate, now that he knew where to get one? But his joy was not unmingled, since he had just learned that the dead girl had a sister. Who was the father of that unexpected sister? That was the essential point, and Monsieur Paulet was anxious to clear it up.

"Pia's name is also Astrodi," continued Freneuse. "That was their mother's name."

"Then everything's all right. My brother never spoke of that second daughter. Therefore she's not his. And as he lived one day longer than Bianca, the model has no right to his estate," thought the blood relative heir of the defunct Monsieur Francis Boyer.

"But, father," Mademoiselle Marguerite said, smiling, "We didn't come to Monsieur Freneuse's studio to establish the relationships of the Astrodis. Since you're forgetting to tell him, I remind him that he promised to show us the curiosities of his studio. I ask to see them, because I've already seen an Italian girl in a red skirt stretched out on a green couch."

Freneuse had a very pronounced attraction for Mademoiselle Paulet. He was delighted to see her, but the tone she took when she spoke of Pia had finally shocked him. There was dryness, almost cruelty in that ironic way of treating a young girl who didn't deserve such disdain. That Pia he reproached himself for having dismissed so brusquely was neither proud nor silly. She only knew how to suffer without complaining and to love her benefactor. The beautiful Marguerite, on the contrary, showed more self-assurance than sensitivity. If she deigned to let it be seen that Paul Freneuse pleased her, she wasn't afraid of wounding him and taking a high moral tone concerning a child in whom he was interested. The artist had a good heart and he couldn't help mentally making comparisons which were not at all to the rich heiress's advantage. But she was so beautiful that he was disposed to pardon her these faults.

"*Mon Dieu,* Mademoiselle," he said, making an effort to respond graciously to her advances. "I'm afraid I was bragging when I spoke to you about interesting things in my studio. I wanted so much to have you come, that I exaggerated when I said there were marvelous things, in hopes of attracting you here... These marvels don't exist. There are only sketches, studies, curious old things that I picked up while roaming the Roman countryside, some tattered pieces of old tapestries, some extremely dilapidated furniture inset with ivory. Monsieur your father has some a great deal more beautiful."

"But your paintings, dear master," Monsieur Paulet exclaimed. "We came expressly to admire them." He was delighted to have said 'dear master' because that expression wasn't used by the bourgeois.

Binos, who was watching him with the intention of mocking him, grasped this intention and bit his lips in order not to laugh.

"My paintings don't merit your admiration," Freneuse said modestly, "but I would be happy to show them to you. Unfortunately, I can't keep them in my studio...because I sell them."

"You sell them very well, and I congratulate you for it." exclaimed Monsieur Paulet. "You have a fortune at the end of your fingers, and painting is the king of professions. If I'd had a son, I'd have made an artist of him."

"Peuh!" said Binos. "There're overhead expenses. Colors are overpriced. As I am right now, I'm ruining myself in buying raw Sienna and Chrome Yellow."

"Ah! Monsieur is a painter?"

"I flatter myself I am. I have been one since my earliest youth. I was born with talent. So I have never had a teacher. I'm self-taught. Paul, please introduce me."

"Pierre Binos, my schoolmate and my friend," murmured Freneuse, who would have given a lot for this awkward dauber not to be there.

"Very glad to meet you, Monsieur," Monsieur Paulet pronounced gravely. "Do you paint portraits?"

"I paint everything...except advertisements...and yet, if I were asked to, to oblige an unfortunate business man, I would go so far as to dishonor my brush. But if I were given the honor of immortalizing Mademoiselle's features by fixing them on canvas, I'm sure I'd paint a masterpiece."

This grotesque compliment exasperated Paul, but it didn't seem to displease Mademoiselle Marguerite, who recompensed it with a smile.

"You have at least one picture remaining," she said, addressing Freneuse, "the one you finishing for the Salon. Is it forbidden to look at it?"

"No, certainly not," answered the artist eagerly. "And I swear to you Mademoiselle that if it has the good fortune to please you, it wouldn't matter to me if the jury refused it."

At that, the father and daughter came to stand in front of the canvas and the father exclaimed:

"Well, there's the little Italian girl who's lost her sister. You may flatter yourself, my dear fellow, that you've caught the resemblance. It's striking."

"I think you've flattered her," said Mademoiselle Paulet. "She has beautiful eyes, but the lower part of the face lacks distinction. If I dare say all I think,

I could add that the race which furnishes models sins by the absence of breeding."

"That's what I keep repeating everyday to Freneuse," exclaimed the facetious Binos. "They stubbornly keep bringing Roman women built expressly for exportation, and they fall into overuse. If Rubens had wanted to paint a shepherdess seated at the foot of Cecilia Metella's tomb, he would just have chosen a beautiful Flemish woman, and the Citadel at Anvers would have represented the tomb. Ah! My dear Paul, if Mademoiselle consented to pose in the place of Pia, you would have a real portrait, a painting which would have a stamp of great originality."

"But," said the beautiful Marguerite. "Supposing I consented, Monsieur Freneuse wouldn't consent, I fear, to erase the face of that young girl from his canvas. If he chose her, it's because she pleases him."

Freneuse certainly felt that the success of a project dear to him depended on the response he was going to make. Mademoiselle was looking at him with eyes that clearly said: 'If marrying me is important to you, you'll certainly sacrifice a painting and an Italian model for me.' Not that she intended to lend her person to try out Binos' ridiculous imaginary theories. She had too much taste to have herself painted as an Abruzze shepherdess, but she wanted to make her future husband submit to a test. It wasn't the model that displeased her; it was poor Pia, whose incontestable beauty contrasted with hers.

"You're crazy," said Monsieur Paulet. "Our friend Freneuse can't miss the Exposition to satisfy one of your caprices."

"If Mademoiselle would be kind enough to permit me to paint her portrait, I would be the happiest of men," murmured Freneuse, who hoped to avoid embarrassment by that evasion.

"And I myself would certainly be the happiest of women," the haughty Marguerite replied dryly, "but I would reproach myself the rest of my life for having deprived that little girl of the immortality you're going to give her."

"I assure you, Mademoiselle, that I don't claim to believe that my works will survive me…no more than Pia expects that her features will pass on to posterity. The poor girl works to earn a living…and I do too; after all I sell my pictures. But I love my art passionately, and if you consented to serve as a model, I am certain I could paint a beautiful portrait. It's inspiration that's most lacking to all of us artists who are obliged to live by our talent. In order to earn more money, we chose subjects which best please the buying public. Italian scenes are sold advantageously. I paint a young girl guarding her sheep in the Roman countryside, just as I would paint a Transteverine kneeling before a Madonna. But if I could paint the picture I am dreaming of, it's then that inspirations would come to me. I would paint it for myself."

"And for me, also, I hope," said Mademoiselle Marguerite. That declaration disguised as a profession of artistic faith had reassured her. She added, smiling, "I warn you that if I decided to pose for you, I wouldn't leave you my portrait."

"I would be delighted to give it to you," Freneuse said quickly, "but I don't swear I won't keep a copy."

"I wouldn't object to that. The question is to know if I would pose. My father pretends that you would make the biggest mistake in abandoning a picture almost finished."

"But I can finish it and paint your portrait at the same time," replied Freneuse, who could certainly see where Mademoiselle Paulet was going.

"That is to say, you would divide your time and your studio between me and Mademoiselle Pia. You would have two canvases and two easels. The shepherdess would pose in one corner, and I in the other, and each of us would take turns posing. I'm very obliged to you, Monsieur, for your good will, but you must allow me not to accept such an ingenious arrangement."

This was said in such a dry tone that the face of the artist turned red.

"I'm not suggesting any such thing, Mademoiselle," Freneuse answered coldly. "I understand very well that you couldn't give me séances here, because I am forced, myself to receive people that it wouldn't be pleasant for you to meet. But if Monsieur, your father, would authorize me to work at his house..."

"What's that!" exclaimed Monsieur Paulet. "But with the greatest pleasure."

"You aren't thinking about it, father," interrupted Mademoiselle Marguerite. "The light in your apartments is detestable for painting. Besides, if I'm going to have my portrait painted, I would like to begin to pose tomorrow, and Monsieur Freneuse is forgetting that he promised to take that girl to the cemetery where they buried her sister. That promise is sacred, and God forbid that I prevent his keeping it."

That was too much, and Freneuse, wounded, gave back blow for blow.

"I would be heartless not to keep it," he said, looking Mademoiselle Paulet straight in the eyes. "I am, and always will be, on the side of the weak."

"That's very generous on your part," said the haughty Marguerite ironically. "But sometimes generosity is expensive."

"I'm not concerned about the cost," countered the artist.

"Marguerite, you're going too far," cautioned Monsieur Paulet. "Monsieur Freneuse is certainly free to spend his time as he pleases, and to make you both agree, I propose..."

That attempt at peace making was interrupted by a violent ring of the bell. Binos, since the war of the words had begun had been content to judge the blows without interfering. At bottom, he was on the side of Mademoiselle Paulet, that he was examining with the eye of a connoisseur and finding superb in her attitude of angry lioness. He was even thinking of scolding Freneuse somewhat later and pointing out to him that he was wrong to argue with such a beautiful person and a rich bourgeois over the beautiful eyes of a little model. But he quickly seized the opportunity to cut the dispute short by going to open the door without the authorization of his friend.

It was a gentleman who had rung, a gentleman freshly shaved, dressed all in black, with a white tie. Binos, whose head was crammed with memories of the omnibus crime, took him to be a police commissioner. After bowing almost to the ground, he began a discourse about a matter of judicial investigation.

"Pardon, Monsieur," interrupted the man who had just come in, "I've arrived from the country to see Monsieur Paulet. They told me he was at Monsieur Freneuse's, a painting artist, Place Pigalle, and I took the opportunity..."

"Here I am," cried Monsieur Paulet, rushing toward the door.

"Monsieur," continued the visitor, "I'm honored to greet you. I'm master Drugeon, notary, and I've come from Amélie-les-Bains to bring you..."

"My brothers' will...I know...I know. I ordered that you come for me and I thank you for having taken the trouble to pass by here. My dear Freneuse, please excuse me. I was expecting Monsieur with impatience... to take care of a family affair. I'm in a hurry to talk to him, and I must take leave of you."

"That's understandable," said the artist, bowing.

"But we'll see each other again soon, and I hope everything will be arranged to your satisfaction and ours. This first visit doesn't count. Come, Marguerite," added Monsieur Paulet, who had somewhat lost his head. Marguerite hadn't waited for her father to ask her to do so. She made her way to the door. She left without looking at Freneuse, but she honored Binos with a smile, which made him very proud.

The notary was already on the stairway. He hadn't come to Paris to see paintings, and painters hardly interested him. Freneuse conducted the father and daughter to the first step, cooling with a glance the ardor of Binos who had wanted to escort them a great deal further, and came back with him into the studio.

"Well, Monsieur Drugeon," began Monsieur Paulet, who had taken the notary's arm to go down, "you're going to show me this will, because your telegrams gave me only a very short, rough estimate. All the same, you can pride yourself on giving me a nice scare. You know it's not pleasant to lose an inheritance of that importance which comes to me legitimately."

"Who are you telling that to, Monsieur?" sighed the notary. "I did everything I could to ward off the blow. You must believe me if it had depended on me, you wouldn't have been disinherited from this magnificent fortune."

"Yes, yes,... I know that and I hold it so much less against you for not succeeding, as Providence has done what you couldn't."

"How's that?"

"You telegraphed me bad news. I've good news to tell you. My brother's will isn't worth anything."

"Pardon, Monsieur, I saw it, and unfortunately I can assure you that it is, on the contrary, perfectly regular. It is dated, signed, and written entirely in the hand of the testator, who even took the precaution of having it read to several persons, declaring to them that it really was the expression of his last will. Nothing was missing. You would be wrong to hope that..."

"It doesn't lack anything, so be it! but it is *Caduc*," continued Monsieur Paulet, using the legal term Monsieur Blanchelaine had taught him that same morning.

"*Caduc!* " repeated the notary. "Do you know the exact significance of this word?"

"*Parbleu!* That means that the woman named Bianca Astrodi, the named heiress, having died a day before my brother, can not inherit from him."

"You have proof of this death?"

"I'll have it tomorrow. So you see everything is for the best."

The notary shook his head and didn't seem convinced.

"You won't doubt any longer when I show you the death certificate."

"It's not that, Monsieur," Master Drugeon said sadly. "Bianca Astrodi wasn't the only named heiress. Monsieur Francis, has, by his will, left his fortune to his two illegitimate daughters, Bianca and Pia. If one is dead, the other is named to inherit the total estate, unless she also died before your brother."

"Ah! *Mon Dieu!* Everything is lost. Because this Pia is alive. I've just seen her, the miserable..."

Marguerite was following her father closely and she had heard everything.

"I'm losing even more," she murmured. "May she also die, the odious creature who has taken the man I love and a fortune that belongs to me."

VII. The St. Ouen Cemetery

In Paris, the poor people live mainly in the outlying areas, the areas which were, before the city walls were torn down, located outside the limits of the city and therefore outside taxation of goods entering the city, and where, as a consequence, it was cheaper to live. And when poor people leave this world, they prefer to bury them outside the fortifications. The large cemeteries situated inside the city are reserved exclusively for the privileged, who have the means of acquiring a permanent grave site. They do reserve a spot for a common grave pit, just as they are obliged to endure the indigent who walk about on the great boulevards. But the dead middle class, those who can afford only a temporary resting place, aren't admitted there. They are relegated to the two suburban cemeteries: Saint-Ouen and Ivry. In villages, the fields of repose belong to everybody. The farm worker sleeps in the same earth as the lord of the chateau. Social distinctions end at the tomb. And in Paris, the egalitarian city par excellence, only the rich have the right to dispose of their bones. They still tolerate the poor for a short time, just as, during their lifetime, public charity gave them hospitality for a night; but they aren't slow to break up their sad sepultures to make place for others. The common people protest by baptizing with bizarre names the faraway enclosures where their dead were exiled. They called *Cayenne* the Saint-Ouen cemetery; they called that of Ivry *Champs des navets*. Ivry is sinister. That's where they throw those who have been guillotined. Saint-Ouen is just sad. The Père Lachaise, Montmartre and Mont-Parnasse have character. The cypress trees have had time to grow; the grave stones don't all resemble the framework of new buildings; moss makes the tombs of the generations preceding ours green. There are memories in the air.

Saint-Ouen dates, you might say, from yesterday. Saint-Ouen has no history. It's a new cemetery, an ordinary cemetery stripped of all majesty. In the desolate plain which extends to the north of Paris, they've taken an ordinary piece of land, enclosed it with walls, and given it over to the gravediggers. There are no trees which separate it from the neighboring fields. It's dry and naked, and it's not quiet. You can hear the whistle of locomotives, the trumpet of tramways, and even the orchestras of dance halls, because, outside the gate, the road leading there is bordered on both sides by cabarets and country dance halls.

About noon, on that dusty road, the day after Monsieur Paulet and his daughter's visit to the studio, rolled a rented carriage, its interior occupied by Paul Freneuse and Pia Astrodi. Binos, perched on the outside seat, chatted with the coachman. Freneuse would have greatly preferred to do without the company of this amateur artist whose unbecoming behavior and careless tongue had become insupportable. But Binos had been present at the burial of Bianca and without him Freneuse wouldn't have been able to find the spot where the victim of the omnibus crime was buried. Or at least he would have had to ask for information from the cemetery custodian, and found it simpler to be led there by Binos, who had, however, sworn the evening before to behave properly, to respect Pia's sorrow, and above all not to add to her sorrow by telling her that Bianca had been murdered.

After the brusque departure of the beautiful Marguerite, the two artists had had an animated, and even stormy, conversation together. Freneuse had reproached Binos for having told Pia brutally about the death of her sister. Binos had mocked Freneuse for his sensitivity and for the preference he gave to the little model, who, according to him, wasn't worthy to be a lady's maid to the splendid and opulent Mademoiselle Paulet. Binos declared that he had to be crazy to disdain this Rubens escaped from its frame, and to burn his bridges as Freneuse had done in taking the side of the poor Italian girl. Upon that, Freneuse became very red with anger and told him clearly that he should no longer meddle in his affairs and never again speak to him about the murder, real or supposed, of Bianca Astrodi.

Binos didn't ask anything better than to be silent, since he had promised Piédoche to keep his past and future operations secret. Binos had accepted the conditions his friend imposed on him with bad grace, and they had ended by coming to an agreement. It was arranged that the next day they would all go together to Saint-Ouen, and that after the visit to the grave site, Binos would leave Freneuse alone with Pia. The unfortunate child was horribly changed. She never stopped crying, no matter what her friend did to dry her tears. He had gone to get her at the Rue des Fosses-Saint Bernard at Old Man Lorenzo's house early in the morning. She had almost fainted on seeing him appear on the threshold of the tiny bedroom that she occupied on the uppermost floor of the house. That was the first time Freneuse had set foot in that bedroom whose modest furnishings had been bought with the money that Pia earned posing for him, and at any other time—the evening before—his presence would have bought joy.

But the child was no longer the same since she learned the terrible news Binos had brought. She turned pale on seeing Freneuse. She shook, but she had enough strength to step back when he advanced toward her to take her in his arms. She stood in front of him, immobile and silent. You could see her heart was broken.

Her friend told her softly that he'd come to ask her to accompany him to the cemetery where he was going to put flowers on Bianca's grave. But he abstained from mentioning Monsieur Paulet's visit and the strange attitude of his daughter, who had behaved in the studio as if in a conquered country. He also thought he should refrain from telling her the scene which took place in the omnibus and the part he had played in it. What did it matter to Pia whether or not her sister was avenged? Besides, Freneuse still doubted that death was the result of a crime. He preferred to think the contrary.

Pia got ready rather quickly, but, to the great surprise of the artist, she hesitated at first to follow him. To make her decide to do so, he had to remind her that without him, she would never find the grave where her sister was buried. The trip was silent, right up to the moment that the *fiacre* stopped at the Place Pigalle, at the door of Freneuse's house and two steps away from the place where, some days before, Freneuse had noticed that the young girl leaning on his shoulder was a cadaver. But there, as Freneuse got out of the carriage to call Binos, waiting in the nearest café, Pia began to whisper:

"No, no, I won't go."

The artist guessed that she had sworn to herself never again to enter the studio where Mademoiselle Paulet might return, and that reflection gave him something to think about. Binos had come forward, but he voluntarily seated himself outside, beside the coachman. Freneuse found himself alone with his protégée, who persisted in remaining silent.

Without exchanging a word they arrived at the entrance of a very short road that left the main highway to led to the cemetery. Binos jumped to the ground and opened the carriage door. Pia avoided taking his arm to get down. Freneuse wasn't too surprised at her repugnance to accept the help of this wicked fellow who, the day before, had eyes only for the beautiful Marguerite.

There are people of various professions who live off death: marble workers operate boutiques selling funeral urns and truncated columns; gardeners sell pots of flowers; official guides show strangers the *beauties* of the cemeteries, without counting the drivers of the hearses busy refreshing themselves in the corner bar.

Pia's appearance started everyone talking. The poor child hadn't put on mourning clothes. She couldn't put them on to conform to the custom. It would have been necessary to dress in the French fashion and she possessed no other clothes but those of her native country. Therefore she was wearing the white headdress and the red skirt of Subiaco. That's a costume often encountered on the streets of the Martyr neighborhood, but very seldom at the entry to cemeteries.

The daughters of the Abruzzes die, however, just like Parisian girls. You would've thought that this one had come to wait at the Saint-Ouen cemetery gate for the funeral cortege of one of her countrywomen, but Freneuse's presence hardly agreed with that supposition. His elegant dress didn't allow anyone to believe he was related to little girl in the scarlet petticoats. Nevertheless he had gotten out of the carriage with her. Binos with his cardigan and soft hat could really pass for a model of casualness.

Freneuse noticed that people were looking at him a little more than he would have liked, and he hurried to make his purchases. He had a wide choice. Open air merchants spread out all sorts of objects of bad taste: crowns of daisies, crowns of false pearls, glass frames holding artificial bouquets. Nothing of all that pleased him. He talked to a gardener who sold him four pots of fresh flowers and provided a workman to carry them.

But Pia had stayed behind to bargain for a little cross of black pearls that she paid for with her own money. Binos, who didn't buy anything, for good reason, had gone on ahead. He was already in the cemetery. Freneuse was rather surprised to see that, in a loud voice and with gestures, he called to a woman walking in front of him, a woman dressed up in an old out-of-fashion tartan and wearing an extravagant hat, a hat like those they wore in the time when mutton sleeves were in fashion.

Is he going to start his antics again? Freneuse wondered. *Who is that old witch decked out like those trained donkeys they show at country fairs? And he's begun his farce just at the moment we're entering the cemetery. Really, that animal doesn't respect anything. I was really wrong to bring him. But actually I couldn't do without him. Well, there! He's bringing his fortune teller over to me. On my word of honor, he's crazy!*

Binos had in fact put his arm under that of the old woman and was dragging her rather than leading her. She didn't seem very willing to follow him. Pia, however, was coming forward to join Freneuse, but she stopped as soon as she saw the amateur artist retracing his steps, flanked by that strange companion.

He's capable of making that poor child run away, Freneuse said between his teeth. *I'm going to stop these out of place jokes.*

And he went straight to Binos, who exclaimed:

"I present to you Madame Sophie Cornu, who honors me with her friendship and who paid out of her own pocket the ground where Bianca reposes. Madame Cornu, I present to you my friend, Paul Freneuse, a first-rate artist, exhibiting at all the Expositions and a three times medal winner."

The old woman stared at Frenuese, who damned Binos and his introductions.

"Well, what do you know!" she growled. "That's what's called an artist. Are you the one who has his studio in the big house on the Place Pigalle? I know you well. I know the whole neighborhood. Is it true that you're the friend of this good-for-nothing Binos?"

Freneuse was red with anger and he almost turned his back on Sophie Cornu. But she didn't give him time to answer.

"Good!" she continued. "Silence implies consent. I ask you that because you seem to be a gentleman, you, and not Binos. So, maybe you let him clean your palette? And the little one over there is a model, *hein?*"

"What! Respectable Madame Cornu," said the amateur artist, "Can't you guess who it is? Look at her a little closer and you'll see the resemblance."

The landlady began to examine Pia, who didn't dare take a step, and she exclaimed:

"You're right, my boy. She's the living image of my dead lodger. Why didn't you tell me right off that it was her sister? You talked about her enough, however, at Bianca's burial. Then at least call her so that I can embrace her."

The Cornu woman had a carrying voice, and Pia must have heard what she was saying. Freneuse broke in to stop the old woman's effusions.

"Madam," he said severely, "that poor child is crushed with sorrow. I beg you to watch your words. I know your charity paid for the burial of her sister at your own expense, but you must understand that you'll torture her by recalling this sad memory."

"I don't have any intention of causing her pain. To prove it, I'm not going to breathe another word...so long as we're in the cemetery. But afterwards I really must talk with her. She must even come to my house to pick up her sister's baggage. But, Ah! Torment her! There's no danger of that. You, you don't know me, but you can ask Binos if I'm mean. Look! Do you know why I came here this morning? I've come to speak with a marble worker so he'll make a nice headstone to put on her grave."

"That's a care that belongs to me," Freneuse said quickly.

"Ah! No. If you wish we can share the expense, but I still insist on paying. And while I'm here, you can't keep me from going to see if the gardener has brought the flowers that I ordered from him yesterday. Oh! Don't worry. I won't bother you. I'm going to walk ahead. Binos will give me his arm. You can follow us with the little girl."

Freneuse had more than one objection ready, but that arrangement got rid of the old woman and the amateur artist. He let them walk ahead and he went back to pick up Pia, who hadn't budged. He found her in tears, and he hadn't the courage to launch into explanations. Together they followed the path that Sophie Cornu and Binos had taken. Carrying the pots of flowers Freneuse had bought, the workman brought up the rear.

Pia had dried her tears and was walking with a steady step, but she didn't say anything and she didn't lift her eyes.

After having passed a rond-point placed some distance from the cemetery entrance, they followed Binos and the old woman into a path bordered on one side by three rows of modest graves and on the other by a vast field in the middle of which there was a long trench which had just been recently opened. This trench was the common burial pit. In the distance there was something like a forest of black wooden crosses, miserable crosses, squeezed one against the other, just as the poor had been in the big city, where there was no room for the poor whose graves they marked, dejected, bent over crosses, almost pulled out of the ground by the wind. You could see in the distance women wandering through this funeral labyrinth, searching for the spot where a beloved husband reposed. You could see them bend down to read the names half-effaced by the rain and fall on their knees on the freshly turned earth.

Paul Freneuse remembered that without that old woman that he had treated so badly, Bianca's body would have been thrown in this common ditch which served as a grave for those who're abandoned. He told himself that if Pia could come to pray at a private grave, she owed that consolation to Sophie Cornu. The landlady of the Rue des Abbesses appeared less ugly and less ridiculous to him.

He looked at her more closely. He even discovered that her face wasn't without attractiveness.

She's right, he thought. *Pia can't avoid going to pick up Bianca's baggage and papers...because, after all, it's important that child be sure the dead woman is really her sister. It's absolutely necessary that I persuade her to take certain indispensable steps. She seems little disposed to listen to me. I could almost be persuaded to believe she's taken a dislike to me. She hasn't opened her mouth since we left Old Man Lorenzo's house. She's done nothing but cry. It might be Binos' presence that's upsetting her. Let's hope he doesn't let out some reference to Bianca's tragic end. Fortunately, I won't need him anymore when he leads us to the place where she's buried. I'll simply ask him to leave. I could even send him away right now, but he would ask me why. I don't want to start explaining to him so long as we're in the cemetery.* Besides, Binos had gotten ahead. He was walking so quickly that the old woman had a great deal of trouble keeping up with him. He was without doubt regaling her with interesting speeches, because he never stopped gesticulating with extraordinary animation.

What the devil could he be saying to her? Freneuse wondered. *He's capable of telling her the drama of the omnibus. I can see right now what would come from his indiscretions. The Cornu woman would carry the story around the whole neighborhood. The gossip would finally come to the ears of the Commissioner, who would open an investigation. The police would get mixed up in it.... They might order the exhumation of that unfortunate Biance. Pia would die of sorrow. And God knows what good that abominable ceremony would do! I would now bet there wasn't a crime, that neither the man on top of the bus nor the woman inside has to reproach themselves with the death of that young girl. They were together at the theater, although the evening before they didn't seem to know each other. What does that prove? That they made each other's acquaintance in the street when they got off the omnibus. Besides, I can find out the man's name and address whenever I like. I'll just have to ask Monsieur Paulet for that information. As for the hat pin, Binos dreamed that it was poisoned. Mirza must have simply died from a convulsion. That's a sickness of cats.*

While thus giving rein to his imagination, Freneuse continued to walk beside Pia, who was more taciturn than ever. He tried not to let himself get too far behind Binos, who was walking ahead like a torch bearer, with Sophie by his side. Soon the *avant guard* turned to the right. Freneuse followed it into a side path bordered by stunted cyprus trees. That path must lead to Bianca's grave, because they saw that they were already entering the section reserved for temporary rentals. The neighboring grounds no longer had the desolate aspect of the field dedicated to graves for the indigent. Nevertheless, this wasn't a section belonging permanently to the opulent dead. There was hardly anything there but wooden surroundings; no marble, no mounds of stone. What good was there for monuments for the dead who were lodgers for only five years? But many of the graves had recently had flowers put on them. They encountered women going about, watering pot in hand, caring for the little garden they had planted on the grave of an infant. After having taken 100 steps in this narrow path, Binos and the old woman stopped and disappeared behind a cypress tree a little straighter than the others. "There it is," said Freneuse, looking at Pia, who was horribly pale, out of the corner of his eye. "Have courage, my child! Lean on my arm, and let's stop here if you think you don't have the strength to go on."

"Thank you," whispered the Italian girl. "I'll go to the end...I'll go alone."

At this moment, Binos appeared at the edge of the pathway and signaled them to approach. They were only a few steps from the grave site. Soon Freneuse heard the hoarse voice of Sophie Cornu, who was saying:

"What! It's you Madame Blanchelaine! "May my house burn down if I expected to find you here!"

What the devil's wrong with that old fool! wondered Freneuse.

The curtain of cypress tress made it impossible to see the person Madame Cornu was addressing, and the name Blanchelaine was completely unknown to him. But he was furious at Binos for having contact with an old gossip who accosted a woman two steps from Bianca's grave. He promised himself to part company with the landlady from the Rue des Abbesses as soon as possible. He continued, however, to go forward, and the amateur artist, who had placed himself as sentinel at the side of the path, pointed a finger at the stone mound that had already been surrounded by a low wooden wall, paid for without doubt by the generous Sophie. At two feet from that enclosure was a gaping ditch, freshly dug; and further on another, and still another. There was a dozen in a row, regularly spaced and ready to receive the day's dead. It was a horrible sight and Freneuse did his best to hide this ghastly sight from Pia. The poor little girl was very pale, but she had the strength to go right up to the side of her sister's grave and plant in the ground the little cross she had bought at the cemetery entrance. Then she began to pray with joined hands, her forehead against the low wall.

Freneuse softly backed away so as not to bother her and went back to the pathway where he had left the workman with the four vases of flowers.

"Help me carry them," he said to Binos, pulling him by the sleeve of his sweater. "I don't want the workman to come disturb Pia's prayer."

"All right! I'll carry them all myself," answered the amateur artist. "But that good Sophie has been robbed. The gardener she paid yesterday to put flowers on the grave didn't do anything."

"She's unendurable, your Sophie. Do people come to a cemetery to chat as if in a shop? Who's that woman chatting with her?"

"*Ma foi!* I have no idea. All I can tell you is that she's decked out like a princess. The Cornu woman has beautiful acquaintances. Hey! Fellow! Come forward so I can take charge of your vases."

While Binos was taking over the vases, Freneuse, who had stepped back to let him pass, found himself leaning against the cypress, behind which the two women were standing. He heard these words pronounced in a clear voice:

139

"Is it really true, what they told me, my dear Mademoiselle Cornu...that one of your lodgers was carried to the morgue? You remember that the last time you came to consult me, I told you about a misfortune. I'd rather this hadn't fallen on you. But I was worried, and I went to your house. There, they told me you'd left for Saint-Ouen. I wanted to see you so much that I took a carriage to catch up with you. I arrived before you did."

"Parbleu!" exclaimed the Cornu woman, "me, I came on the omnibus. But...then you knew where the little girl was buried?"

'They told me her name. I went to see the cemetery superintendent, who pointed out the spot to me. But I see you're not alone."

"No, I met an individual I knew at the door...this skinny fellow with a dirty beard...He's the one who told me day before yesterday that the little girl was at the morgue."

"Is the girl praying at the grave with him?"

"Yes, and with the other one...a painter... Where the devil did he go?"

"A painter?...In fact that child is dressed like an Italian girl, a model probably?"

"As you say, Madame Blanchelaine, and she's the sister of the dead girl."

"Her sister! That's not possible!" exclaimed the lady.

"Oh! Yes, it is. She's named Astrodi, like the other one...and she looks like her, so much you'd think it was she."

"That's strange!"

Freneuse hadn't missed a word of this dialogue, which didn't tell him anything about Sophie Cornu's friend. He was astonished that she took so much interest in Bianca's death, and he wanted to look at her. He went quietly back up the pathway and slid between two cypress trees, in a way so as to put himself on the same line as the two women, but some feet from them.

Pia was still praying, and Binos was taking a great deal of care to put the vases of flowers between the openings in the low wall. To the left, Freneuse first saw the tartan of the Cornu woman, whose shoulder was turned toward him, then an elegantly dressed woman facing him. And at the first sight of that woman, it seemed to him she was not unknown to him. He noticed also that she was staring at him and he guessed she was asking Mademoiselle Sophie his name, very softly. Suddenly, he remembered something.

"That's the woman I saw at the Porte-Saint-Martin, the evening they presented Les Chevaliers du brouillard." he murmured.

The encounter was more than unusual and it threw Freneuse into infinite perplexity. For several days he had not believed in the omnibus crime. A short time ago he had just found excellent reasons to demonstrate to himself that Binos' ideas were absolute fantasies and that Bianca had died a natural death. And now all his suspicions came back. Why was that woman there near Bianca's grave? The explanations she gave to Sophie Cornu seemed to be imaginary pretexts to justify her presence. Why also did she cry out: 'That's not possible!'

when the landlady had declared that the young girl praying was the sister of the dead woman? Freneuse made all these reflections in a second, and he wondered at the same time what he was going to do about it. To go up to that woman and question her? What right did he have? He had no proof against her, and she didn't have to answer him. And then a scene two steps away from Pia, who would see and hear everything! That would be enough to kill the poor child, whose sensitivity was already overexcited. No, wouldn't it be better to hide his impressions, and observe with a disinterested air the conduct of the lady he had so many motives to suspect?

By way of the Cornu woman, who has connections with her, I can always find out where she lives and what she does, he thought. *And I wouldn't have to do the investigation myself. Binos would very willingly take charge of it.*

This very correct reasoning decided him to refrain from interrupting them. He satisfied himself with maneuvering himself so as to approach the two women who were still chatting. Although they were talking rather low, he could grasp this sentence by the unknown woman:

"Because you are with people, my dear, I'm going to leave you, but we'll see each other during the day."

"I'll go to your house," the landlady exclaimed. "I have a lot of things to tell you, and besides, you haven't given me a consultation in a long time."

"I'm at your service, dear Sophie. Only come alone."

And then leaning over to Sophie's ear, the lady added another recommendation that Freneuse couldn't hear, but he guessed.

She forbidding her to give me her address, he thought.

On that, the two friends shook hands in the English fashion. The mysterious person left without showing by her expression that she knew there were two men there examining her. Binos had also finally taken notice of the appearance of that woman just at the moment they arrived and he promised himself to question the providential Cornu woman about her.

During this time, Pia finished her prayers and rose in tears. She remained several instants leaning against the little balustrade, her eyes fixed on the earth covering her sister's body. Then she turned toward Freneuse. She was no longer crying, and her pale face had taken on an expression her friend had never seen.

"Thank you," she said to him in a firm tone. "Thank you and good-bye!"

"What do you mean, good-bye!" exclaimed Freneuse. "I hope you're not going away without me. The *fiacre* which brought us will take us back to the Place Pigalle. You'll have lunch at the studio, and afterwards we'll resume the séance interrupted yesterday."

"No, I won't pose anymore."

Freneuse was going to protest, but he remembered in time that Bianca's grave was in front of him and that this wasn't the moment to argue with an overexcited girl, who probably wouldn't be slow to change her mind.

"All right," he said. "I'll take leave of you today. You are deeply pained and it's right you take a little rest. I'll wait until your sorrow has somewhat eased. But please promise me you'll come back to the Rue des Fosses Saint-Bernard."

"Going by way of the Rue des Abesses," said the Cornu woman, who'd approached stealthily. "She really must come see about the effects and the papers of her sister. I don't wish to keep them."

"It's useless, Madame," the child murmured, without changing expression. "I won't claim anything that belonged to her."

"It will be useless for you not to reclaim her baggage. I know now where you live and I'll send it to you. But I don't have anything else to do here for a quarter of an hour. I must get on the way to the Saint-Ouen road to shake up that scoundrel of a gardener who took my money and didn't even deliver a vase of cheap flowers. I'm dashing off."

"Not without me, Mademoiselle," exclaimed Binos. "I'm sticking to your heels." He offered her his arm and she accepted mumbling words which certainly weren't compliments.

Pia gave a last look at the grave where Binos had put the flowers bought by his friend and went back down the path.

"In a little while I'll find out what's wrong with her," Freneuse said, staying near her. Pia walked with her eyes lowered and persisted in her silence. Freneuse, determined to go to great lengths to make her speak, waited until they were outside the cypress pathway, and then said softly to her:

"Little girl, you are causing me great pain."

"I?" murmured the child, not daring to look at him.

"Yes, you. I understand that you're sad and that you want to rest for a few days, but why won't you come back to my studio? Do you have some complaint against me?"

"No, Monsieur Paul. I've had only kindness from you."

"You don't owe me gratitude. How could I not have been interested in you who were alone in the world...or at least, so I thought, and now that's only too true. But to leave me like this...I haven't done anything to deserve it...that I know of. Come now, explain yourself. Did I hurt you without knowing it?"

Pia turned her head away to hide her tears.

"There! You're crying. Then I guessed it. I've hurt you and didn't know it. Well, tell me what I did, so that I won't do it again."

"Nothing, Monsieur Paul. You've always been good to me, only a poor girl. I might have died of hunger if you hadn't picked me up in the street. I have never been so happy as when I've known you...and I'll never be so happy again."

"Then, why do you want to leave me?"

"Because I must."

"Well! This isn't serious. Why must you leave?"

"I want to go back to Subiaco."

"And what will you do in Subiaco? Do you think you can pose for painters who set themselves up there in the summer? You won't earn enough to live on. In the mountains all the women are so beautiful that artists have a wide choice."

"No, Monsieur Paul. I won't pose anymore for anybody. I'll go back to my old work. I'll herd sheep."

"You're crazy. If your mother were still there, I could understand that silly idea, but you don't even have relatives in your country. You've often told me that."

"And here no one loves me any more."

"Then I don't count, it seems! Listen, Pia, it's very wicked of you to talk this way. If I didn't know you as well as I do, I'd be tempted to believe you heartless. Well! I've always treated you as a friend. I've given you 1,000 proofs of my esteem and my affection...and you come right out and tell me you can't see me any more. Truly, I no longer recognize you. I could remind you that your departure would put me in the most embarrassing position, because, if you no longer pose, I can't finish my painting."

Pia burst into tears and Freneuse continued with sincere emotion.

"But I'd rather tell you that it's not only the model I'd miss, if you persist in your decision. I'm attached to you, and my studio would horrify me if you never came back."

"I can't! ...I can't!" the child said in a stifled voice. "I would like to, but it's stronger than I am. You saw how I almost died yesterday."

This time Freneuse understood. The truth he'd somewhat suspected appeared clearly to him and it was his turn to be silent. He looked for some way to calm Pia without promising her to close his door to Mademoiselle Paulet. To be just to him, he was thinking a great deal less of the Exposition he would miss than the touching sadness of the poor Italian girl who'd fallen in love without hope. They walked silently as far as the rond-point of the cemetery.

Binos, who had long legs, had gone ahead with Sophie Cornu, who was trotting like a rat.

"Would you agree to still pose for me somewhere other than in my studio?" Freneuse suddenly asked.

Pia shook her head sadly.

"In a place where I'd see no one but you for six hours a day? I'm behind and it will take long séances to be ready for the opening of the Exposition," he added, smiling.

"If I thought that was possible," the young girl answered.

"You won't fly off toward the country of orange trees," Freneuse ended gaily. "Very good. I don't ask for anything else. Just swear to me that you won't leave without seeing me again, and that you will wait to hear news from me in your bedroom on the Rue des Fosses-Saint-Bernard."

"I swear it to you on the soul of my sister!" answered Pia, lifting her big eyes bathed with tears.

"That's good. I'm going to get rid of Binos and that old woman for you. You'll go with me as far as my door…only as far as my door, and then the *fiacre* will take you to your house."

Freneuse had had an idea. Pia didn't yet guess it, but she had stopped crying.

VIII. The Rue de la Sourdière

The Rue de la Sourdière is one of those streets that the transformation of old Paris hasn't touched. It borders the Butte-des-Moulins that they razed, but it's still today what it was a hundred years ago, although everything around it has changed.[23] In vain the Rue Neuve-des-Champs and the Rue Saint-Honoré make noise in the north and the south and the Saint Honoré market vainly swarms with people, the Rue de la Sourdière remains peaceful like a grand-mother bent over in the corner of her fire. People come there when they have business, but they don't pass on to other streets. It doesn't lead anywhere. It's a good street, an honest street. Disreputable people never lodge there, and the loose girls who roam around everyday don't even know it exists. It has *respectability* as the English say. That doesn't mean that it's inhabited by millionaires, but all the honest folk who live there have enough to live on and gentle life styles. In the evening, in the summer, they play shuttlecock from one sidewalk to the other. They carry chairs out to the street and sit and talk. Grass grows between the paving stones, and sometimes you see chickens pecking there. It's the country in the middle of Paris.

The houses which line it make a good show with their high coach door-ways, their quiet courtyards, and their wide stone staircases. They seem to have been built to house former magistrates, retired clergymen, and simply wise people disgusted with the world.

Auguste Blanchelaine had taken up residence here three years ago. He was neither the least peaceful nor the least respected of this well-known neighbor-hood. On the second floor of an important house, you could read on the right his name on a brass plaque, followed by this qualification: *Agent d'Affaires*. On the left, on a door directly across from his, shone an inscription which wasn't clear to everybody: —*Stella, Student of Mademoiselle Lenormand.—Consultations from noon until five o'clock*. Consultations about what? Many people couldn't have guessed, but many others knew what it was about. There are still in Paris many old gossips who remember Mademoiselle Lenormand, the fortune-teller of the Rue Tornon, and who firmly believe that fifteen years before the crowning of Napoleon, she had predicted that Josephine would become Empress. Stella, the student of that illustrious sorceress, had as clients a great many maids, many kept women, some little middle class women, and even some ladies, some great ladies, who could have come to see her in carriages with servants in livery, and they wouldn't have feared compromising the coat of arms painted on the panels

---

[23] Reference to Baron Hausmann's renovation of Paris, cutting through streets, installing a new water and sewage system, and modernizing Paris at the command of Napoleon III.

of their carriages. Stella belonged to the great school of fortune tellers of the past. She didn't work by somnambulism. She prophesized only with cards, or even without cards when she was inspired. And inspiration came when the person consulting paid well.

The two apartments, that of the fortune-teller and that of the business man, occupied the entire second floor. They had two separate entries. The clients of Monsieur Blanchelaine had nothing in common with those of Madame Stella. Serious people rang the bell on the right. The believers rang the one on the left and the ones on one side paid no attention to those on the other. But the two apartments were actually only one, in the sense that you could go from one to the other without going out into the hallway. In both the arrangement of the rooms was exactly the same: a waiting room, a dining room, a drawing room, a bath and a bedroom, but the furnishings didn't resemble each other at all. In Stella's side all the décor was dark. You could see only strange objects, sideboards in the style of the Middle Ages, armchair copies of Roman magistrates' chairs, and chests filled with second-hand oddities; a bookcase filled with dusty books of magic, some skulls and a sufficient quantity of stuffed owls. The curtains were never opened. Artificial light was needed in full daylight.

The lair was lit by three candle holders on old wrought iron chandeliers suspended from the ceiling.

In Blanchelaine's apartment, on the contrary, everything was full of light, clean and modern. Mahogany and walnut, wallpaper at twenty *sous* a roll, a buffet decorated with Creil porcelains, a desk with drawers and a chair with a green leather seat, six-drawer file cabinets, and busts of doctors of jurisprudence in the corners.

A twelve-year-old Negro girl answered the door for Stella's clients. Blanchelaine's clients were introduced by a little clerk. However, the two offices were separated by only a thin partition, in which the two renters had, by common agreement, set a louvered window and a door, cleverly hidden in the woodwork.

The afternoon of the day Freneuse had begun by conducting Pia to the Saint-Ouen cemetery, Monsieur Paulet and Sophie met each other at the foot of the stairway which led to the sorceress' lair and the business agent's office. Sophie Cornu had already mounted three steps of the stairway when Monsieur Paulet entered the vestibule and stopped an instant to wipe his feet on the doormat. They didn't know each other and naturally didn't speak, but they observed each other out of the corner of their eyes. Marguerite's father found Sophie Cornu's dress prodigiously ridiculous, and as he had never been to Blanchelaine's office, he was tempted to take her for a client of the business agent.

"What nice people come to see this drole fellow!" he grumbled very low.

Sophie didn't like bohemian artists, but she loathed well-dressed middle-class men.

146

"What's that weird man doing here!" she said between her teeth. "He looks like a law court bailiff who's made his fortune pumping money out of poor people."

They were in these amiable attitudes toward one another when they arrived at the landing of the second floor. There Monsieur Paulet had the satisfaction of seeing the old woman ring at one door just as he saw, on the other, the plaque on which shone in black letters on a brass background the name Blanchelaine.

"Thank Heaven!" he thought. "I won't have the disappointment to go in following that creature. She must be a concierge somewhere."

A small boy who had tousled hair and a pen behind his ear came to open when he rang and let him enter without asking his name.

"The boss is in. I'm going to tell him you're here," said this little urchin with badly combed hair.

Monsieur Paulet remained alone in a waiting room furnished with caned-bottom chairs and decorated with placards spread out in order of date, illustrating the administrative officials of the Department of the Seine.

You'd think you were in a lawyer's office, on my word of honor. That schemer gives himself airs. But that's not something that will keep me from telling him off. When I think he had the audacity to ask me for 100,000 francs! Fortunately, I haven't given them to him, he said to himself, shrugging.

"The boss is waiting for you," yelped the little clerk, motioning with his pointed snout the entry to a corridor.

He found Monsieur Blanchelaine standing, almost leaning against a partition where there was hanging an engraving of Hippocrates refusing Artaxerces' presents. The business agent didn't seem too surprised to see him and greeted him with respectful attention.

"I wasn't expecting, Monsieur, the honor of having you in my modest domicile," he said, bowing. "And I'm sorry you took so much trouble, because I intended to come to your house tomorrow to give you the copy of the death certificate of Bianca Astrodi as was agreed."

"I don't have any need of your copy now," Monsieur Paulet said brusquely. "You were joking with me, or rather you deceived me unworthily."

"I have nothing of the sort to reproach myself," Monsieur Blanchelaine replied calmly. "Please explain yourself, Monsieur... and sit down," he added, bringing forward a chair.

Monsieur Paulet took it with hesitation and brusquely installed himself there like a man who was preparing himself to break into a series of reproaches.

"You dare say you didn't deceive me!" he began. "I commissioned you to investigate a girl my brother had in Italy. You discovered that girl was dead, but you were very careful not to tell me she had a sister."

"I couldn't tell you that because I still didn't know it yesterday."

"Then I'm the one telling you?"

"No, I've known it for some hours. But I don't see why the existence of that sister can alarm you. Bianca Astrodi, dying before Monsieur Francis Boyer, cannot inherit from him."

"Yes, but you, who claim to know everything, you don't know my brother's will."

"I don't think anyone knew it before your brother's death."

"Well, I myself know it. The notary who received it arrived and he showed me a copy of it. My brother left his entire fortune, to be divided equally between his two illegitimate daughters, Bianca and Pia Astrodi. Bianca is dead, but Pia is alive. Therefore, I am well and truly disinherited."

The business agent changed expressions. Evidently he didn't doubt that Pia was an heiress as was her sister.

"I'll get over it," continued Monsieur Paulet, "but I wanted to point out to you that our agreements are henceforth without purpose. I've come to ask you to give me back the contract I signed. You can have no use for it."

"I can no longer use it...now, " Blanchelaine, who had already reflected, said slowly. "But the situation could change."

"What do you mean by saying that?" asked Monsieur Paulet with irritation. "It's a question of positive facts, and not fanciful suppositions. You can't hold me to a contract which depends on a condition which is no longer possible. You therefore have no reason to keep it, and you must give it back to me."

"Please let me ask you what interest you have in wanting it back," Monsieur Blanchelaine asked coldly.

"I don't want any traces to remain of a contract that I regret having made."

"I could answer you that it's important to me that these traces remain. They can't constrain me to restore to you a document you freely signed. But I would prefer to show you that that document may still be useful... later. Do you remember the terms."

"I've never forgotten them. It says that as payment for acts undertaken by my orders, and not spelled out on paper, I owe you the sum of 100,000 francs payable the day...please note...I would inherit the portion which would come to me as a blood relative, in the will of Francis Boyer, my half-brother."

"That's perfectly right, Monsieur, and I hold to the terms of our arrangement."

"Very well. You will never claim your 100,000 francs because I will never come into a *sou* of the inheritance."

"How do you know?"

"Oh! No equivocations, please. I don't think you would have the audacity to tell me that if this little Pia disappeared from this world like her sister, the inheritance would revert to me. Pia Astrodi survived the person making the will; therefore she is the heiress; therefore her death would not make my brother's fortune revert to me. That fortune would pass on to any of her relatives. If she didn't have any relatives, to the State, because the Italian law is probably copied from the French law."

"I believe so."

"Then what do you expect to happen?"

"That's my secret."

"I have a right to know your secret. I don't want to lend a hand to the plot that you're probably meditating to muddy up a business which is very clear…too clear."

"You won't be responsible for what I'll do."

"I certainly hope so."

"Then leave me alone to act as I intend."

"I can't prevent you from doing it, but I declare to you that you won't be paid for your pains. I won't think any more about the inheritance. I will consider it as lost. I don't want to hear any more about you."

"You won't hear any more from me until the moment I will be in a position to demonstrate to you that the situation has completely changed. And I will begin by telling you that this won't be in a week nor in a month, not even in a year. I add that I will again be in a position to call your attention to recompense the service I have already done you."

"If that's how it is, what do you want to do with the paper I signed?"

"To show it, if ever you…or anyone else…quibble with me about the means I used. This paper, Monsieur, that's my guarantee. It proves that we've always been in agreement. The nature of the actions you commissioned me to do, are not specified there. You've just admitted that yourself. It necessarily follows that everything I did, I must have done by your orders."

"In other words, you're pointing out to me that if the law gets mixed up in your business, you would try to compromise me. I warn you that you won't succeed. I am too honorably known to be accused of having authorized illegal activities. Let's leave it there, Monsieur. You won't give me back that contract?"

"No more than the letter you wrote me a month ago giving me your instructions concerning Bianca Astrodi, that it was a question of preventing…at any price… coming to France, or, if she was already there, staying there."

"Very well," Monsieur Paulet said angrily. "Keep everything; I don't care about it;…and I'm not afraid of you."

"I'm convinced of that," Monsieur Blanchelaine answered calmly. "but you won't be uninterested in the 600,000 francs that were going into your pocket if your brother hadn't had a second daughter and you're very afraid of losing them. Well! Monsieur, instead of quarreling with me and imputing to me intentions I don't have, you'd be better advised to leave it to me to arrange things. It'll take me time, but I'll answer to you for its success. A day will come when I'll bring you the inheritance of the late Monsieur Francis Boyer on a silver platter, like the keys to a conquered city, and you won't have to be mixed up in the conquest. I will only ask you then for what you're pleased to give me, and I ask you now only for information, simply information."

"Information!" repeated MonsieurPaulet."I don't have any information to furnish you. Get it wherever you can. That's none of my business."

"There's some that only you can give me," continued the business agent, without emotion, "and which you won't refuse me, I'm sure, because it's not of nature that would compromise you. Several persons already know, isn't that true, that Bianca Astrodi was the sister of that Pia who makes her living posing for painters."

"That means everybody knows it, or will know it. That came out yesterday in the studio of an artist who's using that girl as a model...in the studio of Monsieur Paul Freneuse."

"The young man who was at the Porte-Saint-Martin play with you?"

"Yes, and he has no motive for keeping a secret of that relationship. What's more, there's one of his comrades, an amateur artist named Binos, who gives me the impression that he's a great talker. You can count on the fact that right now all the studios in the neighborhood know the news."

"That's probable. But that matters very little to me. I only want to clear up one point."

"What's that!" brusquely asked Monsieur Paulet, who was letting himself, little by little, answer the questions of that man with whom he had just broken off relations.

"Does anyone other than you know that Monsieur Francis Boyer left his estate to the two Astrodi girls?"

"The notary knows it. He's the one who told me about it. My daughter also knows it. She was there when he told me about it."

"But the others...the ones you just named...Monsieur Freneuse... Monsieur Binos?"

"They don't know anything about it, *parbleu!* I didn't waste my time telling them the news"

"Naturally. And you won't tell them. But the sister...but Pia?"

"She doesn't know anything either. But she will know everything."

"Who will inform her? It won't be you, I think."

"It will probably be the notary."

"Then he knows she's in Paris?"

"Yes. I told him I'd just seen her. She was just then at Monsieur Freneuse's studio when this notary, who'd looked for me everywhere, came in."

"The devil! That's annoying. But then he doesn't know that girl's address?"

"No more than I do. However, all he needs to do to get it is ask Monsieur Freneuse for it."

"And do you believe he will do that?"

"I don't know. But it seems to me that would be his duty."

"Why? Is he the executor of the will?"

"No. He wasn't even the one who drew up the will. My brother wrote it by hand without consulting anyone. And this damned will, it was the Tribunal President who opened it."

"Then this notary is not charged with looking for the heirs?"

"No. Although he always looked out for my interests while my brother was alive. I reimbursed him for the expenses of his trip. I don't think he intends to stay long in Paris."

"Can you tell me what hotel he's staying in?"

"Rue du Bouloi, 75. I certainly hope you aren't going to discuss with him your projects...that I don't know and don't want to know."

"I'll certainly avoid doing so, you must believe me, although my plans aren't anything that couldn't be admitted. I just want to be sure that before leaving he doesn't get in touch with Pia Astrodi. And I can't get information on this point without getting in touch with Monsieur. May I ask you his name?

"Drugeon," answered Monsieur Paulet, drawn in spite of himself into confidences. Monsieur Blanchelaine's self-confidence fascinated him, his protestations of honesty calmed him, and, although he claimed the opposite, he hadn't completely renounced hope of again regaining the inheritance rights. To salve his conscience, he didn't want to be mixed up in anything. But, everything considered, he judged it useless to break off definitively with the man who was working hard to restore the lost inheritance to him.

"I thank you, Monsieur," said the agent, "and I swear that you won't regret having made it possible for me to serve you."

Monsieur Paulet didn't acknowledge that statement. He limited himself to saying:

"Remember that it can no longer be a question of this business between you and me."

And he rose with a dignified air. Blanchelaine bowed very humbly and conducted him right to the door of the apartment without saying a word. The clever fellow knew how much to believe about Monsieur Paulet's protestations of lack of interest. He dismissed his little clerk, who was nibbling hazelnuts in the waiting room. He returned to his office. Instead of sitting down at his desk, he glued his ear against the partition, and a minute afterward, he knocked on it three times at intervals in a certain way. Three discreet taps, placed at equal intervals soon answered this signal. Blanchelaine stretched out his right hand and pressed a brass button hidden in the molding of the woodwork. Immediately a panel on tracks slid back and revealed an opening wide enough for a man to pass through. It was a woman dressed in a long black robe with a turban of red silk who slid through that secret door into Blanchelaine's office. Under that strange get up, Paul Freneuse would've had great difficulty recognizing the woman he had seen at the Saint-Ouen cemetery and in the orchestra seats at the Porte-Sainte-Martin Theater. Nevertheless, it was really the same one, and, really, her fortune-teller costume didn't look bad on her. The color of the head dress made her complexion appear less red, and the loose-fitting robe accentuated her stature. However, she seemed worried.

151

"I've just seen her," she said, with no other preamble.

"Who?" Blanchelaine asked impatiently.

"Sophie Cornu, *parbleu!* She came to consult me, and I took advantage of the opportunity to ask her details. But those she gave me aren't very interesting."

"Well, what did she tell you?"

"It was Binos who told her yesterday, at the burial, that Bianca had a sister. Only, Sophie had never seen that sister. She met her today at the cemetery."

"You already told me that a while ago, and if you don't know anything more..."

"I know how Binos discovered the relationship of the model. He explained everything to Sophie, who has just repeated to me the story that bohemian painter delivered to her. It seems he went day before yesterday to see a painter who lives in the Place Pigalle, Paul Freneuse, the one who had the idea to chase us the other evening when we were leaving the theater, and that we tricked so well. I'm still laughing about it. I'm the one who thought up the ploy with the *fiacre*. Well! Binos, as soon as he got to his friend's studio, started yelling at the top of his lungs that he knew the name of the girl stretched out in the morgue, and that her name was Bianca Astrodi."

"Ah! The scoundrel! I had forbidden him to talk about it."

"Hearing that, Pia, who was posing, became ill. She fell in a faint on the floor, crying out: 'That's my sister!' That's how they knew about it."

"Ah! I hope that brute Binos didn't mention my name in front of Freneuse!"

"At least he didn't brag about it. Sophie Cornu would have told me."

"And did he say my name in front of that old woman?"

"As for that, no, for sure. Sophie doesn't know you. She always calls me Madame Blanchelaine. She would've recognized your name..."

"Binos doesn't know my name. To him and the people who frequent the *Grand-Bock* my name is Piédouche."

"That's true. I wasn't thinking about that."

"And he's never known where I lived. Provided your Sophie Cornu doesn't take a notion to point out my domicile to him!"

"Not on your life. Why do you think she'd go poke around in this business? She believes you don't even suspect the existence of all those people."

"So much the better. Because if she started talking, we'd have one more bad card in our game. Binos would put the match to the powder. He's tied to this Freneuse, who's already spied on us, and who by a miracle just missed catching us. If he finds out that Piédouche is named Blanchelaine, and if he finds out that he has an agency on the Rue de la Courdière, there'll be nothing left for us but to pack our baggage."

"Bah! That won't happen. That Bianca has a sister is not important. That Paulet fellow will nonetheless inherit and you'll collect your 100,000 francs."

"Do you think so?" Blanchemaine asked with an angry gesture.

"What! What's wrong then?" Stella asked, very upset.

"What's wrong is that Paulet left here. He's just told me his brother had two daughters, Bianca and Pia, and that imbecile left his estate equally divided between them; and now that the elder has left for the other world, everything goes to the younger one."

"Ah!" murmured the fortune teller. "It was a lot of trouble to risk so much!"

"Yes, it's a hard blow. But I don't consider myself beaten. If I'm going to lose the 1000,000 francs that Paulet agreed to pay me the day he inherited, I'll recover some other way. It won't be said that I compromised myself for nothing."

"I would never get over it. But what can be done? You aren't thinking about beginning the Bianca story again, I hope? That's too dangerous."

"And that would gain nothing. But there's more than one way to neutralize a woman who's in the way."

"I don't know but one," Stella said with a somber air. "And we've already used it. If we try it again, we'll be taking too great a risk."

"It's not a question of that," Blanchelaine answered quickly. "The situation is no longer the same since the father is dead. If Pia died tomorrow, she would nonetheless inherit and if she had no relatives, the State would claim her inheritance. We are, on the contrary, interested in her remaining alive. I'd rather deal with her than the Italian government."

"What do you expect to get out of that little girl?"

"For the moment, nothing. Later, that'll be different. It'll take a long time for the business to mature."

"I don't understand your idea."

"My idea is to exploit that Pia Astrodi directly to our profit. My plan is based on this: She certainly knows Bianca was her sister, but she doesn't know about the will. Nobody knows it except Monsieur Paulet and the notary from the country. Paulet will certainly avoid telling the little one, and the notary is going to return to the country. The inheritance will remain open, and no one will inherit if the heiress doesn't come forward. And we'll keep her from coming forward."

"Good! And after that?"

"Afterwards, we'll have to play our cards close to our chest. A great deal of diplomacy is the key."

"Diplomacy? I don't understand."

"You have to understand, because I am counting on you to guard the little girl. And I'm sure you'll succeed if you go about it in the right way."

"You forget that I don't know her."

"You've seen her, and she's seen you."

"Yes, at the cemetery, but I didn't speak to her."

"That doesn't make any difference. You'll go visit her, as soon as I find out where she lives."

"I know. She lives on the Rue des Fosses-Saint-Bernard. The painter said that in front of Sophie Cornu, who repeated it to me."

"Then it was to her place that Bianca went every evening. If we'd know this detail earlier, we'd have maneuvered in a different way. But it's done. Let take the situation as it is and let's try to make the best use we can of it."

"Good! But what pretext will I use to get in touch with that Pia?"

"Under the pretext that you used to go see her sister in the garret she lived in on the Rue des Abbesses. She'll be delighted to talk to you about the dead girl."

"Very well, but what'll I say to her?"

"You'll start by coaxing her. You'll feel sorry for her; you'll swear that her sister loved you a great deal. You'll try to console her."

"That'll be difficult. At Saint-Ouen she cried like a Mary Magdelaine. When she knelt on the grave, I thought she wouldn't have enough strength to get up."

"That's what we need. She must be excitable, like all Italian women. You won't have any trouble getting in control of her head."

"To lead her where?"

"First of all, to make her change professions. The main point is to keep her from returning to Paul Freneuse, who must want to help her. I leave it up to you to invent a story. Which one? I don't know. You'll feel out the situation. If you can see she's in love with him..."

"She is. Binos told Sophie Cornu that."

"Then that will progress by itself. You'll tell her he doesn't care anything about her."

"Binos claims she is jealous, and you'll never guess of whom...of Mademoiselle Paulet."

"Not possible!...But, yes, it is. Freneuse makes a lot of money, and that idiot Paulet is thinking of giving him his daughter in marriage. Freneuse was in their box in the theater."

"And Mademoiselle had her father take her to Freneuse's studio. There she found Pia, who left furious. Binos is certain she swore not to pose any more."

"Admirable! Our business is in the bag. You'll find her completely ready to listen to you and you will easily gain her confidence. You'll ask her to let you transfer to her the affection you had for her sister. You'll offer to help her, if she needs it, and, finally, you'll suggest she come live with you, or to take her back to her own country, if she wants to return there."

"What! You want to send me to Italy?"

"No, I prefer a great deal more that we have the heiress at hand, but we have to foresee everything. The important thing is to remain in communication with her, wherever she is, and to lead her to break off with the people she knows. I don't want her to see either Binos or Frenesue any more. I want the executor of the late Francis Boyer's will never to know what's become of her."

"Very well! But supposing that we succeed in doing all that, what will we get out of it?"

"I'm going to explain my plan to you," Blanchelaine said. "It has two aims, and it can be modified, according to the way things go. As you know, Monsieur Paulet signed the contract to pay me 100,000 francs the day he came into possession of his brother's estate. He can only do that if Pia abandons it."

"And that will never happen."

"Why? You can always renounce benefiting by a will...to renounce it by a notarized document, the effect of which restores the blood relative their legal rights."

"And you think you can lead Pia to give up her rights in favor of a man she doesn't know?"

"If she did know him it would be a lot more difficult, since she's jealous of Mademoiselle Paulet. But she's absolutely ignorant of the fact that her natural father is the half-brother of Monsieur Paulet. I'll arrange it so she never knows it. I can add that, to legally sign a document, you must be of legal age, and, probably, that girl isn't."

"She seems to me to be scarcely sixteen-years-old."

"Then we'll have to wait several years, and this way we'll have time to reach our ends. We might, for example, push her toward becoming a nun."

"Bad method. She'd give all her worldly goods to the convent she entered."

"No, because she wouldn't know she was rich."

"Then how could she renounce a fortune she doesn't know exists?"

"We'll tell her the truth at the last moment, after we've prepared her properly. It will be necessary to stir up her generous sentiments, persuade her that Monsieur Francis Boyer committed a wicked act by disinheriting his brother, and that she must make up for that wicked act."

"I doubt very much that she'll listen to that."

"That depends on a number of things. You can get everything from an overly excited girl when you go about it cleverly. If, as Binos, claims, she is in despair because Freneuse doesn't love her, she'll listen to the advice of those who support her, who treat her gently, and who will try to console her."

"That's possible...with time...but really it wouldn't be worth the trouble to take so many pains and to work for so many years to finally get 100,000 francs commission...that Monsieur Paulet might refuse to give you."

"I would defy him to do that. I have his written promise and a letter which compromises him. He would never dare sue. However, you're right to say that a 100,000 is little, since this Paulet fellow would inherit 600,000.

"Why couldn't we inherit in his place?"

"You see! You finally understand. We can just as easily make Pia decide to will us her money as to renounce it. And that's the end I'm aiming at. But why wait? We must get started on the main methods."

"Which ones?"

"First of all, leave Paris with her."

"Exactly! It seems she wants to return to her country. Sophie Cornu heard her say to the painter; 'I don't want to pose anymore.'"

"Very good! We'll accompany her to Italy."

"In what capacity?"

"As friends, *parbleu!* You'll gain her confidence by offering to pay her way. I imagine she's not rolling in gold. You'll tell her that, intending to spend two years in Rome for your health, you need a young girl companion who speaks Italian, and that you're asking her because the good landlady who lodged her sister recommended her. You'll add, of course, that you're going with your husband, because I'll be along on the trip."

"Then you'd leave your business affairs?"

"I don't have any that would bring me as much as this one. And, besides, it would be good for us to leave Paris for a while. I fear Binos' indiscretions, and I'm afraid of Freneuse. If he found us, and above all if he found out we live together, he'll remember the Place Pigalle omnibus, and he won't go easy on us; whereas in two years, the accident that happened to Bianca Astrodi will be ancient history."

"What! We're going to stay there two years!"

"Two or three or more, if necessary. We'll return as soon as the little girl is old enough to legally testify, that is to say, at eighteen."

"And you believe that she'll get the idea to make her will?"

"I'll take charge of whispering it to her. And to whom would she leave all she possesses if not to her benefactors? She doesn't have any relatives."

"Good! But will she live longer than we do?"

"I don't believe so," said Blancelaine, laughing. "You forget that imbecile Binos gave me the hat pin you lost."

IX. The Rue des Fossés-Saint-Bernard

The house on the Rue des Fosses-Saint-Bernard where Old Man Lorenzo lodged his boarders didn't look like anything special. It was an old, black, six-story building, much taller than wide, with narrow windows set irregularly, not one of which was the same dimension as its neighbor. With its weather-beaten façade and strangled between two buildings of better appearance, it somewhat resembled a slice of mildewed paté. The entry to that hovel was through a dark passageway closed by a chest-high door which led into a humid courtyard, with as little light as the bottom of a well. There were two rooms on the first floor. One was a cabaret whose door opened directly onto the street. Lorenzo sold drinks to passers-by there. The other served as a dining hall for the models for both sexes who lodged with that clever fellow.

In the evening, near nightfall and in the morning from sunrise, you could see a nice reunion there of Calabrian thieves and country women from the Abruzzi. There were entire families there, from grandfathers with white beards right down to little four-year-old girls sitting on the knees of robust matrons with heavy shoulders. They spoke an incomprehensible patois there and let off odors of garlic and tobacco which could be smelled as far away as the Jardin des Plantes. All these people slept in rooms laid out like dormitories and lived there in rather good fellowship. Knife fights were rare, but they quarreled often.

Old Man Lorenzo controlled his lodgers and inspired them, if not with respect, at least with a healthy fear. Still vigorous, despite his sixty-five years, the good man didn't stand for any joking either about morality or the payment of rent. He'd been in business fifteen years and he'd never had any slip up with the French police. He was thought, however, to have terrorized the countryside as the head of a band that robbed travelers and extorted money from landowners in the Terracine area. But wealth changes men. Having amassed a nice living in that profession, and a price having been put on his head by the Roman States, one fine day he became disgusted with sleeping out in the open and being nourished by raw chestnuts. And since he was ambitious, instead of retiring peacefully from business, he took passage to Naples on the Marseille mail boat. From there he came to Paris to invest his savings.

God had blessed his efforts. The establishment he directed was completely prosperous. He had bought the building with the profits he made lodging and feeding his countrymen. And he was never lacking for lodgers. He had business associates in all the villages in the south of Italy and from time to time he went there himself to recruit. He was not at all a mean man. He gave reasonable credit and he lent small sums to models out of work. He himself tried to find them work, since he had contacts with all the painters. He sometimes went so far as to send back to Italy, at his own expense, models the painters would no longer use.

157

It was with him that Freneuse had negotiated for Pia's room and board. And as Freneuse's arrangement was very advantageous for Lorenzo, that good bandit treated the young girl with infinite regard and consideration. He finally had even become attached to her. He would have risked his skin to defend her if some scoundrel had tried to get too close to her, or even insult her.

And Pia had settled very comfortably into living in this dirty *caravanserai*, where the poorest Parisian girl wouldn't have wanted to live. It's true she lived completely apart, although she didn't think herself too good to speak to the other inhabitants of this barracks when she met them on the stairs. She occupied a bedroom with a mansard window under the roofs on the top floor of the building. It had sheltered organ grinders and monkeys, during the time they still allowed poor people from southern Italy to send their children to France to beg. She had made a charming nest of this poor retreat. The attic room where Pia was so happy didn't shine by the splendor of its furnishings. An iron bed, some caned-bottomed chairs, an unpainted table, a mirror, a chest where she put her folded linens and clothes, a large pitcher and bowl for washing; on the white-washed walls two crayon sketches by Paul Freneuse. That was all.

But Pia had made good use of the water drain outside her only window.

Disobeying all police ordinances, she had made a little aviary and a garden. A box held the entire garden, and the aviary housed a single finch, but the flowers were fresh and the finch sang all day long. And from that window there was a marvelous view. Old Man Lorenzo's house faced the north-east. To the right, on the other side of the street, were lined up shops, sidewalks and wine warehouse complexes. A little further off, the old trees of the Jardin des Plants were beginning to turn green. To the left, beyond the bridges and above the uneven roofs, rose the Père Lachaise hill, crowned by cypress trees, whose dark silhouettes stood out against the clear sky, a whole corner of Paris, seen from the sky, as the birds of heaven see it.

The day following her trip to Saint-Ouen, Pia, who had gotten up before dawn after a sleepless night, was dreaming, leaning on the wrought-iron bar safety bar on the window. The air was cool, and the morning mist was dissipating with the first rays of the spring sun, which were turning the roofs gold. A beautiful day was beginning, one of those festivals that God sometimes gives to the disinherited of the great city, to those who can't offer themselves any other sight but the reawakening of nature. The merchants were chatting away on the steps of their door, and children were playing in the street.

Old Man Lorenzo's lodgers were preparing to take flight to arrive before noon at the studios on the Place Pigalle and in the Luxembourg neighborhood. You could hear the rushing about on the stairs, and through the dormitory windows joyous bursts of laughter exploding like pistol shots which made passers-by look up.

The former bandit who had become a landlord was smoking his pipe on the threshold of his cabaret and smiling comfortably into his flowing beard, computing very low the payments he was going to put in the till in the evening. This was the season when all those with lodgers earned money, and those due money didn't have to wait. Lorenzo was somewhat surprised not to see Pia, who was always the first to come down. But he never went into her room unless she invited him. But Pia was hardly thinking about inviting him, any more than she was thinking about going to buy her frugal breakfast. Her thoughts were flying away to that square where Paul had left her the evening before, making her swear not to leave without seeing him. And she had wondered what he meant in speaking to her about posing somewhere other than in his studio. To continue posing for him, to pose alone with him, that was the only hope she had remaining, and she scarcely believed it possible.

He's understood what I'm suffering and he's taken pity on me, she thought sadly. *He's so good! He promised to let me hear from him soon. He promised me that to calm me, to keep me from leaving. He thinks I'll have second thoughts, that I don't have enough courage to flee from him and that I'll come back. But he himself isn't coming. Why should he come? I'm only a poor girl who lives off his kindness. It's up to me to go ask him as a favor to let me come back. And I won't go. I'd find that woman there and I'd rather die than appear in front of her. No, I won't go. I'll wait two days, and if I don't see him, I'll write him to say good-bye. I'll go pray one last time on Bianca's grave, and then....*

Pia was at that point in her reflexions when someone knocked gently at her bedroom door.

"What if it's he!" she whispered, nailed to the spot by emotion.

There was a silence and then someone began to knock a little louder. She wanted to answer, but she wouldn't speak. Then she suddenly thought that this couldn't be Freneuse who was knocking. Freneuse wasn't patient and the key was on the outside of the door. Freneuse would have come in. At that moment, the key turned in the lock, and the door opened slowly. Pia had guessed correctly. It wasn't Freneuse. But the surprise she felt when she saw the person who came in was no less great. That person was a woman very elegantly dressed in black, who looked very attractive and had a rather pleasant face. You could have thought her a lady of charity on a visit to the poor. Pia, who wasn't used to receiving visits of this sort, thought there was a mistake. She was going to say so then the unknown woman came up to her, took both her hands and kissed her on the forehead. Pia, completely dumbfounded, didn't dare pull herself away from these unexpected caresses.

"I can see, my dear child," said the lady, sitting down in one of the three caned chairs which furnished the attic room. "I can see by your astonishment that you can't place me... However that's understandable; you've hardly seen me."

"Excuse me, Madame, I don't remember it," said the young girl.

"Yesterday I was very near you. It pains me to remind you of those very cruel moments. I was near you when you were praying for the one who is no

159

more."

Pia shivered and looked at the woman with more attention.

"In the Saint Ouen cemetery...near your sister's grave."

The memory came back to the young girl. She had hardly noticed, the day before, the person chatting with Sophie Cornu, but it seemed to her that she was really the same one.

"I also came to pray over the resting place of our dear Bianca..."

"You, Madame!" Pia, stupefied, said.

"That surprises you because you don't know that I loved her as if I had been her own mother."

"You knew her?"

"For two years. I met her at Milan at the home of friends of my husband who was traveling at that time with me in Italy. I became fond of her and she came to give me her full confidence."

"She never talked about you."

"No more than she told you why she came to Paris."

"Pardon me, Madame. She told me."

The lady bit her lips, but she didn't change expressions.

"So," she continued. "You knew Bianca was looking for her father, who was also yours."

"I knew that."

"But didn't know that it was thanks to me that she found him."

"Our father! What! She saw him again...and I didn't know that! No. No. That's impossible."

"She didn't see him again, but after long investigation I learned that he lived in a little village in the south of France...and Bianca, informed by me, wrote to him."

"And she hid that from me!...That's strange."

"She certainly hid from me that she had a sister...from me who had given her so many proofs of my friendship and of my devotion. It was only by chance yesterday that I learned who you were. She carried discretion, or rather reserve, to an excess. So, she never told you where she lived."

"No, although I asked her often."

"I'm the one who sent her to that good woman who keeps a furnished house on the Rue des Abbesses, and who took flowers to the cemetery yesterday. Bianca had never talked about you to her either, to that excellent Madame Cornu. Bianca told her she was going to a singing lesson whenever she came to visit you. As for me, I didn't know she went out in the evening. She came to see me only in the morning. And she talked to me only about your father. She thought only about seeing him again."

"But...she didn't see him again?" the young girl asked with emotion.

"Alas! No. That's what killed her."

"What do you mean?"

160

"Did they tell you how your sister died?" the lady asked after a silence.

"They told me she died suddenly," whispered Pia, with tears in her eyes.

"She died from sorrow."

"What!"

"She had a weak heart…and her heart broke. She had just learned that your father refused to see her…that he denied her."

"Is that possible?"

"It's only too true. To the begging letter she wrote to him reminding him that he had two daughters, he replied with a very hard letter. The poor child didn't have the strength to endure this blow."

"Ah! That's terrible!" sobbed the girl, fainting, falling into a chair which fortunately was near, or she would have fallen as she fell in Freneuse's studio.

The lady rose, wiping the tears flowing down Pia's face with a batiste handkerchief saying to her gently:

"Don't despair, my child. Men are forgetful, and your father probably gave way to a first fit of anger on learning that the girl he had abandoned had become a singer in order to live... But his heart may change; I hope so. What he refused to the older daughter, he won't refuse to you. He'll come to your aid."

"No, because I won't ask him for anything," said Pia, lifting her head. "He'll never hear anything about me."

The lady, hearing these words, changed expressions.

"I love your pride," she said after a silence. "And I won't have the courage to disapprove of you if you persist in your resolution not to ask help that your sister wasn't able to obtain. But it's time I tell you who I am and why I've come. My name is Madame Blanchelaine. My husband has a fortune. We live in Paris, but we travel every year during the good weather. We've been three times to Italy, and we will certainly go again, because we love your country more than anything. It was, as I told you, during one of our trips that we met your sister and that I became attached to her. The news of her death upset me. I blessed chance which made me learn that my dear Bianca had a sister. I swore to transfer to that sister all the affection with which the one we mourn for inspired me. I found out where you lived. Madame Cornu told me. She learned it yesterday at the cemetery. I ask her to find out information about you. An artist you know, a Monsieur Binos, told her that you had no other resources on which to live but to pose for artists. So, I thought about offering you a better position."

"I thank you, Madame, but I don't need anyone," whispered the young girl.

"I know that, my child. I know you are wise, well behaved, that you have always led an exemplary life, and by working you have been able to lay aside some money. But pardon me for telling you this…I don't see any future in the profession you're following. You won't always be beautiful, and when you've reached the age when you can no longer serve as a model for artists…"

"I won't get to that age. I have decided not to pose any more."

"Then what do you expect to do?"

"I'm going back to Subiaco where I was born and where my mother died."

"To Subiaco! What an extraordinary coincidence! We went there two years ago, my husband and I. We only passed through, but we found your mountains so charming, that we decided to take a house there this spring and stay until the end of the summer. Why don't you come with us?"

"Me, Madame! You can't know that I'm only a poor girl. Back there I'll take up again what I did before coming to France. I herded goats."

"Ours, then," said Madame Blanchelaine with a nice smile. "We'll buy a herd on purpose. My husband does everything I want. It's important to me not to be separated from you. Listen to me, my dear Pia. You are alone in the world, because your father has pushed Bianca away, and you don't want to appeal to his heart..."

"Never!" said Pia quickly. "He'll never know I exist."

"Well! As for me, who has everything that is necessary to be happy in this world, I'm not happy. I have no children. That's the great sorrow of my life...I had a dream which sadly disappeared. I dreamed about adopting your sister if her father didn't recognize her...to treat her and to love her as my daughter. My husband shared my ideas. We would have seen her married one day, and later we would have left her our fortune. Death took Bianca from us, but you're still here. It's just up to you to give me back the hope I lost. Pia, my dear Pia, would you like to have me as your mother?"

"My mother," repeated Pia, lowering her head. "Alas, I lost her."

"I'll take her place," the lady quickly said. "Your sister that I loved so much would not have refused the happiness that just depended on her to give me. I hadn't dared to suggest to her that I adopt her, because I thought her father would agree to recognize her. But when I recognized that man was heartless, that he denied his daughter, my resolution was quickly taken. If death had surprised Bianca, I'd have gone to her to say: 'Come, our house is open to you. Come, you won't leave us again.' And I'm certain she would have come."

"My sister would not have abandoned me."

"Oh! No. She would have talked to me about you. She would have brought me here. I would have asked you not to leave her. You would not have resisted my prayers and hers. You would have agreed to live with her at our house. And I would have had two daughters instead of one. God called her to him, but you, you are alive, Pia. You are an orphan as she was, alone in the world, without friends, without parents, since your father had the barbarity to deny his children. You won't flee from the new family which opens its arms to you."

"I thank you for your kindness, Madame," murmured the child, "but I've told you, I want to return to Italy."

"And I've told you that we're going there, my husband and I, that we plan to spend the summer precisely in your native valley. So it's logical that we make the journey together. When are you going to leave, my dear Pia?"

"I don't know."

"We'll choose the day convenient for you, my child."

"You are too good, Madame, but I can't promise to go with you."

"Why? Haven't you decided to leave France?"

"Yes."

"Then it would be better for it to be as soon as possible, especially if, as you've just told me, you don't intend to pose in studios any longer. If you remain here, you'll quickly exhaust your money, since you're no longer working."

"I won't stay here. It's possible that I'll leave tomorrow. But I can't leave before seeing someone who's supposed to come tell me goodbye."

"Someone who takes an interest in you! Ah! You make me happy. I would like to meet that friend who remains faithful to you in adversity. I would like to meet him to talk to him about my plan for a trip to Italy and to promise to take his place near you."

"Then," said Pia, hesitating an instant, "You don't find it a bad idea that I consult him."

"Not only do I not find it a bad idea, but I strongly urge you to. And if you will give me his name and address, I'll go to him, I'll beg him to join me and persuade you to accept my proposition. If he is truly attached to you, he'll support me, because he'll see that it comes from the heart."

"Well, Madame, it's the painter who accompanied me yesterday to Saint-Ouen."

"What! That Monsieur Binos," exclaimed the lady, who knew very well what she was doing. "But he's not a serious artist. Madame Cornu, who was your sister's landlady, told me he spent his time running from one café to another instead of working. And really, my dear Pia, if you want to ask advice of this poor boy..."

"He's not the one, Madame. I know him. I know what he's worth. I hope never to see him again. I'm talking about Monsieur Paul Freneuse."

"The painter who lives on the Place Pigalle?"

"Yes, Madame."

"It was in his studio that you learned about the death of your sister. You have been posing for him since you came to Paris?"

"Who told you that?" ask Pia, rather astonished.

"Madame Cornu, who had it from Binos."

"Well, he should also have told her that I owe everything to Monsieur Freneuse. That I have lived only by his kindness, that without him..."

"Monsieur Freneuse also owes you something. Where would he have found a model worth as much as you? But...did he really tell you he would come before you left?"

"He promised so firmly that he made me promise not to leave without seeing him."

"And you're waiting for him?"

"Evidently. Why would I doubt his word?"

"*Mon Dieu!* I'm not suggesting he won't come, but I'd be very surprised if he found the time to keep his word. Don't you know he's going to be married very soon?"

"You say Monsieur Freneuse is going to be married? No, that's not possible," murmured Pia, very pale.

"I assure you, my child, that he's getting married," said Madame Blanchelaine. "The bans have been published and the ceremony will take place the day after the opening of the Exposition."

"How do you know that?"

"It was Monsieur Binos who told Madame Cornu and she repeated it to me. Monsieur Freneuse is marrying Mademoiselle Paulet, the daughter of a rich land owner. It's a good marriage for him, who has only what he earns, because his fiancée will bring him a considerable dowry. What's more, she's charming. But what's wrong with you, my dear child?"

"Nothing, madam," answered Pia, hold back with difficulty the sobs which were choking her.

"You're fond of Monsieur Freneuse...I thought that news would please you... But I see I was wrong."

"I don't believe it. If he was to be married, he wouldn't have promised me that he would come."

"Why? On the contrary, isn't it very natural that he'd want to finish the painting he's begun? This painting, it seems, is supposed to be a great success, and it's very important for Monsieur Freneuse that he not miss the Exposition. How can he finish it if you refuse to pose?"

"So, it's because he needs me that..."

"That shouldn't astonish you, dear little girl. Great artists are egotistical. Monsieur Binos explained all that to good Sophie Cornu... He even added a number of other details. You know him... You must know he's very talkative...that he tells everybody his business, and even that of his friends."

"Then, what did he say?"

"Some things I would be wrong to repeat."

"Don't be afraid, Madame. I'm ready to hear everything. If you're my friend, you'll enlighten me as to Monsieur Freneuse's intentions."

"*Mon Dieu!* My dear Pia, You embarrass me a great deal. It would pain me to strip you of an illusion. And from another direction, if you should sacrifice the future I suggest to you, sacrifice it for a man who thinks only of using you."

"Tell me, please!"

"I'm afraid not only of saddening you, but still more of wounding you."

"I'm already wounded," Pia said in a low voice.

"Well, my poor child, it seems Monsieur Freneuse has perceived, ...or thought he perceived...I really don't know how to tell you this...finally, he imagined he had inspired in you a sentiment which..."

"Finish, Madam. He believed I was in love with him."

"Just as you say."

"It's true. I love him."

"Alas! I suspected that. And I thank God who gave me the idea to come here. There is perhaps still time to save you from yourself, to cure you of a fatal passion. I was hesitating to tell you the cruel truth; now I no longer hesitate. You should know that if that man hid from you the fact that he was going to be married, it was because he was afraid you'd leave him on the spot. After the scene which happened in the studio, Mademoiselle Paulet made another one in front of Monsieur Binos. She's jealous of you and she forbade her future husband to see you. He swore that you would never again set foot in his studio, that is to say, he would dismiss you."

"No, I don't believe that... That would be unworthy... Besides, I saw him the next day."

"Because it was to his best interest not to break off with you. Monsieur Freneuse is playing a double game. As a man, he manipulates his fiancée, who's rich; as a painter, he manipulates his model, whom he can't replace. And I can guess his plan. Come, Pia, be frank, admit that he has suggested to you that you pose in some studio other than his own?"

"He hasn't talked about another studio. He asked me if I would consent to pose for him in a place where he would be alone with me."

"And you accepted?"

"No, I answered that I would wait to hear from him."

"And that you wouldn't leave without having seen him. That's what he wanted. He's going to come."

"Here?" asked the young girl, shivering.

"Without a doubt. He knows that in this bedroom you'll be at his command, until he's finished his painting…at his orders and at his mercy…"

"I won't wait for him here," Pia said resolutely.

Pia got up brusquely, and as she was shaking, good Madame Blanchelaine had passed her arm around her waist to support her.

"You are right, my child," she said in her gentlest voice. "Monsieur Freneuse must not find you here. We must outwit his villainous schemes. Let him marry Mademoiselle Paulet, because she's rich, but at least he won't take advantage of your giving up your reputation. To pose, to help that man who unworthily made fun of you, that would really be too much weakness. If I'm to believe what Monsieur Binos, who knows him well, reports about him, he would be capable of profiting from your isolation to try to seduce you. He couldn't try that in his studio, where his fiancée might come at any minute, but here…"

"I want to leave," interrupted the young girl. "To leave this evening…"

"This evening might be too late. It was yesterday that he told you about his visit. He will certainly come today. If you want to avoid him, you don't have a minute to lose to leave this house. Mine is open to you, Pia. I'm going to take you there, and I swear I won't try to influence your plans. You can stay with me as long as you want to…always if that's what you want… only a few days if that's that you choose…the time needed to get rid of the furnishing of this bedroom and to pick up those the poor dead woman left with Madame Cornu."

"Why?" murmured Pia.

"You must, my child. You can't abandon what belonged to your sister. Just think that they will sell her clothes, her linens, at auction. That would be profanation and then there are some papers…which you may need later. I understand that you don't have the courage to enter the house where she lived, but you don't have to go there. I will alert Madame Cornu, who'll have everything brought to you."

"All right! I'll do it!" said Pia, who wasn't thinking of anything but fleeing from Paul Freneuse, since she believed he had deceived her. "Take me away, Madame, I am ready to follow you, if you promise me I can leave Paris tomorrow."

"I promise you, and whatever it costs me to separate from you, I won't try to keep you from traveling alone, if you don't want to wait until my husband has finished his preparations for departure. You'll be free, Pia, absolutely free. We'll meet you in Subiaco. I hope down there, you won't refuse to join us. But time's going by, my child. Come, I beg you."

Pia was in a state of exaltation which didn't permit her to reason.

"I'm ready, Madame," she said, rushing toward the door that Madame Blanchelaine had just opened.

She let that woman go out first. Without even taking care to remove the key, she went down the stairs. She didn't meet anyone there. The Italian birds had taken flight. Père Lorenzo was smoking his pipe at the door of the cabaret. He greeted Pia in a friendly way, but he wasn't given to chatting, and he didn't ask her where she was going. Well dressed people inspired him with respect. And the woman leading his lodger was wearing a silk dress. She had come in a *fiacre* which was waiting at the door. She had Pia get in. She jumped in after her. She gave an address to the coachman, and she lowered the shutters just as the horse began to trot toward the quays. This precaution was wise because another rented carriage came from the opposite direction, a carriage on top of which were loaded various objects, and which carried two gentlemen. The two *fiacres* crossed each other. If Madame Blanchelaine noticed the travelers who passed her by pulling back the shutters slightly, these saw neither the lady nor the child she was spiriting away. A moment afterwards, these two men jumped to the ground in front of the lodging house door, to the great surprise of Lorenzo, who wasn't accustomed to so much coming and going.

"Hello, old bandit," the first one down, smoking a clay pipe and holding a box of paints, yelled to him. Don't you recognize me, *birbante?* You can at least recognize the *illustrissimo signor* Freneuse, the benefactor of one of your lodgers."

"Well! It's you, Monsieur Freneuse!" said Lorenzo, in fairly good French.

This retired bandit spoke a little of all languages, having had the opportunity to learn bits and pieces, from the travelers of all the nations that in the past he had led into the mountains to hold for ransom, following the custom of those like him, who treated their prisoners very friendly right up to the day they cut off their ears or their head, if the ransom wasn't paid.

"Yes, old Fra Diavolo, it's me," the artist said gaily. "Do me the favor of helping the coachman take down the easel on the top of our *fiacre.*"

Lorenzo obeyed without speaking, while Freneuse paid for the trip.

"You weren't expecting this, venerable thief," continued Binos, still joking. "Your *cassine* has never been honored by the visit of two talented painters. It'll have that honor everyday for three weeks. I advise you to light up the building in the evening. And while waiting, if you have an old bottle of Capri wine, you can serve it to me. I want to propose a toast to you and to your lodgers. Why aren't they at the windows, your lodgers? Flown away, *hein*? They're all on the way to pose?"

"There's nobody here but Mamma Carlotta. Her little one has a fever," grumbled Lorenzo, placing the easel and a canvas covered with a cloth against the wall. The *fiacre,* its travelers and their burdens taken off, was already rolling toward the quays.

"Then, is business good?" continued the talkative dauber. "Admit that this profession is better than the other one, ...the one you had , between Rome and Naples. That's all right. Don't disturb the Carlotta woman. She's too ugly. When I paint a picture where there's a witch, I'll hire her. The two of us will drink the bottle. Signor Freneuse will pay but he won't drink any of it. Do you have a boy to carry the things upstairs? How many floors? Six at least, without counting the ground floor and the basement."

"Then you're coming to work here?" asked the good man.

"Yes, Père Lorenzo," said Freneuse. "I have to finish my painting."

"You're looking at it, that painting," interrupted Binos. "Touch it with respect. It's a masterpiece, and he'll finish it at your place."

"When the model won't go to the painter, the painter must come to the model," Freneuse finished for him.

"Ah! Pia!" said Lorenzo, "That's true. She's full of sorrow because her sister died."

"You knew her, the sister?"

"I saw her every evening. But she didn't answer when I spoke to her. There was one who would've earned money if she'd wanted to pose. But no. She was wild as a thrush."

"And when she left, she took the Boulevard Saint-Germain omnibus, didn't she, papa?" Binos asked.

"That's very possible, but I don't know anything about it. And I never knew where she lived. She had forbidden Pia to tell me."

"Not at all. Pia didn't know it any more than you did."

"What!'

"How is Pia?" asked Freneuse, that these chats hardly interested.

"She's not sick, *Signor*, but she's very sad. She cries from morning to night, and she doesn't eat anything."

"Her appetite will come back, I hope, and her gaiety too. I'll take charge of making her well. A six-hour séance everyday, old fellow."

"What! In her bedroom!

"Yes, Papa Lorenzo, It's not very big, but there'll be enough room to set up my easel, and the light is probably better there than in my studio. Only, old fellow, I don't want people in the house to gossip. Not a word to your lodgers. They won't see me, since they're gone all day."

"*Capito, Signor...* Understood, Monsieur Freneuse."

"Very good. Put the easel on your shoulder; Binos will carry the canvas; me the colors. Pia's going to be very surprised to see us come loaded down like moving men."

"Yes, when she comes back."

"What! She's gone out?"

"Not five minutes ago. And I'm astonished you didn't see her. The *fiacre* she was in passed beside yours."

"What! She taking *fiacres* now!" Binos exclaimed. "After what's happened, I can understand that she no longer likes the omnibus."

"That's unusual," said Frenuse. "She promised me..."

"She left with a lady."

"What! She didn't go out alone?"

"No. The lady who took her away came in a carriage. She stayed up there almost three-quarters of an hour, and she came down with Pia. She had kept the *fiacre* and they got in just at the moment yours came around the corner."

"Then we passed them."

"And I know why we didn't see them. The shutters of their *sapin* were lowered," said Binos.

"That's true, I remember," murmured Freneuse, pensive.

"What did the lady look like?" asked the amateur artist, addressing the landlord. "Was it a lady, first of all, or a little girl painter, who had gotten wind of the fact that Pia had nothing to do and had come to get her to pose?"

"She had a silk dress and a velvet cloak. And this isn't the first time she's been here."

"Then she knew Pia?"

"No, I don't think so. One evening when her sister was up there, that lady arrived. She asked me who that person who had just arrived had gone to see. I told her that was none of her business, and she left complaining. But this morning she knew very well who she wanted, because she gave me the name of Pia Astrodi. She told me she was expected up there. "

"She was obviously lying. Pia wasn't expecting any one but me," Freneuse

168

exclaimed.

"You can't answer for that." said Binos. "The little girl doesn't tell you her business. The proof is that she never talked to you about Bianca. And it's probable that she didn't want anybody to know where she was going, since she took the precaution of lowering the *fiacre's* shutters."

"Are you very sure she was the one who lowered them? The brusque departure smells a little like kidnapping, and I suspect the lady in question. Pia didn't say anything when she left?" Freneuse asked, addressing the landlord.

"Nothing at all, *Signor.* She hardly looked at me."

"Then she's going to come back," concluded Binos. "She's settled in and when you're settled in, you don't leave like that, footloose."

"You're right. Let's go up to her place. We'll wait for her," Freneuse said, rushing toward the ladder stairway which led to the mansard room on the top floor.

Binos followed without worrying about the comments of the landlord, who was grumbling in his beard.

It bothers that old fogey to be used as a porter, thought the amateur artist, who was explaining everything in his own way. He didn't realize that Lorenzo was telling them that when she went out Pia always carried the key to her room and they would probably find the door locked. In that, however, Lorenzo was wrong, because the key was still in the lock. Binos noticed that, going in after his friend, who hadn't been aware of this rather strange fact.

"That's funny," he said. "I would have thought her more careful. She leaves her bedroom open to whoever comes by. Still, if she had gone to run an errand in the neighborhood, that would explain it...but she left in a carriage, which seems to indicate that she'll stay a certain time outside. It's true that here in her bedroom there's not much to steal."

Freneuse was silent. But seeing that little empty bedroom, he had felt something like a tightening of his heart. He began to look around for a letter with his address. A foreboding warned him that Pia had flown away forever. It seemed impossible to him that she had left without writing him, if only to tell him good-bye. He also wondered who that woman was who came to take her away and that Lorenzo had already seen one evening trying to get information about Bianca Astrodi. And vague suspicions began to grow in his mind.

"We're here; that's the main thing," continued Binos, who was walking up and down, counting his steps, as if he wanted to measure the room. "You don't need anything else to start work but the model. But I would also be curious to know how you're going to arrange things. This box is so small that there's hardly room for your easel. Provided this scoundrel Lorenzo doesn't keep us waiting... Ah! Somebody's knocking. Ah! He's here. He's so loaded down he can't open the door. Don't get up. I'll go."

He did in fact go, while Freneuse leaned out the window to see if he couldn't locate Pia in the street. It wasn't Père Man Lorenzo that he found on the landing. Brusquely opening the door, Binos almost collided with the person knocking. That person was a very well dressed gentleman of a most respectable appearance. Such a gentleman as was seldom seen in Père Lorenzo's house. He hardly had time to step back to avoid the shock. He seemed very surprised and even a little annoyed when he saw the bearded face of the amateur artist appear on the threshold. "Pardon," he stammered. "I must have made a mistake..."

"Who do you want?" Binos shouted at him in a thundering voice. 'I'm looking for a young girl..."

"What! At your age?"

"An Italian girl whose profession is modeling..."

"Come now! You're not going to make me believe you're an artist with a *binette* like yours."

"Monsieur!"

"Oh! Don't be angry. That's a compliment. You look too proper to be a painter. You look like a lawyer appearing before the court. What's the name of your Italian girl?"

"Pia Astrodi."

"Ah! bah!"

"The man who owns this house told me she lived on the top floor, and I..."

"That's no joke. It's here. What do you want with Pia Astrodi?"

"I need to speak to her about some business which concerns her personally."

"That means you don't need me. I understand that, but I can't do anything about it. The little girl has gone out."

"Then, I'll come back."

"Wait! Wait!," Binos suddenly shouted, looking closely at the visitor. "I seem to have a vague idea that I've seen you somewhere before."

"That's very possible, Monsieur, because it seems to me that I've also met you before...only I don't remember in what circumstance."

"I've got it now! You're the one who came to the Place Pigalle...to the studio...to ask about Monsieur."

"True, Monsieur...and I remember now that you also opened the door there."

"That's right. I hate doormen, but I sometimes replace them. Then, come in, Monsieur. Pia is out, but she's going to come back. While you're waiting you can chat with two of her friends. "*He!* Freneuse!" Binos shouted.

Freneuse wasn't far away. He'd heard this dialogue and he'd approached without any noise. As soon as he showed himself, the visitor took off his hat and assumed another air. Evidently he found that Freneuse had nothing in common with the badly informed comrade who had first presented himself, and that he was someone he could talk with.

"Monsieur," he said politely. "I've already had the honor of seeing you, and I'm very happy to meet you here, because I'm just come from your studio."

"If I'm not mistaken, Monsieur, you're Monsieur Paulet's notary," said Freneuse, who recalled perfectly this person's first visit.

"His notary, no. I was the notary of his brother, Monsieur Francis Boyer, who recently died at Amélie-les-Bains."

"Ah! Yes. Monsieur Paulet spoke to me about the loss he'd just had… but…I haven't seen him since the day you came to my studio to find him, and…"

And you're wondering what my motive is for wanting to see you. Here's what it's about…"

"No, no, not here," exclaimed Binos, drawing the visitor into the bedroom. "I met you on the landing because I didn't know who I was dealing with…The first time I took you for a police commissioner. From the moment you're a notary, that's different."

The administrative officer entered without being asked twice. Freneuse's presence reassured him.

"Monsieur," he said to him, "my name is Drugeon. You probably know I came to Paris to consult Monsieur Paulet about his brother's will, but you don't know, I suppose, that the will disinherited him."

"In fact, I didn't know that," said Freneuse, very surprised at this beginning.

"Monsieur Boyer left all his estate to two illegitimate girls that he had in Italy, and that he had never recognized, carrying the name of their mother, Bianca and Pia Astrodi."

What!" Freneuse exclaimed. "Pia is Monsieur Boyer's daughter… Monsieur Paulet's niece!"

"Legally, no," answered Master Drugeon."Her father never recognized her. If he had recognized her, he wouldn't have been able to leave her all his estate, because French law prohibits willing a natural child what it allows willing to a stranger."

"It's better to inherit than to have bourgeois relatives," Binos said sententiously, "especially if the inheritance is a big one."

"More than 500,000 francs."

"A half million falling into Pia's lap! Ah! She amazing, that one…more amazing than you'd imagine. And that little scatterbrain goes out taking a ride in a *fiacre* just at the moment they bring her a fortune. What a look there're be on her face when she returns! Say, Paul, I have an idea that you'll never finish your painting. It's a sure thing now she won't pose any more."

And in order to express the joy that news gave him, Binos danced a jig in the middle of the floor, to the great stupefaction of Monsieur Drugeon, who took him for a fool.

Freneuse, less demonstrative than his friend, but more genuinely moved, said,

"Monsieur, I'm very happy to learn that child is going to be rich, because she deserves all good fortune. This good fortune comes just at a time to compensate for the misfortune that's just struck her. Her sister died suddenly."

"Bianca Astrodi, co-heiress with Pia. Monsieur Boyer's will made the two daughters of Bartolomea Astrodi, domiciled at Subiaco in the Roman States, co-heiresses with equal portions. And following the death of the elder, the entire legacy falls to the younger."

"Pia didn't know that."

"She might have been forever ignorant of the good fortune befalling her, because no one knew it. Monsieur Boyer never took any notice of his daughters. When he did remember them, at the last moment of his life, he couldn't say where they were. It was completely by chance that I had news yesterday of the one surviving. The information is still incomplete. You may remember, Monsieur, that I came to your studio to speak to Monsieur Paulet, who was there."

"Perfectly. And you almost met Pia there. She had just learned of her sister's death."

"On leaving the house where I was, Monsieur Paulet told me that. He had just seen the heiress of his brother at your studio."

"Who had disinherited him in favor of his natural daughter. That was very generous of him, because without the information he gave you, the relationship of Pia would never have been discovered."

"Never, very likely, Monsieur. But it was necessary also to find the person of the heiress. It wasn't through Monsieur Paulet that I would succeed."

"What! Nothing was simpler for him, however, than to tell you where she lived. He had only to ask me."

"That's what I asked him to do, but he answered me that it wasn't up to him to see that a will disinheriting him to the advantage of a foreign girl was executed."

"That's what's strange. You just told us a while ago that without him you wouldn't have known that Pia was posing at my studio."

"Yes. The first reaction is always the good one. But his bad disposition soon got the upper hand. Monsieur Paulet really had no reason to be happy. He couldn't be expected to take to heart the interests of a young girl who was inheriting to his detriment."

"Then he refused to tell you how to get Pia's address?"

"Absolutely. He told me he didn't want to hear any more about the heiress. Mademoiselle Paulet, who came in unexpectedly during our interview, strongly approved her father's resolution. She ordered me to no longer have anything to do with this affair. She even added that Pia was a vagabond like her sister, and that she had probably left Paris and there would be no use my looking for her."

"Well! Well!" Binos said between his teeth. "She's not the daughter of a bourgeois for nothing. A Rubens! Who would've believed that?"

"Fortunately, Monsieur, you didn't follow this advice," Freneuse said, very moved.

"No," said the notary, "I would have thought myself lacking in my duty as an honest man, if I hadn't done whatever I could to inform Pia of her natural father's will. I delayed my departure on purpose. I went, yesterday, to get information at the Prefecture of Police."

"To the Prefecture!" Binos exclaimed. "Ah! They couldn't tell you very much. Pia's sister died in a peculiar fashion, and they saw only the dead girl."

"Pardon, Monsieur," the notary continued. "It was precisely the death of that sister that put me on the trail. They told me Bianca Astrodi, recently deceased, lodged in Montmartre in a rooming house. I went there this morning and the person who owns that house told me that Pia lived in the Rue des Fosse-Saint-Bernard."

"That's very fortunate. Yesterday before going to the cemetery, she didn't know it."

"She couldn't give me the number of the house, but I met a young Italian girl in costume at the corner of the quay...I got information."

"And she pointed out to you Père Lorenzo's hovel," interrupted Binos. "What astonishes me is the old brigand let you come up, since he had just seen Pia leave."

"He seemed rather astonished when I asked what floor Pia lived on, and he hesitated to answer me...but he finally told me the sixth, without adding that the person wasn't there. I imagine he took me for a policeman."

"Monsieur," Freneuse said, motioning the amateur artist to be quiet. "I thank you for your generous intervention. It comes so much timelier since I have reasons to be worried about the absence of that young girl. I've come here to finish a painting for which Pia was modeling. She had promised to wait for me. The landlord has just told us she left unexpectedly in a *fiacre* with an elegantly dressed woman without saying when she was coming back, or if she was coming back. That's very strange, and I'm beginning to believe that she's been kidnapped."

"That wouldn't be an irreparable misfortune," said Monsieur Drugeon, smiling. "Girls that are run-away with are always found."

"Oh! It's not a matter of a kidnapping like you mean. Pia doesn't have a lover. But she is rich now...and someone perhaps covets her fortune."

"She's rich, but very few people know it. If you were thinking someone was threatening her life, I would point out to you that her death wouldn't benefit anyone but Monsieur Paulet."

"And assuredly Monsieur Paulet is incapable of committing a crime in order to inherit...that's true. However, there are some facts you don't know, and might very well be related to this will. They didn't tell you how Bianca died."

"Suddenly, I believe...and the day before the day Monsieur Francis Boyer died at Amélie-les-Bains, so as far as Bianca was concerned, the will was null and void. Monsieur Paulet was already rejoicing about an event which gave him the fortune as a blood relative...I was the one who informed him that there was another heiress, that one very much alive. He couldn't doubt it, since he had seen her."

"Bianca was murdered," Binos cried out. "And the ones who killed her will kill Pia. That's as clear as day. If they didn't killer her earlier, it was because they didn't know she would inherit."

"Murdered!" repeated the notary, dumbfounded. "But Monsieur, you don't know what you're talking about. The police investigated and they determined that the young girl died from a ruptured aneurism."

"Ah! Yes! Let's talk about the police! They don't know anything. But me, I was there. I have proof and with the help of a comrade I know, I'll nab the scoundrels before they have done away with the younger as they did away with the elder."

"That's enough! Let me speak," Freneuse said impatiently.

And he continued, addressing Monsieur Drugeon, who was greatly troubled by Binos information.

"Monsieur, here's what happened. Bianca Astrodi died one evening in an omnibus where I was, died in a most strange way, without crying out, with one movement. No one realized she was dead until the moment the carriage arrived at the station. I picked up a long hat pin of a woman seated beside Bianca, which was lost or thrown away after being used. The next day, I learned by chance that hat pin was poisoned. A cat stuck with it fell down dead."

"Ah! *Mon Dieu!* But then…if that woman killed the sister…"

"She may also kill Pia. And I'm almost sure now that's the woman who has just taken away the unfortunate child you're looking for."

"But, Monsieur," exclaimed the notary, "if you're not mistaken, your duty is to inform the police immediately of facts that you know. I'm astonished that you're so late in doing so."

"I was wrong. I can see that now," said Freneuse, "But I didn't think it was a crime. I didn't know then that the dead girl was Bianca Astrodi, and that Bianca Astrodi was to inherit a considerable fortune. The murder of a young unknown girl seemed inexplicable to me, because I couldn't see why anyone would be interested in killing her. The news you've just told me clears up this dark story. Evidently, it's Monsieur Francis Boyer's heirs that they're after."

"As for me, I guessed it," Binos exclaimed, "So I confiscated the poisoned, murderous hat pin."

"What did you do with it?" Freneuse asked quickly.

"Ah! Ah! It seems you no longer forbid me to talk about my operations. You recognize that I was right. As you're making honorable amends, I won't hold you to account. Then let me tell you that I passed on that hat pin to a man who took charge of having it examined by a first-rate chemist, solely to determine the nature of the poison the point was dipped in. The experiment should now be complete and perfect. There's nothing left for us to do but unearth the woman who stuck Bianca, and my friend is in charge of that. It's as if we already had her, because he is first-rate in investigations. It took him only half an hour to discover the rooming house where Bianca lived."

"Ah! He's the one who took you there?"

"You'd have known it a long time ago if you'd taken the trouble to ask me. But whenever I opened my mouth to pronounce the name of this worthy Piédouche, you told me to be quiet."

"Very well! Speak now. At what point is this clever man. I hope he didn't limit himself to discovering Bianca's lodgings."

"I hope so also, but there's the devil! I haven't seen him since the day he took me to the Rue des Abbesses."

"And you didn't go see him to find out how far along he is?"

"No, for an excellent reason. He forgot to give me his address."

"What! You gave the hat pin to an individual whose address you didn't know?"

"Oh! I know his café. He didn't come there yesterday, but he'll come back. He's a regular customer of the *Grand-Bock.*"

"And you're counting on this peculiar fellow to find the guilty persons! Let's not talk any more about it. Sit down and be quiet. I'll find them myself. I saw the woman of the omnibus one evening in the theater. She was with her accomplice, the man who climbed on the upper section of the omnibus to give her his seat...and that man is a business agent that Monsieur Paulet has employed."

"A business agent? Then wait a moment," said Monsieur Drugeon. "Monsieur Paulet did in fact tell me that before his brother's death, foreseeing the will he feared, he used an agent to obtain information in Italy concerning Bartolomea Astrodi and her two daughters."

"Did he tell you his name?"

"No, but he will name him to me, I don't doubt."

"And me, I hope so. Do you wish us, Monsieur, to go immediately to Monsieur Paulet's."

"Gladly, if you think he can give us any useful information...excuse that restriction. The story about the omnibus and the poisoned hat pin are so new to me that I'm confused."

"I'll explain them to you on the way. But we don't have a minute to lose."

"And me?" asked Binos.

"You! I advise you to run over to your café to see if your friend Piédouche is there," answered Freneuse, who didn't want any of Binos' cooperation.

Opening the door, he found himself face to face with Lorenzo, bent double under the weight of the canvas and the easel.

"The woman who came to pick up Pia, didn't she have pockmarks on her face?"

"Yes, and eyes black as coal, with a big nose, a Roman nose," said the old man. "If she wanted to pose as Medea, I could find work for her."

"Then she's really the one," murmured Freneuse. "Listen old fellow.

You're going to put down here what you're carrying, lock the door and take out the key. If Pia comes back, you're to keep her from leaving and you're to go find me on the spot. And if the woman who took her away dares to come back, then the police will be necessary. Do you understand?"

"*Si, Signor,*" said Lorenzo, who was never surprised at anything.

Freneuse was already on the stairs. The notary followed. He had taken the affair to heart and he wanted to clear it up.

"Go ahead, my children," Binos grumbled, remaining behind. "Go consult your bourgeois. There still isn't any body but Piédouche to clear this up for you...when I've laid my hands on him."

X. Pigache

Binos had followed the advice Freneuse gave him when they parted at the door of Père Lorenzo's house. While his friend and the notary went on a chase on their side, he went immediately to the bar-café of the *Grand-Bock,* where he hoped finally to encounter Piédouche. Thanks to that clever assistant, he was counting a great deal on arriving first in the race for information organized by Pia's defenders. It was a question above all of finding her and delivering her, if, as everything indicated, she had fallen into the hands of the enemy. The pursuit of her sister's murderers came only in second place.

Binos had a very high opinion of Piédouche's talents. He thought he could do anything, and he was in a hurry to set him off on the disappeared Pia's trail. Piédouche in less than an hour had been able to discover the place where her sister lodged. Binos, in addition, had a number of things to ask this precious comrade, because he hadn't seen him since their excursion to the Rue des Abbesses. He didn't even know if the chemist who was supposed to examine the hat pin had finished his experiments. Therefore he arrived running and full of illusions at the *Grand-Bock,* where he found only the owner seated, melancholy, at his counter. He questioned him and he learned that Piédouche no longer came to the establishment.

Père Poivreau, who as usual was between two absinthes, wanted only to go into his worries. He told the astounded amateur artist, that for the past several days, his clientele had vanished. There was a strike in the billard room; the café stayed empty. The retired druggist, Pigache, the most faithful of his regular customers, no longer came. And Poivreau attributed that desertion to certain rumors that had been spread about among the regular drinkers. They said very quietly that a Sûreté agent frequented the establishment and those gentlemen who didn't like the police went to drink and play pool elsewhere. Nobody could point out that agent, but they claimed he came every day, and that he arranged it so that he couldn't be recognized for what he was. As a result of this, they suspected everybody, and particularly the peaceful bourgeois who didn't rub shoulders with the Don Juans of the area, for whom the *Grand-Bock* served as a rendezvous site. They suspected the sculptor; they suspected the druggist; they suspected Piédouche, and the owner thought that these good people, having gotten wind of the stories circulating, stayed at home for fear of being insulted by the inventors of this calumny. As a result, the unfortunate Poivreau had only ruin to look forward to.

When I think they accused you…you also!" he shouted, striking the counter with his fist. "Ah! If I knew what scoundrel invented these stories to harm me, I would gladly kill him."

Binos wasn't bothered very much by the bartender's confidences. The things they'd said about him touched him very little. Poivreau's problems touched him even less. But he thought the habitual customers weren't wrong, because he'd always been convinced that Piédouche belonged to the police, or had in the past. And the annoying side of the affaire was that Piédouche, probably warned of what was being said, wouldn't return. Where could he be found now? Binos bitterly regretted not having insisted on knowing where he lived. He didn't know any other way to get his address but by going to ask for it at the police station. Still, he doubted they would give it to him. As there was nothing more to be gained from the owner of the bar-café, he left after having asked him to tell Piédouche, if by chance he came back, that his friend Binos wanted to see him as soon as possible. He was also to tell him that he would wait for him every morning on the Rue Myrrha, on the fifth floor above the entry hall. To tell the truth, he was counting very much on his visit. He thought that for the moment the best thing would be to go nicely to Sophie Cornu, tell her about the disappearance of Pia, and try to obtain some useful clues from her.

Very thoughtful, he went along the Boulevard Rochechourt. He had already passed the Elysée-Montmartre when he noticed, sitting on a bench, chatting with two rather shady looking individuals, the former druggist, Pigache, whose absence poor Poivreau missed so much. The idea immediately came into his head to go up to him to ask if he could give him any information about Piédouche. Pigache had his shoulder turned to Binos, and didn't see him coming, but Binos had recognized him from far off by his shape and, above all by a huge hat with turn up edges. He was the only person to wear one in that neighborhood where the most popular hat was the silk cap.

Who the devil is he talking with? he wondered, examining the two men stopped in front of the druggist. *For a former businessman, he has evil-looking acquaintances.*

Those people were, if fact, rather badly dressed, and they were probably conscious of their social inferiority, because they were standing up, and Pigache, on a municipal bench, seemed to be giving them orders. Binos, who couldn't be intimidated by so little, went forward without worrying about whether he was going to disturb the good man by interrupting the conversation. And it didn't take him long to notice that the two individuals facing him were observing his movements. They must have alerted Père Pigache that a gentleman was approaching, because this respectable old man turned his head, and immediately recognized Binos, greeting him with an engaging smile. Immediately, the two men chatting motioned good-bye and started walking with slow steps toward the Place Pigalle.

Good! thought Binos. *Now the old man is alone, I'm going to ask him if he's seen Piédouche. I'll have to shout, but that's all the same to me. Nobody is passing by on the boulevard, and, besides, I don't have any secrets to confide to him.*

"Hello, dear Monsieur Binos," said the retired druggist. "I haven't seen you in a hundred years. And I'm very happy to see you."

"Me, too, Papa; I'm happy. But you don't come to the *Grand-Bock* any more. And right when I wanted to talk to you," answered Binos, raising his voice as loud as he could. "And about that, tell me, ancient one, why did you leave Old Man Poivreau? I've just left his bar, and I found him in a tête-à-tête with a bottle of absinthe. He's in the process of emptying it to console himself for having lost you."

"*Mon Dieu!* I'll tell you. Poivreau isn't a bad man, but he takes in villainous people. And just between us, the society that you find in his bar doesn't suit me. I went there to speak to you and to speak to Monsieur Piédouche. But for several days he has deserted the establishment. And I had an idea that you wouldn't be slow to do the same."

"As for me, that depends, and as for friend Piédouche, I've looked for him everywhere, to bring him back there. And I can't lay my hands on him."

"Really? Then you don't know where he lives?"

"No, and you?"

"No more than you do. And that doesn't astonish me. I've never been around him except in the bar, and then, he didn't chat very often with me…you understand. It's not amusing to chat with a deaf man."

"Who're you telling that to, animal," grumbled Binos.

"It seems you have the same opinion he does," said Pigache with a nice big smile.

"You can see that's not true, because I've stopped on purpose to have a conversation with you," said Binos.

"That's very nice of you, but that doesn't amuse you, because you called me animal."

"What! You heard?"

"Yes, that surprises you because you've never lived around deaf people."

"No, thank God!"

"If you had lived among them, you would know that out in the open, their hearing is not so bad as inside four walls, and inside a carriage they can hear everything."

"Good! The first time I have something to tell you, I'll take you in a *fiacre,* and we'll take a ride inside, only you'll pay for the time spent."

"Oh! very willingly, but while we're waiting, we can always talk a while here. I'm having one of my good days, since the weather is dry. You won't need to shout yourself hoarse."

"That suits me, because I don't want to stir up the passers-by. I want to know if you could give me some news of Piédouche. You don't know his address, but maybe you've run into him."

"No, unfortunately. Because I like this fellow a lot, although he hardly seeks out my company. And if I had seen him in the street, I swear to you I would have stopped him. But I have an idea he doesn't live in this area."

"Bah! He always holed up in the *Grand-Bock*. He must be perched not far away. And to know where, I would give my best colored pipe."

"Then you really need him? Let's bet I can guess why."

"Ah! I defy you to, Papa."

"*Parbleu!* That's not hard. You want him to give you back the gilded hat pin that you lent him the other day at Père Poivreau's."

"The hat pin! What! You noticed..."

"The deaf notice everything. *Dame!* That's understandable. They have no distractions, because they can't understand anything."

"Then you didn't understand what I said to him?"

"Ah! As for that, no. The room where we were has a very low ceiling. And you understand, we deaf need a lot of air to open our ears. But sometimes we can guess, by gestures, by the movement of the lips, by the expression on the face..."

"And you guessed the other day what Piédouche and I were talking about? You were well situated to observe us, because we were sitting at your table."

"Oh! I'm not saying I guessed. I got an idea, but I could very easily have been wrong. I thought to myself that you were telling him that someone had killed, or wounded someone with a hat pin, and that he'd promised you to have it examined to see if it was poisoned."

"You found that out? Ah! That's unbelievable!"

"Oh, no. It was very simple, on the contrary. I wanted to touch it, and you held back my arm. I immediately thought you were afraid of an accident. Understand! It was the same with the torn letter that you showed him. So I thought you had found it the same time as the hat pin."

"My word, Père Pigache, I'm beginning to believe you're a magician. And me who took you for an innocent! Some one naïve!"

"Bah! Go ahead and say for an imbecile. That would be closer to what you think."

"*Ma foi!* That's possible," Binos cynically replied, "but I admit I was wrong. A man who can understand without being able to hear is capable of anything."

"You're really very kind. Then it was true. Someone used the hat pin to commit a real crime?"

"Someone murdered a young girl in an omnibus."

"In the Place Pigalle omnibus, maybe. I read something like that in the *Petit Journal.*"

"Exactly, old fellow. And since that day, my friend Freneuse and I, we've been searching for the hussy who did the deed and for her accomplice. Freneuse was in the carriage. He saw them. Unfortunately, he thought it was an accident, and he didn't take any more notice of them. I, who did take notice of them, I reported it to Piédouche, so well that we were in agreement. And during this time, the scoundrels continued their operations. They've just carried away the sister of the poor girl they killed. If we don't manage to get our hands on them, they're going to do something bad to her."

"Why? What do they have against these children?"

"That would take too long to explain to you, and it wouldn't interest you. It was a matter of an inheritance. A bourgeois who was the natural father of the two little girls and who left them his fortune when he died."

"Eh! Then the relative of this bourgeois paid some rogues to get rid of them for them?"

"That's possible...although...no...the dead man had only one brother, a Monsieur Paulet, who's very rich, and who wouldn't get involved in such an affair."

"You never know. Money can make a lot of things happen. You say his name is Paulet. In that case, I'd look there... You probably have his address?"

"No, but Freneuse has it. Freneuse knows him very well. And you remind me of something he said this morning in front of me. It appears that Monsieur Paulet in the past used a business agent who might be the accomplice of the woman with the hat pin. Freneuse saw that man at the theater, the day after, or two days after, the crime...and he recognized that he had traveled with him in the omnibus...only he doesn't know his name."

"He just has to ask Monsieur Paulet for it."

"That's what he's supposed to do right now, today. When I spied you, I was going to the Rue des Abbesses to see a woman who was the landlady of the dead girl. I was intending to go on from there to Freneuse's to find out where we are."

"Would you like us to go there together?"

"What! Père Pigache, are you thinking about getting mixed up in this! That's something new, for sure. I can understand that would amuse you, but I wonder how you could be of use to us."

"You've just told me I'm capable of anything. Well! Try me. Put me to the test. You'll see what deaf men can be good for. First of all, people aren't afraid of them. And then what chance are you taking? It's just a question of pointing out to me that business agent's house. I'll drop in on him for a visit, and when I've chatted with him, I may let you know something new."

"*Ma foi!*" exclaimed Binos. "I don't see why I shouldn't use you, if only for the novelty of the fact. Freneuse will make fun of me again, but that doesn't matter to me. Beside, I have a perfect right to investigate on my side while he's investigating on his. And you'll be as artful as the notary who's investigating with him."

"Ah! There's a notary?"

"Yes, a notary from the country, who was given the will of the two little girls' father. Ah! That one, he's a good man. Without him we'd never have known that the last daughter was the heiress. Since he's learned she's disappeared, he thinks only about finding her. Hold on! He may be right now at Monsieur Paulet's house to ask him that business agent's address."

"Very well, but will Monsieur Paulet give it to him?"

"And you think that if he refuses to give it to him, he'd give it to you."

"Maybe. Anyway it doesn't cost anything to try."

"No, and I'm curious to see how you'll go about it. I don't exactly know where the bourgeois lives, but Freneuse will tell us. The Place Pigalle isn't far. Let's go, Papa."

Pigache was already standing. He had risen with youthful energy. Binos couldn't believe the change made in the wink of an eye in the carriage of the retired druggist, and even in his physique. His bent-over stature had suddenly straightened up, his face had taken on an intelligent expression, his little eyes were shining. He was no longer the same man.

"Pigache, my friend, you're unrecognizable," said Binos. "If dear old Piédouche were to meet you, he would take you for someone else. And me, I would never have believed, if I hadn't seen it, how the open air could change deaf men to this degree."

"You'll see a lot of other things," said the good man, smiling gently. "But let's not waste time. Monsieur Paulet may live very far away, and who knows where he'll send us to find his business agent? We'll have to take a carriage, because..."

"Look! Your two friends are following us," interrupted Binos, pointing with his finger at the two individuals that his arrival had put to flight.

"Don't worry about them, my dear fellow. These poor men worked for me when I had a shop, and when they meet me, they always come to ask me about my health."

"Why did they run away when they saw me?"

"Because they aren't very clever. That makes them timid."

"And I'm fashionable! Actually, it seems they think I'm rich. That flatters me."

These words and some others no less insignificant enlivened the trip to the Place Pigalle.

Père Pigache, more and more nimble, was walking so fast that Binos had trouble keeping up with him. Just as they arrived at the painter's house, a *fiacre* stopped at the door, and two gentlemen got out.

"Good!" exclaimed Binos. "There are Freneneuse and the notary now. *Diable!* Their faces look turned inside out. What's happened to them? Hopefully they haven't learned that Pia has been shipped off like her sister!"

"Go ask your friend what's happened," said Pigache. "While you're talking with him, I myself will go talk to the notary."

That was done. Bios drew Freneuse aside, and the good druggist, his hat in his hand, went up to Monsieur Drugeon, who didn't seem surprised to see him. They seemed to know each other.

"Well," Binos began, "do you have the address?"

"No," Freneuse answered with irritation. "Monsieur Paulet claims he doesn't remember it. There's only one thing left to do; that's to go find that landlady on the Rue des Abbesses. She knows the woman in the omnibus, because she spoke to her at the cemetery. She'll have to tell us where she lives. What did you do on your side? Nothing, right? Your man from the bar took advantage of you."

"I didn't see him, but I recruited an intelligent helper."

"That little old man who's talking to Monsieur Drugeon?"

"He doesn't look very smart, but I believe he is, even so."

Freneuse was about to call out to him when his eyes fell on a fat woman coming toward him, balancing on her haunches, as a ship balances on the waves.

"It seems to me, if I'm not mistaken," he murmured. "That's the orange merchant, the one who was in the omnibus and the one I met the other evening in front of the Porte-Saint-Martin."

"You can't place me, it appears," said the old gossip. "*Dame!* That's understandable; today I'm not selling oranges. As for me, I recognized you right off, and if I may speak to you, it's because I now know where the little girl on the omnibus lived."

"Me, too, I know."

"Rue des Abbesses, *hein?* At Sophie Cornu's. Then I'm not telling you anything you don't already know, but that's not all. Can you imagine that I've located the woman who was in the omnibus beside the little girl. You know, the one who left the theater at the same time as you and who was holding on to the man from the upper story of the bus. And you'll never guess what she does, that fancy woman."

"No, but if you could give me any information about her, you'd render me a great service."

"She tells the future...She interprets cards. Madame Stella, Rue de la Sourdière, 79. The Cornu woman is one of her regular customers. Yesterday, I met them talking together on the Boulevard Rochechouart... and since I've known that good Sophie a long time, I went up to her. And that other one, who didn't remember my face, suggested giving me a full séance...I asked for her address, and she gave it to me."

"You didn't speak to her about the omnibus business?"

"*Ma foi,* no. That would have caused explanations that would never end. But I promised to go consult her."

"Would you like us to go there together?" Freneuse asked quickly.

"If that pleases you...as for me, I don't believe very much in these stupid things, but that would amuse me all the same. Only, you understand, I'm not rich."

"Oh! I'll pay for the consultation."

"Then that suits me. Tell me what day and time you want."

"Now. I'm going to take you there in a carriage."

"That suits me even better. Perfectly! I don't have anything to do until this evening. I don't sell my merchandise except at theater doors."

"Good! Wait for me five minutes. Just give me time to say a word to that Monsieur over there."

"The one wearing a white tie. He has a nice face. He reminds me of the Justice of the Peace in my country. But the other one has a bad stamp to him."

"You go talk a little with Monsieur, while I go arrange something with Monsieur Drugeon," Freneuse said, motioning to Binos, who had already guessed his meaning.

"So, Mother," Binos began, while his friend went to join the notary who was carrying on a very animated conversation with Père Pigache. "So, you know that good Sophie?"

"That's not difficult. Everybody in the neighborhood knows her. I'll have to tell you I live on the Rue Müller."

"And me Rue Myrrha. We're neighbors. And when you want to have your portrait done..."

"Then you're a photographer?"

"Not on your life. I'm a painter...not buildings."

"An artist, then? I prefer that. Your friend is an artist too, *hein?*"

"Artist number one. He earns money as big as you are. And this isn't to pay you a compliment, but you're really robust."

"But, of course...not bad...and you? ...Say, without being too inquisitive, why is it so important to him, you friend, to consult the sorceress?"

"To know what sickness killed the little girl on the omnibus."

"Well! That's a strange idea. As for me, I'll ask her for a remedy: to cure the pains of my man who's been in bed a month. Ah! There's your comrade who's finished talking with the two old men."

"He's coming to get you, mother."

Freneuse came up, his eyes shining, his face animated. Binos was totally dumbfounded by that sudden change. He looked as happy as if he had found Pia.

"My good lady," said Freneuse. "These gentlemen over there want to talk to you."

"They're very nice. What then do they want with me?"

"They need a piece of information. They're going to explain their business to you."

"Let's go," exclaimed the fat woman.

And while she started off, Binos was saying between his teeth:

"I would really like somebody to stick my nose with the hat pin I gave to Piédouche, if I can understand what all this means."

"You'll understand later. Do me the favor of going to find me a *fiacre.*"

"And the one that brought you that you kept? Look! Old Man Pigache and the notary are helping the fat woman get inside, and they're getting in after her. There's no room for us. *Fichtre, no!* There won't be. Now Pigache's two friends are leaving on the same train...one on the top and one on the driver's seat. Where the devil are they going?"

"You'll see in a little while...because we're going to follow them."

XI. The Inhabitants of the Rue de la Sourdière

That day the people who lived on the Rue de la Sourdière who were relaxing on the steps of their doors had a spectacle to which they were not accustomed. Two *fiacres*, following each other closely, stopped at the corner of the Rue Gomboust, to which they had arrived by way of the Rue Saint-Roch, and parked in a row beside the houses. From the first, four men and a fat woman got down and separated themselves into three groups. At the same time two other men got out of the second carriage and started with slow steps toward the Saint-Honoré market. The woman went into the Rue de la Sourdière. Ten steps behind her walked a little old man wearing a hat with turned-up edges. A little further behind came two tall devils with nasty-looking faces who were walking single file and with measured steps. The fifth traveler from the first convoy took the same path as the two who had turned in the direction of the market. That one was dressed in black and wearing a white tie, like a funeral director.

All these people, who didn't seem to know each other, were, however, part of the same expedition. An observer would've guessed that immediately. But the little merchants who saw them pass by didn't see any harm in them, and no one came to look out the windows at them.

The woman went into a courtyard that stood in front of a rather handsome house, and began a conversation with the concierge. The little old man who followed her arrived before the conversation was over. And as both of them addressed the same person, the porter gave them both the same answer.

"On the second floor, the door to the left. But I don't know if Madame is seeing anybody today. She's leaving on a trip."

They climbed the stairs together, without saying a word. When they arrived on the landing, that was different.

"You've understood exactly what you're supposed to say, haven't you?" asked the old man, lowering his voice. "You're the sister of my housekeeper. I'm deaf and I've tried everything to cure my deafness. You told me about Madame Stella, who gives consultations about all types of maladies, and you've brought me to see her so she could prescribe a treatment."

"Understood! Understood!" answered the fat woman.

"And when you've introduced me, you'll let me talk."

"That suits me, because I wouldn't know what to say."

"Here's the door," continued the good old man, pointing to the plaque where the name of Madame Lenormand's pupil gleamed.

"Ring, my maid."

And while the old gossip pushed the brass button, he noticed another plaque across from this one.

"Good!" he murmured. "There's a business agent across the hall. He's the

186

associate, I'll bet. And I have an idea that I'll make a double catch."

"Nobody's coming to the door," said the woman.

"Ring louder."

She did so again, but with no more success.

"The regular customers must have a special way of being recognized," the old man said very low. "Keep ringing at short intervals. We'll see."

The short peals didn't produce any effect. Nothing budged in the apartment of the fortune teller. But the deaf man, who was deaf only inside a building, thought he heard someone walking up and down in the business agent's apartment. He went over very softly to hear better. He was going to stick his ear against the door, when the door partially opened.

"Well!" he exclaimed. "Monsieur Piédouche!"

At the same time he put his head and arm inside to keep the door half-opened.

"What! Is that you, Père Pigache?" asked the man who had opened the door.

"Ah! I'm really glad to see you, because I have a lot of things to tell you. Some peculiar things have happened at the *Grand-Bock* since you stopped coming there. And I didn't expect to find you here. I came up with my maid to consult Madame Stella."

"She isn't there," Piédouche shouted, making a megaphone of his two hands.

"Ah! I'm very disappointed. I was told she would give me a remedy which would rid me of my infirmity. I'll come back another time. But since you're here, I'd like to chat with you."

"I don't have time."

"Oh! This won't take long. You can certainly give me five minutes. Some things you'll find interesting. Can you imagine that for the past two days Old Man Poivreau's establishment has been full of cops?"

Piédouche was still holding the door half-opened and didn't seem disposed to let Père Pigache enter. He looked at him suspiciously. He also looked at the fat orange merchant who watched their conversation from a distance. But at the word 'cops' he changed his attitude.

"What's happening at the *Grand-Bock*," he asked, yelling at the top of his lungs so as not to have to repeat the question.

"It seems they're looking for an individual who found himself mixed up in an affair of murder, and who frequented the bar under a false name. I can give you all the details. But it may bother you to talk to me because you're not in your own place," Pigache said, pointing to the plaque where the name Blanchelaine was inscribed.

"I'm at the apartment of one of my friends who's running errands, and who asked me to take his place for an hour."

"Then I won't bother you and we'll have time to talk. I'm going to tell the

187

maid to wait for me in the street."

That last suggestion decided Piédouche. He wasn't eager to bring a woman he didn't know into his domicile, but the deaf man inspired no fear in him. He thought it useful to interrogate him at length about the police's actions in Poivreau's bar.

"We can't talk here," Pigache continued. "My infirmity obliges you to shout and we'll wind up drawing the attention of the neighbors. Go away Virginie. If you get bored standing below, you can go sit down in the Tuilleries, in front of the great fountain. I'll join you there in a little while."

He was perfectly aware that Virginie understood without his saying so, that she was not to go so far. The orange merchant obeyed him blindly, since she knew who she was dealing with. She didn't ask any other explanation. She went down the stairs faster than she had mounted them.

"Come in, old fellow," said Piédouche, standing aside.

Pigache went in. Piédouche locked the door and conducted him into his study where there was a woman walking up and down that Freneuse would have recognized without any trouble, if he had been there, because she was dressed exactly as she was the evening of the *Chevaliers des brouillard* play. She frowned on seeing the old fellow her accomplice was bringing in, and her eyes asked who he was.

"Don't worry," Piédouche told her in a low voice. "I need to worm information out of this imbecile. If I find out he's a spy, he won't leave here alive."

While talking thus, Piédouche glanced aside at Pigache, who didn't move. The old man's expression remained as smiling and silly as usual.

"Good! I'm convinced," continued the so-called Blanchelaine. "I was afraid that he was only pretending to be deaf. Now, I'm sure he isn't. We can talk as if he weren't here."

"But, really, who is this man and why has he come here?"

"He's an idiot who frequents the *Grand-Bock* and he didn't come to see me. His maid brought him to consult you about his deafness."

"Then he was the one who was ringing?"

"No, that was his maid, and when I half-opened my door I found myself face to face with him."

"All right, but why did you let him come in?"

"Because he told me he'd seen Sûreté agents in Père Poivreau's bar and I wanted to know what was going on."

"Get rid of him quickly then, because I don't want to leave the little girl alone. She's talking about leaving this evening. To calm her down I had to promise her that we would go pick up her sister's baggage at Sophie Cornu's."

During this exchange of explanations, Pigache had remained in contemplation in front of the lady and was preparing to greet her.

"Madame is the wife of the friend who asked me to watch over his office,"

Piédouche shouted to him.

"My compliments to Monsieur, your friend," said Pigache, bowing very low.

"That's good! That's good! Sit down and tell me your story. So, the police are looking for a murderer at Poivreau's place?"

"Yes, and I have an idea they won't nab him because nobody ever comes there any more. He's suspicious, you see, and he'll never set foot back in the Grand Bock."

"But, who did he murder? The newspapers haven't mentioned a murder in a week."

"They say it was an old crime. A young girl somebody killed in an omnibus."

That answer, made in the most natural and indifferent tone, considerably troubled the fortune teller and her acolyte. They were hardly expecting to hear this bewildered old man speak to them about Bianca Astrodi's death and speak to them as if everybody knew that Bianca had been murdered. And it didn't take that much to make them suspicious. They looked at each other and the woman acted as if she was leaving.

"How do you know that?" Piédouche said the former druggist, without raising his voice.

"You asked me the name of the murderer they're looking for," answered Pigache, making a hearing trumpet with his hands. "Unfortunately, I don't know any more about it than you do. The usual customers at Père Poivreau's aren't worth much, and the suspicions fall a little on everybody, especially those you don't see any more at the bar. But I can name you the animal who caused all this. It's that wicked amateur artist who plays piquet with you. ...The one named Binos. It seems he went to the Prefecture of Police to start an investigation."

"That wouldn't surprise me," grumbled Piédouche, speaking to his companion. "The old man probably told the truth, and I'm more and more certain that he's deaf, because he didn't answer my question, or at least he didn't answer it directly. He hasn't heard, and he's not hearing a word we're saying."

"I believe it. But that doesn't keep what he's just told us from being very serious. I have an idea that Binos probably turned you in. You were terribly wrong to talk to him about this affair."

"It was necessary to get back the hat pin and the letter. But I wouldn't be surprised, not seeing me come to the bar any more, that he didn't finally suspect me, not counting the fact that his friend Freneuse probably pushed him to do it. This Freneuse saw us, and if by some bad luck the Paulet fellow gave him the address of Monsieur Blanchelaine, a business agent, we'd be in a bad fix."

"That is to say that we'd be sleeping in prison right today. If you'll believe me, I don't think we should run the risk. I'd like to leave this evening with Pia."

"But you've just told me she absolutely insists on getting her sister's baggage."

"If that was all it was, I'd go get it myself without her. But she also wants to go once more to the Saint-Ouen cemetery."

"And after that she'll agree to leave?"

"That's all she asks."

"Well! Take her to Sophie Cornu's. Take her to Saint-Ouen. It doesn't take three hours to make the trip. You'll still have enough time to get ready to take the 8:00 p.m. express train. The less time you stay in Paris with her, the better it will be, since the painters will know that she is no longer at Lorenzo's and they are capable of getting on the road to find her. We're at the mercy of chance…the chance of an encounter."

"Oh! I'll take care to lower the shutters of the *fiacre*…besides, no one is looking for her yet."

"No, but they may be looking for her tomorrow. So, get going toward Marseille this evening. I'll join you there the day after tomorrow."

"I think you're right, and in order not to lose time, I'm going to send the little Negress to find me a carriage."

"Fine! But just wait until I get rid of this stupid old beast who's just done us an enormous favor."

And, turning toward the good fellow, who had remained standing, he screamed at him as loudly as he could:

"Excuse me, Pigache, Madame has just told me she's heard that story about the omnibus. As for me, I don't think there's enough in all that to kill a cat. I'll try to reassure that poor devil Poivreau. Would you go wait for me at the *Grand-Bock*? I'll be there in an hour."

"With great pleasure," responded the deaf man. "You're like me. You don't abandon the people you know just because they're in trouble. But I don't want to keep you any longer and I give you my good wishes as well as my humble compliments to Madame. I will come back tomorrow to consult Madame Stella," added Pigache, backing out. Piédouche accompanied him as far as the hallway, telling him good-bye with a vigorous handshake, and barricaded himself in his study.

As soon as he had closed his door, Pigache straightened up, descended the stair steps four at a time, quickly went through the courtyard, and began to run as fast as he could toward the Rue Gomboust, where the two *fiacres* were waiting for him.

XII. Stella the Sorceress

In her position as a sorceress, Stella was always well served. She didn't have to wait ten minutes for the return of the Black messenger she had sent to find a carriage. The closest station wasn't too near. However, the little Negress had been lucky enough to find a carriage which was coming back empty and which was coming slowly down the peaceful Rue de la Sourdière.

Pia was always ready to leave. Having only one change of clothes, she didn't waste time getting dressed. When the lady suggested going that day to the Rue des Abbesses and to the Saint-Ouen cemetery in order to take the evening train, she didn't have to be persuaded. She didn't want anything else. What did it matter to her to leave alone or with a companion, provided she left Paris as soon as possible? What she feared was running into Paul Freneuse because she was afraid she would let herself relent if he begged her to stay.

Stella, who had very different fears, was careful to go out before her when they came to the carriage doorway, and to glance rapidly on both sides of the street. She saw nothing suspicious there. The *fiacre* was parked against the sidewalk, and the coachman had left his seat to chat with a man who must have been one of his comrades, temporarily not on duty, because he was wearing an oil cloth cap and a red scarf under his work shirt.

"Are you the one my servant, a Negress about twelve-years-old, brought?"

"Yes, Madame, and if Madame will get in," answered the driver opening the door.

"I'll hire you by the hour and if you make good time, you'll get a good tip."

"Oh! Madame will be satisfied. We're going to..."

"Rue des Abbesses, in Montmartre. You'll turn to the left at the top of the Rue des Martyrs. I'll stop you when we're in front of the house."

"Right, Madame. But if Madame will allow me, I'll take my friend over there on my seat with me. He lives right on the Place de la Mairie, two steps from where Madame is going."

"Do as you like," responded the so-called student of Madame Lenormand.

She was in a hurry and she was thinking only of getting Pia into the carriage, getting in behind her and lowering the shutters.

"You don't want to be seen, do you, my dear child?" she asked Pia.

"You know very well I don't," murmured the little girl.

"The precaution I'm taking is indispensable, because we'll be forced to pass through the painter's quarter. There's no other way to get to Sophie's."

"What does it matter? I'm very well hidden…and besides no one up there thinks about me any more."

Stella had strong reasons for believing the contrary, but she kept them to

191

herself, and the trip was made in silence. Pia was gloomy and beaten down. She let herself be led like a condemned criminal carried by vehicle to the place of execution. The woman conducting her had no interest in bringing her out of that torpor which kept her from answering embarrassing questions. She was saying to herself:

"Everything is going well. The Cornu woman knows we're coming. She must come down into the passageway. We won't be five minutes at her place. At the cemetery we'd really have bad luck if we met anyone we know. This evening at 8:00 p.m. we'll be rolling toward Marseille."

The *fiacre* went like the wind. The sorceress was thanking herself that she'd made out so well. They went at a trot down the paved side which led into the outside boulevard. When they had crossed it, they started to dash with unusual speed. Stella was so well sheltered from the regards of the passers-by that she at first didn't see the direction the driver was taking.

But she had only to lift the corner of a shutter to recognize that he was going the wrong way. And instead of climbing straight ahead to the Rue des Abbesses, he had turned to the left.

She tapped on the front window to warn him of his error. She rang. Nothing happened.

"This driver must be deaf like Père Pigache, because he stopped at the Place Pigalle."

Stella, astounded and furious, lost all patience and lowered one of the windows so as to grab by the tail the overcoat of the driver who was doing her such a bad turn. But, in a semi-circle on the sidewalk against which that run-away *fiacre* had stopped, she saw a group of people who appeared to be waiting. Then she understood because she recognized Freneuse and Binos.

At that, she thought only about getting away. Naturally she sought to flee from the side of the Place Pigalle. She opened the door; she jumped, and she fell into the arms of the man in the work shirt, who had gotten down from his seat just to catch her. She tried to escape from him, but he lifted he like a feather. He carried her into the vestibule of the painter's big house. He put her down in the concierge's apartment, which was occupied by two city policemen. This was so quickly done that she scarcely had time to cry out. The passers-by thought it was a matter of a woman who'd had a stroke.

Pia, absorbed in her sad thoughts, hadn't so much as seen anything, but almost at the same moment, the other door opened, and Paul Freneuse showed himself.

"Ah!" she murmured, moving backward, "That woman lied to me. She brought me to your studio. Let me go!"

"That woman," Freneuse shouted, "is the one who murdered your sister. She would've killed you the way she killed her, if we hadn't succeeded in snatching you out of her claws. I can't explain that to you here. Binos is going to take you to the studio, and I'll join you there in an instant. First I must confront that scoundrel."

"To the studio! Never!" Pia said in a stifled voice.

"Why? What have I done to you?"

"Good! I can guess!" exclaimed Binos who had come forward. "She's afraid she'll encounter Mademoiselle Paulet up there. Well, little one, I swear that blonde will never again set foot there. If her respectable father takes a notion to show himself there, I'll take charge of showing him the door."

"Me too, I swear it to you," Freneuse added.

And his eyes told so well that he wasn't lying that Pia, pale and trembling, took the hand Binos offered to help her out and let herself be led into the house.

"It's just the two of us now, Madame Piédouche," Freneuse said between his teeth.

"Ah! The low life!" the orange merchant cried out. "Just let her claim in front of me that she wasn't in the omnibus."

"Oh! She won't dare deny it," the notary Drugeon said. "But will they catch her accomplice?"

"He must already be in jail, yelled the man perched on the driver's seat. The boss took charge of getting him wrapped up. He'll be here in ten minutes. How do you like the way he handled this?"

"Marvelously. The idea to disguise you and your comrade as coachmen, was priceless."

"The real drivers had a funny expression on their faces when he ordered them to change their coats with us. But the witch has really been brought down."

Freneuse and Virginie Pilon left Monsieur Drugeon singing the praises of the false Pigache, who was none other than a senior agent of the Sûreté police. They dashed to the porter's lodge where Stella was under surveillance. She looked like a wild beast caught in a trap. When she saw the two witnesses she couldn't challenge appear, a flash of anger passed through her eyes, and she didn't budge. She refused to answer the questions of Freneuse, who soon got tired of questioning her. He had gone to find Pia when Pigache arrived. The clever man had finished his work at the Rue de la Sourdière. Auguste Blanchelaine, arrested at his home by a police Commissioner assisted by four policemen, was on the way to the Prefecture holding cells. Pigache's entry into the concierge's lodge was a sensational event. Stella understood she was lost. The false deaf man had heard her conversation with her associate. He knew all about the guilt of both of them.

"Where is the poisoned hat pin you used to kill Bianca Astrodi?" he asked her right off. "You must have it on you. If you don't give it to me, Madame, who was in the omnibus with you, is going to search you."

"That won't be necessary," the terrible creature said with a hoarse voice. "I'm going to give it to you. Here it is."

She had kept it hidden in her glove since she had been dragged into the concierge's lodge. She closed her hand quickly and she fell over dead. The murderous tip had penetrated the skin on her wrist. Bianca was avenged.

"She avoided the need for a trial," Pigache said philosophically, while the city police hurried to lift up the dead woman. "I'll bet that low life Piédouche won't have the courage to do as she did. Actually, he has some chance of getting out of it. Now that his sweet companion is no longer in a position to kill, the complicity will be hard to prove. I'm still going to stow away the hat pin. Without that evidence, a jury wouldn't condemn him." He picked it up from the floor of the lodge and carefully wrapped it in a newspaper.

The orange merchant had rushed out when she saw the fortune teller fall. At the door of the corridor, she bumped into Monsieur Drugeon, who was talking to someone they hardly expected. From a *fiacre*, this one driven by a real coachman, Monsieur and Mademoiselle Paulet had emerged. The notary, who was walking up and down on the sidewalk, was not a little surprised to see them. An hour before Monsieur Paulet had refused to give him the business agent's address, and they had left each other with very cold feelings.

Now Paulet knew that Freneuse was working hand in hand with Monsieur Drugeon. What had he come to do in the painter's studio?

"I know the name," he shouted in getting out of the carriage. "His name is Blanchelaine and he lives..."

"Rue de la Sourdière. You aren't telling me anything I don't know," interrupted the notary. "He's been arrested."

"Arrested! Oh! *Mon Dieu!* Then it was true... He was involved in a crime! You're my witness that I brought his address to Monsieur Freneuse as soon as I had it... You hadn't been gone ten minutes when I found it among my papers."

Monsieur Paulet wasn't at all at ease. He was thinking about the letters and the contract he signed that they probably seized at Blanchlaine's office. He had changed his mind and he was taking his precautions, so that he could never be suspected of having ordered this scoundrel to commit murder. In coming to see Freneuse, he had been careful to bring his daughter, to give a pretext for his visit.

"Let's go up, Father," said Mademoiselle Marguerite, more beautiful and haughtier than ever. "Monsieur Freneuse will explain what happened to us."

"I warn you he's not alone," murmured Monsieur Drugeon.

"Ah! Well! That's one more reason," she answered. "We'll get complete information."

She had guessed that the Italian girl was there and she was not a girl to retreat. She went into the house and Monsieur Paulet followed.

"Don't look into the porter's lodge," Virginie Pilon shouted to them.

They didn't notice. The father was as much in a hurry as the daughter to get to the painter's studio. They didn't need to knock. The door was open, and they were able to view a totally unexpected picture. Pia was seated on the green couch where Mademoiselle Paulet had seen her the day she had driven her away. But Pia was no longer crying. Pia was listening with delight to the protestations

194

of Paul Freneuse, kneeling in front of her. Pia had given her hands to the artist, who was covering them with kisses. And Binos, always facetious, was giving the gesture of benediction. He was the first to notice Monsieur Paulet and his daughter halted on the threshold, and he had the impudence to shout to them:

"Isn't that touching? Daphis and Chloe, don't you think!"

Freneuse was on his feet in an instant and went straight to them. Pia was waiting, pale and anxious. It was her fate that would be decided.

"Come, Father," the proud Marguerite said dryly. "My place isn't here, since Monsieur welcomes a creature who has stolen your brother's estate."

"You're insulting a child who's better than you are," replied Freneuse, carried away by his anger. "Leave! And you, Monsieur," he continued, speaking to Monsieur Paulet, "Let me tell you that Mademoiselle Astrodi, renounces the inheritance that you covet. She doesn't want the fortune of a man who abandoned her mother. I hope the law doesn't hold you to account for your shameful dealings with a scoundrel, and I hope never to see you again."

The father and daughter bowed their heads. Pia also was avenged.

Three months have gone by. Blanchelaine, known as Pièdouche, will be brought up on charges at the next court session. He hopes to plead extenuating circumstances. Pigache got advancement in rank; that case set him above his peers. He may one day be head of the Sûreté.

Monsieur Drugeon returned to his notary office, heaped with blessings from Freneuse and Pia, who left for Italy. They'll be married at Subiaco, and they don't need Monsieur Francis Boyer's fortune to be happy. Freneuse didn't show a painting at the Exposition that year, but the happiness which awaited him was well worth the sacrifice.

Binos consoled himself for the absence of his friends by drinking beer. Monsieur Paulet didn't get in trouble with the law, and his daughter will have a half million francs more. But she won't find any suitors. Everybody in Paris knows about it. She has been blamed for the omnibus murder.

THE FERRY MURDER

I. The Accident

Germonière isn't a chateau. Germonière has neither towers, nor moats, nor parapets from which to shoot arrows, nor a main house flanked by two wings. Neither is it a chalet, in the Arcachon fashion, nor an English cottage, much less a farm. It's a large country house, built under the bourgeois reign of Louis-Philippe by a druggist grown rich who loved his ease and who disdained architecture. There are no artistic ornaments, no charming roof tops with sculptured weather vanes and overly-elaborate water drains, no projecting stones at the base of the walls, no decorative gables, no moldings. There's nothing but a cube of masonry pierced with symmetrically spaced windows standing one level over the other, on the top of a terrace in the Italian style. As a consequence, there are three floors, with the ground floor elevated. This resembles a *sous prefecture* or a barracks—the ideal of the ugly. But the whole thing is made of dressed stone. It's an orgy of granite, an orgy which didn't cost very much. The stone quarry is two steps away.

So the economical builder gave himself the luxury of two flights of steps with ramps and balustrades, one on the courtyard and one on the gardens. Because it does have gardens, and even gardens like one seldom sees. Trees abound there, hundred-year-old trees that the druggist didn't have time to cut down and that the new owners respected. A little river encircles this park designed in the French style, a real little river holding a boat, although it isn't classified among the navigable waterways, and a great deal deeper than is necessary for someone to drown there.

The druggist who created this domain found this out at his expense. *When the house is finished, death comes in*, says a Turkish proverb. One evening, when this notable business man had dined too much, after having adjusted his builder's expenses to his advantage, he had taken the fancy to stroll along the bank of his little river, and they fished him out of it the next day, completely dead from drowning. His heirs didn't worry too much about how he had fallen in, and having no taste for country life, they tried to sell, but found no buyer, and Germonière remained thirty years uninhabited.

After the war of 1870, Madame Daudièrne (without an apostrophe after the

197

d) bought it for half of what it was worth from the last descendant of the druggist, and Madame Daudièrne regularly spent the summer and part of the fall there. She was a widow. She had what's in the country called a nice fortune, 40,000 pounds of income; that is to say, in Paris, only a moderately comfortable income, especially when one also has two daughters to marry, and a son who has just finished his obligatory military service and is already doing stupid things. These children, it's true, had an uncle on their father's side who could be considered an uncle from whom one could inherit, because he had never married and he had in the past earned a great deal of money in California, where, after a tumultuous youth, he had gone to search adventure. But that uncle was a peculiar man who held disturbing opinions in the matter of inheritances. He claimed that a man always had the right to dispose of his wealth however he wanted to and to will it to whomever seemed right to him, or even to spend it all during his lifetime, if his heart told him to.

However, he was a good relative, indulgent towards his nephew, affectionate toward his nieces, and very devoted to his sister-in-law, all the while gladly making fun of the good lady's ideas on the education of young ladies and on the dangers which the virtue of young boys encountered in Paris. Uncle Armand was in addition a gay companion, wearing his fifty years lightly, and very much appreciated in the circle of Moucherons, his Paris Club, where he spent a good third of his existence. There they were somewhat afraid of him because he had a biting wit and he didn't refrain from using it on people he didn't like. But, because he was amusing, he was pardoned for being caustic.

He wasn't seen too often at his sister-in-law's home when she was in the country. He used as an excuse that Germonière had no women, and, at his age, that was pure fatuousness to put forward such an excuse. But he swore that criticism had no misplaced, hidden meaning, and that he missed women only for their conversation. Men, he claimed, didn't have enough taste for finely phrased unkind spiteful remarks.

That year, however, instead of going back to Biarritz in September, where he usually went to join some of those like him and several ladies very capable of answering him in kind, he came, at the opening of hunting season, to get established at Germonière, to the great astonishment and the great joy of his sister-in-law. He had even announced that he counted on staying there for a long visit.

It was now November. He was still there, and he was not talking about leaving. He, who hadn't hunted for the last ten years, had developed a fine passion for all the sports of the gun. He killed partridges during the month of September, pheasants during the month of October, and after All Saint's Day, he began to kill woodcocks. There was nothing to prove that he wasn't waiting for the arrival of wild ducks.

Everything had changed appearances in the household since he had become established there. He had now and then attracted likeable Parisians there. He'd chased away the too boring country people and he'd been able to make use of the others. The little village of Arcy-sur-Beuvron is only seven kilometers from Germonière. This intelligent man of leisure had awakened it. It was really the one most asleep in the *Sous-Préfecture* of Orne-et-Sarthe. He made it a branch of Trouville and of Aix en Savoy. They started playing Baccarat in the *Chambre Littéraire*, where, as long as anybody could remember, they had only played Boston.[24] They came yoked together four at a time to visit Madame Daudièrne. They were talking about putting on a comedy that winter in the conservatory of the chateau—because now they were saying *the chateau*, and the lady let them say it.

The old people of the countryside shook their heads and claimed that she was ruining herself, but the mothers, silently, approved it. They were hoping to profit from this worldly change in the household in order to get their daughters settled. And Madame Daudièrne, who had two of them, probably thought like all the mothers, because she had given her carefree brother-in-law carte blanche. He made use of it to organize parties almost every day.

Nevertheless, by dint of putting on all sorts of parties, he had become somewhat calm. He had thoughtful moments, and he fell sometimes, after dinner, into prolonged meditation. He dined copiously, that's true, but it could be seen that he was preoccupied with something other than his digestion. With what? That was what no one had been able to find out, because no one dared question him.

His sister-in-law wondered if he had lost a large sum of money, and his nieces suspected that he was in love. The youngest, named Germaine, audacious and sure of herself, claimed that she knew how to get out of him the name of the woman he preferred. But, Laurence, who was the oldest and the most reasonable, leaned toward believing that he had too much wit to give over to the ridiculous fault into which many superannuated rakes fall. Their brother, Alfred, took on mysterious airs, saying that Mademoiselle Coralie of the *Fantaisies-Comique* had just bolted off to Russia, and he insinuated that Uncle Alfred's melancholy had no other cause than that unexpected flight. Whatever the cause, that very outgoing uncle had become suddenly silent and was concentrating. He didn't come out of that abnormal lethargy except to throw out bitter words, and that particular evening, a sad autumn evening, he appeared rather out of sorts.

He was sunk into an enormous armchair in the corner of the huge chimney of the drawing room, and Madame Daudièrne was sitting across from him. They had had a family dinner at home, but they were expecting guests. They always expected them. The elegant young men from Arcysur-Beuvron didn't have to be invited to come about 9:00 p.m. to drink a cup of tea, a visit which often ended in a hop over to the piano.

Lawrence and Germaine had gone upstairs to their bedroom to freshen up a bit. Alfred had gone to Paris under the pretext of settling terms with a coach for

---

[24] A card game with four players and 52 cards.

lessons in law. At that moment, he was probably showing off his fashionable waistcoat behind the scenes at a little theatre where he was known by everybody.

The brother-in-law and sister-in law had been alone for twenty minutes and they had not yet exchanged a word. Nothing could be heard but the far-away cracking sound of the park trees shaken by the stormy wind. It wasn't raining; it was snowing leaves and there was a bitter cold. But the drawing room was well insulated, well heated, well lighted. There were flowers everywhere. Winter stopped at the door. It's pleasant to make fun of the icy mist with your feet on the andirons.

"What a gale!" grumbled Uncle Armand, after having passed his hand across his forehead, like a man waking from a short nap.

"It's frightful," said Madame Daudièrne. "I really believe that we won't have any visitors this evening."

"The fact is, my dear Queen, that if these carefree fellows from Arcysur-Beuvron risk their lives coming to flirt with these young ladies today, they'd have to fear neither God nor the Devil. *Only crime can go out in such weather,*" the late Ducray-Duminil wrote in the past."

"Who is this Ducray-Duminil?" asked the Chatelaine distractedly.

"A novelist who was very fashionable under the first Empire and who had style; you may judge that by that scrap of his prose. I don't believe that our little gentlemen from the village are taking advantage of the storm to be lax in their commitments, but I doubt that they'll decide to brave it for your daughters' beautiful eyes."

"My daughters can do very well without them…and you can also, I think."

"Oh! There're two or three of them who amuse me, and I'll bet that Laurence and Germaine will regret not seeing them, Germaine most of all. She adores music and she dotes on dancing. It's time to get her married."

"Still it's necessary to wait until I've married her older sister. So, my dear Armand, it's easy for you to talk about it. Do you think that's so easy?"

"Yes, but of course! …Especially for Germaine, who pleases at first sight. Laurence charms those who get to know her, but many people judge by appearances!"

"Laurence has some serious qualities," said Madame Daudièrne, a little annoyed, "and I don't see why she wouldn't find a suitable match."

"She'll find ten of them…unless she's too demanding."

"It seems to me she has the right to be so."

Instead of answering, Uncle Armand began whistling a fanfare very softly.

"Really, my friend," continued the mother, obviously offended, "I don't know what's come over you, but you seem to be trying hard to torment me about my children."

"Me! I love them, your children; I cherish them as if they were my own…even including that ridiculously elegant little Alfred, who's anticipating

200

your inheritance…and mine. Only, I don't have your maternal illusions, and I see the situation as it is. How much dowry are you giving to each of your daughters?"

"You know very well, 150,000 pounds, and you also know I can't give any more."

"Good! And after you, they'll have the same amount again…if my pretty nephew doesn't whittle away at their portions by running up debts that you'll have the weakness to pay. But for the moment, they have nothing, given the fact that their father left them nothing when he died. He had no fortune when you determined to marry him…under the *régime dotal*.[25] No more fortune than did I, who made my fortune in San Francisco. In sum, these young ladies are marriageable parties with a 100,000 *écus*, including their expectations, as the matrimonial prospectuses say. Therefore, they must be united with millionaires."

"What ideas you have! You push everything to the extreme. Certainly, I believe Germaine would be very happy with a very rich husband."

"And you think Laurence would be content with a poor husband?"

"Perfectly, if he pleased her. She has simple tastes, a thoughtful character, and a never failing even temper.. She's neither capricious, nor ambitious, nor…"

"Nor silly, nor carried away by passion. I grant you that…although I've seem in my travels volcanoes covered by snow."

"Now there you go comparing my poor Laurence to a volcano! Decidely, my dear Armand, you're trying to make fun of me."

"I've no desire to do that, I swear to you. And since the volcano shocked you, I take back the volcano. I know the excellent qualities of your older daughter, and I ardently hope she finds a husband worthy of her. But at the present moment, I don't see in this country anyone suitable for her. That isn't because of a lack of suitors. Since I've taken up my autumn quarters at Germonière, all the masculine youth of Arcy has paraded before me. I've counted a half-dozen unworthy fellows who aspire to become your sonin-law. But not one meets the conditions I require. There is the weather vane rooster…the handsome Arthur du Pommeval. He's not bad looking; he's not too much a fool, and it seems to me he hasn't displeased these young ladies; but a gentleman who gets mixed up with horse racing in the provinces and who has at the most an income of 15,000, offers only insufficient guarantees."

"He's supposed to inherit from an uncle," Madame Daudièrne said in a soft voice.

"An inheritance from an uncle, that's a fat prize which can never be counted on. Let's talk about something else, dear sister. Who're you expecting this evening?"

"Everybody and nobody. Whoever wants to can come from 9:00 p.m. until

---

[25] Rules governing marriage which concerned the conservation and the restitution of the woman's dowry.

midnight. But the weather's so bad! We may have no one but that good doctor."

"So much the better. His philosophy agrees with mine."

"It could also be that our neighbors from the other side of the water might decide to pay us the visit their nephew, Monsieur de Pommeval, told us to expect about three months ago."

"The Vignemals? They'd have to be crazy because the storm is turning into a cyclone...But...did you hear"

"What's that?"

"Something that seems to come from the bottom of the garden. You'd swear someone was calling for help."

"You must be mistaken, my friend," said Madame Daudièrne, without being too upset. "Nobody goes for a walk in the garden at this hour and in such abominable weather."

"I assure you, my dear, that I heard a cry...a cry of distress," answered Uncle Armand, who had gone as far as the French doors opening onto the garden steps, and was listening, his ear glued against the panes.

"It's the whistling of the wind."

"No, it isn't. I know what I'm talking about. It's the voice of man...or of a woman."

"Are you going to believe that someone is being murdered near the house? You're going to windup making me afraid with your gloomy imagination."

"I don't say that, but there may have been an accident. The little river is 200 meters from here, that pretty little river where in the past the former owner drowned. Who knows but that one of your household people hasn't fallen in there?"

"The people who work for me don't go prowling around at night on dangerous paths."

"Oh! There are sentimental maids who give their lovers a rendezvous in solitary places...in moonlight. The moon has just become full. But I don't hear anything any more."

"Because nothing happened."

"Or because the person who cried out is no longer in this world."

"Armand, you're unendurable this evening. You know that I'm very nervous and you take pleasure in frightening me."

This dialogue was interrupted by an explosion of silvery laughter. The drawing room door opened noisily and two young girls entered, holding hands. They hardly resembled each other. One was pink and blond, of an adorable ash-blond, with dark eyes which sparkled with malice and gaiety. The other was brown and pale with big eyes of a difficult to define nuance. Uncle Armand claimed they were violet, which annoyed Madame Daudièrne a great deal. What was certain was that they were superb, although less lively than those of her sister. They had an expression of touching resigned softness and sometimes glances which shone like flashes of lightening and which were as quickly extinguished. This evening they told nothing. The blonde Germaine burst out with laughter in vain. The dark Laurence's expression did not light up.

"You, little one, you're very happy," said Armand.

"That's because I'm happy for two," retorted Germaine. "My older sister can't be cheered up. I've just told her some stories which would make you bend double with laughter. I even went so far as to mimic the old Baroness Verton when she gets angry with her partner at whist. Nothing worked. Mademoiselle is in a set melancholy just as the barometer is in a set ugliness since yesterday. And I'd like to ask you why. She's had dazzling success. This week Monsieur du Pommeval, who sets the tone for golden youth of Arcy, waltzed with her seven times, while he honored me with only three sad mazurkas."

"Four, I counted them," Laurence said softly. "And, then, you know very well that Monsieur du Pommeval had to take me as second best because he arrived late and you were already taken for the whole evening."

"Oh! I forgive him. But I really wish he'd bring some of his friends today, because for two days I've amused myself doing crochet. I feel the need to change exercise."

"Then, play a little music for us," said the uncle, "because we aren't going to have anyone. The wind is blowing enough to throw off all the ridiculous, elegant young dandies of the neighborhood."

"Well! That's true," Germaine cried out, running to the window. "And it's snowing in the bargain. So much the better! I adore snow. You'd think that the trees had gotten dressed to go to a white ball, and that they were bowing, the way they bowed in the time when they still danced the Lancers' Quadrille. And then, if the fountain in the garden freezes, we can go skating. That's what's amusing! But those little Arcy gentlemen are afraid of the cold. If I had a lover, I'd want him to come serenade me under my balcony in thirty degrees below zero weather."

"Germaine! Will you please be quiet" asked Madame Daudièrne. "Your sister is already at her work. Help her finish that lap rug. It isn't getting any further along."

"On my word, no. Tapestry work bores me. I prefer to play my piano. I'm going to play you a quadrille of Offenbach and I'll imagine myself dancing it."

"Not too loud, all right?" grumbled Monsieur Armand. "I don't like music that sounds like cannon fire."

"Don't worry, Uncle. I'll use the soft pedal," Germaine answered, taking her place on the piano stool.

Laurence was already at work and didn't look up. Monsieur Daudièrne, who no longer thought about listening for noises outside, had just taken his place standing up in front of the chimney when a domestic in brown livery announced in a discrete voice:

"Doctor Subligny!"

"It's about time!" cried out Uncle Armand. "You at least, you're not abandoning us under the pretext that the roads are bad."

"To brave the storm to see us, that's beautiful, that's great, that's sublime," said Germaine, clapping her hands.

"Good evening, dear sir," continued Madame Daudièrne. "Come near the fire. You must be frozen."

"Ah, do that. How did you get here?" asked the uncle.

Everyone was talking at the same time except Laurence, who just gave a friendly smile to the visitor. The doctor who was given such a friendly welcome was more than sixty, but he was as straight as a poplar tree and as robust as an oak tree. He had been a military doctor when he was young and he still kept a certain brusqueness of manners from his former life which social life had tempered. He was a well educated and, which was more important, an excellent man. His face expressed frankness and goodness with a slight touch of mischievousness. They loved him in the village and they welcomed him at Germonière where he came without an invitation whenever he liked and where he gladly spent his evenings, especially since Monsieur Armand had elected to live there. Subligny had never married and these two old bachelors understood each other marvelously.

"*Mon Dieu!*" he answered after having greeted Madame Daudièrne and her daughters. "I came very nicely on foot. My mare's old and I was afraid she'd break a leg in this snowy weather."

"And you preferred to expose your own," the uncle said, laughing.

"Bah! I saw a lot more in the retreat from Constantine."[26]

"That doesn't matter. If I'd known that you were on the road, I would've believed it was you who cried out for help a while ago."

"Somebody called for help? Let's go. I have with me everything necessary to dress a wound."

"Calm yourself, dear friend. Somebody cried out, but no one's calling out any longer. And besides, I'm not absolutely certain that somebody cried out.

"Let's hope that you were wrong. Anyway, I think that, this evening, nobody is running along the roads. I left Arthur du Pommeval and his happy band in the Arcy Club. They had intended to come here in their coaches, but they were afraid of turning over and right now they're playing baccarat to console themselves."

"The cowards!" Germaine exclaimed; "to play baccarat when there're two poor girls at Germonière who haven't waltzed in forty-eight hours!"

"I admit they're very guilty. But these gentlemen have expensive horses and they take care of them. The young Pommeval boy has just bought a pair which cost him 300 *louis*."

"And he'd rather let us stay vainly waiting in our solitude than to risk such

---

[26] Constantine, Algeria. The French tried unsuccessfully to take it in 1836. They overcame it in 1837, but with terrible losses.

precious animals! People aren't gallant any more."

"Ah, as for that," asked Uncle Armand, "then he's indeed rich, this Arcy-sur-Beuvron Beau Brummel?"

"Rich? No. He has enough to live on, and yet...the way he's going..."

"But there is in our neighborhood a millionaire relative from whom he's supposed to inherit, I'm told."

"Monsieur Vignemal, his mother's brother. That inheritance won't bring him any income. It's Madame Vignemal who's a millionaire. Monsieur didn't possess very much when he married a widow almost as old as he is. It's true that since their marriage they made a will giving their wealth to the last one alive. But the good man is rather sickly and his wife is strong as steel. She'll bury him; you can be sure of that and the Pommeval boy won't get anything. She can't stand him. I'm sorry about that because he has more good qualities than faults, and if he inherited he would be a good catch," the doctor concluded, looking at Laurence from the corner of his eyes. Their eyes met and he could certainly see that she hadn't lost a word of the conversation. But she lowered her eyes almost immediately and began work again on her tapestry. Germaine was leafing through the musical scores and didn't seem to be a great deal interested in Monsieur du Pommeval's financial future.

All the while he was talking, the Doctor had taken an armchair and was warming himself with a very understandable satisfaction.

"These Vignemals are strange neighbors," said Madame Daudièrne after a silence. They live three-quarters of a league from Germonière. I went to pay them a visit visit last year, but I wasn't able to see them and they haven't yet returned my visit."

"They don't do anything like other people," answered Doctor Subligny. "They have horses and carriages but they never use them."

"Then they're misers?"

"The nephew is prodigal; that a compensation," murmured Monsieur Armand.

"No, it isn't because of avarice that they stay at home. It's for a great deal more amusing reason. Would you believe that Madame Vignemal is as jealous as a tigress of her husband, who is fully fifty-five years old and who wears a wig? I'll have to tell you she married him for love a quarter of a century ago. She still sees him as he was then and she's afraid that someone will lead him astray. So she keeps him incommunicado in a private prison, and he lets her do it. However, I know on good authority that they won't be long in paying you a return visit. They've been getting ready for it for three months, because, for them, the shortest trip is a big affair. But you'll see them appear at the moment you least expect them...in the evening, most probably. Vignemal consulted me the other day to find out what time it would be decent to arrive at your house and I amused myself by telling him that at Germonière people never went to bed before three o'clock in the morning."

"What if they came today, what a party!" Germaine exclaimed. Those good people must be something to die laughing at. I'd be very amused to study them."

A severe glance from Madame Daudièrne silenced the young girl, who started playing softly the first measures of Fortunio's song.

"*Parbleu!*" her uncle said to her, "You don't need the Vignemal couple to find something to satisfy your instinct for mockery. In this charming countryside, there's no lack of ridiculous people."

"No, these are run of the mill."

"What do you mean, by saying they are *ordinary*?"

"I mean they aren't faces which don't at all resemble all those in the streets, the contrasted characters, those who are unique, to sum it up."

"*Peste!* Mademoiselle, my niece, how well you express yourself. I'd be curious to know where you've picked up these sophisticated terms."

"In the newspapers, when Mama lets me read them. But admit that I'm right. All the elegant young men of Arcy dress and speak in the same way. All the bourgeois are cut from the same pattern. If you know one, you know a hundred. I was hoping for something better from country people, but I have been hoaxed. I have yet to see one who doesn't have light yellow hair, a pale complexion, a red nose, stooped shoulders and a sneaky attitude. Here the race is ugly and common."

"I think that you make an exception of Monsieur du Pommeval."

"Oh! That man is a being apart. He has Parisian characteristics and he would make a very passable hero of a novel if he didn't have a ridge in the middle of his forehead and if he didn't comb his sideburns so carefully."

"Ah, so that's it. You're dreaming about a Fra Diavolo?"

"Maybe."

"Well, Mademoiselle, I have something for you," said Doctor Subligny, smiling.

"What! Are there Italian brigands from Calabria in the area around Germonière?"

"No, very fortunately. But there is a wild man who camps on your land without your knowing it."

"Tell me where he is so I can dash over there."

"He's sometimes in your woods, sometimes on your river. He's a nomad who lives off your game and off your fish."

"And…is he young?"

"He's twenty-years-old and has superb good looks."

"Good! We'll paint his portrait; not me, I draw too poorly, but Laurence, who has artistic talent."

"Thank you, no!" her elder sister said quickly. "I don't like savages and I have no interest in reproducing the features of this Mohican."

"I doubt very much, besides, that he would consent to pose," Monsieur Subligny added.

"That doesn't matter. I would really like to see him," Germaine murmured.

"And so would I, to fill out a verbal complaint against him," added the uncle. "Because, after all, this displaced Red Skin is hunting and fishing without permission on Germoniére... But...what is it, Baptiste?" Monsieur Daudièrne continued, addressing an old valet who had just entered.

"Why do you look so frightened?"

"Monsieur," the servant stammered, "Something bad has happened."

"Something bad! Where's that...and to whom?"

"On the river, Sir."

"*Parbleu!* I was sure I heard someone cry out...a drunken county man who fell into the water, probably."

"No, Monsieur... It seems Monsieur and Madame Vignemal took the ferry to cross the Beauvron... The wind broke the rope and the vessel overturned."

"Ah! *Mon Dieu!*" Madame Daudièrne cried out, "and they drowned! drowned coming to see us!...because they were coming here, I'm sure...the ferry is at the end of the garden. This is terrible!"

"But we have to go there," said Germaine. "It may still be time to help them."

"Roch says not, Mademoiselle. He saw the accident...twenty minutes ago."

"Roch, who's this Roch?"

"Roch Ferrer, the savage I was telling you about," answered the Doctor. "If he didn't rescue them, it was because rescue was impossible because he swims like a fish and he dives like an otter. The husband and the wife died at the same time, there's no doubt of that."

"The Devil! Here's a strange event...an event which could very well improve Arthur du Pommeval's situation."

"It really concerns Monsieur du Pommeval!" exclaimed Germaine. "It's a question of hurrying to the place where the accident occurred and trying to resuscitate these poor people. People who've drowned have been known to return to life after having been an hour under water, isn't that true, Doctor?"

"Rarely, Mademoiselle, very rarely," answered Monsieur Subligny, not without smiling a little. "But nothing should be neglected, even in hopeless cases. I'm going there. The question is to know if they've recovered the bodies."

"Roch tried, Monsieur," the valet sighed. "But the current is so strong... the river carried everything away. They didn't even see the boat again."

"I was very sure that brave boy risked his life to save them. He's as courageous as a lion."

"Then I forgive him for having alerted us so late," interrupted Monsieur Armand. "It's my opinion we ought to attempt new searches. I'm going with you, Doctor...and we're going to take all our servants with us. They'll help us explore all the banks of the Beuvron. Your heroic poacher can serve as our guide."

"Roch has gone back there, sir," said the old valet. "He wants to dive again."

"Good! He'll have to come up for air, and we'll see him. There's a marvelous clear night. Come, Doctor. And you, my dear sister-in-law, don't torment yourself here, please. When one is as nervous as you are, emotions are very dangerous. Ask our friend about that."

"How could I not be upset?" whispered Madame Daudièrne. "I can't get it out of my mind that I'm partly the cause of the death of these unfortunate neighbors."

"Because you imagined they left home to come visit you. Nothing proves that. But this is not the time to argue about it. Come, Doctor…and you, Baptiste, go down to the kitchen…get together the coachman, the gardener…get some lanterns and let's go."

"You'll take me with you, won't you, Uncle," asked Germaine. "I just ask you for time to put on a coat and a little hood."

"Take you along! Not on your life. There's nothing for you to do there. I certainly hope your mother is going to keep you from going out."

And not waiting to reprimand his fearless niece, Armand Daudièrne left the drawing room. The doctor did the same. He picked up in the hallway his broad-brimmed hat and his wolf-skin overcoat while the uncle put on his wool insulated overcoat and a fur cap. Germaine really wanted to follow them, but Madame Daudièrne held her back, addressing a serious admonition to her. Lawrence, wise Laurence, took advantage of the fact that no one was paying attention to her, to leave the door ajar and to say softly to those gentlemen:

"You'll come back quickly, won't you? I didn't say anything because I didn't have the strength to speak. I was overcome, but I still want to hope. And I beg you to bring us news…good or bad…promptly. Uncertainty is the worst of all bad things."

"Rest easy, my dear child. We won't lose a minute. Only, I must commit myself to not lulling you with any illusions. Monsieur Vignemal is at the bottom of the water, Madame also, and they won't come out of it alive."

Having spoken, the uncle rushed toward the staircase. Monsieur Subligny was already on the ground floor. There weren't twenty steps to descend and he was still as limber as a young man. Baptiste was waiting for them. The servants were ready with torches.

"March straight ahead!" Monsieur Daudièrne told them. They obeyed and they left the house and went down the steps. The storm was at the height of its violence and swept about whirlwinds of fine snow which didn't stay on the ground because the wind was carrying it away. The chestnut trees in the park bent so as to almost break under the strength of the intermittent gusts which came from the north like flashes of lightening and the high branches of the great pines shook with noise which recalled the faraway murmur of the rising tide. The sky, hidden by the flakes of snow, was lit up at intervals and then the full moon lit up with melancholy clarity that winter landscape. The park extended a great distance on both sides of the house but it wasn't large. The little river cut through it two or three hundred feet from the steps. A narrow alley led to the river bank; that is to say to a long earthen levee bordered with Tamaris trees. These formed a rather agreeable promenade in the summer which was disagreeable in the bad season, because the valley through the Beuvron flows is enclosed almost everywhere and the cold wind blows furiously there. There are also a great many trees and the thick brush undergrowth which covers the left river bank hides from the inhabitants of Germonière the view of the rather run-down manor house where the Vignemal couple live.

This manor house, called Fougéray, actually belonged to Madame, who inherited it from her father, and who had never had it renovated either before or after her marriage. The fields around her chateau produced very little. The husband got involved in improving them, although he understood nothing about agriculture. The woods, for lack of paths to explore them, grew haphazardly, so much so that on the other side of the Beuvron you found yourself in a wild country, while on the right side of the river bordered by Madame Daudièrne's property, you could have thought yourself in a villa of the great Paris suburbs. Uncle Armand preferred civilized country sides; thus he had never wanted to go across the river. That evening, however, he went forward bravely without paying attention to the snow which lashed his face. He seemed willing to do everything he could to bring help to some people whom he cared very little about. It's true that the doctor, older than he by fifteen years, set him the example. This excellent doctor, he ran rather than walked. It was a question of saving two lives and in cases like this he never spared his pains.

"Before we left, I should have given orders that they get some woolen covers warm to roll our drowned people in, if we fish them out…and to bring some rags to rub them with," he was saying between his teeth. "That's elementary. But I forgot. That's what getting old means. And then, the news of this bizarre catastrophe has troubled me so much…"

"It really is very bizarre," Monsieur Daudièrne shouted. "What the devil made those Vignemals decided to embark on a bad boat to come see us? Aren't there any bridges in this country?"

"There's one upstream but it requires a detour of two leagues to find it, whereas the ferry is very close to their house. They didn't want to have a team hitched up for fear of tiring out their horse."

"And this is the weather they chose to go visiting! On my word of honor, these rural people have their head on backward. And if it costs them their life, which is more than probable, they'll get just what they deserve. Between us, that's just about all the same to me. Only, I'm very sorry for my sister-in-law, who is impressionable to an excess…and unfortunately her daughters take after her."

"Especially the older one," murmured Monsieur Subligny.

"Oh! Germaine too, although it's less apparent. Laurence still feels more passionately because her feelings are contained, and I fear all violent emotions for her. She's my favorite, that one. One of these days I'll tell you why…but our people are already on the levee. I see their lanterns going up and down. Let's hurry."

In a few strides, they reached the foot of a grassy slope which inclined gently toward the park and in three leaps they came to the top of that dike, at the bottom of which flowed the Beuvron. The waters, swollen by the rains which had preceded the first cold spells, rolled impetuously between two steep banks and the storm was raising veritable waves there. That river, ordinarily very peaceful, had suddenly taken on the looks of a torrent.

"*Parbleu!*" Monsieur Daudièrne exclaimed. "I'm not surprised that Philemon and Baucis [27] were swept along God knows where. They've fallen into a real windmill flood gate. I flatter myself I'm a good swimmer and I'm not sure I could manage to do it. If your savage gets back out of this current, he'll have to have remarkable strength. Speaking of that, I don't see him. Has he stayed at the bottom, this time?"

"Baptiste," shouted the doctor. "Where is Roch?"

"Monsieur, we're looking for him," answered the old valet.

"He's capable of having gone across the river to get back to his shelter."

"His shelter? Then where does he lodge?"

"I think that for some weeks he's arranged for himself a kind of hut made of foliage on the left bank. He's even had some trouble about that illegal installation with Madame Vignemal, who doesn't take lightly any infringement on her property rights. But he doesn't pay any attention to her and to the gendarmes. Nobody has been able to lay a hand on him. I'm probably the only man to whom he shows certain deference and to whose opinion he sometimes listens. I'll have to tell you that I set a fractured bone for him and he's grateful to me for it."

"That's really very fortunate. Where does he come from, this Robin Hood? Was he born in the countryside?"

"No, but he came here when he was very little. His father was a gypsy who probably came from Spain and who went around the countryside buying old scrap iron and grooming horses. Those are the two jobs the people of his race most willingly practice. That man was found dead one morning at the corner of a boundary marker in the vicinity of Arcy. The child had stayed seated beside the cadaver but he was not crying. The Brothers of the Christian Doctrine took him in and raised him up to the age of fifteen."

"I can guess the rest. As soon as he was old enough to support himself by pilfering, instinct got the upper hand and he made off. But I'm chatting very much off the subject, and we have better things to do."

---

[27] In classical mythology, two peasants who gave hospitality to Zeus and Hermes, who were in disguise.

"I can hardly see what. We aren't in a position to drag the river and, besides, the bodies must be far from here right now. I was somewhat hoping that Roch would have succeeded in bringing them to the bank, and in that case, I would have attempted to work a miracle. If he's given up trying to recover them, we're not going to manage to do so."

"I fear so, but if you'll trust me, my dear Doctor, we'll follow the levee right to the end of the park to be sure our drowned victims didn't come aground at the edge of the water. The Beuvron makes some very sharp bends and a cadaver carried along by the current could be stopped by a natural barrier."

"You're right. We have to explore all the corners."

"Downstream, of course. Here's where the ferry was, if I'm not mistaken."

"Yes, Monsieur," said Baptiste. "Here's the pathway to go down to it, and the rope which goes from one side to the other is still holding by one end to the piling where it was attached on this side. It must have broken in the middle. It wasn't too solid and it should have been replaced by a new one...but the ferry was used so seldom."

"Oh! A ship's cable wouldn't have held in a storm of this strength. However, the boat couldn't have sunk where it was; we must search lower. Walk ahead to light the way, Baptiste, and be careful of your lantern."

"Monsieur," exclaimed the gardener, who had gone ahead, "there's Roch coming here running."

"Right," murmured the Doctor. "I recognize him by his height. He's tall."

"And he's running as fast as he can; evidently he's bringing news or he wouldn't be in such a hurry."

Thirty seconds later Roch Ferrer stopped short two feet from Monsieur Subligny and out of breath said to him:

"I found the woman."

"Is she still alive?" the doctor asked quickly.

"I don't know."

"What do you mean, you don't know! You only saw her pass by at the edge of the water?"

"Pardon me; I touched her. I even tried to lift her to carry her to you on my shoulder, but I wasn't able to."

"What! As strong as you are!"

"It's not strength that's needed. Her legs are caught in the roots of an old willow tree...impossible to get her free by myself."

"At least we must not abandon her. Supposing she wasn't already dead, she must be now if you left her in that position."

"If she is, it won't be my fault. I put her head and her torso out of the water and I stretched her out on the bank that's sloping."

"Her head on a plane higher than her feet, that's good. Without knowing it, you did what was the best thing to do. There's still one chance in a hundred that the asphyxiation isn't complete. But let's hurry. Is this place far?"

"A hundred feet from here! You know it very well. It's the first bend in the river, a point of land sticking out."

"Perfectly. The former proprietor drowned there."

"Oh! That's a bad spot. There's a whirlpool there and when someone falls in, they can't get out."

The dialogue ended quickly and Armand Daudièrne hardly had time to look at this unusual boy who appeared to be more a gentleman of the open road than a savior. He could see only by the uncertain light of the moon that he was very tall, well proportioned and that he was clothed from head to foot with animal skins, like an Eskimo or a Samoyed.[28]

Every one walked faster. The gusts had not lessened. The snow was still falling and the wind whistled with an unheard of violence, but was blowing down river and they had it at their backs.

"And Monsieur Vignemal, you didn't find him?" shouted Monsieur Daudièrne, using the familiar *tu* to Roch, who was walking ahead of him. [29]

"No," the boy answered dryly, turning around to size up this monsieur whom he had never seen and who had begun by treating him as an inferior.

"Then he's dead. Let's see what we can do for the woman."

"I'm very afraid she won't be in any better shape than he," murmured Monsieur Subligny. "The body being on dry ground doesn't mean much. Well! We'll soon find out what we're dealing with."

"Here's where she came aground. There's the willow tree, down below us. The lady is stretched out beside it, on the gravel."

The doctor went down first and Uncle Armand followed him closely, yelling out:

"Baptiste, my boy, bring us your light. The moon has just gone behind a cloud and we can't see anything there."

Then, an instant later he continued, addressing Monsieur Subligny: "But, *Sacre bleu!* The body isn't there. Your savage is joking with us."

"Let's look around," said the doctor. "Give us some light, Baptiste... and you Roch, come help us. Let's see now. Where did you leave Madame Vignemal?"

"There...on the bank," answered Roch, "who had jumped from the top of the levee to the edge of the water with just one leap. "It's true she isn't there any longer. I can't understand that at all. The big rock I put under her head hasn't moved at all. The current must have carried the body away... yes, look here! The roots of the willow tree have been pulled up. The body followed. And the tree's going to follow because it can't hold any longer."

"That's true...nothing can hold out against that damned river when it's

---

[28] A Ural-Altaic people living in N. W. Siberia.

[29] The French *tu* is used rather than the formal *vous* for children, animals, family members and inferiors.

swollen and the wind is blowing from the northeast. But, really, my boy, you had a very bad idea to leave that poor woman there. You should have stayed near her and called out."

"That's true. I recognize now that I was wrong. That'll teach me to rely on the solidity of old willow trees."

"*Mon Dieu!*" the doctor continued, "it's clear that the poor woman was dead because before coming up on dry land here she spent a good twenty minutes under the water. But I would have liked to try to bring her back to life...just to have a clear conscience. Now all hope is lost, and there's nothing more for us to do but leave."

"Not before I tell this droll fellow what I think of him," exclaimed Monsieur Daudièrne.

"Is that me you're talking about?" Roch asked, lifting his head.

"Yes, you, vagabond. Explain your conduct to us instead of being insolent. You conduct was suspicious and nothing proves to me that you didn't contribute to the drowning of these people that you claim to have wanted to save."

Roch drew forward two steps and resembled a race horse which was preparing to jump a ditch. But the doctor, who knew him, threw himself in front of him and it took only a gesture to stop him.

"Then you don't see that I risked my skin," said the young man, going near Baptiste, who held the light. His face, his hands and his clothing were dripping with water.

"I dove three times and I could have stayed peacefully on the bank. Nobody would have held that against me, because nobody knew I was there. You do the same, if you have a mind to. You may recover Monsieur or Madame Vignemal."

The retort was sharp and Uncle Armand was silent. Roch's tone and attitude had impressed him. This wasn't the way guilty people defend themselves. The proud savagery of that unusual being didn't displease him, and he began to be interested in him.

"Let's go back up on the levee," said Doctor Subligny, "the ground isn't solid and if we stay here the Beuvron might finally wash us away also."

"Without adding that we're freezing and the snow is cutting off our voices," Monsieur Daudièrne grumbled while painfully climbing the rather steep slope of the dike.

"Roch," said the doctor, "you're going to come to Germonière with us. There's a good fire in the kitchen and you're very much in need of drying off."

"I don't need anything, monsieur, and I'd prefer to go back to my place."

"Where is that, your place?"

"Very near here. In the woods above the spot where the ferry was."

"On the other side of the river, then...and you'll have to swim across it to go lie down in your burrow where a fox would die of cold. I forbid you to do that, my boy."

"But, monsieur..."

"Don't say anything. This is my order and if you don't follow it, I swear to you that the first time you break an arm or a leg, which will hardly be very long from now, thanks to the pretty life you lead, I'll let you take care of it all by yourself. Besides, it's absolutely necessary that you tell us how the accident happened, since you were there."

"Ah! That won't take long. I had just stretched out in my hut when I heard steps and voices. I slid on my stomach right up to the edge of the pathway. I thought that was the two guards from Fougéray who were making a round to nab me, but I recognized Monsieur Vignemal and his wife who were coming down, followed by their servant and I understood that they wanted to go across the water."

"Ah! There was a servant," grumbled Daudièrne. "What happened to that one? Did he drown like his masters?"

"No, his masters had gotten in the boat and he was going to get in also, but he stayed on the bank in order to detach the chain which was mooring the ferry. He had no sooner done that than the current picked up the barge and the rope broke. Then he began to cry out for help."

"Then it was he! He cried out so loudly that I heard it in my sister-inlaw's drawing room."

"Possible. The wind at that moment was carrying from the Germonière side. But the good fellow didn't cry out very long. When he saw the boat running off adrift, he lost his head and ran away."

"Then he went back to Fougéray," said the Doctor. "He should have at least gone to bring people back here to try to save his masters. But they say their servants didn't like them very much."

"They're right. And that's why after having done all I could to fish them out I went to Germonière instead of going to their house."

"But you first threw yourself into the water, my brave fellow?"

"Oh! Without losing a second, and I really thought I was going to get them out of trouble, because the end of the broken rope was trailing in the water. It was just a matter of swimming and getting hold of it and very nicely bringing the boat back to the bank."

"Hum! That wasn't easy."

"Even so, I would have succeeded. The boat was spinning like a top and me, swimming straight ahead, I was gaining on it. I had come so near them that I saw them as I'm seeing you. The husband was seated in the bottom and was hiding his face in his hands. The woman was standing up, and I really think she was getting undressed because she had unbuttoned the upper part of her dress. It even seemed to me that she was taking I don't know what out of it."

"Her purse, maybe. She had, they say, a mania for carrying her rent receipts and her bank bills on her."

"All I can tell you is at the moment I was shouting to them, 'Don't be afraid!' the boat slammed against a pointed rock that was right in the middle of the river. Ah! That didn't take long. It sank where it was and I saw nothing else."

"But you dived?"

"Yes...and I promise you that if I came back up without bringing anything with me, it was because I couldn't stay down any longer. I was out of oxygen, but I dived again further on...and then again even further on... everywhere I thought they could have gone down and you know that I know the bottom of the Beuvron as well as I do the surface. I didn't find anything. That was my fault. I should have gone as far as the old willow tree, but I was at the end of my strength."

"Anyone would be at least that," said Monsieur Daudièrne, whom the simplicity of the story had touched.

"I know very well that you didn't abandon them," exclaimed the Doctor. "You did more than your duty."

"No, I thought too late about that pointed rock which was brought out of the water by the current and which stopped the woman. And I also see that I should have foreseen that the roots would break...and nevertheless they were holding strong."

"Nothing resists water. Now, tell me, when you lifted Madame Vignemal, did she still have any warmth...was she still breathing?"

"I don't think so. It seems to me however that she made a movement just as I was putting her down on the bank...but I could be mistaken. The only thing I'm sure of is that her fists were closed. She seemed to have something clutched in her hand and she was holding it tightly...her arms were as stiff as iron bars."

"Good! I'm sure...the asphyxiation was complete. The help I would have been able to give her wouldn't have been of any use. That thought consoles me a little. Walk straight ahead, my boy, and when you've gotten your strength back at the chateau, you'll be free to go wherever you like. But I require you to come with us. I still have a few words to say to you and I don't care to prolong the conversation outside in this kind of weather."

Roch hesitated. Evidently the perspective of drying off by the kitchen fire didn't please him, but he venerated Monsieur Subligny and he didn't dare displease him. Without saying a word he went to join Madame Daudièrne's servants who were going ahead of the rest of the party.

"You were right, Doctor," Uncle Armand said. "This poacher is somebody."

"To be accurate, he doesn't really poach because he doesn't sell either the game he takes or the fish he catches. He does nothing but eat them. He prepares roasts and fish cooked with wild onions. I even tasted his cooking out in the open air once, and I can assure you that it was excellent. But he doesn't think about money. Because he wouldn't know what to do with it. He clothes himself with fox skins and, to cover his head, he fabricates caps made of otter skins."

"That fellow there is a Leather Stockings in person.[30] He was born to live in Canada. I'd like to suggest to my sister-in-law that she make him a game keeper."

"He wouldn't accept it. His freedom is too important to him. Madame Vignemal tried to enroll him in her service. He would never agree. He preferred to live at war with her and she finally got tired of tracking him down."

"Between us, Doctor, that life he leads, it's not very edifying and it's a good bet he'll wind up poorly. I admit to you that I even thought for an instant that he had helped our unfortunate neighbors to drown."

"He told you the truth on all points. I'd stake my life on it because since he's been in the world he's never lied. Besides the Vignemal servants were there when the accident occurred. He'll tell what he saw."

"Oh! Now I no longer suspect your gypsy. How old is he?"

"He doesn't know anything about himself. He must have been born on the open road or at the depth of some wood and he didn't find any civil servant there to register his birth. He owes the fact that he's never been called up for military service to that circumstance."

"That's a shame, *ma foi!* He was cut out to carry a sword, and although I didn't see his face very well, it seemed to me that he had the true head of a model. But, to come back to the gloomy end of the Vignemal couple, don't you think there's something else we have to do? Not for saving them... because they're both dead and gone. But there are some people we should alert as soon as possible."

"I'll be in Arcy in an hour. And I'll make it my duty to inform all those with an interest in the event: the mayor, the Procurer of the Republic... They'll give orders that the bodies be looked for and they'll probably designate me to examine them. So I'm going to take leave of Madame Daudièrne and your charming nieces..."

"You won't have to climb the stairs to the drawing room to tell them goodbye, because I see those little ladies on the threshold of the kitchen door. They're wearing their hoods, and I suppose their mother isn't far away. Well! They're in parley with Baptiste. I'm not sorry about that. We won't be the first to tell them the sad news. Ah! They're going back into the house...our servants are going in after them and Roch is following them without having to be asked too much. Let's do as they do, Doctor. We'll be better inside."

The kitchen was as vast as the guard room of a fortress from the Middle Ages and whole trees were burning in the monumental fireplace. Three great lamps suspended from the ceiling inundated that immense room with light that the fire burning on the hearth already lit sufficiently.

Madame Daudièrne hadn't come down there, but her daughters hadn't lost

---

[30] Allusion to James Fenimore Cooper's hero Natty Bumpo, aka Leather Stockings, in the novel *Last of The Mochicans*.

any time in interrogating the old valet. And when Uncle Armand appeared they already knew what to make of the fate of the Vignemals.

Laurence was paler than usual and had tears in her eyes.

"Is it really true, Uncle, that there's no more hope?" she asked in an emotional voice.

"Absolutely none, my dear child. They did everything humanly possible to save them. That *they* wasn't me because I arrived a great deal too late and this dear doctor didn't have an opportunity to use his medical skills, for lack of anyone to use his medical skills on. The river swept the bodies of our unfortunate neighbors very far from here. But I'm going to introduce you to a brave boy who risked his life. Well! But where is he, my hero? Look! He's gone to hide in the shadow of the chimney corner. Come now, Roch, come forward a little so people can see you. What the devil, you're good to show off."

Roch decided, much against his will, to leave his refuge and he came out into the full light. He had taken off his otter skin cap and the brown curls of his naturally curly hair fell haphazardly on his rather low but well defined forehead. He had a straight nose, the nose of a Greek statue, a complexion inclined toward olive, strong lips, but red as the pomegranate flower. His immense eyes shone like black diamonds, expressive eyes which stayed obstinately fixed on Laurence.

"*Sacre bleu!* How handsome he is," exclaimed Monsieur Daudièrne. "He never hides what he thinks and he doesn't mind expressing it strongly."

"What the doctor told us was right," Germaine continued thoughtlessly, while approaching to better see the gypsy, whom this movement of childish curiosity didn't at all disconcert because he made no effort to avoid it. Roch had eyes only for the elder sister, who was looking at him as one looks at a rare bird or a Japanese bronze, with interest but without emotion. Germaine had become even more animated but she didn't stop looking at the features and the physique of that young savage who resembled an Indian Bacchus. She immediately thought about the heroic action which Uncle Armand had briefly sketched.

"You risked your life, Monsieur," she said warmly. "I'm very happy to meet you. I like people such as you...and I certainly hope that you'll come back often to Germonière. My mother, I'm sure, will be anxious to thank you herself."

Roch, a little surprised that someone called him Monsieur, bowed without answering. He seemed to be waiting for a word from the mouth of Mademoiselle Laurence. That word didn't come and Monsieur Daudièrne began talking again in order to cut short admiration and compliments.

"My friend, I hope you won't refuse to come hunting with me one of these days. Monsieur Subnigny has told me how good you are at it and I'm dying with envy to see you shoot my sister-in-law's game."

"You're very kind, Monsieur," Roch stammered, "but..."

"I warn you that if you don't come I'll go looking for you. I absolutely insist that we go hunting together. If the snow keeps us from going out, my nieces will draw your portrait."

"That means that my sister will do it," said Germaine, smiling. "Me, I'll be content to be present at the sittings."

"We first must know if our mother will approve of this project," the calm Laurence answered evasively.

"I'll take charge of arranging that," continued the uncle. "And I'm counting on you my dear fellow."

"I'll come, Monsieur," Roch said after a silence.

"That's good! Don't let us wait for you very long or I'll really believe you hold it against me for certain sharp words that I regret having thrown out."

"Roch is too intelligent to remember them," added the doctor. "And if you'd be willing to take my advice, my boy, you'll take supper this evening at Germonière and you'll sleep there. Otherwise, look out for pleurisy. Besides, tomorrow morning you must come pick me up at Arcy. I'll need you to explain the facts to the magistrate who'll be in charge of the inquest and to avoid the disagreeableness of being severely interrogated. You don't have a smell of saintliness to the officers of the court, and if I don't guarantee your sincerity, these gentlemen could very well not accept your deposition except as an invention for profit."

"I'll be at your house before noon," answered Roch, without adding that he would take advantage of the hospitality which had been offered him for the night. He took leave with rather good grace and went to lean against the chimney.

Laurence simply returned his salutation, but Germaine smiled at him and sent him a gesture with her little white hand which meant: *Au Revoir*.

"Have you finally found the lover you've been dreaming about?" her uncle asked her gaily as he was climbing the stairs. "It seems to me that fellow over there answers your requirements rather well.

"He answers them too well. I maintain I'm going to marry according to my own notions, but I can't adjust myself at all to a husband who lives in the forest."

"Oh! You would do well to give up that one," replied Monsieur Daudièrne to continue his joke. He hardly looked at you while your sister literally fascinated him. He devoured her with his eyes and he no longer dared move."

"I didn't notice the effect I was causing," Laurence murmured.

"Well?" asked the anxious voice of Madame Daudièrne, who had come forward as far as the landing.

"Bad news, my dear sister-in-law."

"What! Lost! Both of them!"

"Irretrievably; God knows when they'll be found…maybe never. The Beuvron is nothing but a big stream but it could pass for a river, since it empties directly into the sea."

"Oh! the bodies won't go so far. The flood which caused this misfortune won't last and as soon as the water begins to subside, they'll come to ground somewhere. Let's hope so, because it would be very troublesome if the deceased couldn't be legally declared..."

"Troublesome for this boy who acted so generously and who they would perhaps accuse. Bah! I'll help you defend him. He didn't at first inspire me with any great confidence, but now I'll answer for him."

This dialogue, begun outside the drawing room, finished near the fire. Madame Daudièrne was all atremble and her daughters were hovering attentively around her.

"You're really distressing yourself too much," her brother-in-law said to her. "I pity Monsieur and Madame Vignemal with all my heart, but, after all, I've never seen them...nor have you."

"I should have had this cursed ferry repaired."

"Why? You never used it that I know of, and the other day when I was examining your property titles, I discovered that the upkeep of the crossing was the responsibility of your neighbors. You have nothing to reproach yourself and the care of weeping for them will have to be left to their inheritors," Uncle Armand concluded philosophically.

"I doubt they'll shed a great deal of tears," murmured the Doctor. "I know of only one of them and that one had half broken off relations with his uncle Vignemal. He had completely done so with his aunt by marriage. She'd taken a dislike to him, and since she led her husband around by the nose..."

"The young du Pommeval wasn't in good standing at Fougéray. I suspected as much from the way he talked about them. But how the devil would he be able to inherit. Only an hour ago you were saying the contrary. You even went into this subject in very precise details. These loving spouses each gave everything to the last one living by a well drawn up will and the whole fortune was on the wife's side. She has just died at the same time as her husband. Would you be able to tell me which of the two was the last one alive?"

"No, but the law has foreseen the case. Lacking certainty on which to base the order of inheritance, they set it up according to the age of the deceased."

"Actually, I now remember having known that, but I had completely forgotten it and I no longer have very clear in my mind the framework of the Civil Code. It seems to me however that the younger must be presumed to have survived. That's logical."

"Not always. So over the age of fifteen it's supposed that the oldest is the strongest."

"Fine! Our neighbors were a great deal older than fifteen."

"The husband must have been fifty-five, the wife fifty-four at least. I'm certain there wasn't six months difference between them."

"What does that matter? If the husband was the oldest, it's the wife who inherits."

"I don't know anything about that because I'm not very strong in legal matters. It certainly seems to me however that in determining the legal presumptions of survival, they took into consideration not only age but sex."

"Really, gentlemen," said Madame Daudièrne, "I wonder how you can, in the presence of such a misfortune, discuss a question of inheritance... which doesn't interest any of our family."

"It strongly interests someone we know, and as I didn't at all know the deceased, it's very natural that I should inform myself of the chances that Monsieur du Pommeval could have to become a millionaire. Aside from some little faults, he's a charming boy."

"He leads the cotillion better than anyone," Germaine said maliciously.

"We have seen conductors of cotillions who made excellent husbands, Mademoiselle," retorted the uncle with droll gravity. "But right now it's a matter of knowing if he's called upon to become the lord of Fougéray."

"I'll be able to tell you after tomorrow," answered Monsieur Soubigny. In a small town uncertainties in the matter of inheritance aren't of long duration. The news of the accident will no sooner be spread about Arcy than the question will be settled. In Normandy everybody is a lawyer."

"I don't doubt it, but if there was a copy of the Code at Germonière we could settle it immediately. Unfortunately these young ladies don't read anything but novels, and me, I read only newspapers."

"A copy of the Code? My brother has one of them," Laurence said softly.

"Indeed! That's true! He's supposedly studying for the law. I had forgotten about that. But he's in Paris, your studious brother..."

"Oh!" Germaine exclaimed. "When he goes there he carries only amusing books."

"I'm very convinced of that. It's a question of finding out where he has stuffed away this Code that he's probably never read."

"I saw it this morning on the night table," Laurence murmured.

"Because he used it to put him to sleep."

"Do you want me to go get it for you, Uncle?"

"I'd be glad for you to, my dear child." And when the elder sister had left the drawing room, "You wouldn't be the one, Germaine, who'd know how to bring us a law book. Let's bet that you don't even know what a Code is."

"I beg you pardon, my dear Uncle. It's a fat book shaped like a chopping block, with the spine in several colors. I admit that I've never opened it. Laws aren't at all for me. My Code is here," said Germaine, placing her hand on her breast over her heart.

"If you govern yourself after that Code, you'll do nothing but stupid things. Don't listen to this little girl, Doctor, and tell us who the heirs of Madame Vignemal are."

"Oh! She has several...cousins and cousins, all poorer one than the other. Her father earned a lot of money in real estate but his contemporaries remained peasants and she didn't want to associate with them. However, there was one of them in the past in whom she took an interest. He was an orphan and as he seemed to have good instincts, she decided to pay for his education. She enrolled him in a *lycée* in Paris and she got it into her head that he would become a magistrate. Maybe she hoped that he would one day sit on the Arcy court and see to it that she won her case. The good lady spent her life in lawsuits. She had trouble with all her neighbors."

"Except with my sister-in-law."

"Oh! She would have had sooner or later. She was given to squabbling and changeable to a point of which you can have no idea. But to come back to that great nephew she'd taken a liking to. I won't surprise you by telling you she quickly got tired of looking out for him. This devil Roger had no calling for the profession of magistrate. When he left the *lysée* he didn't return to the region and since then no one has heard anything of him."

"His name if Roger?...His first name, I suppose?" asked Germaine.

"Yes, Mademoiselle, Roger Pontac."

"That's short. It's simple and pleasant to the ear, Decidedly Roger Pontac pleases me. Then nobody knows what happened to him?"

"Because nobody tried to find out. Me, I've always believed he joined the military. I'd not be at all surprised if he had made a successful career. He was an intelligent boy and he wasn't afraid of anything. You'll see one of these days that he's been made a general. That would be better still than inheriting from Madame Vignemal. "

Madame Daudièrne was opening her mouth to interrupt these exchanges which she found improper given the circumstances, when Laurence reappeared loaded down with a massive octavio volume.

"Thank you, little one," her uncle said to her. "Pass me this interesting collection quickly, because I see you're bending double under the burden. That Alfred bought a book of first-class dimensions, but he's never used it. The pages haven't yet been cut. Do you know what to look for in it, Doctor?"

"I'm going to try to remember," murmured Subligny. "What we want to know should be found in the chapter which deals with inheritances."

"This dear Arthur du Pommeval doesn't have any idea that at this moment we're taking care of him," continued the uncle while the doctor was leafing through the book.

"I've got it," said Monsieur Subligny. "*Book III, Title II, Article 720.*"

"Read us Article 720, my dear friend."

"Here's what it says: *If several persons having equal rights to the inheritance, one another perishing in the same event, without it's being possible to find out who died first...*"

"That's exactly the case. Monsieur and Madame Vignemal had each willed his estate to the last one living, and the devil knows which one was the last one alive."

221

"I'm reading further," read the doctor: "*The presumption of survival is determined by the factual circumstances...*"

"They would seem to be in favor of Madame, the factual circumstances, because, after all, we aren't absolutely sure she was dead when the body came to dry ground on the bank."

"*By the factual circumstances, or lacking that, by the prime of life or of sex...*"

"You understand that: *of sex*."

"Let's see what follows."

"The following is Article 721, which states that under fifteen-years-old, the oldest is presumed to have survived, and below sixteen years old, it's the youngest."

"Go on! Go on! That situation doesn't at all concern the Vignemals. Between fifteen and sixteen-years-old, it's still the youngest, isn't it?"

"Yes, Article 722 says that in this case the inheritance is open, *following the order of nature*."

"Therefore, it's Madame who inherited from Monsieur and Arthur du Pommeval won't get a *sou*."

"You didn't let me finish: There is: *If they are of the same sex...*"

"And if they are of different sexes?"

"*The male is always presumed to be the survivor if they are of the same age, or if the difference in age doesn't exceed a year*."

"The Devil! That changes everything if, as you've just read to us, Monsieur Vignemal was only six months older than his wife."

"Barely six months."

"All right, but he has perfectly arranged things, this wise legislator. Thanks to him, our friend du Pommeval is going to become a great Monsieur. What fortune do the Vignemals leave?"

"They are reputed to have a fifty thousand franc income and as they never spend half of their revenue, they must have doubled their capital. Their nephew will be the richest land owner in this area, because the Articles I've just read to you are very clear and I don't doubt that his rights to the inheritance will be recognized without difficulty. Madame Vignemal's cousins will contest it, but they'll lose their lawsuit. As for Roger Pontac, he won't claim his right. He doesn't know his relative is dead, and even if he learned it, he wouldn't claim it. He's a careless fellow who cares nothing about money and that money would be better placed in the hands of Arthur du Pommeval than in his."

"*He! He!* Doctor, It seems to me that he's rather a spend-thrift, this handsome Arthur."

"Yes, because he's sowing his wild oats. But I know him...he'll change. Economy is in the blood of people in the province. It would only take marriage to make him a steady man, especially if he had the good fortune to meet a serious and well brought up young girl, a girl whose firm character..."

"Don't think you can reproach me for not having those virtues," interrupted Germaine, bursting with laughter.

Laurence blushed; Madame Daudièrne pinched her lips together; her brother frowned, and the good Doctor, sensing that he had gone too quickly and too far, consequently continued with:

"But I find that's it's late. Please allow me, good Madame to take leave of you."

"You won't go back on foot," Uncle Armand exclaimed. "Here's Baptiste who's bringing tea. You'll have a cup with us while they hitch up the surrey to take you back to Arcy."

And speaking to the valet. "Speaking of that, the boy, has he had supper?"

"No, Monsieur. He didn't want to eat anything. He left running like a mad man."

"We'll have trouble getting him to pose for his portrait," said Germaine.

The doctor raised his arms to heaven. He despaired of civilizing his savage and he decided to accept his host's offer.

"Serious matters can be taken up tomorrow," he murmured, sitting back down.

He wouldn't have believed he'd predicted so accurately.

II. The Lemon Rock

In the northwest of France, great cold spells don't last very long. The sea isn't far away and the warm current of the Gulf stream constantly warms the climate of these humid regions. It rains often but it rarely freezes, especially in autumn, and toward the middle of November the Saint-Martin summer [31] seldom misses beautifying the late season.

The sun came out the day after the storm that had been fatal to the country neighbors of Madame Daudièrne. Its first rays had melted the snow and the sky was almost blue; the breeze was gentle, and the Beuvron, returning from overflowing its banks, began a well-behaved entry into its bed. They got up late at Germonière and ate a family breakfast rather sadly. Each one was thinking of the gloomy events of the evening before, and they could hardly talk of anything else.

They'd had no news of Doctor Subligny; the young savage hadn't reappeared at all and the servants hadn't found any trace of the drowned victims although they had inspected the river banks for more than a league down stream from the park. All that wasn't cheerful and as a diversion, Uncle Armand had proposed to his nieces that they go for a long horseback ride. Madame Daudièrne had raised some objections. The moment seemed to be badly chosen to go galloping across the countryside watered by that accursed stream where the Vignemal couple has just found death. But her brother had pointed out to her that all the lamentations in the world wouldn't bring them back to life, that the young ladies had great need of exercise, that they weren't at related to the deceased, and that, in addition, riding was mourning. This last argument had made the lady smile and Germaine, taking that smile for consent, lost no time running to the stables to order the coachman to saddle up the three horses which made up the household cavalry. Germaine was always prepared for any kind of moving activity and if she didn't follow Monsieur Daudièrne to the hunt that was because Monsieur Daudière had always formally opposed it.

Laurence showed less enthusiasm for very active sports, but she never opposed Germaine's wishes, even less the desires expressed by Uncle Armand and she had consented with good grace to be part of the group. So it happened that about one o'clock, the two sisters, in great Amazonian dress, put their feet in the stirrups, under the somewhat worried eyes of their mother, who watched the departure from the top of the steps and who didn't spare them prudent advice.

Germaine was charming under her felt hat with wide brims, an antique Gainsborough which she had modified to fit the situation, since she never rode horseback very often, and wearing her deep blue outfit which showed off her

---

[31] Indian summer.

224

curves.

Madame Daudièrne hadn't reared her daughter for the *high life*, although she had allowed them to take lessons in a respectable riding school. She intended to marry them into the upper middle class, where she came from. She reckoned that in order to find them suitable mates, it wasn't necessary to send them prancing around the Bois de Boulogne like Americans infatuated with movement and eccentric pleasures.

Laurence had put on a certain low-crowned hat that her brother wore in the summer time on Normandy beaches and which suited her marvelously.

As for Monsieur Armand Daudièrne, he simply wore the suit he put on to go through the underbrush in his sister-in-law's woods: a round cape, a short jacket, trousers with velvet patches on the inside leg seams, and strong boots. He also wasn't given to parade equitation that used to make one shine on the Champs Elysees. He was, however, very much at home on horseback, having practiced a great deal in his youth, and he still had a very good seat in the saddle. Tall, slim and muscular, bright eyes, a full mouth of teeth, a beard with hardly any silver in it, at first sight you would have thought him forty-years-old at the most.

He rode one of the two gray mares that they hitched to Madame Daudièrne's calèche, two animals with stamina that could serve two purposes, provided they were never asked to gallop too far, since they were accustomed to a respectable and measured pace. The other one had been assigned to Laurence, who got on very well with its gentle gait and its well behaved character. But Germaine had reserved for herself a pretty brown half thoroughbred bay that her brother Alfred claimed to have trained himself and of whom he claimed miracles. To hear him tell it, this exceptional horse jumped five-feet high hedgerows without faltering and hunted twelve hours at a time without tiring.

Monsieur Daudièrne, who scarcely believed the exploits his nephew recounted, distrusted this very much touted hunter and he would have preferred to ride it himself, but the animal wasn't strong enough to carry heavy weight and Germaine wanted so much to ride it that her debonair uncle had consented to let her have it that day.

To complete this cavalcade, there should at least have been a groom in livery, but at Germonière, they didn't pique themselves with conforming to the fashions of Parisian high society, and Baptiste, the old valet, would have made a very poor figure in a groom's livery and on a farm horse.

"Please don't come back too late," said Madame Daudièrne, who was not too reassured since she had seen the younger of her daughters making the brown bay prance around pawing the ground.

"Don't worry, my dear sister-in-law, we'll be back before night fall," answered Monsieur Armand. "These little ladies are all on fire at the departure but when they've trotted an hour or two, they'll have had enough."

"We'll see about that," Germaine said under her breath.

And the little troop began to walk up the avenue which led to the Departmental road at the end of the park which the former owner had enclosed with a wall. On the opposite side, the river marked the limit of this well enclosed domain.

Monsieur Daudièrne kept to the left of the group, Germaine to the right, and Lawrence walked between her sister and her uncle.

"Where are we going ladies?" leader of the expedition asked. "It's very nice to go riding but we still must have a goal. Why don't we go as far as Arcy? We could go surprise Doctor Subligny, who might tell us some news."

"It seems to me it wouldn't be very proper to show ourselves in town today," Laurence murmured.

"Why not?"

"The misfortune which has just struck Monsieur du Pommeval is so recent that they might accuse us of indifference."

"Hum! I haven't been shown that this boy considers the accident by which he could inherit a great fortune a misfortune... But you may be right. People would be capable of saying that we're in a hurry to know if he will inherit... It would be better not to give them a subject to gossip about. However, if we're not going to Arcy, I don't see any other road to follow but the one which goes down along the Beuvron."

"You're not thinking about that, Uncle!" Germaine exclaimed. "We might just discover the bodies of those poor people. That would be a lot worse than meeting Monsieur du Pommeval. First of all, me, I'm terribly afraid of drowned people."

"I thought you weren't afraid of anything. But, all right, I agree that the prospect of finding oneself face to face with a cadaver isn't the thing to tempt you. It's not impossible that that misadventure could happen to us, because the river has gone down enormously this morning. I come back to my question: What road are we going to take? I don't have any preferences, but I don't know a great number of practical excursions in the area. This country is rocky and filled with ravines like the devil. It's very picturesque, but it's not very easy for horses and if one of ours came back lame with skin scrapped off both knees your mother would say it was my fault. I would be free from moral obligation by replacing it, but as a guide for young ladies I would no longer inspire confidence in my sister-in-law."

"If you let me direct the expedition, we'll have the most charming ride you can imagine, and I'll take responsibility for everything," Germaine said.

"*Ma foi!* Nice guarantee! Where do you intend to lead us?"

"To the Lemon Rock."

"What's that?"

"What! You've never heard of Lemon Rock since you've been living at Germonière?"

"Never, absolutely never. I know the Tertre Woods which belongs to your mother and which is excellent for woodcocks...the Bretêche forest, where I don't have permission to hunt to my great regret, but as for the Limon Rock..."

"Lemon, please. My rock doesn't at all have a ridiculous name and I'll have to get you reconciled with it. We're at the end of the avenue here. We turn to the right. I'm going to tell you the legend, because there is a legend."

"A legend! That's charming. But is it far from the house, this poetic rock?"

"A league, more or less. And the path that leads there is delightful. We're going to cross exactly the woods that are dear to you because of the woodcocks. After that we'll go into a wild gorge. There's a waterfall which flows at the bottom and enormous blocks which overhang both sides."

"You think that's pretty, you! Overhanging blocks!"

"Adorable. And that's nothing compared to the beauties of my rock. Imagine a wall of granite which rises above a curtain of green, a lacy curtain which shuts off the horizon—the Alpes or the Pyrénées in miniature. And when you climb to the end of this escarpment, you stand above all the Bretêche forest. You can even see the Duke de Bretteville's chateau. It's the most beautiful view there is for ten leagues around."

"This chateau is not much more than a pavilion, and the duke, who's too old to hunt, doesn't come there very often. It seems, however, that he's there at the moment. Monsieur du Pommeval told me so the other day. He even asked me to go see this Seigneur to ask him for authorization to shoot his deer. But that service would be a little hazardous and I won't risk it...especially since they say he's just lost his only son."

"Yes, in Tunisia. The newspapers spoke of his death. He was killed while charging at the head of his squadron. We are going to the rock, aren't we, Uncle."

"Since there's no way to go elsewhere, I give up, on condition that you won't do any foolish equestrian feats."

"I swear it. Besides, look! Ralph is behaving in an exemplary way. Since we've been gone he hasn't tried to rear or shy once. Alfred doesn't know how to control him and he'll wind up making him hard to ride. Me, I can make him do whatever I like. But here's the moment to put in my legend."

"Somebody told you about it?" asked Laurence.

"I have it from Monsieur du Pommeval. That astonishes you because he hardly talks about anything but races and jockeys. But since he saw that conversations about horses bored me, the other day he launched into more interesting stories, and here's one of them. There is, right in the middle of the Lemon Rock, a fissure which splits it from top to bottom like an enormous gash. You've already guessed that that fissure is only an opening to hell, or something approaching that. Fairies live in this granite palace and God knows what treasures they have hidden there—shovels full of diamonds, rubies, emeralds. But no one can enter there without their permission and when they're in a bad mood they unleash terrible storms on the countryside. The wind which blows across their mountain uproots trees, overturns houses..."

"And drowns people who cross rivers in boats," interrupted Uncle Armand. "By the way, Germaine, your legend is not unpublished. Fairies run throughout Brittany."

"Wait! I haven't finished. When a young girl wants to know whom she will marry, she approaches the fissure and she whispers her name. Laurence or Germaine, I suppose...and then she hears a soft voice like a heavenly voice, the voice of the fairies, which answers her: Georges, or Ernest, or Edmond. She's immediately committed. She'll fall in love with the man the fairies have named and she'll be loved by him in return, which is a very important point because it wouldn't be worth the trouble to become engaged to an ungrateful man."

"*Parbleu!* That ploy is ingenious. The aspiring lover has only to hide himself behind the rock and if he's a little bit a ventriloquist, the deed is done."

"Oh! Uncle, don't you believe in anything?"

"I believe there are some little girls silly enough to consult the oracle, but I hope you're not one of them."

"Hee! Hee! I wouldn't swear to it."

"That sounds like you. Your sister isn't the one who'd go confide her love problems to the Lemon Rock."

"Because she doesn't have any."

"Then you do have some?" the uncle asked.

"No, but I wouldn't be bored if I did have. That would give me something to do."

"Then, if I was a handsome young man, like, for example Monsieur du Pommeval, I know very well what I would do. I would hide out very near the devil's telephone and..."

"You might waste your time. Not every name pleases the fairies. But here we are in the middle of the Tertre woods. It's rather beautiful, isn't it? These tall beech trees which stand like columns of white marble above the yellowing autumn leaves! You could say: "*The sun and the rain have turned the forest to rust.* Where did I read this verse? Laurence, you should know. You know everything."

"It's by Victor Hugo," said the older sister.

"I was sure of that. Ah! If he'd seen the Lemon Rock, how many admirable verses wouldn't he have written about it! I'd have learned them by heart."

"And I don't doubt you'd recite them to us all day long," said Monsieur Daudièrne. "But at the moment you'd please me if you let me listen. It seems to me someone is walking in the woods there...very near us."

"In the woods," repeated Germaine; "yes, I heard something like branches rustling... But now I don't hear anything. We must have disturbed a deer and he's already far away."

"There aren't any deer here, unfortunately," grumbled Monsieur Daudièrne. The Bretêche forest is full of them but they never leave it. The brushy area which belongs to your mother is not extensive enough."

"Then it was a rabbit in his hiding place we disturbed and he's run off."

"I rather think it was a man."

"A poacher maybe... And who knows? The wild man Monsieur Subligny introduced us to yesterday?"

"Why would he hide? I've invited him to hunt with me."

"True, he'd be wrong to hide, because he's superb. He has, most of all, eyes like I've never seen...eyes which light up...eyes which flame. If he'd looked at me as he looked at Laurence, I would have been on fire."

"I'm safe from fire," Laurence murmured.

"And me," said Uncle Armand. "I now regret having almost made advances to this bad character. I thought about it last night, and the more I thought about the Beuvron accident, the more the Doctor's protégé seemed suspect to me. This odd fellow claims he risked his life to save our unfortunate neighbors, but nobody saw him dive and he has to be taken at his word. Now, there are huge, quite unlikely, things in the story he told us. So he claims that Madame Vignemal's body came aground at the bottom of the levee, and the body was no longer there when we arrived. Nothing proves that the gypsy didn't throw it back in the water."

"But that would be a crime," exclaimed Germaine. "And why would he have committed this crime? So Monsieur du Pommeval would inherit from our neighbors! Come now! He doesn't know Monsieur du Pom-meval...and as a consequence he has no reason to wish him well. Besides," she added, laughing, "I suppose he hasn't studied the Civil Code and he doesn't know what the... What do you call that?... Ah! The presumptions of survival."

"That's probable. But he had it in for Madame Vignemal, who had him hunted down by her guards. If I were a magistrate, instead of setting up the handsome Arthur in possession of the inheritance, I'd begin by sending the Roch Ferrer we're talking about to prison. And I'd let him stay there until he told us the truth about the ferry accident."

"That's an opinion the handsome Arthur wouldn't agree with."

"I can hardly believe this Roch is a murderer," Laurence said gently. "Your friend the Doctor wouldn't have taken an interest in him if he thought him capable of..."

"Quiet!" whispered Monsieur Daudièrne, suddenly halting his gray mare. "This time I certainly heard something and I'm sure I heard someone walking in the thicket...there...on our left. Let me look and listen."

The two girls were immediately quiet and the little troop halted in the middle of a pathway that was scarcely wide enough for the three horses to go through side by side. The underbrush which bordered this pathway was not very extensive and there were openings from place to place where there grew an abundance of grasses high enough to hide the ground, those dry grasses into which game animals gladly recede in autumn. They were undulating, gently blown about by the wind, but there was nothing to make it seem they hid a man, and the woods had again become silent.

"You were mistaken, my dear Uncle," Germaine said very softly after waiting a minute. "There's no one here but us."

"I maintain the contrary," grumbled Monsieur Daudièrne. "Somebody has been following us since we entered this little road."

"Who could be following us? Robbers? That's not believable. Nobody, so far as I know, has any interest in spying on us. We aren't conspiring about anything."

"I can't guess any more than you can the motives for this espionage, but I repeat to you that someone is following us very closely, and if this cane brake weren't so thick, I'd pass a sword blade through it. But I have another plan to catch the individual who lets himself spy on us, a plan I'll put in operation in a little while. Let's go on, Mesdemoiselles."

"I don't ask for anything better," exclaimed Germaine. "Ralph is getting impatient and if we stop every minute I soon won't be able to hold him in check."

"We'll pick up a trot a little further on. The terrain here is too bad. Ah, as for that, are you sure you haven't gotten lost while leading us to the fairies' rock. I think you've never been there before, have you?"

"No, but Monsieur Subligny described the road to follow so well to me that I don't need a guide."

"What! The doctor also got mixed up in getting you excited about this Lemon Rock? I didn't think he had a mind inclined toward poetry. Well, since I was weak enough to embark on this voyage of discovery, I'd like to go to the end of it…after I've taken care of the prowler who's dogging our footsteps. First of all, he needs to know who he's dealing with."

"Would you suppose, by chance, that it's about Laurence or me? A lover then. That would be very amusing; but among the eligible young men of Arcy, I don't know one who has the strength to run through the woods just for the pleasure of looking at us at a distance through the leaves. In any case, I'll answer for it's not being Monsieur du Pommeval."

"Why do you always make fun of him?" asked the elder sister.

"To give you an opportunity to defend him," Germaine answered gaily. "You've always been fond of the handsome Arthur."

"Be quiet little ladies and listen to me," interrupted the uncle, lowering his voice. "You see that crossroad just in front of us. There's a rather wide road there which intersects the path we're following. You're going to go in front of me and continue straight ahead. Me, I'm going to dismount and appear to be tightening the girth of my mare. Then, I'll remount and hide behind that big oak growing right at the intersection of the two roads. If this rascal who's had the audacity to follow us crosses the pathway I'll see him and I'll show him a chase which will end, I can guarantee you by overtaking the beast. If, on the contrary, he doesn't show himself, that means that he has it in only for me and I'll soon outdistance him. This gray mare is sure-footed and she's good for some gallop. You'll wait for me on the edge of that last enclosure. I'll join you there and as soon as we're out of the woods we'll take off at a speed the scoundrel can't follow. Do you understand?"

"Perfectly," Germaine said very low." But that man may have bad intentions and if he takes it into his head to attack you..."

"Í won't need anyone to hold him off. I never go out without a good revolver in my pocket. That was a habit I picked up in America. But I'll bet the affair will end differently. Don't worry about me."

Germaine was going to insist; Monsieur Daudièrne motioned her to be quiet, and suddenly raising his voice:

"*Diable!*" He shouted so as to be heard twenty feet away, "My saddle is slipping. That devil of a coachman has girthed my mare poorly. I'll have to dismount to put the cinch the girth to the right notch. Don't wait for me, ladies. I'll catch up with you later on."

The two young girls decided to obey, a little against their wishes. But when they had passed the side road they looked back more than once. They soon saw Monsieur Daudièrne remount and take a position under a tree whose trunk was wide enough to hide him.

"What an unusual idea our uncle has had," Laurence said.

"And not practical at all, that idea," continued Germaine. "If there really is a man hidden in the cane brake, that man must have guessed the reason for the clever maneuver that our bodyguard has dreamed up to throw him off the track and he won't have any trouble getting away from him. He'll just have to retrace his steps."

"Well, we're rid of his presence."

"That's too bad. I would have liked to see him."

"Not me. This strange chase is beginning to frighten me, and I'd be delighted if it ended."

"Why? It's almost an adventure and adventures are so rare! Only I don't really know what to think of this one...because somebody was following us. That can't be denied. I heard very distinctly walking on the ground cover. And it wasn't a poacher walking. A poacher would have hidden himself instead of escorting us. That's all very clear, and I'm almost tempted to believe that one of the two of us has turned the head of some handsome shepherd who takes her for a goddess."

"Always romantic ideas. You have no common sense."

"And you, you are a great deal too rational. And so I advise you to get married as soon as possible. And since we're talking about marriage...just between us...will you marry Arthur du Pommeval?"

"That's a question I've never asked myself."

"I can certainly believe it. But I believe that someone will ask it to you one of these days. Arthur has been very attentive to you lately and now that he's suddenly rich he won't be long in declaring himself."

"I'll wait until he has declared himself."

"Naturally. But you must already know how you'll answer our mother when she comes to tell you that the Vignemal heir has come to ask for your hand."

"What would you do if he asked for yours?"

"Isn't this rather Normand, the dodge you've found there to avoid telling me what you think? And aren't you secretive! Well, I want to be more open than you. I admit that if Monsieur du Pommeval preferred me, I would be very embarrassed. I don't have anything against him and I would never find such a handsome match. However, this would only be a marriage of reason and nothing more, because I don't love him. They claim that these sorts of marriages succeed better than others but I'm not anxious to make that experiment. Nevertheless, I would agree perhaps if I were pushed into it. In short, I haven't taken a position."

"Neither have I."

"Good! But you're the older. It's up to you to go first. And you'll see they'll hardly be very long in nailing you to the wall. That's why I advise you to start thinking about it. Oh! Oh! Ralph wants to run. He's clamping on his bit. It's hurting my hands to rein him in and I'm very afraid he won't be patient enough to wait for my uncle at the edge of the woods."

"We're coming to it."

"Let's hope he joins us soon. If he doesn't hurry I can't be responsible for anything. Do you see him?"

"No, he's still behind the huge oak tree. You made a mistake to ride that horse."

"Bah! If I'm having trouble with him, I'm the one who'll be stronger. And then, I would have preferred to accompany you on foot rather than to perch on the shoulder of that fat carriage horse you're riding. Spur her a little. Try to make her trot, so I'll be able to give Ralph his head."

Laurence kicked her mare with her heels, but the peaceful beast increased her gait only a little.

It must be said that the path became more and more difficult, especially for the horses. The Tertre woods isn't spaced and planted like a State forest and it covers the backside of a hill, the slope of which isn't easy to climb even for someone walking. Beyond that there's open ground but it's not less hazardous because after leaving Germonière one enters a bristly region of sheer hills furrowed with deep cuts, a true Normandy Switzerland which contrasts in the most bizarre fashion with the grassy plains of the low country.

The Lemon Rock, so praised by Germaine, is the highest point of this chain which divides water between the Seine basin and the Loire basin. And Madame Daudièrne never directed her walks in any direction but on the Arcy side which is infinitely more accessible. Her daughters finally reached the edge where Uncle Armand had told them to wait for him. They were a little surprised to see in front of them piles of rocks as far as they could see. There had been a rather wide road which went alongside the woods, but the road they had followed continued straight ahead across scattered rocks which had probably been deposited there by some antediluvian disaster. Laurence was hastening to turn the gray mare which wanted only to stand on more level ground. But Germaine was struggling with her horse. Ralph, as a half-thoroughbred didn't think he should have to obey like a simple Percheron mare. He couldn't stay in one place, he breathed with wide-open nostrils and he tried to get the bit between his teeth. Germaine pulled back with all her strength, but her arms weren't made of iron and she began to tire.

"Sister Anne, my sister Anne, don't you see anything coming?" she asked laughing. "If our dear uncle stays on guard duty back there three minutes more, Ralph's going to run away."

"Run away?" Laurence repeated, astonished.

"That means to take off...since you have to be explained to in the most used terms of sports language. I'd like to calm him down by a good gallop."

"No, please... We wouldn't be able to follow you. Besides, my uncle is coming. I hear some noise."

"Yes, under the trees. Ralph hears it too and he's going to rear up if I don't give him his head."

That noise rapidly grew louder and it wasn't the noise of a horse walking. It came from the cane brake. The branches were cracking and breaking as if they had been run through by a wild boar about to break cover. The brown bay made a frightening rear complicated by a half turn to the right, and Germaine judging it was time to give him his head or be unseated let him leave at full speed, his stomach to the ground. This was done so quickly that, frightened, Laurence, didn't see in which direction her young sister had raced. At the same instant a man left the woods and jumped into the road. The apparition was so sudden and so loud that the gray mare, the calm gray mare jumped violently.

Laurence remained in the saddle however, although she was not a very good rider, but she was so frightened she closed her eyes. When she opened them again, a man was standing in front of her, his hands placed on the reins of the mare that he was holding still by applying pressure on the bit, a man she immediately recognized. Roch Ferrer, whom she had hardly seen the night before, wasn't somebody one forgets. And Roch Ferrer, bare-headed, his hair blown by the wind, his mouth half opened, was looking at Mademoiselle Daudièrne with glowing eyes which didn't at all reassure her as to the intentions of this disturbing bohemian. She immediately understood that this encounter was one of those which had to be met with boldness.

"Turn loose of my horse's bridle," she said in the calmest tone she could manage.

Roch released the bridle but he didn't step back a foot.

"You've been following us since we entered the woods," said Laurence. "Why are you following us?"

"You were the one I was following. And I was following you to look at you. I follow you every time you go out."

"If I had been aware of that earlier..."

"You would have forbidden me to follow you. I know that. That's why I hid myself."

"But I'm forbidding you to do so now,...and I warn you that Monsieur Daudièrne, my uncle, will be here in a minute."

"I've just escaped from him. I'll still escape from him. But before I run away, I must talk to you."

Laurence trembled. She was alone with this young savage, whose excited behavior didn't promise anything good. Uncle Armand wasn't on the way and Germaine, on a runaway horse, had disappeared. She must already be far away because Ralph's rapid gallop could no longer be heard. Laurence remained then at the mercy of Doctor Subligny's protégé and the information that the good Doctor had given her wasn't of the kind that would calm her. Whether or not he had risked his life to save the Vignemal couple, Roch was none the less a prowler with neither house nor home, a man in revolt against society's laws, who gave in only to his passions. This wasn't the time to lose one's head, and the courageous girl was calm enough to ask coldly:

"If you want to speak to me, why not come to Germonière?"

"Because at Germonière I can't speak to you freely. Your mother, your sister, or your uncle would be there."

"What do you have to say to me that they couldn't hear?

"I have to tell you that I am in love with you," the gypsy answered boldly.

That impudent declaration made Mademoiselle Daudièrne blush and anger drove back fear. It seemed to her monstrously ridiculous that this barefoot person allowed himself to use such language to her and her feminine instinct told her at the same time that the danger wasn't immediate because she was dealing with a sentimental poacher.

"You...in love with me! You!" she exclaimed, throwing Roch a disdainful look.

"Madly," he murmured without lowering his eyes.

"You would have to have gone mad to dare to speak to me in this way. What is there in common between you and me, I ask you? By what right do you insult me? You'll be sorry about this, I swear to you."

"No, because I'm not free not to love you and I ask you nothing but to listen to me. After you've heard me to the end you'll never see me again if you forbid me to show myself to you. But I have to tell you everything. I've looked for an opportunity to see you alone for three years."

"Three years! What is this silly joke? I saw you yesterday for the first time."

"Me, I've seen you every day."

"Even when I was living in Paris?" Laurence asked ironically.

"No, when you lived in Paris, I didn't live. But here I live by you and for you. If you didn't spend the summer and the fall at Germonière, I would have left the country a long time ago."

"I'm very obliged to you for having stayed here," Laurence said with a disdainful smile, "but I would be even more grateful if you told me what you expect to gain by persecuting me like this. "

"Nothing."

"What do you want of me then?"

"I want to obey you as a dog obeys his master."

"I don't know what to do with your obedience, and I see that you're more mad than I thought. Let's leave it there, please…and let me go join my uncle, who's not far away, I warn you."

"He won't find me here, because I have nothing more to say to you. You know now that you can do whatever you like with me as you would a slave. Whatever you command me to do, I'll do it…even if you were to command me to kill someone."

"That's a commitment I'd never hold you to," said Laurence, still joking. "I don't wish anyone's death."

"If you wished for mine, you'd find me ready to die. My life is yours. I risked it yesterday to spare you sorrow."

"For me!"

"I detested the Vignemals but I knew they had only crossed the river to pay you a visit at Germonière. If I hadn't thought that their death would cause you pain, I would not have tried to save them."

This time, Mademoiselle Daudièrne, although she had regained complete control of herself, didn't find an immediate reply. The unusual claim that Roch had just uttered surprised her very much and touched her a little.

"You'd have been better advised to have prevented them from getting into the boat, since you were there when they embarked."

"That's true. I thought about you too late."

That answer startled the young girl and made her think differently. The Beuvron accident appeared to her in a new light and so did Roch. But she didn't have time to think about what she had just learned. Her uncle was coming at a trot down the path she had followed with her sister. She couldn't see him because she had turned left on leaving the woods but she heard the noise of his horse's hoofs striking the pebbles.

"Leave," Laurence said quickly. "I don't want Monsieur Daudièrne to find you here."

"I'm going," murmured the gypsy, who hadn't stopped devouring her with his eyes. "I'm going and I'll only come back when you call me. When you have an order to give me put a light near your window in the evening and come to the Beuvron levee…walk along it to the place where the cane brake ends."

"How do you know where my window is?" Laurence asked, without letting it appear that she had taken notice of the rendezvous that Roch had permitted himself to set up.

"It was there I saw you for the first time three years ago. And since that time I've spent many nights watching it."

The noise was coming closer. And in a few seconds Uncle Armand was going to emerge from the narrow road which cuts the Tertre road into two equal parts. Roch seized one of the young girl's gloved hands, the hand which held her riding whip, and covered it with kisses before she could think about pulling it away. He jumped with one leap to the other side of the ditch and disappeared in the thick cane brake. It was just in time. Monsieur Daudièrne, was spurring his gray mare, which the rapid climb had greatly exhausted, and yelling at the top of his lungs:

"The scoundrel has gotten away. He saw that I was watching out for him beside the road and he swerved to throw me off the track. Let him go get himself hanged somewhere else. I'm not going to chase after him. It's enough for me that he doesn't prowl around after us. It doesn't matter. I'll have to make our servants make rounds searching for him. Your mother would be very wrong to allow suspicious unknown people to prowl around her land and so near her house. They'll wind up coming at night into the park. But what's wrong? You're absolutely white."

Laurence was probably about to tell about the encounter and the scene which she'd just undergone, but her uncle added:

"And Germaine? What's become of her?"

It was very natural that she should first answer that question and following that she thought she could dispense with answering the real cause for her pallor.

"Germaine's horse has run away with her," she murmured. "That devilish animal was too impatient to wait. She couldn't hold him back and he dashed off a mile a minute."

"Ah! The Devil! Your sister rides well and she's not afraid... But who knows where Ralph might've taken her? This delightful country if full of sheer drop-offs. I'm surprised that you stayed calmly here while Germaine was running a real danger."

"My mare isn't up to matching Ralph's speed."

"Neither is mine, unfortunately. And I should've foreseen what has just happened. But, then, if we can't gallop, we can trot and we'll finally catch up with that foolish girl who imagines you can control a half thoroughbred as you do a working horse. I hope she's stayed on and that Ralph calmed down two or three kilometers from here. In cases like this the best thing to do is to let the horse run until he's had enough. The question is to find out which direction he took."

"That happened so quickly and I was so upset I didn't see anything. However, it seems to me he ran down that road...on the right."

"It's certain he didn't go back into the woods. I would've met him. And it seems to me impossible that he climbed this rocky path which goes up that steep bluff there in front of us. Having thought about it, I think we have only to follow the Departmental road which goes around the Tertre woods. Your sister has already tried it and I think she'll have common sense enough to go back to Germonière by way of the levee which begins at the park grille. She won't see her Lemon Rock today. That'll be her punishment. But if her mother suspected what had happened, she would be terribly upset and I absolutely insist on taking Germaine back to her. Let's go, Laurence. Give the gray mare a good swat with your whip and let's be off. This entire charming ride has all been spent chasing people, but I'd prefer running after my niece than after that scoundrel who's made so much fun of me. I hope we won't miss her and I can scold her at my convenience."

Uncle Armand was flattering himself. It was written that day, nothing would succeed for him. While he was dashing down with Laurence the only practical road which presented itself, Germaine, in spite of herself was galloping across obstacles before which the most intrepid fox hunters of old England would have recoiled. At the moment she felt herself powerless to dominate Ralph. She still possessed all her logic and she understood that it was necessary at any price to prevent her horse taking a road where there was nothing to stop him. She knew that road which went down by very sharp and very rapid turns right to the edge of the river. She also understood the devilish brown bay that her extravagant brother had probably bought expressively to show off by bravely risking his skin before the handsome Arcy Messieurs. She knew this horse jumped to perfection, that he had stamina and speed, but he was hard to control, and above all, very inclined to run away at the first pretext that presented itself. He had more than once almost broken Alfred's shoulder. He had confided these misadventures only to Germaine and this sly girl who longed to ride this dangerous animal had been very careful not to speak of his faults. She had even sworn to her mother and her uncle that Ralph was as gentle as a lamb and she had gotten what she wanted.

She was beginning to reflect on the consequences of her foolhardiness, but she was resolved to fight as much as she could and the course she had immediately taken was assuredly the best. Ralph, held in check by the nervous hands of that twenty-year-old child, hadn't been able to turn right and he had jumped into a cross road, or rather she had jumped him there, and from that side the ascent was so steep that he must inevitably calm down before long. For the imprudent Germaine it was only a question of not letting herself be thrown off by the horse shying and she was hoping to succeed. Everything went well at the beginning of that mad race.

Ralph was keeping up a furious gallop but it was evident that he couldn't keep up that speed very long. However much a horse bolts, he runs out of breath quickly when he climbs a steep slope. Unfortunately that slope was only the first step in a staircase cut out in the rock by nature. That entire region seemed to have been overturned in the past by volcanic eruptions. At the edge of the Tertre woods there began a series of escarpments stacked one above the other cut at certain places by deep depressions in the terrain.

When Ralph had jumped the first stepping stone, Germaine saw a veritable abyss opening at her feet. The road continued on the other side of the hill; the incline formed a forty-five degree angle with the horizon. The enraged brown bay, that had already gotten his breath back, dashed forward blindly. Only then did Germaine understand the danger she was running. Her life depended on a false step by Ralph. If he made a misstep on one of the round stones which littered the path, the young girl, violently thrown from the saddle, was going to crush her head against a rock. She instinctively closed her eyes because she hadn't been able to ward off a first impression of fright. But she didn't turn loose of the reins and she didn't at all give up, as many riders better than she would have done in a similar situation.

Germaine had heart, in all the meanings of the word. She was loving, compassionate, sensitive, as they said under the Directorate. She had charm, gaiety, the silliness of her age, but she could have been able to show more serious qualities that no one knew she had and that she didn't herself know. There was a virile quality in that joyous and tender nature. If she had remained a child in her character that was because there hadn't been an opportunity to prove what she was worth. For a young girl that opportunity is love and she could only speak about that sentiment by hearsay. She didn't really have a very clear idea about it, having been brought up by a mother steeped in the respectable principles of the honest middle class, which didn't understand the usefulness of a preventive education. They had willingly omitted warning her of the dangers a woman runs in life and they had let her believe that marriage was only a platonic association of convenience and interests, a port where it was necessary to land because it was the custom. In this system it's never a question of passions which upset young hearts. It's understood that a well-bred girl must not think of pleasing men who are not in a situation to marry her and she must never be tempted to place her affections elsewhere.

Germaine had reserved her own and didn't rebel against the ideas inculcated in her since her childhood. The future they told her about seemed acceptable to her and she had resigned herself in advance to marrying acceptably but she wasn't in any hurry to do so. The life she was leading didn't weigh heavily on her at all. Her mother left her completely free to do as she liked. She took advantage of that permission only to follow innocent pleasures: she adored dancing, music, dressing up; to sum it up in one word: society. It could be believed she would never adore anything else. Her sentimental wishes came out in words. It sometimes happened that she burst out in words which came out like

238

rockets, which very much amused Uncle Armand. She said: "I would like to fall in love," as she would have said: "I would like to see Niagara Falls." And a minute later she had forgotten it. But she also calmed down by violent exercise. She was never happy except at Germonière where she could wear herself out running in the park, while her sister sketched under her mother's eyes. Horseback riding days were her holidays.

She had been plotting to ride Ralph for three months and she had not yet regretted her lack of caution. Her vanity was involved and she didn't want to be afraid. The danger was not any the less great because of that and it took an exceptional courage to look it in the face without falling apart. Ralph had picked up his furious speed and was descending at full speed the terrifying slope of a path parallel and very near to a sheer drop into a ravine. It was a miracle he hadn't rolled down this precipice because the soil was covered with pebbles which gave way under his feet and a slip would have been mortal.

Germaine, having recovered from her fright, was thinking of nothing but controlling and guiding him. Her body leaning backward, her two hands clutching the reins, she remained firm in the saddle and she was beginning to hope she would get herself out of that adventure successfully.

The slope was climbed without accident, but Ralph didn't slow down his speed. The effort he'd made to climb the opposite back side had excited him more rather than calmed him. Where and when would this crazed brown bay stop? It was impossible to foresee, and Germaine put herself in the hands of God, who calms storms after having unleashed them.

It didn't displease her to be carried to an unknown end. It was a new sensation for her which wasn't without charm. She forgot the danger she was running and her imagination flew toward dream-land. She imagined she was going to go through a dark forest and suddenly see appear a mysterious chateau. The door would open before her, a chateau inhabited by the Prince Charming of fairy tales. It seemed to her that until that time she hadn't lived and that unknown horizons were opening before her. The wind whipping her cheeks revealed ideas sleeping at the bottom of her young heart. She understood the poetry of danger. She felt sorry for her sister Laurence, who was very satisfied with a calm horse. Movement made her drunk. She was almost at the point of hoping that this mad ride would never end. She wanted to use her riding whip on Ralph to excite him even more and to push him to the point that he fell, even if his fall crushed her.

A tragic end was only too much to be feared because there was no longer any reason for the devilish horse to stop. The scarcely visible path on which he galloped ascended, descended. Nothing stopped him. Ralph still went at breakneck speed. And if, by chance, at some turn in the path, he found himself in front of some precipice he jumped so that he couldn't miss clearing it.

Germaine was in the clouds. She no longer thought about admiring the site which was becoming savage and grandiose. She heard the murmur of a stream at the bottom of a ravine but she no longer saw it. It had disappeared in the inextricably interlaced thorny underbrush. In the distance loomed enormous blocks of granite which seemed to have been thrown down one on top of the other by the hand of a Titan. Tall pines twisted by the wind contrasted like black stains with the grey background. On the right, on the left, straight ahead, behind, the view was blocked by escarpments. It seemed as if there was no way out of that gorge and as if the world ended there.

So then, after having jumped a last summit at a galloping charge, Germaine came out on a level plateau. She wondered for an instant if she was still dreaming. No more stone wall on her left, no abyss on her right. And in front of her a prairie extended right up to an isolated rock which rose up three hundred meters above the crest she had just reached. She didn't have to direct Ralph to that obstacle which couldn't be jumped. It wasn't difficult because a runaway horse always goes in a straight line. Besides, the animal was beginning to tire out. He had just finished a race which would have exhausted an Arab stallion. And Germaine could stop reining him in without running any risk. By a superabundance of good luck that narrow moor rose by a gentle slope which this bizarre rock crowned as if placed there as a goal. Ralph had still been crossing the moor at a gallop, but when he reached the top he was winded, and after a last effort he stopped short.

Germaine didn't waste a second to jump to the ground and she had the presence of mind not to drop the reins in case the brown bay took a notion to run away. That was a useless precaution because he was in no state to abuse his freedom. He couldn't do anything more and he was trembling all over. You might have said he was sorry for his madness and by looking sadly at the young girl he seemed to be asking her forgiveness. Germaine would gladly have beaten him but she was too happy to have gotten out of that adventure safe and sound without thinking of applying this merited punishment. She also told herself that the first wrongs were her own fault. She should have foreseen that Ralph, never having been ridden by a woman, would try to get free as soon as he didn't have two calm mares on either side of him. Germaine, who had a good soul and who never feared to do things right, snatched up a large handful of ferns and began to rub him down with as much zeal and skill as a stable man would have been able to. When she had finished, she spoke to him.

"Do you understand, bad beast, that you almost broke my neck?" she said, caressing him with her small hand. "I'll tell your master about your wild behavior and he'll make you rue the day." The horse answered with a neigh of thanks which made her smile.

"And now," she continued, "how are we going to get back to the house, you big fool? I'm not going to be so silly as to get back on your shoulders.

You don't inspire me with the least confidence in you any longer. I'd really like to leave you in this desert. The wolves will eat you and you can't fly off it. All right! Come on! I'm going to begin by staking you out like a stubborn nag. Ralph probably understood this language because he let himself be led gently by the bridle which Germaine attached firmly to the trunk of a wild gorse bush.

"Now," she murmured, "the question is to decide what I'm going to do. I don't have any desire to sleep here and I don't want to abandon Ralph. Monsieur my brother would make a nice scene if I lost his half thoroughbred. So I must lead my horse by the muzzle back to Germonière. That's not easy. Without counting on the fact that I'm not very sure of how to find the way back. I've forgotten to sow the path with little pebbles like Petit Poucet. I was so busy trying to avoid the precipices I didn't see which way I was going. I don't know at all where I am."

She started to look around her and she soon recognized that the ravine she had skirted so near was not very far from the big rock that dominated the moor. This ravine made a bend at almost a right angle and extended well beyond the last summit she had climbed.

"*Impossible to get out by that way*," Germaine thought.

Her charming face clouded but cleared up very quickly.

"I'm wrong to torment myself. Laurence saw Ralph run away. She'll have told my uncle about this serious situation and they're on the way to search for me. I have only to wait for them. I'll be in for a sermon. But God knows when they'll arrive. The two Percherons could only take tiny steps over these devilish roads. I'll have a lot of time to contemplate the landscape. *Ma foi,* it's worth the trouble. I've never seen anything like it. That gray rock which menaces the sky looks like a fortress. It has everything: towers, battlements, everything, even to a long crack which forms a groove from top to bottom. Could that be…? But, of course, that crack, that's the fairies air hole…Ralph didn't have the wrong idea. He's led me to the Lemon Rock. It's really as I imagined it."

It didn't take anything more to change the direction of her thoughts. She was seized with a mad desire to complete that accidental excursion by a climb and to verify the legend accredited in the region. Everything invited her to attempt the trial. The access to the famous rock wasn't very difficult. It rose at the top of a bank that Germaine was strong enough to climb. Ralph was hanging his head humbly low and wasn't asking for anything but not to budge any more. There was no sound and that was certainly the proof that no one had come to consult the oracle that day.

"I want to make the pilgrimage right to the end," she exclaimed. "And my uncle would keep me from it if I waited on this moor. He'll be angry when he sees me up there, but I'll explain to him that I climbed up there just to see if he was coming to my aid. I'll only be half-way lying because once I'm perched on that observatory, I'm very sure I'll be able to see him in the distance riding alongside Laurence. Too bad! I'm going to climb."

And without any more thought, Mademoiselle Daudièrne, lifting her Amazonian skirt with one hand, rushed bravely forward to the assault of the palace of the fairies who arranged the marriages of young girls daring enough to come question them. It took a quarter of an hour. She was as agile and skillful as a young goat and the brambles didn't discourage her. Holding back the gorse bushes, she often got her dress caught and stuck herself. But she only laughed about it and her perseverance paid off. Hardly had she reached the base of the rock when she saw before her a marvelous panorama. At her feet there extended as far as she could see an immense forest of stately oaks above which rose the towers of a chateau. Her dream had become reality, the dream she'd had while Ralph was running away with her.

"That's the Bretêche forest and the chateau of the Duke of Bretteville," she whispered. "I didn't think I was so near it. Our park would make only a sorry show beside these tall stately trees. If they were mine, I'd walk through them night and day. But there you are! They aren't mine and the old duke would never think to ask for my hand. Bah! Everything is for the best because I don't want him, even with his forest. I want a young husband…whether he's rich or poor, that's all the same to me, provided I like him. But I wouldn't be upset to know his name…if the fairies deign to tell it to me. I'm not counting on it, but I don't risk anything asking them what it is. However," she said laughing, "If they decide to tell me: *Arthur*, I believe I'll really be trapped because I'm hardly interested in marrying the handsome Arthur du Pommeval."

Germaine interrupted her monologue to discover if she could see her uncle and her sister coming up. But turning back toward the moor where she had left Ralph, she saw that the closest ridge was high enough to hide the stepping stone path she had followed. From that direction the horizon was limited and she had to give up hope of seeing the two gray mares. This was a disappointment and Mademoiselle Daudièrne became concerned. She started to be worried about the situation in which her thoughtlessness had thrown her. She had never found herself alone, far from all habitation, out of the range of all human help and this debut into the adventurous life which had so seduced her worried her a little. The silence weighed heavily on her. She would have liked to hear a bird sing, but birds weren't singing in that desert.

"They're afraid of waking the fairies," Germaine said to herself. "I'll be more courageous than they are because I don't want to have come here for nothing. But I don't want to wait here. If night comes on before I know it…I'll never see Germonière again. And the daylight is beginning to fade."

Daylight hadn't yet fallen, but the sky was becoming cloudy and fog was rising from the depth of the humid valleys.

"*Right now you'd think you were in Scotland*," she murmured. "*A grey sky, rocks, moors. Macbeth's witches would like it here.*"

She had reached the crack in the rock. Germaine had to take only one step to put her hand on it, but she hesitated. By dint of dreaming about the legend, she had wound up half-way believing it. Besides, the aspect of that unusual fissure was such as to inspire a young girl with superstitious fears. The rock seemed to have been split from the top to the base by the saber of a giant, and the cut was large enough for a man to go through but its depth couldn't be seen.

It needed only a little imagination to fancy that this corridor lead to a cavern inhabited by supernatural beings.

Germaine was ashamed of being afraid and approached the opening. She was not a little surprised to find placed there on a ledge inside the rock dried bouquets of flowers, faded ribbons, gold plated rings, and little wooden crosses. Evidently all these stray remnants had been left there by naïve consultants who thought to draw the protection of the fairies to them or who were anxious to thank them for having granted their wishes. The oracle was much patronized and it could be concluded that he had not deceived those who had faith in him. Assuredly, Mademoiselle Daudièrne lacked that faith but curiosity took its place. For nothing in the world would she have missed pushing childishness right to the point of throwing out her first name into the subterranean echoes. She put her head forward into the air hole and she shouted very distinctly:

"Germaine!"

A burst of cold air struck her in the face and made her draw back. She wondered where that cold breath could have come from and she was already laughing at the silly idea that had pushed her to speak to rocks when a sonorous voice answered her:

"Roger!"

That unexpected reply cut short her gaiety and frightened even more than it startled her.

The voice had nothing infernal to it. It was a well timbre and very masculine voice. Germaine was not so silly nor so fearful as to believe for one instant that she had just entered into conversation with a malicious spirit. Evidently, a man was there, in flesh and blood, a man who had thought it amusing to reply to the imprudent request thrown out by a girl aspiring to an approaching marriage. And that farce in rather doubtful taste was not reassuring to Mademoiselle Daudièrne as to the intentions of this false prophet. So, she thought first of all about fleeing but she didn't have time to avoid the encounter.

The unknown man who had just given the reply showed himself suddenly and that apparition had nothing terrifying about it. It was a tall young man, elegantly turned out and correctly dressed, although he didn't look at all like those handsome fellows that you see represented in the fashionable pictures used by tailors. He was in hunting dress but he wasn't carrying a gun and as soon as he saw Germaine he politely took off his cap to greet her. She then saw that he had close-cropped hair, a long blond mustache, silky and fine, a complexion tanned by life in the open air, and a forehead marked by a scar which didn't spoil that military and likeable face. Evidently he hadn't expected to find a young girl dressed like an Amazon beyond the Lemon Rock, since he seemed as astonished as Germaine. But his embarrassment wasn't clumsiness.

"Forgive me, Mademoiselle, for having frightened you," he exclaimed. "I was there on the other side of the rock and I couldn't resist the temptation to answer. I thought I was dealing with a credulous peasant and I was amusing myself by acting like a sorcier. I was greatly mistaken and I beg you to forget my involuntary mistake."

This was said in a tone of good fellowship and with an accent of frankness which reassured Germaine.

"I admit I was afraid but I would be bad-mannered to hold it against you because I gave way to a silly fantasy in questioning the oracle and merited someone make fun of me. It's the legend that's at fault."

"Since you know it, Mademoiselle, I don't have to go into explanations which would make you smile. It's enough for me to know that you won't accuse me of having premeditated a scene of selfish comedy. I couldn't guess when I left Bretteville that I would meet you here."

"You live in the Bretteville chateau?" Germaine asked quickly.

"Just for a few days and I'm only passing through."

"The Duke is your relative, probably?"

"No, Mademoiselle, I was the comrade and the friend of his son, who was killed at my side in Tunisia."

"You're an officer, Monsieur?"

"Just barely. I was promoted to First Lieutenant three months ago and it seems to me that I'm still a sergeant. You could have seen it a while ago Mademoiselle, because in honor of my new epaulette I should have forbidden myself that barracks joke. Would you excuse me now if I allow myself to ask by what happy circumstance I owe the honor of introducing myself...after an unhoped-for meeting?"

Germaine understood that it was now time to give her name and even to explain her presence at the foot of the Lemon Rock without running the risk of being taken for what she was not.

"I live very near here, at Germonière."

"The property that was bought ten years ago by Madame Daudièrne?"

"You know that?" Germaine exclaimed, very astonished.

"I was born in this region, Mademoiselle. It's true I left it when I was very young and I haven't been back for a long time. But I was still here when Germonière became the property of..."

"Of my mother, Monsieur. We've been living there since the beginning of the summer and nevertheless I've never come here. We undertook this excursion today, my uncle, my sister and I. Unfortunately, Ralph ran away and dragged me right to this rock which stopped him."

"By what road, *Grand Dieu!* On this side there's only a path scarcely usable for goats. And your horse didn't fall with you in the ravine you skirted?"

"No, because here I am," said Germaine smiling. "I tethered him down there on the moor and nothing's broken. However, that race exhausted him and I'm afraid he's in no state to take me back to the house. So I've decided to wait for my uncle and sister, who are undoubtedly looking for me and won't be long in joining me."

Germaine stressed these last words. She was anxious to state that she had not left alone and that someone was coming to help her.

"I wouldn't presume, Mademoiselle, to dissuade you from waiting for them," said the young man, who understood what this speech meant. "But I'm afraid you'll wait for them a very long time. Your uncle surely wouldn't be foolish enough to expose himself to the dangers that you've confronted."

"Oh! Certainly in spite of myself." Germaine said laughing. "It was Ralph who faced them. He has good blood and he's very sure of himself."

"There's a great deal easier but a great deal longer road to get to the Lemon Rock. Your uncle will have taken it."

"I don't think he knows about it."

"However that may be, Mademoiselle, I swear to you that you'd be risking your life if you returned by the road you took. And I add that to stay here would be unwise. I see certain signs that the weather is going to change. Night comes on early in this season, and if you're surprised outside in one of those storms which, our country people claim, come out of the caves in this rock, you'll have a great deal of trouble getting back to Germonière."

"Then what should I do?" asked Germaine, somewhat frightened.

She sensed that the unknown man was telling the truth but she also suspected that he might have something else in mind. She raised her eyes and she was reassured in looking at him. Reliability was painted on his face. He had doubtlessly guessed that she was afraid because he said to her gently:

"You'd be wrong not to trust me, Mademoiselle. I'm only thinking of helping you out of a difficult situation. I would limit myself to pointing out to you the road you must follow to get back without an accident if I thought you wouldn't get lost. But that road forks several times and you might choose the wrong one. I dare then offer to act as your guide. I commit myself on my honor to leave you as soon as my presence is no longer useful to you."

"I thank you, monsieur," stammered Germaine, moved and still more perplexed. But I...I can't leave my horse."

"No, certainly not. And I certainly hope he'll carry you all the way to Germonière. The road which runs along side the edge of the Bretteville forest is excellent. And if you'll follow my advice, you'll ride at a walk. I'll escort you on foot, and if it's necessary I'll help you control Ralph."

"You know the name of my horse!"

"You told it to me a while ago, Mademoiselle, and I can see from here that Ralph has good blood," said the young man, pointing to the indefatigable brown bay that was already snorting and pawing the ground with his foot. All he wanted to do was to get in motion.

"Yes, he's a brave beast and I'm very content because I was afraid of having foundered him. I would be less satisfied if I thought he was going to run away with me again," Germaine added gaily.

"I'd be there to keep him from doing it and I'm going to begin by bringing him here," said the young man, starting toward the slope at the bottom of which Ralph was tethered. He was already far away before Mademoiselle Daudièrne thought to raise new objections against the arrangement he had just proposed. She remained alone near the enchanted rock, somewhat embarrassed and almost worried about the turn that adventure had taken. It had become a little more romantic than she would have hoped, but deep down she was very happy because the weather was menacing and the day was far along.

"*After all*," she thought, "*it wouldn't be my fault if I returned escorted by a cavalier I met. My uncle and my sister have evidently lost trace of me. I really can't push virtue to the point of spending the night on these summits. Besides, I'm dealing with a well born and well brought up man. The Duke de Brettsville's guest can only belong to the best society. I'll introduce him to my mother when we arrive and that will be the end of it. My uncle will probably owe me thanks, because I will have furnished him a pretext to introduce himself at the chateau and the old Duke will invite him to hunt in his forest.*"

Germaine wasn't admitting to herself that the young officer had made a strong impression on her. But that impression had something to do with the decision she had just made.

He returned, leading by the bridle Ralph that had followed him without any trouble. Horses have sure instincts and they recognize right off those who are their friends.

"Now that I've examined him close up," said the obliging stranger, "I can answer, Mademoiselle, for his not stumbling on the road and that he won't run away either. His legs are excellent and fatigue has calmed him. He's in perfect condition to do what you want him to do today. I think that tomorrow he'll need rest and care."

"Oh! I'll see that he gets good treatment," interrupted Mademoiselle Daudièrne. "He belongs to my brother but I already love him as if he belonged to me since he...since he valiantly got me out of a bad spot."

Germaine also had managed to get out of the embarrassment into which a thoughtless answer had thrown her because she knew that it was also thanks to Ralph that she'd been led to the Lemon Rock. She would have been embarrassed to show all of her thoughts.

The young man perhaps understood because he was discreet enough not to let anything appear and he spoke again with a brisk completely military air.

"Since you've been willing, Mademoiselle, to put me in command, I would like you, please, to go down on foot this slope which leads to the main road. It wouldn't be safe to go down it on horseback. I'll lead Ralph by his bridle to the bottom of the slope."

He arranged the means and the path of the expedition as if this two- person trip had been something agreed to, and even though Germaine had not yet said anything, he took her silence for tacit consent. And he wasn't wrong.

"You're going to find me very curious," she said with embarrassment, "but

I'd like to know how you were able to hear my name. I spoke so low!"

"That's very simple, Mademoiselle. The hollow into which you pronounced your charming name isn't very deep, but it's cut at a right angle by a crack which opens onto one of the other sides of the rock. I was leaning exactly on the lateral fissure. You couldn't see me...I couldn't see you either...and I took advantage of the situation to answer as one of the country boys answer when they're spying on one of their girl friends. I should now introduce myself in a more serious...and more proper...fashion. Roger Pontac, First Lieutenant of the 9th Hussards."

"Roger Pontac!" Germaine repeated.

"Yes, Mademoiselle. My name surely could hardly interest you and doesn't mean anything to you because I don't have the honor to know you."

"It seems to me I've heard it pronounced recently."

"I'd be very proud not to be completely unknown to you, but I doubt that there's anyone in this region who still remembers me, and if I told you my name, it was to be polite. I should even have done that at first, but you're not an English woman. I hope you'll excuse me."

"I'll excuse you even better because you started by introducing yourself...half-way," the young girl said, laughing. "Before I saw you, I already knew your name was Roger. And at the foot of the Lemon Rock, I don't have the right to require anything more."

"You remind me, Mademoiselle, that I've been unmannerly, and I'm afraid you'll never think better of me."

"Oh! I don't hold that against you at all...and the proof is that I'm putting myself in your care to take me back to the house."

"This road is going to take us there, Mademoiselle, and you can already see it hardly resembles the terrible trails you came over."

Ralph, lead by Lieutenant Pontac, had just set foot on a tarmac road that Mademoiselle Daudiere hadn't seen when searching the horizon from the top of the hill that served as a base for the rock of the fairies. This road, kept up at the expense of the Department, went along side the Bretêche forest and after a great detour came back to the edge of the Tertre woods. The engineer who designed it had evidently proposed to avoid the construction of a bridge to cross the ravine that Germaine had skirted at great peril to her life. As the bird flies, Germonière wasn't far from the Lemon Rock but it took an hour to get back by a passable road.

"We have no time to lose because the sky is clouding over more and more," said the young officer. "Allow me, Mademoiselle, to help you back into the saddle."

Mademoiselle Daudièrne had gone too far to refuse. She put her small foot in the hand that Monsieur Roger Pontac held out to her without having to be begged. Ralph raised his head and made ready as soon as he felt the pull of the reins, but he made no effort to recommence the madness that had almost cost

Germaine so dear. You would have said the intelligent animal was trying to make her understand that he was still in a state to carry her but he would obey her docilely.

"Really, Monsieur," she said, "I'm very sorry to give you so much trouble. My horse has a very long stride and you're going to tire yourself out following him."

"Oh! Don't be afraid of that, Mademoiselle. I've always served in the Calvary, but my childhood was spent running through our woods and mountains. I would still easily do ten leagues to have the happiness to escort you."

"Actually," murmured Germaine without noting this warm compliment, "you told me you were from the province where we spend the summer…from Arcy, undoubtedly?"

"No, Mademoiselle. I was born on a farm which belongs to the Brettevilles…a farm where my father was the farmer. I was twelve-years-old when they put me in a secondary school in Paris."

Germaine wasn't expecting to learn that her cavalier was the son of a peasant, because he had the appearance and the manners of a gentleman. But that discovery didn't bother her at all. She would almost have been annoyed if he were noble. Where did she get this feeling? That's what she hadn't yet disentangled. Perhaps she thought her mother and her uncle would willingly welcome a well-bred boy who had earned his promotion by his own merit while they would have thought themselves obligated to be reserved with someone representing the privileged class. Madame Daudièrne insisted on staying in her social class and Uncle Armand didn't seek out petty country gentlemen. If he accepted Monsieur du Pommeval, that was because the handsome Arthur was at bottom only a bourgeois whose father had taken the name of a piece of land.

"You see, Mademoiselle, that Ralph isn't outdistancing me," Lieutenant Pontac continued gaily. "That's the result of having learned to use your legs while very young. Really, I'd prefer to accompany you on horseback but I'm very happy to stay a good walker since you're allowing me to serve you as guide."

"And I, Monsieur," Germaine said quickly, "I certainly hope we'll now have the pleasure of seeing you often at Germonière. Since you're living at the Bretteville chateau, we're neighbors and my mother will be very anxious to thank you."

"Oh! Mademoiselle, it's I who should thank you for having entrusted yourself to me."

"You will come, won't you?" asked the young girl, astonished at that evasive reply.

"I don't dare agree to that," said Roger Pontac, visibly embarrassed.

"Why?"

"But…I'm going back to my regiment, which is in Tunisia. I got a furlough for a month and I have so little time left."

"You still have some days."

"And then…I promised myself not to visit anyone. I left ten years ago and no one thinks about me any more. If I show myself, many people will recognize me. They will know that I'm at the Bretteville chateau and they'll blame me for not leaving it."

"Is it so important to you not to displease the inhabitants of Arcy?"

"I'm indifferent to their opinion. But I still have relatives…not in the town, that's true, relatives I don't want to see and that I don't want to offend either. That's why I intend to remain incognito and I can do so only by staying at the Duke's house. His servants came from Paris with him and they don't know I'm from the region."

"Ours come from Paris also and I don't believe your compatriots spy on visitors who come to Germonière."

"Absolutely not. But the relations I told you about are your neighbors."

"Really?"

"The closest neighbors there are. Le Fougéray is two kilometers away from your mother's dwelling."

"Le Fougéray! But that's Madame Vignemal's chateau!"

"Precisely, Mademoiselle, and Madame Vignemal is my cousin."

"Ah! *Mon Dieu!*" Germaine exclaimed, much moved and still more troubled.

"That astonishes you, Mademoiselle," Pontac said, smiling. "And there's something there to astonish you, because Madame Vignemal is very rich and I have only my army pay. But it's precisely because I have nothing that I don't desire to renew my connections with her. We quarreled with each other in the past and I think she believes me dead. If I tried to get back in her good graces, I'd be accused of coveting her inheritance, which I scarcely think about. I don't care to give rise to unjust suspicions."

Germaine had on her lips the sad news it was only up to her to tell Lieutenant Pontac and she didn't dare speak. How could you tell this young man that his relative had just perished, the victim of an accident, and that his relative, ill-disposed toward her kin, had left all her fortune to her husband?

"What a sad memory of our encounter he'll keep if I make myself the messenger of bad news!" she thought. *"No. No, I won't tell him Madame Vignemal is dead and that she's disinherited him. He'll know it only too soon because the news of a catastrophe like that one will finally get as far as Monsieur de Bretteville's chateau."*

"It will cost me, I swear to you, not to see you again," Roger continued in a voice betraying strong emotion, "but I'll never forget I saw you and I won't say that I'll never go back to the Lemon Rock."

"Me, I can't answer that you'll never see me again," murmured Mademoiselle Daudièrne. "I'll certainly have to tell my adventures and God knows when they'll let me get on a horse again. Above all, they'll want to know why you stay away and my uncle won't take seriously the reasons you've given me. He's capable of imagining that I'm not telling him the whole truth."

The officer trembled. Germaine had hit the nail on the head in giving him to understand that they might suppose she'd been compromised.

"If you require it, Mademoiselle," he said after a silence. "I'll come to Germonière before returning to Africa."

"Why not today? If you come into the house with me I won't be at all embarrassed to explain what happened to me...whereas your absence will seem unusual. Wouldn't it be better to act frankly...above all since no one has anything to reproach himself? You've done what every gallant man would have done in a similar case...unless you have some motives I don't know about to hide from my mother's gratitude."

"I have one...and that one, I'm astonished you haven't guessed it, since you know now that I'm..."

"I know that you are an officer in the army fighting against the Arabs and that the Duke de Bretteville honors you with his friendship. That's enough to open the doors of our house to you."

Roger Pontac was silent, to the great stupefaction of Mademoiselle Daudièrne and the conversation stopped abruptly. They had made the trip while chatting and they had arrived at a place where the road turned to the right, moving away from the forest.

"Mademoiselle," the young man said suddenly, "when we have gone over this rocky hill which hides the view, you'll see the Germonière trees and you can't get lost any longer. The road we're following ends at your garden's fence."

"You're going to abandon me?" exclaimed Germaine.

"I have to. But you won't say I shouldn't when you have heard my confession."

"Your...confession!"

"Didn't you ask me to tell you why I have condemned myself never to see you again?"

"No doubt..."

"Well! I would have wished not to have to answer, but I don't know how to lie. I'm fleeing from you because Lieutenant Pontac who has neither a name, nor a family, nor a fortune, can't marry Mademoiselle Daudièrne."

"I...I don't understand," said Germaine, blushing.

"If I introduced myself to your mother, I wouldn't have the courage never to reappear and if I were imprudent enough to go back there I would prepare bitter disappoints for myself."

"But, Monsieur, it's not a question of marrying me...and I admit that I'm understanding less and less."

"What! Don't you understand that I'm afraid of falling in love with you," Roger said, lowering his voice.

With that admission, which she somewhat foresaw perhaps, Germaine became very pale and clenched in her left hand the reins which she had let dangle on Ralph's neck. She finally felt that the danger in taking the wrong road wasn't the only one she ran, and her first thought was to cut short a talk that was becoming a great deal too stressful.

"Don't be afraid, Mademoiselle," Lieutenant Pontac continued in a different tone. "I've said everything. The only thing left is for me to ask you to forgive me for my brutal sincerity...and also for my caution. You'll be left with a sorry opinion of me and you surely will have no doubt that there exists an officer of the Hussards wise enough to take precautions against getting his heart involved. I lack all the traditions of my military profession, but fortunately I'm an exception."

That time Germaine wondered if the officer had simply wanted to make fun of her, but she had only to look at him to dismiss that idea. Roger Pontac was trying to turn his declaration into a joke, but his eyes gave the lie to his smile. Only then did she guess that he was affecting that casual attitude to reassure her and such delicacy touched her deeply.

"He would love me as I would like to be loved," she thought, and she no longer thought about reining in Ralph, who wanted only to take up a faster trot.

"I warned you that if you force me to say what I think, you'll send me away after having heard me out," Roger continued gaily. "The time has come to submit to the fate I foresee...and you'll see, Mademoiselle, that I don't lack courage because I'm going to go away without complaining."

"And without going back on your resolution never to enter Germonière?" exclaimed Mademoiselle Daudièrne. "You must agree, Monsieur, that that's pure childishness and that you're giving a great deal too much importance to a very simple incident. You've gone to the trouble to take me back to the house. Without you, I would have perhaps been reduced to spending the night under the beautiful stars. It's very natural that a service rendered should become an opening of relations between you and my family. But it's a long way from there to the consequences that frighten you. And if you persisted in being set against us, you'd wound me, I swear to you, because I'd at last believe that I've inspired you with an invincible antipathy...and I have a completely different feeling for you. I hope that I too am frank," Germaine added gaily. "Ah! You believe that we've met as people meet in novels and that's all it takes! No, no, I don't want to fall out with the Lemon Rock fairies. They'd be doing me a bad turn if I was content with the pretexts you're giving me. You'll come, Monsieur, and you'll see that you're wrong to be alarmed. Besides, I warn you, if you don't come, my uncle will go look for you at Bretteville. I mean to say to thank you, and you'll have to return his visit. You'll be received cordially and you'll go away as you came...with your heart free."

"I'll try," murmured Pontac, vanquished. "I would give my life for you. I can certainly sacrifice my peace of mind for you."

"Then, I'm relying on you and I'm allowing you to leave me here. It would be better if you didn't come visit this evening. You'd seem to be asking a reward for returning a lost object. But, starting tomorrow, I'll expect you any day."

The Hussard officer bowed without replying and Germaine set her horse on the road without looking back. She was delighted with having gotten out of a rather dubious situation, but she was afraid she had said too much. However, she was thinking more than she had said.

III. The Marriage Proposal

Arcy-sur Beuvron has always been the most peaceful of provincial villages. In coming to live at Germonière, Uncle Armand had done what he could to wake it up, but he had only half-way succeeded. The youth there were a little more active than in the past, but the old bourgeoisie hadn't budged. Set in unchanging habits, they defended themselves vigorously against innovations. They persisted in taking their main meal at noon and if they read the newspapers, it was to find something there to repeat and to add something to conversations. They loved to make fun of Parisians and to appear well informed. In depth, they took an interest in literature, even in politics, a little like a fish takes an interest in a flower. Money, that was the only business. They considered the supreme happiness, the veritable goal of life, was to die rich. They thought only of money; they talked of nothing but money. They spent their time amassing money and computing other people's fortunes. They evaluated inheritances; they added up revenues; they audited expenses, and whoever did not hoard was accused and convicted of an unpardonable crime. They declared he was bankrupting himself and people who go bankrupt are doomed to public disdain. To mortgage one's land, even to buy others, was to lower oneself. To go into debt was equivalent to theft in the opinion of the citizens of Arcy.

They had one reason for their existence, which was to gossip and amass *ecus*. It was a city of people of independent means who disdained commerce and knew nothing about industry.

You had to see the main street, the National Highway, which had changed names three or four times in a half-century, but which had not changed its appearance. People walked along it two by two, slowly, silently, self-assured. They were not in a hurry and they had no ideas to exchange. They counted the paving stones and that activity was enough for them. Merchants strolled about and yawned on the threshold of their open shops. The houses themselves seemed to be bored. And nobody wondered what time it was. The city hall clock could stop and the citizens of Arcy wouldn't be aware that it wasn't working.

But when big news, especially local news, fell into the middle of this silence, Arcy quickly wakes up from its sleep and becomes active, like an ant's bed into which a pebble has been thrown. They get together at the tobacco shop; they chat in front of the pharmacy counter and the balcony club is stuffed with the curious who keep watch on the comings and goings of the people that the day's event directly concerns. If it's a matter of a marital scandal they wait until the husband passes by to see on his face how he's taking it. And if it's a question of some business in which the law can intervene, they're on the lookout for the emergence of the Procurer of the Republic.

The day after the catastrophe of the Germonière ferry, the entire population of that drowsy Sous Prefecture was on foot. The literary room was always full and the commentaries went full speed. Some of the imaginative claimed that the tragic death of the Vignemals wasn't the result of an accident but the great majority was only concerned about the consequences of that death from the point of view of the transmission of the inheritance. They knew about the wills of the last survivor. They knew to which notary they had entrusted them, and those who knew something about law, declared that Arthur du Pommeval was going to collect the opulent inheritance of his aunt by marriage by virtue of Article 722 of the Civil Code. One can easily believe that his slightest activities were carefully watched, and his compatriots were not slow to congratulate him on his new fortune.

But Monsieur du Pommeval respected propriety and conducted himself like a well brought up nephew. To mark his sadness, he abstained from appearing in the street and even from receiving his friends at the elegant little house he inhabited at the entrance to the suburbs. They took note of a visit he made in the morning to Doctor Subligny, a very natural visit since Monsieur Subligny had been called the evening before to certify the double death, the bodies having been recovered in the afternoon very far from Germonière. But nobody had talked with the young heir, who had become in the last forty-eight hours the most important person in the area. And nobody had caught sight of the hat with the wide brims of the doctor, who had stayed in his office, probably in order to write his medical report.

He lived in the least inhabited street of Arcy, this good doctor, and he was lodged according to his tastes. The house that he had bought after ten years of practice wasn't large but it was amply suitable for him, since he didn't intend to give parties. For housekeeping he had only one servant, a former canteen keeper of his regiment who was a good cook—Monsieur Subligny liked good food—and who also knew how to groom a horse. The garden, all the houses in Arcy had one of them, the garden was taken care of by a daily man who successfully cultivated vegetables and flowers, vegetables especially, because at the house of the Ex-Surgeon-Major of the 1st African Chasseurs the useful was never sacrificed to the pleasant.

That day, about two o'clock, if the seekers of information had dared to penetrate into the doctor's office, they would have gathered enough unedited information to entertain for a whole week the circle meetings and the gossip of good families who take pleasure in maligning their neighbors in the evenings by the fireside. It wasn't luxuriously decorated, this office, and a Paris doctor would have been so scandalized that he would never have wished to see his patients there. But the consultations that Monsieur Subligny gave there were well worth those for which fashionable practitioners were highly paid. They were worth even more because he took the trouble to examine his patients and he often cured them. The desk was walnut and the doctor didn't spread out gold pieces there with the sole aim of stimulating the generosity of his consultants. The leather armchair had twenty years of service as did its master, and the black marble pendulum clock dated from Louis-Philippe's reign. White wooden shelves filled with books and four chairs with rush seats, almost always littered with pieces of paper, completed that scant furniture.

The classic engraving representing Hippocrates refusing Artaxerces' presents didn't adorn the pine paneling and this was assuredly a case which fit the saying: *A bon vin pas d'enseigne,*[32] because Monsieur Subligny was certainly the most disinterested of doctors. He took care of the poor for free and he was content with whatever the rich wanted to offer him. Since he had set up practice among them, all the inhabitants came to see him, and all got what they came for. But they didn't consult him only as a doctor. He had a well-deserved reputation for being a wise man and many people came to ask his advice on occasions where his professional knowledge had nothing to do with it.

And this time precisely it wasn't a sick man who had an appointment. The man seated in front of him radiated good health. His stoutness, his full face, his relaxed looks would have done honor to a Canon. But a magistrate rather often looks like an ecclesiastic and this magistrate was President of the Arcy Tribunal, a local man who had spent his whole career in the same place and who didn't desire advancement. He was a judge like one seldom sees any more and the likes of which soon one won't see at all. Sufficiently rich, and related to the most honorable families in the countryside, this model President was without doubt the most esteemed person in the city and seemed to have been created and put in the world to render justice to his fellow citizens. He knew all of them without exception. He knew their antecedents and the moral value of each one and, in addition, he understood business. The most complicated law cases never bothered him because he judged them with the good sense with which nature had amply supplied him. He had a high regard for Monsieur Subligny and he must have had a particular esteem for him because he had gone out of his way to have recourse to his insight on a rather difficult subject.

"So, my dear doctor," he said after a short introduction to the subject, "you're sure that the death of these poor Vignemals is due only to being under water too long?"

"Absolutely sure, my dear President," answered the ex-military doctor in the most affirmative tone. "First of all, the bodies show no sign of violence. Madame Vignemal certainly had some scrapes and some bruises, but she got her legs caught in the roots of a willow tree and that's enough to explain the superficial injuries I certified I found. What's more, yesterday evening at Fougéray I did an autopsy of the two bodies and I'm in a position to swear that the husband and the wife were alive when they fell into the water. They were for good and all drowned and I don't know why the Procurer of the Republic requires that I proceed to a medical-legal operation which seems to me superfluous."

---

[32] *Good wine doesn't need an advertisement.*

"Me, I know why."

"You mean like all beginners he has zeal, too much zeal."

"That's true, but there's something else. He suspects a crime has been committed."

"By the fellow who's camping on the Fougéray land. He hasn't hidden his opinion from me, this Procurer, but he's wrong. I'll answer for Roch Ferrer."

"Just between us, he's a vagabond who's not worth much."

"I can agree to that, although he has some qualities you don't know about. Nevertheless, it's not possible to accuse him. There was a witness at the landing, a witness whose testimony can't be suspected because he detests Roch…this witness is the Vignemals' servant. They questioned him and he stated that at the moment that his masters got into the ferry there was no one on the Beuvron bank."

"That is to say, he didn't see anyone, but your bohemian was there… hidden in the underbrush. He admitted it."

"I'll point out to you, my dear President, that after having examined and re-examined him in every way, your head of the local court let him go free, and certainly it wasn't from lack of a desire to send him to prison. I add that Roch came of his own free will to Fougéray as soon as he knew the law was there. It would have been very easy for him to hide from the interrogation because he has no set dwelling and he could easily do fifteen leagues on foot from evening to morning."

"Oh! If he'd taken a notion to flee, the gendarmes would have picked him up. He'd be arrested everywhere because of his appearance and his hurry to come forward was perhaps only a clever calculation."

"I see you're prejudiced against this boy, and it's not my place to defend him. But I surely have the right to ask you to what cause you can assign these guilty acts which you suspect him of without specifying them. There's an axiom that's cited in Latin which expresses a very accurate idea: When someone commits a crime it's because they have a motive to commit it. And I don't at all see the benefit that Roch Ferrer could derive from the death of the Vignemal couple."

"He would not directly benefit from it, but others than himself could benefit. Madame Vignemal has poor relatives that this gypsy probably knows because they are peasants from the Arcy area."

"And you would suppose that one of them paid this poor Roch to… Ah! I can guarantee that he didn't take on such a commission, moderately recompensed. He despises money. Besides these people don't have any. Would you say he did it for the pleasure of rendering a service to a friend? No, right? Then the accusation is null and void."

"But, my dear doctor, I'm not accusing your protégé. I'm trying to enlighten myself by talking with you. The question of inheritance will surely be brought up and I'll certainly be called on the judge it. Now, if a criminal case came before the civil case, that would change the situation considerably."

"There won't be any criminal case. There can't be because the two victims' deaths were purely accidental. I've certified it...My report is there and I don't believe there can be a civil case. The Code has provided for this situation...Article 722."

"You're citing an Article of the Code!" the President said, laughing. "Could you also be a Doctor in Jurisprudence? I wouldn't doubt it."

"I'll be content to be a medical doctor, but I've read the law which governs the rules of inheritance. I read it because I'm interested in the young du Pommeval, and I saw that, according to the requirements of that law he'll inherit the entire Vignemal fortune."

"You've read the law, my friend, but you've interpreted it badly. It doesn't apply to the provisions of a will and as Vignemal was an heir only in virtue of his wife's will..."

"The Devil! Are you sure of that?"

"Perfectly sure. The question has been settled by numerous judgments. The last one set down in the Dalloz Registry is, I believe, from 1850."

"Ah! *Mon Dieu!* But that completely changes the situation of my young friend. And the poor boy doesn't suspect it. He's losing everything."

"Why should that be? He could depend on the factual circumstances. And if he can prove that his uncle survived, if only by a minute, he will win his case. Only it's up to him to prove it."

"How do you expect him to prove that his uncle survived?"

"I don't know anything about that and it's not up to me but there are lawyers practicing at the Arcy bar who would willingly take the case. I even know one of them who would take the case on a contingency basis, because the case is very winnable. And that's why I want to inform myself on the morality of the vagabond who saw the accident. They will probably try to trap him, because if he swore, for example, that Madame Vignemal was still breathing when she came to dry ground on the bank..."

"He told me the contrary and I can answer for the fact that he won't lie in front of a tribunal. Besides, he described to me the state of the body when he found it and I'm convinced. The poor woman was dead. It is even probable that she died before her husband."

"Why?"

"Because she was a great deal more courageous than that poor Vignemal. She must have tried to save herself when she fell into the water, splashed around, fought, made violent efforts to breathe. In cases like that, water fills the lungs and asphyxiation comes in thirty or forty seconds. Vignemal, on the contrary, was half dead at the moment the boat capsized. The syncopation would have happened at the same time as the immersion and a man in syncope can live more than half an hour under water. There are some examples. By the act of fainting the respiratory functions are suspended and you can do without air for a certain time."

"I don't contest the value of these scientific hypotheses, but…how can you know that before the catastrophe the husband was paralyzed by fright, while the wife had kept her head?"

"Roch saw everything. He recounted the scene to me."

"Roch! Always Roch! Decidedly this good for nothing played a major role in the Beuvron drama…a role which doesn't seem clear to me."

"Roch conducted himself very courageously, and I swear to you that it isn't his fault if the Vignemals perished, because he risked his life trying to save them. It was while diving, trying to stop the boat being carried away by the current, that he witnessed the last moments of these unfortunate people. The husband was sunk down in the bottom of the boat, overcome by fear to the point that he was no longer conscience of his acts. The woman, on the contrary, stayed upright and began to take off her clothes. She probably wanted to dive into the water and try to reach the bank. She had already opened the top of her dress when the boat suddenly capsized."

"You're repeating to me, my dear doctor, what your bohemian told you," answered the President, shaking his head. The President was skeptical by nature. "I hope he's told the truth and that they leave him alone. As for that, it's not a question at the moment of arresting him, but I can certainly assure you that the court authorities are going to keep an eye on him. If it's not a question of catching him in the act fishing at night or hunting with prohibited weapons, they'll find something. There's nothing to all that, but the Procurer of the Republic suspects that this Roch Ferrer is in collusion with another bad character who, he himself, is found to be a relative of Madame Vignemal, close enough to be in the line of inheritance."

"But that's an absurd supposition. One of the Fougéray servants was there. You know that, and he swears that…"

"I believe he's not in a position to attest to much of anything because he scuttled off at his masters' first cry of distress and he saw almost nothing. But if the vagabond might have sawed only half way through the ferry rope the evening before or the morning of the accident, he would still be in the case to be followed with criminal charges."

"Ah! For the report, my dear President, here's what the facts are: Supposing that Roch wanted to send the Vignemals into the next world, he couldn't guess that they would cross the Beuvron that evening. And then, why would he have so much interest in drowning them? To make a scamp who's the cousin of Madame Vignemal rich? But there's nobody in the area who doesn't know that the husband and wife each willed their estate to whoever lived the longest. Roch certainly didn't know that the rules governing inheritance are not applicable in the case of inheritance though a will. He hasn't studied law, this Robin Hood of the woods."

"Agreed, and it's possible that's why the vagabond fished out Madame

Vignemal and didn't fish out Monsieur. He fished her out and he threw her back into the water after having found she wasn't yet dead."

"But he would have said that,…that she wasn't dead. Then he would have cried it from the roof tops. To achieve his purpose, it was necessary to prove that she'd survived her husband. He thought so at least."

"He might have had motives to keep quiet that I don't know about; for example, fear of being implicated in a criminal affair. And he's holding back speaking until the moment comes that he judges will serve the interest of his comrade without compromising himself."

"Really, you astound me. You're painting a picture for me there of a Roch Ferrer that I've never known and who doesn't exist. The Roch Ferrer that I've observed is a violent man, very capable of killing someone in a moment of anger and completely incapable of premeditating an evil action…above all incapable of calculating the pecuniary consequences of it."

"He comes, however, from a race in which trickery is in the blood."

"His father was a gypsy, that's true, but education modifies instincts and Roch has been elevated by the Brothers, who have seen him at close hand, and think about him exactly as I do. And then, this boy could not be part of a plot for the excellent reason that he never sees anyone. He lives in the fields and in the woods. He hasn't even constructed himself a cabin like Robinson Crusoe. The peasants take him for a mad man and don't associate with him. Some of them fear him and the others look down on him. I'll never believe that one could be found who'd suggest a bargain to the Fougéray savage, as they call him."

"My dear doctor," the President said after a short silence. "I have absolute confidence in your discretion, and I'm going to prove it to you by repeating to you what the Procurer of the Republic told me. Someone has recently pointed out to the local court the presence in the area of an individual who disappeared in the past leaving behind sad memories…and this individual is actually a cousin of Madame Vignemal."

"Would that be little Roger you're talking about?"

"Yes, Roger Pontac, the son of a poor devil who farmed land of the Duke de Bretteville and who ruined himself there."

"But I knew him very well, this Roger. He was a fine and remarkably intelligent boy. I took an interest in him and I went to see him several times at the St.Louis College where he was studying at his aunt's expense. I was sorry to learn that he'd left at the end of his philosophy year, but I wasn't very surprised by it. Madame Vignemal wanted to force him to take up a career that didn't suit him, and, what's more, she was very stingy with the small allowance she gave him. The young man, who didn't want to live on charity, got the key to the open fields one day and he hasn't been seen since. I thought he became a soldier. That was his real vocation. And you say he's been seen in Arcy?"

"In Arcy, no. He didn't dare. But people have seen him prowling around Fougéray and the Procurer of the Republic has been informed."

"By whom?"

"By the Vignemals' gardener, who surprised him looking at the house."

"And he didn't speak to him?"

"No, that man ran off when he saw someone was watching him."

"That's strange, and even stranger because he doesn't, so far as I know, have any reasons to hide. His cousin didn't have any serious grief against him. If he had gone to see her, I really believe she would have received him coldly, but she certainly wouldn't have thrown him out. And nothing keeps him either from coming back to Arcy. He's almost unknown here and he hasn't left behind any debts here since he hasn't been here since his childhood. I'm even rather astonished that he hasn't tried to see me, and I admit to you that his visit would please me."

"I urge you, my dear doctor, not to count on it. A man of that type has nothing to discuss with you."

"But then, where has he been living since he's been in the neighborhood?"

"Nobody knows anything about it. Maybe he's already made off. But they will find him."

"Then your Procurer of the Republic imagines that Roger Pontac has come expressly to enroll Roch Ferrar into a conspiracy against the life of the Vignemal couple?"

"That's his idea. I tell it to you for what it's worth."

"This magistrate of the new school has no common sense, please allow me to tell you. Roger Pontac has never seen Roch Ferrer in his life and doesn't know he exists, seeing that Roch came into this region while Roger was studying in Paris. How then could these two poor devils get together to commit this crime?"

"They might have met at the corner of a wood or on the bank of the Beuvron and as they were made to understand each other, they had no trouble falling into agreement."

The doctor reflected an instant and then said with conviction:

"I'll never believe that. Roch is an eccentric, a vagabond, a poacher… Roch is not a murderer. As for Roger, I can't answer for him as I'm answering for my savage. I've lost sight of him for ten years and he might have spoiled himself in leading a life of adventure, but if he's stayed such as I knew him, he hasn't gotten mixed up in anything infamous. He had an upright character, prompt to give in to a first inclination, but that first inclination was always good. And besides,…I always come back to this…I don't see how Roch could have set up the accident so that Monsieur Vignemal would have been forced to drown before his wife. These sorts of schemes are too complicated. And I would certainly bet that neither he nor his suspected accomplice have ever opened the Civil Code."

"In what concerns the man called Pontac, you could be wrong, my dear doctor. But let's drop this painful subject. I only brought it up to give you an opportunity to tell me what you know favorable about the background of a boy in whom you take an interest. Now that I've heard you out, I admit that they're probably wrong to suspect him, and I won't occupy myself with him any more."

"Then you think that du Pommeval will not lose his uncle's inheritance?"

"Pardon, my dear doctor. I can't give you my opinion on the outcome of a lawsuit that I'll be called on to judge. If I gave it to you, I'd be forced to recuse myself. All that I can tell you is that the law is not content with testimony without foundation and that of Roch Ferrar will be infinitely suspicious. It would be useless for your protégé to swear that Madame Vignemal spoke to him when he found her under the willow tree... That won't be enough."

"My dear President, I'm delighted with what you've told me. Your language is a good sign for Arthur du Pommeval, who came to see me this morning."

"Really?" asked the President with an ironic smile. "I suppose he wanted to know what his chances were of inheriting."

"No, he came for something else... I won't tell you that he's very unhappy. You wouldn't believe me. But he's not showing an indecent joy. What's more, he doesn't doubt that the inheritance will come to him with being contested."

"If it comes to him, he won't save it as his uncle did. But God knows how he'll use his fortune. It will be squandered on buying horses, betting on races and having dinners with young ladies."

"That was really what I was afraid of, but since I've talked with him I'm reassured. He has a project...that I strongly approve and which will cut short these youthful follies."

"A marriage then?"

"Excuse me, my dear President, for not telling you any more about it. It's still a secret...a secret that all of Arcy village will soon know, but I've promised to keep it...and..."

"The doctor didn't finish what he was saying. The office door opened and Jeannette, the before-mentioned canteen worker for the African troops, entered, holding in her hand a visiting card that she put under her master's nose. Monsieur Subligny glanced at the square of Bristol paper and remained totally absorbed in reading the name of Roger Pontac.

"A patient probably," said the President. "I'm leaving, dear doctor. We mustn't keep clients waiting."

"Oh! As far as that's concerned, there's nothing pressing," murmured Monsieur Subligny. And speaking to the ex-canteen worker who had stayed there at attention:

"Jeannette," he continued, "Show this gentleman into the drawing room and let him know I'll be with him in an instant."

The good doctor didn't intend, and for good reason, to put Roger Pontac in the presence of a judge who didn't seem look favorably on this homecoming. He didn't intend to give out his name either and he quickly slid the visitor's card into his pocket. The President was already standing and buttoning his overcoat, ready to leave. Jeannette gave a military salute and turned on her heels.

"I'm very obliged to you for informing me about the intentions of these gentlemen of the court," said Monsieur Subligny. "I'll find out all Roch knows."

"Don't forget, I beg you, that my information is strictly confidential," interrupted the President. "It was the friend talking to you and not the magistrate."

"Don't worry. It's my business to be discreet. I'll use caution informing myself and I think I can promise that I'll soon know something to consider about the suspected relations that my gypsy has formed with this poor Roger, who has never harmed anyone but himself. I'm actually obligated to go to Germanière today and Roch seldom goes far from Madame Daudièrne's park."

"How is she, that good lady? And how are her charming daughters?"

"The day before yesterday they had a strong shock...the accident happened at the end of their garden...and the purpose of my visit is to find out how they are."

"If the young du Pommeval were wise, he'd marry the older one. But he has in mind, probably, marrying into the Parisian financial world."

"I have reasons to think otherwise," said Monsieur Subligny, smiling. "And I'm delighted to know that you aren't without hope that he'll come into possession."

"It's still as a friend that I'm speaking. It's understood that I'll follow my conscience when I judge."

"I'm very sure of it," exclaimed the doctor, shaking the hand of the President whom he had conducted to the door to the street. "And that's exactly what reassures me, because this dear Arthur's cause is a good one."

"I hope so," answered the President, "and I won't look any further into this little cousin of Madame Vignemal who's come back into the country three days before the tragic deaths of his relatives."

The ex-military surgeon closed his door and returned, very thoughtful, into the corridor which separated the ground floor of his little house into two equal parts.

"The fact is," he was saying to himself, "the sudden return of this boy is rather extraordinary. I've always had a good opinion of him, but I don't know how he's been living the past ten years. What can he want from me? Maybe he's come to ask me for help. *Ma foi!* I won't refuse to give it to him but I'll advise him not to cool his heels very long in our countrside. It's always troublesome to get crossways with the Procurer of the Republic, even when you haven't done anything wrong."

And noticing Jeannette at the end of the corridor:

"What's this monsieur who's waiting for me in the drawing room like?" he asked her.

"Dressed like a prince, Major, and a nice looking young man; that's all I can tell you. By his physique you can see he's served in the military. If he hasn't yet been decorated, that's because he's too young, but he wouldn't have stolen it because he has a scar across his face and I recognize it. It's from a blow by a Turkish saber."

"Ah! Really!" murmured the doctor, calmed by that description."Well! Bring him in to me and I won't see anyone until he's left."

An instant later, Roger Pontac came into the consulting room of Monsieur Subligny, who was struck dumb with surprise on seeing him. The child he had known in the past, pale, puny, and unbecomingly dressed in a too tight and too short tunic of a secondary school uniform, had become a handsome young man, tall, vigorous, tanned by the sun and elegantly dressed in a black frock coat made by a good tailor.

"You don't recognize me, Monsieur Subligny," the newcomer said while smiling.

"Then have I changed very much?"

"Yes! my boy. Changed to your advantage. You're superb. *Ah ca!* Then you've made a fortune?"

"Me! Oh! No. I'm not very much richer than when you came to see me at St. Louis."

"The Devil! Then you owe money to your tailor because you're dressed in the latest fashion. Let's see. What profession have you chosen?"

"Then you didn't look at my visiting card?"

"I saw only your name, which astonished me greatly, because it's ten years since I've heard anything of you. And I didn't know if you were living or dead. But, your card, I have it," said Monsieur Subligny, rummaging around in his pocket, "and since you don't want to state your profession aloud, I'm going to look at this piece of paste board... What! First Lieutenant of the 9th Hussards! Is that really true? You're an officer."

"For three months...and as I signed up in 1873, you can see that I've put in enough time there. That's not my fault. I didn't avoid risking my skin."

"And officer! But that's magnificent!" exclaimed the doctor, whose face was expanding more and more. "You've managed take down the epaulette in eight years, you who had neither protection, nor a family, nor any money to spend. Ah! Me, I really knew you were a fine boy and that you'd make your career in the army. Give me your hand, Roger, and sit down so we can talk."

The young man clasped both the doctor's hands with enthusiasm and took a seat in the chair where a magistrate who thought nothing good of the poor relatives of Madame Vignemal had just been sitting.

"If you knew how happy I am to see you," he said, with an emotion he didn't try to hide. "You were so nice to me in the past. I have never forgotten your visits to the college where I was so abandoned that they left me there even during the holidays."

"That's very good, but why have you never shown me any signs of life since the escapade with which you crowned your studies? I was told you've come back into the country very recently, but I didn't know any more than that and I didn't want to believe it."

"I swore to myself not to come back until the day I had atoned for my wrongs and earned the rank I wanted to get. I was in Tunisia when I was promoted to First Lieutenant, and I didn't lose a minute asking for a leave. But I didn't foresee that I would learn on arriving the news of my cousin's death...and what a death!"

"Ah! You know she accidentally drowned," said Monsieur Subligny, frowning. "How did you find it out? Did you go to Fougéray?"

"No, Doctor. I didn't dare go there although I really wanted to, because Madame Vignemal had taken care of me during my childhood and I owed her gratitude. I even went once to the garden gate but I didn't have the courage to ring the bell. I was afraid of being badly received."

"It seems the gardener saw you."

"That's very possible. I wasn't hiding. And I'll have to tell you why I didn't go in. The day after the day I received official notification of my promotion, I wrote my cousin a letter in which I explained to her the reason for my great deal too prolonged silence. I begged her to forget the past and to allow me to see her when I got back to France. She didn't answer me."

"*Perfect!*" thought the doctor, speaking to himself. "*Maybe that letter can be found and it will prove that... But it's not a question of that for the moment.*"

He continued: "Where have you been living since your arrival? You didn't stop at an Arcy inn, I suppose."

"I'm living at the Bretteville chateau."

"What! At the Duke's house?"

"*Mon Dieu.* Yes. I've agreed to be his guest for the duration of my stay in France."

"And to what circumstance do you owe the honor of being housed by this great seigneur who doesn't deign to receive the Arcy citizens?"

"To a very unfortunate circumstance. His son, who was a lieutenant in my squadron, was killed leading a charge against the Arabs. In defending him I received a saber blow where you see the scar. And if I wasn't able to save his life, I was at least able to retrieve his body, which had remained in the hands of the enemy. I had the consolation of bringing back his Legion of Honor cross to his father."

"And the Duke received you as a friend... That's good... That's very good, Roger, what you did there. I was right to maintain that you were a man of heart."

"Then you've been told the contrary?" asked the young officer, smiling.

"No, not exactly...but when I think that that imbecile of a Procurer... Let's talk about something else, my boy. I can understand why you hesitated to present yourself at the Vignemals. But I tell you frankly, I hold it a little against you not to have come to see me. Bretteville isn't far, and..."

"Then think, Doctor. Someone would have recognized me if I had shown

264

myself in the streets of Arcy and the news of my presence in the area would have reached Fougéray."

"Right! I understand. You were afraid that your cousin would have held it against you for having seen me first."

"You guessed it. I don't have that fear any longer, alas! because the poor woman is dead. So I came running. I was late in telling you I have never lost the memory of your kindness...to ask for your friendship...your advice..."

"My friendship you have. And when I know what you want to consult me about...not about your health, I hope. Are you still healthy?"

"I haven't been in the hospital twenty-four hours since I joined the service. But I'd like you to point out to me how I should behave. Everybody knows that Madame Vignemal withdrew her protection and even her goodwill toward me."

"That's not any reason not to go to her funeral, which takes place tomorrow. I even urge you very strongly not to miss it."

"I'll go, Doctor, and I can even tell you it won't be hard for me to do this duty, because I'm sincerely sorry to have lost her."

"You probably know," Monsieur Subligny said after a pause, "that by a very old will she left all her property to her husband."

"No, I didn't know that," Roger said with indifference.

"Yes, my boy, her fortune will probably pass to Monsieur Vignemal's nephew, Arthur du Ponneval."

"The little du Pommeval boy who was always dressed so neatly while the other kids his age were tearing their pants climbing trees? Well, so much the better. If he turned out to be what he promised, he must love to spend money for his clothes. Monsieur Vignemal's inheritance will suit him very well."

"But, unfortunately, that fortune belonged to your cousin and it's to your detriment that it reverts to du Pommeval."

"Then I was the heir?"

"An heir to part of it, big innocent boy. But that part is enough to be sorry not to have it. Your cousin must have left between one and two million and on her side there are between six and seven of you in line for the inheritance."

"*Ma foi!* I didn't know that. I thought my cousin had relatives more closely related than I...or rather I had never worried about knowing who would inherit her estate. And, really, I swear to you that I don't regret it. My army pay is enough for me."

"You are actually what I knew you to be in the past," said the doctor, looking at Roger with a sort of affectionate admiration. "You have faith in yourself and you expect nothing from those quirks of fate which enrich a man. You're right because I'm certain you'll succeed by your own merit. I like your courage and I sincerely ask you to count on me at all times."

"Well, Doctor," the lieutenant of the Hussards said gaily, "I actually have a favor to ask you."

"So much the better. Speak, my boy. What can I do for you?"

265

"You can, I believe, introduce me to Monsieur Daudièrne…the brother-in-law of Madame Daudièrne, who bought Germonière about ten years ago."

"If that's all it is," said the Doctor, "there's nothing easier. I'm the family doctor. But what the devil do you want with Monsieur Daudièrne. Where did you meet him?"

"I don't know him," Roger answered. "And it's precisely because I've never seen him that I'd need someone to introduce me to fulfill a commission I've been charged with."

"By whom?"

"By Monsieur le Duke de Bretteville. He's learned that Monsieur Daudièrne is a great hunter and would very much like to be authorized to hunt in the Bretteville forest, which is full of game. The Duke would like to please him and would go himself to invite him to shoot his goats and pheasants if he were not in mourning. Since the death of his son, he doesn't want to see anyone…but me, who can talk to him about his poor Henry."

"And he's sent you as an ambassador to his neighbor at Germonière. That's so much more gracious of him since he's always avoided having anything to do with the people of the area. They say he's very aristocratic."

"They're wrong, Doctor. He keeps his social position, but he has no class prejudices."

"The proof of that is that he's offered you hospitality, you, who're the son of one of his farmers. The exception he's made in your favor honors you, my boy…and I approve your having accepted. So you are living in the chateau. You're the messmate, almost the friend, of one of the greatest seigneurs of France, of a Duke who has three hundred thousand francs income. And me who thought for an instant that…"

"Then what did you think?" Roger Pontac asked gaily. "That I was sleeping under the beautiful stars?"

"Not precisely, but I was supposing that you had found food and shelter with some country person in the neighborhood of Fougéray. I knew that you'd been seen and I didn't know that you'd become a brilliant officer. And you have some relatives among the farmers of the canton…"

"Relatives that I hardly know and who've never done anything for me. *Dieu merci,* I don't need anyone and I don't intend to rake up kinship with them. If the Duke hadn't insisted so much to have me stay at Bretteville, I would just have come to take lodgings at the Hotel de Bretagne in the main street of Arcy and my first visit would have been to you. I would have asked you to try to get me back into Madame Vignemal's good graces."

"And I might have succeeded in doing so. Your promotion, bravely earned, would have flattered her vanity… Your repentance might have touched her. In short, it's very unfortunate for you that she died. But to come back to your other cousins. I warn you that they very well might soon come back to badger you at Bretteville."

"Oh! I'm not ashamed of them, and even if I can't be useful to them, I..."

"It's not that. But it's claimed that du Pommeval will have to file suit against them to have the inheritance come to him."

"Well, they'll sue without me."

"Really? You'll refuse to be reunited with them if they sue."

"Certainly. Yes. I have a horror of chicanery."

"You can count on the fact that they'll come to you to propose an association."

"I'll send them packing, I sincerely ask you to believe it. It would be useless to see an officer of the Hussards spend his life running around to notaries and to lawyers' offices. I'd prefer to go back to Africa."

"And you're right, Roger, a hundred times over, and so much more so because those people will lose their lawsuit; I'm certain of it. They'll be out their costs and I very strongly approve your remaining outside their process. Besides, if they should win, your rights are still there. You'll inherit with the others."

"Inherit? Me! I don't care to. Money would inconvenience me."

"As for that, my boy, you're wrong. Money doesn't do any harm even to a military man. I've known some who were millionaires and who didn't sulk by the fireside any more than others. And if you couldn't use money for any thing but to contract a good marriage..."

"You're forgetting, Doctor, that I'm a First Lieutenant."

"Right! But when you're a superior officer, or only a captain, you perhaps won't be sorry to marry a woman who pleases you...and when you don't have a *sou* you don't have a choice... You marry whoever you can. While waiting for your marriage bells to chime, you want to be introduced to Monsieur Daudièrne, don't you?"

"Yes, that would be more proper, I believe. I won't have to state my name and my position myself. If I went alone, Monsieur Daudièrne might take me for the Duke's attendant."

"He has too much tact and too much knowledge of the world to make that mistake, but that doesn't matter. It would be better if I introduced you. And this comes at a good time. I have business today at Germonière. Do you want me to take you there?"

"Please, Doctor...on condition that my presence won't bother you."

"Not at all. I'd be delighted to take you. My Tilbury has two seats and my mare is probably harnessed up. Jeannette had orders to have the carriage ready at three o'clock. And Jeannette is as exact as an old trooper. You know she comes from the cavalry?"

"I don't doubt it, since you turn over the direction of yours to her."

"Oh! My cavalry is comprised of a single horse and Jeannette's enough to take care of it. Then you're ready to accompany me to my friends over there? Yes, because you're already in visiting clothes. Give me time to put on a coat for the outside weather, and we'll leave. Wait for me here and don't worry about smoking a cigar. My patients are used to the smell of tobacco. I always have my old pipe from the regiment and I don't deprive myself of smoking it when I work in my office in the evening."

That said, the doctor went out and Roger Pontac was left to his thoughts. The welcome that Monsieur Subligny had just given him had moved and charmed him. He felt himself stronger now that he was assured he had not lost the friendship of this worthy man who had supported and consoled him in the past. It seemed to him that he was no longer alone in the world and that his life was going to take a new direction. He would find at last what he had missed the last ten years, affection, support, almost a father. He couldn't add 'a confident,' because he hadn't dared tell him that if he wanted to go to Germonière it was not only to get Uncle Armand invited to hunt in the Bretêche forest.

The evening before, after his adventure, Roger Pontac had returned to the Bretteville chateau in a state of agitation which hadn't escaped the clairvoyant eyes of the old Duke. And Roger, gently questioned by the most kindly of hosts, had hidden nothing from him. He had even allowed himself to consult him on what he should do, and, to his great surprise, the Duke had advised him to go see his country neighbors without being concerned about what might come from that abortive novel at the foot of the Lemon Rock.

"You must be bored here, my dear boy," the indulgent lord had said to him. "Why don't you go to Germonière and take your mind off our sad conversations? If I could forget for an instant the misfortune which has struck me, I'd go there with you. But please tell Monsieur Daudièrne that my game fields are at his disposal. Your scruples in regard to his niece are exaggerated. An officer like you is on a level footing with the daughter of a bourgeois, however honorable. Whatever happens will happen with relationships that chance has brought about. So go where your destiny calls you."

Roger was only too willing to follow this advice given by a man that his rank, his age, and his experience authorized to speak this way. He gathered courage little by little and he managed to ask Monsieur Bretteville the proper way to approach Madame Daudièrne. Should he tell her about the encounter and the trip with her daughter or, instead, use the convenient pretext of the invitation the Duke had commissioned him to carry to the lady's brother-in-law? The Duke had pronounced in favor of the pretext.

"You never know what a young girl will do in such a case," he had answered smiling. "Mademoiselle Daudièrne told you she would admit everything to her mother. She might change her mind from one day to the next. You'd do better to wait until her mother brings up that story. If she doesn't mention it, it's because she doesn't know about it and it's not up to you to tell her about it."

On this point Roger Pontac thought the same as his noble protector. And he wasn't about to raise objections to a plan which was his. It seemed to him the next day would never come and he hardly slept. For the first time in his existence, his heart opened up to an unknown feeling. Certainly this wasn't his first taste of love. Eight years spent in the regiment had taken away the naïve illusions of adolescence, and his make-up being what it was, regarding easy successes he'd had an embarrassing number of choices. But he had grown tired rather quickly of these inglorious conquests and he'd never had anything but a modest taste for gross pleasures. And then, he hadn't become a soldier to be a Don Juan of the garrison. He had put on the uniform to fight and to earn promotion at the point of his saber. And after having heroically fought in Algeria and in Tunisia, he had finally left the ranks. He was somebody in the great army family and he already saw, in the very distant future, the stars of generalship, this dream of the soldier now that the Marshall's baton is nothing but a memory. He had arrived at that moment when life is decided. And there it was that God had put in his path an adorable young girl that he would never have dared approach if he had met her in society. That society had always been closed to him and he now had the right to enter it, his head held high. She was in debt to him, that charming Germaine, who'd made him promise to see her again. There was almost already a secret between them. It was too strong. The caution of that twenty-seven-year-old boy couldn't hold out against the temptations of that force. And the Duke's motto: *Come What May: Let Honor Be Saved*, had triumphed over his last hesitations.

Roger had gone early in the morning to prepare for his first visit to Germonière. He wanted to go there on one of the saddle horses Monsieur Bretteville had put at his disposal, and he was going into the stables to give his orders when he overheard a conversation between two grooms that informed him about the sad ferry accident. No one in the chateau knew that Monsieur le Duc's guest was Madame Subligny's cousin, and the young officer had the presence of mind not let it be seen that the event had anything to do with him. But that news modified his projects somewhat. He told himself that it imposed duties on him and he thought immediately of going to see that good doctor he reproached himself for having neglected so long. He wanted to tell him his story, explain to him his perplexity, and ask him if he ought to go to his cousin's funeral services. Then he also had the idea of asking him to introduce him at Germonière. He knew that Monsieur Subligny took care of Madame Daudièrne, her daughters and her servants since she'd bought the property created by the druggist. He thought that the patronage of the family doctor wouldn't be without use on that occasion.

And he didn't regret having gone to see him. The doctor had received him as one receives an old friend. The doctor was going to open wide to him all the doors to the household, support him, recommend him. And later, if the poor Lieutenant's dreams took shape, if the encounter at the foot of Lemon Rock should have serious results, the doctor wouldn't refuse to speak in favor of his protégé.

Roger Pontac was at that point when Monsieur Subligny reappeared dressed all in black, even to tie and gloves, he who usually didn't take much thought of the correctness of his dress.

"You've never seen me so handsome, *hein?*" he said, laughing. "Don't you find I have a solemn look? This doesn't amuse me, I assure you, but for today it's what's required."

"Naturally, because you're going to visit Madame Daudièrne," Pontac murmured.

"Oh! That's not it. I'm received very well at Germonière in my everyday clothes. The lady of the house is not at all formal, and her brother, whom you're going to invite, treats me as a comrade. But this time it's an exceptional situation. Well, my boy, I can certainly tell you this, you who're outside the gossip of our little city. I'm charged with a mission. I'm going to officially ask for the hand of one of the young Daudièrne girls—not for me, of course," explained the doctor, bursting with laughter.

At that unexpected declaration, Roger turned pale and remained silent. His trouble was so apparent that Monsieur Subligny noticed it and asked:

"What's wrong with you, young man? What an expression you have on your face! You'd think I'd just told you some bad news."

"Me," stammered the First Lieutenant. "Nothing's wrong with me, I assure you. I've become very hot. It was so warm in your office..."

"That's because Jeannette has a mania for lighting a fire hot enough to roast an ox, as if I were still on bivouac in the Kabylie Mountains. And I don't know where my mind was to imagine that my mission to Germonière would interfere with you. You're hardly concerned with the marriage of the Daudièrne's girls, whom you've never seen."

"Actually, no...but I'm afraid of being in your way if I go with you. In circumstances like this one, a stranger is out of place."

"First of all, you're not completely a stranger.I've known you since you came into the world and you'll soon be introduced to the people at Germonière. You won't be in my way at all, I assure you."

"Nevertheless, I can't be a third party to the matrimonial conversation that you're going to have with Madame Daudièrne," Pontac murmured with a forced smile.

"That wouldn't be very proper, in fact," the doctor said gaily. "Those sorts of things take place in private and the most absolute secrecy is needed...right up to the day the marriage is announced by a blast from a trumpet. I should not even have told you what I was going to do at Germonière. But you aren't going to pass on this story because you see only the Duke de Bretteville, who, I think, is very little interested in the little tattling of the countryside. And, besides, I'm sure you're discreet. No matter; I'll not say any more to you. As to any inconvenience that would come from your being in the chateau while I make my request. Be reassured, my boy, everything will be arranged wonderfully. Those at Germonière enjoy complete freedom. Madame Daudièrne keeps to the drawing room, the young ladies walk in the garden or draw in their attic. Monsieur

Daudièrne shoots rabbits on the Beuvron levee and the visitors do what they please. You are just like at home. I'll introduce you to the mistress of the house; you'll lay out for her the purpose of your visit. If her brother is outside, you'll go look for him, unless you prefer to chat with the young ladies, who are both quite pretty and very intelligent. Once I've introduced you, I'll ask to speak to Madame Daudièrne privately. This will take about a half-hour. If I obtain a favorable answer, you'll be the first to know because we'll come back together. Will you have dinner with me?"

"That would be a pleasure, my dear Doctor, but I promised Monsieur de Bretteville to return at seven o'clock."

"Then that will be for another time. Let's go relieve Jeaneette, who's on guard duty with the Tilbury and the mare."

Roger really wanted to raise new objections, because the trip to Germonière was appearing a great deal less pleasant since Monsieur Subligny had explained the reason which took him to Madame Daudièrne's. But how could he refuse the Doctor's help after having asked for it? That would almost be the same as betraying his secret hopes. The ex-Surgeon-Major was very perceptive despite his frankness and his brusque behavior. He would have been able to guess what his young protégé absolutely wanted to keep from him. And, then, Roger flattered himself he could make him talk during the trip. One of the young Daudièrne girls was going to marry, but which one? The poor love-sick man preferred to know it while there was perhaps still time to repress at the bottom of his heart the feelings stirring in him.

The carriage which had been hooked up was waiting in front of the garden door under the watchful eye of the servant of long military service. The doctor drove this bizarre vehicle which did not resemble any known model as being a Tilbury. It bore some resemblance to the Phaeton, to the Victoria, and the antique Cabriolet of our fathers. The chassis rested on four wheels, with a seat in front, a seat behind, a moveable cover and a pull-down seat.

"She's not fashionable, my little jalopy," said Monsieur Subligny, "but she's solid and that's the primary quality needed to run over the roads in this bitch of a rocky country. That's what I was repeating once again to Monsieur du Pommeval, who won't believe me. He has to have a Parisian carriage maker...and one of these days he'll turn it over going to Germonière. Get in, Roger, it's time to leave!"

"*I understand now,*" thought Roger. "*It's this du Pommeval who's asked the Doctor to present his request...and he won't be refused now that he's so rich. Pray God he's chosen...the other one.*"

Monsieur Subligny already had the reins in his hands. Roger had to take a seat to his left and wait for him to finish his indiscretions by naming which of the two sisters the wealthy heir of the Vignemal couple would honor with his preference. The mare the doctor drove carelessly, sitting on the seat destined to an absent coachman, left at a slow trot, and after several detours turned into National Street. There were numerous people strolling about there and it was easy to believe that Monsieur Subligny, passing by carrying an unknown young man in his jalopy, was commented on in all tones of voice. The direction the carriage took indicated well enough that the travelers were making their way to Germonière. And the curious concluded very quickly that the stranger was a suitor for the hand of one of the daughters of Madame Daudièrne. The news spread with electric rapidity and three-quarters of an hour later, all of Arcy knew it. But no one had recognized the little Pontac boy who in the past raced through the Fogèray woods in his peasant shirt and country shoes.

"You see, my boy," exclaimed Monsieur Subligny. "They don't remember you, these paving stones stompers. I'm delighted about that because you have nothing to gain frequenting them. Country people have more memory, unfortunately, since one of them reported your walk around your cousin's property."

"Unfortunately Why! I certainly have the right to go where I wish," murmured Pontac, somewhat astonished.

"Without a doubt…but goodness isn't the distinctive trait of Arcy's inhabitants. You have no ideas of the absurdities they dream up. But you don't care anything about that, and you're right. And, speaking of their inventions, tell me, then, have you ever encountered Roch Ferrar?"

"Roch Ferrar? I don't know that name."

"Good! But you may know the individual who wears it. A fellow about twenty years old who camps out in the woods like a Huron Indian and poaches everywhere. You could have run into him tending his snares on the Duke de Bretteville's land."

"He wouldn't risk it there. The Bretêche forest is too well guarded. And to keep this homeless man from destroying the game there, I'll turn him in this evening to Monsieur de Bretteville's manager."

"Don't do that, please. That boy interests me. I've set his broken bones two or three times and I have the weakness of becoming attached to my patients, as if I were still in the regiment."

"Why doesn't he join the army instead of being a vagabond? That's the advice I'd give him, if I found him in my path."

"He wouldn't follow it, and I urge you very strongly not to speak to him if you ever see him."

"I don't intend to start a conversation with your protégé, but how will I know it's he?"

"Oh! You can't make a mistake about it. He resembles neither a peasant nor a monsieur. He has a bronzed complexion, hair black as jade…"

Monsieur Subligny wasn't telling the truth because it wasn't at all by chance that he had casually thrown out Roch Ferrar's name. He wanted to be sure that the suppositions of the Procurer of the Republic were not well founded and Roger's frank and clear answers had just informed him on this point. But he didn't think he had to tell this fine boy the ridiculous suspicions of which he'd

272

been the object. He thought an instant about telling him how Roch had been present at the death of the Vignemals. That would have been rather natural, but nevertheless he kept his silence. He thought it useless to create an opportunity for a meeting between these two men that a newly appointed magistrate had so unlikely accused of being in complicity to commit a crime. He even wondered if it wouldn't be better, when introducing Roger at Germonière, not to speak of his relationship to Madame Vignemal.

"What would be the use?" he said to himself. *"When the Daudièrnes learn that he's coming on behalf of the Duke of Bretteville, they'll no longer remember that day before yesterday I named him as one of the wronged heirs. If they do remember it, they may believe they're obligated to express their condolences, which would embarrass him. And it would be a matter only of the accident. That would be very sad. Decidedly. I won't say anything. It's up to him to see if it's proper to pass himself off as a put upon cousin."*

The mare was trotting at a steady pace and they had made good time.

"We're coming to Germonire," said Pontac. "I can see the tops of the trees of the Tertre woods."

"You must have played around her from your early childhood," said the doctor.

"I came every day to run about the park in the time when the house was not lived in. I could still walk about it with my eyes closed."

"Madame Daudièrne bought the land and the chateau in 1871, but for the first three or four years she seldom lived here. Her daughters' education kept her in Paris."

"She has two of them, I believe."

"Yes, and a son, who's not worth as much as his sisters."

"Are they about the same age," Roger asked, to start the doctor on the way to clearing things up.

"The oldest is past twenty-three; the youngest is twenty and a half. You can see it's time for them to marry, the eldest especially."

"And that time's not long off, you've told me."

"You can never be sure about those things. It's not enough just to ask for the hand of a young girl of good family. These young ladies have the right to be demanding...Laurence, particularly...and their mother is not a woman to force them to marry."

Roger trembled in hearing that name of Laurence which wasn't the one the echo of the Lemon Rock had repeated. Monsieur Subligny's words seemed to indicate that his mission concerned the elder of the two sisters, the one it was time to marry. Was Germaine the younger? Roger didn't know and he didn't intend to find out without giving up his secret.

"Mademoiselle Laurence, that's...the youngest probably?" he asked timidly.

"No," answered the Doctor. "She's the oldest and I find her even more attractive than Germaine, who's three years younger than she is. Both of them are adorable young girls, but Laurence will be a perfect woman."

"While her sister..."

"Mon Dieu! Her sister has the germ of all the qualities which will assure the happiness of a family. It's just a question of developing them, and that'll be up to her husband. If he knows how to make her love him, he'll be the happiest of men. But if he goes about it backward, I wouldn't guarantee anything. Germaine is giddy, willful and her mind is turned toward the romantic. She'll correct herself later of these small faults, but Laurence is already mature enough for marriage."

"No more doubt," Roger said to himself, completely reassured. *"It's the eldest who's going to become Madame du Pommeval."*

"I don't know why I'm going into all these details," Monsieur Subligny continued. "You're not a suitor and you're not even thinking of getting married. You'll wait to get married until you're a captain, and you'll be right. It's better to remain a bachelor than to make a bad marriage and a First Lieutenant always marries badly. When I think that, on leaving the Val-de-Grace with the rank of Assistant Aide Major, I almost married a lingerie maker from the Rue St. Jacques, I still shake."

Pontac gave a hearty laugh. The Doctor had just, without knowing it, pulled him up short and brought him suddenly back to reality.

"We're coming into the avenue," said the ex-military surgeon after a rather long silence, "and there's Baptiste. He seems to be going to put a letter in the post box and he'll inform us as we pass by."

"Is Madame at home?" he shouted to the old valet, who greeted him respectfully.

"Madame is in the garden with the young ladies," Baptiste answered. "I think they've gone in the direction of the periwinkle lane. Monsieur Armand has gone out with his gun to shoot ducks on the river."

"I like it this way," the doctor said very low. "The uncle would have bothered me. You'll go join him after having paid your compliments to the lady of the house and you'll keep him busy while I take care of the mission I've been charged with."

The arrangement proposed by Monsieur Subligny pleased Roger only slightly. He was a great deal less interested in inviting the uncle than in talking freely with the younger of his nieces. He felt strongly that that interview would decide his fate. The encounter at the Lemon Rock was only a beginning. A well-brought up young girl doesn't show her true feelings in a first tête-à-tête. And everything depended on the welcome Germaine would give to First Lieutenant Pontac, properly introduced by a friend of the family. However, it was necessary to hope for the best and to step down with the doctor in front of the service buildings where the coachman, who had seen them come down the avenue, was waiting for them to unhitch the carriage and lead the mare to the stables.

"Madame Daudièrne is in the garden with her daughters. That's very nice," grumbled the Doctor, "but the devil if I know where to find the periwinkle path."

"I know where it is," Roger said quickly, "and I'll take you there. You should begin by introducing me to Madame Daudièrne."

"That's the proper order. And even if Monsieur Armand has gone hunting too far away, you can still explain to his sister-in-law the purpose of your visit. After that you'll be free to leave or to stay. If you stay, you won't be bored. The young ladies are very likeable."

"I don't have a set schedule," Roger stammered.

The house built by the druggist was situated between the courtyard and the garden in the old-fashioned way, but the new owner had had the walls separating them torn down.

"Do you recognize this place?" asked Monsieur Subligny as they both came into the grand alley which lay in a straight line from the steps right down to the river.

"Perfectly," murmured the Hussard officer. "I find the park just as I left it. There, to the left is the Orangerie; a little further on, the cage for the hunting hawks. Here's the little artificial lake with its wooden bridge to the kiosque decorated with colored glass. And to the right, the great mass of ancient trees."

"Yes, Madame Daudièrne was right not to go to the expense to arrange her domain in the English fashion by planting artificial grass lawns and planting cottages constructed in the Champs Elysees here. There's nothing changed here but us, my boy. But it's a matter of taking the shortest tangent to reach the periwinkle walk."

"We just have to go through this grove of larch trees."

"These larch trees have grown since you've seen them. But the grotto is still where it was. The druggist was generous with artificial grottos and plaster figures. Here's a Flora who's lost an arm and a Faun who's no longer on his pedestal."

Roger was looking distractedly at the rocks entwined with ivy and the statues turned green by the moss. His mind was elsewhere. Fate shortened for him the agony of waiting. At the turn of a shady pathway, the First Lieutenant and the doctor saw Madame Daudièrne, who was walking straight toward them with one of her daughters that Pontac recognized very quickly under her blue flannel hood. Monsieur Subligny found his legs of twenty-years before to spare them half of the walk and he reached them saying:

"Good morning Madame. Good morning, Mademoiselle Germaine. You're surprised to see me at this hour, aren't you? But doing it once won't make it a habit. I deserted my office to come to Germonière. My patients will have to get on the best they can. Today, I'd like to introduce you to my young friend, Roger Pontac, an officer of the Hussards, whom I haven't seen in a long time and who finds himself at the present time your country neighbor. He's living in the

Bretteville chateau and he's brought Monsieur Armand an invitation from the Duke."

"My brother-in-law will be infinitely flattered," stammered Madame Daudièrne, very surprised. "He doesn't have the honor of knowing Monsieur de Bretteville, and..."

"Monsieur de Bretteville knew, Madame," said Roger, "that Monsieur Daudièrne would enjoy hunting in the Bretteville forest and he's asked me to..."

"Oh! Monsieur," Germaine interrupted, "you can't imagine what pleasure you're going to give my uncle. He thinks only about the little Bretteville goats. He dreams about them and if you're bringing him permission to shoot them..."

"As many as he likes, Mademoiselle. Monsieur le Duc will put game-keepers and beaters at his disposal."

Roger had gotten back his self-possession since he had understood the situation. Evidently, Mademoiselle Daudièrne had said nothing about her adventure. Or if she had spoken about it, she'd taken care not to mention the most characteristic incident of the trip to the Rock of the Fairies. Her mother had shown no reaction when Monsieur Subligny had said the name Pontac. This was not, however, the first time she had heard this easy to remember name. The Doctor had said it in front of her apropos of the Vignemal inheritance, but she had completely forgotten it. Germaine was the only one at Germonière who remembered it. Madame Daudièrne didn't suspect that the Duke de Bretteville's ambassador was not a stranger to the younger of her daughters. That amiable Germaine wasn't at all troubled on seeing her cavalier appear. You might have said she was expecting him. And her discretion as far as her mother was concerned seemed a good sign to Roger.

"My brother-in-law will be very sorry not to have been here to meet you, Monsieur," Madame Daudièrne said. "He's gone hunting rather far from here and I doubt that he'll return before nightfall, but he'll certainly go to thank Monsieur de Bretteville and he'll have the honor of seeing you at the same time."

"While waiting, dear Madame," began the Doctor, who wanted to get to his purpose quickly. "My young friend and I wouldn't like to interrupt your walk. I need to talk to you about a serious matter, but I think we can deal with it very well outside. The weather is like springtime and the private talk I ask for won't take long."

"As you like, Doctor," said the lady, not without glancing out of the corner of her eye at her daughter and the handsome young officer, who had come to them out of nowhere.

"Laurence won't be long in coming to join us, I think?" she asked, addressing Germaine, who was quick to answer.

"She would already have been here if she hadn't stopped to pick up faded periwinkles. She is mad about herbs. Me, I detest them. Herbs are the cemeteries for flowers. But she walks faster than we do, and she'll catch up with us her in five minutes."

"Dear Doctor, I'm yours," continued Madame Daudièrne, walking faster, so as to leave the young people a little behind. "The gentleman will please excuse me for a few minutes. Germaine is going to show him our magnolias. They're the most beautiful in the whole country and I don't know if you could find any in Paris any taller."

Pontac didn't ask for anything better than to stay behind alone with Mademoiselle Germaine and he blessed the older sister's absence. The uncle wasn't there either. Everything was coming together to help him with an explanation, just the thought of which made his heart beat.

"I really knew that you'd come," Germaine said to him with an encouraging smile.

"Then, Mademoiselle, you'll forgive me for using a pretext," he murmured.

"That pretext, I was the one who pointed it out to you the day before yesterday. It wouldn't be very gracious of me to reproach you for having used it. But I wasn't sure you'd agree to use it and it was because I wasn't sure that I didn't tell here about our meeting and our trip. Now that you've come, I no longer have the same reasons to be silent and my mother will be told how you got me out of dangerous situation. As soon as she's finished with that excellent Doctor, I'll tell her the story of my adventures. But I can't imagine what he has to say to her in secret that's so important."

"I believe I know, Mademoiselle," Roger said timidly.

At the same moment, Monsieur Sibligny, who always came to the point, broached the big question after a short preamble.

"Yes, dear Madame," he was saying, "it's very serious. Arthur du Pommeval came to me this morning, expressly to ask me to present his request. He could have chosen a better go-between, because as a bachelor I'm very inexperienced in these things. But you know he hasn't even one relative left in the world and that's I'm his doctor and his friend. Therefore I agree to represent him and I have the honor of being closely enough tied to you for you not to hesitate to answer me frankly...and immediately, because I won't hide from you the fact that this young man is very much in a hurry to become your son-in-law."

"In too much a hurry," Madame Daudièrne answered, smiling. "His uncle Vignemal isn't yet buried. The request you're making me flatters me a great deal, but it seems to me premature."

"I'm not saying the contrary, but men in love jump over social customs with both feet, and du Pommeval is crazy in love."

"I was aware of that the last time he came to Germonière. He danced with my daughter the whole evening."

"He would have proposed a year ago if he had dared. But then he possessed only a modest income. He's rich now...at least, he's going to be. And you will probably be touched with his speed to put his fortune at the feet of Mademoiselle Daudièrne. His first thought was for her."

"I certainly understand that he could have changed feelings when his fortune changed. I'm persuaded his love is sincere and that he has everything which could make my daughter happy. However, I still have to consult my daughter before I answer for her."

"That's only too right, dear Madame, and the sooner the better because I don't doubt the answer will be favorable."

Madame Daudièrne was very moved and Monsieur Subligny was silent in order to give her time to compose herself. Ten steps behind them another dialogue was following its course.

"So," Germaine was saying, "The Doctor admitted to you that he came to deliver a proposal of marriage?"

"He didn't admit it to me, because I didn't ask him about it. He told me about it spontaneously."

"And...did he tell you if it was a matter of my sister or me?"

"No. Mademoiselle. And I didn't want to ask him because I was shaking that I might learn it was for you."

"If it were for me, the marriage would never be concluded like that. I'll marry whom I want to, I assure you. But at least Monsieur Subligny told you the name of the suitor?"

"Not that either, Mademoiselle, but I think I guessed it. The Doctor had a visit today from Monsieur du Pommeval."

"Good! Then it isn't my liberty he wants to take away. Monsieur du Pommeval is very much in love with Laurence, who, I think, is well disposed toward him. And I would be delighted if this marriage took place."

"And I. I ardently hope that you're not mistaken about Monsieur du Pommeval's intentions."

"I can't be mistaken. First of all, for some time he has shown more strongly his preference for my sister. Then, she's the elder, and she must marry before the younger. The opposite would be ridiculous. And besides, if it was about me, Monsieur Subligny would have awaited a better time to present his request. He's taking advantage of the moment Laurence is absent. You'll see. As soon as she comes, the marriage interview will stop. The Doctor will come join us very nicely and my mother will call Laurence to let her know the honor Monsieur Vignemal's heir is doing her."

"Pray God you're right, Mademoiselle," Roger murmured.

While they were exchanging guesses and wishes in a low voice, Madame again said in a firmer tone:

"You know me, my dear Doctor, and you know I don't understand forced marriages. I chose Monsieur Daudièrne, who had no fortune, and I did the right thing in marrying him. I won't apply pressure on my daughter's decision."

"You can at least give her advice."

"Absolutely, but I'll leave her free to accept or refuse Monsieur du Pommeval."

"That's as I would expect it to be. I just ask you to put to her, right now, the proposition of this poor fellow who's dying of impatience."

"Gladly, and as soon as Laurence has joined us, which shouldn't be very long, I'm going to ask her to tell me what she thinks of..."

"Pardon, dear Madame," interrupted Monsieur Subligny, "but...I don't follow you. You're talking to me about Mademoiselle Laurence..."

"Naturally, I can't decide anything without her."

"Why? I've just asked you for the hand of Mademoiselle Germaine for my young friend. It's not necessary for you to ask her sister's advice."

"Germaine!" Madame Daudiere exclaimed. "It's Germaine that Monsieur du Pommeval wants to marry?"

"Yes, dear Madame," the Doctor said, smiling. "I was wrong not to name her at the beginning of our talk, but I didn't think you could misunderstand my friend's intentions."

"My misunderstanding was completely natural. Your friend was openly courting Laurence, who certainly noticed it. How could I have guessed he was thinking of her sister?"

"He certainly did the wrong thing there, because he's completely smitten with Mademoiselle Germaine. That's how lovers are. They're always afraid of betraying the secret of their preference, and to hide it they play little comedies which society takes seriously. But I'll bet Mademoselle Germaine is not deceived."

"And I, on the contrary, believe that she doesn't at all suspect having inspired passion in this young man. He paid attention to her as he paid attention to many others, but he certainly didn't propose. Germaine would have told me."

"She's perhaps going to tell you if you'll please tell her of the proposal I bring."

"Yes, certainly, I will. The situation my daughters find themselves in can't be prolonged."

"Your two daughters, dear Madame? Ah! I understand. You're saying it's painful for the elder to see her sister married before her. That's true,... but these things happen every day...and besides, Mademoiselle won't at all lack suitors. She's charming, and I can certainly admit that if du Pommeval had consulted me, I would have counseled him to try to please her. But people who are smitten don't consult anyone."

"Smitten!" Madame Daudeirne repeated. "Is he so much in love as that?"

"No one could be more so. He can no longer sleep; and he might die of sorrow if I bring him back a refusal."

"I didn't think him so passionate. He seemed to me to love only luxury...horses, social life."

"He was trying to drown his sorrows because he despaired of being accepted because of his mediocre fortune. Now, he's a totally different man. He's thinking only of happiness for two."

279

"That's good…that's very good. If he can come to an agreement with Germaine, I won't try to prevent them from being happy. But after all, Monsieur du Pommeval isn't flattering himself that my daughter's going to say yes without thinking about it. She doesn't know him, although she's seen him often. She can judge his dress in a drawing room; she hasn't been able to study his character. And I'm sure she won't decide except after a longer and more decisive test."

"Oh! He'll accept all the tests that can be imposed on him. What he asks for the moment is authorization to begin his courtship trying to obtain the consent of the one he loves and whom he hopes to make love him. For the rest, it wouldn't be decent for him to get married before the end of his required mourning. Mademoiselle will have a lot of time to decide, knowing what she's doing."

"With these reservations, my dear Doctor, I'm ready to tell my younger daughter the proposal you're making on behalf of Monsieur du Pommeval. I'm going to call her. Also, is it very proper that I've left her alone with the young man you've introduced us to?"

"Oh! You don't need fear that he will put himself forward as a suitor. He's an honest boy and he knows that a soldier of fortune, or rather without a fortune, cannot place himself in the social rank to marry one of the Daudièrne young ladies. I'm going to go join him and I'll keep him busy while Arthur du Pommeval's future is decided. Besides, I see Mademoiselle Laurence, who'll help me show him the beauties of your park."

While using this reassuring language to the mother, Monsieur Subligny slowed his walk to wait for the young people, and Laurence joined the group standing in the middle of the larch tree path. She held in her hand a bunch of periwinkles, those false violets which sometimes bloom again in autumn. She looked curiously at Roger Pontac and Monsieur Subligny quickly introduced him. Madame Daudièrne took Germaine's arm and gently led her away while the doctor, to occupy the Hussard officer and the elder sister, made an effort to have them admire the giant magnolias, famous twenty leagues away.

"My dear child, I have great news to tell you," the chatelaine of Germonière said, leaning to whisper in her daughter's ear.

"My dear mother, I believe I've guessed that great news." Germaine gaily replied. "This dear Doctor has put on his kid gloves and a dress coat. That get-up means a marriage proposal."

"You're gifted with second sight. Monsieur Subligny has come on behalf of…"

"On behalf of Monsieur du Pommeval."

"Precisely."

"To ask you to give him the hand of Mademoiselle Laurence Daudièrne."

"No, yours."

"That's not possible!" Germaine exclaimed, sincerely astonished. "The Doctor must have misunderstood. It's Laurence Monsieur du Pommeval wants to marry. He's been in love with her for three years and the last time he spent the evening here, he no longer took any pains to hide his passion. He had eyes…and waltzes…only for my dear sister."

"You didn't see very well or you interpreted his conduct badly. Monsieur Subligny explained himself very categorically. And he's waiting for your answer to report it to his young friend. It's only up to you to become Madame du Pommeval."

"What! Immediately, on the spot! But I don't love him, this handsome millionaire, and all I know about him is that he's a good dancer."

"Then…you don't like him?"

"No, and I believe he would displease Laurence less. What made him propose to me? Young girls should marry in the old-fashioned order. It's not my turn."

"Don't say silly things and listen to me. It's not a matter of getting engaged exactly at this moment. Monsieur du Pommeval only asks permission to pay court, and to come often to Germonière…"

"But he comes whenever he wants to. He doesn't budge from Germonière and it's not as if he lacked opportunities to propose What's got into him to make him want to play the boring role of an official candidate? He must be very timid if he needs your permission to tell me what he thinks of me…and what he wants. I don't know if he adores me as he claims to, but really he's going about it all wrong."

"But think a moment, Germaine. In the social world we live in, things are always done this way. You'd be the first to be offended if a young man offered you his heart while dancing with you. Monsieur du Pommeval is following custom, which means first addressing a young girl's parents."

"Good! But it's still necessary that the young girl is somewhat expecting to be asked. And I wasn't expecting it at all. I thought he was in love with Laurence, and as she's not at all like me, I can't suppose he could pass quickly from the brunette to the blonde, to the well-behaved to the silly one. In short, I'm not prepared to answer."

"Nevertheless, I have to answer. Would you be displeased if I encouraged Monsieur du Pommeval's hopes?"

"To say 'encourage' would be saying too much. It's enough to allow him to continue his visits."

"Then you're not absolutely turning down his proposal?"

"I'm holding on to my liberty."

"You know very well I'm not thinking of taking it away from you. Just let me tell you that this young man is very rich…"

"A great deal too rich for me."

"Also that the magnificent land he's going to inherit is adjacent to our Germonière property that we all love."

"The neighborhood has nothing to do with it."

"Last of all, this marriage would insure you the first social rank in the country where we spend several months each year..."

"I don't doubt I'd dazzle the inhabitants of Arcy, but..."

"As to the person attributes of Monsieur du Pommeval, that's up to you to decide what they are...to you alone. And you can't estimate them except by at least letting him demonstrate them. All I ask you is not to refuse without examining a proposal you may perhaps later regret."

Madame Daudièrne had taken the right tact and her moderation brought Germaine's hesitations to an end.

"Well! I won't refuse, but I want to set my conditions."

"Provided they are acceptable, I..."

"The first is that nothing about our relations with Monsieur du Pommeval will change. He'll come as in the past...more often if he wants to. He'll lay siege to my heart as he means to. I won't promise to give in, but I won't resist on purpose. It's up to him to conquer me, and if he really loves me, I believe he'll succeed because I believe love must be contagious. But if, by chance," Germaine added bursting out laughing, "he comes to see it's Laurence he's in love with, I won't hold it against him."

"You can never be serious. I don't consider the conditional engagement you describe any the less an engagement and I'm going to transmit the answer to Monsieur Subligny. Let's go join him."

So it was done. The two groups merged. However, Madame Daudièrne took the Doctor's arm and whispered in his ear:

"You didn't hope, nor did I, that Germaine would say yes right off. She asks to think about it, but she would see Monsieur du Pommeval continue his visits to Germonière with pleasure."

"That's all he can hope for at the moment, and I'll hasten to tell him my mission has succeeded," murmured the Doctor. "So I'm going to take leave of you and take away my young officer, who must be in your way. You must need to chat with Monsieur Armand...and with the young ladies."

"Yes, I need to consult my brother-in-law and I can't hide from my elder daughter the fact that Monsieur du Pommeval has asked for the hand of her sister."

Laurence approached just at the moment her mother was speaking of her.

"Could you please tell me, dear Doctor," said the jilted girl, "why those gentlemen from Arcy have abandoned us? Nobody has come for three days."

While Monsieur Subligny was explaining to her at great length that the recent mourning of the head of the elegant youths had upset all the projects for evenings of dancing. Germaine was saying to Roger Pontac:

"I've changed my mind. I won't ever tell my mother about our encounter at the foot of the Lemon Rock."

"I know why you've changed your mind, Mademoiselle," Roger said sadly, "and I think as you do that the only thing left for me is to try to forget you."

"You've guessed that Monsieur du Pommeval has asked me to marry him,"

Germaine answered quickly, "but you can't know what I answered. You have to know it. I answered that I would decide later and in the meantime I'd receive Monsieur du Pommeval on the same footing as in the past."

"Isn't that as if you were engaged?"

"He might think so, but what does that matter? I have a reason for preventing our house being closed to him...and I really want to confide this motive to you...if you promise me to keep to yourself what I'm going to tell you."

"You mistrust my discretion?"

"No, and to prove it, here's my secret. I'm sure that my sister loves Monsieur du Pommeval and I want him to marry her."

"But he doesn't love her. It's you he loves."

"He imagines he does; I intend to prove to him that he's mistaken. You see I don't have any doubt about anything. And now that you've been brought up to date on my projects, I hope we'll see each other again. My uncle, by going to thank Monsieur de Bretteville, is sure to invite you to Germonière. It's useless for you to wait for him today. He won't come back before nightfall."

Roger, pale with emotion and joy, was looking for an answer, when the Doctor stepped in saying to him:

"Good fellow, it's late and I'm expected in Arcy. Your commission is completed. I'm going to take you back in the Tilbury right up to the first turn in the Bretteville Road."

"I'm counting on your returning soon, Monsieur," Madame Daudièrne added graciously. "My brother-in-law will go pick you up."

In any other circumstance the good lady wouldn't have let a stranger leave without offering him to sit down in comfort in the drawing room. However, Monsieur Subligny's declarations had so troubled her that she passed over the most elementary rule of politeness for chatelaines. Besides, no one wanted to prolong these interviews in the open air. Germaine had done what she intended. Laurence suspected that between her mother and Monsieur Subligny, she was the one it was about. She wanted to clear up her doubts. The Doctor was in a hurry to report good news to his candidate and Roger only asked to be alone to regain possession of himself. The poor Lieutenant was carrying away hope. He didn't dare yet believe that Mademoiselle Daudièrne would perhaps decide to prefer the cape and sword of the disinherited cousin of Madame Vignemal to the millions of Arthur du Pommeval. The future was reserving more strange surprises to all the characters of this drama, the first scene of which had been acted out at the Beuvron ferry.

IV. Arthur du Pommeval

Socially speaking, the human species is subdivided into different categories. Each one has its manners, its tastes and its particular instincts. In France there are people who have good manners and those who don't. There are people who live in the provinces and those who live in Paris, without counting several sub-genres which differ essentially one from the other. A pure-blooded *boulevardier* has more in common with a Russian than with someone who lives in a small village.

Arthur du Pommeval belonged to a variety which tended to merge, because he pretended to be the cock of Arcy and to play at the same time a certain role on the pavements of Paris, where he spent six months of the year. In general, young rural men who intend to shine tip to one side or the other. Some of them, disdaining the success of the Sous Prefecture, launch themselves hardily and without hope of return into the great furnace where patrimonies melt like wax. Almost all of them burn their wings there, but there are also some who finally stand on their feet on the slippery boulevard pavement and make a place for themselves. The latter, after some years, lose the taste for the soil and become more Parisian than the Parisians themselves and remain Parisians forever. Others, and these are the most numerous, recognize rather quickly that they will never get used to being lost in the crowd. They lower themselves to the easier and less costly triumphs awaiting them in their native soil. They content themselves with astonishing their fellow citizens with follies which don't exceed certain limits, and by luxury which doesn't bankrupt them. Then, when the psychological moment comes, they marry and they resign themselves, without too much trouble, to dividing their existence between twelve-course dinners, whist at five *sous* a point and hunting parties where you have to walk six hours in order to shoot a partridge. There were others who lower themselves even to spending their evenings at the Café au Commerce with traveling salesmen and civil servants.

Arthur du Pommeval wasn't yet at that point and he hoped never to be there. He wasn't at all renouncing being the first in Arcy but he also attached great price to not losing his Parisian associates.

Arthur got from his father a very pronounced tendency to rise above his social condition and to push himself into society. In the past his father flaunted claims to nobility and elegance. It had cost him half of his fortune to shine in Paris and to be on friendly terms with the country squires. But Arthur also took after his mother, the sister of Monsieur Vignemal, with a solid foundation of order and prudence, two qualities essentially provincial. Orphaned at fifteen, of age at eighteen, he had begun by making a hole in his capital, driving a four-horse team in the summer down the grand Rue d'Arcy-sur-Beuvron Avenue and in appearing in the winter at the first nights of Parisian theatres. But he had always thought of marrying advantageously, as soon as he found the opportunity. That opportunity hadn't yet presented itself and his fortune had already undergone notable losses when Madame Daudièrne began the habit of spending the good season every year at Germonière with her children. Arthur told himself that he might find there what he was looking for. The two girls were charming, perfectly brought up and had serious qualities. The mother was said to have a very nice fortune, and the Uncle Armand, who was very rich, didn't seemed disposed to disinherit his nieces. For a boy who'd eaten into his fifteen thousand income, these young ladies were very good prospects. As a result, du Pommeval had begun to maneuver. He saw them often during their stay in the country and he got himself invited to the drawing rooms in Paris where they went. His first efforts at an approach hadn't moved his affair very far. They gladly invited him but a close relationship wasn't making any progress when Monsieur Armand Daudière's coming to live at his sister-in-law's chateau had offered the enterprising Arthur new methods of attack. The fine young man had pleased the old bachelor, who was trying to recruit lively young people to entertain him in his spare time on country holiday. And Monsieur du Pommeval, with a permanent invitation, having put himself on the footing of coming almost every day to Germonière, had finally initiated serious operations.

He lacked neither intelligence nor tact, and he was very careful not to present himself immediately as a suitor. He felt it was first necessary to gain the confidence of Madame Daudièrne and to be sure of the support of Uncle Armand, who had something to say in the matter. Then, discreeetly doing his utmost to please the two sisters, testing the water before going any further, and finally choosing the one who seemed to respond to his advances, he found both of them very much to his taste and he couldn't make a choice.

It should be said that at the beginning of his amorous campaign, he wasn't in a position to choose. The less endowed of the two young girls would have done him great honor by consenting to marry him. It was very difficult to decide which of them had the most merits before knowing them better. They were equal in beauty although that of Germaine was perhaps the most attractive. And the marriage he was trying to achieve could only be a love match because these young ladies were in a position to find husbands in Paris richer and nobler than Arthur du Pommeval. Above all, it was a matter of inspiring in one of them a strong enough feeling to lead her beyond the inconvenience of a marriage with a young man who brought only an embarrassingly small fortune.

Therefore he had carefully avoided showing a preference and he thought only of showing off the advantages nature had endowed him with. He was a pretty boy, distinguished in looks and manners; he was a marvelous dancer, and he knew how to talk to women, which is rarer. He didn't lack conceit, but he hid it, and although he had a practical mind, he was very capable of being carried away by emotion. To sum it up, his good qualities outweighed his faults a great deal.

With so many advantages and that sophistication which society gives, he could scarcely fail to succeed at Germonière, and he had succeeded there. But from that combined system he'd put in practice, there had resulted two things he hadn't foreseen. Laurence had fallen in love with him and he had fallen violently in love with Germaine, who didn't love him at all. His careful calculations were turning against him. He was being severely punished for having shilly-shallied instead of frankly declaring himself. Love is an emotion which can't adapt to compromises and hesitation. Love has nothing in common with opportunism and gets revenge on those who try to hold it back or make it agree with self-interest.

Arthur du Pommeval's clever maneuvers had resulted in nothing but placing him between two troublesome alternatives: to give up a young girl he adored to marry a young girl who only half-way pleased him, or not to marry anyone. Now, he understood very well that they intended for Mademoiselle Laurence Daudièrne to marry first. They wouldn't, to please him, go against the rules of marital hierarchy. Anyone else would have considered himself beaten and would have chosen to retreat. He'd had the courage to stay and to suppress his feelings, in order to hold on the future. He began to pay court to Mademoiselle Laurence assiduously without ceasing, for all that, being very attentive to her sister. Laurence was deceived, but Germaine saw through it. She had guessed that this perpetual suitor was tactfully handling, as they say, the *chèvre et le chou*,[33] and finally, rather than remain a bachelor, he would accept whichever of the two girls they would give him.

Things were at that stage when the ferry accident had made Monsieur Vignemal's nephew a millionaire. And he has to be given credit for the fact that he hadn't for a single minute thought of placing his choice and his new fortune elsewhere, although now he could marry someone much richer. But he told himself that nothing now stood any longer in the way of his showing his preference for Germaine. Among the most virtuous bourgeoisie, when an exceptional opportunity presented itself, they didn't hesitate to get the younger established in marriage before the elder. "Exceptional opportunity," that's the phrase the advertisers use in fashion magazines. And it can accurately be used for marital affairs.

Behaving this way, du Pommeval didn't betray any vow. He had made Mademoiselle Laurence think that he was hoping for her hand, but he had very carefully not committed himself by too ardent speeches, by those words which escape sincere lovers and which are the same as a promise. He thought himself free in very good faith, and it seemed to him very natural to follow his preference, now that he had the means, as they say vulgarly. He became a provincial again. His mother's lessons bore their fruits. She had taught him from his youth

---

[33] Holding a cabbage in front of a goat to manipulate him.

that money was the king of the world and that you can do anything when you're rich. He was sincerely sorry for Laurence, whom he was dropping, and he had no doubt he could make himself pleasing to Germaine, who didn't yet love him but would certainly love him soon. She couldn't help but be flattered to see the king of the golden Arcy youth place his heart and his wealth at her feet. He even thought himself very generous and very chivalrous in behaving this way. If he hadn't been in love, he would never have returned to Germonière. He would have gone to take up quarters in Paris, where money opens wide drawing room doors to heirs looking for a wife.

On the contrary, he hadn't lost an instant to propose, since the day after the death of his uncle, he had sent Monsieur Subligny as an ambassador. The Doctor had brought him back an encouraging answer, but at the same time he hadn't hidden from him the opinion of the President concerning the point of law relating to the interests of the heirs of Monsieur and Madame Vignemal. The presumption of survival wasn't applicable in this instance and it was up to Monsieur du Pommeval to prove that his uncle was the last one to die. If he couldn't do this, Madame Vignemal's will was null and void and all her fortune would go to her near relatives, cousins, uncles, aunts, etc.

This was a lightening bolt out of the blue for poor Arthur. It was useless for Monsieur Subligny to affirm that the President thought the lawsuit very winnable, to such an extent that he, Jean Subligny, ex-Surgeon-Major and Chevalier de la Legion d'Honneur, hadn't thought he should delay fulfilling his mission to Madame Daudièrne. He added, in vain, that he was strongly persuaded he could demonstrate with medical proof that the husband must have survived the wife. Nothing would do. Arthur, his illusions lost, fell into deep discouragement.

Four days had gone by and he had gotten over this blow, so much harder for him, since the reversal in the situation wasn't yet known in Arcy. The Doctor had kept the secret and when following the funeral procession of the couple who would rest side by side in the cemetery of their native village, du Pommeval had been very aware of the looks full of hatred directed at him by his aunt's cousins, who thought themselves disinherited by the law. He was considered everywhere as the heir and he didn't dare confide his worries to anyone.

But the truth wasn't long in coming out. Madame Vignemal's poor relatives weren't people to renounce their cousin's inheritance without consulting a lawyer. And lawyers don't commit blunders when it's a matter of interpreting three Articles of the Civil Code. These kinds of errors are pardonable only to lay people and doctors who haven't studied law.

It was time for du Pommeval to take a position and above all to decide how he was going to present himself at Germonière. He hadn't showed up there since the Doctor had reported the authorization to come there as often as he liked. The death and burial of the victims of the accident excused an absence of several days, but the moment had come to go back on stage, to leave his house where he had been confined by decency and, above all, by fear of learning bad news. It was absolutely necessary to reappear in Arcy streets, to confront the questions of curious Arcy citizens, under pain of letting people think he had given up the inheritance. It was also necessary to go thank Madame Daudièrne, to begin the probation that Germain had imposed on him, and to put himself on guard against Laurence's resentment. Worse than all that, he must talk business with Uncle Armand, who would be sure to bring up the serious question of when he would come into possession. What should he say to him? Lying was repugnant to du Pommeval, and, besides, the truth was going to burst out any day. The Doctor wasn't there to advise him. The Doctor had been called away for a consultation by one of his usual patients who happened, by chance, to be in Paris. Du Pommeval, after a number of hesitations, decided to ask the President what he thought of his case. The step was delicate because the President had the very well-deserved reputation of being a magistrate strongly attached to his professional duties and very little accessible to solicitations, from whomever they came. What's more he didn't have a very high opinion of handsome Arthur, who had a reputation for throwing money out the windows and for leading a hardly edifying life. But after all, the President had been somewhat close to Monsieur du Pommeval, who had been somewhat prodigal himself and father of this prodigal boy. He could hardly refuse to advise his son. Besides, according to what Monsieur Subligny said, he was well disposed toward Monsieur Vignemal's heir. He had even let it be seen that the case would be judge in a sense favorable to his claims. Du Pommeval had too much tact to presume on a confidence the Doctor shouldn't have repeated, and he would be very careful not to allude to it when speaking with the President. But nothing prevented him from talking to an old friend of his father about his painful situation and to ask him how he should go about introducing an *instance* in this rather unusual case.

His resolution taken and his topic decided on, Arthur alerted the coachman to have the coupe that he used only on important occasions ready, and to get ready to leave for Germonière. He had to go there or run the risk of being thought impolite whatever advice the President gave about the procedure to follow. And then, even if his case was lost in advance before the tribunal, Arthur didn't despair of keeping in the good graces of the Daudièrne family. At this point, frankness was cleverness. He plan was to tell everything, and if it came to it, to state clearly that the Vignemal inheritance wasn't going to come to him. Then, once the admission was out, to elaborate sentimental variations on this very easy to develop motif.

"When I learned I was going to be rich, my first thought was to ask for Mademoiselle Germaine's hand, which I couldn't aspire to when I was poor. I learn today that I was mistaken, that the law is against me and that I remain what I was. My duty is to tell you what has happened and to take back my proposal without taking advantage of the authorization you've been good enough to give me. It costs me to renounce my dearest hope but honesty obliges me to."

Arthur knew Madame Daudièrne and her daughters well enough not to doubt the answer they would make to that opening. He knew they wouldn't want to be less generous in hospitality and that the chateau doors would not be closed to him. It was up to him to take advantage of that new situation. He could flatter himself that his correct and disinterested conduct would assure him Germaine's sympathy first of all.

Du Pommeval, heir to a great fortune, didn't have that romantic side which pleases young girls. Misfortune was giving it to him.

The President, who was to clear things up, didn't have any meetings that day and when he wasn't at the law courts, he could almost always be found at his home. However, he lived at the other end of the town and du Pommeval had to travel from one end to the other in order to see him. He could have had himself taken there by carriage but his visit would have been noticed because in Arcy a carriage that stops in front of a house is an event. It would be better to go there on foot at the risk of being approached by troublesome and indiscreet people.

Arthur, in full mourning dress, then made his way through back streets toward the less frequented quarter to the residence of President Lestrigon —an old name in the country, a bizarre name which suited this magistrate of the old school very well. And the heir everyone one was talking about since the ferry accident was counting on not meeting anyone on the way. Going this way there was only one dangerous passage, that of the Rue Nationale, which absolutely must be crossed, very near the plaza circle,[34] but du Pommeval hoped to cross it incognito. He was walking at a good pace and he quickly reached the heart of the city, to that large street which was the rendezvous of loiterers. By chance there was no one that day on the pavements and the balcony overlooking the plaza was empty when du Pommeval came out in front of the house where his oldest friends often passed their nights. But just at the moment when he reached the opposite sidewalk, a voice coming from above called out his name. He raised his head and saw, at a window on the second floor, young Alfred Daudiérne, who was motioning him to come up. In his present state of mind, du Pommeval could have well done without meeting Germaine's brother.

He hadn't seen him for several days. Alfred had left some hours before the gloomy accident which had troubled the peace of the Germonière inhabitants. They hadn't expected him back so soon, because, when his mother permitted him to go to Paris, he was never short of pretexts to stay there as long as possible.

"What luck to surprise you here!" this *gommeux en herbe* shouted.[35] "I was

---

[34] Small towns in France are frequently built around a central plaza often with a fountain, and provide a convenient place for the idle to loiter.

[35] An elegant 19th century young man wearing tight-fitting clothes, shoes with pointed, tipped-up toes, walking with affectation. Also the name given by women in the barrier cabarets to effeminate men who cut their absinthe with gum.

just asking myself whether I should go to your place before returning to the maternal domicile. Here you are! That decides me to stay here until tomorrow morning. Come on up, my friend."

"Impossible right now," du Pommeval answered. "I'm going to pay a visit."

"A visit! Are you still getting mixed up in that rot? You, a total *boulevardier*! Me, I've given that up. You can pay your visit later."

"No, no, I have an appointment and it's a matter of important business."

"Me, too, I need to talk to you about a matter...important to me."

"Can't you come down? I'd prefer not to be seen by our friends"

"Come down? Not on your life. My uncle just might pass by. I'd get an unforgettable beating. And then, you can't talk quietly in the street."

"And up there even less. We'd be interrupted every instant."

"No we won't. There's not a soul...three or four old codgers who'd make one good dead man or who're reading newspapers. That's all. Come on up, please."

"Absolutely not. That wouldn't be proper. I'm in full mourning."

"Ah! Yes. Your uncle Vignemal has given up the ghost and the aunt Vignemal too. I've just learned about that. And you're inheriting a nice pouch you weren't counting on. You have all the luck. That's luck I'd never have and nevertheless I would really need an inheritance to get back on my feet. In the name of your millions, my dear du Pommeval, in the name of God, come up. I have a favor to ask you... a great favor."

Du Pommeval wished the young Daudièrne and his insistence were miles away but he didn't want to miss the opportunity to be helpful to Germaine's brother. And he told himself he could spare ten minutes conversation in a corner.

"There's nothing I wouldn't do to oblige you and since it's a matter of doing you a favor, I'm at your service."

After having sent up that answer that his situation as a suitor imposed on him without raising his voice too much, du Pommeval slid into the passage way which served as a vestibule for his circle of friends that the old inhabitants of Arcy stubbornly called the Literary Room, although very little involving literature went on there.

This circle recalled only vaguely Parisian Clubs. The antechamber wasn't peopled with footmen in livery and the furnishings were remarkable by their simplicity: five paneled rooms, a number of rush chairs, and a dozen caned armchairs, gaming tables whose covers needed renewing, and a billiard table bought second-hand from a café which went bankrupt. This hardly luxurious locale was nonetheless very frequented and the most respected people in Arcy wanted to get into it, every bit as much as a the son of a family who comes out in elegant life wants to be admitted to the Jockey Club. And not just anyone could join.

But this wasn't the hour when the young people gathered there to celebrate the mysteries of baccarat. Betting games were played only behind closed doors, after the grandparents had left to go to bed. And for the moment there were only respectable bourgeois there, civil servants or people living off their savings, as they say in the provinces, some tied to a peaceful game of whist, others sleeping under the morning newspaper which had just arrived from Paris. The entry of Alfred and du Pommval therefore went almost unnoticed. Alfred, who had met him at the door, could therefore seize him in order to drag him into the billiard room, where they found themselves alone.

"I didn't know you'd returned," said du Pommeval. "When did you arrive?"

"Today at twelve-thirty, dear boy. I have five hours of train ride in my back and as I didn't sleep last night, I can't stand any more."

"Then you haven't yet seen your mother?"

"No, and I'm not in a hurry to turn up at Germonière. It will always be too soon for the reception waiting for me there. I'm at the point of asking myself if I'm going to rent a room in town in order to postpone the problems hanging over my head. My mother and my uncle are going to out-do each other trying to get at me when they find out the trouble I'm in, and my sister Laurence is capable of getting mixed up in it. Not Germaine, she understand life, she does."

"Is it indiscreet to ask you what crime you've committed?"

"Indiscreet? No *pardieu*! That's why I called you. Old fellow, I made the stupid mistake of betting against the bank in a gambling house where I've been going since last winter. And I took on one of those losing one's shirt events that come up in the life of a minor. First of all, the four *sous* that little Pauline of the Follies left me stayed there…and what's worse is that I owe a hundred and fifty *louis* to the croupier. A hundred and fifty *louis* that I have to pay without delay, under penalty of being kicked out of the establishment."

"That wouldn't be a great misfortune."

"No, but that would come out and if my uncle, who goes everywhere, happened to learn about it…"

"He wouldn't leave you in a bad fix, I'm sure."

"Him! You can really see you don't know him. He has rules in life that cut like razor blades. He'd stick one in my face and that's all I'd get from him. I can hear him now: 'My boy, you're on the way to dishonoring yourself. If I pay your debt, you'd only make another of the same kind. It's better for you to suffer dishonor immediately. That would cost less and would keep you from starting again.' "

"I can hardly believe Monsieur Daudièrne wouldn't relax his principles in a case like this."

"There's no circumstance that would make him; I'm sure of that. He wouldn't hand me over a penny. It would be easier to make my mother come around, but there'd be a tearful scene that I want to avoid at any price. Ah! If Germaine had enough money, she'd get me out of this mess. But I'd be willing to bet she hasn't sixty *sous* in her little savings. And, considering everything, my dear friend, I can no longer see anyone but you who can help me out of the mess I've got myself into."

Du Pommeval was expecting that conclusion, but it hardly delighted him. The sum was hefty and in the present state of his finances, it was unpleasant to risk it. On the other hand, he was aware that a refusal would cause a falling out with Alfred, and he wasn't anxious to make himself an enemy at Germonière.

"What I'm doing is stupid as everything," Alfred continued, somewhat disconcerted by the length of time du Pommeval took to answer. "You shouldn't borrow from a friend; I know that very well. And I beg you to believe that if I were of age, I'd go to a money-lender…but my signature isn't worth anything right now…and I thought you wouldn't miss four thousand francs for a few months. I'm saying four thousand so as not to find myself broke after paying the croupier.

"I'll gladly lend them to you," said du Pommeval, who had made his decision and had just thought of a plan suggested by the demand for a loan.

"Thanks, old boy," young Daudièrne exclaimed, shaking his hand vigorously. "I really knew you were a good fellow and that I wasn't wrong to count on you. Ah! if anyone over there at Germonière consulted me, I don't need to tell you what I'd advise them. We're close enough for me to dare speak to you from the heart. So, I swear to you that if you ever think of entering our family, I would be more than happy to have a brother-inlaw like you."

The opening was crude, and du Pommeval had never foreseen that Alfred in his enthusiasm would go so far as to offer him his help in making his mother look favorably on an offer of marriage.

"I seem to be throwing my sisters at you," continued that foolish nineteen-year-old youth. "But I know what I'm talking about, and I have eyes that can see things clearly. I can certainly tell you that I've guessed your feelings."

"If you had passed through Germonière before coming to Arcy," du Pommeval answered gravely, "you'd have learned, my dear Alfred, that last Thursday, Doctor Subligny went there on my behalf and he asked Madame Daudièrne for her daughter's hand for me."

"Really! Well, I'm delighted…and Laurence must be happier than I am because I won't hid from you any longer that…"

"I've asked for the hand of Mademoiselle Germaine," du Pommeval interrupted.

"Ah! Bah! Well! That's funny. I had thought that…but that doesn't matter. I hope they answered: Agreed!"

"Things aren't at that stage. Mademoiselle Germaine did me the honor of not refusing me. She's very willing to let me come to Germonière every day."

"Good! That's what all families do. You have to get to know each other before getting married…as if you didn't know each other well enough! But don't worry. You'll be married after Lent. If my little sister didn't like you, she wouldn't have authorized you to court her. My mother would have gone back to Paris to cut short the meetings, whereas we may be stuck in the country until New Years. That's annoying, but I can resign myself willingly since you're going to marry Germaine. And I'm not sorry for her, nor for you either. She's charming; she's good; she has every good quality. As for you, old boy, I don't want to overwhelm you with flattery to your face, and, besides, you know what I think about you. And here it is that in the bargain you're becoming a millionaire."

"I'm not one yet."

"It's just as if you were. Old man Sourdas, who'se over there playing dead, has just explained your situation to me. He's clumsy at whist, that good old man over there, but he's boned up on the Civil Code, and it seems in virtue of I don't know what Article, your uncle having been presumed to have survived his wife..."

"Monsieur Sourdas is mistaken, my friend...and others have made the same mistake, me first of all. But I'm better informed now, and if I'd been so sooner, I wouldn't have dared ask for Mademoiselle Germaine's hand. The step was taken, to my great regret, because now Madame Daudièrne may accuse me of not having told her the truth about my situation."

"What! You're not inheriting! But that's impossible. The law is there."

"The law harms me. I'll inherit if I prove that Madame Vignemal died before her husband."

"All right, you'll prove it."

"That would be difficult. Only one man was there when the accident happened. He saw them go under at the same time when the boat capsized... Some minutes afterward he found Madame Vignemal. She had come up on dry ground at the foot of the levee which borders the Beuvron River on the side of your park and she no longer gave any sign of life. But the body of my uncle was only found the next day very far from where the Fougéray ferry was. You can see that the circumstances of the facts are against me."

"I don't see that at all. Your uncle could have swum for a half hour and drowned when he ran out of strength,"

"I don't think he knew how to swim. And if he had known how, that wouldn't prove anything. There would have to be a witness, I tell you, a believable witness who would swear before the court that he saw Monsieur. Vignemal supporting himself in the water a long time after the capsize of the boat, that he had heard him...cry out...call for help."

"The devil! Those are some conditions!"

"So long as this witness doesn't come forward, I remain in an uncertainty which depresses me...not for me, because I would resign myself to stay as I am, but I can't endure the idea of having unwillingly deceived Madame Daudièrne."

"Wait a second then, old fellow," murmured young Alfred, hitting his forehead. "A conversation I heard is coming back to me...and if the details of the event agree with the story told to me…I'll furnish your witness."

"Are you speaking seriously?" asked du Pommeval, who scarcely believed in the value of a witness picked up by young Daudièrne.

"Ah! Look here, you're taking me for an idiot! I was taken at baccarat, that's true, but I'd be the last of cretins if I was joking when it was a matter of a friend's interests. And I repeat to you, old fellow, that chance has given me information which will make you win your lawsuit."

"I'm delighted about that, but they don't back what I said. You've been absent several days and this morning coming back to Arcy you didn't even know my uncle and his wife had drowned."

"That's true. I learned the event in the club. I certainly regret not having known it sooner because if I had known it there wouldn't be a gap in the story I'm going to tell you. But first, you have to give me some details about the accident. I don't want to cause you false joy and I need to focus on certain points to know if the story I heard has any bearing on your affair. It was last Tuesday, wasn't it when the Vignemal couple fell in the water while crossing the Beuvron ferry?"

"Tuesday, about nine o'clock in the evening."

"Your mother and Monsieur Daudièrne, your uncle, can verify, within a few minutes, that they heard a cry the moment the misfortune happened. Very well. Now, where did they find the cadavers?"

"They found them the next day, in the afternoon; that of Madame Vignemal on the right bank about a kilometer down stream from your park's fence. I've just told you it halted the first time under the walk way of the tamaris and, the current having risen, it disappeared."

"That doesn't matter to me. I need to know where the husband went."

"He came up on dry ground on the left bank, but a great deal lower down, about a stone's throw from the Mouettes Bridge."

"Perfect! And the boat, has it been seen again?"

"Only its debris has been seen. It must have gone down the river between two currents and broken apart against one of the piling of the bridge because they fished out the planks under the first arch. The violence of the flood waters had formed a whirlpool which held back the pieces of the wreck."

"Better and better. Now, dear friend, I've got my bearings. The business is in the bag…that means: the inheritance is yours."

"It would please me very much if you consented to explain yourself more clearly."

"Gladly. Here's what happened to me, not any later than this morning, on the train. I was seated in a first-class compartment, where I counted on going to sleep, since there was no one there but me. Ah,well! I was no sooner stretched out on the cushions than a sort of pompous gent came in…protruding chin, a hooked nose, gold-rimmed glasses, everything was there. This grotesque character hauled himself into the train compartment and took over the other corner. I

294

was already furious, but I hadn't reached the end of the unpleasant things re-served for me. A minute later here comes another fellow to sit across from the first one…a little old man who looked like country bailiff or a village money-lender. I was furious. I lit a big cigar without asking their permission to smoke. I hope to put them to flight. Not at all. The little old man coughed. Monsieur Pompous threw me angry glances over his glasses. But they stayed put, both of them, and we were off."

"Your adventure is amusing, but I'm on pins and needles and if you could shorten it a little…"

"I'll skip to the denouement and you won't lose anything by waiting. I had finished my cigar and I was trying to sleep when my creatures started a conver-sation. Note that they didn't know each other and they exchanged boring com-monplaces. I wanted to start to sing: *Too Bad for Her!*[36] in hopes of making them shut up. Finally the man with the glasses asked the man across from him if he knew the newspapers had spoken of an accident which happened near Arcy-sur-Beuvron. The other one answered he hadn't…and in fact I hadn't read any-where the story of the Vignemal shipwreck."

"Neither did I… But how did that man know about it?"

"He played a role in it, old fellow."

"Impossible. My uncle's servant had followed his masters right up to the ferry and he hadn't seen anyone. There was a vagabond there who acted rather suspicious, but…"

"This vagabond had nothing in common with this majestic traveler who told, in my presence, the moving narration here. Listen to me closely. It'll be as if you were there. I have a particular talent for imitating."

Du Pommeval was cursing the untimely chatting of his future brother-in-law but he wouldn't have gained anything by interrupting him. He resigned him-self to suffering this flow of words in hopes of getting useful information from it.

"I must tell you, Monsieur," began the incorrigible Alfred, counterfeiting the invented voice of Henry Monnier, "I must tell you that I own a modest coun-try house not far from that little town where I often come to get a breath of fresh air, even in winter, the pure air of the fields. This little get-away place is situated on the edge of a stream, which even though not very big, is nonetheless impetu-ous at certain times."

"Alfred, my friend, please!"

"Calm down! I'm coming to the facts. Monsieur Pompous continued like this: 'I had been there a week when, Tuesday evening, I was called back to Paris by a pressing matter. Although the weather was terrible, I got ready to take the train which leaves at 9:45 from the station at the Mouettes Bridge.' Ah! This is beginning to interest you."

---

[36] Scandalous song of the period.

"Could that man, by chance, have seen..."

"Old Boy, you owe your uncle's inheritance to that imbecile. Just as he was going across the bridge, he heard cries of distress. He looked through the parapet and he saw an unfortunate man clinging to an overturned boat. It seems there was a superb clear moon. Almost immediately after that the boat smashed up against one of the pilings and everything disappeared."

"But that imbecile was a scoundrel. He should have dived into the water to try to rescue the drowning man or at least go look for help. He calmly went on his way?"

"*Mon Dieu,* yes. He didn't know how to swim and he was afraid of missing the 9:45 train. He ran to the station, which is three meters away from the bridge. The train was in the station. He had just enough time to get on. But before leaving, he took care to alert an employee who was closing the station doors and who didn't think it fitting to leave his post to go drag the river. That's unbelievable, but that's how it was. Well! What do you say about my story?" Alfred continued. "Do you doubt that your uncle was still alive a half hour after the accident?"

"No...although that bohemian said he had disappeared the moment the boat capsized."

"Your bohemian lied or he didn't see very well. You fall into the water, but you come back to the surface and you grab onto whatever you can. Your uncle would have found under his hands the boat floating with its keel in the air. He grabbed on to it and he was carried away with it. He might have been saved if the current hadn't thrown it against the bridge. However that may be, don't suppose that my pompous gentleman invented that story, which doesn't do him honor. In general, when you've acted like a cad you don't brag about it."

"That's true... Only you really should have asked him his name."

"*Ma foi!* I really didn't think about it. You understand that if I had guessed it was a question of your uncle... But when I'm in Paris I arrange things so that I don't get any letters from Germonière and the narration of this old man hardly interested me. I listened to him because his ridiculous accent amused me and it's a miracle I remembered it."

"What's to be done to find that man?"

"That won't be difficult."

"You would recognize him?"

"Oh! A mile away. Heads like his are rare."

"Good! But where is he?"

"At his country place, *Parbleu*! At this get-away where he comes to breathe the pure air of the fields, in winter. I forgot to tell you that he got off at the Mouettes Bridge station."

"Then I'm going there," du Pommeval said quickly.

"Go there if you like, dear friend. But I believe that it's not worth the trouble since I also forgot to add that this respectable, dotty old man came back here expressly to inquire about the drowned man he left there for fear of missing the train…and most of all of risking his skin. He declared in a high and intelligible voice that he had resolved to make his deposition before the Arcy authorities, and you can believe he wouldn't miss such a beautiful opportunity to make himself look important. I wouldn't be surprised if he didn't go today to see the Mayor, the *Sous-Prefet*, the Procurer of the Republic, and everybody below them. He thinks there was a crime. And for nothing but the pleasure of seeing his name in the *Gazette des Tribunaux*, he would gladly have gone two hundred leagues."

The heir's hope was reborn. His case was won in the court and at Gemonière. The fortune which had almost escaped him was his, thanks to providential luck. And he could, in all confidence, take advantage of what Germaine had granted him. He thought for an instant of going, even so, to his visit to the President, but he reflected very quickly that the visit no longer had a purpose and it might be awkward. It would be better to let this blessed civil servant take the initiative and spontaneously proclaim that Monsieur Vignemal had survived his wife. Doubt was no longer possible, since they had recovered the body and the debris exactly at the place where a landowner, a person worthy of belief, had the wreck sink and the drowning. The distance between the Fougéray ferry and the Mouettes Bridge was such that Madame Vignemal must had perished at least twenty minutes before her husband, while granting that she was still alive at the moment Roch Ferrer left her on the river bank.

"My dear Alfred," du Pommeval said after a silence, "It's nice to learn through you that I can affirm to Madame Daudièrne without worry and without remorse of conscience that I am bringing to Mademoiselle Germaine a fortune worthy of her. You can bear witness to that if need be."

"Have you talked to them about your doubts?"

"No. I was thinking of admitting to them today that the question of inheritance wasn't yet settled, and I would have offered to take back my proposal if…"

"Don't admit anything at all, dear friend. You are now sure of your claim. What's the good of going back over the past? My uncle is meticulous as the devil and he would ask you no end of questions. If you take my advice, we'll take ourselves together to Germonière. I'm no longer afraid to reappear there since you've promised to get me out of trouble."

"I have the four thousand francs at my house," the future brother-inlaw said quickly. "Do you want to go by there?"

"I certainly do think I want to. Thank you, old fellow, you're going to restore my credit, which certainly needed it. Tomorrow that scoundrel of a croupier will be paid. This is an enormous favor you're doing me and I swear I'll pay you back. Then, is it agreed, we'll dash off to Mama's house?"

"My carriage should be harnessed up. We'll be there in half an hour. On the way back we'll pass by the Moulettes Bridge."

"Well! That's an idea. I'll get information at the station about the man with the gold-rimmed spectacles, and if he's at home, I'll introduce him to you."

That was exactly Arthur's plan and Arthur was beaming with joy. He now had an ally at Germonière. And he didn't yet know that he had an enemy there. He took the arm of Germaine's brother and they went out together under the nose of the whist players, who said to each other:

"Well! The marriage is settled. The Vignemal fortune will be squandered in Paris."

V. Roger Pontac Visits Germonière

"My dear Pommeval, I present to you Monsieur Pontac, Officer in the Hussards, our country neighbor since a few days ago and for some days still, I hope. Monsieur Pontac, I present to you Monsieur Arthur du Pommeval, a friend of the family whom you will often meet at Germonière. I don't present my nephew Alfred Daudièrne to you. You'll have occasion all too often to see this scamp here at Germonière," said Uncle Armand, after having correctly fulfilled the formalities imposed by custom on the chatelaines hosting two gentlemen strangers to one other.

Monsieur Vignemal's heir had gotten down from his carriage in the court of honor a quarter of an hour before the arrival of Madame Vignemal's cousin, who had come on foot through the park gate.

Chance is a great master. It develops situations; it leads up to scenes; and it hastens the denouement. The two rivals were meeting each other at a place in the drawing room where the whole Daudièrne family had come together and it was clear they had not premeditated that encounter.

Du Pommeval, free from a terrible worry, hadn't lost a minute to rush over to Germonière in the company of young Alfred, who has just given him precious information.

Pontac, more tormented than ever, had decided, after long hesitation, to follow the advice given by Germaine, advice which resembled an order. He was returning the visit that Monsieur Armand Daudièrne had made to Bretteville, and beginning that day he set up relations from which he expected only grief. He didn't flatter himself they could end in an engagement between him, a poor First Lieutenant, and a young girl as gifted in relations as by nature.

However, he had an advantage over his millionaire competitor. He had known about du Pommeval a long time and he knew that du Pommeval a few days before, had become an official suitor, agreed to by the mother and allowed by the daughter to pay court, while du Pommeval didn't suspect that this hand-some blond cavalier who fell out of the blue at Germonière was madly in love with Germaine, and that Germaine had done nothing to that point to discourage him.

Du Pommeval didn't even remember ever having seen him and the name Pontac didn't mean anything to him. However, they must have run into each other in the main street of Arcy in the past during vacations when Roger was studying at St.-Louis secondary school and Arthur was studying the art of tying his tie at a boarding school in the Saint Honoré suburb. But at that time they were both children; and ten years in Africa changes a man. Besides, handsome Arthur would never have paid attention to a badly clothed youngster living off the charity of a cousin, who was only indirectly related, and that by marriage, to the Pommevals. Arthur hadn't even noticed him in the crowd that followed the Vignemals' funeral procession. Roger was present at the burial but he hadn't talked to anyone and no one had paid any attention to him. At least he thought so, and he had reasons to think so, because he hadn't recognized a single one of his co-heirs among the peasants he saw there.

But du Pommeval had many other superiorities oven Pontac: knowledge of society, the way to dress, the talent of saying in well-chosen terms the most commonplace things. He possessed the fashionable jargon and that ease that's acquired only by being around women. Looking at him, Roger found himself awkward. He blushed to be dressed like an officer on leave, and he was certainly wrong because his character's natural elegance set off the simplicity of his dress, and reserve is not awkwardness.

Nevertheless du Pommeval had the good luck that day to arrive first at Germonière. He was already established in front of the fireplace between Madame Daudièrne and her daughters when Pontac made his entrance into that drawing room where he was setting foot for the first time. Du Pommeval had been able to enjoy the rather natural embarrassment that the newcomer's somewhat stiff attitude betrayed. He had already dropped anchor in the port while the other one had yet to go through the channel.

What's more, du Pommeval knew the territory in depth. He had dealt with Madame Daudièrne and Uncle Armand for a long time. He knew what to do to please them. And with these young ladies, he didn't lack subjects of conversation. He wasn't reduced to sighing like a suitor without experience. He could develop a compliment in a memory recalled for the occasion, a burning declaration in a discreet allusion to words exchanged one evening at a ball.

Roger, on the contrary, had landed in a county almost unknown to him and caution condemned him to silence for fear of saying the wrong thing. What would he have been able to say, even to Germaine? Their love had no past, since it dated only from the trip to the Lemon Rock, that trip that the young girl had told no one about.

Madame Daudièrne came to the Lieutenant's aid, without suspecting the favor she was doing him

"I'm glad to be able finally to thank you, Monsieur," she said in her most gracious way. "My brother-in-law is in debt to you for the welcome given to him by Monsieur le Duc of Bretteville, and as for me, I'm grateful to you for not having forgotten the way to Germonière. I can even tell you we're counting on you to help us spend our still remaining weeks in the country. We aren't leaving until the end of the year and during the month of December we'll be almost alone here. Our young men from Arcy are flying off to Paris, and Monsieur du Pommeval who certainly doesn't want to abandon us is in mourning. We won't give any parties, but we will take great pleasure in welcoming our friends...and you are one of those."

Roger answered these words of welcome as was proper and that time he didn't at all excuse himself by saying that he would very soon be recalled to his regiment. He had read in Germaine's eyes that she wanted him to accept without restrictions.

The de Bretteville name had had their effect. Du Pommeval had never been invited to the chateau, and he knew the Duke only by sight. He looked with more respect at that officer who was the friend of the great Seigneur. And he promised himself he would profit by the opportunity to have the doors of the aristocratic world opened to him.

Young Alfred was no less desirous than his friend to become friendly neighbors with the highest ranking man in the whole province. He also felt the need to be reconciled with Pontac, whom he had at first taken as a nuisance.

"You've served in the cavalry, Monsieur," he said point blank. "You must love horses. Me, I adore them. I did my compulsory service in the 19th Dragoons and I flatter myself that I ride rather well. It wasn't in the regiment that I learned, *Dieu merci!* Because if it had been I wouldn't know anything. The military instructors' methods are detestable."

"I'm not at all of your opinion, Monsieur," Roger modestly answered.

"*Parbleu!* That's your profession. You would never agree that the worst sportsman in England knows more than all the French cavalry. But that's not what it's about. I'd be delighted to go hunting with you to show you the skill of a half-thoroughbred that I bought this year at Tattersall...Ralph out of Rob-Roy and Gypsy."

"I'll advise you to praise your Ralph," Uncle Armand exclaimed. "He was carrying Germaine the other day and he almost broke her neck."

"That would have served her right. Why did she ride him without my permission?"

"I did without your permission and I'll do without it again if I take a notion to ride Ralph," Germaine retorted.

"My two saddle horses are at your disposal, Mademoiselle," du Pommeval immediately said.

"Thanks. I had too much fear the other day. All's well that ends well. My forced ride ended very well but I no longer am proud of riding the half-thoroughbred. I'll do like Laurence. I'll be content with one of our Percherones. There's no danger they'll run away, those two. They're made of wood."

Alfred started to laugh and to sing between his teeth a refrain popular in café-concerts:

Because he's made of stone, of stone...

Pontac was on hot coals while that foolish youth was talking about Ralph and his face almost showed it. Germaine's intervention helped him recover and her words gladdened his heart.

"We've had much excitement for several days," Madame Daudiène said to him after he had taken his place in front of the fire, facing her and beside her brother-in-law. "My daughter got lost through the fault of this confounded horse who almost threw her over some precipices and we were very worried for an hour."

"Monsieur Pontac will believe you without any trouble when he finds out that Laurence and I together looked for Germaine on all the roads and night was falling when we came back without finding her," exclaimed Uncle Armand.

"And the evening before," Madame Daudièrne continued, "the uncle and the aunt of Monsieur du Pommeval drowned while crossing the river at the end of our garden. You've certainly heard about that terrible accident."

"Yes, Madame, the day after...by way of Monsieur de Bretteville's servants.

"It hasn't been proved that this was an accident," said Monsieur Daudièrne. "There's a strange fellow who played an unexplained role in this drama. It's the gypsy I pointed out to the Duke asking him to again order his guards to keep a look out. But I'm afraid my warning won't come to anything. The Duke doesn't seem to me disposed to do what it takes to put an end to the depredations of this marauder."

"He always finds it repugnant to deal severely with the unfortunate... and at this time more than ever. He's inclined to indulgence. He's thinking only of his sorrow."

"That doesn't prevent him for having remained the most courteous gentleman I've ever seen. He welcomed me as if I were of his social rank. I'm overcome by what he offered me...his forest, his game keepers, his horses, his game. I hardly dared accept. You had something to do with that reception, my dear Lieutenant, but that doesn't matter. I'm beginning to reverse the prejudices I had against the old nobility."

"Say, Uncle," Alfred interrupted. "When you go to hunt at Bretteville, will you take me with you?"

"You! Never, my boy. You get off shots too quickly. I don't want to get lead destined for a little goat through my body. What I'm telling you is for your own good. You might be accused of having killed me on purpose in order to inherit from me."

"Armand!...My friend!" murmured Madame Daudièrne.

"Alfred knows very well that I'm not talking seriously. But the truth is he's not invited and I won't take it on myself to take him along."

"Monsieur de Bretteville will be happy, I have no doubt, to please everybody in your family. Monsieur your nephew will be welcome in the chateau, and if it pleases these ladies to be present at a big deer hunt..."

"Oh! That would be charming!" Germaine exclaimed. "What do you say, Laurence?"

"Me! I don't have an opinion," said the elder sister, stealing a glance at Madame Vignemal's heir.

And Monsieur du Pommeval will be a member of the party," Germaine continued. "There's no rule of mourning that forbids firing guns."

"I don't have the honor of knowing Monsieur le Duc de Bretteville," murmured handsome Arthur, delighted with this opening.

Roger Pontac was hardly interested in inviting his rival, but he thought he read in Germaine's eyes a prayer that he interpreted in his own way.

"She's afraid that Madame Daudièrne will refuse to be part of the group if the son-in-law of her choice is left to one side," he thought.

He quickly answered that the Duke was inviting his Germonière neighbors and their friends and he had the satisfaction of receiving warm thanks from a man he had no reason to like.

"That's perfect," exclaimed Uncle Armand. "If Monsieur Pontac will please let us know the day that Monsieur de Bretteville will fix the party will be complete because we're all going. Decidedly, good news comes in bunches. I've come back from Arcy and I bring from there which will very much interest you, my dear Arthur."

"You didn't tell me you were going into town, my dear friend, and if you had told me," murmured Madame Daudièrne.

"You would have given me a multitude of errands and that was just what I wanted to avoid, my dear sister-in-law. I needed to talk with Monsieur Lestarigon, President of the Tribunal."

"You've seen him?" du Pommeval quickly asked. "I spent an hour with him and I don't know why I should hide from you the fact that we spoke only about you."

At the first words of this unexpected speech, Arthur, put on guard by the name Monsieur Daudièrne had just spoken, had picked up his ears, and when he learned that it had been a question of him between the President of the Tribunal of Arcy and Germaine's uncle, he was visibly troubled. He was going to learn his fate, because Monsieur Lestrigon must already have formed an opinion about the probable outcome of the lawsuit and the heir feared to learn that his lawsuit was already lost in the mind of the knowledgeable magistrate.

"Don't get upset," the uncle continued, smiling. "I told you just a while ago that today was the day of good news and I'm not going to say differently. Your affair is on the right road. But you don't know what danger you've run."

"Danger?" repeated Madame Daudièrne, very surprised.

"Yes, the danger of being deprived of the Vignemal inheritance."

"It seems to me, my dear Armand, that the moment is badly chosen to bring up a subject which interests only Monsieur du Pommeval...and us."

"Why should that be, my dear sister-in-law? Monsieur Pontac is a stranger to this area, and it matters very little to him to find out who will receive inheritance of our neighbors of Fougéray. But he's one of us now and he'll be happy to know that our friend du Pommeval will receive that fortune coveted by the cousins, who, I believe, aren't worth very much, greedy and avid peasants. Isn't it true, Lieutenant, that you're happy with us?"

Roger made a sign of agreement, and he should be given credit to take in that fashion the bad compliment Monsieur Daudièrne had given him without knowing it. He himself was one of those cousins so harshly described by a man who did not know them. And if he didn't covet his aunt's wealth, he couldn't really rejoice that the inheritance would pass to his rival. He told himself that if fate hadn't made Monsieur du Pommeval wealthy, Madame Daudièrne wouldn't marry her daughter to this almost gentleman who was in debt. His unselfishness wouldn't go so far as to be happy about an event that ruined his hopes.

"What's more," Uncle Armand continued, "the story is amusing and won't bore anyone. Let me tell you, Mesdames et Messieurs, that we were all mistaken from beginning to end about the meaning of the famous Article 722... A great many others than we were also mistaken about it. What do you expect?" Uncle Armand continued, looking at this nephew with a mocking air. "Alfred wasn't here and if he'd been with us he would have explained to us the rule about inheritances."

"Me!" said Alfred. "Ah, Well, no, not at all. I'm still preparing for my first examination, and that section isn't part of the program."

"Then your knowledge didn't mislead us, and, besides, I don't regret the error into which we all fell. If Monsieur du Pommeval had known his real situation, he would have spent some very bad nights."

"I did know it," said Arthur, in an emotional tone which wasn't false even though he was already very reassured.

"And you hid it from us?"

"I came today especially to tell you the law was against me, and that I was no richer than a week ago. It costs me to make that admission here, but for reason you'll understand, I couldn't leave you in uncertainty."

"My dear du Pommeval, that's a sentiment that does you honor, and I'm certain that my sister-in-law and my nieces thank you for it."

Madame Daudièrne gave her agreement with a gesture, Germaine with a smile, but Laurence, who was embroidering, didn't raise her eyes. She was listening, however, with great attention and she didn't lose a word of the dialogue. Roger was also listening, and afraid of letting his impressions be seen, he stayed absolutely impassive. He stood straight and stiff, like a soldier on sentry duty, and his eyes didn't leave Germaine.

"Fortunately," continued the uncle, "you didn't have to give us that proof of honesty that I was almost expecting, because I won't hide the fact that I've had some doubts. I didn't trust my ability nor that of Doctor Subligny. I needed to consult a competent man, and I couldn't find a better one than Monsieur Lestrigon, who has the reputation of being a first rate jurist. I had the luck to meet him, and I've been completely convinced. The first thing that he told me was that you wouldn't automatically legally inherit. And that, in order to inherit, you would have to establish absolutely and unconditionally that your uncle had lived longer than his wife. I was, on my part, convinced of the contrary, because I was relying on the testimony of that gypsy who saw Madame Vignemal some minutes after the accident. It was very probable that at that moment she was still breathing. And she would probably have come out of her unconscious state if the one named Roch hadn't abandoned her. Now, the result would have been that his testimony would have been *caduc*, that's the acceptable term, and that means useless. You can't inherit when you're dead before the reading of the will and I was very inclined to believe that Monsieur Vignemal found himself in exactly that situation."

Madame Daudièrne didn't seem to understand very much about her brother-in-law's explanations. But it was apparent she was worried and that it wasn't a matter of indifference to her that her future son-in-law might lose the two millions he would bring to the marriage. Alfred was laughing to himself. He thought he knew what was behind all this and he was promising himself to startle his family by recounting the story of the encounter he'd had on the train. Pontac himself understood very well that he had almost received a part of the inheritance and he wasn't at all sorry to learn to what unexpected circumstance he owed remaining poor. Germaine and Laurence evidently took the greatest interest in their uncle's story. They held back from interrupting him or making comments, but it was easy to guess that they were impatiently waiting for the end of the story. Germaine fidgeted in her chair and Laurence made little nervous movements which caused a great deal of harm to her embroidery design's regularity.

"Well, my dear boy." Monsieur Daudièrne went on, "we were wrong to be alarmed. The President, who's very clever, guessed, I believe, why I insisted so much on being informed about the chances which remained to you. He amused himself by keeping me on the grill for a full quarter of an hour. And after considerably drawing out the legal difficulties which might come up in the course of a lawsuit of this kind, he smiled me and asked me if I hadn't met an old gentleman in the corridor of his house. I told him I had and that the gentleman in question was totally unknown to me. He then told me that he was a business man who'd retired after making a fortune, and as that thought didn't seem to interest me very much, he added that this gentleman, who lived in Paris, had built a kind of bungalow a hundred feet from the Mouettes Bridge."

"I'll bet that that gentleman had the profile of a Polichinelle and wore gold-rimmed glasses," exclaimed young Alfred.

"Absolutely. Where the devil did you learn that?"

"I know him, your retired grocer. I spent five hours this morning in his amiable company. I could repeat to you what he must have told Monsieur Lestrigon. It's only his name I didn't know, but I know the story by heart. Old man Vignemal held on to the boat which broke into pieces against one of the bridge pilings. Old man Vignemal was calling for help, and the heroic grocer went on his way in order to get to the train on time... And Arthur knows all about the adventure...I've just told it to him at the Arcysur-Beuvron Club."

"Then, my dear du Pommeval, I haven't told you anything new?" asked

Uncle Armand, a little vexed at having been outdone by his nephew.

"You overwhelm me with joy," the heir quickly answered. "Alfred wasn't able to tell me what had happened to this providential traveler... I hope to get in touch with him, but I wasn't sure as to how to go about it. And here it is that you tell me he went to see the President of the Tribunal of his own accord. I couldn't hope for anything better."

"No, because that former businessman is a very honorable man and his testimony will be decisive. You don't owe him any gratitude because he helped you without wishing to. But it has to be admitted that he did it with zeal because he came back from Paris just for that. It even seems that when he arrived at Mauconseil Street, where he lives in a house he owns, he wrote to the President to tell him about the shipwreck which he had just witnessed."

"That now explains why Monsieur Lestrigon had led Doctor Subligny to believe that I shouldn't despair about winning my lawsuit."

"I must tell you that he's known Monsieur Grandminard a long time and he thinks highly of him."

"His name is Grandminard, that old geezer," nephew Alfred exclaimed. "Well! That fills it in."

"I forbid you to make fun of him. He's positively a savior. The President confirmed to me that nothing would take precedence over the sworn testimony by a witness worthy of belief, of a witness who saw and heard Monsieur Vignemal surviving and crying out thirty minutes after the ferry accident. Our dear President even thinks that our friend's rights won't be contested and there won't be any difficulty to his taking ownership."

"May he not be mistaken!" murmured du Pommeval. "It would be very painful for me to be a litigant against poor people."

"They wouldn't risk it. Just remember that they would have to prove that Madame Vignemal had lived three-quarters of an hour under water... or almost, since her body stayed only a short time on the bank. And the only witness they could produce would be Roch Ferrer, that nobody would believe. Besides, what would he say? That he saw her drown. We know that. It could be that things happened differently from the way he told it. But he wouldn't have the audacity to swear before a tribunal that his first story was a lie."

"I've always thought that he didn't tell you the truth," Laurence murmured without lifting her eyes.

"You're very severe towards one of your admirers," Germaine said gaily, "Because he loves you, this boy. The other evening, in the kitchen, he never stopped staring at you. You petrified him."

"Oh! The rascal is daring." Uncle Armand continued. "but if one of you, Mesdemoiselles, wants to paint his portrait, she'd do well to hurry, because one of these days they're going to lock him up. The Attorney General suspects him of misdeeds more serious than poaching. It seems they've opened an investigation into the role he played in the drama which cost the life of the Vignemal couple. And if that investigation goes against him, they'll arrest him."

"I would be extremely sorry about that," Germaine exclaimed. "A protégé of the Doctor couldn't be a rascal."

"Me, too, I'd be very sorry," said Monsieur Daudièrne, "but not for the same reason. I am, on the contrary, very inclined to believe that excellent Subligny is mistaken about that boy. And if Roch is taken into custody apropos of the ferry accident, this criminal trial, or prison would complicate our friend du Pommel's affair. At least that's the opinion of President Lestrigon, as he understands it."

"Why don't we talk about something else," said Madame Daudièrne. "What pleasure can you find, my dear Armand, in making me remember an event which I can't think about without emotion? I'm persuaded these gentlemen would prefer a subject of conversation less gloomy."

"Oh! I really think these young ladies would prefer to waltz, but it's not the right time for that, and what's more we lack people to waltz. Besides, du Pommeval is in full mourning."

"We could play a little music," suggested Germaine.

"Do you like music, Monsieur Pontac?" asked Uncle Armand.

"Very much, Monsieur. Only I don't know a note of music."

"You must know Arab songs. If you would sing some of them to us, my nieces, who are first rate at the piano, would accompany you. And that would give me rest from symphonies, sonatas, and other kinds of sophisticated music they inflict me with too often. What do you say about that, Laurence?"

Uncle Armand's suggestion pleased everybody, except the man and the girl he asked to go to the piano. Madame Daudièrne was glad to put an end to a conversation concerning the death of her neighbors and their heirs which had gone on too long. Alfred counted on taking advantage of that pause to go lock away in his secretary the four thousand franc bills that he had just borrowed. Du Pommevel was hoping to court the younger girl while the older one was accompanying the oriental songs. And Germaine was delighted to hear that soft and grave voice that she had heard for the first time at the foot of the Lemon Rock. But Roger didn't at all intend to amuse the company that evening and Laurence had other projects that evening.

"I don't know how to sing," the First Lieutenant of the Hussards, "and African songs would hardly please serious musicians. They jar at every moment and the words would scorch French girls' ears."

"As for me," murmured Laurence, "I must beg off. I can't accompany very well anything but what I understand. And I don't know a word of Arab."

"That's an answer taken from *Les Femmes Savantes*, of Molière," the uncle exclaimed. "*Excusez-moi, Monsieur, je ne sais pas le grec.*"

"Well, me, I'll risk it," Germaine said, getting up. "It's too bad if I don't follow in the right key. Monsieur Pontac will have to be obliging and begin again, and I'll finally get it right"

"Mademoiselle," begged Roger. "I swear to you that my songs are going to bore you. They're monotonous singsongs that we tolerate in the Moorish cafes because they put us to sleep a little like the tobacco they smoke in the *narghileh*. Here, they'd seem absolutely ridiculous to you."

"I don't believe that at all. I love flowing melodies."

"By virtue of the law of contrasts, then," said Monsieur Daudièrne. "I don't know any mind clearer than yours. Is that any reason not to enjoy the charm of Oriental poetry? I've often listen to the *Desert of Felicien David*, and I was delighted with it. Admit, instead, that you're the one who detests music."

"I don't detest it, but I fear it. If I were a husband or a father, I would forbid my wife and my daughters to play the piano and to listen to pianists. I wouldn't be less charmed hearing an Arab song sung by an officer of the army of Africa and accompanied by a Parisian girl. That's an opportunity that doesn't present itself often in these parts in Arcy-sur-Beuvron."

"Monsieur Pontac," Germaine said gaily, "Since my uncle himself asks you to sing, you can't refuse. "Come! You're going to see how I can acquit myself of the accompaniment."

Roger was obliged to do it, whatever it cost him to make a spectacle of himself in front of Monsieur du Pommeval.

There was certain compensation to this disagreeable business. That was to be alone with Germaine in the middle of this drawing room where she hadn't yet been able to say a word to him which was not overheard. But he wasn't expecting anything from this apparent tête-à-tête. Every eye was going to be fixed on them and it was more important to him than ever not to betray by his attitude the feelings which moved him.

Germaine had already taken her place at the piano. He had to follow her and Roger soon was aware that he would not be very much watched so long as the improvised concert lasted. Uncle Armand had gone to sit on a couch at the other end of the drawing room. He didn't intend to stay in the immediate vicinity of the sonorous instrument he dreaded. Alfred was already maneuvering to slyly reach the door. He had just arrived in traveling clothes and the well-filled wallet. He was in a hurry to go up to his bedroom and deposit his money and then to go down to the stable to inspect Ralph's legs, because he suspected Germaine of having exhausted him. Laurence was absorbed in her embroidery and du Pommeval, who didn't mistrust the Lieutenant of the Hussards, had the good taste to move near her under the pretext of complimenting her on her needle work. He knew he had some wrongs to be pardoned for.

Madame Daudièrne had taken a seat beside her brother-in-law. She too didn't distrust Pontac. She also felt that some explanation between her future son-in-law and the girl not chosen was almost indispensable and that the situation was marvelously suited for it. She didn't want to bother them and, on the other hand, she had some additional clarification to ask the dear uncle who had brought such good news. This was arranged so, very naturally, the family and the suitors found themselves grouped two and two and far enough away from one another to be able to speak freely, on condition of not speaking too loudly.

"My uncle has had a good idea," Germaine said, letting her fingers run over the keyboard. If you were singing a love song or a fragment of an opera, I'd be obliged to spread a stack of music in front of me, and I'd need someone to turn the pages, since you can't read the notes. The Arab song, having never been written down, we're going to be enough ourselves."

"And I'm going to be able to tell you."

"Everything you like...between two songs. But begin by giving me the key. Sing the first phrase to me."

"*La thir ennouba*," Roger murmured, in a slow and melancholy rhythm. He had a good voice and he sang with emotion.

"I've got it," Germaine continued, playing some cords. "That's charming. That's like the Italian. And I thought Arab was a harsh language. Let's see how the rest goes."

"*Sir ou sellem alá el mahbouba...*"

"*Mahbouba* is a little hard because of the aspirate a. That means?"

"Very beloved."

"Perfect. Translate what comes before for me."

"*Ois au mélodieur, va saluer ma bien aimée.* The rest isn't worth my explaining to you. It's only a paraphrase of the beginning and the same motif occurs over and over again."

"Good! I now know enough of it to follow you. I'm going to give you an energetic accompaniment. Try to see that there are a lot of couplets. I have a lot to say to you."

Roger started the song in a well-chosen pitch: rather low in order to let him hear Germaine's words, rather high to prevent those words from reaching ears which shouldn't hear them. The difficulty was to answer. It's impossible to sing and chat at the same time. But that trial African concert required frequent interruptions which gave those executing it the ability to exchange some words.

"Well, fate's started its work," Germaine whispered while Roger was singing in Arab the verses the message sent to the beloved by the melodious bird: Monsieur du Pommeval is inheriting. My sister will have a millionaire husband. Yes, my sister. Don't you see that I've managed a têteà-tête for them? Laurence will know how to get him back. I believe the conversation is already taking the right turn. They're doing the same thing we are. They're speaking in a confidential tone. My brother has slipped away. My mother and my uncle are engaged in a furtive dialogue and won't disturb themselves. Besides, I know Mama really wants to marry my older sister before me. Everything will work out. Monsieur du Pommeval will see that he took a caprice for a serious passion and he'll come back to the one he really loves and who suits him. It's that damned inheritance that turned his head. He imagined that I would help him to spend his fortune better than Laurence would. He takes me for a totally worldly person... me who wants only private happiness. I'm right, aren't I, to despise money. I saw very well a little while ago that we have the same ideal in life. You didn't wince when my uncle told you your cousin's fortune would go in its entirety to a stranger."

"You knew that Madame Vignemal was my cousin?"

This was said so quickly and so low that the words blended with the repetition of the first couplet, that Roger was competing at the same instant.

"Go on with the song," Germaine murmured, drumming her nervous fingers on the piano keys. "I haven't finished. I want to give you some advice. Doctor Subligny talked to us about you, here, the evening of the accident. He even said your name. My mother, my uncle and my sister forgot what he told us about your childhood and your sudden disappearance. As for me, I remembered, but I didn't say anything. What would be the use of acting as a competitor to Monsieur du Pommeval who's inheriting to your detriment? The Doctor thinks as I do that it's completely useless, because when he introduced you to my mother he was very careful not to speak of your relationship to Madame Vignemal. Imitate his caution if you want to please me."

Roger would have willingly cut short the second couplet to answer, but Germaine quickly continued:

"Not a word, please. My uncle is looking at us."

The uncle was looking at them, in fact, but it was without an ulterior motive, because he wasn't thinking about them.

"Does du Pommeval have anything private to say to your older daughter?" he asked his sister-in-law. "He paid attention to no one but her this evening."

"I'm glad he's doing so, my friend," Madame Daudièrne answered. "Laurence might have believed in the past that Monsieur du Pommeval was courting her. And perhaps she wasn't without returning his advances, which were for a time very marked. Most certainly she is not jealous of Germaine's happiness, but, after all, she's a woman…and Monsieur du Pommeval probably thought he owed her an explanation."

"In such a situation, explanations are useless, my dear sister-in-law. It's not with excuses that broken hearts can be cured. But I hope Laurence's hasn't been touched."

Madame Daudièrne and her brother-in-law were both wrong, and they would have reconsidered their error if they had heard the conversation the young people held in a low voice.

"So, you dare deny that your new wealth has changed your feelings!" Laurence said, while counting the stitches of her embroidery.

"I swear to you that I regret not having shown them to you more clearly, since you were able to misunderstand my true intentions," stammered du Pommeval.

"Your repentance won't repair the wickedness you've done to me. And I know why you've acted out an outrageous comedy. Before the accident which made you rich, you didn't think you'd be given my younger sister's hand, and of necessity you were glad to marry me, since you couldn't do better. I was a substitute. I pardon you for that odious calculation, but I pray God Germaine will refuse to be your wife, because I love her, and you will deceive her as you've deceived me. She will refuse, I hope, when she knows what you're worth. Your betrayal won't bring you happiness; I predict it."

The heir, troubled by that declaration of war, was going to try again to justify himself, but the Arab song was finished and silence suddenly fell in the drawing room. Germaine was closing the piano; her mother and her uncle rose to thank the Lieutenant for having shown them a bit of primitive poetry and savage music. Laurence herself abandoned her embroidery; and du Pommeval had to leave it as it was.

"That's charming," Monsieur Daudièrne, who'd only half-way listened, said with conviction. "Ladies, you should give up Beethoven and Mozart, who put me to sleep. I prefer the airs which have never been written down. The American Redskins have some very pretty ones."

"The gypsies also," retorted Germaine. "Do you want us to go look for Roch Ferrar?"

"I certainly hope that rascal will never again set foot here at Germonière. He'll sleep in prison one of these days, and he'll have deserved it. Did I tell you the Attorney General suspects him of having drowned our neighbors, that he claimed he wanted to save?"

"Yes, but I'll never believe that."

"Because I didn't tell you everything. It seems he was paid by a cousin of Madame Vignemal who had left the country and who came back just to do this job. They're looking for that one and as soon as they've found him, they'll open an investigation, which will take the two accomplices to be charged."

Roger Pontac trembled. The cousin they suspected of an abominable crime, that evidently was he. No other relative of Madame Vignemal had left the area and had come back unexpectedly. The accusation was absurd and wasn't worth his taking it into account. However, forgetting Mademoiselle Daudièrne's instructions, he almost betrayed his incognito status that she had asked him to keep for the moment. Germaine broke in just in time.

"But that's a novel, this relative who reappears at a set time to drown people," she exclaimed. "I didn't know magistrates had so much imagination. They invent theatrical effects."

"President Lestrigon is incapable of lying and it's from him that I got this information," said Uncle Armand. "Madame Vignemal had, through charity, reared a little scamp, who paid her poorly for her goodness. He ran away from school about ten years ago and he's never been heard of again."

"It seems to me," Madame Daudièrne murmured, "that the Doctor told us that story."

"Exactly. I even believe he told us the name of that individual, but I've

311

forgotten it and I didn't think to ask the President for it. What's certain is that that man was seen prowling around, the evening of, or the evening before, the accident, the Vignemal property. The gardener recognized him. Unfortunately, he didn't think to follow him."

"And since that encounter, the fantastic cousin has not shown himself," Germaine said ironically. "He may have a talisman which makes him invisible."

"You're laughing, little girl. You're wrong. They know, without a doubt, that he's hidden somewhere in the vicinity of Fougéray, and they're looking for him undercover in order not to raise his accomplice's suspicions."

"His accomplice, that's Roch Ferrer, I suppose?"

"*Parbleu!* These two scoundrels must have come to an understanding when they first spoke to each other."

"Then they know each other?"

"Nobody knows, but however that may be, they could have come together on a road or in a wood. The gypsy doesn't have fixed living quarters. He spends his nights outside and he never sleeps twice in the same place."

"Oh! He never goes very far from Germonière and I'd gladly bet that if Laurence would paint his portrait, they wouldn't have any trouble ferreting him out."

"That's possible, but I don't want to," the elder sister said dryly.

"Well," said Germaine, "why don't they question this poor gypsy, since they suspect him. I have no doubt he would clear himself."

"They're waiting until the other one is caught before they arrest him. If they put Roch in prison, the cousin they're looking for would be quick to skip out, and they'd no longer be able to confront the two of them."

Frowning, Roger Pontac listened to Uncle Armans's indictment and held himself in check in order not to cry out: "That cousin, that's me, and what you're saying doesn't make sense."

A glance from Germaine once again prevented him from losing control. And the young girl, who was maintaining Roch Ferrar's innocence found an unexpected ally. Arthur du Pommeval wasn't at all interested in their arresting people about the event which made him an heir. He knew that a criminal trial would slow down his entering into possession and in the course of this trial something could again come out about the events which would put in question the validity of Monsieur Grandminard's testimony.

"It seems to me," he said, "that the law would be acting without due consideration if they had men imprisoned on vague information. I don't know this uncatchable cousin of Madame Vignemal, but I scarcely believe what they say of him. If he'd had evil designs on his relative, he would have carried them out all alone. And, above all, he wouldn't have gotten in touch with this gypsy who is incapable of committing a crime. Doctor Subligny confirms it."

"Doctor Subligny takes an interest in him and in my opinion he's wrong," grumbled Monsieur Daudièrne. "But we've certainly talked enough about this villainous affair. Monsieur Pontac has sung us an Algerian song. I won't take advantage of his kindness by asking him to do another, but I hope he's going to give us some details about African hunts. Have you killed lions, my dear Lieutenant?"

"Never, Monsieur," Pontac answered. "I even admit to you that I have little taste for hunting. Since I've been at the Bretteville chateau I haven't fired a shot. But I would be delighted to make my debut with you...and if these ladies will please fix the date for the great deer hunt in the Bretteville forest, I'll give orders to make everything ready."

"It's up to Monsieur le Duc to choose the day that's convenient for him," said du Pommeval, just to remind people that he considered himself as invited.

"Monsieur de Bretteville has turned everything over to me. I have carte blanche to organize the party. He just asks these ladies to excuse him if he doesn't come. He's still overwhelmed by his sorrow and I reproach myself for having left him alone too long. So I'm going to take leave of you, Madame," said Roger, bowing to Germaine's mother.

"What! You're not going to give us the pleasure of having you dine with us at Germonière?" exclaimed Uncle Armand.

"Please excuse me. Monsieur de Bretteville is waiting for me and if we're going to hunt this week, as he wishes us to, I have things to do, beginning this evening."

"Would you like us to hunt day after tomorrow. I'm asking my nieces and our friend du Pommeval. Alfred doesn't vote, because he thought fit to give our company the slip."

"Yes, yes, the day after tomorrow," Germaine exclaimed, clapping her hands.

"Perfect," said du Pommeval.

Laurence approved by nodding her head and Madame Daudièrne raised no objection, although the project didn't please her very much. Any other time she would have opposed it. But Germaine's marriage seemed to her so likely that she didn't want to deprive the fiancés of a diversion which would please both of them and which must give rise to opportunities to speak freely without going against social conventions, since Uncle Armand would be a member of the party.

If Roger had decided to cut short his visit, it was because he had read in Germaine's eyes that she was advising him to leave. He understood this mute language, easier to interpret than the language of flowers. And he guessed why Germaine wished him to leave. The intelligent young girl understood what Lieutenant Pontac must have suffered while Monsieur Daudièrne was accusing him without naming him, and she was afraid he would lose patience. This wasn't the time to bring things out in the open. It would be better to keep silent until the law became aware that it was on the wrong track.

They insisted that he stay. Du Pommeval, who didn't want to be outdone in politeness, offered him his carriage to return him to Bretteville. He even went so far as to suggest that he himself take him there. Roger refused everything except a handshake from his rival, which he was obligated to submit to. They separated, promising to get together two days later.

The rendezvous for the hunt was set by common accord on the edge of the Bretêche forest, at the foot of the Lemon Rock. The guests would come there by carriage, taking the Departmental road that Germaine, carried away by Ralph, hadn't followed, and it's easy to believe that this arrangement didn't displease the heroine of that equestrian adventure.

Roger had come on foot. He had left his horses in Tunisia and he rarely rode those the Duke put at his disposal. Besides, Germonière was only six kilometers from the chateau and the First Lieutenant of the Hussards was as good a walker as a horseman. He went there by the way he preferred, that is, by going across the garden and climbing the Beuvron levee to reach the park gate, which they closed only in the evening. And the narrow pathway led him right to the place where the ferry had been before the storm carried it away. He had seen this ferry in the past, set up as a temporary measure by the proprietors who seldom used it and who didn't like to spend any money on it. He remembered the worm-eaten boat, hardly perpendicular pilings on each side of the river which held the two ends of the cable worn out by the repeated rubbing of the rope which attached the boat. He certainly thought that Madame Vignemal had never had anything repaired, and he was astonished that all that equipment, so badly kept up, had lasted so long.

The idea come to him to look around while there. He went down to the edge of the Beuvron, and he saw that a fragment of the broken rope had remained attached to the post on the right bank and was dragging in the water. He drew it to him and, examining it closely, he found that the hemp, rotted by the water, no longer had enough strength to resist the pull of a heavy boat pushed by a very violent current.

"It was just a simple accident," he murmured, *"an accident they should have foreseen. That cable had been in service 20 years, perhaps. If it broke, it wasn't the fault of the gypsy the law suspects. And when I think that they suspect me also, I'm tempted to believe that all those people there are mad, including Monsieur Daudièrne, who repeats their stupid inventions. I remember now that Doctor Subligny asked me the other day if I knew Roch Ferrer. They probably told him the same story. Evidently he didn't attach any importance to it. But I really can't stay under the threat of an accusation of this type...however absurd it may be. It's a miracle that nobody in this area has discovered that Roger Pontac is living in the de Bretteville chateau. I'm not going to wait until they come looking for me there. Monsieur Subligny wrote me from Paris that he'd come back to Arcy tomorrow or the day after tomorrow. As soon as he's back, I'll ask him to go with me to President Lestrigon, who informed Monsieur Daudièrne so well. We'll explain ourselves at length. I want to be finished with*

false rumors."

Night was coming on. He didn't stop to contemplate the dangerous stream which had swallowed up the Vignemal couple, nor the Fougéray roofs, which could be seen on the other bank, on the other side of a waving plain. He went back up the levee. He found the park gate open, and he started on the way to Bretteville thinking about the happenings in his visit to Germonière.

He had just found himself face to face with that Arthur du Pommeval, who had taken a fortune from him and who expected to marry Mademoiselle Daudièrne. He had seen him. He had spoken to him. And he recognized that that heir had all that was necessary to please Germaine's relatives. Between an elegant millionaire and a poor First Lieutenant, the fight wasn't equal. And nevertheless Roger didn't despair yet. Germaine hadn't yet told him she loved him, but assuredly she didn't love Monsieur du Pommeval, since she wanted him to marry her sister. Mademoiselle Laurence had chatted a long time with the handsome Arthur while Germaine was playing an accompaniment on the piano to a song favorable to confidences. Was this a double omen, these two tête-à-têtes that neither the mother nor the uncle had interrupted. Roger didn't dare believe so, but he certainly felt that it was no longer up to him to escape his destiny. He was in love and he was ready to sacrifice everything for his love. War, military glory, advancement, he no longer thought about them. The wind of passion had blown through all the dreams of his youth. It seemed to him now that he had never begun to live until the day the Lemon Rock repeated the sweet name of Germaine. The daydreams preoccupying him kept him from paying attention to the noises heard on a road bordered by trees and underbrush: the branches cracking, the dry leaves whirling around, birds flying away. He walked with a steady and rapid step without being distracted and without letting his thoughts be led astray by the snatches of views which each turn in the road presented. Le Beuvron wasn't far away and its grey waters mirrored the last lights of a clear autumn day.

Roger didn't pay any attention to a black dot staining the middle of the river's current approaching little by little from the right bank. Roger was walking straight ahead and he was approaching the spot where a few days before he had left Mademoiselle Daudièrne, when a man appeared standing on the river bank, ten steps away from him. That time, the Lieutenant, suddenly drawn from his thoughts by that apparition, stopped short and confronted the enemy. Of a certainty, Roger wasn't easily frightened and his campaigns in Africa had accustomed him to surprises. But he had learned in fighting a war with the Arabs that it's always better to begin by taking a defensive stance when one suddenly finds oneself face to face with a man on a lonely road. He immediately took a pretty revolver from his pocket, and after having loaded it, he walked calmly forward to meet that almost fantastic apparition, because it seemed to have risen from the river. Night was falling. Objects were beginning to merge with each other in the half clarity of the twilight. It was becoming difficult to estimate their proportions exactly. The silhouette standing out in black against the gray sky appeared gigantic.

Coming closer, the Hussard Lieutenant saw that he was dealing with a tall fellow dressed in skins like a native of Siberia and dripping with water. That strange fellow traveler stared at him but didn't budge. It almost seemed that he didn't intend to go far from the Beuvron, which was probably his line of retreat. His attitude was not threatening and he seemed to have come there out of curiosity, for the pleasure of seeing a well-dressed man. Roger didn't need to tax his memory to remember what they had just told him at Germonière. He very quickly guessed that fate had put him in the presence of the gypsy they suspected of having played a villainous role in the ferryboat tragedy. He also remembered they had accused that gypsy of having acted in agreement with a cousin of Madame Vignemal who was in a hurry to inherit her wealth. The cousin they didn't name was himself, Roger Pontac, and the occasion was a good one to explain himself to his supposed accomplice.

"Good Evening, Roch," he said to him coldly.

"You know me!" exclaimed the bohemian.

"No, but people claim that you know me."

"Me! A little while ago I saw you from a distance...when you were examining the broken rope."

"Ah! Really. Then, where were you?"

"In front of you...on the other side of the Beuvron."

"And I find you here! Then you came across the water? I didn't know there was a bridge."

"I swam across."

"Í can see that. You're wet from your head to toe. It seems you aren't chilly and you aren't afraid for your skin. "

"I'm not afraid of anything at all."

"Not even of the law, or so it appears."

"If you're talking about the Duke's gamekeepers or the Commune's rural property guards, it's true I laugh at them. They can look for me as much as they want to. They'll never catch me."

"Others might catch you. The gendarmes, for example. And you'll go to prison in Arcy."

"Why? I've never killed anybody. And I've never stolen."

"Are you very sure about that?"

"Trapping forest rabbits and river carps, that's not stealing."

"Go ask Monsieur Daudièrne what he thinks of your case."

"You're coming from Germonière?"

"You know that I am, since you saw me on the levee at the end of their garden."

"This is the first time you've been there?"

"No, the second."

"You're from Arcy?"

"You're too curious, but I'm willing to answer your questions…on condition that you answer mine. No, I'm not from Arcy but I'm from the region and I know a number of people there, Doctor Subligny, among others."

"Doctor Subligny! Did he talk to you about me?"

"Yes, and he said nothing but good things about you. But everyone doesn't agree with him. Monsieur Daudièrne claims that you helped the Vignemals drown."

"He certainly knows the contrary. He was there when I tried to save them."

"The Republic Prosecutor wasn't there and he accuses you."

"That's possible. He questioned me the other day at Fougéray and I really suspected that he wanted to have me arrested, but he didn't dare. There was nothing against me."

"Do you know the heirs of the Vignemals?"

"The heirs?"

"Yes, the relatives who'll get the estate of the husband and his wife?"

"I've heard it said that the husband had a nephew and that the wife had some cousins, but I've never taken any interest in them."

"Then you don't know one of them named Pontac?"

"Not even the name."

"Nor a Monsieur du Pommeval?"

"That one, I've seen him many times. He's come almost every day to Germonière for the last six months."

"Then you're mounting guard around Madame Daudièrne's property?"

"No, but I see all those who're invited to the chateau come and go."

"You've never seen me, then?"

"It was to see you up close that I swam the Beuvron. "

"You spy on the guests, so it seems. Well! What do you think of me now that you've spoken to me?"

"I think that if you're Monsieur Subligny's friend, you're a good man."

"You're right. The doctor has only good people for his friends. And he's also the friend of Monsieur du Pommeval."

"Oh! That man, I detest him!"

"Bah! Then what's he done to you?"

"Well, he doesn't even know I exist. But I don't like him."

"Then you won't be happy to learn that through the death of his uncle Vignemal he's become the owner of Fougéray?"

"That doesn't make any difference to me."

"And that he'll be an even closer than ever neighbor of the Daudièrne family and that he may end up marrying one of the young ladies."

"Which one?" the gypsy asked quickly.

"Ask him when you meet him," Roger Pontac answered, smiling. "He can inform you a great deal better than I can. I'm not in on the secrets of Madame

Daudièrne's projects."

"Then," Roch continued, "you yourself haven't come to marry?"

"No, me, I'm not an heir and they wouldn't want a poor devil who has nothing but his rank."

"Ah! You're a soldier?"

"An officer in the Cavalry and I enlisted as a simple soldier. You really ought to do the same."

"I've thought about it more than once…but I don't want to."

"Why? You're built to ride horseback, you're strong, clever, and daring…and you're used to privations. The life of an African calvary soldier would fit you like a glove."

"Later, maybe…now, no. I want to stay what I am."

"A vagabond and a pilferer. You'll be sorry, my boy, because the life you're leading will end badly. And that sooner than you think. You're being watched and one of these days they'll arrest you. You'll be able to prove, I can well believe, that you had nothing to do with the accident which cost the lives of two people, but they'll condemn you for having hunted and fished without a license. And when you've spent your time in prison, you'll start over again. People with previous convictions, that leads very far. Believe me, Roch, don't waste any time. Come to see me tomorrow at the Bretteville Chateau. I'll give you a letter to the officer who commands my regiment's post at Castres and some money to make the trip. They'll enlist you immediately and in six months they'll send you to my squadron. You'll see the country. You'll shoot a gun…that's amusing, that is, and the next year you'll be promoted to corporal. The gendarmes who're looking for you to lock you up, will be very fooled."

"At the Bretteville chateau? Then you're the Duke's son?"

"No! Not even a relative. But I live at his house. I'll expect you tomorrow and if you think it necessary to consult Doctor Subligny before making a decision, we'll go to Arcy to see him together."

Roger Pontac had forgotten one of the recommendations of the ex-Surgeon-Major, who knew the whole situation better than he did and who had advised him to avoid the Beuvron savage. Roger was no longer thinking about the ridiculous suspicions which Monsieur Daudièrne had just told him about. He didn't recognize that they could seriously accuse a French officer of having paid a scoundrel to drown a cousin from whom he could inherit. And now that he had talked with Roch Ferrer, he took him to be a good eccentric fellow, incapable of committing such a cowardly crime. He didn't ask himself why it was so important to that odd fellow to stay on Madame Daudièrne's property, nor why he had swum the river with the sole purpose of seeing close up a Monsieur who was leaving the Germonière garden. He was thinking only of putting him on the right road by opening up to him an honorable career.

"It's agreed. You'll come."

Roch, instead of answering, turned around to dive into the water. He jumped quickly into the water and swam vigorously toward the opposite bank.

"Well!" said Roger, astounded. "Decidedly this boy has no calling for the military. That's too bad. He would have made an excellent soldier. But the devil if I can guess why he swam the Beuvron just to find himself on my pathway. I forgot to ask him that. And judging by the questions he asked me, I'd be tempted to believe that he'd set himself up to spy on the Messieurs who frequent Germonière. He asked me if I'd come to get married, and he detests du Pommeval. He's capable of having fallen in love with one of the Daudièrne young ladies. I can't do anything more and I've done my best to make him decide to leave. But I'll alert Mademoiselle Germaine and I'm sure she'll approve."

Roger wasn't wrong and in truth he could not guess that Laurence was going to come on stage in this intimate drama where he was acting the role of first lover.

VI. Laurence the Jilted One

At Germonière whether there were invited guests or they dined as a family, dinner was always a happy affair. There were abundant dishes, the cooking was praiseworthy, and what was even better, all the Daudièrnes had a good appetite, a good stomach and very few cares. Numerous enough to be sufficient unto themselves, they took pleasure in retorting to one another and conversation was never lacking. Uncle Armand was speaking easily and drinking a great deal. He had filled the wine cellar of his sister-in-law, who knew little about the matter, with first class wines, and as he had seen a great deal and retained a great deal, he was never short of interesting stories.

His nephew Alfred did what he could to imitate him, but he was not up to it. At the third glass he couldn't tell the difference between a first rate local wine and an ordinary table wine, and he launched into Parisian stories which drew him frequent calls to order. Even so, he took his part in these agreeable concerts, because his sisters were amused by his transgressions and Uncle Armand wasn't bothered by making fun of him when he began to recount his luck in love affairs.

Germaine was always given to laughter; Laurence, more serious, wasn't sad, however, and their mother possessed, among other qualities, evenness of temperament.

Thus, everyday was a party at the chateau in the dining room charmingly decorated by the chatelaine, who had a wonderful understanding of interior and exterior design. Everything at her house was carefully taken care of, from the garden right up to the attics. When there were guests, as there frequently were in good weather, joy was at its heighth. Madame Daudièrne, breaking with the provincial tradition, didn't give large dinner parties. She didn't send out invitations two weeks in advance. And she didn't think herself obliged to regale her guests with a four-course feast. People came when they wished and they were always nicely treated.

The Arcy ladies, who didn't practice this system, and for good reason, thought that she didn't go to much trouble and that she didn't live up to her fortune. They accepted, however, when they were asked after paying a visit, but it was to see how people dined in Paris. And Monsieur Armand, always a candid talker, didn't miss that opportunity to tell them about the customs of a society whose prodigious blunders they didn't know anything about. He even amused himself by announcing to them that the next time he proposed to invite the new Sous Prefet, that good society of the little village had put in quarantine. The gentlemen had to be begged less to dine, above all the young, who knew the evening would be interesting.

And when only particular friends were dining at Germonière, they had the pleasure of passing in revue the Arcy bourgeois and their ridiculous behavior. But the jokes never went too far and when they fell on the invited guests, those who were the butt of the jokes were the first to laugh about it.

Arthur du Pommeval had often been among those because he was received on an intimate footing, and in those happy times he was liked by all the men and all the women. They were pleased that he preferred the pleasure of family reunions to the emotions of baccarat and to the excitement of horse shows. It has to be added that he was then taking advantage of his situation as a perpetual marriage candidate. And he brought off with a great deal of ease and happiness this role difficult to sustain for long. He behaved in such a way as to let it be thought that he esteemed himself too honored to enter into the family life and if he didn't say so openly, it was from an excess of modesty. And by not stating his preference for one or the other of the Daudièrne young ladies, he had chosen the best method of making both of them kindly disposed toward him.

The youngest, who wasn't at all thinking about marrying him, found him amusing and pleasant. She recognized that his absence made a difference at all the parties, that there were no good little intimate dances without him, and the older sister didn't say anything different.

The tragic death of the Vignemals had changed all that. The heir had been forced to make a decision, and as it always happens to hesitant people who make a sudden decision, he hadn't satisfied anyone. Laurence, wounded to the heart, didn't forgive him for having deceived her, and Germaine, too clear-sighted, wasn't at all grateful to him for the late preference with which he'd decided to honor her. There was no one, right up to Madame Daudièrne, who didn't feel herself made uneasy by this unexpected change. She almost held it against du Pommeval for having made a mistake by supposing her to have intentions which were not hers. There was hardly anyone but Uncle Armand who wasn't unhappy with the choice made by his protégé, and he would have been embarrassed if he'd had to say why. Alfred, on this question, had no firm opinion. He congratulated himself on being the brother-in-law of a good fellow who understood life and who made loans easily. It mattered little to him if that obliging friend married Laurence or Germaine.

And in the new situation created by the offer of marriage officially presented by Doctor Subligny, Roger Pontac counted only as a friendly country neighbor, a valuable recruit to occupy the leisure of a winter stay in the country. He had pleased everybody. Monsieur Daudièrne praised him to the skies. Madame Daudièrne praised his perfect manners and his reserved language. Laurence found him to her taste, although she had noticed him very little and listen to him even less. Alfred dreamed of dazzling him by his hunting exploits and his equestrian prowess. Du Pommeval was particularly impressed with him because of the interest the Duke de Bretteville had taken in him.

Germaine didn't say as much good about him as these enthusiasts, but she thought a great deal more and no one had guessed what she thought. It was easy to believe that when the officer of the Hussards met Arthur du Pommeval for the first time at Germonière, it was a great question of him after his departure.

Arthur had remained behind. His mourning did not prevent his spending the evening in a small group now that he was almost a part of the family. It was important to him to take advantage of the privilege accorded to suitors paying court in such a case. He made an effort to be likeable, but in vain. The dinner was cold. However, Germaine showed her usual liveliness. She, her mother, and her uncle bent over backwards to enliven the gathering. But it takes just one false note to disturb the most perfect accord and Laurence gave hers, very gently, without apparent bitterness. She limited herself to throwing out at appropriate times words which fit provincial "Gommeux" dandies in general and the handsome Arthur in particular. She praised the merit of those fearless individuals who owed nothing but to themselves and who didn't rely on the fortunes of others to make a place for themselves in life.

She said so much about it that Monsieur Daudièrne wondered if Lieutenant Pontac hadn't made a very lively impression on her, and he allowed himself to tease her about her romantic notions. Madame Daudièrne, who knew her better, attached less importance to it, but she saw very well that the poor child was using this language only to hide cruel suffering. And she almost began to reproach herself for having tolerated, if not encouraged, Monsieur du Pommeval's betrayal. She even vaguely thought about going back on the consent that had been snatched from her a little by surprise and of attempting to bring back the flighty heir to his first love. But the guilty man didn't appear to be repentant. He was flirting openly with the youngest without worrying about the vexation of the older. It was easy to see that he believed himself in a position to choose and he didn't regret having chosen.

Germaine maneuvered in such a way that it was almost impossible to understand if she was flattered by the attentions of her neighbor at the table or if she simply took pleasure in exciting him so that he would give way to some silly flattery and to ridiculous compliments.

And when they got up from the table to go into the drawing room, du Pommeval himself was rather embarrassed by his behavior. It wasn't a question of playing music. It was good for a First Lieutenant from Africa to sing Arab songs. Arthur's new fortune kept him far from the piano. And when indifferent topics of conversation had been exhausted, when the Duke de Bretteville's courtesy had been praised by every voice, and everyone stopped talking all at one time about the arrangements for the big hunt in the La Bretêche forest, the fiancé felt it was time to take leave.

They didn't try to persuade him to stay, but they separated on very good terms. Uncle Armand and Alfred accompanied him as far as his carriage. And Madame Daudièrne having left an instant to give an order to a chamber maid, the two sisters found themselves alone.

"You mauled handsome Arthur soundly," Germaine said, laughing. "You did well. He asked for it. I didn't want to help you out. But one of these days, I'll get into it myself also, and you'll see that with both of us, we'll put him back on the right road."

"He took the one that suits him," Laurence answered. "And I'm not the one who'll turn him away from it."

"Then it will be me, big sister. I would tell you how I'll go about it, but... it's a secret you'll allow me to keep a few days more."

"Oh! As many as you'd like. I won't try to guess it. And I won't do Monsieur du Pommeval the honor of thinking about him."

"And you'll be right. That would be the way to bring him back. Because you love him and..."

Laurence made a gesture of protest, but Germaine continued gaily:

"And me, I don't love him. Do you believe I'm bragging? What if I told you I love someone else?"

Madame Daudièrne reappeared at this moment and Uncle Armand wasn't long in showing himself. Alfred had gone to bed to get some rest after a night of playing baccarat. And, although it was scarcely 10:00 p.m., nobody wanted to prolong the evening,

"Our friend is definitely a charming young man," Monsieur Daudièrne said.

"Who are you talking about, Uncle?" Germaine asked maliciously.

"About Arthur, *Parbleu!* The Hussard officer is very likeable also, but he's a migrating bird, whereas du Pommeval is and will remain in perpetuity Seigneur of Fougéray."

"He isn't that yet. His Seignorial position depends on Roch Ferrer. If the savage comes to swear that Madame Vignemal was still alive when he left her on the bank, the inheritance will go up in smoke. You told us so."

"Don't be afraid little girl. That won't happen, and when the gypsy has paid for inventing lies, nobody will give any credence to the saying of such a bizarre fellow."

"So be it!! Let's go to bed. I won't dream of the inheritance of our poor neighbors."

On that declaration that nobody disagreed with, each went to his own bedroom, after the usual ceremony of good nights and embraces.

All the family lived on the second floor, with the exception of Alfred, who had established himself on the ground floor to be freer to go out at night whenever the fancy took him to mount Ralph and ride to Arcy to play baccarat.

Madame Daudièrne's apartment was situated between that of Laurence and that of Germaine and did not communicate from the inside with theirs. The druggist, when he had his country house built, had arranged it like an army barracks. One interminable corridor, off of which a dozen doors opened, went across the entire building to end, on one side at the central main stairway, and, at the other, the service stairway. It was ugly but it was convenient from the point of view of privacy. The uncle inhabited the courtyard side, the mother and the daughters the garden side.

"Finally I'm going to be able to cry," Laurence told herself, after having locked the door. And falling into an armchair, she burst into tears. Those who had seen her at the dinner table and in the drawing room didn't suspect that she had fled to her bedroom to sob like a child.

So long as that cruel trial imposed by the false situation in which she found herself lasted, she'd had the strength to control herself. She didn't want to make a spectacle of her sadness. Her mother and her uncle had certainly understood that her ego was suffering, but they didn't believe her heart was wounded. Du Pommeval himself had seen in her attitude and in her language only the effects of a very natural petulance. He imagined she was pouting and that, with time, she would console herself of his loss.

Germaine wasn't mistaken about that, but Germaine had her plan and judged it useless to temporarily dress a wound that she flattered herself she would soon heal.

The jilted one was therefore reduced to swallowing her tears. She was proud and she didn't want anyone to pity her. Her straight forward personality revolted against the betrayal and felt repugnance at the concession society imposed on females. She preferred to die of sorrow rather than try to bring back the man who had abandoned her, or even let him believe she took lightly his bad faith. Dissimulation and coquettishness were not her weapons.

But, nevertheless, it was her life which was being broken when Roger Pontac was singing in Arab, *"the melodious bird which flies toward the beloved."* Just at the decisive moment when she found herself free to explain herself fully to the forgetful Arthur, Monsieur Subligny had come to ask for Germaine's hand for the Vignemals' heir. But that action was so unexpected that everybody concerned had asked themselves if it had been thought out or if had to be seen as a rash act inspired by a passing feeling of spite. Monsieur du Pommeval had perhaps been peaked by having made advances to which Laurence had responded only with reserve. The place he held in Arcy society and some successes in Paris had given himself a high opinion of himself. He might have figured that to make the elder submit, it was necessary to appear to be courting the younger. These tactics succeed with certain women and he perhaps judged Laurence according to those he had known.

The injury was serious and the noble girl that he confused with heartless creatures had sharply resented it. But neither the mother nor the sister had seemed to attach much importance to this quick change of tactic. Madame Daudièrne had answered evasively. Germaine had only laughed about it. And in repeating to Laurence the words of the good Doctor, they were eager to ask her opinion about the new situation created for all three of them by the mission Monsieur Subligny had just filled in such a free and easy way.

Unfortunately, Laurence had a lofty soul, and however lightly it was touched, she retreated into herself like a sensitive blossom. She thought complaining unworthy of herself and she wanted before anything else to hear Monsieur du Pommeval himself be forced to confess that he had committed himself and that his words were deceiving; to tell him, without recriminations, what contempt his conduct inspired in her and then to leave him to his remorse.

Laurence, closely pressed, had been wrong to answer by protesting that Monsieur du Pommeval was free to marry whomever he pleased, and her mother, believing her, was satisfied with that too vague declaration. In this way the poor child prepared a more bitter deception for herself.

It was done now. The unfaithful man, having settled himself into his decision, had hardly defended himself, and his embarrassed protests had only snatched away the abandoned girl's last illusions. There was nothing left for her to expect from this provincial Lovelace who changed his affections when he changed his fortunes. To tactfully handle in his own interests a marriage suitable to the mediocrity in which he was vegetating before the ferry catastrophe, he wasn't afraid of faking a passion which he was incapable of feeling.

It had taken Laurence only a five-minute meeting to judge him. She had shone light on his self-interested calculations, his shabby ambitions, his compromises with his conscience. She knew he wasn't worth her regret. She reproached herself for ever having loved him, and she was afraid she still loved him.

"No," she murmured, drying her tears, "I no longer love him... I hate him. I curse him and I'll get revenge. I don't want him to deceive Germaine as he deceived me. She's just sworn to me that she's indifferent to him and she isn't lying...she never lies...and nevertheless she lets him come here... She doesn't discourage him. She didn't cry out when our mother told her he'd asked to marry her. Should what she told me be believed... that she wants to bring him back to me? If she's sincere, she's mad. She could refuse him, but as impudent as he is, he wouldn't have the audacity to come back to me. He'd understand that I want nothing to do with him now that I know what he's worth. And who knows whether Germaine may be taken in by the comedies he plays so shamelessly? Who knows whether he might manage to persuade her that he's always been in love with her? Why wouldn't she be as credulous as I was? A while ago she gave me to understand that she was engaged to someone else... That wasn't serious. Who could she have given her heart to? All the young men who come here seem ridiculous to her. To that officer she accompanied on the piano? That's not possible. She hardly knows him. She's seen him twice, and they haven't exchanged ten words. She said that to reassure me and nothing prevents her falling into the traps this traitor is going to set for her. She'll fall into them even more easily than everybody else would, except me. My mother, my uncle, my brother approved Monsieur du Pommeval's intentions and supported him. She'll resist, but, tired of fighting, she'll finally give in.

"God is my witness that if I thought he sincerely loved her, I could only *hope that he wouldn't make her the most unhappy of women; I could forget the outrage I'd suffered and I'd sacrifice everything for my sister... everything... even my resentment. I'd pardon Monsieur du Pommeval for having preferred Germaine to me. But he sees nothing in this marriage but the satisfaction of a caprice. He's rich. He wants the pleasure of marrying a young girl that he finds prettier than I am. And when this fantasy is past, he'll drop her as he dropped me. No, No, that won't happen. I don't want that to happen,"* Laurence said, rising.

The bedroom was decorated in light grey. A wood fire was burning in the white marble fireplace, and the soft glow of a night light lit the virginal bed, at the foot of which a Great Dane was sleeping. He was dear to the two sisters, who let him sleep wherever he pleased. This spotted representative of an almost disappeared race alternately guarded Laurence and Germaine. That night it was Laurence's time, and she must have been terribly preoccupied not to have responded to his caresses. Discouraged, Belt had gone to stretch out on a swan skin brought back by Monsieur Daudièrne from a hunt in the cypress hedges of the Somme River, occasionally lifting his head to follow his mistress' movements with an attentive look.

She slowly walked aimlessly around the small apartment where she had spent so many happy hours before knowing Arthur du Pommeval. Less outgoing than her sister, she had always had a pronounced taste for solitude and she loved to shut herself up in this pretty and cosy nest where no one could come trouble her. She stayed there entire days, copying old engravings or painting, using as models flowers she had grown herself which were in beautiful vases given to her by Uncle Armand.

She also often sat down at her window and lost herself for a long time dreaming, while looking at that countryside which was made for pleasing the eyes: close at hand the huge trees in the park: further off, the Beuvron with its clear waters, and in the background, well beyond the tile roofs of Fougéray, the chain of bluish hills which barred the horizon. She wasn't romantic as was her sister. She had no taste for adventures. Adventures at the depth of a forest didn't tempt her, and the incident at the Lemon Rock would have left her cold. Her type of poetry was meditative. She dreamed of her own kind of happiness, and she had a different view of life than Germaine. She kept her heart in reserve, for fear of placing it lightly. Before loving, she wanted to be sure of being loved. And it was only after having studied for a long time the character of Arthur du Pommeval that she had responded to the advances of this king of the elegant youth of Arcy. He pleased her, but she wanted to put him to the test, and the test had been favorable to this fortunate boy. Laurence could never have doubted, no matter what he might have said, that he had developed for her a respectful and discreet love. Even less had she suspected that he was thinking about Germaine. And little by little, she came to love him, without, for all that, being blinded by his imperfections. She was very aware of them; she felt that he lacked energy, a head for management, and stability in his ideas. So, left to himself, he would probably end up like his father, who had ruined himself in provincial vanities. But she forgave him all those faults because she thought him loyal and good. Perhaps she wasn't annoyed that he had them since she hoped to correct them. She flattered herself that he would sacrifice his tastes for her and it would be her pleasure to convert him. A more perfect suitor wouldn't have been able to give her that satisfaction so dear to all women. Besides, du Pommeval led her to believe that he was hoping to lead a family life, the winter in Paris, the summer in Germonière. He made fun of the false pleasures and the empty existences of the young fools who didn't understand that true happiness is in marriage. And, as he was sincere at the moment he was speaking, Laurence had believed in his profession of faith and had sworn she would marry no one but him. She was waiting for nothing more but an opportunity which would allow him to declare himself, even, to commit himself to open his heart to her mother, whom she somewhat reproached herself for not having consulted. A single day was enough to drive away these deceptive illusions. The dream vanished. Laurence fell from the height of her illusions and the only feeling she had left was the desire to punish the traitor who had reduced her to despair.

"Yes, I want him to atone for his betrayal," she murmured. *"Germaine will lure him with promises which commit to nothing and will finally send him away. He'll be repaid for the shame of having deceived me and his pride will be hurt. But that's not enough. He has to be struck in what's dearest to him...that fortune which perverted his heart has to be taken away. He thinks he can do anything, since chance has just thrown him millions. If he falls back into mediocrity from which an accident has lifted him he'll feel all the bitterness of chastisement. The inheritance...it's the inheritance that he must be made to lose...and my uncle is sure that it won't even be contested.*

Laurence had gone to the window and was looking distractedly at the space extended in front of the house. The night was clear enough to see the Beurvron waters, marked by a long train of fog.

"And," she continued, *"there's where that gypsy saw Madame Vignemal wash up on the bank. Was she dead? Only he could say so, and if he said she was still alive at the time he saw her, everything would be put in question... My uncle has just said a while ago that Monsieur du Pommeval had nothing to fear but Roch Ferrer's testimony, and, if I wished it, Roch Ferrer would speak... Didn't he tell me in the Tertre woods that he was ready to do everything I commanded him to...and it's just up to me to call him. He's waiting for the signal, and if I shone a light in my bedroom windows, he'd come to the levee at the end of the garden."*

Laurence became excited while talking to herself, and perhaps not to give herself any time to reflect, she took the lamp which was lit near the bed and she put it on the window sill. The Great Dane got up and came to rub his muzzle against Laurence's hand which had just placed the lamp. You would have said that he understood the gravity of that very simple action. His gentle, intelligent eyes seemed to say: "I'm ready to follow you everywhere and to defend you against everyone."

She also understood that in giving the signal the gypsy was waiting for, she had just started down a bad pathway, and that this first step might lead her further than she wanted to go. To communicate with Roch Ferrer, with that insolent gypsy who had the audacity to love her, was to be compromised already. To go join him at the rendezvous that he had allow himself to give her, was even worse still. It was to go against all the rules that a well brought up girl had willingly followed.

As thoughtless as she was, Germaine would not have done as much. It was true that Germaine had not been able to size up Roch Ferrer. She knew him only by having talked to him an instant, the evening of the accident. She had not, as had her sister, heard his protestations of submissive and passionate devotion. It wasn't to Germaine that he'd said: "You can treat me as you would treat a slave. My life belongs to you." Germaine didn't know that this savage was capable of respecting a woman and of obeying her blindly.

"Down there, on the edge of the Tertre woods," Laurence was saying to herself, *"I was at his mercy. I had lost my head when he took hold of my horse's bridle. My sister, on a run-away horse, was galloping down the road and my uncle was still far away. Roch could have carried me off before anyone came to my aid. And it was enough just to look at him for him to lower his eyes, to order him to leave for him to disappear. I have nothing to fear from this excited exalté. At the first disdainful word I threw at him, if he were to forget who he is and who I am, he would fall on his knees and he would ask my forgiveness. And, after all, the Beurvon levee is at the end of the garden, two steps from here. If I called out, they would hear me at the house. Besides, I'll take Belt.*

"You'll protect me, Belt, isn't that right?"

The Great Dane showed his white teeth and growled softly. It was as if he had answered in his dog language: "Count on me!"

Laurence was reasoning this way to give herself courage, but she was well aware that this nocturnal excursion was dangerous folly and that she risked at least her reputation in going through with it, alone, at such an hour, on an out-of-the-way path, to meet up with a gypsy who defied the law and the gendarmes.

"I would expose myself uselessly. Roch doesn't spend all his nights looking at my window. He might not see the signal. How could I believe that he was at a certain point on the Beuvron bank? The revenge I was dreaming of is escaping me. Nobody will trouble Monsieur du Pommeval's security."

Resigned, Laurence was going to leave the window when she saw a light shining at the end of the garden. It was only a shining point but that point was raised and lowered alternately.

"He's seen my lamp and he's answering that he's there," she told herself. *"I was wrong. He has waited without giving up and he's ready. And he, he's*

keeping his promise. He'd give his life for me if I asked it. And I would recompense his heroic devotion by letting him believe that I gave the signal just to test him and to make fun of him! That would almost authorize him to come call to me from under my window and to scale the wall to come to where I am. And he would do it... No obstacle would stop him. No, I don't want to be the cause of a misfortune or of a scandal. If my uncle caught him trying to break down a door, he would kill him by shooting him and if he met him in the house, he would suspect me of having brought him there. It's better to go confront the danger than to wait for it here. Come, Belt!"

She withdrew the lamp quickly, lit a small lantern which she used in the evening to go down the long corridor when the wind was blowing more than usual. Throwing a shawl over her shoulders, she slipped outside her bedroom and started walking noiselessly toward the service stairway. The dog went ahead of her, walking cautiously. He had guessed that she didn't want to be heard.

The walls were thick and there was a mat in the corridor. The stairway let onto a little door opening into the garden, beside the main steps, a door which the servants never took the key out of.

Laurence could leave without waking anyone. The most difficult thing was done. She had only to follow the right path which leads to the river, a five-minute trip on open ground. The young girl no longer hesitated. Her resolution was taken. And she was not afraid. She was sure that Roch would not take advantage of the situation. What did she base that certainty on? She would have been very puzzled to say. It was a sort of intuition which those who have fought in a war understand. There are days when one goes into combat saying to himself: "I won't be killed"; and one isn't killed that day.

The moving light she had seen was no longer visible, but that disappearance didn't bother Mademoiselle Daudièrne. In the Tertre woods, Roch had told her: "Come to the levee and walk to the spot where the Tamaris bushes end. She remembered his words and she didn't doubt that she'd find him at the spot indicated.

Belt was already lifting his nose in the air and at the moment his mistress reached the bank which dominated the Beuvron, he left without barking.

"Then he knows him." Laurence said to herself.

That fact had a good side because a barking dog would have drawn the attention of a gardener or a guard. But, on the other hand, she could no longer count on Belt's protection. The Great Dane was going over to the enemy. She soon saw him come back, still silent and gambling happily around her, then dashing again toward the levee where he was lost in the shadows, to reappear again an instant afterward and begin the same trick again, which evidently meant: *"I've found a comrade. I'm taking you to him."*

"His instinct isn't mistaken," she thought. *"He knows that the man who's petted him more than once doesn't intend me any harm."*

However, before going any further, she stopped an instant to listen and to look about. The night's silence was disturbed only by the murmur of the western wind which bent over the tamaris trees. There was no longer any light shining from the chateau windows. Everybody was already asleep.

Mademoiselle Daudièrne could expect no help except from her own strength, her cool-headedness which had already gotten her out of a difficult step. But she didn't doubt herself and she began to go bravely forward again. She had hardly taken ten steps when she saw Belt on alert, his head turned toward the river. She still went forward, calling softly to the dog, that didn't move. By the light of the lantern she was carrying she saw Roch Ferrer, standing, leaning against the trunk of an oak that marked the edge of the tamaris trees.

"I've come because I think I can trust you," she said, in a voice that trembled a little.

"Thank you," whispered the poacher, much more moved than the young girl. "I was hoping that you'd remember me. Now, whatever you ask of me, I'm already repaid, since you haven't forgotten that I was ready to do anything to help you. The people here fear me and hate me. You're not afraid of me and you speak to me nicely. That's all that's necessary to pay for my life, if you want to take it."

"It's not a matter of any such thing. Let me first explain why you've inspired confidence in me. Monsieur Subligny has vouched for you, and I would already have asked you to come to the house if, the other day, in the Tertre woods, you hadn't spoken words to me that made very little sense."

"I'm mad. I know it."

"I pardon you because I hope you'll get over it. If I didn't hope so, I wouldn't be here. And I see that I was right not to listen to those who spoke badly of you. If you were a wicked boy, my dog wouldn't have let you come near."

Laurence felt she had nothing to fear. In dangerous encounters, the situation becomes clear as soon as the dialogue begins. The poacher's language and attitude had nothing threatening. Roch Ferrer was really what she had judged him to be at their first encounter.

"It seems you know good old Belt," she continued.

"He comes to see me every evening before going back to Germonière," the gypsy answered softly. "Animals love me."

"To see you! Then he knows where you live? We didn't know that?"

"He knows that I never go very far from your garden at night. He looks for me and he finds me. For the last seven days he's had to swim the Beuvron to eat with me."

"Then you've set yourself up on the left bank?"

"Yes, right across from your garden. There're some bushes from which you can see everything that happens in the chateau. I can tell you what time your window lights up each night…what time your light goes out."

"I can understand now why it didn't take you very long to answer my lamp's signal. That was you, I suppose, that moved the lamp about."

"That wasn't a lamp; it was a torch that I made myself. The Fougéray land isn't lacking in pine trees. I notched some of them to draw out some resin. You can see that I'm not worth any more than my reputation says I am. I take things belonging to others."

"That's very bad and if you want to see me again, you must live different-ly. But it's time I told you why I came. I want to ask you for some information."

Roch lowered his eyes and made a gesture of disappointment. He was hop-ing that Laurence was expecting something more of him than information. If he had been in a state to reflect he would guessed without difficulty that Mademoi-selle Daudièrne would not have risked that nocturnal walk to get information.

"You were present at the death of my poor Fougéray neighbors," she con-tinued.

"Yes," said the poacher, lifting his head quickly. "I was there when the fer-ry rope broke."

"And you dived into the water to save them. You even found Madame Vignemal's body and the river reclaimed it, unfortunately."

"Yes, it took it back."

"I know that, but I would like to know if…things happened exactly as you told them to my uncle and to Doctor Subligny."

"Then you think I lied?"

"I believe that you perhaps had a motive…an excuse for not telling the truth."

Staring at the young girl, Roch trembled.

"Oh!" continued the young girl, "I don't have the right to question you, and you're free not to answer me."

"I've sworn to obey you. Ask me; I won't hide anything from you."

"Well! The thought came to me that perhaps Madame Vignemal was still alive when you found her. And for fear that they would reproach you for having abandoned her on the bank, you let it be understood that you didn't know if she was dead, when you were certain she was not."

"The judge who questioned me at Fougéray spoke to me as you're speak-ing to me," murmured the gypsy, visibly troubled.

"And you persisted in your first testimony. That was very understandable, but it's no longer a judge you're answering. It's to a…friend who asks you for a sincere confession. Was Madame Vignemal still alive?"

"Yes," Roch Ferrer answered without hesitating.

"You've sure of that?"

"Now…yes, I'm sure of it."

"Now, you say? Did you doubt it when you saw her?"

"I didn't doubt it, but…I couldn't prove it. Since then, I have the proof."

"And you could furnish that proof?" Mademoiselle Daudièrne exclaimed.

"To you, yes," Roch Ferrer answered. "I can prove that Madame Vignemal regained consciousness while I was going for help at the chateau."

"Well, prove it to me, "Laurence said quickly. "Explain yourself in a more intelligible way. How do you know what happened on the Beuvron ferry when you were no longer there?"

"Will you believe me if I explain it to you?"

"Yes, I'll believe you. Why would you lie when you can remain silent?"

"And I would keep quiet if anyone other than you questioned me because if I made the admission to anyone else I'm going to make to you, it would cost me dearly. But I've told you that if you asked me for my life, I'd give it to you. I'm giving it to you, since after having heard me, you'll have horror of me, and I'll die."

Laurence turned pale. She wasn't expecting that admission and she understood its importance very well. Evidently the suspicions of the Procurer of the Republic had a foundation, as Uncle Armand had said.

Roch Ferrer had committed a crime and he was going to admit it to Mademoiselle Daudièrne. She was looking for someone to help punish Arthur du Pommeval and she fell onto a murderer. The idea of becoming his confident revolted her. She no longer thought of anything else but cutting short the meeting, for fear of learning what she didn't know.

"No. No," she cried out. "Don't tell me anything more. You've already said too much."

"Too much and not enough," the poacher immediately replied. "If I stopped there, you'd take me for a murderer. You must know everything. You can judge me afterwards…and if you condemn me, I'll let you arrest me without complaining."

The situation had changed faces. Laurence could no longer refuse to listen to Roch Ferrer now that he was asking to justify himself. And she began again to hope that he wasn't as guilty as she had believed him after having heard him begin with a disturbing preamble.

"Speak," she whispered.

"I didn't kill them," Roch said in a steady voice, "but I could have kept them from dying and I didn't do it."

"What! My uncle and Monsieur Subligny told us that you jumped into the water and that you dove several times…"

"That's true! But before the accident I was hidden in the bushes some steps from the pathway they came down to embark. They didn't see me, but I saw them. I understood that they were going to cross the river. At that moment it was up to me to save their life. I had only to show myself and warn them."

"You couldn't have foreseen the accident that was going to happen to them?"

"I knew that the ferry rope was rotten and that it wouldn't hold in the force of the current. I knew it so well that for a month I seldom went very far from the landing. If a man from the country or one of your servants had come to get in the boat, I would have prevented it."

"If you had warned us, we would have had it repaired."

"I wasn't afraid that anything would happen to you or yours. The ferry was anchored at the other side. It would only be used by the Fougéray people and I was at war with them."

"At war! Because they forbade you to hunt on their land! And it was to avenge yourself on their forest wardens that you let them go to their death?"

"No," the poacher said quickly. "If that had been all it was, I would have stopped them and I'd have shown them the danger."

"Then what had they done to you?"

"Nothing...but when I saw they were going to Germonière, I thought..."

"What then!"

"I thought that Monsieur Vignemal was going to ask for you in marriage for his nephew."

That answer, more troubling than all the others, troubled Laurence profoundly. She strongly felt that Roch wasn't lying and she recognized with fright that the insane love she had inspired in this gypsy had been the indirect cause of a lamentable catastrophe.

"His nephew!" She stammered. "Then you know him?"

"I see him come to the chateau almost every day. It's said everywhere that he wants to marry you. The Vignemals never go to see you. I figured that their visit had no other purpose than to ask your mother to give you to du Pommeval. I'd have killed him rather than see him become your husband. I let the Vignemal go to their deaths. It was a crime, I know..."

"A crime that the law can't touch, but that your conscience will reproach you for eternally."

"I repented immediately and I jumped into the Beuvron to try to get them out."

"So, it's really true that you really tried to save them?" Laurence, very moved, asked.

"Your uncle himself didn't doubt it. He found me dripping with water, shivering with cold, worn out with fatigue after twenty minutes fighting against a current nothing could resist. At the moment the rope broke, when I saw their cowardly servant abandon them, I couldn't stay there. I forgot the guards' law cases against me, the nephew's projects, and I no longer thought about anything but bringing help to the two living beings who were going to perish. I would have brought them to ground if the boat hadn't sunk. You know how that happened. Monsieur Daudièrne and Monsieur Subligny must have told you what I told them, on the levee, the place where we are now. And I told them only the truth."

"Not the whole truth, because you've just told me that Madame Vignemal was alive when you saw her and you let them believe she was dead."

"You guessed why. I was afraid that they would reproach me for having acted badly. And I did act badly in fact because I gave way once again to a bad

333

feeling."

"I'm afraid to understand," Laurence whispered, struck down by this new admission. "Then that poor woman was still breathing when she came up on the dry ground of the bank, and instead of getting her away from the current, you pushed her back..."

"Into the river! Ah! If I had done that, I would be a murderer. But I didn't do that. I didn't touch Madame Vignemal except to help her. I freed her legs, which were caught in the roots of a willow tree, the one you see there below us. I stretched her out on the bank, which slopes. I knelt near her; I touched her heart and I felt it was beating. Her right hand was holding in her clenched fingers an object she was clasping tightly. I tried to open it. I couldn't. I called out. Nobody came. I didn't know what to do to get her to come back to life. I thought for a moment about picking her up in my arms. I didn't have the strength because she was very heavy, and I couldn't do anything more. On the other hand, I didn't want to stay near her body. I was afraid. It seemed to me that she was going to rise up to curse me and I was tempted to throw her back into the water. I decided to leave her there and run to the chateau to look for help."

"And when you came back here, the body had disappeared. The current had then carried it away?"

"The current couldn't have carried it away. I had left the poor woman two meters from the river bank. When I saw that she was no longer there, I wondered if the devil hadn't carried her away. And not knowing how to answer those Messieurs who pressured me with questions, I told them that I hadn't been able to drag her but half-way out of the water, that her feet were still entangled, and that the roots holding her had given way and that she had gone back into the current. It was only the next day that I understood what had happened during my absence."

"The next day!" Laurence repeated. "Everything that you've said is so astounding that I don't know if I ought to believe you."

"I swear to you that everything is true. When I left Germonière, I came back to the bank. I spent the rest of the night there and as soon as daylight came, I examined closely the place where Madame Vignemal had come to the bank. The traces the body had left on the wet ground were very visible. And I had no trouble recognizing that Madame Vignemal had come to herself, that she had dragged herself on her knees right up to touching the top of the talus bushes and that there she had tried to stand up. Her feet had slid. To catch herself she had grabbed a branch of tamaris which broke off in her hand and she fell over backward. The slope is very steep. She rolled right down to the bank, which is straight down and she plunged in. And that time it was finished. She drowned completely."

"You're swearing to this as if you had seen it. But these are only suppositions because you weren't there."

"It was just as if I had been there. Her two feet had sunk deeply into the soil at the moment of the slide. The broken branch was still fresh."

"And you didn't come looking for my uncle to show him these discoveries?"

"I didn't know they would interest you. Besides, they don't prove anything...now that the prints have been wiped out. Do you insist on being certain that everything happened as I've just told you?"

"Yes, because I strongly doubt it."

"Would you believe me if I showed you an object that Madame Vignemal was clutching in her hand when the boat sank and that I found under the tamaris bushes, fifteen feet above the edge of the river?"

"An object!"

"Yes, a little sack locked like a billfold. She was carrying it in her bosom and when she saw she was in peril, she undid the front of her dress to take it out. She hadn't turned it loose when the current threw her up on the river bank. But she let it fall when she was trying to grab onto the tamaris bushes which border the top of the levee. There's where I picked it up, and nobody can say it got there all by itself. Madame Vignemal, who lost it there, had recovered, and she'd had the strength to climb right up to there, and she'd still be alive if she hadn't had the misfortune to fall back into the Beuvron."

"And...this little sack...you kept it?"

"Yes, but I didn't open it, and if they accuse me stealing it, I can show that it's just as I found it."

"Then, you carry it with you?"

"No, I hid it in a place nobody will go to look for it. But if you want it, you'll have it tomorrow."

Mademoiselle Daudièrne wasn't prepared to answer that proposition, which certainly merited that she think about it. Was Roch's story sincere? She was beginning to believe it and she concluded that Madame Vignemal really could have survived her husband, who had died only twenty or thirty minutes after the ferry accident. Now, more time than that must have elapsed between the time of the ferry capsized and the time when she fell from the top of the bank. Besides, whatever was thought about these points of fact, Roch's declarations, brought to the attention of the tribunal, must put everything back in question.

It was a matter of making him decide to reappear before the Magistrates called to judge the case. That was what Laurence was thinking, but she found it repugnant to become further embroiled in that scabrous affair.

"No," she said, after a rather long silence. "I don't want to see what you found. It's enough for me to be sure you can prove what you're putting forth."

"I'll prove it to whomever you wish. What do I have to do?"

"The truth has to be known. People have to know that Madame Vignemal wasn't dead when you left her fainting at the foot of the talus... Let them know it at Germonière, at Fougéray, at Arcy...and only you can tell it, since you were there. You're the only one who saw it. If I myself told it, they wouldn't believe me."

"No," Roch Ferrer whispered sadly, "because you wouldn't add that you had come here to question me. I'll speak then. You're commanding me to go tell your uncle what I did? To Monsieur Subligny?"

"To the President of the Tribunal, who will decide between the heirs of the Vignemal fortune."

"You're asking me for the sacrifice of my liberty, of my life, maybe."

"What to you mean?"

"I mean that the President of the Tribunal will send me to the Attorney General of the Republic and the Attorney General of the Republic will send me to prison. He already suspects me. I saw that very well when he questioned me. After he's heard me, he'll doubt me even more. He'll accuse me of having drowned Madame Vignemal. Everyone will accuse me because appearances are against me. I'll prove that Madame Vignemal was still alive when I found her, that she had the strength to climb up the levee. I'll show the little sack that she dropped and that I picked up...but I can never prove that I didn't snatch it from her and that I didn't throw her into the river from the top of the talus."

"If you had murdered her you would keep silent. You wouldn't go tell the Attorney General the facts he doesn't know. And you wouldn't turn over to him Madame Vignemal's billfold."

"They will tell me I should have told that at first, and they won't believe a word of my story. Do they believe a poacher? It's enough that a game warden makes a claim against him for them to condemn him. And this time, I'll admit right off that I could have prevented the accident. They'll retain the admission and they won't enter my explanations for the rest. No judge can be found who'll find me innocent. And when they've found me guilty, there'll be nothing left for me to do but die. But I've sworn to obey you, whatever you may command me. Tomorrow morning I'll go give myself up."

Laurence hadn't foreseen that the admissions she pushed Roch Ferrer to would have such serious consequences. From the moment a legitimate resentment had hurled her into a hazardous action, she had met only difficult stumbling blocks she had not been aware of the moment she decided to get revenge against Arthur du Pommeval.

She had her revenge, because the poacher's admission would without a doubt put the inheritance again in question. But it was also very clear that Roch ran a great risk of being put in jail, judged, and finally condemned, if he put himself at the mercy of a judge prejudiced against him. He would be condemned at least for involuntary manslaughter and perhaps for theft. And Roch was very capable of committing suicide if sentenced to some years, or even some months in prison. Birds that live in the forest can't live in a cage.

Certainly Mademoiselle Daudièrne didn't wish the death of the poacher, and she would have bitterly reproached herself for having made him the victim of a judicial error. She couldn't help feeling sympathy for the boy who devoted himself in this fashion without complaining, without hesitation, without asking what good the sacrifice would do, and how it would be repaid.

She would have preferred a million times over that du Pommeval inherit. What's more, Laurence understood that it was time for her to stop. She had reached the extreme limit of the imprudence a young girl could commit without contracting dangerous obligations. She even regretted having gone so far.

"No, no," she said quickly, "I don't want you to expose yourself to the severity of a judge ill-disposed toward you. When I asked you to go to the President and to explain to him how Madame Vignemal died, I wasn't thinking that it could cost you dearly to confess the truth. You've just enlightened me. I now think like you that your new statements would make you suspect and they wouldn't believe you. It's therefore completely useless for you to make them before the law. You've told them to me, but I'll keep them to myself. Things will stay as they are and you won't be bothered. That's what I want more than anything."

"Then you don't despise me now that you know what I did?"

"I'm sorry for you and I'd like to bring you to understand that you've taken the wrong pathway in life. If you led an ordinary existence no one would think of accusing you of a crime and you could have, without a risk, rendered me the service I asked."

"What does the danger I run matter? If I pointed it out to you, it wasn't to pride myself on confronting it. But when I was in the hands of the judges they wouldn't let me go, and I'd never see you again. I need to tell you again that I would think myself more than happy to die to serve you, and my last thought would be of you. I'm telling this and tomorrow you wishes will be done."

"Whatever may happen?"

"Whatever may happen. Tomorrow I'll go to Arcy and it's probable that I'll stay there."

"You won't go to Arcy and if you've seriously decided to obey me, you'll leave this region."

"You're chasing me away?"

"No, I'm saving you. If you stay here, you'll come to a bad end and you won't exist any more for me. I had the courage to come here, to trust myself to you, and I'm not sorry for it. But what I did once, I can't do again if you don't change your behavior. It depends on you whether you see me again. I won't talk any more to a poacher. I'll talk to a soldier."

"You want me to sell myself?"

"People don't sell themselves any more. I want you to enlist…in an African regiment. I want you to make up for your past by serving France. I want you to go to war and someday become an officer. On that day you won't be forced to hide yourself in the bushes to look at our house. You'll come into Germonière and we'll all be very proud to receive you there…as we receive one of your country neighbors who wasn't, I think, any richer than you are when he became a soldier."

"The young man who lives in the de Bretteville chateau?"

"Yes. How is it that you know him?"

"I saw him yesterday on the road which goes along the river. He was leaving your garden and he spoke to me."

"That's unusual. Then what did he have to say to you?"

"He told me everything you've told me, that I'm wrong to poach, that I'd do better going into his squadron. He even added that if I'd come to see him at Bretteville, he'd take care of sending me over there, where they're fighting."

"What did you answer him?"

"That my freedom was too important to me for me to follow the advice he was giving me."

"But you'll follow mine. I'm counting on it. Besides, this isn't advice, it's an order. And you've sworn to obey me."

"I'll obey!"

"Without waiting. Tomorrow you'll present yourself at the Duke's chateau and you'll ask Monsieur Pontac to do what he promised you. I hardly know him, but I have a good opinion of him. Besides, he's going to return to his regiment soon, and when you're there, he'll look after you. He'll protect you. In a few years, you'll come back to us a second Lieutenant, just as he came back, he, who left without any hope of returning."

"No, I'll never come back. It would hurt me too much to see you again… married."

"I'll never marry," Mademoiselle Daudièrne said quickly.

"I thought that Monsieur du Pommeval was going to marry you," Ferrar whispered.

"Why did you think that?"

"Because he came every day to Germonière…because he's noble, because he's handsome, because he's rich."

"Rich? He's not that yet. But he's going to be. He will have to be given the Vignemal inheritance.

"Then was he threatened with losing it?"

"They're asking him to prove that Monsieur Vignemal survived his wife. And that's not easy."

"No, because the opposite is true."

"I don't know anything about it. There was a witness who saw Monsieur Vignemal clinging to the boat, which broke apart on one of the pilings of the Mouettes bridge, twenty minutes after the accident."

"And me, I saw Madame Vignemal living thirty minutes afterward… and it was a good quarter of hour more before she fell back into the water."

"That's possible, but you can't say that for fear of compromising yourself, and I don't want you to say it. The cousins of our unfortunate neighbors will

338

lose a nice fortune, but at least they won't accuse you of a crime."

"And that man will inherit?"

"Without a doubt, since his claim won't be contested."

"And if I talked there would be a lawsuit between him and the other heirs?"

"A lawsuit he would probably lose…and that would be justice."

"Then you would hope that he'd lose?"

"I don't need to answer you…but I do want to tell you frankly that I'm a great deal less interested in Monsieur du Pommeval than his adversaries, who're poor peasants."

"And who are worth more than he is. They won't use their cousin's inheritance to take advantage everywhere."

"I don't know what use Monsieur du Pommeval will make of his uncle's inheritance. It's probably that he's thinking of getting married and it's certain that his fortune will be a great help in that. Every mother would like to have him for a son-in-law."

"And all the girls would accept him as a husband," Roch said between his teeth.

"Perhaps, if they were forced to. But don't think any more about Monsieur du Pommeval and let me remind you of your promise. I'm counting on your going to see Monsieur Pontac tomorrow. I'll know if you've seen him because day after tomorrow we're going hunting with him in the Bretêche forest."

"With him, alone?"

"My mother, my uncle and my sister will be there. My brother also. Why that question?"

"To know if Monsieur du Pommeval will come."

"He's invited. And he's accepted. What difference does that make to you?"

"Oh! nothing. Only I was thinking that if tomorrow I went to tell the Arcy Judges what happened on the bank of the Beuvron, this handsome monsieur wouldn't be very happy…and maybe he wouldn't marry anyone."

"That's probable, because they say he's ruined. But you would pay a great deal too dearly for that satisfaction, and as for me, I attach no importance to it."

"You! Then why did you order me a while ago to swear before the law everything I knew…everything I haven't dared to admit, even to Doctor Subligny, who wants only good things for me."

"I gave way to a fantasy I had to test you. I thought you hadn't told everything and I sympathized with Madame Vignemal's relatives. You've made me see that you couldn't intervene in the lawsuit without seriously compromising yourself. That's enough to make me give up my idea. I don't regret having had it, because I've gotten a commitment from you that you'll keep, I don't doubt. You'll be a soldier and Monsieur du Pommeval is going to become the richest proprietor in the country. Don't envy his fate. Your future is worth more than his."

Roch trembled and didn't answer. He preferred to be silent than to be put in the position of renewing a solemn promise that he no longer wished to keep since he had learned that the presumptive heir of the Vignemal depended on his testimony.

"And now," continued Mademoiselle Daudièrne, "I must go back to the house. Forget we've seen each other if you want me to see you again. As for me, I'll remember. And whatever happens to us, I'll remain...your friend."

On this last word that she somewhat hesitated to pronounce, she held out to Roch her hand, that he kissed as respectfully as the handsome Arthur would have in the Germonière drawing room.

And Roch said nothing more. Roch made no move to follow her. He let her walk away, without even petting Belt.

"I had a bad impulse and I've done a good deed," Laurence told herself. *Monsieur du Pommeval will inherit and that independent being will go back into the right path. I'm the only one who'll be unhappy."*

And she would have thought differently if she had been able to read the heart of the poacher, that she thought she had converted.

"I've guessed it," he whispered, threatening the absent enemy with his raised fist. *"Her mother wants to force her to marry that man because she'll have the property and the money of the Vignemals. She has a horror of him and she resigns herself to give in rather than let me run the risk of being condemned by the judges who detest me. Well! It's up to me to save her from Monsieur du Pommeval. I'll go to prison, to the galleys, to the guillotine, if they send me there. What does that matter to me? Mademoiselle Daudièrne wants nothing to do with Roch Ferrer, even if that Roch Ferrer earns the epaulettes of an officer. She'll never be mine, but she won't be the wife of the other one, since he won't inherit."*

VII. Roch Ferrer and Doctor Subligny

The Minimes Garden is one of the two promenades in Arcy, and the less frequented of the two. It was formerly the garden of a convent whose buildings were transformed after the Revolution into law courts. The soil is humid, the pathways gloomy. It lacks air and sun. Mothers don't send their children to play there and hardly anyone goes there except those who have business at the tribunal.

The day following his interview with Mademoiselle Daudièrne, Roch Ferrer walked through it about noon, took a sloping path and walked with a fast pace right to the square where they had built the Sous-Prefecture which holds the law courts and dominates the pathways where the Arcy citizens never walk.

Arriving at the esplanade, he paused to gather his thoughts before giving himself up, and also perhaps to look one last time at that wooded and hilly country where he had lived free for so many years.

An immense distance could be seen from that platform. The Germonière woods and the rocky hillsides where the Beuvron begins its course extend to the horizon.

And Roch was thinking that he'd never see them again because he had no illusion as to the outcome of the steps he was taking to ruin a detested rival. He had thought about it all night. He had tried to persuade himself that he would be better advised to follow the advice given by Mademoiselle Daudièrne than to sacrifice his liberty to his vengeance. He had wondered if he would have the courage to survive the marriage of this du Pommeval and he had told himself:

"No! I'd kill him at the door of the church and I'd kill myself afterwards. If I keep him from inheriting, he won't marry. I'll be in prison, but she'll know what I did. She'll know that I sacrificed myself to get rid of that man that they want to make her marry."

He had told himself all that and he was saying it again, while leaning on the balustrade which surrounds the square. At that moment a hand fell on his shoulder and a voice that he knew well exclaimed:

"What the devil are you doing here, my boy?"

"Monsieur le majeur," Roch exclaimed, turning around quickly.

"Well, yes, it's me," Doctor Subligny answered with a nice smile. "You seem surprised to see me. I'm even more surprised to see you coming 300 feet above the Beuvron valley."

"I wasn't hoping I'd have the good luck to see you here. I went to your office. They told me you had come back from Paris yesterday evening, but that you'd gone out. I wanted to wait for you, and..."

"And Jeanette showed you the door. She claimed that you had a bad appearance. In Africa, however, she served drinks to zephyrs who looked worse than you do. But what do you expect? That's how she is and at her age she won't change. Everything's all right since here I am. It was just by chance. I have been to see President Lestrigon, who lives very near here and as it's fine weather, I took the long way around to go home. So! you must really need me if you've left your burrow to come into town."

"No, Major," murmured the poacher, who had the habit of calling the Doctor as he was called in the regiment. And that habit didn't displease the ex-Military Surgeon.

"Then what brings you here?" he asked him. "Has someone made trouble for you down there? A citation by a game warden, *hein! Ma foi!* I wouldn't be upset about that. It might make you change your life style."

"No, Major, that's not it. The game wardens are leaving me alone...and besides...for the last week I haven't tended traps or fishing lines."

"Bah! Really? You've converted. But...what have you been doing with your time. You're not a man to work in the fields."

"I wouldn't know how."

"You can't expect me to believe that. You can learn, *parbleu*! I agree however that you'd never be anything but a bad laborer. You dream night and day in your den like a hare in its burrow nest. And I find you in Arcy, dreaming on the esplanade. Are you in love?"

"In love?" Roch repeated, turning red right up to his ears.

"Why not? That happens at your age."

"What woman would want me?"

"I know of more than one. You're too modest, my boy. If you decided to go to work for any farmer, his daughter would marry you just for your beautiful eyes."

"I don't want to get married."

"Oh! You'll have enough time. But I advise you not to lose any time to get started on the right path. Do you know where the nice life you've been living has gotten you? Everybody suspects you of having done something bad when the Vignemals drowned in the Beuvron. It didn't do any good to say that you risked your skin trying to fish them out. Nobody wants to believe me. *Tiens!* Even Monsieur Daudièrne, who was praising you to the skies the evening of the accident, now distrusts you."

"He told you that?"

"Oh! He didn't take any trouble not to, and one of these days you'll get yourself put away by the people at the de Bretteville chateau. You've been pointed out to them as a suspicious character that has to be watched. In the city, it's even worse. The most troublesome gossip about you is getting about. And we have a new Attorney General of the Republic who does nothing but try to dig up harmful things. He'd be delighted to lay the death of the masters of Fougéray on your shoulders. He even tried to make you contradict yourself. I was there the day of the autopsy and I must say you didn't get mixed up in your answers. But he wasn't satisfied with them. And it would only take an anonymous denunciation for him to unleash criminal proceeding against you. Ah! He's a gentleman I wouldn't want you to have anything to do with. I've just met him in the Tribunal courtyard. He seems like a tiger."

"Then he's in his office?"

"I suppose so. He was going in when I was crossing the courtyard. But I'd be curious to know how it can matter to you whether or not he's in the court room."

"That's because…I want to talk to him."

"Ah! Well that's something new! Then he had you summonsed?"

"No, I came to Arcy of my own free will."

"And especially to see a man who wishes you no good. Then you've lost your head."

"No, Major. I know very well what I'm doing. Only I wanted to see you first. That's why I went to your office."

"Well, you found me here. It comes to the same thing. What do you have to say to me?"

"That I lied to you."

"Lied! About what?"

"About what happened on the river bank."

"What, unfortunate man, you tricked us, Monsieur Daudièrne and me! Did you murder the Vignemals?"

"No, but I could have saved their lives and I didn't do it. The ferry rope was rotten. I knew that, and I didn't say anything to them."

"If that's all it is," murmured the Doctor with a sigh of relief. "That already very bad, but after all they don't hang you for not having warned people who're running toward a precipice. Especially since you have only to keep quiet. Nobody would accuse you of a crime because of bad intentions, because nobody would guess it."

"I've come to find the Attorney General to confess to him."

"Obviously you're crazy. Then you want to be locked up! They won't send you there for not having warned those poor people, but they'll believe that's only the beginning of the confession. They'll grill you with questions and they'll turn you every which way but loose until they've snatched a compromising word from you. Believe me, my boy, hold your tongue and if you have only that to reproach yourself with…"

"I have something else."

"What? So speak. You're giving me goose pimples with your half revelations."

"I reproach myself for having left Madame Vignemal at the foot of the talus."

"In fact, it would have been better to have dragged the body further until it was out of danger and the proof is that the current carried it away from the place

343

you left it. But after all, that's only a blamable lack of foresight. And then, you didn't go away except to look for help. Besides, the poor woman showed no signs of life, and you could have thought she was dead."

"No, Major. On the contrary, I was sure she was alive. Her heart was still beating."

"And you didn't tell me that!"

"I didn't dare. I wouldn't have hidden the truth from you if you'd been the only one there when I came back to the river bank and I'd seen she wasn't there any more. But I was afraid to say that in front of Monsieur Daudièrne."

"I didn't believe you were so timid. And you are very guilty. You don't act that casually when it's a question of a human creature. It's almost as if you had killed Madame Vignemal, because I could probably have saved her if you had taken the simplest of precautions. I thought you knew better than that."

"I didn't know what I was doing."

"What I find the most serious in your case is your lack of frankness. I feel contempt for, and I despise, lying. You're repenting, because you're admitting your mistakes. But it's very late and the admission doesn't fix anything.

"Ah ça! I hope you aren't going to go repeat it before the Attorney General of the Republic. "

"Pardon, Major. That's why I came to Arcy."

"But your admission doesn't mean anything, or it mean too much. A Magistrate as set against you as this Attorney General would never admit that this new story is true. You deceived him the first time, when he questioned you in the basement of Fougéray. He'll think you're still deceiving him and he'll treat you as if you were."

"I'm expecting that."

"Then you're absolutely insisting on getting a taste of prison! What is this temporary madness, or rather, what's your purpose, because you won't persuade me that you're giving yourself up just for the pleasure of being jailed."

"I don't have anything to hide from you now, Major. My purpose is to prevent Madame Vignemal's cousins from losing their inheritance."

"Oh! Now there's an answer I wasn't expecting. You're getting mixed up in deciding the outcome of an inheritance in litigation. That's wonderful! And what can you do about it, I pray?"

"I can do a lot…because I will prove that the wife lived longer than the husband, and then…"

"The devil. So you know the law these days? Now all you need to do is recite the Articles of the Code. Where did you study law? Was it in running around in the woods and thinking it over by the edge of the water?"

"I didn't know anything…but someone told me that the case depended only on one thing…"

"Good! I don't doubt that someone instructed you. You couldn't have guessed all that by yourself. Who was it then who informed you so well?"

"People around here," Roch replied, visibly embarrassed.

"Tell me their names."

"I don't know them by their names."

"Stronger and stronger. To do a favor to fellows you met by chance, you're going to run the risk of losing your freedom. I give you a charitable warning that this nice devotion to them will be completely useless. You don't know that Monsieur Vignemal was still alive when the boat he was hanging onto went down under the Mouettes bridge twenty minutes after the first accident."

"And ten minutes before his wife rolled from the top of the levee into the Beuvron."

"What! From the top of the levee! You left her at the bottom."

"She regained consciousness while I was going for help at Germonière and she dragged herself that far."

"Truly, I'm astounded. I can easily admit that you're not making up a story, but I wondered why you waited so long before you told me about it."

"Because I was ashamed of my negligence which cost the live of a person I didn't like, but that I had tried to save."

"You aren't telling the real reason. Let's bet that you've just learned what your testimony is worth if there's a lawsuit between the heirs."

"I learned it...yesterday."

"Very well! And seized with admirable zeal, you are running to enlighten the judges. And you can imagine nothing better than to throw yourself at the feet of the head of the court, whose job it is to grab people who seem the least bit suspicious to him."

"I would rather submit to my fate than let an injustice be committed."

"A noble sentiment that'll cost you dearly. Then you're very concerned about Madame Vignemal's relatives?"

"They're poor..."

"They're less so than you who own nothing but your skin. There's even one who has a good position, because he's earned the rank of officer... Roger Pontac..."

"The man who lives at the de Bretteville chateau?"

"Ah! Ah! You know him, so it appears. Would he be the one who gave you this advice?"

"No, Major. I met him yesterday for the first time. He spoke to me on the road...but he didn't tell me he was an heir. He just told me he was your friend and that..."

"*A la bonne heure!* I certainly thought that Roger wasn't capable of pushing you into dangerous behaviour through self-interest. But I'm understanding less and less. Then who is it you want to sacrifice yourself for?"

"Nobody, Major... But there is...the other one...Monsieur Vignemal's nephew."

"Arthur du Pommeval. Well, when he has the Fougéray land and the rest?

345

You're figuring he'll declare war on you and the domestics will track you down?"

"I don't care anything at all about him and them., but he's going to marry one of the Germonière young ladies..."

"Well, yes. He's marrying Germaine...the youngest... What can that have to do with you?"

"Germaine! Did you say Germaine?" Roch cried out.

"Exactly, " replied the doctor. "And I think you could say: Mademoiselle Germaine."

"The youngest of the Daudièrne girls."

"Well, yes, the younger one. And I come back to my question: What does that have to do with you that the Germonière lady is marrying one of her daughters?"

"Nothing, Major...I...yes...I'm very glad about that."

"You wouldn't think so. You seem completely upset."

"I swear to you, Major, it's with joy."

"Joy! Because Monsieur du Pommeval is becoming part of the Daudièrne family. *Parbleu!* That's hard to believe. A while ago you were hoping he'd lose the inheritance of his Aunt Vignemal."

"Now it's all the same to me if he inherits."

"Why now?"

"Because a while ago I didn't know what I now know. You wouldn't be deceiving me?"

"Deceive you? What does that mean?"

"It's really Mademoiselle Germaine this gentleman's going to marry?"

"Yes, my boy. And the proof is that last week I, who am talking to you, went to ask her hand in marriage for him."

"And she agreed to be his wife?"

"Almost. He's allowed to come to Germonière every day. He's very much in love with her and he's everything that could please her. The marriage will be settled before Madame Daudièrne returns to Paris."

"If I was sure of it!" Roch muttered under his breath. And lowering his head he was absorbed in thoughts that Monsieur Subligny began to guess.

The two of them were alone on that esplanade that dominates the countryside. The Arcy inhabitants are blasé about views which draw tourists. In winter they prefer to stroll down the Rue National rather than to expose themselves to the western wind in order to admire the countryside.

"Roch," the Doctor said gently after a silence, "you've promised not to hide anything from me any more and you're still hiding something."

"Me, Major!" the gypsy stammered. "I swear to you..."

"Don't swear. You'd be lying. Instead admit to me that you've developed a ridiculous passion for Mademoiselle Daudièrne, the elder."

Roch Ferrer was silent, but his blush was enough.

"That's why, the other evening in the kitchen of the chateau you looked at her so steadily. I certainly noticed it, but I never imagined that you had lost your head to the point of falling in love with a young girl who doesn't think any more about you than about her gardener."

"I know that for her I don't exist," Roch said in a gloomy voice.

"And you're in love with her, even so. You're going to tell me it isn't your fault, and I won't argue about that. These sorts of things happen every day. However, it cooks poor devils who fall in love with a woman above their social level. To adore Mademoiselle...you might as well adore the daughter of the Emperor of China. It's a case of mental sickness and I want to cure you of it. First of all, tell me when and how that happened to you."

"When! The day I saw her for the first time...a long time ago. She was walking on the Beuvron levee... I was hidden behind the tamaris bushes. How, I don't know, but I knew that until that moment I hadn't lived..."

"Words! You're even sicker than I thought. What did you do after having been sturck by lightning?" Monsieur Subligny asked in a joking tone.

"I followed her...without being seen...where she went...I went."

"And you never spoke to her?"

"Never."

Roch had hesitated only a second before answering, but the Doctor had noticed it. and his face darkened somewhat. He was skeptical enough not to believe blindly in the good behavior of the best brought up young ladies. And he was wondering if this young savage was sincere or simply as discreet as a man of the world.

"I'd like to believe you," he said, "and I praise you very strongly for having been so reserved. It's nonetheless true that you're playing a very dangerous game, not only for yourself but for the girl who turned your head. You're aware, I suppose, that she can't marry you?"

Roch agreed with a nod.

"So, your night stalkings, your walks under the woods, and your ambushes can only compromise her and you must give it up. Now, since you admit that your outrageous passion can only end by making you lose the little reason you have left, will you please tell me what you'd gain by keeping Monsieur du Pommeval from marrying?"

"It's no longer important to me to prevent him. I've already told you that."

"Because it is a matter of Mademoiselle Germaine. But when you thought he wanted to marry Mademoiselle Laurence, you decided to accuse yourself of a lot of villainous things you didn't do. I'm persuaded of that. You were coming to give yourself up to justice like a criminal driven by remorse. And all that just to ruin a gentleman who has never done you any harm."

"Yes...I'd prefer to die rather than to suffer."

"You'd only succeeded in going to prison, because despite your admissions, Monsieur du Pommeval would have won his lawsuit and you'd have a very bad action on your conscience."

"Is telling the truth doing something bad?"

"No, but you won't make me believe Madame Vignemal came back to life on the river bank and climbed to the top of the talus bushes."

"It's so true that she dropped a billfold she was clutching in her hand. I found it the next day and I picked it up. I put it in a hiding place where it still is."

"The devil! That changes the situation. If this billfold contains valuables...or a will...or only some papers belonging to Madame Vignemal, unexpected things will come out. That would be a Pandora's box...but you don't know anything about Pandora's box and you'd understand me better if I told you that they'd start to accuse you of having killed her."

"That's probable," Roch said with indifference.

"And that's why I advise you to leave it where you've put it." Monsieur Subligny said quickly. "I don't want to take on the responsibility of keeping it, especially right now. Later, when you're beyond the grasp of people who have something against you, we'll see. I could take care of giving it to the proper person...because after all that's the key to the process, if there is a process. But first, let's take care of you. I think you've given up your absurd idea of going before the Attorney General of the Republic and telling him a story, the conclusion of which would be an order to enroll you in the Arcy prison."

"I've given it up...because you've told me that it's not a question of marrying Mademoiselle Laurence to that man."

"Again! Ah! You're stubborn, you are! Do I have to give you my word of honor?"

"No, Major, I know you wouldn't want to deceive me."

"Then, you have confidence in me. That's perfect. You'll follow the advice I'm going to give you and everything will turn out all right. Listen to me, my boy. You know that you can't stay in this land."

"Why? I've lived here up until now. I'll still get along."

"You've lived here because people have tolerated you. They've seen you here as a child. They're used to you. And they let you get by with pranks they wouldn't have tolerated from anyone else. The country people don't like you, maybe, but they don't turn you in. The Vignemals troubled you sometimes, but didn't really wish you any harm, because they never followed through on the complaints they made to the authorities. The local authorities were informed of your little misdeeds. They knew you'd declared war on the the game and the fish but they also knew you didn't sell the game and the fish you caught and so they closed their eyes. That wouldn't have lasted very long. One overlooks in an adolescent what one wouldn't overlook in a grown man. But then the danger of getting into trouble wasn't immediate. Unfortunately for several days we haven't been at that point. An event occurred which has drawn the attention of a number of people and the truce has been broken. People will look for a reason to quarrel with you before long. If you're silent, you'll have against you Madame Vignemal's cousins, who'll suspect you of having known a lot about the death of their relative. If you speak, you have the lawyers against you, and those people won't wear kid gloves to treat you like a criminal. That would already have happened, if their Chief hadn't gotten it into his head to incriminate a good boy who is more innocent than you. And you can't count on a long reprieve. I came just in time to stop you on your way to prison, but they'll come looking for you in your den. That's a word that a political speech has made fashionable, and that can be applied to you, since you live like a wolf. My conclusion is that you have to leave."

"You want me to become a soldier, don't you?"

"See! You guessed it."

"The officer who lives at the de Bretteville chateau has already advised me to do that."

"That doesn't surprise me. We talked about you, and he was of my opinion. You were born for war and it would be a shame to miss your vocation. Nothing is holding you here, I think?

"No, nothing," Roch Ferrer said sadly.

"That's the right idea! Chase away the thoughts that are troubling your head. Act like a man, and I'll answer for the future. Pontac will open up a career for you. Go find him and tell him I sent you."

"He's expecting me today."

"You'd have done better to go there than to show yourself in the city. But what's put off isn't lost. And besides, I myself want to see this dear Roger. I need to discuss things with him…about you first of all. Also for something else, because, after all, he would inherit if du Pommeval doesn't inherit. I'll write him to ask him to come around to my office. Together we'll arrange the business of your enlistment. Come back day after tomorrow. Everything will be ready for your approaching departure and Jeanette will have orders to let you in. While you're waiting, I ask you to stay in hiding. Try to be seen as little as possible. From this moment, you'll have to begin to make yourself forgotten.

"Take my advice, Roch, don't sleep this evening at the edge of the Beuvron. Change your den; don't go out in the daytime. Come to see me day after tomorrow between 11 p.m. and midnight. And right now, make a dash by way of the path that goes under the old city. Get going, my boy, and don't do anything stupid, *hein*?"

The doctor wound up, honoring his protégé with a vigorous handshake.

Roch wasn't thinking about disturbing Laurence Dauièrne's tranquility. He was no longer afraid that she'd marry Monsieur du Pommeval and he'd decided to join the army, but he went away with a heavy heart. And he was not resigned to leave without seeing her one more time.

349

VIII. The Hunt

For the peaceful inhabitants of Germonière, including Uncle Armand and nephew Alfred, a hunt in the Ducal forest of la Bretêche was an event. And the project agreed on in Roger Pontac's presence was the starting point for deliberation which occupied all the next day. It didn't matter that it was agreed. Madame Daudièrne had nevertheless objections to present. Mothers always have some when it's a question of allowing their daughters an unusual diversion. She also had some scruples in accepting from a country neighbor who had never paid her a visit such a marked point of politeness. But the rank, the age, and most of all the recent and so sad bereavement of Monsieur de Bretteville certainly merited that on this occasion she overlook the customary formalities, the Duke having apologized when he received Monsieur Daudièrne at the chateau. And then, the suggestion had been made on the spur of the moment, and the lady, caught off guard, hadn't found, on the spot, any good reasons to refuse.

The commitment once made, there was nothing to do but keep it. But how many details there were they'd totally neglected to attend to! How many difficulties to overcome they hadn't foreseen!

The invitation was general. So general that Monsieur du Pommeval hadn't been counted out. Uncle Armand had answered yes for everybody present, and his prudent sister-in-law hadn't had time to set limits. First of all, it remained to be decided if she would be part of the group. She didn't like to move about. And the diversity of sports that foreigners have made fashionable in our country hardly tempted her. She would never have considered following a hunt a *courre* or *rallye-papier*, even less to send these young ladies. Bourgeois manners didn't at all lend themselves to such fantasies, and Madame Daudièrne was a bourgeoise right down to the marrow of her bones. *Lawn tennis*, that game so dear to adolescent English girls seemed to her more suited to developing the muscles of young boys than to forming the mind and heart of young girls. And perhaps she wasn't wrong to forbid at Germonière that exercise that the best brought up *Misses* on the other side of the channel played without impropriety. The handsome Arcy Messieurs would have been able to take advantage of it. Pleasure in France is never innocent pleasure. It's a matter of climate or of temperament.

But this time it was impossible to go back on a promise and Madame Daudièrne found herself between two alternatives which pleased her very little. She would either have to be part of the great hunt or let her children go without her. And this last arrangement suited her even less than the first. Uncle Armand was certainly at an age to be used as a chaperon, but Uncle Armand was also a passionate hunter, very capable of forgetting his nieces while waiting for deer to break cover. He himself admitted that, and to bring together the convenience and the maternal worries of his sister-in-law, he suggested a compromise.

The Bretêche forest had admirable openings and nothing prevented the family carriage, with the top down for the hunt, to roll along at the speed of two calm mares that would carry it along and halt at the main roads the hunters would take. Nor did anything prevent its parking in a crossroad while the beaters hunted through an area, and while the vigilant mother, comfortably seated on nice cushions, followed at a distance the various stages of the hunt and the movements of the hunters of both sexes.

The idea was simple and practical. Madame Daudièrne came around even more willingly when Laurence declared she wanted only to be a spectator like her mother. She had never touched a gun and she wasn't anxious to massacre poor inoffensive animals. Neither was she anxious, perhaps, to find herself in contact with Monsieur du Pommeval, who was supposed to take part in the work of destruction.

Since her meeting with Roch Ferrer, the noble girl had realized that it was unworthy of her to take vengeance on a betrayal. She resolved to no longer show the traitor anything but indifference and disdain.

A seat was reserved for her in the calèche which could carry everyone to the place of the rendezvous: Madame Daudièrne and her brother-in-law in the back, Laurence and Germaine up front, Alfred on the seat beside the driver. They didn't have to make a place for handsome Arthur, who was to come directly from Arcy in his dog cart.

The uncle and the nephew knew what they had to do, once they were on the terrain, the uncle most of all because the nephew had more enthusiasm than experience. He had too much enthusiasm to be relied on to shoot or to watch.

Monsieur Daudièrne suggested consigning this beginner to the end of the line and far enough away so that his nearest neighbor would be out of range of his bullets. It wasn't in his power to get him to take care of his sister somewhat.

So Madame Daudièrne was relying only on herself to prevent Germaine from doing something unwise. After a rather lively discussion, during which she was alone in her opinion, she finally gave in to the fancy of her younger daughter, who wanted to play an active role in that expedition organized by Roger Pontac.

She had been tormenting her uncle for a long time, asking to go hunting with him. The uncle resisted. He claimed there wasn't much game around Germonière and that Germaine wasn't strong enough to endure the fatigue of long waits in the woods or interminable walks across difficult terrain. However, he didn't refuse to teach her how to shoot. He had even brought her from Paris, a gun made especially for her, a charming little gun with central percussion, and not a lot heavier than a child's toy.

Uncle Armand was a good teacher. He gave his niece lessons on the bank of the Beuvron, a river very frequented by water birds. And in a very short time, the student had become a very good shot. She could very easily bring down a gull in full flight and she could accurately hit a duck showing his head after a dive.

Given these precedents Monsieur Daudièrne would have been hard put to it to forbid his niece to come along. The hunt with beaters is certainly the least trying of all hunts because it requires only patience and a cool head. All you have to do is not budge from one spot and wait for the game to come to you...and not shoot the trackers who're sending the game to you.

It was agreed that Germaine would go carrying a gun and that she could use her gun. She had solemnly sworn to be as calm as an old guard, never to blast away at anything just for the pleasure of making noise, to strictly follow the directions of the hunt coordinator, who was in charge of placing the hunters, never to leave her post under any pretext; in short, to behave more wisely than many experienced hunters do.

There remained the big question of dress. To practice at the edge of the water, Germaine made do with putting on a smock on top of her dress, but that get-up absolutely lacked distinction. One had to be put together which answered the requirements of an exceptional outing.

Madame Daudièrne was strongly opposed to women dressing like men. She naively believed that a woman who was mad enough to go hunting could very well go into the woods in morning dress and her brother-inlaw had a great deal of trouble showing her that dresses and little walking boots wouldn't hold up under the bramble tears and contact with sharp rocks. Hearing that, young Alfred, who had a penchant for new fashions, dived into a collection of *La Vie Parisienne* and discovered in it an abundance of designs appropriate to the occasion. The fashions pictured there were all ravishing, each more than the next. It was just a matter of choosing the one best suited to the height and figure of his little sister.

This discerning boy at first suggested a Louis XV outfit in corduroy cord with grey-blue embroidery on the pockets and the cuffs, big buttons made of marquisate, similar panties, a prune colored satin vest, gloves and boots in grey suede, sleeves and shirt front decorated with expensive Ma-lines lace, a tricorn hat embellished with rose-colored plumes. And when his sisters laughed in his face, he came down to a Tyrolean costume, a little less theatrical: a long coat, fitted trousers, waistcoat of fawn-colored material, leather leggings, big hob-nailed shoes and a maroon soft felt hat ornamented with a gyrfalcon feather.

That one had no more success than the one before. A Polish fur outfit lined with beaver, with fluffy myrthe green trousers, boots à la Souvarov [37] and a felt hat decorated with small chains was also blackballed unanimously.

Madame Daudièrne first and foremost declared all of them improper. Uncle Armand took the trouble to explain to his nephew that the journal of elegant style didn't claim to govern the dress of modestly brought up girls. That was

---

[37] Russian general who put down the Polish insurrection of 1794,

Germaine's opinion also, and, besides, these extreme creators of high fashion couldn't complete such fabulous outfits in one day. It took time and work by a knowledgeable dressmaker. Alfred offered to be off to Paris and to bring back a *chef-d'oeuvre* of dressmaking skill created in one night by a fashionable couturier, but that absurd proposition had no success.

Germaine suddenly remembered that she possessed at Germonière everything needed to put together a hunting costume with a decent appearance and suited to the occasion. The year before the girls had brought back from an excursion to the coast of Finistere a complete Breton peasant costume which seemed made to fit Germaine. She often put it on to pose for her sister, who had undertaken, in memory of this trip, a small painting showing a child kneeling at the foot of a calvaire. It was just a matter of lengthening the big buttoned vest and the waistcoat covered with bright embroidery and enlarging still more the vast dark blue flannel trousers, of closing the canvas leggings at the knee, and of replacing the wooden shoes with solid walking shoes.

This took several hours and Laurence wanted to help work on it. In the evening it was tried on in the drawing room. Madame Daudièrne had to admit that her daughter could wear it in the daytime without going beyond the permitted limits of eccentricity and without making an exhibition of physique. The jacket went down so far that it hid three-quarters of her torso.

And that scarcely coquettish get-up suited her marvelously. She had tied a red scarf around her beautiful blond hair and put a Breton hat with wide borders on that coiffeur full of local color. The only thing missing to make her look like a young Chouan [38] was an old flintlock rifle and a big sword hanging from her belt. And she had, nevertheless, lost none of her feminine grace.

Uncle Armand didn't find anything about it to criticize and the problem of Germaine's dress was resolved to everyone's satisfaction. Everyone went to bed early so as to rise at daybreak. The rendezvous was set for 10 a.m. and it took a good forty minutes to get there without straining the grey mares' pace.

Daybreak comes late in December and everyone was up before dawn. As a chatelaine who thought of everything, Madame Daudièrne had given orders for a quick breakfast and everyone did it justice. She was even thinking about storing snacks in the trunk of the calèche, but her brother-in-law decided that it would be wiser to return to Germonière for lunch after the hunt, advancing dinner by two hours and inviting Monsieur du Pommeval and Monsieur Pontac.

The program settled, they left.

Laurence, somewhat pale, was even more charming because of it. Her big dark eyes had never shone so brightly, and her dress was in perfect taste. Madame Daudièrne, dignified and calm as always, had put on a huge coat trimmed with expensive fur. She wanted to make her daughters proud. Monsieur Armand,

---

[38] An insurgent in the Britanny, Normandy, Vendée rebellion under the first Republic.

who didn't want to go to any trouble, hadn't changed anything about his hunting costume: a soft hat, shoes with leather leggings, and a suit of checked material. But his nephew had set himself up in a costume most in vogue. With his tight-fitting knee britches, his ammunition bag in fawn-colored leather and his pointed hat, he looked like a Calabrais brigand.

The carriage was rolling along the Departmental road that Germaine had taken one evening to return to Germonière after a romantic adventure. They had already gone some distance when loud barking made the two Percherons prick up their ears.

"That's Belt following us!" young Alfred exclaimed, turning around on the seat where he was perched. "What the devil's wrong with him! He's going to ruin our hunt."

Monsieur Daudièrne said, "Nobody has ever seen a Great Dane brought to a hunt. Who had that bad idea? Is that bad idea yours, Germaine? If it is I'd disown you as my niece."

"Not at all," Germaine answered quickly. "Belt slept in my room last night. It was my turn to keep him. But I understood very well that he would be useless at the hunt and I was careful to lock him up when I left my room."

"That's what I call a useless precaution. You should have thought about the fact that the maid who waits on you would open the door. He has to be sent to the kennel and tied up."

"I'm strictly against that," said Germaine. "Belt is our friend and I don't want anybody to put him on a chain."

"All that's well and good," cried young Alfred, "but we can't hunt with that beast on our heels. Monsieur Pontac would take me for an imbecile. I have a good mind to shoot your Great Dane."

"Don't even think about it," replied Germaine. "I'm sorry he's come, but that's not a reason to harm him. I'm taking him under my complete protection."

"Monsieur, my nephew," continued Monsieur Armand, "I advise you to get down, take him back to Germonière, and lock him in the stable. That's a lot better than murdering an animal who loves all of us."

"Right! And I'll have to go two leagues on foot to come back to you. The hunt will be over when I get back."

Monsieur Daudièrne, who liked to tease Alfred, said, laughing: "You'll mount Ralph and you'll come back at break-neck speed."

"In the costume I'm wearing!" exclaimed the young man indignantly. "Not on your life. I would be ridiculous. Du Pommeval would tell the gentlemen in Arcy about that ride without spurs and they'd have a good laugh about it. I prefer not to take the trouble caused by the negligence of these young ladies. There'll certainly be a guard at the hunt to muzzle him and tie him to a tree by his four feet."

"I won't endure that," Laurence said. "Belt isn't used to such treatment, and I don't see any reason to inflict it on him. We'll keep him with us, my mother and I."

"And you think he'll stay there!"

"Absolutely. He does everything I tell him to. And when I order him not to budge, he obeys me. Don't you, my old Belt?" Laurence added, looking at the Great Dane, that had caught up with the Percherons and was gamboling joyously around the calèche.

"And he'll defend us if a wolf attacks us," Madame Daudièrne added, smiling.

"There aren't any wolves in the Bretêche forest, my dear sister-in law, murmured the uncle, "but I agree my niece should hold her favorite herself and I hope she can."

"Yes, then do it!" grumbled the nephew. "All right! Since there's no way to do otherwise, we have to tolerate his presence. Too bad for him if he dashes into the woods when he smells the game and he gets shot. That'll teach him to meddle in things he has no business in."

No one reacted to that indirect threat, but Laurence's face clouded over. She was grateful to Belt for having come and she promised herself to watch out for the security of this faithful friend that had gone with her on a nocturnal excursion of which she recalled all the incidents.

"Without him," she was thinking, *"I'd never have had the courage to go find Roch Ferrer. I wouldn't have known there was a man in the world ready to sacrifice himself for me. And if I'd wished it, that miserable man who deceived me would lose that fortune he was counting on to dazzle my sister and steal her consent. I don't regret having spared him. His fall wouldn't have consoled me for the unhappiness of that brave Roch. But I'm happy to think that I hold Monsieur du Pommeval's fate in my hands. And I may give myself the satisfaction of letting him know that he's at my mercy."*

"The weather's in our favor," said Germaine, who couldn't hold still for joy. "It's as mild as springtime and the hunt will be magnificent. It seems to me Monsieur Pontac is bringing us good luck. We've all been sad since the death of our Fougéray neighbors. He comes one fine day to Germonière and everything takes on another face. I don't want to return to Paris until New Year's."

"This Hussard is a charming boy. Too bad he doesn't have anything!" added Uncle Armand.

"It's a misfortune he carries lightly. And really I don't pity him too much. He likes war and he wouldn't change his situation with that of the richest landowner around here. Besides, he'll become a general, and when he's at that rank, he won't have any more need for money. "

"Good! But while he's waiting, he wouldn't mind it if he got married. He'll make, *Ma foi!* the kind of husband I'd wish for my daughter, if I were a father. He needs only two or three hundred thousand francs. Unfortunately, when you don't have a *sou* you can hardly marry anyone but a laundress or as seamstress."

"Why is that? If it was an absolute rule, you would only have to match equal fortunes and all you'd have to do is get the information at the notary's office. The fiancés would see each other for the first time when they entered the mayor's office."

"You're exaggerating. I recognize that marriages of inclination can sometimes turn out well. But you can be allowed to regret the fact that a young man who has everything pleasing is not rich. You were lucky to stumble on to du Pommeval. That's perfect. But suppose that the Bretêche forest and the de Bretteville chateau belonged to Monsieur Roger Pontac, wouldn't that be a perfect match for your sister? Look what would surround the Germonière domaine. Fougéray on one side, la Bretêche on the other. What hunts, *Bon Dieu!* I'd stay forever at your mother's house, Mesdemoiselles."

"That would be charming, but that's only a dream," sighed Germaine. "Let's be satisfied with the permission that Monsieur le Duc de Bretteville has graciously granted us."

"Well said, little one. Truth sometimes comes out of the mouths of babes. Wisdom consists of enjoying what you have, without desiring what you don't. But it seems to me we must be getting close. I recognize over there on our left the escarpments I noticed the other day when I went to thank the Lord of this Canton. The forest isn't far off."

"That's the Lemon Rock you see and the rendezvous is at the crossroad that's located right at the foot of the chateau of the fairies."

"How are you so well informed? I thought you had never come this way."

"The day before yesterday, at the house, Monsieur Pontac described the famous rock to me. There's no way not to recognize it. It's the one that stands up like a tower at the summit of the hill."

"It does seem to have an unusual appearance and I'd like to see it up close. But today we have better things to do than climb up there."

"You, yes…and me too. But if I were in Laurence's place, I'd undertake this pilgrimage instead of cooling my heels in the calèche."

"I have nothing to ask the fairies," Laurence replied sadly.

"Bah! What would you risk by throwing your name at them? When they don't have any husband to offer to the person consulting, they don't answer. But they're discreet, and they don't take advantage of the secrets confided to them. Just try. You never know what can happen."

"I see Arthur du Pommeval's dog cart," young Alfred shouted. "Arthur has already gotten out and the beaters are set up for battle on the road. They're just waiting for us to begin. That's what happens when you hitch up two old mares that move like tortoises."

"They don't run away like Ralph, who almost broke your sister's neck and I'm grateful for that," said Uncle Armand. "We're the last to arrive. What a good misfortune! It's the duty of lovers to arrive first, and du Pommeval hasn't missed doing so."

"I see Monsieur Pontac," said Germaine, who had stood up to look in front of the calèche.

"He certainly should be there to meet us, since he's the one we owe for the Duke's permission to hunt. I see him also. He's talking with a servant in livery."

"He's the first huntsman," explained Alfred. "An old man smartly outfitted. The Duke has four of them: two dog handlers, six horses and sixty tracking dogs. From Vendée, admirably trustworthy."

"You, my little man, want to throw dust in our eyes by spouting hunting terms and what you reel off doesn't make sense. Monsieur de Bretteville keeps a very nice crew; we all know that, but today we're not going on a cross-country hunt and the Duke's huntsmen and dog handlers stayed at the chateau."

Uncle Armand was right. The man taking Roger Pontac's orders was a simple forest guard and the men assembled a little further off were peasants recruited to beat the underbrush.

Madame Daudièrne's calèche soon reached the point where, on the road running around the rocky crest of Lemon, four roads came together in the shape of a fan. There an opening cut through the undergrowth in a sort of half-moon where ten carriages and fifty guests would have been very comfortable.

In the center of this crossroad a little granite obelisk was set up in front of which three footmen were guarding a table filled with pates, galantines, and other cold meats. They had forgotten neither generous wines nor refreshing liqueurs. Bottles of champagne in gilded containers placed opposite long vials of old brandy looked like quills.

Seeing this preparation Monsieur Daudièrne exclaimed: "This Hussard First Lieutenant is a first rate organizer. He's taken care of everything. And there you are, my dear sister-in-law, a big problem solved. You won't need to advance the dinner hour, since we'll find everything here to satisfy the most demanding appetites."

"You'd better ask Monsieur du Pommeval," Germaine added, pointing to handsome Arthur, who was putting down his glass after having swallowed a large full glass of the Duke's cognac.

"He's right to get some strength. Would you want him to drink water?"

"That's for lovers shaking with cold, but that one there, you hardly worry about him…nor Laurence either, I suppose."

Laurence didn't answer and she turned her head to avoid greeting Arthur du Pommeval who was coming forward, his hat in his hand and a smile on his lips.

The calèche had just stopped. Alfred had already gotten down and opened the door. In an instant everyone was standing on the ground and the Vignemal heir had started shaking hands with the uncle and the nephew, who returned the handshakes warmly. Madame Daudièrne and Germaine were less reserved, but they greeted him politely. Laurence alone was very cold.

Roger, who had finished giving orders to the head guard, arrived during these polite exchanges.

"From what I can see, we're late," Monsieur Daudièrne said to him after the required banalities. "Your people, I'd bet, have been up since dawn, and I apologize for having made you wait."

"I'm the one who should apologize for having set such an early hour," Pontac replied. "Unfortunately, when you start late in this season, there's hardly time to beat out a few hiding places of the game, and since these ladies really wanted to come, I want to assure them of a completely successful hunt."

"We shoot everything, don't we?" asked giddily Germaine, who was already had out her little pistol.

"Yes, Mademoiselle. No one has hunted in the Bretêche forest this year and the guards are of the opinion that there're too many she goats and too many pheasant hens. So there's nothing wrong with shooting some of them. Monsieur le Duc de Bretteville only asks that you spare an old buck that his son had often hunted on horseback and that he was never able to catch."

"To kill a buck, that would be murder," said Uncle Armand.

"Especially that one, who is truly the king of the forest," replied Roger. "What's more he's easily recognized in his woods. He has ten points on his antlers."

"I'd be unhappy if anyone one wounded him," Germaine said, "but I'd really like to see him. I've never see bucks except in the zoo. And I imagine that a buck in the wild must be superb."

"So is a lion," Monsieur Daudièrne grumbled.

"Do you mean it? If I went to Africa, I'd certainly go lion hunting."

"I say, Pontac," Uncle Armand exclaimed, "you must have killed some lions, since you've been in the army in Algeria for eight or ten years."

"Never, Monsieur," the Hussard officer responded modestly. "My duties took all my time and I seldom thought about hunting. But it's good that Mademoiselle knows that an old buck is almost as much to be feared as a lion."

"You're exaggerating a little, Lieutenant, but it's certain that these animals with horns aren't mild mannered. It's not good to attack them too close up. *To be hit by a buck is to be thrown into a coffin*, is a saying that all foresters know. The pointed antlers of a ten-point buck defending himself can totally rip open a man's stomach. That's why, my niece, if the beast comes toward you, I strongly advise you to let it go past."

"Oh!" Germaine replied, "I don't have the least desire to harm him."

"And besides," Uncle Armand added, "it's understood that no one will shoot at him. Now, my dear Pontac, we await your orders. Please show us what we must do. I must tell you that my sister-in-law and her elder daughter intend to follow the hunt in the carriage."

"That's very easy. We have three underbrush enclosures to beat out and we'll begin, if you're ready, with the most distant one so as to come back here where lunch is waiting for us."

"Any lunch would be too much. We ate before leaving and we really hope you're going to come dine with us at Germonière."

"I thank you very much, Monsieur, but I don't know if..."

"Good! We'll deal with that question after the hunt. Right now we have four guns to put in place, one of which, that of my nephew, is dangerous and one that's harmless, that of my niece."

"Harmless!" exclaimed Germaine. "In just a little bit you'll see if I miss a good shot. Let's bet that I'll kill more than you do."

"Provided that your brother kills only the game, I'll be satisfied."

"You think I'm a child," Alfred retorted, very vexed.

"No, but I suspect your skill and your level-headedness. So, we'll put you between Pontac and me. We've often been under fire, and we'll watch out for you."

"Please excuse me, Monsieur," Roger replied. "I must direct the trackers and I'll walk with them."

"Is that why you haven't brought a gun?"

Pontac, in fact, wasn't carrying any weapon but a hunting knife attached to a faun-colored leather belt.

"Yes, I might have been tempted to use it, and I'll be more useful to you directing the beating myself. The guard that I brought from Bretteville wouldn't be able by himself to command beaters recruited a little here and there among the local peasants. But, may I ask you what this dog's doing here?" Pontac asked while petting Belt, who had recognized a friend in him and was holding out his intelligent head.

"He came without our permission," replied Germaine, "but he won't bother us. My sister will take charge of watching him."

Roger bowed and du Pommeval, who was also surprised to see that they had brought along the Great Dane, didn't dare raise any objection against the clearly expressed wishes of the Mesdamoiselles Daudièrne. Besides, he was more silent than usual, this brilliant heir, and he seemed to have lost a little of his usual self-assurance. Obviously something was bothering him: maybe the presence of Laurence, Laurence who, the evening before had openly declared war on him and who had good reasons to be hostile toward him. Perhaps he had also begun to be jealous of Roger Pontac. That day the representative of the golden youth of Arcy had flaunted everything: his dog cart came from one of the greatest Paris carriage makers; his horse had cost him two hundred *louis*; his groom seemed to have come in a box directly from England; his gun was a choke-bore bought in London at Purdey's, the fashionable arms-maker; his suit, made by a tailor in vogue, was in perfect taste. In brief, nothing was lacking to hold on to his rank as a first class young man in a superior way.

However, he was feeling that the simplicity and the natural distinction of Lieutenant Pontac was more pleasing than all that affected elegance which dazzled the provincials.

Pontac had come on foot. Pontac wasn't dressed like those Messieurs pictured on the engravings of the fashionable magazines. Pontac showed off nothing pretentious, not even that of showing his skill at the hunt. But with his reserved attitude, his almost haughty coolness, he could have been taken for a landed gentleman showing the bourgeois from a little village the wonders of the forest. And under that apparent indifference, fiery passions and an iron will seemed hidden. His eyes showed that he knew how to command and that he knew how to love.

"It's very fortunate that this First Lieutenant doesn't have a sou," handsome Arthur, humiliated with the comparison, was thinking, to console his ego.

Besides, Mademoiselle Germaine Daudièrne didn't seem to be paying too much attention to the officer on leave. She was delighted to be handling her pretty gun and she was impatience to be using it.

Laurence had taken a seat at the back of the calèche, beside her mother. She called to Belt, who leaped through the door and lay down obediently at the feet of his young mistress.

The beaters in work shirts and heavy shoes spread out, sticks in hand, led by the head guard.

"Mesdemoiselle, would you like first of all to shoot at some hares?" Roger asked.

"I like everything today," replied Germaine.

"Near here there's a little plain shut off in the corner of the forest which is used as a resting place for small game. We could begin there."

"That's an idea," exclaimed young Alfred. "This year I've only gone on cross-country hunts. I wouldn't mind getting in practice again."

"Are there any partridges?" Uncle Armand asked.

"Two or three covies, the guards tell me."

"Well! We could spend a pleasant quarter of an hour there, while waiting to shoot the big game."

They took the road to the left. The calèche followed slowly. Germaine found a way to position herself between her uncle and Roger. Alfred took the point ten feet ahead of the group. Monsieur du Pommeval, who didn't want to stay too near the carriage, thought it a good idea to go join him.

Ten minutes later, Monsieur de Bretteville's guests entered the woods and came to the edge of a clearing longer than it was wide. Some brushwood growing very far apart separated that clearing from the carriage road which was scarcely fifty meters away so that Madame Daudièrne and her elder daughter could follow from the top of their calèche everything that happened in the prologue to the action.

Roger understood Monsieur Daudièrne's intentions and he took care to place the nephew on the extreme left of the line of huntsmen, at least sixty feet from the uncle. He put Monsieur du Pommeval to the extreme right and Germaine in the center, closer to her uncle than to her fiancé.

Her mother observed these evolving preparations with interest, but her sister didn't seem to take any pleasure in it. She looked distractedly at the Great Dane sleeping with his paws extended and his muzzle pressed against the rug, like those marble dogs crouched at the feet of a chatelaine on the tombs of the Middle Ages. And she looked so sad that Madame Daudièrne couldn't pretend not to be aware of it.

Since Arthur du Pommeval had officially asked for Germaine's hand, the good lady had purposely abstained from questioning Laurence. She had carefully avoided all opportunities to be alone with her. And certainly it wasn't by indifference that she shut herself off this way. She strongly felt that Laurence must have been hurt by the behavior of that young man who had shown himself so eager around the older daughter and suddenly declared himself in love with the younger. But she was persuaded that a discussion between her and her daughter would revive a sorrow which would quickly pass if it wasn't brought up to the offended one.

Madame Daudièrne hadn't foreseen the depth of the hurt. She had never asked herself if Laurence's affections had been involved, and she preferred not to ask herself that, being one of those natures who decide not to believe in wickedness except at the last extremity.

It must be said also that Laurence's attitude had begun to reassure her. Neither Laurence's expression nor her behavior had appreciably changed. She was as calm as always, affectionate toward the family, and she made not the slightest mention of her sister's marriage.

"What's wrong with you today, my dear child?" Madame Daudièrne asked her. "You haven't said three words since we left Germonière. Are you sick?"

"No, Mother," Laurence replied quietly. "I haven't said anything because I don't understand anything about hunting. These *messieurs* have talked of nothing else."

"This outing doesn't amuse you very much, does it?"

"Oh! Not at all, but it amused Germaine, and I didn't want to spoil her pleasure by staying at home."

"It's true she would have been extremely sorry to leave you alone. She loves you so much!"

"I love her the same."

"Then you're glad about her happiness?"

"I would gladly resign myself to suffering my whole life if I was sure she'd be happy."

"And do you doubt she will be. I've never seen her so happy."

"She always is, and she never worries about the future."

"I know you don't have the same personality, and just between us, you lean a little too much toward the opposite. Luck causes your sister to marry before you. That's not a reason for you to despair of meeting a match as suitable as Monsieur du Pommeval."

"Do you think I regret him?"

"I think you could have thought of him…in the past."

"I would have been very wrong," Laurence said evasively. "And it seems to me that Germaine should think twice before marrying him."

"That's my opinion…and hers, since she hasn't yet said yes. She wants to get to know him."

"She doesn't seem to be studying him very much. Nevertheless the test can't go on indefinitely."

"No, certainly not. If the marriage hasn't been decided on before we go back to Paris, it never will be. And we go back the first of the year."

"If I were in Germaine's place, I would decide immediately."

"Why? You've just said the opposite."

"Not exactly. I said that she would do well not to commit herself in a heedless way. She asked to think about it and I approve. But she hasn't thought about the unusual situation Monsieur du Pommeval finds himself in. He's counting on the inheritance of his uncle, and it's going to be contested. You seem to be waiting to make a decision until he has won his lawsuit... If he loses and Germaine refuses him afterward, people will say that the marriage for her was only a question of money."

"That's true," Madame Daudièrne murmured, "and I didn't think about that…nor did your sister. I'm sure of that."

"Me, I'm persuaded that Germaine doesn't want Monsieur du Pommeval and that she'll refuse him when she's mocked him enough."

"That would be very bad, and if I were certain that you're not making a mistake…"

"You'd stop this dangerous childish game. Well! Question Germaine; question her at length…She's incapable of lying…and she'll tell you her entire secret. She only told me half of it."

"A secret!... Germaine has secrets now!... You almost scare me."

"Would you like to know what I know?"

"Yes, absolutely."

"Well! Germaine imagines that I love Monsieur du Pommeval…and she confided in me that she doesn't love him at all. She even almost admitted to me that she's in love with someone else. "

"Someone else!" Do you know what you're saying? And she encouraging Monsieur du Pommeval's hopes... No, that's not possible... Germaine is sometimes flighty, inconsiderate…whatever you like…but this would be more than flightiness."

"Germaine has an excuse in her own eyes," Laurence said quickly. "She claims…she believes she can convince Monsieur du Pommeval to marry me. She's got it into her head that I love him, that he loves me, and that he'll come back to me when he finds out she doesn't want him."

"And that's why she keeps him around," exclaimed Madame Daudièrne.

"Then she's mad. Doesn't she understand that that young man can no longer be your husband after having been her suitor, officially agreed on? All the city of Arcy knows it."

"She's not mad, but she listening to her heart and not to her reason. It was useless for me to tell her that I'd rather die than to be Monsieur du Pommeval's wife. She didn't want to listen to me. She's even managed not to be alone with me, for fear she'll understand me."

"Why didn't you warn me earlier, my dear Laurence?"

"Germaine told me that day before yesterday. And why would I not admit it...I was hesitating to repeat it to you."

"You were wrong. It's necessary to put an end to an...inconvenient... situation. This evening I'll confront your sister, and if she admits that she's playing with Monsieur du Pommeval, she'll just have to tell me what she intends to do about it. And, if she's in love with someone else...well, she'll have to name him...and then..."

"She'll name him. Don't doubt that. The dissimulation is not her fault. I ardently hope she has chosen well. And I hope she won't be let down."

"Deceived...as you were, my poor child," murmured Madame Daudièrne, who was beginning to read her older daughter's heart.

The gunfire which broke out along the whole line of hunters kept Laurence from answering. The beaters had surrounded the clearing and were coming forward shouting to frighten the game sheltered in the dry grass or crouching in the furrows. The hares, disturbed in their burrows, fled before this noise. Trying to get back into the woods, they were killed at close range. The partridges were flying away in group, passing forty feet in the air as rapidly as the shots were fired. There was constantly firing, a rain of lead which didn't hit all of them, since hitting birds in flight is not easy. The hunters hardly had time to recharge and there rose a constant cloud of white smoke above them. It resembled a vanguard attack. Nothing was missing to this tableau but red trousers in the plain and Prussian helmets in the edge of the undergrowth.

Germaine did her part in this effort with extreme ardor and astonishing ability. It was marvelous to see her open her little gun, dip into her cartridge case, slide cartridges into the barrels, aim, empty the two barrels, and begin the same exercise again, as if she had never done anything else all her life.

Madame Daudièrne couldn't get over it. She had never seen such a sight. She could scarcely believe the pleasure her daughter took in this murderous activity.

Laurence didn't see anything. She was busy holding Belt, who had gotten up at the noise of the first shots. He seemed to want to run toward the firing.

However, that skirmish didn't last very long. Shooting in a two hectare open space ends quickly. The trackers were soon coming in range of the hunters' guns. They had to stop shooting for fear of an accident. Alfred got off some shots too many, but, fortunately, he didn't wound anyone.

Roger Pontac, seconded by the guard, had conscientiously directed the beaters and gave orders to pick up the hares that had fallen on the field of battle. There were only two partridges there and it was Mademoiselle Daudièrne who had killed them.

She came back triumphant, the gun on her shoulder, the Breton hat tilted over her ear, her expression animated, her eyes shining, her gestures rapid. The men followed her at a distance, chatting about the episodes of the massacre, and Pontac hurried his steps to rejoin them.

"I shot nine hares myself," she shouted to her mother, jumping onto the road where the calèche was parked. "It seems to me that's a good beginning. My uncle didn't miss a shot, but Alfred hit something one time out of ten. He might as well not have come and he should give over his choke bore gun to Monsieur Pontac."

"Really, I don't recognize you," Madame Daudièrne said severely. "You aren't talking like a woman."

"On a hunt, there're only hunters," Germaine replied, laughing.

"Calm down, please, or you'll make me cut short this outing you make me regret having accepted. What's more I want to get back to Germonière early, because I want to talk to you about serious things."

"I couldn't ask for anything better, but you're forgetting that we'll have guests. My uncle has invited Monsieur du Pommeval, Monsieur Pontac... and he'd invite the Duke de Bretteville if he dared."

This attitude was not one to please Madame Daudièrne and she would probably have gotten angry, but the men were arriving just in time to keep her from reprimanding her daughter.

Pontac was the last one to come in and Germaine was in such a hurry to thank him that she retraced her steps to shout to him:

"Marvelous! Admirable! I've never had such fun."

The Lieutenant turned red and stammered a somewhat badly phrased compliment. He seemed embarrassed to the point that Laurence said to herself:

"Could it be this officer she's in love with? She's almost throwing her arms around him... and you'd say that by looking at her he's afraid of betraying the feelings she inspires in him."

"Well, my dear sister-in-law, what do you think about this pastime?" Uncle Armand shouted. It's a Royal hunt the most likeable of Lieutenants has prepared for us. But you don't seem enthusiastic."

"I'm afraid that Laurence is not very well," replied Madame Daudièrne, who was looking for an excuse to take her daughters back to the house.

"Really? She probably got chilled by staying seated in the carriage, and the same could happen to you. You should walk about a little. Why don't you climb up to the Rock of the Fairies?"

"The area we're going to attack now is precisely on this side," Roger Pontac said. "It borders the Departmental Road."

"Which goes by the base of the Rock," Monsieur Armand interrupted.

"I don't like hunting very much, but I like difficult climbs even less," stated Madame Daudièrne.

"Then I don't insist. But we would be very sorry to impose a burden on you and Laurence. If you'd like the calèche to take you back to Germonière, don't hesitate, please. We're all strong enough to make the trip on foot... Aren't we Germaine?"

"I certainly think so!" exclaimed the niece."I never feel tired when I'm happy...and today I'm bursting with joy."

"And it was easy to see that was true. She appeared so happy, that her mother, who adored her, didn't dare scold her, nor even oppose her.

"We'll stay until it's over," she said. "I only ask you not to finish too late."

"It will be the matter of an hour or two, my dear sister. Our friend Pontac is going to direct the three beaters in a military way."

They had come back to the half-moon area where lunch was still waiting, and Roger stationed the shooters on a narrow band of ground which overlooked the public highway and extended right up to the edge of the forest. That the Bretêche forest Germaine had in the past admired from the top of the Lemon Rock escarpment had an imposing aspect on that side. There was no longer the underbrush that is seen everywhere. The Duke de Bretteville's ancestors had in the past applied a system of judicious cutting, which hardly suits anything but private lordly holdings. They cut down everything every twenty years, leaving only trees of a certain dimension to grow to a great height. These chosen trees have room to grow, each having its own section of land and sun. With time they become magnificent trees, at least those still standing after fifty years, because they begin the eliminations again every ten years and the weakest disappear. The monumental trees left at Fontainebleau and Compiègne owe their existence partly to this procedure. But an industrialist wouldn't profit by it, because the wood in a well-managed forest is sold every year, while these giants of the earth, until the day they're cut down, serve only to delight landscape painters.

The section they were going to invade next was planted entirely in beech trees, almost all time-honored. Their white trunks rose from place to place like enormous columns supporting endless domes. In the spaces between them, long carpets of moss extended and crossed in places healthy tree fern high enough to shelter little deer. And those of the Bretêche forest were so seldom hunted that they gave them cover thicker than the bushy corners of the forest offered. They could often be seen wandering about in little bands and sometimes even coming as far as the edge of the seldom-used road which went from Germonière to Bretteville.

The calèche had parked along that road and Pontac had gone to rejoin his men. They had a rather long detour to make to get on the good side of the enclosure to include in the beating area certain game cover where the large game preferred to rest and to push it toward the corner where the hunters were waiting.

These were posted in the same order: Albert and Monsieur du Pommeval at each end of the line, Germaine and Uncle Armand in the center.

And this time Madame Daudièrne and Laurence were going to witness at close hand the killing being prepared. This was the moment when experienced hunters themselves feel emotion, the emotion of anticipation. They don't know if luck will be with them. They are absolutely like the roulette players who watch the cylinder whirling around. Just as the ivory ball falls by chance into one of the numbered slots, a little deer might come out almost under the legs of a clumsy person who would miss him, or, on the contrary, show itself in the right position for the best shot of the gathering. It's a matter of luck, and the best shot can easily come back empty-handed if the game doesn't come under his lead. That even happens rather often, and in those cases, it's the hunted animals that are lucky.

Each one prepared himself to profit by the fortunate circumstances fate would send him. Germaine, her gun poised, her eyes and ears open, felt her heart beat with pleasure and hope. But the demon of the hunt didn't possess her to the point of making her forget Roger. She was grateful to him for the modest role he had chosen. The more she compared him to Monsieur du Pommeval, the more she found him superior to this provincial dandy who had never done anything but spend his money to shine in regional waters and who thought himself irresistible. She had begun to wonder if it wasn't time to tell her mother that she didn't want at any price to marry the new lord of Fougéray and that she was dreaming of giving over that honor to her older sister.

There was another confession she could have made, but that one was more difficult. It would have cost her terribly to admit that she was in love with a Hussard on leave for a few months, a bird flying through, almost a stranger. She had seen him four times. The time hadn't come; she knew that very well. She had to wait. For what? She didn't know. Perhaps for one of those events that hardly ever happen except in novels, a fairy's wand transforming the poor officer into a millionaire, the son of a laborer into a landed property owner.

Germaine had no doubt that Madame Daudièrne had resolved to put her, that same evening, in a position to have to make a decision. And Germaine had been careful not to return to the side of the calèche. Motionless and leaning on the trunk of a colossal beech tree, she was watching out for one of those first signs which signal the game's appearance, the noise of leaves rubbing together, movement in the high grasses.

Suddenly the silence of the forest was broken by the far-away cry of the trackers. And soon, thirty feet from the edge, above a large tuft of fern made yellow by the autumn, rose the fine head of a young deer.

The fawn didn't see Germaine, but Germaine saw it very well. She put her gun to her shoulder quickly and she was going to fire, when the graceful animal turned its head to the side where she was. He showed three-quarters of himself. He looked at her with his big, black gentle eyes, and he didn't run. Maybe he took her for one of those little herdsmen who lead their cows to pasture across the back of the road's ditches.

"No," she told herself, lowering her weapon. "I won't have the cruelty to kill him while he's resting. I'll wait until he gets up to leave and if he has the strength to save himself on the beaters' side, so much the better. I don't intend to murder him. I even hope that Alfred doesn't see him. Alfred would shoot at him and since he shoots badly he could lame him.

Germaine was moved and yet she had just massacred with enthusiasm hares and partridges, all as interesting as this little deer. Pity is a very complicated sentiment which depends a great deal on circumstances. It's very easily stifled and becomes very quickly dulled. At the end of a fierce combat, the least ferocious soldier willingly cuts the throat of a man he would have helped if he'd met him the day before the battle. And murders en masse are less impressive than an isolated murder.

In essence, it's a matter of nerves. The cries of pain touch the hardest hearts. But too bad for those who suffer without complaint. Nobody would feel pity for the horrible torture the lobster feels when he's thrown still alive into boiling water. And then, there's the influence of the exterior form. You don't kill a beautiful butterfly, but you take pleasure in crushing a hideous spider. And besides, Germaine's feelings had never been put to a serious test. The hare which dashes away, the partridge that flies away are felled by a gun shot, rather far from the hunter who isn't present at its last convulsions. In a hunt with beaters, he doesn't even have to soil his hands with their blood since the paid servants who flushed them out of hiding take care of picking them up. But it's not exactly that. It's a matter of shooting an animal who isn't thinking about running away. When the action hasn't yet begun, a sentry doesn't amuse himself by shooting at the enemy sentry who's across from him. There's a sort of implied truce between these soldiers that the sound of the drums beating the charge will pit, one against the other, with fixed bayonets. So it is in the hunt. It's agreed that one must not abuse his advantages by taking aim at a still target. It would be the same as shooting the target. A deer that doesn't budge is a creature of the *Bon Dieu*. You admire and respect him. When he dashes away he's game and you shoot him without scruples and without remorse.

This time the halt in firing wasn't very long. The shouts of the peasants became more distinct and you could soon make out the dry sonorous noise of their clubs hitting the branches of the willow shoots and the trunks of the baliveau. Two or three deer that were grazing near there hidden by the dry grass, jumped out at the same time and dashed in all directions. The best advised ran across to the forest and so avoided the lead of the hunters posted on the edge. One, the one Germaine had been looking at for several instants, had the unfortunate idea to break through the line and rushed past between her and her brother. She didn't have the time, and maybe the courage, to shoot at him, but Alfred shot at him once, at the risk of wounding Germaine, and by chance hit him.

The poor beast, hit in the flank at the moment she jumped onto the road, fell, got up, and dragged itself, dying, as far as the calèche where Madame Daudièrne and Laurence were sitting.

"He's mine! He's mine!" cried out the novice hunter at the top of his lungs.

"Will you shut up!" riposted Uncle Armand from a distance. "If you continue to yell like that, we won't see even another rabbit. *Allons!* Well!" he continued, "Now he's left his station. That urchin is going to ruin our whole day. "

That was true. Forgetting the fundamental rule of beating hunts, and the wise advice of Monsieur Daudièrne, Alfred had nothing more important to do than to run to his fawn. Was it to pick him up or to finish him off? He didn't know himself. Joy had turned his head.

The fawn, dealt a death blow, was lashing out desperately and moaning like a child.

"Ah! This is horrible," Laurence said, turning away her eyes. "I don't want to see any more." And she opened the door to get out. Belt didn't lose a second. Before his mistress had gotten up he was already on the ground.

"Call your dog," screamed Alfred. "Get him away or I'll kill him."

"Jean," Madame Daudièrne said to her coachman, "Go forward a little. We're too close to the hunters, and we're probably bothering them. Go park at the entry to the crossroads."

"Madame is right," replied Jean, who was an old servant of the house and had the right to speak freely. "I've just heard some buckshot and my mares could very well be hit by some."

And changing places was certainly not a useless precaution, considering Alfred's wild behavior and clumsiness. But if Madame Daudièrne wanted to get further away, it was above all to flee the sad spectacle of the agony of an inoffensive animal. She didn't like to see blood spilled any more than her daughter did. And the deer that was fighting against death was pouring forth waves of it.

"I won't stay here another minute," Laurence said as soon as the calèche had parked where the roads met.

"I wouldn't ask anything better than to leave," Madame Daudièrne said softly, "but I can't let Germaine finish this stupid day without me. She's overexcited to the last degree, and she'll wind up doing something foolish."

"I really think you'd be right to watch over her, and over others. But my presence here doesn't serve any use and I can do without watching scenes which I find repugnant. I'm going to climb up to that rock."

"Alone?"

"I'd rather climb up there with you, but you couldn't get to the top without tiring yourself out. And I won't run any risk. Belt will go with me, and, besides, I won't be out of your sight."

The escarpment which crowned the Lemon Rock dominated the road, just across from the obelisk where lunch was set up. Madame Daudièrne could, in fact, from the carriage where she was seated, watch her daughter climb that slope that Germaine, aided by Roger Pontac, had come down one evening. And she had only to look in the other direction to keep an eye on her younger daughter, posted a hundred feet to her right.

"If you promise me to be careful and not go too far away," she said, "I won't oppose your trying that climb, even though it seems to me wiser not to attempt it."

"I won't go past the crest you can see from here, and I'll be back when the carnage is over."

"Unfortunately, it's only beginning."

That was true. The trackers were closing in and some deer were already coming within range, greeted by a fusillade still more murderous.

"Come, Belt!" Laurence called to her dog, that seemed to hesitate. "Come with me. They would kill you."

The Great Dane was not a hunter and, at a sign from the young girl, he followed her without regret.

"Why did I come," she asked herself, as she climbed rapidly toward her chosen destination, although she didn't have the least interest in consulting the oracle.

"These methodical exterminations break my heart. Germaine must be crazy to enjoy them, even crazier than when she dreamed of making a pilgrimage to the chateau of the fairies. I'm going there myself, but it's to get away from that odious hunt. They won't tell me the name of my husband, because I'll never marry."

Laurence climbed without looking around, even when she had to stop to take a breath. She didn't want to see those tidbits set out for lunch, that white smoke which smelled of gunpowder, those carriages, those servants in livery who reminded her that Monsieur du Pommeval was there, and whose company she was undoubtedly going to be forced to endure on the return trip.

She was climbing to find forgetfulness and her thoughts gradually took another direction. The pure air of the summit refreshed her burning face and she began to admire the grandiose tableau under her eyes. The forest no longer appeared to her as anything but a dark mass and instead of the fracas of the guns firing, she could only hear a faraway crackling.

The Rock rose up before her silent and unadorned. The sky was blue, that pale, sad blue of clear day at the end of autumn. An eagle soared above the granite tower and gusts of wind moved through the heather which carpeted the ground of that solitude.

Laurence felt herself revive. She was now in a hurry to see up close that fissure made poetic by a legend which began to interest her. Belt also seemed impatient to reach the top of that wild hill. He was running, his nose lifted to the wind, and from time to time he stopped to bay joyfully.

He was the first to reach the top of the Rock, just at the spot where Roger had stood while Germaine was questioning the fairies at the entrance of the vent which opened on the other side of this stone cube. He took a position of alert, his head lifted, as dogs do lying in front of an apple tree where a covey of red partridges have lit.

"What's wrong with you?" asked Laurence, who knew his behavior.

Five feet above the base of the blue square, there began a fissure as narrow as the openings for projectiles in the wall of a chateau of the Middle Ages. That sort of window was placed too high for the girl to look at it. Roger Pontac had used it as a megaphone to answer Germaine, but Roger Pontac was tall enough to have enlisted in a cavalry regiment.

Laurence, very astonished to see that Belt was not moving, wondered if he smelled someone he knew there. But as it was hardly likely that the interior of the rock was inhabited, she didn't hold that supposition very long. She began to make herself walk around and examine this dungeon not built by man. Before attempting this tour, she looked down below her and saw the calèche, the footmen and the hunters at the place she had left them. Her mother was waving a handkerchief, probably to show her that she was watching all her movements. That signal reminded her that she had promised not to go past the crest. And she gave up attempting a complete examination of the fairies' palace. She also again began to feel a vague uneasiness. She limited herself to going around the side of the massive Rock and she was no little surprised to find herself in front of a crevice a great deal larger than the first one and a great deal more accessible.

The look of this black hole seemed sinister to her. She was careful not to approach it as had Germaine, more curious and less timid. She called to her dog, that could defend her if, in the unlikely case that she would need defending.

Belt didn't obey as quickly as usual. But he finally decided to leave his observation post, and he came to her, searching and smelling the moss as if to find there the traces of a friend who had passed by. He soon ended this maneuver. He stopped short in front of the gaping opening, gave a sonorous bark, and made one leap into the depths of the cavern.

Belt had disappeared. Belt gave no sign of life. He had forced the fairies subterranean entrance and the fairies were keeping him prisoner to punish him for his audacity.

That idea, which probably would have amused Germaine, didn't at all bother Laurence's calmer and more reasonable mind. But all the same, she wasn't reassured. Evidently there was a man there, a man Belt knew.

"If it's Roch Ferrer," the young girl was thinking, "that would explain why Belt dashed into that hole... but what would Roch Ferrer be doing there? He swore to me that he'd go find Monsieur Pontac at the de Bretteville chateau, and he was supposed to go there yesterday. And even supposing that he didn't go, what motive could have made him hide himself here. Could he have learned that they're looking for him to arrest him and take him to prison? No, because I didn't tell him we were going hunting today in the Bretèche forest... and then, even if he'd known it, he couldn't have known that I'd climb up to this rock."

Laurence was at that point in her reflections when her dog took a great leap out of the cavern and came to fall down at her feet.

"Where did you come from, you wicked beast?" she asked him.

Belt couldn't bark to answer her because he held an object in his mouth he didn't want to release. But he was obviously bringing it to his mistress, because he willingly let her take it from him. It was a kind of sack, or rather a money holder in suede leather, held shut by a steel clasp which probably held a secret lock. The object was square and it must have been worn like an amulet, because the ends of two pieces of leather hung from the two rings affixed to the two top corners.

How did this find its way into the hole in the rock? Who could have hidden it there? And what deep-seated instinct made Belt go there to look for it? All these questions coming at one time, Laurence didn't know how to answer them when, fingering the sack, she saw two initials stamped in black: two V. Then she suddenly remembered that Madame Vignemal was named Virginia. Germaine had joked many times about this sentimental given name which hardly suited the very prosaic proprietor of the Fougéray domains. And she also recalled the story that the poacher had told her on the Beuvron levee.

"This is the money holder that he picked up in the brush where Madame Vignemal had thrown it." she said to herself. *"He told me he put it somewhere nobody would find it. And in fact nobody would have thought about coming to search for it here in this rock crevice. Roch Ferrer, who roams around every-where must be familiar with the Lemon Rock. He came here on purpose to hide that dead woman's relic. He couldn't know that Belt would bring it to me."*

All that couldn't be more likely. But what should be done with this bag which evidently held important papers, perhaps deeds belonging to the woman who was carrying it. Throw it back into the black hole where the Great Dane had unearthed it? That was the first thought that came to Mademoiselle Daudièrne, but she quickly realized she didn't have the right to do this. This remnant belonging to Madame Vignemal was valuable to the named heir or to the natural heirs. To abandon it would be to prejudice someone's claims because two things would happen: one, it would rot there without benefiting anyone, or, two, it would fall into the hands of a peasant who had come to the Rock to consult the fairies. And in the latter case, you could hardly count on the object being restored to its rightful owner. Roch Ferrer had certainly renounced using it because he had gotten rid of it. And besides, Roch Ferrer was going to leave the country for a long time, probably forever.

"The secret of the inheritance is probably there," Laurence told herself, while tapping that little leather sack, *"and it's up to me if this secret is ever known. But if chance brought me here, it's God who wants me to intervene. How could I intervene? For nothing in the world would I agree to break open this envelope that a poacher respected. To give it to that du Pommeval, who'd have no scruples about opening it and destroying it if he saw it was beneficial to him*

to do away with it? No, no, never! I don't want to be the cause, even indirectly, of the ruin of people worth more than he is. And on the other hand, if I show my findings to one of the magistrates who'll judge the lawsuit between those who claim the inheritance, I'll have to answer questions they'll surely put to me, and since I can't lie, I'll have to repeat what that unfortunate boy told me. That would mean his doom and seriously compromise me. They would remember nothing of my declaration but the admission of our nocturnal meeting. They wouldn't take note of the explanation he'd furnish to justify himself."

Belt, crouching on the ground, was looking at his mistress. It almost seemed as if he were waiting for the command to take the bag back to where he had found it. Laurence thought for an instant about using this dog as a messenger, of putting that object in his mouth and leaving him free to go wherever his instinct took him. That would have been a rather unusual way of getting rid of all responsibility. But this would not have solved the problem, because Belt might leave the money holder in the brush or on the road. And he could just as easily let it be taken by the first person who petted him—Uncle Armand, for instance, or Monsieur du Pommeval, which would be much worse.

At the height of her indecision, she looked up and saw two eyes shining in the gloom of the crevice looking at her. A man was there wedged between the walls of the rock, like a saint's statue in a niche. He had come forward as far as the entrance to the corridor of the fairies. He was in full daylight. But she didn't at first recognize him. She saw only his eyes and she drew back, frightened.

"Don't be afraid, Mademoiselle," said a voice which made her tremble. "I want to talk to you, but I won't show myself to those watching us."

"You!" exclaimed Laurence. "What are you doing here?"

"I'm hiding. I know they're looking for me. They won't find me. Tomorrow I'll be far away. But I didn't have the courage to leave without seeing you again. I guessed that you would climb up to the Lemon Rock. If you hadn't come, I'd have asked Monsieur Subligny to take you to the Beuvron levee this evening."

"Monsieur Subligny! Then you told him..."

"Nothing...only that I love you. For years I've followed you everywhere you went. And I swore to him that I never dared approach you."

"It's too much...a great deal too much he knows..."

"What does that matter since I'm leaving. I'm going to Africa and I'll never come back."

"Then you've seen Monsieur Pontac?"

"Yes, this morning, here where we are. He comes here every day and I slept last night in the fairies' hole. He promised me that he'd give me money this evening, some clothes, and a letter of recommendation to his colonel. In a week I'll be a soldier."

"What you've done, that's good, Monsieur," the young girl, very touched, said softly. "I forgive you for the fright you've just caused me and I'll pray for

372

you."

"Then I can hope you won't forget me?"

"Forget you! Oh, no. I'll always remember that you offered to sacrifice yourself for me to satisfy a fantasy I had and that I no longer have."

"Is it true that you no longer want that man to lose the inheritance he hopes for?"

"It's so true that I'm going to give you back Madame Vignemal's bag. You can do whatever you like with it. I'm indifferent to Monsieur du Pommeval."

"I know you're not the one he's going to marry. The Major told me so."

"The Major?"

"Yes, Doctor Subligny. But he told me also that he was going to marry your sister and that's why I gave the sack to Belt. You might have refused it from my hand, and I can't keep it. If you don't want to open it, give it to Monsieur Subligny."

"It's fitting that you be the one to give it to him."

"I won't see him again. I was supposed to go to his office tomorrow, but if I go into Arcy, I'll be arrested. They're lying in wait for me. Monsieur Pontac has promised to explain to Monsieur Subligny why I'm leaving tonight. I'm sure the Major will agree with me. If you don't want to tell him that we met, tell him that your dog found the sack in the crevice where I hid it. Monsieur Subligny now knows the whole truth of the ferry accident. He knows that Madame Vignemal, just as the ferry broke away, thought first of all about the little sack she carried around her neck. She tore it from her neck; she clutched it in her right hand, and she didn't turn loose of it when she fainted. If it was so important to her that it didn't stay at the bottom of the river, it was because she had locked up something precious in it. That's what the Major thinks…and me too, I believe that. So I told myself I couldn't keep the thing. It seems that if Monsieur du Pommeval doesn't inherit, it will be Monsieur Pontac and others who'll inherit."

"Monsieur Pontac! You must be mistaken."

"No, Mademoiselle, Monsieur Pontac is a relative of Madame Vignemal."

"And we didn't know that," Laurence said under her breath. "That's strange. "

"The Major could have told you so, because he knew Monsieur Pontac during the time he was in school. His cousin had put him there and he escaped to join the army."

Yes!… I remember. The doctor told us that story. It even seems to me that he told us the name of Madame Vignemal's protégé…and none of us remembered it. But then, you must give what you found to Monsieur Pontac. It's to his advantage more than to that of anyone else to know if his aunt remade her will."

"I thought about that…only I was afraid of displeasing you."

"Me! What does it matter to me if Monsieur du Pommeval is rich or stays as he is?"

"To you nothing, probably, but…to your sister?"

"My sister doesn't love him."

"And they may make her marry him! Ah! I was right to offer the sack to Monsieur Pontac."

"You did that?"

"Yes, I admit it. I detest this Monsieur du Pommeval, I would have been happy to hurt him. That's bad. I should have asked you before talking to Monsieur Pontac."

"And you told him how this object fell into your hands?"

"I told him everything."

"Well?"

"Well, he refused."

"That might have been a fortune he was refusing."

"He has his commission and he doesn't care anything about money. It was useless for me to say anything. He didn't even want to listen to me. I told him I'd send the sack to Monsieur Subligny who'd open it. He told me I could do whatever I wanted to with it, so long as he didn't hear any more talk about the inheritance. And he turned down all the other cousins who were trying to persuade him to join them in a lawsuit."

"There are noble hearts," the young girl said softly.

"Do you still refuse to refer it to Monsieur Subligny's judgement?" Roch Ferrer asked gently.

"No," Laurence answered in a firm voice. "Whatever happens, I've done my duty…and it would be pleasant to think that you were out of the reach of the pursuits…and of those who say evil things about you."

Roch fell on his knees. He was weeping.

"Good-bye," Mademoiselle Daudièrne continued. "And if we never see each other again, think that in France, a country you love, someone is praying for you. And now," Laurence went on, "get up, Monsieur, you should kneel only before God."

Roch Ferrer obeyed. He straightened up, motionless, his body rigid, his head thrown backward, his eyes fixed on the young girl, his big eyes still wet with tears, eyes that could talk.

"You're leaving," he asked in a stifled voice.

"I must. They're calling me," replied Mademoiselle Daudièrne.

And that wasn't a pretext to cut short an improper meeting. Her mother was making repeated and almost commanding signs to her from below to get her to go down.

"Don't you have anything else to say to me?" whispered the gypsy.

"I have one word to say to you: Courage!"

"Courage! I have that, since I'm giving up seeing you. But I have a favor to ask you."

"Tell me what it is."

"I beg you to allow me to write to you. Oh! Not directly. I'll address my letters to Doctor Subligny, who'll read them to you. That's to let you know they won't contain anything which would offend you."

"The Doctor! Then he knows..."

"He knows that I love you with an insane love, and if I'm agreeing to change my existence, to forfeit my liberty, it's because you wish it. He won't be astonished to see that I'm consecrating my life for you, the new life I'm accepting to obey you. You've commanded me to redeem my life. You've shown me the road to follow to merit your pardon. Won't you allow me to tell you from a distance: 'I'm walking in the path you pointed out to me?'"

"Nothing that happens to you would ever be indifferent to me. I would be happy to learn that you'd become a brave soldier...and when you've earned a commission like Monsieur Pontac, I would be proud to have guessed that you were a man of valor. Then I must always know where you are," Laurence continued gaily. "Write to the Doctor. Write to him often. He'll give me news of you...and...he'll answer you for me. Don't you have to know if I'm still alive?"

"Yes, because if you died, I'd kill myself not to survive you."

"I have no desire at all to die, and I'm sure I'll see you again. It was God that inspired you with the beneficial thought of leaving. God will bring you back one day to this country where you've left behind friends. And nothing would then keep me from saying to my mother that when Lieutenant Ferrer was still only a poacher, I had a long meeting with him at the foot of the Rock of the fairies."

This was said in a casual tone which was unlike the emotion that Laurence was feeling and that she was afraid of showing. She was no longer even sure enough of herself to go through a scene of passionate good-byes, and she didn't want Roch to leave desperate. In these thorny situations, upbringing and the habits of the social world, even the bourgeois world, are a great help. Mademoiselle Daudièrne had found right off the right thing to say. And she was quick to take advantage of this success to cut short a situation which wasn't without peril and which was in danger of becoming ridiculous. If Roch disappeared into the depths of the cavern or if he came out completely to kiss Laurence's hand, as he had already done on the edge of the Tertre, the adventure would have turned into the grotesque. He knew that very well because he didn't move. But it had to come to an end.

"Good-bye, Monsieur," she said, petting Belt and motioning him with her finger toward the crevice.

Belt understood. With a bound he jumped the distance and standing up on his hind feet, he held out his head to Roch, who covered it with kisses. He too had understood.

"Yes, Good-bye," continued the young girl. "In two years, in five years, in ten years, we'll meet here, don't you wish? I'll wait until you give me a rendez-vous by the intermediary of our friend the Doctor. We may not recognize each other, because I won't be young any longer and you'll be a handsome officer. It's only hearts that don't change."

"No, they don't change," whispered Roch. "I'll always love you, and you'll never love me."

"Who knows?" replied Laurence.

The retort had a double meaning and couldn't compromise her. She regretted, however, having let it come out and to keep from explaining it, she started quickly to descend the slope of the hill.

Roch had the courage not to follow her. He had taken what she said as encouragement and he still had hope.

Mademoiselle Daudièrne assuredly hadn't committed herself, but she didn't leave as she had come. Her meeting with the poacher had troubled her. She was seeing him now in a new light. He was no longer that vagabond, that man running through the woods whose first sight had frightened her so much. He was a strong and loyal young man who only asked to live for her and to die for France. And she was praying that he would live.

And, then, she was carrying away that little mysterious bag that had only to be opened to know the last and definite wishes of Madame Vignemal. She didn't yet know what she would do with it, but she had no intention of throwing it into the bushes where the first peasant passing by would pick it up. She had slid it into the top of her dress without remembering that the dead woman had also carried it that way. She was too preoccupied to think of the forebodings which ought to have come with that memory.

Madame Daudièrne hadn't gotten down, but the calèche wasn't in the same place. It was parked on the other side of place where all the roads come together, as far as possible from the big clearing where the great beating was taking place. And the compassionate Germonière chatelaine was seated so as to have her shoulders to the massacres.

The scene of the fawn dying under her eyes had almost been repeated two or three times since Laurence's departure and her mother didn't want to see it in spite of herself.

At the edge of the woods there was constant shooting. The beaters were finishing their work and the poor beasts they were chasing came, exhausted, to throw themselves under the legs of the hunters, who didn't miss them very often. Even Alfred killed with almost every shot. That butchery began to disgust Germaine, and she had already spared more than one fawn that she could have cut in two if she had wanted to. Fortunately, the carnage was drawing to a close. The line of trackers was coming forward. They could be seen through the trees, Roger Pontac at their head.

Laurence came to the bottom of the hill, covering her ears and turning away her eyes, going across the half-moon area to rejoin her mother.

"This hunt absolutely revolts me," Madame Daudièrne said, "and I won't stay right up to the end. At the first intermission of this abominable tragedy, I'll call Germaine back, and I'll take her with you to Germonière. These gentlemen can well do without us."

"But Germaine will have some trouble doing without them."

"Nevertheless, she'll have to do so. And I'll get some serious explanations from her this evening. Our relationship with Monsieur du Pommeval can't continue on the same footing as it is now. Since you told me what your sister has in mind doing, it's time for me to get back to the house and I was waiting for you with impatience. What were you doing up there? You stayed there a long time."

"The time to examine that rock, which is very unusual. And, then, Belt would have run away, as he usually does. He can't be controlled as you wish."

Madame Daudièrne agreed. "I was watching him from here and he ranged very far away, since he disappeared for a rather long time."

"There's a cave in the Fairies' Rock. Belt ran into it, and I thought for a moment I'd never see him again. I finally got him back. He won't leave us any more. He doesn't like the smell of the gunpowder."

"I'm glad he doesn't...but, do you hear?"

"What's that?"

"Those shouts. Ah! *Mon Dieu,* Is one of our people in danger?...Who knows if those people haven't disturbed a wild boar...or a wolf?"

"No, no, the other day, my uncle said in front of me that there're no wild boars in the Bretêche forest. And the only thing the wolves have in mind is running away when they see so many people assembled."

Laurence was right, but if she had listened more closely, she would have understood the situation. The last deer had spread out and the hunters had gotten off a last salvo, when Roger's sonorous voice had shouted:

"A buck! Attention!...don't shoot."

The command wasn't useless because the psychological moment had arrived when guns go off by themselves. The buck had jumped out suddenly from the depth of a group of bushes where he was resting without paying too much attention to all that noise. He didn't hear a group of pack hounds barking and he knew very well they weren't after him. But Roger Pontac having walked almost right up on him, he had made off, in not too much of a hurry. He was going in a direction so as to come out at the outside opening of the enclosure, so he was going to pass under the sights of the hunters, one after the other. And Pontac, who had perfectly recognized the ten-point buck pointed out to him before the beating began, wasn't satisfied with just shouting to stop the fusillade. He didn't trust the cool-headedness of his guests and to better protect the king of the forest, he began to follow him, running very fast, reiterating at the top of his lungs, the warning not to shoot.

Everything went well at first. The buck, always going obliquely to the left, because the trackers were obliquely to the right, passed within thirty feet of Monsieur du Pommeval, within twenty feet of Monsieur Daudièrne, and within ten feet of Germaine. All of these behaved correctly. Handsome Arthur and Uncle Armand knew how to observe a rule of the hunt. Germaine, less experienced, thought of nothing but admiring that noble beast who hardly deigned to flee and who didn't turn to avoid her. He was running straight toward Alfred, posted thirty meters further off. It was easy to see that he intended to jump into the road, to follow it peacefully, and to go back into another enclosure. That tactic, familiar to old bucks, would have succeeded, but it was written that the day would end in a drama.

At the exact instant that he was going to run past Mademoiselle Daudièrne, a shot went off, and the ten-point buck, wounded in the left shoulder, stopped in his tracks. He didn't see the imprudent Alfred, who had shot him, but he saw Germaine and he rushed on her with his head lowered. That would have been the end for the poor child if she hadn't had the presence of mind to hide behind the trunk of the beech tree where she had been leaning. The buck, which had gone beyond her, turned around, and, retracing his tracks, began the attack with even more fury.

Alfred had completely lost his head; du Pommeval was at the other end of the line; and Monsieur Daudièrne, who was in a good position to shoot, didn't dare, for fear of hitting his niece. In addition, his gun was loaded with Number 4 lead, excellent for killing a doe, but a great deal too small to hit a buck.

Germaine continued to move in a circle around the tree. That maneuver had been successful and it was the only chance for safety which she had left. If she had tried to flee, the ten-point buck would have reached her in one leap. He followed her furiously and he still missed her. But at each try, his jump carried him less far, and he came back more quickly to the charge, whereas, the young girl's strength was running out. The terrible antlers had already scraped her. She already had a tear in her Breton jacket and she wasn't discouraging him. Unfortunately, her feet slid on the moss and she fell. At that point she understood that she was lost. But before closing her eyes in order not to see the blow coming, she saw Roger Pontac running, and she started to hope he wouldn't let her die this way.

"Help me!" she said in a failing voice.

For the spectators of that emotional scene, there was a terrible moment to get through. Made powerless by the lack of proper weapons, and paralyzed by emotion, they all understood that Lieutenant Pontac was the only one in a position to help Germaine. Roger didn't have a gun, and if he had had one he wouldn't have dared shoot for fear of hitting the girl, because the buck was almost on her. But he did have a knife, not one of those parade knives that those novice huntsmen carry hung on their belt in an elegant sheath, but a real knife the head guard had lent him, a solid knife, filed and sharpened, which had killed several bucks at bay and wild boars standing off dogs. As soon as the ten-point buck stood before him, Roger thought about the danger which would eventually menace Germaine. It took just a shot fired in spite of the orders and badly directed for the animal to throw himself on the hunter closest to him.

And foreseeing this situation, Roger had begun to follow him at racing speed, knowing very well that if the buck got out without an accident, he wouldn't catch him, but he would be in time to intervene if the buck stopped to charge.

The situation he foresaw happened, and it was Mademoiselle Daudièrne who was threatened. Fortunately she was cool-headed enough to avoid the first attacks. When she fell, Roger was only a few feet from the buck and at the moment she screamed: "Help!" Roger grabbed the furious animal by the horns and turned away the blow that was going to slit open poor Germaine's stomach. Held by those steel hands, the ten-point buck's front legs buckled and he fell on his knees. But he wasn't vanquished. He tried to get rid of his enemy by shaking his antlers and to get up in order to nail him to the ground. If Roger turned him loose, he was doomed, but he held firm. Kneeling, the hunting knife between his teeth, he put his full weight on the buck, forcing him to lie on his side. He succeeded after a five-minute battle which would have saved the young girl if she had wanted to flee, because she was back on her feet, and she could have gotten out of danger while her defender was fighting for her. The buck, hit by the imprudent Alfred's shot, wasn't seriously wounded, but he was losing a lot of blood and his strength was slacking. He finally gave in and Roger was able to put his knee on his throat, seize his knife with his right hand and strike at the right place. The weapon went in right up to the hilt and he didn't take it out. The beast was stone dead. The last death throes almost knocked Pontac down, but that was all. He got up slowly and ran to Germaine. She waited for him, pale and trembling. Her uncle came, followed at a distance by du Pommeval. Alfred, mad with fear, had gone to tell Madame Daudièrne.

"Thank you," she whispered, holding out her hand to the man she loved. She couldn't do less, but she involuntarily did much more. Her strength suddenly gave way, and she would have fallen if Roger hadn't caught her in his arms. She let herself to without resistance, and her mother, her sister, her uncle, her brother, and her fiancé arrived just in time to see her head resting on the shoulder of the Lieutenant, who was holding her by the waist.

It would be difficult to describe exactly the scene which followed. Madame Daudièrne's fright, Laurence's astonishment, Alfred's frightened looks, Uncle Armand's emotion and Arthur du Pommeval's crestfallen looks. The hero of that adventure didn't know what to make of it, nor what to listen to, because everyone was talking at the same time. Fortunately, Germaine came around and got down to run and throw herself on the shoulders of her mother, who cried out in fright on seeing her all covered with blood.

"You're hurt! You're hurt!" she stammered.

"No, no," Germaine murmured, "I'm all right."

"And you, my friend?" Monsieur Daudièrne asked, squeezing both of the brave Lieutenant's hands.

"Nothing, Monsieur, that's the buck's blood."

"Then everything's for the best. You've saved my niece's life in exposing your own. We can never do enough to repay you, but I ask you to believe you can count on me, always and in any situation. And I'm counting on seeing you, beginning this evening, at Germonière. Our hunt is finished. My niece isn't standing any more. I don't suggest you follow us."

"I'll go find out how Mademoiselle is," Roger said timidly, "but right now I'm afraid of bothering you..."

"Alfred," Madame Daudièrne interrupted, "Run to the calèche and tell Jean to drive here. Your sister is in no state to walk."

"Me!" Germaine exclaimed. "I'm capable of climbing up to the Fairies Rock."

At this moment the noise of wheels grating on the tarmac of the departmental road and the cheerful cracking of a whip announced the arrival of a carriage.

"It's the Doctor," Uncle Armand cried out. "He's come at the right time."

"I assure you I can do without his help," Germaine said.

Monsieur Daudièrne, who wasn't of that opinion, jumped onto the road and stopped Monsieur Subligny's dilapidated old carriage.

"I knew very well I'd find you here," began the Doctor, "and I came to see you operate. I'm not a hunter, but I still like to hear the guns firing."

"That's what it's about!" shouted the uncle. "My niece has been rammed by a buck...which didn't hurt her, since she's coming with us, but she must have been very frightened. And if you don't mind, we're all going back to Germonière and I'd feel a lot better if she were looked at."

Germaine, completely restored, came up leaning on her mother's arm and stated that in fact she needed nothing but rest. The calèche was there. They got in: Madame Daudièrne, Uncle Armand, and Alfred sat beside her. Everyone had lost his head a little and they were forgetting Laurence, who, instead of protesting, said to Monsieur Subligny:

"Do you want to let me ride with you, Doctor?" and she added in a low voice:

"I need to talk to you."

The good man offered her his hand to help her climb up beside him in that bizarre carriage he drove himself. Nobody was thinking about them. Du Pommeval was acting important standing near the carriage and Roger Pontac had stayed modestly at the edge of the woods.

"Messieurs," Uncle Armand cried out to them. "See you this evening. Excuse us for leaving this way; it's doctor's orders."

The coachman whipped up his horses which left at a fast trot. But Germaine had time to send Roger a look into which she put her whole soul.

The tilbury followed and the two rivals, left alone, separated after having exchanged some rather cold polite formalities. Du Pommeval hadn't come off very well that day and he wasn't happy about it.

"Here's a departure that looks like a stampede," Monsieur Subligny said to Laurence. "So what happened?"

"I don't know a lot about it," Mademoiselle Daudièrne replied. "I wasn't there when Germaine was attacked by a buck and Monsieur Pontac killed it. She wasn't hurt, very luckily. But that accident upset all of us, and it's time to go home."

"Yes. The situation must be tense. Because, after all, this dear Pontac has everything that's needed to please a young girl...and he saved the life of Mademoiselle your sister. She owes him gratitude...whereas she owes nothing at all to du Pommeval...and *ma foi!* if my friend Roger only had an independent fortune..."

"He may have one."

"How's that, Mademoiselle?"

"Roch Ferrer found a little sack that Madame Vignemal was carrying on her person."

"You've seen Roch Ferrer?"

"Yes...a while ago. I climbed up to the Lemon Rock. He was hiding there."

"I knew it. I was the one who told him to leave his lair and go away tonight. But he was very wrong to show himself and above all to speak to you."

"You also know that he's in love with me."

"Still that madness! I was hoping he had gotten over that ridiculous passion."

"A touching passion. Roch Ferrer who loves me hopelessly is worth more than Monsieur du Pommeval who deceived me and who would deceive Germaine, if she's weak enough to marry him."

The Doctor didn't say a word. He wasn't prepared to receive that outpouring of confidences.

"But she won't marry him," Laurence continued. "I'm certain now that she's in love with Monsieur Pontac."

"The Devil! That's serious, that's very serious," the Doctor said softly, shaking his head. "Roger has nothing and Madame Daudièrne would have difficulty deciding to accept him as a son-in-law."

"Do you think she'd accept him if he inherited from his cousin?"

"I don't know, Mademoiselle, but it's impossible for him to inherit. Only Roch could testify in his favor if a lawsuit materialized, but it would cost him dearly. And besides, nobody would believe him. Pontac could even be compromised, because a magistrate has been found stupid enough to suspect him of I don't know what complicity in a crime Roch didn't commit. Roch is going to leave the country and things will stay as they are."

"However, if the key to the enigma were there..." said Laurence, taking out of her dress the leather sack Roch had given her.

"So that's where it is, that notorious discovery!" the Doctor exclaimed.

381

"The boy confided it to you!"

"In order to give it to you."

"And what the devil does he want me to do with it?"

"He hopes...and I also hope...that you'd be good enough to ask President Lestrigon to open it."

"That could be done," the doctor replied, after thinking a bit. "But I'm convinced that there's nothing there but unimportant papers. People don't carry their wills on their person. They leave it with a notary."

"That's true," Laurence, who was turning the little sack over and over between her fingers, said softly.

By chance she pressed on the steel button, which opened under that slight pressure.

"Oh! Oh!" Monsieur Subligny cried out, "you've accidently opened the billfold. Nothing prevents you from looking at its contents and closing it afterwards. I'd just ask you, Mademoiselle, to make that inventory. I have to drive the horse and my hands aren't free."

Laurence had resolved to carry it to the end. She took from the leather envelope a paper that she unfolded and read aloud:

"If I should die suddenly, I ask my husband to take the ebony chest in my bedroom which contains our marriage contract and to give it to Monsieur Bernier, my notary, who has the key to it, and who is to open it in the presence of the Arcy Tribunal.

And it was signed, *Virginie Vignemal.*

"Well! Mademoiselle, I was right. This paper doesn't change the situation."

"That's true," Laurence said softly, "and...nevertheless...why then would Madame Vignemal attach so much importance to it?"

"I don't know, but surely if this chest in question contained a change in her will, she wouldn't charge her husband to take it to her notary. However that may be, I don't see any reason not to put this billfold in the hands of my friend, Monsieur Lestrigon. And I don't think I'm obligated to tell him that it has passed through yours. I'll just tell him that Roch Ferrer found it, and I won't be lying. The rest will take its course. They'll break open the seals put on at Fougéray and Master Bernier will open that mysterious box in front of witnesses. Tomorrow, everything will be over, and we'll know what it contains."

"And you'll come let me know?"

"You, Mademoiselle, Madame your mother, Mademoiselle Germaine, everybody this secret can concern. I would bet it's not worth your time thinking about it. Until it's opened I won't say anything to anybody."

That's all Laurence wanted. She gave the little sack to Monsieur Subligny, who put it in his pocket, and that was the end of the conversation.

Laurence was confused by having said so much.

The Doctor didn't want to know anything more about it before having clarified the situation.

And, arriving at Germonière, he was glad to verify that Germaine was doing very well after her dangerous adventure.

IX. The End

Why did the rich druggist who built his country house on the edge of the Beuvron River give himself the luxury of an Orangerie? Nobody ever knew. Perhaps he knew that the Duke de Bretteville had one and he thought that a rich businessman could afford the same amenities as a titled gentleman.

In the time of Louis XIV, German princes ruined themselves building palaces and planting gardens to imitate the luxurious *soverain* who created Versailles. The druggist didn't bankrupt himself at all, but he only half-way succeeded. His Orangerie was immense and superb. Nothing was missing except orange trees. He could have bought young ones. Paris nurserymen sold them. But he wanted time-honored orange trees, historic orange trees like those of the Chateau, almost all of which dated from the reign of Henry IV. The Duke's ancestors got them from that warrior king who came to spend the night at Bretteville while he was traveling across Normandy, and they came from Fontainebleau. The Revolution spared them because the peasants didn't know what to do with them, and they're still doing very well.

Since he couldn't get any like them, with his money the new lord of Germonière had to be content with scrawny pomegranate trees and some big plants of doubtful origin, some cactus from Pantin near Paris and some Montreuil-les-Pêches aloes.

Madame Daudièrne had been wiser and had made the orangerie into a conservatory and kept rare flowers there that her daughters lovingly tended. In the winter, when it was too cold in the garden, and too hot in the drawing room, they preferred to spend their time there. They spent whole days there drawing and painting and their mother sometimes came to be keep them company. Their brother didn't come there often, but Uncle Armand took pleasure in smoking his cigar there after lunch.

Two days after the memorable hunting expedition which had almost ended so badly, the family reunion was almost complete. Only Alfred had not made an appearance. In the morning he had flown off toward Arcy under the fallacious pretext of buying some new novels at the bookstore in Arcy and hadn't reappeared.

Germaine, gayer than ever, was busy using scissors to trim the dead leaves from certain plants she particularly liked. Laurence was making a watercolor copy of some mimosas an old friend of her father had sent from Nice. At the other end of the long glassed gallery, Madame Daudièrne and Monsieur Armand were chatting confidentially on serious matters.

"It's unusual that we didn't see anyone yesterday," the uncle was saying. "Those gentlemen have abandoned us."

"Monsieur Pontac came the same evening as the accident to get news of

Germaine," Madame Daudièrne said distractedly. "He couldn't do less, but I couldn't persuade him to stay until she came down to the drawing room. He left after about five minutes. That boy is charming, but he doesn't do anything like other people. I appreciate his discretion. After what happened at the hunt and in the unusual situation in which Germaine finds herself, the meeting would have been embarrassing."

"Well! And du Pommeval? How do you explain his disappearance? We haven't heard anything from him since we left him on the road…rather brusquely, I must admit."

"He had probably been kept back by business."

"Then you don't think he's angry?"

"I have no idea, but really if he backed out I wouldn't be unhappy about it. And I believe Germaine would be consoled about it too."

"That's my opinion. She's never had an inclination for this marriage, and du Pommeval didn't shine brilliantly yesterday. The Hussard outdistanced the handsome Arthur and I admit I admired his courage and his presence of mind. Germaine assuredly doesn't look at him with an indifferent eye. Have you questioned her to find out all of her thoughts?"

"I haven't dared."

"Because you're afraid she'll tell you clearly her preferences. I'm afraid of that also, but anything is better than uncertainty. If I were in your place, I'd want to know, right today, what to expect. If she flatly refuses du Pommeval, that's her right. You won't force her to marry a man who displeases her. But if she's fallen in love with that officer, what'll you do?"

"I'll try to prove to her that such a marriage would be absurd."

"Because Pontac doesn't have a *sou*? She knows that. And if you think she'll have a taste for your reasoning! She'll answer that money doesn't make happiness, and you won't have anything to say, because you're the one who taught her that fine maxim. That's the result of a sentimental education."

"I don't deserve your reproach," replied Madame Daudièrne, a little piqued. "I've reared my children as I should have reared them. And if I haven't taught them to adore wealth, I've never ceased repeating to them that you can't be happy in this world unless you behave well. For my daughters I've dreamed of husbands who would bring them fortunes about equal to the fortune they'll one day have. It's not my fault if Monsieur du Pommeval is too rich and Monsieur Pontac too poor."

"Yes, you'd like a proper balance. But that's not easy to find. And since you find yourself between two extreme terms, you must opt for one or the other. But what's worse is that nothing is definitive in the financial situation of the two suitors."

"What do you mean?"

"Did you notice the preoccupied air the Doctor had when he left us?"

"Yes, when we came back to Germonière he hardly examined Germaine.

He prescribed something to calm her, advised rest, and then he left."

"Germaine wasn't hurt. Medicine wouldn't do her any good. But when Subligny got back into this dilapidated old carriage to return to Arcy, he said something that made me start to thinking. What he said was: 'You must make Madame Daudièrne agree not to conclude any agreement with du Pommeval before you see me again.' I tried to get some clearer explanation, but he whipped up his mare and was off."

"That's unusual. Then how has it happened he hasn't come back? He must know we're waiting for him impatiently."

"I've told Alfred to go by his office to ask him to dine with us this evening, but I scarcely have faith in your son's reliability. It seems to me the time has come to clarify things with your daughter. Do you want me to call her?"

"Yes, my friend, but you'll help me, won't you?"

"Oh! Gladly. Germaine!"

"Here I am, Uncle," she replied, and she ran forward from the other end of the Conservatory, her eyes shining, her hair a little in disorder and a smile on her lips.

"What serious expressions!" she exclaimed, seeing her mother and her uncle, who had moved to sit side-by-side on a bench. "You seem to have made yourselves into a tribunal to judge me. What am I accused of?"

"I'll tell you after you've promised to answer frankly," retorted Monsieur Daudièrne.

"Have you ever known me to lie?"

"No. Remaining silent is not lying, and you've been silent for some time."

"I've been too often reproached for talking too much."

"Try to be serious just for once, and to begin with, tell us what you intend to make of Arthur du Pommeval."

"A leader of a cotillion, a piano accompanist…whatever you like, except a husband."

"I must say! That's clear."

"You should have told me that sooner," Madame Daudièrne burst out, "because you talked to me in a very different language the day Monsieur Subligny came to ask for your hand. It's useless to lead on this young man with a promise that you don't mean to keep."

"I didn't promise anything at all. I said I'd think about it, and…"

"And you had already completely decided," broke in Uncle Armand. "Why have you shilly-shallied this way?"

"Because I wanted Monsieur du Pommeval to marry Laurence."

"You're mad."

"No, because she loves him, and he did love her, and he'll come back to her. Do you want proof? Look down there, without showing yourself."

Germaine, standing and half-hidden by one of the boxes the druggist hadn't been able to fill with orange trees, was looking at what was happening in the garden in front of the other end of the conservatory. Her mother and her uncle, seated in front of her, had only to lean forward a little to watch Monsieur du Pommeval walk softly the length of the glass windows.

"He's seen Laurence," Germaine continued, "and he believes she's alone. Let's bet he's going to tip-toe in and start up a conversation in order to explain to her. Don't move and don't make any noise. This will be interesting."

With a glance, Madame Daudièrne consulted her brother-in-law, who said between his teeth:

"Why not? Day before yesterday, at the end of the hunt, du Pommeval seemed somewhat unhappy. I wouldn't be unhappy to learn what he has on his mind. With that boy, everything is possible."

"There he is! He's coming in!" Germaine said in a low voice. "Let's hope Laurence doesn't have the silly idea of calling us."

Germaine was right. Du Pommeval had just slid into the orangerie and was moving softly toward the corner where Laurence was finishing her watercolor. Evidently he didn't suspect that the mother, the uncle and the sister were there, since if he had seen them, he would have first come to greet them.

The orangerie was long, like the corridor of a convent. The pyramids of flower pots stacked against the supports masked the little family consulting group. Handsome Arthur didn't have that triumphant air which set him apart from the other Arcy dandies. His eyes were downcast, his face had a worried look, and, a more significant sign than all the others, he wasn't as carefully dressed as usual. He came forward, his hat in his hand, and Laurence, absorbed in her work, didn't see him come in. When she raised her head, he was in front of her. She turned pale, but she didn't change expressions.

"Are you looking for my mother, Monsieur?" she asked him coldly.

"No, Mademoiselle," replied du Pommeval in a low and sad voice. "It's just you I'm looking for."

"Really? Then what do you have to say to me?"

"Can't you guess?"

"Not at all."

"I've come to ask you for forgiveness."

"Forgiveness for what?"

"For having acted out an unworthy comedy. I loved you. I've never stopped loving you and out of spite I decided to feign sentiments for someone else that I didn't feel."

"What!" Laurence said ironically. "You were indifferent to my sister and you asked her to marry you. What was your purpose in trying to deceive her?"

"I was mad...I adored you and I couldn't get a commitment nor even a promise from you. You let me hope and that was all. So, I hardly dare admit it to you: I thought you were acting this way out of coquettishness, and maybe if I could excite your jealousy you would finally give me the consent I had been asking for such a longtime...I was hoping that..."

"You have a sad opinion of me, Monsieur," interrupted Laurence, who had recovered all her cool-headedness. "You care very little about other people's suffering. Breaking Germaine's heart after having broken mine, was that just a game to you?"

"I knew your sister would pretend to accept my courtship and that, finally, she would refuse to marry me."

"How did you know that?"

"I had guessed she was in love with Monsieur Pontac. I was certain she wouldn't continue to hide her love for him. Didn't he save her life at the hunt?"

"And now that you can't expect anything more from her, you come to offer me what she turned down."

"Mademoiselle, I swear to you that I have never changed. Appearances are against me, but I beg you to put me to the test. Authorize me to ask for your hand...today even..."

"You would go talk to my mother?"

"Right now, if you wish. Where is she? I was told I'd find her here."

"She's here. You can foresee, I suppose, how she's going to answer you."

"What! Madame Daudièrne..."

"Is down there at the other end of the orangerie with my uncle and my sister. And I advise you not to attempt to do that, however flattering that may be for me. I believe that I can even predict that if you risk it, the door of our house will be closed to you forever. It would be better to leave immediately and never try to come back."

Du Pommeval blushed right up to his ears on hearing the dismissal he very well deserved. He was probably asking himself what he was going to do when Alfred came racing in crying out:

"I'm bringing news...and really odd news. *Allez! Tiens!* There's nobody there...Ah! yes, there is,...Laurence...and...what! Du Pommeval! Ah! What about that! I didn't expect to meet anyone here. Not you, old fellow. Then don't you know what they're saying in Arcy?"

"In Arcy!" repeated du Pommeval, who had turned pale on seeing young Daudièrne. "No, I don't know anything."

"Then, *ma foi,* I'd rather you learned about it by someone other than me...and I advise you to go back to town without losing a minute. Your lawyer must need to see you to confer with you...because, I still hope everything isn't lost. There's gossip circulating...which may be false."

Du Pommeval didn't ask "What gossip?" He was so distraught it was painful to look at him. He found nothing better to do than give way. He stammered some words of excuse to Laurence and left the orangerie faster than he had entered.

"What! Uncle! He dashes off without saying good-bye to me, without shaking hands! Ah! Then it's true, what they're saying."

"What? What are they saying?" demanded Monsieur Daudièrne from the end of the conservatory.

"*Tiens!* Uncle! You're down there!...and Mother also...and Germaine. Are you playing hide and seek? And du Pommeval didn't see you!"

"We didn't want him to see us. Tell what news you're bringing."

"They aren't happy ones. They're saying in our club that a will of Madame Vignemal has been found that disinherits du Pommeval's uncle."

"The Devil! Your friend du Pommeval is losing big because he's nothing to the lady. To whom did she leave her fortune?"

"They don't know yet. What's sure is that it isn't to poor Arthur. She couldn't stand him."

Uncle Armand added: "She may have simply revoked her first will, and in that case her estate will go to her family heirs, who are a dozen or so, they say. But that matters very little to us, if du Pommeval is cut out. *Sacrebleu!* I'd like to know what to make of all this and I don't understand anything about the Doctor's behavior. He must be well-informed and he knows the situation interests us. He ought to be here to bring us up to date. I told you to invite him for me to come dine this evening. Did you go to his office?"

"Yes, but he was out."

"Will you make yourself useful to your family for once in your life? Yes. Well! Then do me the pleasure of mounting your Ralph, who probably hasn't been unsaddled yet, and gallop to Arcy and send us Subligny. This is his consultation time. You're sure to find him in his office."

"Gladly, but I'll stay in town until tomorrow morning. Ralph has already made the trip both ways today. He'll do it once more, but twenty-eight kilometers hard riding in one day, that's too much."

"Stay as long as you like. We don't need you. But we do need the Doctor. Tell him I beg him to come immediately."

"Don't worry. I'd rather bring him by force," said Alfred, dashing out of the conservatory.

"Do you others understand anything about that?" Uncle Armand asked.

"I understand that Monsieur du Pommeval is ruined," Madame Daudièrne said very softly. "You were right, my dear Laurence. Germaine would have done better to decide sooner, since she won't have him. Now people will say that she accepted him as a suitor only for his money."

"I don't care about that," Germaine retorted. "I'll soon prove that I don't care anything about a fortune."

"Do you know what Monsieur du Pommeval said to me just a while ago?" asked Laurence, looking at her mother and her uncle.

"We were too far away to hear," murmured Madame Daudièrne.

"He swore to me that he had never loved anyone but me and that he was ready to ask you for my hand."

"I really told you he'd come back to you," Germaine exclaimed.

"*Ah ça!* This little Monsieur," Uncle Armand said, frowning. "He passes

389

from the older one to the younger one and from the younger one to the older one. He imagines then that he just has to choose. People don't behave that way. And I'll soon tell him what I think of his conduct."

"*Oh!* We won't see him any more. His plan failed," Laurence said.

"His plan?"

"Do you know why he came to offer me his heart? It was because he knew he wouldn't inherit. He thought I would accept him then and there, and as he wasn't getting the inheritance, he wanted to marry at any price. He became aware day before yesterday that Germaine's preference was not for him. And he found that, since he couldn't do any better, I'd still be a good catch."

"But then he's an abominable scoundrel!"

"No, he's just a vain and self-interested provincial."

"Those are faults that can be excused," Madame Daudièrne said, "but I see now that he has no feelings. May it please God that he not enter our family."

"Do you still hold it against me that I didn't accept him?" Germaine asked maliciously.

"No," Uncle Armand replied. "Your young girl's instinct served you very well. But the time's come for you to explain yourself absolutely. Are you in love with someone?"

"*Mon Dieu!* Yes.

"I was sure of that. But your mother has the right to know who. And you can speak in front of your sister and me."

"Haven't you guessed?"

"Yes I have, or at least I'm afraid I have. It's Roger Pontac."

"Himself."

"Because he killed…courageously, I recognize…a buck that was going to gore you. That's all well and good, but how many times have you seen this young man before the hunt when he saved you?"

"One…two…three times," Germaine said, counting on her fingers.

"*Peste!* Your heart certainly goes to work quickly. You hardly talked to him in the drawing room during his first visits. It's true he sang an Arab song to you about a singing bird."

"Excuse me. I know him a great deal better than you think. The day Ralph ran away with me, I met Monsieur Pontac at the Lemon Rock."

"May the Devil take your Rock and the fairies that live there."

"Me, I bless them, these good fairies. If they hadn't protected me, I don't know what I would have done to get back to Germonière. Fortunately, Monsieur Pontac was there. He's the one who brought me back to the house. Without him I would never have found the way."

"And you hid that adventure from us," exclaimed Madame Daudièrne. "That's bad; that's very bad."

"I was wrong, I admit. But I had decided to marry him and I wanted to give you time to know and appreciate him. It was me who asked him to come see you on whatever pretext."

"Unheard of!" Uncle Armand growled. "That's what the unsophisticated do these days!"

"Would you rather I were a hypocrite? I haven't said anything for a week. Now I'm telling everything. And I'm saying aloud that I've been compromised. Yesterday Monsieur du Pommeval saw me fall into Monsieur Pontac's arms and all of Arcy will know that story. There's no longer any way to back out. If I don't marry my savior I'll risk being an old maid because no one would want me after that."

"On my word of honor, I'm beginning to believe that you had yourself charged by that buck on purpose, unless the Hussard had an agreement with this damned animal. But you talk about marrying Pontac as if it were a sure thing. Are you even sure he wants you?"

"If he doesn't want me, I'll stay an old maid," Germaine said, smiling.

"Very well. You're set on that officer's feelings. It corresponds perfectly to yours. And all I have left to do is ask if you can envisage what will happen after this beautiful marriage. I have nothing to say against the man you've chosen. I'm even willing to recognize that he's worth infinitely more than du Pommeval, considered from any point of view. And the friendship the Duke de Bretteville has honored him with won't harm his future. But, for the moment, he has only his army pay, something around two hundred pounds income, and later, when your dear mother is no longer in this world, when he's knocked down big promotions, together you can enjoy a revenue of twenty thousand. If the fairies you've brought together continue to watch over you, you'll have a lot of children—the happiness they're guaranteeing to their favorites doesn't come without that. Well! My dear girl if they give you just five or six, your daughters will be reduced to marrying cave rats."

"No, Second Lieutenants. They'll do the same as their mother."

Uncle Armand raised his arms to heaven. He had reached the end of his arguments. Madame Daudièrne, nonplussed, said nothing. Laurence came to her sister's aid.

"Monsieur Pontac may not be as poor as you think," she said gently. "Because, if as people say, Madame Vignemal has changed her will, he'll have his part of the inheritance."

"What's that you're talking about there?" asked Uncle Armand, excited.

"Monsieur Pontac is Madame Vignemal's cousin. Ask Doctor Subligny."

"Very definitely a cousin," Germaine said very low.

"You knew this?" Madame Daudièrne asked.

"Yes, since the evening of the ferry accident. And you too should have known it. Doctor Subligny told in front of you the history of a child that Madame Vignemal, his closest relative, had placed in a secondary school in Paris..."

"What! That child...that was..."

"Roger Pontac. The Doctor said his name quite clearly, but you have no memory for names."

"And yourself do, even not counting what your heart remembers," said Uncle Armand. "I remember now, and I admit the Hussard has a chance of inheriting…but only a chance."

"It's not at all important to me whether it comes about. People would think I was making a self-interested marriage."

"There's no doubt, little girl. You're crazy. But I must hurry to see Subligny. That was why he said to me: 'Don't settle anything with du Pommeval until you see me again' …and he hasn't returned, that animal! What's he thinking about to leave us like this?"

"Don't get angry, Uncle. I see him coming," said Germaine.

"That's right; there he is!" Madame Daudièrne exclaimed. "He's buttoned up to his chin in his big frock coat, and he has put on his expression for important occasions. We're going to get some news."

That excellent doctor came and made the rounds with greetings and handshakes the most calmly in the world. By his calmness you might have said that he knew they were expecting him and that he was enjoying exciting his Germonière friends' impatience.

"My nephew has just gone on horseback to look for you," Monsieur Daudièrne began. "You must have met him on the road to Arcy, not very far from here."

"I haven't come directly from Arcy," replied the Doctor. "I left there this morning and right now I've come from Bretteville."

"Ah! Then you also didn't meet du Pommeval, who was going back to his house?"

"No, and I'm glad not to have seen him."

"Then it's true that he's disinherited? Alfred has just come to tell us that the gossip around the town and I didn't want to believe it."

"I've come especially to tell you the great news of the day. Yesterday I was kept away by information I had to gather. But I have it…as complete and as exact as possible, and I'm bringing it to you. It's really going to astonish you."

"Madame Vignemal has revoked the legacy she made to her husband?"

"Better than that. Here's what happened. The young man, there when the couple was drowned, found on the bank of the Beuvron River, a little sack that Madame Vignemal wore around her neck and he didn't tell anyone about that find."

"I really thought he was a contemptible fellow."

"No, he was just an uncivilized fellow who didn't understand anything about ordinary life. He didn't suspect that this sack might contain precious papers and he kept it…without opening it. Note this point. I've taken a great deal of interest in him the last several days and I've persuaded him to leave the country and join an African regiment. He left yesterday."

"So much the better. He was going to get himself hanged otherwise."

"I certainly hope he won't be hanged nor even imprisoned. I've converted him and I can answer to you that he'll make his way in the army. But before he left, he gave the object he had picked up on the edge of the river to me," the good doctor said, looking at Laurence out of the corner of his eyes. He knew that what he was saying might upset her and he wanted to reassure her, showing her by what he was saying that she hadn't been and would never be, implicated in that scabrous story of the discovered sack.

"I understood very quickly," he continued, "the importance of that discovery, and I took that little sack to my friend the President, who opened it with all the formalities required by law. He took out a handwritten note by Madame Vignemal, who asked her husband, in case she died before him, to carry to Master Bernier, her notary, a little box placed in her bedroom. She ordered Bernier to proceed to inventory the papers contained in that box. That inventory was done yesterday and there have been consequences that nobody expected."

"I can guess what they are," Uncle Armand cried out. "Du Pommeval is disinherited, *parbleu!*"

"He's not the one who was disinherited," said the Doctor. "It was the husband, but it comes to the same thing, since du Pommeval was only related to Monsieur Vignemal."

"Then the wife's relatives will divide the fortune."

"No, that's still not it."

"What is it then? Explain it to us, my friend. You're making us die with impatience."

"The little box contained a handwritten will, signed, dated,…in short perfectly legal. And that will, that I read, said just about this:

"My very dear husband won't find it wrong that I modify my last wishes, foreseeing what might happen after my death if I leave them such as I had made them."

"That's a preamble you're repeating to us."

"Yes, but the will follows, and it's good that you know the whole thing. I'll go on.

"My husband has only one heir, Monsieur Arthur du Pommeval, the son of his sister, and I'm sure he wouldn't dare change the natural order of inheritance. Now, I don't want my estate to pass to a man of bad life who would quickly waste everything."

"The Devil! She's hard on that poor du Pommeval, the Fougéray lady."

"Severe and unjust, because this boy will straighten up, I believe. But he didn't know how to please her, and his youthful mistakes will cost him dear. Listen to what follows:

"I have then hit on an arrangement that would conserve the fortune, painfully acquired by my father, and which would change nothing of my husband's situation during his lifetime. That fortune will not leave my family and I have firm confidence that it will be wisely administered, because blood will tell. The

heir that I name has already proven by his conduct that he is worthy of following me."

"Good! She's chosen the most economical and the hardest working of her cousins...a laborer or a usurer from the village."

"Not exactly. The will ends like this...I memorized it."

"I, the undersigned, Virginia Pontac, wife of Monsieur François Vignemal..."

"Pontac! Then, is our neighbor the aunt of your protégé, Roger Pontac?"

"His aunt more or less according to the customs of Britanny. Madame Vignemal's father and Roger's father were first cousins and both were named Pontac. She had several other relatives in the same degree of relationship who might have been named in the inheritance the same as Roger, if she had died intestate. Fortunately, she had foreseen this situation and you'll see that she tried to prevent her beautiful Fougéray estate from being divided."

"I, the undersigned, etc., give and bequeath with this testament to my husband, Monsieur François Vignemal, the use during his lifetime of everything fixed and moveable belonging to me..."

"There's a gift the poor man didn't take advantage of."

"His wife couldn't foresee that he would die at the same time she did. The intention was there."

"All my goods, fixed and moveable I bequeath without conditions to my cousin, Roger-Paul-Joseph Pontac, currently a First Lieutenant in the 9th Hussard Regiment, garrisoned at Gabes, in Tunisia."

"What! Our young friend the sole heir! That's unbelievable! You told us she had disinherited him ten years ago."

"Wait! There's an explanation...and a condition."

"On condition that Roger Pontac leave the military service no later than one year after the death of my husband, and take up his residence at Fougéray. I hope that Roger will accept this condition that I impose on him in his own interest, and that he forget my wrongs against him as I have long forgotten his youthful faults. He has lately written me to tell me about his promotion to the rank of officer and of his coming return to France. I'm waiting for him to let him know the disposition herein, which is the definitive expression of my will.

"It's dated at Fougéray, 19 December 1881," added Monsieur Subligny.

"So that if the accident had happened a month ago du Pommeval would have inherited," Monsieur Daudièrne said between his teeth. "Then everything thing's for the best. Isn't that your opinion, Doctor?"

"Yes...certainly since two days ago."

"We thought you were interested in Monsieur du Pommeval."

"You weren't wrong...and the proof is that I did something for him... that I later regretted. But I'm also interested in Roger. He's a good, charming and honest young man. I've known him since he was a boy, and I can answer for him as I could answer for my son, if I had one."

"So here he is all at once a millionaire, if he agrees to resign his commission as an officer and live in the country, which I doubt," said Uncle Armand.

"I doubt it also, I can tell you…if..." replied the Doctor.

"If what? If he was of a higher rank or if the inheritance was less good?"

"No," replied Monsieur Subligny, looking at Germaine, "if Fougéray weren't so near Germonière."

"Well! Me," Germaine exclaimed, "if he consulted me, I'd advise him to stay a soldier."

"And be as poor as Job," added the uncle, shrugging.

"No. He'd always have his part of the inheritance."

"You're mistaken, Mademoiselle," said the Doctor. "You're mistaken as we were mistaken when we interpreted in our own way the Articles of the Code which regulate the order of inheritance. Since I committed that stupidity, I have doubted myself and I promised myself to consult a lawyer whenever I have a question about the law. I asked President Lestrigon what would happen if Roger preferred to follow the career he had chosen. And the President told me that the condition imposed by the testate not having fulfilled by the designated heir, du Pommeval would ask for and perhaps get the will declared null and void. If it was declared null, a lawsuit would be instituted between him and the natural heirs of Madame Vignemal, who might win it. In that case they would try to have Roger Pontac excluded, claiming that the refusal to execute a clause in the will was equivalent to renouncing any part of the inheritance. That would be another lawsuit to be undertaken against some people who aren't interesting, I swear to you. The league of the cousins would be lead by a certain Pierre Le Masle, who has an agreement with a wicked fellow, a lawyer named Vaurinet, to accuse poor Roch of having drowned Madame Vignemal at the instigation of Roger."

"In fact, he has been accused," Monsieur Daudièrne put in. "I was even one of those who accused him. It's true that I didn't then know that it was a question of our friend Pontac. But, Doctor, don't you think that miraculous find of a will made to his advantage is going to give more weight to some vague suspicions? They will say he had a reason to get rid of his cousin."

"They said that yesterday. The Attorney General of the Republic was the first to bring up this difficult question. But the President proved to him that you had only to read the will closely to be convinced of Roger Pontac's innocence."

"I'm expecting him to let him know the changes in the will I have just made."

"Madame Vignemal wrote the 19 November, that is three days before her death. Now, it's been proved that Roger didn't see his cousin either before or after the redrawing of that will. It has even been sworn to that he came as far as the Fougéray gate and that he hadn't dared enter. It's also certain that the good lady didn't tell anyone about what she had done at the last moment for a boy for whom she'd had affection in the past and who hadn't deserved so much censure, because he had earned his promotion through courage and perseverance. How could he have known he would be the heir? My friend Lestrigon knew so well how to put forth these arguments that the Attorney General finally listened to reason... much against his will. Then I myself took in hand the defense of Roch Ferrer, and I convinced, without too much trouble, this seeker of the guilty to stop the proceedings against our man who enlisted voluntarily. In essence, it was army officers that the head of the legal system wanted to strike by having an officer arrested at the Duke de Bretteville's. He had very little interests in the poacher and he won't take any further interest in him."

"This is excellent news, my dear Doctor," Uncle Armand burst out. "And you can be sure that it will be particularly pleasant to one of my nieces."

"I'm sure it'll be agreeable to both of them," replied Monsieur Subligny, glancing at Laurence, who had trembled with joy on learning that Roch Ferrer had nothing to fear from the law.

"No doubt. But Germaine has personal reasons to be satisfied...reasons you don't yet know, but that you perhaps guess."

"Could it be the insolvency of Monsieur du Pommeval which cheers up Mademoiselle?" Monsieur Subligny asked maliciously.

"No, because you should never rejoice about the misfortunes of your neighbors," answered Germaine. "But I can tell you it doesn't distress me. This pretty Monsieur doesn't deserve to be rich. He cares for no one but himself. I hope the same thing happens to him as to all heartless men."

"What has he done to be treated like this?"

"He mocked my sister and he tried to mock me. God punished him...in the way most painful to him...through money. It was well done."

"It's unfortunately true that I don't know how to excuse Monsieur du Pommeval's conduct. I've decided never to invite him again," said Madame Daudièrne.

"Didn't you tell me, dear Madame, that he's just left here?"

"Yes, and he would have done better not to have come, because he showed his true self. Would you believe, Monsieur, that he had the audacity to tell my elder daughter that he had never stopped loving her?"

"Then he mocked me also," said the Doctor. "Decidedly he's an idiot and this will serve me as a lesson. I'll never again accept a matrimonial ambassadorship."

"You might be more fortunate some other time," Germaine said, lowering her eyes.

"I prefer not to try. Those missions are completely beyond my speciality. I'll leave them to those better at them."

"I understood you were coming from Bretteville," Germaine questioned.

"I do, in fact, Mademoiselle."

"Then," Monsieur Daudièrne questioned, "you've seen Pontac?"

"Yes, I had a long interview with him."

"And naturally you informed him that he was the heir?"

"That's the only reason I went to the chateau."

"Well! How did he take the news?"

"Very calmly, I assure you. He sets more store by honor than by money. I think he would willingly trade his cousin's inheritance for a red ribbon, courageously earned."

"The Devil! Does he intend to refuse the inheritance to stay in the military?"

"He's hesitating. The decision he makes will depend on...something."

"On the advice that the Duke de Bretteville will give him, for example?"

"No...not exactly. The Duke is of the opinion that he should accept the inheritance, but he understands Roger' particular situation and he leaves him free to decide according to the circumstances."

"My dear Subligny, your answers lack clarity. What circumstances are you referring to?"

"Well...to marriage, for example. If Pontac were in a position to marry, and if the woman that he intended to marry wanted him to give up a military career, Pontac would resign himself without any trouble to become Lord of Fougéray. If, on the contrary, he must remain a bachelor, he would prefer to run the risk of becoming a general, one day or another."

That meaningful statement troubled Madame Daudièrne a great deal and Uncle Armand somewhat. Germaine probably expected it and didn't change expressions. Laurence smiled and drew near her sister. She was forgetting her own troubles to think only of Germaine's happiness.

"Doctor," Uncle Armand said, after a silence, "I think that at the point we are now, we no longer have anything to hide. I'll broach big confidences squarely. After that it will be your turn. You won't be very astonished to learn that the youngest of my nieces has given her heart without consulting her mother, and that her choice has fallen to a First Lieutenant with whom you're acquainted. It remains to be seen if the feelings of this First Lieutenant are the same as those of Mademoiselle. No one is in a better position than you to inform us on this important point."

"Oh! Uncle! You're turning the roles upside down. It's up to the Doctor to begin."

Madame Daudièrne didn't say anything, but it was obvious from her expression that she agreed with her daughter that her brother-in-law was moving too quickly.

"I agree with that," replied Monsieur Subligny gaily, "but I've sworn never again to meddle in those things...and besides, here's a visitor coming to see you."

"What the devil does this visitor want? Why does Baptiste permit himself to bring in a visitor without asking if we want to see him?" exclaimed Monsieur Daudièrne.

Uncle Armand continued: "They praise old servants. They're wrong. A young man wouldn't have committed that stupidity and your Baptiste is an idiot."

"I understand his conduct even less, since the gentleman he's bringing in is totally unknown to me," said Madame Daudièrne.

"And to me too," Germaine said very low.

"Can you others see him? I can't. You're blocking my view," grumbled Uncle Armand.

"Some new civil servant who's just arrived in Arcy," said Laurence.

"You must be mistaken, Mademoiselle," replied Doctor Subligny, smiling. "Germonière is on the black list for government employes."

"Oh! And also this gentleman appears too distinguished," Germaine continued. "Doesn't he, Uncle? Civil servants these days don't appear that distinguished."

The family, gathered at the back of the conservatory, was grouped in such a way that the uncle, sitting behind his nieces, couldn't see the person coming in at such an inconvenient time. Monsieur Subligny himself could see him very well, and just as Baptiste was opening the door to the conservatory, he left the group to advance toward the entering visitor.

"Do you know this gentleman?" Uncle Armand asked him in a low voice.

"Yes," answered the Doctor in the same tone. "And you know him also. Then come with me, because it's proper that you be the one to introduce him to Madame Daudièrne."

"Ah! *Mon Dieu!* But that looks like the…!"

"Exactly, That's who it is. I knew he was coming."

Madame Daudièrne and her daughters hearing these stage whispers, didn't understand what it was about. They were looking with uneasy curiosity at that stranger they had never seen before. He was a man who had aged, but he wasn't an old man. The full beard he wore was becoming very gray, but he was still tall and straight, and his face had no wrinkles. His person and his bearing was that of an aristocratic gentleman. He couldn't be mistaken for one of the many landowners in the Arcy environs, rich bourgeois or petty country gentlemen. He looked distinguished.

Madame Daudièrne remained dumbfounded, seeing this imposing lord hold out his hand to her brother-in-law, who overwhelmed him with greetings. Germaine understood immediately. She whispered in her sister's ear:

"Let's leave. This is the right time. You'll understand in a few minutes."

And she led her away running. Their mother, stunned, didn't have time to call them back and still less to ask them for an explanation for their sudden departure.

"My dear sister-in-law," Monsieur Daudièrne said to her, "here is the Duke de Bretteville who has done us the honor to come see us."

"An unexpected honor," said the modest chatelaine of Germonière.

"You're reminding me, Madame, that I owe you apologies" the Duke began, greeting her with that easy politeness, the tradition of which tends to become lost in our times.

"I'm your neighbor for the first time this year, because I've never stayed at Bretteville since the war. I would already have paid you a visit if I hadn't been condemned to live in retirement because of the death of my son."

"I very much appreciate your having come out, *Monsieur le Duc*," said Madame Daudièrne, "and I'm the one who must ask you to excuse me. I was so little expecting to be honored with your visit."

"We might go back into the house," Uncle Armand exclaimed. "The drawing room would be more appropriate to receive *Monsieur le Duc*."

"I'm very comfortable here," Monsieur de Bretteville said, smiling. "I only regret having made Madame Daudièrne's charming daughter's run away. But I can take advantage of their absence to tell you what brought me here. I hope they will come back after they know what I have to say. I've come, Madame, to ask you for the hand of Mademoiselle Daudièrne for the comrade of my unfortunate son, for Roger Pontac, whom I love as if he were of my own blood. Do I need to add, that I wouldn't ask you like this, on the spur of the moment, if I didn't know that my young friend is hopelessly in love. His financial situation now allows him to aspire to an alliance to which he wouldn't have dared claim when he had only his sword?"

The Duke could also have said that Roger knew he could be certain of Germaine's feelings, but he was careful not to commit that indiscretion, which, in the circumstances would have been almost impertinence.

"I couldn't be more flattered by such a request," Madame Daudièrne said very softly. "We know Monsieur Pontac and we appreciate his qualities. But, you understand, *Monsieur le Duc*, I must first of all consult my daughter and I'm going..."

"You know very well, my dear sister-in-law, that's not necessary," interrupted Uncle Armand. "*Monsieur le Duc* is not unaware of what happened in the forest...and elsewhere. Germaine, who can't hide anything, has just declared flat out to us that she's engaged to Roger Pontac and that she doesn't want any other husband but this brave boy, who has all it takes to make her happy. Nothing more is necessary but your own consent. I hope you won't put any obstacle in the way of your daughter's happiness. Me, to start with, if I'm called on to vote, I'll vote yes, with both hands, and so will the Doctor, I'm sure."

"With enthusiasm," exclaimed the ex-surgeon Major.

"If I refused, I would be alone against everybody," Madame Daudièrne said softly.

"But you won't refuse. I'm going to find Germaine."

"Don't go looking for me; I'm here," said a silvery voice. The artful girl hadn't gone very far away and she suddenly came forward, holding on to her sister's arm. She had hidden behind a row of bushes in tubs. Laurence was paler than usual, but Germaine didn't appear at all embarrassed. She made a nice curtsy to *Monsieur le Duc* and said to him gaily:

"I heard everything, *Monsieur le Duc*. But I hope you'll believe I don't make a habit of listening at doors."

The Duke wasn't one of those severe moralists who condemn the slightest infractions of propriety. He had no intention of taking exception to that somewhat too lively entrance on stage. He thought only about admiring that flower of youth and beauty, those eyes shining with joy, that sweet face showing the greatest frankness, that voice which went straight to the heart, and he began to smile. That was the first time since his son died in combat.

"Mademoiselle," he said, holding out his hand to her, "I knew Roger couldn't be in love with anyone but a person with all the social graces. Now that I've seen you, I find him the most fortunate of men."

And he gallantly kissed that little white hand.

"Not yet," said Germaine. "I have some conditions."

"Roger will accept them all."

"Are you sure about that? I want to be the wife of an officer. And as he'll lose his cousin's inheritance if he doesn't resign his commission..."

"A year from now, Mademoiselle," interrupted Monsieur de Bretteville.

"And before a year is out, he'll be decorated," added Doctor Subligny. "He's already been proposed for it. And once he has the medal of honor, I don't see why he would stay in the service. In these day, the army is no longer a career. Our governments are talking a great deal about reprisals for our losses, but they're going to reclaim them using the national guard!"[39]

"The day of reprisals will come, whatever happens," said the Duke, "and on that day Roger will get back his commission, unless they give him a regiment to command."

"That's true," Germaine said very softly. "The will gives him a year to make up his mind. Well, I'll wait, too. And that would be more fitting. What would the handsome Arcy Messieurs say about me if I married Monsieur Pontac a month after he inherited to the detriment of Monsieur du Pommeval? I'd appear to be always going to the richest."

"It would be even worse if you waited until Pontac took possession. People would believe that, having been disappointed in the hopes you were founding on du Pommeval, you intended this time to take your precautions. I can already hear the bourgeois and the dandies of our nice *sous prefecture,* 'It doesn't make any difference who's the husband provided the inheritance goes with him'...and other conversations just as kind toward you."

"You're above such gossip, Mademoiselle," said the Duke de Bretteville, "but please let me plead Roger's cause. You're putting him to a hard test, if you put his happiness off for a year."

---

[39] Reference to the Franco-Prussian War in 1870, which France lost.

"And if you require that he remain a soldier after your marriage, you'll have to go live in military quarters at Gabes," said Uncle Armand.

"I'd gladly go. And that would be charming. I would protect that poor Roch Ferrer, who enlisted so bravely," said Germaine, looking at Laurence.

"Roch will make his way by himself," Monsieur Subligny said gently.

Madame Daudièrne hasn't yet had her say and it was time to hear from her.

"My dear child," she began in an emotional voice. "The reasons you're putting forward are not serious. You're in love with Monsieur Pontac, and I don't blame you for loving him, any more than I'm opposed to your marrying him. But if the present situation continues, it will become intolerable for you...for him...and for us. So I ask you to make your decision immediately."

"Make my decision!" replied Germaine. "But I did."

"Then, Mademoiselle," continued the Duke, "you're authorizing me to carry to Roger the happy news he's waiting for with impatience."

"With so much impatience that he stayed tranquilly at the de Bretteville chateau," the young girl said teasingly.

"It would have been, perhaps, more proper for him to have stayed there, but he couldn't hold out any longer. And do I dare admit to Madame, your mother, that I brought him with me?"

"What! He's here!" Uncle Armand cried out.

"I left him on the road at the end of the avenue...and I'm sure he's counting the minutes, because I promised I'd come back as soon as I'd accomplished my mission."

"It would be better if I went to get him, *Monsieur le Duc*, and I'll run there now," said Uncle Armand.

"May I know, my dear Uncle, what you're going to tell him?" demanded Germaine.

"That you've got a two-pronged idea in your head, but you'll rethink it, I hope, and that you'll marry him with or without a delay. Is that right?"

"Just about."

"Good. The rest is up to him. It's up to him to make you see reason on setting the date and on your trip to Gabes."

"You can add that the wife must obey her husband. I read that beautiful maxim in the Civil Code and I'll obey the law."

"Then the marriage will take place in the chapel of my de Bretteville chateau," the Duke said, smiling. "I intend to leave for Italy in six weeks and Roger wants me to be his witness."

"That would be a great honor for us, *Monsieur le Duc*," Germaine replied ceremoniously. "And I want whatever Monsieur Pontac wants. But before he's here, I still have ten minutes of liberty. I can certainly take advantage of it to talk to my sister."

Nobody objected, since that arrangement suited everybody. Uncle Armand hurried to bring Pontac. Madame Daudièrne found she needed to explain a number of things to the Duke de Bretteville, who asked for nothing better than to put forth the serious merits of his protégé. The Doctor continued to insist on the certainty of the inheritance and to make known President Lestrigon's opinion on this important point. So Laurence wasn't unhappy to be away from this family council, which didn't concern her.

"True? Really true? You don't love him any more?" Germaine asked her when they were alone.

"No, I have too much contempt for him."

"They say that doesn't have anything to do with it. Me, I don't know about that. But, after all, you did love him."

"I was blind. He took care of opening my eyes himself."

"Wouldn't it be rather that you love someone else?"

"You're crazy. Where did you get that idea?"

"If I'm mistaken, that's too bad. I had thought..."

"What indeed?"

"You're going to make fun of me but I don't care. Well, day before yesterday, at the hunt, you climbed up the Lemon Rock...I saw you."

"Our mother also saw me. And what does it matter that I climbed up there?"

"I imagined that you also, you had consulted the oracle..."

"I had nothing to ask him," Laurence said sadly.

"He sometimes answers without being asked. But keep your secret if you have one. Just let me tell you that I want you to marry as I'm marrying, to a man you've chosen. You can't chose badly and if he loves you as you deserve to be loved, nothing more matters. I regret only one thing: that's that Roger is going to be rich. I would have hoped that he owed everything to me. And I'm going to make, in spite of myself, what they call in Arcy, an advantageous marriage. But you can find what I was looking for: a valiant soldier who enlisted for love of you, and who will come back with a commission nobly earned."

"In ten years," Laurence said softly. "There won't be any more time."

"Roger took only eight years to become an officer and he didn't go abroad for me. Roch, who adores you, will have a commission in fewer than five years"

"Roch! What do you mean?"

"I guessed everything. And I have the right to be interested in him, because if he hadn't given to that excellent doctor the sack of our poor Fougéray neighbor, I would have had all the trouble in the world getting rid of Monsieur du Pommeval. Now, not a word more. Nobody will know what I know...nobody except Roger, who won't do anything to stand in the way of Roch Ferrer's advancement. There's my uncle and he's bringing Monsieur Pontac. Come, let me introduce you to my husband."

That was quickly done, although Laurence protested and Germaine was wise enough to spare Roger the embarrassment of expressing what he felt. She didn't allow him to say a word.

"*Monsieur le Duc*," she said happily, "it was on your land that my happiness was decided. The Lemon Rock belongs to you and the fairies living there certainly favored my first meeting with Monsieur Pontac. You'll certainly let us invite them all to our wedding, and later to our children's baptism."

"If God sends you any, I'm the one who'll bring them up," Laurence whispered softly.

"Then I'll bring up yours," exclaimed Germaine, hugging her sister. "You'll get married; the fairies promised me so."

Roger Pontac has not yet resigned his commission, but he will before the end of the year and yesterday he married Mademoiselle Daudièrne.

Roch Ferrer has achieved the entry level rank and will certainly become an officer.

Will Germaine's prediction come true one day? Why not?

www.ingramcontent.com/pod-product-compliance
Lightning Source LLC
Chambersburg PA
CBHW030933020726
47498CB00001B/222